THE WILD CARDS

As the nations struggled through four turbulent decades, from the end of World War II through the sleek New Wave '80s, the bizarre metahumans created by the Wild Card virus used their extraordinary abilities to shape the course of history. Now an investigative committee of Wild Card victims sets out on a world tour to learn how Aces and Jokers are treated in other countries.

In this fourth astonishing volume, here are some of the heroes you'll meet as the Wild Cards travel from the jungles of Haiti to the Great Wall of China:

XAVIER DESMOND—The unofficial mayor of Jokertown. A monstrosity with a pink elephantine trunk adorning his face, he has nevertheless more humanity than most "nots."

PEREGRINE—The winged beauty whose talent is to drive men sexually mad—before flying away.

FATHER SQUID—The kindly pastor of the Church of Jesus Christ, Joker. He delivers his moving sermons through the tentacles that hang over his mouth like a constantly twitching mustache.

FORTUNATO—the handsome half black/half Japanese ex-pimp whose special powers depend on his sexuality.

ACES ABROAD

A Wild Cards Mosaic Novel

edited by George R.R. Martin
and written by
Stephen Leigh
John J. Miller
Leanne C. Harper
Gail Gerstner-Miller
Walton Simons
Edward Bryant
Lewis Shiner
Victor W. Milán
Melinda M. Snodgrass
Michael Cassutt

BANTAM BOOKS
NEW YORK · TORONTO · LONDON · SYDNEY · AUCKLAND

ACES ABROAD

A Bantam Spectra Book / June 1988
2nd printing . . . February 1990

ISBN 0-553-27628-X

Published simultaneously in the United States and Canada

Bantam Books are published by Bantam Books, a division of
Bantam Doubleday Dell Publishing Group, Inc. Its trademark,
consisting of the words "Bantam Books" and the portrayal of a
rooster, is Registered in U.S. Patent and Trademark Office and
in other countries. Marca Registrada. Bantam Books, 666 Fifth
Avenue, New York, New York 10103.

PRINTED IN THE UNITED STATES OF AMERICA

OPM   10 9 8 7 6 5 4 3 2

for Terry Matz,
a treasured friend for longer than
I care to think about

ACES
ABROAD

THE TINT OF HATRED

Stephen Leigh

Prologue

THURSDAY, NOVEMBER 27, 1986, WASHINGTON, DC:

The Sony threw flickering light over Sara's Thanksgiving feast: a Swanson turkey dinner steaming in foil on the coffee table. On the television screen a mob of misshapen jokers marched through a sweltering New York summer afternoon, their mouths moving in silent screams and curses. The grainy scene had the jerky look of an old newsreel, and suddenly the picture swung about to show a handsome man in his mid-thirties, his sleeves rolled up, his suit coat slung over a shoulder and his tie loose on his neck—Senator Gregg Hartmann, as he had been in 1976. Hartmann strode through the police lines blockading the jokers, shrugging away the security men who tried to hold him, shouting at the police himself. Alone, he stood between the authorities and the oncoming crowd of jokers, motioning them back.

Then the camera panned toward a disturbance within the ranks of jokers. The images were jumbled and out of focus: at the center was the ace/prostitute known as Succubus, her body seemingly made of quicksilver flesh, her appearance constantly shifting. The wild card had cursed her with sexual empathy. Succubus could take on whatever shape and form most pleased her clients, but that ability was now out of control. Around her, people responded to her power, grasping out for her with a strange lust on their faces. Her mouth was open in an imploring scream as the pursuing crowd, police and jokers both, bore her down. Her arms were stretched out in supplication, and as the camera panned back, there was Hartmann again, his jaw open in surprise as he gaped at Succubus. Her arms were reaching for *him*, her plea was for *him*. Then she was gone under the mob. For several seconds she was buried, lost. But then the crowd drew back in horror. The camera followed Hartmann closer: he shoved through those around Succubus, angrily pushed them away.

Sara reached for the VCR's remote switch. She touched the pause button, freezing the scene, a moment of time that had shaped her life. She could feel the hot tears streaking her face.

Succubus lay twisted in a pool of blood, her body mangled, her face turned upward as Hartmann stared at her, mirroring Sara's horror.

Sara knew the face that Succubus, whoever she might have really been, had found just before death. Those young features had haunted Sara since childhood—Succubus had taken on Andrea Whitman's face.

Sara's older sister's face. Andrea who, at thirteen, had been brutally murdered in 1950.

Sara knew who had kept that pubescent image of Andrea locked away in his mind for so many years. She knew who had placed Andrea's features on the infinitely malleable body of Succubus. She could imagine that face on Succubus as he lay with her, and that thought hurt Sara most of all.

"You bastard," Sara whispered to Senator Hartmann, her voice choking. "You goddamn bastard. You killed my sister and you couldn't even let her stay dead."

FROM *THE JOURNAL OF XAVIER DESMOND*

NOVEMBER 30/JOKERTOWN:

My name is Xavier Desmond, and I am a joker.

Jokers are always strangers, even on the street where they were born, and this one is about to visit a number of strange lands. In the next five months I will see veldts and mountains, Rio and Cairo, the Khyber Pass and the Straits of Gibraltar, the Outback and the Champs-Élysées—all very far from home for a man who has often been called the mayor of Jokertown. Jokertown, of course, has no mayor. It is a neighborhood, a ghetto neighborhood at that, and not a city. Jokertown is more than a place though. It is a condition, a state of mind. Perhaps in that sense my title is not undeserved.

I have been a joker since the beginning. Forty years ago, when Jetboy died in the skies over Manhattan and loosed the wild card upon the world, I was twenty-nine years of age, an investment banker with a lovely wife, a two-year-old daughter, and a bright future ahead of me. A month later, when I was finally released from the hospital, I was a monstrosity with a pink elephantine trunk growing from the center of my face where my nose had been. There are seven perfectly functional fingers at the end of my trunk, and over the years I have become quite adept with this "third hand." Were I suddenly restored to so-called normal humanity, I believe it would be as traumatic as if one of my limbs were amputated. With my trunk I am ironically somewhat more than human . . . and infinitely less.

My lovely wife left me within two weeks of my release from the hospital, at approximately the same time that Chase Manhattan informed me that my services would no longer be required. I moved to Jokertown nine months later, following my eviction from my Riverside Drive apartment for "health reasons." I last saw my daughter in 1948. She was married in June of 1964, divorced in 1969, remarried in June of 1972.

She has a fondness for June weddings, it seems. I was invited
to neither of them. The private detective I hired informs me
that she and her husband now live in Salem, Oregon, and
that I have two grandchildren, a boy and a girl, one from each
marriage. I sincerely doubt that either knows that their
grandfather is the mayor of Jokertown.

I am the founder and president emeritus of the Jokers'
Anti-Defamation League, or JADL, the oldest and largest
organization dedicated to the preservation of civil rights for
the victims of the wild card virus. The JADL has had its
failures, but overall it has accomplished great good. I am also
a moderately successful businessman. I own one of New
York's most storied and elegant nightclubs, the Funhouse,
where jokers and nats and aces have enjoyed all the top joker
cabaret acts for more than two decades. The Funhouse has
been losing money steadily for the last five years, but no one
knows that except me and my accountant. I keep it open
because it is, after all, the Funhouse, and were it to close,
Jokertown would seem a poorer place.

Next month I will be seventy years of age.

My doctor tells me that I will not live to be seventy-one.
The cancer had already metastasized before it was diagnosed.
Even jokers cling stubbornly to life, and I have been doing
the chemotherapy and the radiation treatments for half a year
now, but the cancer shows no sign of remission.

My doctor tells me the trip I am about to embark on will
probably take months off my life. I have my prescriptions and
will dutifully continue to take the pills, but when one is
globe-hopping, radiation therapy must be forgone. I have
accepted this.

Mary and I often talked of a trip around the world, in
those days before the wild card when we were young and in
love. I could never have dreamt that I would finally take that
trip without her, in the twilight of my life, and at government
expense, as a delegate on a fact-finding mission organized and
funded by the Senate Committee on Ace Resources and
Endeavors, under the official sponsorship of the United Nations and the World Health Organization. We will visit every
continent but Antarctica and call upon thirty-nine different
countries (some only for a few hours), and our official charge
is to investigate the treatment of wild card victims in cultures
around the world.

There are twenty-one delegates, only five of whom are

jokers. I suppose my selection is a great honor, recognition of my achievements and my status as a community leader. I believe I have my good friend Dr. Tachyon to thank for it.

But then, I have my good friend Dr. Tachyon to thank for a great many things.

THE TINT OF HATRED

Part One

MONDAY, DECEMBER 1, 1986, SYRIA:

A chill, arid wind blew from the mountains of the Jabal Alawite across the lava rock and gravel desert of Badiyat Ash-sham. The wind snapped the canvas peaks of the tents huddled around the village. The gale made those in the market pull the sashes of their robes tighter against the cold. Under the beehive roof of the largest of the mud-brick buildings, a stray gust caused the flame to gutter against the bottom of an enameled teapot.

A small woman, swathed in the *chador,* the black Islamic garb, poured tea into two small cups. Except for a row of bright blue beads on the headpiece, she wore no ornamentation. She passed one of the cups to the other person in the room, a raven-haired man of medium height, whose skin glowed a shimmering, lambent emerald under a brocaded robe of azure. She could feel the warmth radiating from him.

"It will be colder for the next several days, Najib," she said as she sipped the piercingly sweet tea. "You'll be more comfortable at least."

Najib shrugged as if her words meant nothing. His lips tightened; his dark, intense gaze snared her. "It's Allah's presence that gleams," he said, his voice gruff with habitual arrogance. "You've never heard me complain, Misha, even in the heat of summer. Do you think me a woman, wailing my futile misery to the sky?"

Above the veils, Misha's eyes narrowed. "I am *Kahina,* the Seer, Najib," she answered, allowing a hint of defiance into her voice. "I know many hidden things. I know that when the heat ripples over the stones, my brother Najib wishes that he were not *Nur al-Allah,* the Light of Allah."

Najib's sudden backhanded cuff caught his sister across

the side of her face. Her head snapped sideways. Scalding hot tea burned her hand and wrist; the cup shattered on the rugs as she sprawled at his feet. His eyes, utter black against the luminescent face, glared at her as she raised her hand to her stinging cheek. She knew she dared say no more. On her knees she gathered up the shards of the teacup in silence, mopping at the puddle of tea with the hem of her robe.

"Sayyid came to me this morning," Najib said as he watched her. "He was complaining again. He says you are not a proper wife."

"Sayyid is a fatted pig," Misha answered, though she did not look up.

"He says he must force himself on you."

"He doesn't need to do so for *me*."

Najib scowled, making a sound of disgust. "*Pah!* Sayyid leads my army. It is his strategy that will sweep the *kafir* back into the sea. Allah has given him the body of a god and the mind of a conqueror, and he is obedient to me. That's why I gave you to him. The Qur'an says it: 'Men have authority over women because Allah has made the one superior to the other. Good women are obedient.' You make a mockery of Nur al-Allah's gift."

"Nur al-Allah shouldn't have given away that which completes him." Now her eyes came up, challenging him as her tiny hands closed over the pottery shards. "We were together in the womb, Brother. That's the way Allah made us. He touched you with His light and His voice, and He gave me the gift of His sight. You are His mouth, the prophet; I am your vision of the future. Don't be so foolish as to blind yourself. Your pride will defeat you."

"Then listen to the words of Allah and be humble. Be glad that Sayyid does not insist on *purdah* for you—he knows you're Kahina, so he doesn't force your seclusion. Our father should never have sent you to Damascus to be educated; the infection of the unbelievers is insidious. Misha, make Sayyid content because that will content me. My will is Allah's will."

"Only sometimes, Brother..." She paused. Her gaze went distant, her fingers clenched. She cried out as porcelain lacerated her palm. Blood drooled bright along the shallow cuts. Misha swayed, moaning, and then her gaze focused once more.

Najib moved a step closer to her. "What is it? What did you see?"

Misha cradled her injured hand to her breast, her pupils wide with pain. "All that ever matters is that which touches yourself, Najib. It doesn't matter that I hurt or that I hate my husband or that Najib and his sister Misha have been lost in Allah's roles for them. All that matters is what the Kahina can tell Nur al-Allah."

"Woman . . ." Najib began warningly. His voice had a compelling deepness now, a timbre that brought Misha's head up and made her open her mouth to begin to speak, to obey without thinking. She shivered as if the wind outside had touched her.

"Don't use the gift on me, Najib," she said gratingly. Her voice sounded harsh against that of her brother. "I'm not a supplicant. Compel me too often with Allah's tongue and you might one day find that Allah's eyes have been taken from you by my own hand."

"Then *be* Kahina, Sister," Najib answered, but it was only his own voice now. He watched as she went to an inlaid chest, took out a strip of cloth, and slowly wrapped her hand. "Tell me what you just saw. Was it the vision of the *jihad*? Did you see me holding the Caliph's scepter again?"

Misha shut her eyes, bringing back the image of the quick waking dream. "No," she told him. "This was new. In the distance I saw a falcon against the sun. As the bird flew closer, I noticed that it held a hundred people squirming in its talons. A giant stood below on a mountain, and the giant held a bow in his hands. He loosed an arrow at the bird, and the wounded falcon screamed in anger. The voices of those it held screamed also. The giant had nocked a second arrow, but now the bow began to twist in his hands, and the arrow instead struck the giant's own breast. I saw the giant fall. . . ." Misha's eyes opened. "That's all."

Najib scowled. He passed a glowing hand over his eyes. "What does it mean?"

"I don't know what it means. Allah gives me the dreams, but not always the understanding. Perhaps the giant is Sayyid—"

"It was only your own dream, not Allah's." Najib stalked away from her, and she knew that he was angry. "I'm the falcon, holding the faithful," he said. "You are the giant, large because you belong to Sayyid, who is also large. Allah would remind you of the consequence of defiance." He faced away from Misha, closing the shutters of the window against the brilliant desert sun. Outside the muzzein called from the village mosque: "*A shhadu allaa alaha illa llah*"—Allah is great. I bear witness that there is no God but Allah.

"All you want is your conquest, the dream of the *jihad*. You want to be the new Muhammad," Misha answered spitefully. "You won't accept any other interpretation."

"*In sha'allah*," Najib answered: if Allah wills. He refused to face her. "Some people Allah has visited with His dreadful Scourge, showing their sins with their rotting, twisted flesh. Others, like Sayyid, Allah has favored, gifting them. Each has been given his due. He has chosen *me* to lead the faithful. I only do what I *must* do—I have Sayyid, who guides my armies, and I fight also with the hidden ones like al-Muezzin. You lead too. You are Kahina, and you are also *Fqihas*, the one the women look to for guidance."

The Light of Allah turned back into the room. In the shuttered dimness he was a spectral presence. "And as I do Allah's will, *you* must do mine."

MONDAY, DECEMBER 1, 1986, NEW YORK:

The press reception was chaos.

Senator Gregg Hartmann finally escaped to an empty corner behind one of the Christmas trees, his wife Ellen and his aide John Werthen following. Gregg surveyed the room with a distinct frown. He shook his head toward the Justice Department ace Billy Ray—Carnifex—and the government security man who tried to join them, waving them back.

Gregg had spent the last hour fending off reporters, smiling blankly for video cameras, and blinking into the constant storm lightning of electronic flashes. The room was noisy with shouted questions and the *click-whirr* of high-speed Nikons. Musak played seasonal tunes over the ceiling speakers.

The main press contingent was now gathered around Dr. Tachyon, Chrysalis, and Peregrine. Tachyon's scarlet hair gleamed like a beacon in the crowd; Peregrine and Chrysalis seemed to be competing to see who could pose most provocatively for the cameras. Nearby, Jack Braun—Golden Boy, the Judas Ace—was being pointedly ignored.

The mob had thinned a bit since Hiram Worchester's staff from the Aces High had set up the buffet tables; some of the press had staked permanent claims around the well-freighted trays.

"Sorry, boss," John said at Gregg's elbow. Even in the cool room the aide was perspiring. Blinking Christmas lights reflected from his beaded forehead: red, then blue, then green. "Somebody on the airport staff dropped the ball. It wasn't supposed to be this kind of free-for-all. I told them I wanted the press escorted in *after* you guys were settled. They'd ask a few questions, then . . ." He shrugged. "I'll take the blame. I should have checked to make sure everything had been done."

Ellen gave John a withering glance but said nothing.

"If John's apologizing, make him grovel first, Senator. What a mess." That last was a whisper in Gregg's ear—his other longtime aide, Amy Sorenson, was circulating through the crowd as one of the security personnel. Her two-way radio was linked directly to a wireless receiver in Gregg's ear. She fed him information, gave him names or details concerning the people he met. Gregg's own memory for names and faces was quite good, but Amy was an excellent backup. Between the two of them Gregg rarely missed giving those around him a personal greeting.

John's fear of Gregg's anger was a bright, pulsing purple amidst the jumble of his emotions. Gregg could feel Ellen's placid, dull acceptance, colored slightly with annoyance. "It's okay, John," Gregg said softly, though underneath he was seething. That part of him that he thought of as Puppetman squirmed restlessly, begging to be let loose to play with the cascading emotions in the room. *Half of them are our puppets, controllable. Look, there's Father Squid over near the door, trying to get away from that woman reporter. Feel his scarlet distress even as he's smiling? He'd love to slither away and he's too polite to do it. We could fuel that frustration into rage, make him curse the woman. We could feed on that. All it would take is the smallest nudge . . .*

But Gregg couldn't do that, not with the aces gathered here, the ones Gregg didn't dare take as puppets because they had mental abilities of their own, or because he simply felt the prospect too risky: Golden Boy, Fantasy, Mistral, Chrysalis. And the one he feared most of all: Tachyon. *If they even had an inkling of Puppetman's existence, if they knew what I've done to feed him, Tachyon'd have them on me in a pack, the way he did with the Masons.*

Gregg took a deep breath. The corner smelled overbearingly of pine. "Thanks, boss," John was saying. Already his lilac fear was receding. Across the room, Gregg saw Father Squid finally disengage himself from the reporter and shamble pitifully toward Hiram's buffet on his tentacles. The reporter saw Gregg at the same moment and gave him a strange, piercing glance. She strode toward him.

Amy had seen the movement as well. "Sara Morgenstern, *Post* correspondent," she whispered in Gregg's ear. "Pulitzer, '76, for her work on the Great Jokertown Riot. Cowrote the nasty article on SCARE in July's *Newsweek*. Just had a makeover too. Looks totally different."

Amy's warning startled Gregg—he hadn't recognized her. Gregg remembered the article; it had stopped just short of libel, intimating that Gregg and the SCARE aces had been involved in government suppression of facts concerning the Swarm Mother attack. He remembered Morgenstern from various press functions, always the one with the hardball questions, with a sharp edge to her voice. He might have taken her for a puppet, just for spite, but she had never come close to him. Whenever they had been at the same affairs, she had stayed well away.

Now, seeing her approach, he froze for an instant. She had indeed changed. Sara had always been slim, boyish. That was accentuated tonight; she wore tight, black slacks and a clinging blouse. She'd dyed her hair blond, and her makeup accentuated her cheekbones and large, faintly blue eyes. She looked distressingly familiar.

Gregg was suddenly cold and afraid.

Inside, Puppetman howled at a remembered loss.

"Gregg, are you all right?" Ellen's hand touched his shoulder. Gregg shivered at his spouse's touch, shaking his head.

"I'm fine," he said brusquely. He put on his professional smile, moving out from the corner. Alongside him Ellen and John flanked him in practiced choreography. "Ms. Morgenstern," Gregg said warmly, extending his hand and forcing his voice into a calmness he didn't feel. "I think you know John, but my wife Ellen . . . ?"

Sara Morgenstern nodded perfunctorily toward Ellen, but her gaze stayed with Gregg. She had an odd, strained smile on her face that seemed half-challenge and half-invitation. "Senator," she said, "I hope you're looking forward to this trip as much as I am."

She took his proffered hand. Without volition, Puppetman

used the moment of contact. As he had done with every new puppet, he traced the neural pathways back to the brain, opening the doors that would, later, allow him access from a distance. He found the locked gates of her emotions, the turbulent colors swirling behind, and he greedily, possessively, touched them. He unfastened the locks and pins, swung open the entrance.

The red-black loathing that spilled out from behind sent him reeling back. The abhorrence was directed toward *him*, all of it. Totally unexpected, the fury of the emotion was like nothing he'd experienced. Its intensity threatened to drown him, it drove him back. Puppetman gasped; Gregg forced himself to show nothing. He let his hand drop as Puppetman moaned in his head, and the fear that had touched him a moment ago redoubled.

She looks like Andrea, like Succubus—the resemblance is startling. And she detests me; God, how she hates.

"Senator?" Sara repeated.

"Yes, I'm very much looking forward to this," he said automatically. "Our society's attitudes toward the victims of the wild card virus have changed for the worse in the last year. In some ways people like the Reverend Leo Barnett would have us regress to the oppression of the fifties. For less enlightened countries, the situation is far, far worse. We can offer them understanding, hope, and help. And we'll learn something ourselves. Dr. Tachyon and myself have great optimism for this trip, or we wouldn't have fought so hard to bring it about."

The words came with rehearsed smoothness while he recovered. He could hear the friendly casualness of his voice, felt his mouth pull into a proud half-smile. But none of it touched him. He could barely avoid staring rudely at Sara. At this woman who reminded him too much of Andrea Whitman, of Succubus.

I loved her. I couldn't save her.

Sara seemed to sense his fascination, for she cocked her head with that same odd challenge. "It's also an entertaining little junket, a three-month tour of the world at the taxpayer's expense. Your wife goes with you, your good friends like Dr. Tachyon and Hiram Worchester. . ."

At his side Gregg felt Ellen's irritation. She was too practiced a politician's wife to respond, but he could feel her sudden alertness, a jungle cat watching for a weakness in her prey. Off balance, Gregg frowned a moment too late. "I'm surprised a reporter of your experience would believe that, Ms. Morgenstern. This trip also means giving up the holiday season—normally, I go home after the congressional break. It means stops at places that aren't exactly on Fodor's recommended list. It means meetings, briefings, endless press conferences, and a ton of paperwork that I can certainly do without. I guarantee you this isn't a pleasure trip. I'll have more to do than watch the proceedings and cable a thousand words back home every day."

He felt the black hatred swelling in her, and the power in him ached to be used. *Let me take her. Let me dampen that fire. Take away that hatred and she'll tell you what she knows. Disarm her.*

She's yours, he answered. Puppetman leapt out. Gregg had encountered hatreds before, a hundred times, but none had ever been focused on him. He found control of the emotion elusive and slippery; her loathing pushed at his control like a palpable, living entity, driving Puppetman back.

What the hell is she hiding? What caused this?

"You sound defensive, Senator," Sara said. "Still, a reporter can't help but think that the main purpose of the trip, especially for a potential '88 presidential candidate, might be to finally erase the memories of a decade ago."

Gregg could not help the intake of breath: *Andrea, Succubus.* Sara grinned: a predator's smile. He readied himself to assault her hatred again.

"I'd say the Great Jokertown Riot obsesses both of us, Senator," she continued, her voice deceivingly light. "I know it did when I wrote my piece on it. And your behavior after Succubus's death cost you the Democratic nomination that year. After all, she was only a whore—wasn't she, Senator? —and not worth your . . . your little *breakdown*." The reminder made him flush. "I'll wager we've both thought about that moment every day since then," Sara continued. "It's been ten years now, and *I* still remember."

Puppetman wailed, retreating. Gregg was startled into silence. *My God, what does she know, what is she hinting at?*

He had no time to formulate a reply. Amy's voice spoke in his ear again. "Digger Downs is heading over at a trot, Senator. He's with *Aces* magazine—covers the entertainment types; a real sleazeball, if you ask me. Guess he saw Morgenstern and figured he'd listen in to a *good* reporter—"

"Hiya, folks," Downs's voice intruded before Amy had finished speaking. Gregg looked momentarily away from Sara to see a short, pallid young man. Downs fidgeted nervously, sniffing as if he had a head cold. "Mind another reporter's nosing in, Sara love?"

Downs was a maddening interruption, his manner rude and falsely familiar. He seemed to sense Gregg's turmoil. He grinned and looked from Sara to Gregg, ignoring Ellen and John.

"I think I've said all I want to—for the moment," Sara answered. Her pale aqua eyes were still locked on Gregg's; her face seemed childlike with feigned innocence. Then, with a lithe turn, she spun away from him, going toward Tachyon. Gregg stared after her.

"Chick's looking damn good these days, ain't she, Senator?" Downs grinned again. "Begging your pardon, of course, Mrs. Hartmann. Hey, let me introduce myself. I'm Digger Downs, with *Aces* magazine, and I'll be tagging along on this little venture. We'll be seeing a lot of each other."

Gregg, watching Sara disappear into the crowd around Tachyon, realized that Downs was staring at him strangely. With an effort he forced his attention away from Sara. "Pleased to meet you," he said to Downs.

His smile felt wooden. It made his cheeks ache.

FROM *THE JOURNAL OF XAVIER DESMOND*

DECEMBER 1/NEW YORK CITY:

The journey is off to an inauspicious start. For the last hour
we have been holding on the runway at Tomlin International,
waiting for clearance for takeoff. The problem, we are informed, is not here, but down in Havana. So we wait.

Our plane is a custom 747 that the press has dubbed the
Stacked Deck. The entire central cabin has been converted to
our requirements, the seats replaced with a small medical
laboratory, a press room for the print journalists, and a
miniature television studio for their electronic counterparts.
The newsmen themselves have been segregated in the tail.
Already they've made it their own. I was back there twenty
minutes ago and found a poker game in progress. The business-
class cabin is full of aides, assistants, secretaries, publicists,
and security personnel. First class is supposedly reserved
exclusively for the delegates.

As there are only twenty-one delegates, we rattle around
like peas in a pod. Even here the ghettoes persist—jokers
tend to sit with jokers, nats with nats, aces with aces.

Hartmann is the only man aboard who seems entirely
comfortable with all three groups. He greeted me warmly at
the press conference and sat with Howard and myself for a
few moments after boarding, talking earnestly about his
hopes for the trip. It is difficult not to like the senator.
Jokertown has delivered him huge majorities in each of his
campaigns as far back as his term as mayor, and no wonder—
no other politician has worked so long and hard to defend
jokers' rights. Hartmann gives me hope; he's living proof that
there can indeed be trust and mutual respect between joker
and nat. He's a decent, honorable man, and in these days
when fanatics such as Leo Barnett are inflaming the old
hatreds and prejudices, jokers need all the friends they can
get in the halls of power.

Dr. Tachyon and Senator Hartmann co-chair the delega
tion. Tachyon arrived dressed like a foreign corresponder
from some *film noir* classic, in a trench coat covered wit
belts, buttons, and epaulettes, a snap-brim fedora rakishl
tilted to one side. The fedora sports a foot-long red feathe
however, and I cannot begin to imagine where one goes t
purchase a powder-blue crushed-velvet trench coat. A pit
that those foreign-correspondent films were all in black an
white.

Tachyon would like to think that he shares Hartmann'
lack of prejudice toward jokers, but that's not strictly true
He labors unceasingly in his clinic, and one cannot doubt tha
he cares, and cares deeply . . . many jokers think of him as
saint, a hero . . . yet, when one has known the doctor as lon
as I have, deeper truths become apparent. On some unspc
ken level he thinks of his good works in Jokertown as
penance. He does his best to hide it, but even after all thes
years you can see the revulsion in his eyes. Dr. Tachyon and
are "friends," we have known each other for decades nov
and I believe with all my heart that he sincerely cares fo
me . . . but not for a second have I ever felt that he consider
me an equal, as Hartmann does. The senator treats me like
man, even an important man, courting me as he might an
political leader with votes to deliver. To Dr. Tachyon, I wi
always be a joker.

Is that his tragedy, or mine?

Tachyon knows nothing of the cancer. A symptom tha
our friendship is as diseased as my body? Perhaps. He has nc
been my personal physician for many years now. My doctor i
a joker, as are my accountant, my attorney, my broker, an
even my banker—the world has changed since the Chas
dismissed me, and as mayor of Jokertown I am obliged t
practice my own personal brand of affirmative action.

We have just been cleared for takeoff. The seat-hoppin
is over, people are belting themselves in. It seems I carr
Jokertown with me wherever I go—Howard Mueller sit
closest to me, his seat customized to accommodate his nine-foe
tall form and the immense length of his arms. He's bette
known as Troll, and he works as chief of security at Tachyon'
clinic, but I note that he does not sit with Tachyon among th
aces. The other three joker delegates—Father Squid, Chrysa
lis, and the poet Dorian Wilde—are also here in the cente

section of first class. Is it coincidence, prejudice, or shame that puts us here, in the seats furthest from the windows? Being a joker makes one a tad paranoid about these things, I fear. The politicians, of both the domestic and UN varieties, have clustered to our right, the aces forward of us (aces up front, of course, of course) and to our left. Must stop now, the stewardess has asked me to put my tray table back up.

Airborne. New York and Robert Tomlin International Airport are far behind us, and Cuba waits ahead. From what I've heard, it will be an easy and pleasant first stop. Havana is almost as American as Las Vegas or Miami Beach, albeit considerably more decadent and wicked. I may actually have friends there—some of the top joker entertainers go on to the Havana casinos after getting their starts in the Funhouse and the Chaos Club. I must remind myself to stay away from the gaming tables, however; joker luck is notoriously bad.

As soon as the seat belt sign went off, a number of the aces ascended to the first-class lounge. I can hear their laughter drifting down the spiral stairway—Peregrine, pretty young Mistral—who looks just like the college student she is when not in her flying gear—boisterous Hiram Worchester, and Asta Lenser, the ballerina from the ABT whose ace name is Fantasy. Already they are a tight little clique, a "fun bunch" for whom nothing could possibly go wrong. The golden people, and Tachyon very much in their midst. Is it the aces or the women that draw him? I wonder? Even my dear friend Angela, who still loves the man deeply after twenty-odd years, admits that Dr. Tachyon thinks mainly with his penis where women are concerned.

Yet even among the aces there are the odd men out. Jones, the black strongman from Harlem (like Troll and Hiram W. and Peregrine, he requires a custom seat, in his case to support his extraordinary weight), is nursing a beer and reading a copy of *Sports Illustrated*. Radha O'Reilly is just as solitary, gazing out the window. She seems very quiet. Billy Ray and Joanne Jefferson, the two Justice Department aces who head up our security contingent, are not delegates and thus are seated back in the second section.

And then there is Jack Braun. The tensions that swirl around him are almost palpable. Most of the other delegates are polite to him, but no one is truly friendly, and he's being openly shunned by some, such as Hiram Worchester. For Dr.

Tachyon, clearly Braun does not even exist. I wonder whose idea it was to bring him on this trip? Certainly not Tachyon's, and it seems too politically dangerous for Hartmann to be responsible. A gesture to appease the conservatives on SCARE perhaps? Or are there ramifications that I have not considered?

Braun glances up at the stairway from time to time, as if he would love nothing so much as to join the happy group upstairs, but remains firmly in his seat. It is hard to credit that this smooth-faced, blond-haired boy in the tailored safari jacket is really the notorious Judas Ace of the fifties. He's my age or close to it, but he looks barely twenty ... the kind of boy who might have taken pretty young Mistral to her senior prom a few years back and gotten her home well before midnight.

One of the reporters, a man named Downs from *Aces* magazine, was up here earlier, trying to get Braun to consent to an interview. He was persistent, but Braun's refusal was firm, and Downs finally gave up. Instead he handed out copies of the latest issue of *Aces* and then sauntered up to the lounge, no doubt to pester someone else. I am not a regular reader of *Aces*, but I accepted a copy and suggested to Downs that his publisher consider a companion periodical, to be called *Jokers*. He was not overly enthused about the idea.

The issue features a rather striking cover photograph of the Turtle's shell outlined against the oranges and reds of sunset, blurbed with "The Turtle—Dead or Alive?" The Turtle has not been seen since Wild Card Day, back in September, when he was napalmed and crashed into the Hudson. Twisted and burnt pieces of his shell were found on the riverbed, though no body has ever been recovered. Several hundred people claim to have seen the Turtle near dawn the following day, flying an older shell in the sky over Jokertown, but since he has not reappeared since, some are putting that sighting down to hysteria and wishful thinking.

I have no opinion on the Turtle, though I would hate to think that he was truly dead. Many jokers believe that he is one of us, that his shell conceals some unspeakable joker deformity. Whether that is true or not, he has been a good friend to Jokertown for a long, long time.

There is, however, an aspect to this trip that no one ever speaks of, although Downs's article brings it to mind. Perhaps it falls to me to mention the unmentionable then. The truth is, all that laughter up in the lounge has a slightly nervous ring to it, and it is no coincidence that this junket, under discussion for so many years, was put together so swiftly in the past two months. They want to get us out of town for a while—not just the jokers, the aces too. The aces *especially*, one might even say.

This last Wild Card Day was a catastrophe for the city, and for every victim of the virus everywhere. The level of violence was shocking and made headlines across the nation. The still-unsolved murder of the Howler, the dismemberment of a child ace in the midst of a huge crowd at Jetboy's Tomb, the attack on Aces High, the destruction of the Turtle (or at least his shell), the wholesale slaughter at the Cloisters, where a dozen bodies were brought out in pieces, the predawn aerial battle that lit up the entire East Side . . . days and even weeks later the authorities were still not certain that they had an accurate death toll.

One old man was found literally embedded in a solid brick wall, and when they began to chip him out, they found they could not tell where his flesh ended and the wall began. The autopsy revealed a ghastly mess inside, where his internal organs were fused with the bricks that penetrated them.

A *Post* photographer snapped a picture of that old man trapped in his wall. He looks so gentle and sweet. The police subsequently announced that the old man was an ace himself, and moreover a notorious criminal, that he was responsible for the murders of Kid Dinosaur and the Howler, the attempted murder of the Turtle, the attack on Aces High, the battle over the East River, the ghastly blood rites performed at the Cloisters, and a whole range of lesser crimes. A number of aces came forward to support this explanation, but the public does not seem convinced. According to the polls, more people believe the conspiracy theory put forward in the *National Informer*—that the killings were independent, caused by powerful aces known and unknown carrying out personal vendettas, using their powers in utter disregard for law and public safety, and that afterward those aces conspired with each other and the police to cover up their atrocities, blaming everything on one crippled old man who happened to be conveniently dead, clearly at the hands of some ace.

Already several books have been announced, each purporting to explain what *really* happened—the immoral opportunism of the publishing industry knows no bounds. Koch, ever aware of the prevailing winds, has ordered several cases re-opened and has instructed the IAD to investigate the police role.

Jokers are pitiful and loathed. Aces have great power, and for the first time in many years a sizable segment of the public has begun to distrust those aces and fear that power. No wonder that demagogues like Leo Barnett have swelled so vastly in the public mind of late.

So I'm convinced that our tour has a hidden agenda; to wash away the blood with some "good ink," as they say, to defuse the fear, to win back trust and take everyone's mind off Wild Card Day.

I admit to mixed feelings about aces, some of whom definitely do abuse their power. Nonetheless, as a joker, I find myself desperately hoping that we succeed...and desperately fearing the consequences if we do not.

BEASTS OF BURDEN

John J. Miller

"From envy, hatred, and malice, and all uncharitableness,
Good Lord, deliver us."
—The Litany, *Book of Common Prayer*

His rudimentary sexual organs were dysfunctional, but his
mounts thought of him as masculine, perhaps because his
stunted, wasted body looked more male than female. What
he thought of himself was an unopened book. He never
communicated about matters of that sort.

He had no name but that borrowed from folklore and
given to him by his mounts—Ti Malice—and he didn't really
care what they called him as long as they addressed him with
respect. He liked the dark because his weak eyes were
unduly sensitive to light. He never ate because he had no
teeth to chew or tongue to taste. He never drank alcohol
because the primitive sack that was his stomach couldn't
digest it. Sex was out of the question.

But he still enjoyed gourmet foods and vintage wines and
expensive liquors and all possible varieties of sexual experience. He had his mounts.

And he always was looking for more.

i.

Chrysalis lived in the Jokertown slum where she owned
a bar, so she was accustomed to viewing scenes of poverty
and misery. But Jokertown was a slum in the most affluent
country on the earth, and Bolosse, the slum district of
Port-au-Prince, Haiti's sprawling waterfront capital city, was
in one of the poorest.

From the outside the hospital looked like a set from a

B-grade horror movie about an eighteenth-century insane asylum. The wall around it was crumbling stone, the sidewalk leading to it was rotting concrete, and the building itself was filthy from years of accumulated bird shit and grime. Inside, it was worse.

The walls were abstract designs of peeling paint and mildew. The bare wooden floors creaked ominously and once Mordecai Jones, the four-hundred-and-fifty-pound ace called the Harlem Hammer, stepped on a section that gave way. He would have fallen all the way through the floor if an alert Hiram Worchester hadn't quickly relieved him of nine tenths of his weight. The smell clinging to the corridors was indescribable, but was mostly compounded of the various odors of death.

But the very worst, thought Chrysalis, were the patients, especially the children. They lay uncomplainingly on filthy bare mattresses that reeked of sweat, urine, and mildew, their bodies racked by diseases banished long ago in America and wasted by the bloat of malnutrition. They watched their visitors troop by without curiosity or comprehension, serene hoplessness filling their eyes.

It was better being a joker, she thought, though she loathed what the wild card virus had done to her once-beautiful body.

Chrysalis couldn't stand any more of the unrelievable suffering. She left the hospital after passing through the first ward and returned to the waiting motorcade. The driver of the jeep she'd been assigned to looked at her curiously, but said nothing. He hummed a happy little tune while they waited for the others, occasionally singing a few off key phrases in Haitian Creole.

The tropical sun was hot. Chrysalis, bundled in an all-enveloping hood and cloak to protect her delicate flesh and skin from the sun's burning rays, watched a group of children playing across the street from the run-down hospital. Sweat trickling in tickling rivulets down her back, she almost envied the children in the cool freedom of their near nakedness. They seemed to be fishing for something in the depths of the storm drain that ran under the street. It took Chrysalis a moment to realize what they were doing, but when she did, all thoughts of envy disappeared. They were drawing water out of the drain and pouring it into battered, rusty pots and cans. Sometimes they stopped to drink a mouthful.

She looked away, wondering if joining Tachyon's little traveling show had been a mistake. It had sounded like a good idea when Tachyon had invited her. It was, after all, an opportunity to travel around the world at government expense while rubbing shoulders with a variety of important and influential people. There was no telling what interesting tidbits of information she would be able to pick up. It had seemed like such a good idea at the time. . . .

"Well, my dear, if I hadn't actually seen it with my own eyes, I'd say you hadn't the stomach for this sort of thing."

She smiled mirthlessly as Dorian Wilde heaved himself into the backseat of the jeep next to her. She wasn't in the mood for the poet's famous wit.

"I certainly wasn't expecting treatment like this," she said in her cultured British accent as Dr. Tachyon, Senator Hartmann, Hiram Worchester, and other important and influential politicians and aces streamed toward the limos waiting for them, while Chrysalis, Wilde, and the other obvious jokers on the tour had to make do with the dirty, dented jeeps clustered at the rear of the cavalcade.

"You should've," Wilde said. He was a large man whose delicate features were loosing their handsomeness to bloat. He wore an Edwardian outfit that was in desperate need of cleaning and pressing, and enough floral-scented body wash to make Chrysalis glad that they were in an open vehicle. He waved his left hand languorously as he talked and kept his right in the pocket of his jacket. "Jokers, after all, are the niggers of the world." He pursed his lips and glanced at their driver, who, like ninety-five percent of Haiti's population, was black. "A statement not without irony on this island."

Chrysalis grabbed the back of the driver's seat as the jeep jounced away from the curb, following the rest of the cavalcade as it pulled away from the hospital. The air was cool against Chrysalis's face hidden deep within the folds of her hood, but the rest of her body was drenched with sweat. She fantasized about a long, cool drink and a slow, cool bath for the hour it took the motorcade to wend its way through Port-au-Prince's narrow, twisting streets. When they finally reached the Royal Haitian Hotel, she stepped down into the street almost before the jeep stopped, anxious for the waiting coolness of the lobby, and was instantly engulfed by a sea of beseeching faces, all babbling in Haitian Creole. She couldn't understand what the beggars were saying, but she didn't have to speak their language to understand the want and desperation in their eyes, tattered clothing, and brittle, emaciated bodies.

The press of imploring beggars pinned her against the side of the jeep, and the immediate rush of pity she'd felt for their obvious need was submerged in fear fueled by their piteously beseeching voices and the dozens of thin, sticklike arms thrust out at her.

The driver, before she could say or do anything, reached under the jeep's dashboard and grabbed a long, thin wooden rod that looked like a truncated broomstick, stood up, and began swinging it at the beggars while shouting rapid, harsh phrases in Creole.

Chrysalis heard, and saw, the skinny arm of a young boy snap at the first blow. The second opened the scalp of an old man, and the third missed as the intended victim managed to duck away.

The driver drew the weapon back to strike again. Chrysalis, her usually cautious reserve overcome by sudden outrage, turned to him and screamed, "Stop! Stop that!" and with the sudden movement the hood fell away from her face, revealing her features for the first time. Revealing, that is, what features she had.

Her skin and flesh were as clear as the finest blown glass, without flaw or bubble. Besides the muscles that clung to her skull and jaw, only the meat of her lips was visible. They were dark red pads on the gleaming expanse of her skull. Her eyes, floating in the depths of their naked sockets, were as blue as fragments of sky.

The driver gaped at her. The beggars, whose importunings had turned to wails of fear, all fell silent at once, as if an invisible octopus had simultaneously slapped a tentacle over each one's mouth. The silence dragged on for a half dozen heartbeats, and then one of the beggars whispered a name in a soft, awed voice.

"Madame Brigitte."

It passed among the beggars like a whispered invocation, until even those who had crowded around the other vehicles in the motorcade were craning their necks to get a glimpse of her. She pressed back against the jeep, the concentrated stares of the beggars, mixed fear and awe and wonder, frightening her. The tableau held for another moment until the driver spoke a harsh phrase and gestured with his stick. The crowd dispersed at once, but not, however, without some of the beggars shooting Chrysalis final glances of mingled awe and dread.

Chrysalis turned to the driver. He was a tall, thin black in a cheap, ill-fitting blue serge suit and an open-necked shirt. He looked back at her sullenly, but Chrysalis couldn't really read his expression because of the dark sunglasses he wore.

"Do you speak English?" she asked him.

"Oui. A little." Chrysalis could hear the harsh edge of fear in his voice, and she wondered what put it there.

"Why did you strike them?"

He shrugged. "These beggars are peasants. Scum from the country, come to Port-au-Prince to beg on the generousness of people as yourself. I tell them to go."

"Speak loudly and carry a big stick," Wilde said sardonically from his seat in the back of the jeep.

Chrysalis glared at him. "You were a big help."

He yawned. "I make it a habit never to brawl in the streets. It's so vulgar."

Chrysalis snorted, turned back to the driver. "Who," she asked, "is 'Madame Brigitte'?"

The driver shrugged in a particularly Gallic manner, illustrating again the cultural ties Haiti had to the country from which she'd been politically independent for nearly two hundred years. "She is a loa, the wife of Baron Samedi."

"Baron Samedi?"

"A most powerful loa. He is the lord and guardian of the cemetary. The keeper of the crossroads."

"What's a loa?"

He frowned, shrugged almost angrily. "A loa is a spirit, a part of God, very powerful and divine."

"And I resemble this Madame Brigitte?"

He said nothing, but continued to stare at her from behind his dark glasses, and despite the afternoon's tropical heat Chrysalis felt a shiver run down her spine. She felt naked, despite the voluminous cloak she wore. It wasn't a bodily nakedness. She was, in fact, accustomed to going half-naked in public as a private obscene gesture to the world, making sure that everyone saw what she had to see every time she looked in a mirror. It was a spiritual nakedness that she felt, as if everyone who was staring at her was trying to discover who she was, was trying to divine the precious secrets that were the only masks that she had. She felt a desperate need to get away from all the staring eyes, but she wouldn't let herself run from them. It took all her nerve, all the cool she could muster, but she managed to walk into the hotel lobby with precise, measured steps.

Inside it was cool and dark. Chrysalis leaned against a high-backed chair that looked as if it'd been made sometime in the last century and dusted sometime in the last decade. She took a deep, calming breath and let it out slowly.

"What was that all about?"

She looked over her shoulder to see Peregrine regarding her with concern. The winged woman had been in one of the limos at the head of the parade, but she'd obviously seen the byplay that had centered around Chrysalis's jeep. Peregrine's beautiful, satin-feathered wings only added a touch of the exotic to her lithe, tanned sensuality. She should be easy to resent, Chrysalis thought. Her affliction had brought her fame, notoriety, even her own television show. But she looked genuinely concerned, genuinely worried, and Chrysalis felt in need of sympathetic company.

But she couldn't explain something to Peregrine that she only half-understood herself. She shrugged. "Nothing." She looked around the lobby that was rapidly filling with tour personnel. "I could use a few moments of peace and quiet. And a drink."

"So could I," a masculine voice announced before Peregrine could speak. "Let's find the bar and I'll tell you some of the facts of Haitian life."

Both women turned to look at the man who'd spoken. He was six feet tall, give or take, and strongly built. He wore a suit of white, tropical-weight linen that was immaculately clean and sharply creased. There was something odd about his face. His features didn't quite match. His chin was too long, his nose too broad. His eyes were misaligned and too bright. Chrysalis knew him only by reputation. He was a Justice Department ace, part of the security contingent Washington had assigned to Tachyon's tour. His name was Billy Ray. Some wit at JD with a classical education had tagged him with the nickname Carnifex. He liked it. He was an authentic badass.

"What do you mean?" Chrysalis asked.

Ray looked around the lobby, his lips quirking. "Let's find the bar and talk things over. Privately."

Chrysalis glanced at Peregrine, and the winged woman read the appeal in her eyes.

"Mind if I tag along?" she asked.

"Hey, not at all." Ray frankly admired her lithe, tanned form, and the black-and-white-striped sundress that showed it off. He licked his lips as Chrysalis and Peregrine exchanged unbelieving glances.

The hotel lounge was doing desultory afternoon business. They found an empty table surrounded by other empty tables and gave their orders to a red-uniformed waiter who couldn't decide whom to stare at, Peregrine or Chrysalis. They sat in silence until he'd returned with the drinks, and Chrysalis drank down the thimbleful of amaretto that he'd brought.

"The travel brochures all said that Haiti's supposed to be a bloody tropical paradise," she said in a tone that indicated she felt the brochures all lied.

"I'll take you to paradise, babe," Ray said.

Chrysalis liked it when men paid attention to her, sometimes too much. Sometimes, she realized, she conducted her affairs for all the wrong reasons. Even Brennan (Yeoman, she reminded herself, Yeoman. She had to remember that she wasn't supposed to know his real name) had become her lover because she'd forced herself on him. It was, she supposed, the sense of power that she liked, the control she had when she made men come to her. But making men make love to her body was also, she recognized with her habit of relentless self-scrutiny, another way to punish a revulsed world. But Brennan (Yeoman, damnit) had never been revulsed. He had never made her turn out the lights before kissing her, and he had always made love with his eyes open and watching her heart beat, her lungs bellow, her breath catch behind tightly clenched teeth. . . .

Ray's foot moved under the table, touching hers, drawing her back from thoughts of the past, of what was over. She smiled a lazy smile at him, gleaming teeth set in a gleaming skull. There was something about Ray that was unsettling. He talked too loud, he smiled too much, and some part of him, his hands or his feet or his mouth, was always in motion. He had a reputation for violence. Not that she had anything against violence—as long as it wasn't directed at her. For goodness's sake, even she'd lost track of all the men Yeoman had sent to their reward since his arrival in the city. But, paradoxically, Brennan wasn't a violent man. Ray, according to his reputation, had a habit of running amuck. Compared to Brennan, he was a self-centered bore. She wondered if she'd be comparing all the men she would know to her archer, and she felt a rush of annoyance, and regret.

"I doubt that you'd have the skill to transport me to the dreariest shithole in the poorest part of Jokertown, dear boy, let alone paradise."

Peregrine squelched a twitchy smile and looked away. Chrysalis felt Billy's foot move away as he fixed her with a hard, dangerous stare. He was about to say something vicious when Dr. Tachyon interrupted by flopping into the empty chair next to Peregrine. Ray shot Chrysalis a look that told her the remark wouldn't be forgotten.

"My dear." Tachyon bowed over Peregrine's hand, kissed it, and nodded greetings to everyone else. It was common knowledge that he was hot over the glamorous flyer, but then, Chrysalis reflected, most men were. Tachyon, however, was self-confident enough to be determined in his pursuit, and thickheaded enough not to call it off, even after numerous polite rebuffs on Peregrine's part.

"How was the meeting with Dr. Tessier?" Peregrine asked, removing her hand delicately from Tachyon's grasp when he showed no inclination of letting it go on his own.

Tachyon frowned, whether in disappointment at Peregrine's continuing coolness or in remembrance of his visit to the Haitian hospital, Chrysalis couldn't tell.

"Dreadful," he murmured, "simply dreadful." He caught the eye of a waiter and gestured him over. "Bring me something cool, with lots of rum in it." He looked around the table. "Anyone else?"

Chrysalis tinged a red-painted fingernail—it looked like a rose petal floating on bone—against her empty cordial glass.

"Yes. And more, um?"

"Amaretto."

"Amaretto for the lady there."

The waiter sidled up to Chrysalis and slipped the glass out from in front of her without making eye contact. She could feel his fear. It was funny, in a way, that someone could be afraid of her, but it angered her as well, almost as much as the guilt in Tachyon's eyes every time he looked at her.

Tachyon ran his fingers dramatically through his long, curly red hair. "There wasn't much incidence of wild card virus that I could see." He fell silent, sighed gustily. "And Tessier himself wasn't overly concerned about it. But everyting else ... by the Ideal, everything else ..."

"What do you mean?" Peregrine asked.

"You were there. That hospital was as crowded as a Jokertown bar on Saturday night and about as sanitary. Typhus patients were cheek to jowl with tuberculosis patients and elephantiasis patients and AIDS patients and patients suffering from half a hundred other diseases that have been eradicated everywhere else in the civilized world. As I was having a private chat with the hospital administrator, the electricity went out twice. I tried to call the hotel, but the phones weren't working. Dr. Tessier told me that they're low on blood, antibiotics, painkillers, and just about all medicinals. Fortunately, Tessier and many of the other doctors are masters at utilizing the medicinal properties of native Haitian flora. Tessier showed me a thing or two he's done with distillations from common weeds and such that was remarkable. In fact, someone should write an article on the drugs they've concocted. Some of their discoveries deserve widespread attention in the outside world. But for all their efforts, all their dedication, they're still losing the fight." The waiter brought Tachyon's drink in a tall slim glass garnished with slices of fresh fruit and a paper umbrella. Tachyon threw out the fruit and paper umbrella and swallowed half his drink in a single gulp. "I have never seen such misery and suffering."

"Welcome to the Third World," Ray said.

"Indeed." Tachyon finished off his drink and fixed Chrysalis with his lilac-colored eyes.

"Now, what was that disturbance in front of the hotel?"

Chrysalis shrugged. "The driver started beating the beggars with a stick—"

"A *cocomacaques*."

"I beg your pardon?" Tachyon said, turning to Ray.

"It's called a *cocomacaques*. It's a walking stick, polished with oil. Hard as an iron bar. A real nasty weapon." There was approval in Ray's voice. "The Tonton Macoute carry them."

"What?" three voices asked simultaneously.

Ray smiled a smile of superior knowledge. "Tonton Macoute. That's what the peasants call them. Essentially means 'bogeyman.' Officially they're called the VSN, the *Volontaires de la Securite Nationale*." Ray had an atrocious accent. "They're Duvalier's secret police, headed by a man named Charlemagne Calixte. He's black as a coal mine at midnight and ugly as sin. Somebody tried to poison him once. He lived through it, but it scarred his face terribly. He's the only reason Baby Doc's still in power."

"Duvalier has his secret police acting as our chaffeurs?" Tachyon asked, astonished. "Whatever for?"

Ray looked at him as if he were a child. "So they can watch us. They watch everybody. It's their job." Ray laughed a sudden, barking laugh. "They're easy enough to spot. They all have dark sunglasses and wear blue suits. Sort of a badge of office. There's one over there."

Ray gestured to the far corner of the lounge. The Tonton Macoute sat at an otherwise empty table, a bottle of rum and half-filled glass in front of him. Even though the lounge was dimly lit, he had on dark glasses, and his blue suit was as unkempt as any of Dorian Wilde's.

"I'll see about this," Tachyon said, outrage in his voice. He started to stand, but settled back in his chair as a large, scowling man came into the lounge and strode straight toward their table.

"It's him," Ray whispered. "Charlemagne Calixte."

He didn't have to tell them. Calixte was a dark-skinned black, bigger and broader than most Haitians Chrysalis had seen so far, and uglier too. His short kinky hair was salted with white, his eyes were hidden behind dark glasses, and shriveled scar tissue crawled up the right side of his face. His manner and bearing radiated power, confidence, and ruthless efficiency.

"*Bon jour.*" He bowed a precise little bow. His voice was a deep, hideous rasp, as if the poison that had eaten away the side of his face had also affected his tongue and palate.

"*Bon jour,*" Tachyon replied for them all, bowing a precise millimeter less than Calixte had.

"My name is Charlemagne Calixte," he said in gravelly tones barely louder than a whisper. "President-for-Life Duvalier has charged me with seeing to your safety while you are visiting our island."

"Join us," Tachyon offered, indicating the final empty chair.

Calixte shook his head as precisely as he'd bowed. "Regretfully, *Msie* Tachyon, I cannot. I have an important appointment for the afternoon. I just stopped by to make sure everything is all right after that unfortunate incident in front of the hotel." As he spoke he looked directly at Chrysalis.

"Everything's fine," Tachyon assured him before Chrysalis could speak. "What I want to know, though, is why the Tomtom—"

"Tonton," Ray said.

Tachyon glanced at him. "Of course. The Tonton whatevers, your men, that is, are watching us."

Calixte gave him a look of polite astonishment. "Why to protect you from that very sort of thing that happened earlier this afternoon."

"Protect me? He wasn't protecting me," Chrysalis said. "He was beating beggars."

Calixte stared at her. "They may have looked like beggars, but many undesirable elements have come into the city." He looked around the almost empty room, then husked in a barely intelligible whisper, "Communist elements, you know. They are unhappy with the progressive regime of President-for-Life Duvalier and have threatened to topple his government. No doubt these 'beggars' were communist agitators trying to provoke an incident."

Chrysalis kept quiet, realizing nothing she could say would make any difference. Tachyon was also looking unhappy, but decided not to pursue the matter at this time. After all, they would only be in Haiti one more day before traveling to the Dominican Republic on the other side of the island.

"Also," Calixte said with a smile as ugly as his scar, "I am to inform you that dinner tonight at the Palais National will be a formal affair."

"And after dinner?" Ray said, openly gauging Calixte with his frank stare.

"Excuse me?"

"Is anything planned for after dinner?"

"But of course. Several entertainments have been arranged. There is shopping at the Marché de Fer—the Iron Market—for locally produced handicrafts. The Musée National will stay open late for those who wish to explore our cultural heritage. You know," Calixte said, "we have on display the anchor from the *Santa Maria*, which ran aground on our shores during Columbus's first expedition to the New World. Also, of course, galas have been planned in several of our world-famous nightclubs. And for those interested in some of the more exotic local customs, a trip to a *hounfour* has been arranged."

"*Hounfour?*" Peregrine asked.

"*Oui.* A temple. A church. A voodoo church."

"Sounds interesting," Chrysalis said.

"It's got to be more interesting than looking at anchors," Ray said insouciantly.

Calixte smiled, his good humor going no farther than his lips. "As you wish, *msie.* I must go now."

"What about these policemen?" Tachyon asked.

"They will continue to protect you," Calixte said depreciatingly, and left.

"They're nothing to worry about," Ray said, "leastways while I'm around." He struck a consciously heroic pose and glanced at Peregrine, who looked down at her drink.

Chrysalis wished she could feel as confident as Ray. There was something unsettling about the Tonton Macoute sitting in the corner of the lounge, watching them from behind his dark glasses with the unblinking patience of a snake. Something malevolent. Chrysalis didn't believe that he was there to protect them. Not for one single, solitary second.

Ti Malice particularly liked the sensations associated with sex. When he was in the mood for such a sensation he'd usually mount a female, because, on the whole, females could maintain a state of pleasure, particularly those adept at self-arousal, much longer than his male mounts could. Of course, there were shades and nuances of sexual sensation, some as subtle as silk dragged across a sensitive nipple, some as blatant as an explosive orgasm ripped from a throttled man, and different mounts were adept at different practices.

This afternoon he wasn't in the mood for anything particularly exotic, so he'd attached himself to a young woman who had a particularly sensitive tactile sense and was enjoying it enjoying itself when his mount came in to report.

"They'll all be at the dinner tonight, and then the group will break up to attend various entertainments. It shouldn't be difficult to obtain one of them. Or more."

He could understand the mount's report well enough. It was, after all, their world, and he'd had to make some accommodations, like learning to associate meaning with the sounds that spilled from their lips. He couldn't reply verbally, of course, even if he'd wanted to. First, his mouth, tongue, and palate weren't shaped for it, and second, his mouth was, and always had to be, fastened to the side of his mount's neck, with the narrow, hollow tube of his tongue plunged into his mount's carotid artery.

But he knew his mounts well and he could read their needs easily. The mount who'd brought the report, for instance, had two. Its eyes were fastened on the lithe nakedness of the female as it pleasured itself, but it also had a need for his kiss.

He flapped a pale, skinny hand and the mount came forward eagerly, dropping its pants and climbing atop the woman. The female let out an explosive grunt as it entered.

He forced a stream of spittle down his tongue and into his mount's carotid artery, sealing the breach in it, then gingerly climbed, like a frail, pallid monkey, to the male's back, gripped it around the shoulders, and plunged his tongue home just below the mass of scar tissue on the side of its neck.

The male grunted with more than sexual pleasure as he drove his tongue in, siphoning some of the mount's blood into his own body for the oxygen and nutrients he needed to live. He rode the man's back as the man rode the woman, and all three were bound in chains of inexpressible pleasure.

And when the carotid of the female mount ruptured unexpectedly, as they sometimes did, spewing all three with pulsing showers of bright, warm, sticky blood, they continued on. It was a most exciting and pleasurable experience. When it was over, he realized that he would miss the female mount—it had had the most incredibly sensitive skin—but his sense of loss was lessened by anticipation.

Anticipation of new mounts, and the extraordinary abilities they would have.

ii.

The Palais National dominated the north end of a large open square near the center of Port-au-Prince. Its architect had cribbed its design from the Capitol Building in Washington, D.C., giving it the same colonnaded portico, long white facade, and central dome. Facing it on the south end of the square were what looked like, and in fact were, military barracks.

The inside of the Palais stood out in stark contrast to everything else Chrysalis had seen in Haiti. The only word to describe it was opulent. The carpets were deep-pile shags, the furniture and bric-a-brac along the hallway they were escorted down by ornately uniformed guards were all authentic antiques, the chandeliers hanging from the high vaulted ceilings were the finest cut crystal.

President-for-Life Jean-Claude Duvalier, and his wife, Madame Michele Duvalier, were waiting in a receiving line with other Haitian dignitaries and functionaries. Baby Doc Duvalier, who'd inherited Haiti in 1971 when his father, François "Papa Doc" Duvalier, had died, looked like a fat boy who'd outgrown his tight-fitting tuxedo. Chrysalis thought him more petulant-looking than intelligent, more greedy than cunning. It was difficult to imagine how he managed to hold power in a country that was obviously on the brink of utter ruin.

Tachyon, wearing an absurd peach-colored crushed-velvet tuxedo, was standing to his right, introducing Duvalier to the members of his tour. When it came Chrysalis's turn, Baby Doc took her hand and stared at her with the fascination of a young boy with a new toy. He murmured to her politely in French and continued to stare at her as Chrysalis moved down the line.

Michele Duvalier stood next to him. She had the cultivated, brittle look of a high-fashion model. She was tall and thin and very light-skinned. Her makeup was immaculate, her gown was the latest off-the-shoulder designer creation, and she wore lots of costly, gaudy jewelry at her ears, throat, and wrists. Chrysalis admired the expense with which she dressed, if not the taste.

She drew back a little as Chrysalis approached and nodded a cold, precise millimeter, without offering her hand. Chrysalis sketched an abbreviated curtsy and moved on herself, thinking, *Bitch*.

Calixte, showing the high status he enjoyed in the Duvalier regime, was next. He said nothng to her and did nothing to acknowledge her presence, but Chrysalis felt his stare boring into her all the way down the line. It was a most unsettling feeling and was, Chrysalis realized, a further sample of the

charisma and power that Calixte wielded. She wondered why
he allowed Duvalier to hang around as a figurehead.

The rest of the receiving line was a confused blur of faces
and handshakes. It ended at the doorway leading into the
cavernous dining room. The tablecloths on the long wooden
table were linen, the place settings were silver, the center-
pieces were fragrant sprays of orchid and rose. When she was
escorted to her seat, Chrysalis found that she and the other
jokers, Xavier Desmond, Father Squid, Troll, and Dorian
Wilde, were stuck at the end of the table. Word was whispered
that Madame Duvalier had had them seated as far away from
her as possible so the sight of them wouldn't ruin her
appetite.

However, as wine was being served with the fish course
(*Pwason rouj*, the waiter had called it, red snapper served
with fresh string beans and fried potatoes), Dorian Wilde
stood and recited an extemporaneous, calculatedly overblown
ode in praise of Madame Duvalier, all the while gesticulating
with the twitching, wriggling, dripping mass of tentacles that
was his right hand. Madame Duvalier turned a shade of
green only slightly less bilious than that of the ooze that
dripped from Wilde's tendrils and was seen to eat very little
of the following courses. Gregg Hartmann, sitting near the
Duvaliers with the other VIPs, dispatched his pet Doberman,
Billy Ray, to escort Wilde back to his seat, and the dinner
continued in a more subdued, less interesting manner.

As the last of the after-dinner liquors were served and
the party started to break up into small conversational groups,
Digger Downs approached Chrysalis and stuck his camera in
her face.

"How about a smile, Chrysalis? Or should I say Debra-
Jo? Perhaps you'd care to tell my readers why a native of
Tulsa, Oklahoma, speaks with a British accent."

Chrysalis smiled a brittle smile, keeping the shock and
anger she felt off her face. He knew who she was! The man
had pried into her past, had discovered her deepest, if not
most vital, secret. How did he do it? she wondered, and what
else did he know? She glanced around, but it seemed that no
one else was paying them any attention. Billy Ray and Asta
Lenser, the ballerina-ace called Fantasy, were closest to them,
but they seemed absorbed in their own little confrontation. Billy
had a hand on her skinny flank and was pulling her close. She
was smiling a slow, enigmatic smile at him. Chrysalis turned

back to Digger, somehow managing to keep the anger she felt
out of her voice.

"I have no idea what you're talking about."

Digger smiled. He was a rumpled, sallow-looking man.
Chrysalis had had dealings with him in the past, and she
knew that he was an inveterate snooper who wouldn't let go
of a story, especially if it had a juicy, sensational angle.

"Come, come, Miss Jory. It's all down in black and white
on your passport application."

She could have sighed with relief, but kept her expression stonily hostile. The application had had her real name on
it, but if that was as far as Digger had probed, she'd be safe.
Thoughts of her family raced poisonously through her mind.
When she was a little girl, she'd been their darling with long
blond hair and a naive young smile. Nothing had been too
good for her. Ponies and dolls and baton twirling and piano
and dancing lessons, her father had bought them all for her
with his Oklahoma oil money. Her mother had taken her
everywhere, to recitals and to church meetings and to society
teas. But when the virus had struck her at puberty and
turned her skin and flesh invisible, making her a walking
abomination, they shut her up in a wing of the ranch house,
for her own good of course, and took away her ponies and her
playmates and all contact with the outside world. For seven
years she was shut up, seven years. . . .

Chrysalis shut off the hateful memories rushing through
her mind. She was still, she realized, walking on tricky
ground with Digger. She had to concentrate fully on him and
forget the family that she'd robbed and fled from.

"That information is confidential," she told Digger coldly.

He laughed aloud. "That's very funny, coming from
you," he said, then suddenly sobered at her look of
uncontainable fury. "Of course, perhaps the true story of your
real past wouldn't be of much interest to my readers." He put
a conciliatory expression on his pale face. "I know that you
know everything that goes on in Jokertown. Maybe you know
something interesting about *him*."

Digger gestured with his chin and let his eyes flicker in
the direction of Senator Hartmann.

"What about him?" Hartmann was a powerful and influential politician who felt strongly about jokers' rights. He was
one of the few politicians that Chrysalis supported financially

because she liked his policies and not because she needed to keep the wheels greased.

"Let's go somewhere private and talk about it."

Digger was obviously reluctant to discuss Hartmann openly. Intrigued, Chrysalis glanced at the antique brooch watch pinned above the bodice of her gown. "I have to leave in ten minutes." She grinned like a Halloween skeleton. "I'm going to see a voodoo ceremony. Perhaps if you care to come along, we might find time to discuss things and come to a mutual understanding about the newsworthiness of my background."

Digger smiled. "Sounds fine to me. Voodoo ceremony, huh? They going to stick pins in dolls and stuff? Maybe have some kind of sacrifice?"

Chrysalis shrugged. "I don't know. I've never been to one before."

"Think they'll mind if I take photos?"

Chrysalis smiled blandly, wishing she was on familiar turf, wishing that she had something to use on this gossip-monger, and wondering, underneath it all, why his interest in Gregg Hartmann?

In a fit of sentiment Ti Malice chose one of his oldest mounts, a male with a body almost as frail and withered as his own, to be his steed for the night. Even though the mount's flesh was ancient, the brain encased in it was still sharp, and more strong-willed than any other Ti Malice had ever encountered. It said, in fact, a lot for Ti Malice's own indominatable will that he was able to control the stubborn old steed. The mental fencing that accompanied riding it was a most pleasurable experience.

He chose the dungeon for the meeting place. It was a quiet, comfortable old room, full of pleasurable sights and smells and memories. The lighting was dim, the air was cool and moist. His favorite tools, along with the remains of his last few partners in experience, were scattered about in agreeable disarray. He had his mount pick up a blood-encrusted flaying knife and test it on its callused palm while he drifted in pleasant reminiscence until the snorting bellow in the corridor outside proclaimed Taureau's approach.

Taureau-trois-graines, as he had named this mount, was a huge male with a body that was thick with slabs of muscle. It had a long, bushy beard and tufts of coarse black hair peered through the tears in its sun-faded work shirt. It wore frayed, worn denim pants, and it had a huge, rampant erection pushing visibly at the fabric that covered its crotch. It always had.

"I have a task for you," Ti Malice told his mount to say, and Taureau bellowed and tossed its head and rubbed its crotch through the fabric of its pants. "Some new mounts will be awaiting you on the road to Petionville. Take a squad of *zobops* and bring them to me here."

"Women?" Taureau asked in a slobbering snort.

"Perhaps," Ti Malice said through his mount, "but you are not to have them. Later, perhaps."

Taureau let out a disappointed bellow, but knew better than to argue.

"Be careful," Ti Malice warned. "Some of these mounts may have powers. They may be strong."

Taureau let out bray that rattled the tattered half-skeleton hanging in the wall niche next to it. "Not as strong as me!" It thumped its massive chest with a callused, horny hand.

"Maybe, maybe not. Just take care. I want them all." He paused to let his mount's words sink in. "Do not fail me. If you do, you will never know my kiss again."

Taureau howled like a steer being led to the slaughter block, backed out of the room, bowing furiously, and was gone.

Ti Malice and his mount waited.

In a moment a woman came into the room. Its skin was the color of coffee and milk mixed in equal amounts. Its hair, thick and wild, fell to its waist. It was barefooted and obviously wore nothing under its thin white dress. Its arms were slim, its breasts large, and its legs lithely muscled. Its eyes were black irises floating in pools of red. Ti Malice would have smiled at the sight of it, if he could, for it was his favorite steed.

"Ezili-je-rouge," he crooned through his mount, "you had to wait until Taureau left, for you couldn't share a room with the bull and live."

It smiled a smile with even, perfectly white teeth. "It might be an interesting way to die."

"It might," Ti Malice considered. He had never experienced death by means of intercourse before. "But I have other needs for you. The *blancs* that have come to visit us are rich and important. They live in America and, I'm sure, have access to many interesting sensations that are unavailable on our poor island."

Ezili nodded, licking red lips.

"I've set plans in motion to make some of these *blancs* mine, but to ensure my success, I want you to go to their hotel, take one of the others, and make it ready for my kiss. Choose one of the strong ones."

Ezili nodded. "Will you take me to America with you?" she asked nervously.

Ti Malice had his mount reach out an ancient, withered hand and caress Ezili's large, firm breasts. It shivered with delight at the touch of the mount's hand.

"Of course, my darling, of course."

iii.

"A limousine?" Chrysalis said with an icy smile to the broadly grinning man wearing dark glasses who was holding the door for her. "How nice. I was expecting something with four-wheel drive."

She climbed into the backseat of the limo, and Digger followed her. "I wouldn't complain," he said. "They haven't let the press go anywhere. You should've seen what I had to go through to crash the dinner party. I don't think they like reporters much . . . here . . ."

His voice ran down as he flopped onto the rear seat next to Chrysalis and noted the expression on her face. She was staring at the facing seat, and the two men who occupied it. One was Dorian Wilde. He was looking more than a little tipsy and fondling a *cocomacaques* similar to the one Chrysalis had seen that afternoon. The stick obviously belonged to the man who was sitting next to him and regarding Chrysalis with a horrible frozen grin that contorted his scarred face into a death mask.

"Chrysalis, my dear!" Wilde exclaimed as the limo pulled away into the night. "And the glorious fourth estate. Dug up any juicy gossip lately?" Digger looked from Chrysalis to Wilde to the man sitting next to him and decided that silence would be his most appropriate response. "How rude of me," Wilde continued. "I haven't introduced our host. This de-lightful man has the charming name of Charlemagne Calixte.

I believe he's a policeman or something. He's going with us to the *hounfour*."

Digger nodded and Calixte inclined his head in a precise, nondeferential bow.

"Are you a devotee of voodoo, *Monsieur* Calixte?" Chrysalis asked.

"It is the superstition of peasants," he said in a raspy growl, thoughtfully fingering the scar tissue that crawled up the right side of his face. "Although seeing you would almost make one a believer."

"What do you mean?"

"You have the appearance of a loa. You could be Madame Brigitte, the wife of Baron Samedi."

"You don't believe that, do you?" Chrysalis asked.

Calixte laughed. It was a gravelly, barking laugh that was as pleasant as his smile. "Not I, but I am an educated man. It was the sickness that caused your appearance. I know. I have seen others."

"Other jokers?" Digger asked with, Chrysalis thought, his usual tact.

"I don't know what you mean. I have seen other unnatural deformities. A few."

"Where are they now?"

Calixte only smiled.

No one felt much like talking. Digger kept shooting Chrysalis questioning glances, but she could tell him nothing, and even if she had a inkling of what was going on, she could hardly speak openly in front of Calixte. Wilde played with Calixte's swagger stick and cadged drinks from the bottle of *clairin*, cheap white rum, that the Haitian took frequent swallows from himself. Calixte drank over half the bottle in twenty minutes, and as he drank he stared at Chrysalis with intense, bloodshot eyes.

Chrysalis, in an effort to avoid Calixte's gaze, looked out the window and was astonished to see that they were no longer in the city, but were traveling down a road that seemed to cut through otherwise unbroken forest.

"Just where are we going?" she asked Calixte, striving to keep her voice level and unafraid.

He took the bottle of *clairin* from Wilde, gulped down a mouthful, and shrugged. "We are going to the *hounfour*. It is in Petionville, a small suburb just outside Port-au-Prince."

"Port-au-Prince has no *hounfours* of its own?"

Calixte smiled his blasted smile. "None that put on such a fine show."

Silence descended again. Chrysalis knew that they were in trouble, but she couldn't figure out exactly what Calixte wanted of them. She felt like a pawn in a game she didn't even know she'd been playing. She glanced at the others. Digger was looking confused as hell, and Wilde was drunk. Damn. She was more sorry than ever that she'd left familiar, comfortable Jokertown behind to follow Tachyon on his mad, worthless journey. As usual, she only had herself to depend on. It had always been like that, and always would. Part of her mind whispered that once there had been Brennan, but she refused to listen to it. Come to the test, he would have proved as untrustworthy as the rest. He would have.

The driver suddenly pulled the limo to the side of the road and killed the engine. She stared out the window, but could see little. It was dark and the roadside was lit only by infrequent glimpses of the half moon as it occasionally peered out from behind banks of thick clouds. It looked as if they had stopped beside a crossroad, a chance meeting of minor roads that ran blindly through the Haitian forest. Calixte opened the door on his side and climbed out of the limo smoothly and steadily in spite of the fact that he'd drunk most of a bottle of raw rum in less than half an hour. The driver got out too, leaned against the side of the limo, and began to beat a swift tattoo on a small, pointed-end drum that he'd produced from somewhere.

"What's going on?" Digger demanded.

"Engine trouble," Calixte said succinctly, throwing the empty rum bottle into the jungle.

"And the driver is calling the Haitian Automobile Club," Wilde, sprawled across the backseat, said with a giggle.

Chrysalis poked Digger and gestured to him to move out. He obeyed, looking around bewilderedly, and she followed him. She didn't want to be trapped in the back of the limo during whatever it was that was going to happen. At least outside the car she had a chance to run for it, although she probably wouldn't be able to get very far in a floor-length gown and high heels. Through the jungle. On a dark night.

"Say," Digger said in sudden comprehension. "We're being kidnapped. You can't do this. I'm a reporter."

Calixte reached into his jacket pocket and withdrew a

small, snub-nosed revolver. He pointed it negligently at Digger and said, "Shut up."

Downs wisely did.

They didn't have long to wait. From the road that intersected the one they'd been driving upon came the cadenced sound of marching feet. Chrysalis turned to stare down the road and saw what looked like a column of fireflies, bobbing up and down, coming in their direction. It took a moment, but she realized that it was actually a troop of marching men. They wore long, white robes whose hems brushed the roadtop. Each carried a long, skinny candle in his left hand and each was also crowned with a candle set on his forehead by a cloth circlet, producing the firefly effect. They wore masks. There were about fifteen of them.

Leading the column was an immense man who had a decidedly bovine look about him. He was dressed in the cheap, tattered clothes of a Haitian peasant. He was one of the largest men that Chrysalis had ever seen, and as soon as he spotted her he headed straight toward her. He stood before her drooling and rubbing his crotch, which, Chrysalis was surprised and not happy to see, was bulging outward and stretching the frayed fabric of his jeans.

"Jesus," Digger muttered. "We're in trouble now. He's an ace."

Chrysalis glanced at the reporter. "How do you know?"

"Well, ah, he looks like one, doesn't he?"

He looked like someone who'd been touched by the wild card virus, Chrysalis thought, but that didn't necessarily make him an ace. Before she could question Digger further, however, the bull-like man said something in Creole, and Calixte snapped off a guttural "Non" in answer.

The bull-man seemed momentarily ready to dispute Calixte's apparent order, but decided to back down. He continued to glower at Chrysalis and finger his erection as he spoke in turn to the strangely garbed men who had accompanied him.

Three of them came forward and dragged a protesting Dorian Wilde from the backseat of the limo. The poet looked around bewilderedly, fixed his bleary eyes on the bull-man, and giggled.

Calixte grimaced. He snatched his *cocomacaques* from Wilde and lashed out with it, spitting the word "*Masisi*" as he struck.

The blow landed where Wilde's neck curved into his shoulder, and the poet moaned and sagged. The three men supporting him couldn't hold him, and he fell to the ground just as all hell broke loose.

The snap, crack, and pop of small-arms fire sounded from the foliage bordering the roadside, and a couple of the men so strangely crowned by candles went down. A few others broke and ran for it, though most held their ground. The bull-man bellowed in rage and hurtled toward the undergrowth. Chrysalis, who'd dropped to the ground at the first sound of gunfire, saw him get hit in the upper body at least twice, but he didn't even stagger. He crashed into the underbrush and in a moment high-pitched screams mixed with his bellowing.

Calixte crouched behind the limo and calmly returned fire. Digger, like Chrysalis, was huddled on the ground, and Wilde just lay there moaning. Chrysalis decided that it was time to exercise the better part of valor. She crawled under the limo, cursing as she felt her expensive gown snag and tear.

Calixte dove after her. He snatched at her left foot, but only grabbed her shoe. She twisted her foot, the shoe came off, and she was free. She scrambled all the way under the limo, came out on the other side, and rolled into the jungle foliage lining the roadside.

She took a few moments to catch her breath, and then was up and running, staying low and keeping to cover as much as she could. Within moments she was away from the conflict, safe, alone, and, she quickly realized, totally, utterly lost.

She should have paralleled the road, she told herself, rather than taking off blindly into the forest. She should have done a lot of things, like spending the winter in New York and not on this insane tour. But it was too late to worry about any of that. Now all she could do was push ahead.

Chrysalis never imagined that a tropical forest, a jungle, could be so desolate. She saw nothing move, other than tree branches in the night wind, and heard nothing other than the sounds made by that same wind. It was a lonely, frightening feeling, especially to someone used to having a city around them.

She'd lost her brooch watch when she'd scrambled under the limo, so she had no way of measuring time other than the

increasing soreness in her body and dryness in her throat.
Hours, certainly, had passed before, totally by accident, she
stumbled upon a trail. It was rough, narrow, and uneven,
obviously made by human feet, but finding it filled her with
hope. It was a sign of habitation. It led to somewhere. All she
had to do was follow it, and somewhere, sometime, she'd find
help.

She started down the trail, too consumed by the exigen-
cies of her immediate situation to worry any more about
Calixte's motives in bringing her and the others to the
crossroads, the identity of the strangely dressed men crowned
with candles, or to even wonder about their mysterious
rescuers, if, indeed, the band that had ambushed their
kidnappers had meant to rescue them.

She walked through the darkness.

It was difficult going. Right at the start of her trek she'd
taken off her right shoe to even her stride, and sometime
soon afterward she'd lost it. The ground was not without
sticks and stones and other sharp objects, and before long her
feet hurt like hell. She cataloged her miseries minutely so
she'd know exactly how much to take out of Tachyon's hide if
she ever got back to Port-au-Prince.

Not if, she told herself repeatedly. When. When. When.

She was chanting the word as a short, snappy little
marching song when she suddenly realized that someone was
walking toward her on the trail. It was difficult to say for sure
in the uncertain light, but it looked like a man, a tall, frail
man carrying a hoe or shovel or something over his shoulder.
He was headed right toward her.

She stopped, leaned against a nearby tree, and let out a
long, relieved sigh. The brief thought flashed through her
mind that he might be a member of Calixte's odd gang, but
from what she could discern, he was dressed like a peasant,
and he was carrying some sort of farm implement. He was
probably just a local out on a late errand. She had the sudden
fear that her appearance might scare him away before she
could ask for help, but quenched it with the realization that
he had to have already seen her, and he was still steadily
approaching.

"*Bon jour,*" she called out, exhausting most of her French.
But the man made no sign that he had heard. He kept on
walking past the tree against which she leaned.

"Hey! Are you deaf?" she reached out and tugged at his

arm as he passed by, and as she touched him, he stopped, turned, and fixed her with his gaze.

Chrysalis felt as if a slice of night had stabbed into her heart. She went cold and shivery and for a long moment couldn't catch her breath. She couldn't look away from his eyes.

They were open. They moved, they shifted focus, they even blinked slowly and ponderously, but they did not see. The face from which they peered was scarcely less skeletal than her own. The brow ridges, eye sockets, cheekbones, jaw, and chin stood out in minute detail, as if there were no flesh between the bone and the taut black skin that covered them. She could count the ribs underneath the ragged work shirt as easily as anyone could count her own. She stared at him as he looked toward her and her breath caught again when she realized that he wasn't breathing. She would have screamed or run or done something, but as she stared he took a long, shallow breath that barely inflated his sunken chest. She watched him closely, and twenty seconds passed before he took another.

She suddenly realized that she was still holding his ragged sleeve, and she released it. He continued to stare in her direction for a moment or two, then turned back the way he'd been headed and started walking away.

Chrysalis stared at his back for a moment, shivering, despite the warmth of the evening. She had just seen, talked to, and even touched, she realized, a *zombi*. As a resident of Jokertown and a joker herself, she'd thought herself inured to strangeness, accustomed to the bizarre. But apparently she wasn't. She had never been so afraid in her life, not even when, as a girl barely out of her teens, she had broken into her father's safe to finance her escape from the prison that was her home.

She swallowed hard. *Zombi* or not, he had to be going somewhere. Somewhere where there might be other . . . real . . . people.

Timorously, because there was nothing else she could do, she began to follow him.

They didn't have far to go. He soon turned off onto a smaller, less-traveled side trail that wound down and around a steep hill. As they passed a sharp curve in the trail, Chrysalis noticed a light burning ahead.

He headed toward the light, and she followed him. It

was a kerosene lantern, stuck on a pole in front of what looked like a small, ramshackle hut clinging to the lower slopes of the precipitous hillside. A tiny garden was in front of the hut, and in front of the garden a woman was peering into the night.

She was the most prosperous looking Haitian that Chrysalis had yet seen outside of the Palais National. She was actually plump, her calico dress was fresh and new-looking, and she wore a bright orange madras bandanna wrapped around her head. The woman smiled as Chrysalis and the apparition she was following approached.

"Ah, Marcel, who has followed you home?" She chuckled. "Madame Brigitte herself, if I'm not mistaken." She sketched a curtsy that, despite her plumpness, was quite graceful. "Welcome to my home."

Marcel kept walking right on past her, ignoring her and heading for the rear of the hut. Chrysalis stopped before the woman, who was regarding her with an open, welcoming expression that contained a fair amount of good-natured curiosity in it.

"Thank you," Chrysalis said hesitantly. There were a thousand things she could have said, but the question burning in the forefront of her mind had to be answered. "I have to ask you . . . that is . . . about Marcel."

"Yes?"

"He's not actually a *zombi*, is he?"

"Of course he is, my child, of course he is. Come, come." She made gathering motions with her hands. "I must go inside and tell my man to call off the search."

Chrysalis hung back. "Search?"

"For you, my child, for you." The woman shook her head and made *tsk*ing sounds. "You shouldn't have run off like that. It caused quite a bit of trouble and worry for us. We thought that the *zobop* column might capture you again."

"*Zobop*? What's a *zobop*?" It sounded to Chrysalis like a term for some kind of jazz afficionado. It was all she could do to keep from laughing hysterically at the thought.

"*Zobop* are"—the woman gestured vaguely with her hands as if she were trying to describe an enormously complicated subject in simple words—"the assistants of a *bokor*—an evil sorcerer—who have sold themselves to the *bokor* for material riches. They follow his bidding in all things, often kidnaping victims chosen by the *bokor*."

"I . . . see . . . And who, if you don't mind my asking, are you?"

The woman laughed good-humoredly. "No, child, I don't mind at all. It shows admirable caution on your part. I am Mambo Julia, priestess and *première reine* of the local Bizango chapter." She must have correctly read the baffled look on Chrysalis's face, for she laughed aloud. "You *blancs* are so funny! You think you know everything. You come to Haiti in your great airplane, walk about for one day, and then dispense your magical advice that will cure all our ills. And not once do even one of you leave Port-au-Prince!" Mambo Julia laughed again, this time with some derision. "You know nothing of Haiti, the real Haiti. Port-au-Prince is a gigantic cancer that shelters the leeches that are sucking the juices from Haiti's body. But the countryside, ah, the countryside is Haiti's heart!

"Well, my child, I shall tell you everything you need to know to begin to understand. Everything, and more, than you want to know. Come to my hut. Rest. Drink. Have a little something to eat. And listen."

Chrysalis considered the woman's offer. Right now she was more concerned about her own difficulties than Haiti's, but Mambo Julia's invitation sounded good. She wanted to rest her aching feet and drink something cold. The idea of food also sounded inviting. It seemed as if she'd last eaten years ago.

"All right," she said, following Mambo Julia toward the hut. Before they reached the door, a middle-aged man, thin, like most Haitians, with a shock of premature white hair, came around from the back.

"Baptiste!" Mambo Julia cried. "Have you fed the *zombi*?" The man nodded and bobbed a courteous bow in Chrysalis's direction. "Good. Tell the others that Madame Brigitte has found her own way home."

He bowed again, and Chrysalis and Mambo Julia went into the hut.

Inside, it was plainly, neatly, comfortably furnished. Mambo Julia ushered Chrysalis to a rough-hewn plank table and served her fresh water and a selection of fresh, succulent tropical fruits, most of which were unfamiliar, but tasty.

Outside, a drum began to beat a complicated rhythm to the night. Inside, Mambo Julia began to talk.

*   *   *

One of Ti Malice's mounts delivered Ezili's message at midnight. It had succeeded in the task he'd given it. A new mount was lying in drugged slumber at the Royal Haitian Hotel, awaiting its first kiss.

Excited as a child on Christmas morning, Ti Malice decided that he couldn't wait at the fortress for the mounts he'd sent Taureau after to be delivered. He wanted new blood, and he wanted it now.

He moved from his old favorite to a different mount, a girl not much bigger than he, that was already waiting in the special box that he'd had built for occasions when he had to move about in public. It was the size of a large suitcase and was cramped and uncomfortable, but it afforded the privacy he needed for his public excursions. It took a bit of caution, but Ti Malice was smuggled unseen to the third floor of the Royal Haitian Hotel where Ezili, naked and hair flying wild, let him into the room and stood back while the mount bearing him opened the lid and stepped from the box as he moved from the girl's chest to the more comfortable position upon its back and shoulders.

Ezili led him into the bedroom where his new mount was sleeping peacefully.

"He wanted me the moment he saw me," Ezili said. "It was easy to get him to bring me here, and easier yet to slip the draught into his drink after he had me." She pouted, fingering the large, dark nipple of her left breast. "He was a quick lover," she said with some disappointment.

"Later," Ti Malice said through his mount, "you shall be rewarded."

Ezili smiled happily as Ti Malice ordered his mount to bring him closer to the bed. The mount complied, bending over the sleeping man, and Ti Malice transferred himself quickly. He snuggled against the man's chest, nuzzling its neck. The man stirred, moaned a little in its drugged sleep. Ti Malice found the spot he needed, bit down with his single, sharp tooth, then drove his tongue home.

The new mount groaned and feebly reached for its neck. But Ti Malice was already firmly in place, mixing his saliva with his mount's blood, and the mount subsided like a grumpy child having a slightly bad dream. It settled down into deep sleep while Ti Malice made it his.

It was a splendid mount, powerful and strong. Its blood tasted wonderful.

iv.

"There have always been two Haitis," Mambo Julia said. "There is the city, Port-au-Prince, where the government and its law rule. And there is the countryside, where the Bizango rules."

"You used that word before," Chrysalis said, wiping the sweet juices of a succulent tropical fruit off her chin. "What does it mean?"

"As your skeleton, which I can see so clearly, holds your body together, so the Bizango binds the people of the countryside. It is an organization, a society with a network of obligations and order. Not everyone belongs to it, but everyone has a place in it and all abide by its decisions. The Bizango settles disputes that would otherwise rip us apart. Sometimes it is easy. Sometimes, as when someone is sentenced to become a *zombi*, it is difficult."

"The Bizango sentenced Marcel to become a *zombi*?"

Mambo Julia nodded. "He was a bad man. We in Haiti are more permissive about certain things than you Americans. Marcel liked girls. There is nothing wrong with that. Many men have several women. It is all right as long as they can support them and their children. But Marcel liked young girls. Very young girls. He couldn't stop, so the Bizango sat in judgment and sentenced him to become a *zombi*."

"They turned him into a *zombi*?"

"No, my dear. They judged him." Mambo Julia lost her air of convivial jollity. "*I* made him into what he is today, and keep him that way by the powders I feed him daily." Chrysalis placed the half-eaten fruit she was holding back upon its plate, having suddenly lost her appetite. "It is a most sensible solution. Marcel no longer harms young girls. He is instead a tireless worker for the good of the community."

"And he'll always be a *zombi*?"

"Well, there have been a few *zombi savane*, those who have been buried and brought back as *zombis*, then somehow managed to return to the state of the living." Mambo Julia plucked her chin thoughtfully. "But such have always remained somewhat . . . impaired."

Chrysalis swallowed hard. "I appreciate what you've done for me. I... I'm not sure what Calixte intended, but I'm sure he meant me harm. But now that I'm free, I'd like to return to Port-au-Prince."

"Of course you do, child. And you shall. In fact, we were planning on it."

Mambo Julia's words were welcome, but Chrysalis wasn't sure that she cared much for her tone. "What do you mean?"

Mambo Julie looked at her seriously. "I'm not sure, either, what Calixte planned for you. I do know that he's been collecting people such as yourself. People who've been changed. I don't know what he does to them, but they become his. They do the dirty deeds that even the Tonton Macoute refuse. And he keeps them busy," she said with a clenched jaw.

"Charlemagne Calixte is our enemy. He is the power in Port-au-Prince. Jean-Claude Duvalier's father, François, was in his own way a great man. He was ruthless and ambitious. He found his way into power and held it for many years. He first organized the Tonton Macoute, and they helped him line his pockets with the wealth of an entire country.

"But Jean-Claude is unlike his father. He is foolish and weak-willed. He has allowed the real power to flow into Calixte's hands, and that devil is so greedy that he threatens to suck the life from us like a *loup garou*." She shook her head. "He must be stopped. His stranglehold must be loosened so the blood will flow through Haiti's veins again. But his power runs deeper than the guns of the Tonton Macoute. He is either a powerful *bokor*, or he has one working for him. The magic of this *bokor* is very strong. It has enabled Calixte to survive several assassination attempts. Though one of them, at least," she said with some satisfaction, "left its mark on him."

"What has all this to do with me?" Chrysalis asked. "You should go to the United Nations or the media. Let your story be known."

"The world knows our story," Mambo Julia said, "and doesn't care. We are beneath their notice, and perhaps it is best that we are left to work out our problems in our own way."

"How?" Chrysalis asked, not sure that she wanted to know the answer.

"The Bizango is stronger in the country than in the city, but we have our agents even in Port-au-Prince. We've been watching you *blancs* since your arrival, thinking that Calixte might be bold enough to somehow take advantage of your presence, perhaps even try to make one of you his agent. When you publicly defied the Tonton Macoute, we knew that Calixte would be driven to get even with you. We kept close watch over you and so were able to foil his attempt to kidnap you. But he did manage to take your friends."

"They're not my friends," Chrysalis said, starting to realize where Mambo Julia's argument was heading. "And even if they were, I couldn't help you rescue them." She held her hand up, a skeleton's hand with a network of cord and sinew and blood vessels woven around it. "This is what the wild card virus did to me. It didn't give me any special powers or abilities. You need someone like Billy Ray or Lady Black or Golden Boy to help you—"

Mambo Julia shook her head. "We need you. You are Madame Brigitte, the wife of Baron Samedi—"

"You don't believe that."

"No," she said, "but the *chasseurs* and *soldats* who live in the small, scattered hamlets, who cannot read and who have never seen television, who know nothing of what you call the wild card virus, they may look upon you and take heart for the deeds they must do tonight. They may not totally believe either, but they will want to and will not think upon the impossibility of defeating the *bokor* and his powerful magic.

"Besides," she said with some finality, "you are the only one who can bait the trap. You are the only one who escaped the *zobop* column. You will be the only one who will be accepted into their stronghold."

Mambo Julia's words both chilled and angered Chrysalis. Chilled her, because she never even wanted to see Calixte again. She had no intention of putting herself in his power. Angered her, because she didn't want to become mixed up in their problems, to die for something she knew virtually nothing about. She was a saloon keeper and information broker. She wasn't a meddling ace who stuck her nose in where it didn't belong. She wasn't an ace of any kind.

Chrysalis pushed her chair away from the table and stood up. "Well, I'm sorry, but I can't help you. Besides, *I* don't know where Calixte took Digger and Wilde any more than you do."

"But we do know where they are." Mambo Julia smiled a smile totally devoid of humor. "Though you eluded the *chasseurs* who were sent to rescue you, several of the *zobop*

did not. It took some persuading, but one finally told us that
Calixte's stronghold is Fort Mercredi, the ruined fortress
overlooking Port-au-Prince. The center of his magic is there."
Mambo Julia stood herself and went to open the door.
A group of men stood in front of the hut. They all had the
look of the country about them in their rough farm clothes,
callused hands and feet, and lean, muscular bodies. "Tonight,"
Mambo Julia said, "the *bokor* dies once and for all."

Their voices rose in a murmur of surprise and awe when
they saw Chrysalis. Most bowed in a gesture of respect and
obeisance.

Mambo Julia cried out in Creole, gesturing at Chrysalis,
and they answered her loudly, happily. After a few moments
she closed the door, turned back to Chrysalis, and smiled.

Chrysalis sighed. It was foolish, she decided, to argue
with a woman who had the demonstrated ability to create
zombis. The feeling of helplessness that descended over her
was an old feeling, a feeling from her youth. In New York she
controlled everything. Here, it seemed, she was always controlled. She didn't like it, but there was nothing she could do
but listen to Mambo Julia's plan.

It was a rather simple plan. Two Bizango *chasseurs*—
men with the rank of hunter in the Bizango, Mambo Julia
explained—would dress in the *zobop* robes and masks that
they'd captured earlier that evening, bring Chrysalis to Calixte's
fortress, and tell him that they tracked her down in the
forest. When the opportunity presented itself (Chrysalis wasn't
pleased with the plan's vagueness on this point, but thought
it best to keep her mouth shut), they would let their comrades in and proceed to destroy Calixte and his henchmen.

Chrysalis didn't like it, even though Mambo Julia assured her airily that she would be perfectly safe, that the loa
would watch over her. For further protection—unnecessary
as it was, Mambo Julia said—the priestess gave her a small
bundle wrapped in oilskin.

"This is a *paquets congo*," Mambo Julia told her. "I made
it myself. It contains very strong magic that will protect you
from evil. If you are threatened, open it and spread its
contents all around you. But *do not let any touch yourself!* It
is strong magic, very, very strong, and you can only use it in
this simplest way."

With that, Mambo Julia sent her off with the *chasseurs*.
There were ten or twelve of them, young to middle-aged.

Baptiste, Mambo Julia's man, was among them. They continually chattered and joked among themselves as if they were going on a picnic, and they treated Chrysalis with the utmost deference and respect, helping her over the rough spots on the trail. Two carried robes they had taken from the *zobop* column earlier that evening.

The foot-trail they followed led to a rough road where an ancient vehicle, a minibus or van of some kind, was parked. It hardly looked capable of moving, but the engine started right up after everyone had piled in. The trip was slow and bumpy, but they made better time when they eventually turned off onto a wider, graded road that eventually led back to Port-au-Prince.

The city was quiet, although they did occasionally pass other vehicles. It struck Chrysalis that they were traveling through familiar scenery, and she suddenly realized that they were in Bolosse, the slum section of Port-au-Prince where the hospital she'd visited that morning—it seemed like a thousand years ago—was located.

The men sang songs, chattered, laughed, and told jokes. It was hard to believe that they were planning to assassinate the most powerful man in the Haitian government, a man who was reputedly an evil sorcerer as well. They were acting more as if they were going to a ball game. It was either a remarkable display of bravado, or the calming effect of her presence as Madame .Brigitte. Whatever caused their attitude, Chrysalis didn't share it. She was scared stiff.

The driver suddenly pulled over and silence fell as he parked the minibus on a narrow street of dilapidated buildings, pointed, and said something in Creole. The *chasseurs* began to disembark, and one courteously offered Chrysalis a hand down. For a moment she thought of running, but saw that Baptiste was keeping a wary, if inconspicuous, eye on her. She sighed to herself and joined the line of men as they walked quietly up the street.

It was a strenuous climb up a steep hill. After a moment Chrysalis realized that they were heading toward the ruins of a fort that she had first noticed when they'd passed through the area earlier in the day. Fort Mercredi, Mambo Julia had called it. It had looked picturesque in the morning. Now it was a dark, looming wreck with an aura of brooding menace about it. The column stopped in a small copse of trees clustered in front of the ruins, and two *chasseurs*, one of them Baptiste, changed into the *zobop* robes and masks. Baptiste courteously motioned Chrysalis forward, and she took a deep breath, willed her legs to stop trembling, and went on. Baptiste took her arm above her elbow, ostensibly to show that she was a prisoner, but she was grateful for the warmth of a human touch. The shaft of night had returned to her heart, but it had grown, had spread until it felt like a dark, icy curtain that had totally enveloped her chest.

The fortress was encircled by a dry moat that had a dilapidated wooden bridge spanning it. They were challenged as they reached the bridge by a voice that shouted a question in Creole. Baptiste answered satisfactorily with a curt password— more information, Chrysalis guessed, wrenched from the unfortunate zobop who'd fallen into the hands of the Bizango— and they crossed the bridge.

Two men wearing the semiofficial blue suit of the Tonton Macoutes were lounging on the other side, their dark glasses resting in their breast pockets. Baptiste told them some long, involved story, and looking impressed, they passed them on through the outer defenses of the citadel. They were challenged again in the courtyard beyond, and again passed on, this time led into the interior of the decrepit fort by one of the second pair of guards.

Chrysalis found it maddening not to understand what was being said around her. The tension was growing higher, her heart colder, as fear wound her tighter than a compressed spring. There was nothing she could do, though, but endure it, and hope, however hopelessly, for the best.

The interior of the fortress seemed to be in moderately good repair. It was lit, medievally enough, by infrequent torches in wall niches. The walls and flooring were stone, dry and cool to the touch. The corridor ended at a railless spiral staircase of crumbling stone. The Tonton Macoute led them downward.

Images of a dank dungeon began to dance in Chrysalis's mind. The air took on a damp feel and a mildewy smell. The staircase itself was slippery with unidentifiable ooze and difficult to negotiate in the sandals made from bits of old automobile tires that Mambo Julia had given her. Torches were infrequent, and the pools of light they threw didn't overlap, so they often had to pass through patches of total darkness.

The staircase ended in a large open space that had only a

few uncomfortable-looking bits of wooden furniture in it. A series of chambers debouched off this area, and it was to one of these that they were led.

The room was twenty feet on a side and lit better than the corridors through which they'd just passed, but the ceiling, corners, and some spots along the back wall were all in darkness. The dancing light thrown by the torches made it difficult to discern details, and after her first glance inside the room, Chrysalis knew that was probably for the best.

It was a torture chamber, lined with antique devices that looked well cared for and recently used. An iron maiden lay half-open against one wall, the spikes in its interior coated by flakes of either rust or blood. A table loaded down with impedimenta such as pokers and cleavers and scalpels and thumb and foot screws stood next to what Chrysalis imagined was a rack. She didn't know for certain because she'd never seen one, never thought she would see one, never, ever, wanted to see one.

She looked away from the instruments of torture and focused on the group of half a dozen men clustered in the rear of the room. Two were Tonton Macoutes, enjoying the proceedings. The others were Digger Downs and Dorian Wilde, the bull-man who had led the *zobop* column, and Charlemagne Calixte. Downs was shackled in a wall niche next to a moldering skeleton. Wilde was the center of everyone's attention.

A stout, thick beam stuck out from the dungeon's rear wall, close to the ceiling, parallel to the floor. A block and tackle hung from the beam and a rope descended from the sharp, wicked-looking metal hook at the bottom of the block and tackle set. Dorian Wilde was dangling from the rope by his arms. He was trying to haul himself up, but lacked the muscular strength to do so. He couldn't even get a proper grip on the coarse hemp with the mass of tentacles that was his right hand. Sweating, wild-eyed, and straining, he swayed desperately while Calixte operated a ratcheted handcrank that lowered the rope until the bottoms of Wilde's naked feet were hanging just above a bed of hot glowing coals burning in a low brazier that had been placed below the gibbet. Wilde would desperately swing his feet away from the searing heat, Calixte would crank him up and give him a brief respite, then lower him again. He stopped when the bull-man glanced

toward the front of the room, noticed Chrysalis, and let out a
bellow.

Calixte looked at her and their eyes met. His expression
was wildly exultant, and he was sweating profusely, though it
was damply cool in the dungeon. He smiled and said something in Creole to the men in the background, who sprang
forward and removed Wilde from the gibbet. He then spoke
to Baptiste and the other *chasseur*. Baptiste must have answered
him satisfactorily, for he nodded, then dismissed them with a
curt word and a gesture of his head.

They bowed and started to walk away. Chrysalis took a
single instinctive step to follow them, and then the bull-man
was before her, breathing heavily and eyeing her strangely.
His erection, she noted sickly, was still rampant.

"Well," Calixte growled in English. "We are all together
again." He came to Chrysalis, put a hand on the bull's
shoulder, and pushed him away. "We were having a bit of
amusement. The *blanc* offended me and I was teaching him
some manners." He nodded at Wilde, who was huddled on
the damp flagstone paving, heaving great shuddering breaths.
Calixte never took his eyes off Chrysalis. They were bright
and fevered, burning with unspeakable excitement and pleasure. "You also have been difficult." He plucked at the scar
tissue that glinted glassily in the torchlight. He seemed deep
in mad thought. "You need, I think, a lesson also." He
seemed to make up his mind. "He'll have the others. I don't
think he'd mind if we used you up. Taureau." He turned to
the bull-man, spoke some words in Creole.

Chrysalis scarcely understood him, even though he spoke
English. His words were thick and blurry, even more so than
usual. He was either very drunk, very stoned, or very mad.
Perhaps, she realized, all three. She was frantic with terror.
The *chasseurs* weren't supposed to leave, she thought wildly.
They were supposed to kill Calixte! Her heart beat faster than
the drums she'd heard sounding through the Haitian night.
The dark fear centered in her chest threatened to flow out
and overwhelm her entire being. For a moment she teetered
on the thin edge of irrationality, and then Taureau came
forward, snorting and drooling, one massive hand unbuttoning
the fly of his jeans, and Chrysalis knew what she had to do.

She clutched the packet that Mambo Julia had given her
and with frantic, shaking fingers pulled off the paper wrapping, exposing a small leather sack closed by a drawstring.

She ripped open the mouth of the sack and with trembling hands threw it and its contents at Taureau.

The sack hit him in the face and he walked right into a cloud of fine, grayish powder that billowed out from it. It coated his hands, arms, chest, and face. He stopped for a moment, snorted, shook his head, then kept right on coming.

Chrysalis broke. She turned with a sob and started to run, thinking incoherently that she should have known better, that Mambo Julia was a conniving fraud, that what was about to happen was nothing compared to what she would experience in a lifetime of domination by Calixte, and then she heard a horrible, bellowing scream that froze every nerve, muscle, and sinew in her body.

She turned. Taureau was standing still, but shivering from head to toe as every massive muscle in his body spasmed. His eyes nearly bulged from his head as he stared at Chrysalis and screamed again, a horrible, drawn-out wail that wasn't even remotely human. His hands clenched and unclenched, and then he began to rake at his face, tearing long furrows of meat away from his cheeks with his thick, blunt fingernails, howling all the while like a damned soul burning.

A memory flashed through Chrysalis's mind, a terse recollection of a cool, dark bar, a delightful drink, and a short Tachyon speech on Haitian herbal medicine. Mambo Julia's *paquets congo* contained no magic powder, no concoction compounded during a fearful ritual and consecrated to the dark voodoo loa. It was simply some herbal preparation, a fast acting, topically effective neurotoxin of some kind. At least that's what she told herself, and almost believed.

The awful tableau held for a moment, and then Calixte barked a word to the Tonton Macoutes who were watching Taureau with astonished eyes. One stepped forward, put a hand on the bull-man's shoulder. Taureau turned with the speed of an adrenalized cat, grabbed the man by his wrist and shoulder, and ripped his arm from his body. The Tonton Macoute stared at Taureau for a moment with unbelieving eyes, and then, blood fountaining from his shoulder, he fell weeping to the floor, trying unsuccessfully to stanch the bleeding with his remaining hand.

Taureau brandished the arm above his head like a gory club, shaking it at Chrysalis. Blood splattered across her face and she choked back the bile that rose in her throat.

Calixte roared an order in Creole, whether at Taureau or his other man Chrysalis didn't know, but the Tonton Macoute ran from the chamber as Taureau whirled in a mad circle, trying to watch everyone at once from crazed, fear-distended eyes.

Calixte kept shouting at Taureau, who was shaking and trembling with terrible muscle spasms. His face was the face of a tortured lunatic, and his dark skin was turning darker. His lips were becoming distinctly blue. He shambled toward Calixte, screaming words that Chrysalis, even though she couldn't understand the language they were spoken in, knew were gibberish.

Calixte calmly drew his pistol. He pointed it at Taureau and spoke again. The joker continued to advance. Calixte squeezed off a shot that hit Taureau high in the left side of his chest, but he kept coming. Calixte shot three more times before the maddened bull covered the distance between them, and the last shot hit him right between the eyes.

But Taureau kept coming. He dropped the arm he'd been brandishing, grabbed Calixte, and with a final spasm of incredible strength, threw him at the chamber's rear wall. Calixte screamed. He reached out to grasp the rope hanging from the gibbet, but he missed. He missed the rope, but not the meathook from which it hung.

The hook took him in the stomach, ripped up through his diaphragm, and skewered his right lung. He showered screams and blood as he kicked his legs and swung in counterpoint rhythm to the spasmodic jerking of his body.

Taureau staggered, clutching his shattered forehead, and fell onto the brazier of burning coals. After a moment he stopped bellowing and there came the crisp sizzle and sweet smell of burning flesh.

Chrysalis was violently sick. After she finished wiping her mouth with the back of her hand, she looked up to see Dorian Wilde standing before the limp, swaying form of Charlemagne Calixte. He smiled and recited:

> "It is sweet to dance to violins
>   When Love and Life are fair:
> To dance to flutes, to dance to lutes
>   Is delicate and rare:
> But it is not sweet with nimble feet
>   To dance upon the air!"

Digger Downs rattled his chains impotently. "Someone get me out of here," he pleaded.

Chrysalis heard the snap of small-arms fire in the upper reaches of the fortress, but the Bizango *chasseurs* were too late. The *bokor*, swaying from the meathook above the dungeon floor, was already dead.

It was hushed up, of course.

Senator Hartmann asked Chrysalis to be silent to help diffuse the fear of the wild card virus that was raging back home. He didn't even want there to be a hint of American jokers and aces mixing in foreign politics. She agreed for two reasons: First, she wanted him in her debt, and second, she always avoided personal publicity anyway. Not even Digger filed a story. He was recalcitrant at first, until Senator Hartmann had a private talk with him, a talk from which Downs emerged happy, smiling, and oddly close-mouthed.

The death of Charlemagne Calixte was ascribed to a sudden, unexpected illness. The other dozen bodies found in Fort Mercredi were never mentioned, and the two-score odd deaths and suicides among government officials over the next week or so were never even connected to Calixte's death.

Jean-Claude Duvalier, who suddenly found himself with a sullen, poverty-stricken country to run, was grateful for the lack of publicity, but there was something he discovered at the end of the affair, something puzzling and terrifying that he carefully kept secret.

Among the bodies recovered from Fort Mercredi was that of an old, old man. When Jean-Claude saw the body he blanched nearly white and had it interred in the *Cimetière Extérieur* in haste, at night, without ceremony, before anyone else could recognize it and ask how it was that François Duvalier, supposedly dead for fifteen years, was, or had been until very recently, still alive.

The only one who could answer that question was no longer in Haiti. He was on his way to America where he anticipated a long, interesting, and productive search for new and exciting sensations.

FROM *THE JOURNAL OF XAVIER DESMOND*

DECEMBER 8, 1986/MEXICO CITY:

Another state dinner this evening, but I've begged off with a plea of illness. A few hours to relax in my hotel room and write in the journal are most welcome. And my regrets were anything but fabricated—the tight schedule and pressures of the trip have begun to take their toll, I fear. I have not been keeping down all of my meals, although I've done my utmost to see that my distress remains unnoticed. If Tachyon suspected, he would insist on an examination, and once the truth was discovered, I might be sent home.

I will not permit that. I wanted to see all the fabled, far-off lands that Mary and I had once dreamed of together, but already it is clear that what we are engaged in here is far more important than any pleasure trip. Cuba was no Miami Beach, not for anyone who cared to look outside Havana; there are more jokers dying in the cane fields than cavorting on cabaret stages. And Haiti and the Dominican Republic were infinitely worse, as I've already noted in these pages.

A joker presence, a strong joker voice—we desperately need these things if we are to accomplish any good at all. I will not allow myself to be disqualified on medical grounds. Already our numbers are down by one—Dorian Wilde returned to New York rather than continue on to Mexico. I confess to mixed feelings about that. When we began, I had little respect for the "poet laureate of Jokertown," whose title is as dubious as my own mayoralty, though his Pulitzer is not. He seems to get a perverse glee from waving those wet, slimy tendrils of his in people's faces, flaunting his deformity in a deliberate attempt to draw a reaction. I suspect this aggressive nonchalance is in fact motivated by the same self-loathing that makes so many jokers take to masks, and a few sad cases actually attempt to amputate the deformed parts of their bodies. Also, he dresses almost as badly as Tachyon with his ridiculous Edwardian affectation, and his unstated preference for perfume over baths makes his company a trial to anyone with a sense of smell. Mine, alas, is quite acute.

Were it not for the legitimacy conferred on him by the Pulitzer, I doubt that he would ever have been named for this tour, but there are very few jokers who have achieved that kind of worldly recognition. I find precious little to admire in his poetry either, and much that is repugnant in his endless mincing recitations.

All that being said, I confess to a certain admiration for his impromptu performance before the Duvaliers. I suspect he received a severe dressing down from the politicians. Hartmann had a long private conversation with "The Divine Wilde" as we were leaving Haiti, and after that Dorian seemed much subdued.

While I don't agree with much that Wilde has to say, I do nonetheless think he ought to have the right to say it. He will be missed. I wish I knew why he was leaving. I asked him that very question and tried to convince him to go on for the benefit of all his fellow jokers. His reply was an offensive suggestion about the sexual uses of my trunk, couched in the form of a vile little poem. A curious man.

With Wilde gone, Father Squid and myself are the only true representatives of the joker point of view, I feel. Howard M. (Troll, to the world) is an imposing presence, nine feet tall, incredibly strong, his green-tinged skin as tough and hard as horn, and I also know him to be a profoundly decent and competent man, and a very intelligent one, but... he is by nature a follower, not a leader, and there is a shyness in him, a reticence, that prevents him from speaking out. His height makes it impossible for him to blend with the crowd, but sometimes I think that is what he desires most profoundly.

As for Chrysalis, she is none of those things, and she has her own unique charisma. I cannot deny that she is a respected community leader, one of the most visible (no pun intended) and powerful of jokers. Yet I have never much liked Chrysalis. Perhaps this is my own prejudice and self-interest. The rise of the Crystal Palace has had much to do with the decline of the Funhouse. But there are deeper issues. Chrysalis wields considerable power in Jokertown, but she has never used it to benefit anyone but herself. She has been aggressively apolitical, carefully distancing herself from the JADL and all joker rights agitation. When the times called for passion and commitment, she remained cool and uninvolved, hidden behind her cigarette holders, liqueurs, and upper-class British accent.

Chrysalis speaks only for Chrysalis, and Troll seldom speaks at all, which leaves it to Father Squid and myself to speak for the jokers. I would do it gladly, but I am so tired. . . .

I fell asleep early and was wakened by the sounds of my fellow delegates returning from the dinner. It went rather well, I understand. Excellent. We need some triumphs. Howard tells me that Hartmann gave a splendid speech and seemed to captivate President de la Madrid Hurtado throughout the meal. Peregrine captivated all the other males in the room, according to reports. I wonder if the other women are envious. Mistral is quite pretty, Fantasy is mesmerizing when she dances, and Radha O'Reilly is arresting, her mixed Irish and Indian heritage giving her features a truly exotic cast. But Peregrine overshadows all of them. What do they make of her?

The male aces certainly approve. The *Stacked Deck* is close quarters, and gossip travels quickly up and down the aisles. Word is that Dr. Tachyon and Jack Braun have both made passes and have been firmly rebuffed. If anything, Peregrine seems closest with her cameraman, a nat who travels back with the rest of the reporters. She's making a documentary of this trip.

Hiram is also close to Peregrine, but while there's a certain flirtatiousness to their constant banter, their friendship is more platonic in nature. Worchester has only one true love, and that's food. To that, his commitment is extraordinary. He seems to know all the best restaurants in every city we visit. His privacy is constantly being invaded by local chefs, who sneak up to his hotel room at all hours, carrying their specialties and begging for just a moment, just a taste, just a little approval. Far from objecting, Hiram delights in it.

In Haiti he found a cook he liked so much that he hired him on the spot and prevailed upon Hartmann to make a few calls to the INS and expedite the visa and work permit. We saw the man briefly at the Port-au-Prince airport, struggling with a huge trunk full of cast-iron cookware. Hiram made the trunk light enough for his new employee (who speaks no English, but Hiram insists that spices are a universal language) to carry on one shoulder. At tonight's dinner, Howard tells me, Worchester insisted on visiting the kitchen to get the chef's recipe for *chicken mole*, but while he was back there he concocted some sort of flaming dessert in honor of our hosts.

By rights I ought to object to Hiram Worchester, who revels in his acedom more than any other man I know, but I find it hard to dislike anyone who enjoys life so much and brings such enjoyment to those around him. Besides, I am well aware of his various anonymous charities in Jokertown, though he does his best to conceal them. Hiram is no more comfortable around my kind than Tachyon is, but his heart is as large as the rest of him.

Tomorrow the group will fragment yet again. Senators Hartmann and Lyons, Congressman Rabinowitz, and Ericsson from WHO will meet with the leaders of the PRI, Mexico's ruling party, while Tachyon and our medical staff visit a clinic that has claimed extraordinary success in treating the virus with laetrile. Our aces are scheduled to lunch with three of their Mexican counterparts. I'm pleased to say that Troll has been invited to join them. In some quarters, at least, his superhuman strength and near invulnerability have qualified him as an ace. A small breakthrough, of course, but a breakthrough nonetheless.

The rest of us will be traveling down to Yucatan and the Quintana Roo to look at Mayan ruins and the sites of several reported antijoker atrocities. Rural Mexico, it seems, is not as enlightened as Mexico City. The others will join us in Chichén Itzá the following day, and our last day in Mexico will be given over to tourism.

And then it will be on to Guatemala...perhaps. The daily press has been full of reports on an insurrection down there, an Indian uprising against the central government, and several of our journalists have gone ahead already, sensing a bigger story than this tour. If the situation seems too unstable, we may be forced to skip that stop.

THE TINT OF HATRED

Part Two

TUESDAY, DECEMBER 9, 1986, MEXICO:

"I stand in *El Templo de los Jaguares,* the Temple of the Jaguars, in Chichén Itzá. Under the fierce Yucatan sun the archway is impressive, two thick columns carved in the likeness of gigantic snakes, their huge, stylized heads flanking the entrance, their linked tails supporting the lintel.

"A thousand years ago, the guide books tell us, Mayan priests cheered the players in *El Juego de Pelota,* the ball court twenty-five feet below. It was a game that would be familiar to any of us. The players struck a hard rubber ball with their knees, elbows, and hips, scoring as the ball caromed through rings set in the long stone walls flanking the narrow field. A simple game, played for the glory of the god Quetzalcoatl, or Kukulcán, as those here called him.

"As his reward, the captain of the victorious team would be carried to the temple. The losing captain would behead his opponent with an obsidian knife, sending him into a glorious afterlife. A bizarre reward for conquest, by our standards.

"Too different to be comfortable.

"I look out on this ancient place, and the walls are still brown with blood; not of Mayans, but of jokers. The wild card plague struck here late and virulently. Some scientists have hypothesized that the mind-set of the victim influences the virus; thus, from a teenager fascinated by dinosaurs, you get Kid Dinosaur. From an obese master chef such as Hiram Worchester, you get someone who can control gravity. Dr. Tachyon, when asked, has been evasive on the subject, since it suggests that the deformed jokers have somehow punished themselves. That's just the kind of emotional fodder that reactionaries such as fundamentalist preacher Leo Barnett, or a fanatic 'prophet' such as Nur al-Allah, would use for their own purposes.

"Still, perhaps it's not surprising that in the ancestral lands of the Mayans, there have been no less than a dozen plumed serpents over the years: images of Kukulcán himself. And here in Mexico, if those of Indian blood had final say, perhaps even the jokers would be well-treated, for the Mayans considered the deformed blessed by the gods. But those of Mayan descent don't rule.

"In Chichén Itzá, over fifty jokers were killed only a year ago.

"Most of them (but not all) were followers of the new Mayan religion. These ruins were their place of worship. They thought that the virus was a sign to return to the old ways; they didn't think of themselves as victims. The gods had twisted their bodies and rendered them *different* and holy.

"Their religion was a throwback to a violent past. And because they were so different, they were feared. The locals of Spanish and European descent hated them. There was gossip concerning animal and even human sacrifice, of blood rites. It didn't matter if any of it was actually true; it never does. They were *different*. Their own neighbors banded together to rid themselves of this passive threat. They were dragged screaming from the surrounding villages.

"Bound, pleading for mercy, the jokers of Chichén Itzá were laid here. Their throats were slit in brutal parody of Mayan rites—splashing blood stained the carved serpents red. Their bodies were cast into the ball court below. Another atrocity, another 'nat vs. joker' incident. Old prejudices amplifying the new.

"Still, what happened here—though horrible—is no worse than what has happened, *is* happening, to jokers at home. You who are reading this: You or someone you know has probably been guilty of the same prejudice that caused this massacre. We're no less susceptible to the fear of the *different*."

Sara switched off the cassette recorder and laid it atop the serpent's head. Squinting into the brilliant sun, she could see the main group of delegates near the Temple of the Bearded Man; behind, the pyramid of Kukulcán threw a long shadow over the grass.

"A woman of such obvious compassion would keep an open mind, wouldn't she?"

Panic crawled her spine. Sara whirled about to see

Senator Hartmann regarding her. It took a long moment to recover her composure. "You startled me, Senator. Where's the rest of the entourage?"

Hartmann smiled apologetically. "I'm sorry for sneaking up on you, Ms. Morgenstern. Scaring you wasn't my intention, believe me. As for the others—I told Hiram that I had private business to discuss with you. He's a good friend and helped me escape." He grinned softly as if at some inner amusement. "I couldn't quite get away from everyone. Billy Ray's down below, being the dutiful bodyguard."

Sara frowned into that smile. She picked up her recorder, placed it in her purse. "I don't think you and I have any 'private business,' Senator. If you'll excuse me . . ."

She started to move past him toward the temple's entrance. She thought for a moment that he might make some move to detain her; she tensed, but he stepped aside politely.

"I meant what I said about compassion," he commented just before she reached the stairs. "I know why you dislike me. I know why you look so familiar. Andrea was your sister."

The words battered Sara like fists. She gasped at the pain.

"I also believe you're a fair person," Hartmann continued, and each word was another blow. "I think that if you were finally told the truth, you'd understand."

Sara gave a cry that was half-sob, unable to hold it back. She placed a hand on cool, rough stone and turned. The sympathy she saw in Hartmann's eyes frightened her.

"Just leave me alone, Senator."

"We're stuck together on this trip, Ms. Morgenstern. There's no sense in our being enemies, not when there isn't any reason."

His voice was gentle and persuasive. He sounded kind. It would have been easier if he'd been accusatory, if he'd tried to bribe her or threaten her. Then she could have fought back easily, could have reveled in her fury. But Hartmann stood there, his hands at his sides, looking, of all things, *sad*. She'd imagined Hartmann many ways, but never like this. "How . . ." she began, and found her voice choked. "When did you find out about Andrea?"

"After our conversation at the press reception, I had my aide Amy run a background check. She found that you'd been born in Cincinnati, that your family name was Whitman. You lived two streets over from me, on Thornview. Andrea was what, seven or eight years older than you? You look a lot like her, like she might have grown up to be." He steepled his hands to his face, rubbing at the corners of his eyes with his forefingers. "I'm not very comfortable with lying or evasion, Ms. Morgenstern. That's not my style. I don't think you are either, not from the blunt articles you've written. I think I know why we've been at odds, and I also know it's a mistake."

"Which means that you think it's my fault."

"I've never attacked *you* in print."

"I don't lie in my articles, Senator. They're fair. If you have a problem with any of my facts, let me know and I'll give you verification."

"Ms. Morgenstern—" Hartmann began, a trace of irritation in his voice. Then, oddly, he leaned his head back and chuckled loudly. "God, there we go again," he said, and he sighed. "Really, I read your articles. I don't always *agree* with you, but I'll be the first to admit that they're well written and researched. I even think that I could like the person who wrote them, if ever we had the chance to talk and know each other." His gray-blue eyes caught hers. "What's between us is the ghost of your sister."

His last words took the breath from her. She couldn't believe that he'd said them; not so casually, not with that innocent smile, not after all those years. "You killed her," she breathed, and didn't realize that she'd spoken the words aloud until she saw the shock on Hartmann's face. He went white for an instant. His mouth opened, then clamped shut. He shook his head.

"You can't believe that," he said. "Roger Pellman killed her. There was no question at all about that. The poor retarded kid . . ." Hartmann shook his head. "How can I say it gently? He came out of the woods naked and howling like all the demons of hell were after him. Andrea's blood covered him. He *admitted* killing her."

Hartmann's face was still pale. Sweat beaded on his forehead, and his gaze was withdrawn. "Damnit, I was *there*, Ms. Morgenstern. I was standing outside in my front yard when Pellman came running up the street, gibbering. He ran into his house, the neighbors all around watching. We all heard his mother scream. Then the cops came, first to the Pellmans', then taking Roger into the woods with them. I saw them carry out the wrapped body. My mom had her arms around your mother. She was hysterical, wailing. It infected all of us. We were *all* crying, all of the kids, even though we really didn't understand what was going on. They handcuffed Roger, hauled him away...."

Sara stared, bewildered, at Hartmann's haunted face. His hands were clenched into fists at his side. "How can you say I killed her?" he asked softly. "Don't you realize that *I* was in love with her, as infatuated as an eleven-year-old kid can be. I would never have done anything to hurt Andrea. I had nightmares for months afterward. I was furious when they assigned Roger Pellman to Longview Psychiatric. I wanted him to *hang* for what he'd done; I wanted to be the one to pull the damn switch on him."

It can't be. The insistent denial pounded in her head. Yet she looked at Hartmann and knew, somehow, that she was wrong. Doubt had begun to dampen some of the fiery hatred. "Succubus," she said, and found her throat dry. She licked her lips. "You were there, and she had Andrea's face."

Hartmann took a gulping, deep breath. He looked away from her for a moment, toward the northern temple. Sara followed his gaze and saw that the tour group from the *Stacked Deck* had gone inside. The ball court was deserted, quiet. "I knew Succubus," Hartmann said at last, still looking away from her, and she could feel the trembling emotion in his voice. "I knew her at the end of her public career, and we still saw each other occasionally. I wasn't married then, and Succubus..." He turned around to Sara, and she was surprised to see his eyes bright with moisture. "Succubus could be *any*one, you know. She was anyone's ideal lover. When she was with you, she was exactly what you wanted."

In that instant Sara knew what he was going to say. She had already begun to shake her head in denial.

"For me, quite often," Hartmann continued, "she was Andrea. You were right, you know, when you said we're both obsessed. We're obsessed by Andrea and her death. If that hadn't happened, I might have forgotten my crush on her six months later, like every pubescent fantasy. But what Roger Pellman did engraved Andrea in my mind. Succubus—she roamed in your head and used what she found there. Inside me, she found Andrea. So when she saw me during the riot, when she wanted me to save her from the violence of the mob, she took the face she had always shown to me: Andrea's.

"I didn't kill your sister, Ms. Morgenstern. I'll plead guilty to thinking of her as my fantasy lover, but that's all.

Your sister was an ideal for me. I wouldn't have harmed her at all. I couldn't."

It can't be.

Sara remembered all the strange links she'd found in the months after she'd first seen the videotape of Succubus's death. Sara had thought that she'd escaped the cloying Andrea-worship of her parents, that she'd left her murdered sister behind her for the rest of her life. Succubus's face had shattered all that. Even after she'd shakily written the article that would eventually win her the Pulitzer, she'd thought it had been a mistake, a cruel trick of fate. But Hartmann had been there. She'd known all along that the Senator was from Ohio. She discovered later that not only was he from Cincinnati, but he'd lived nearby, been a classmate of Andrea's. She'd done more research, suddenly suspicious. Mysterious deaths and violent acts seemed to plague Hartmann: in law school, as a New York City councilman, as mayor, as senator. None of them were ever Hartmann's fault. There was always someone else, someone with motive and desire. But still . . .

She dug further. She found that five-year-old Hartmann and his parents had been on vacation in New York the day Jetboy died and the virus was loosed on the unsuspecting world. They'd been among the lucky ones. None of them had ever shown any signs of having been infected. Still, if Hartmann were a hidden ace, "up the sleeve" in the vernacular. . .

It was circumstantial. It was flimsy. Her reporter's instinct had screamed "Objectivity!" at her emotions. That hadn't stopped her from hating him. There was always that gut feeling, the certainty that he was the one. Not Roger Pellman, not the others who had been convicted, but *Hartmann*.

For the last nine years or more she'd believed that.

Yet Hartmann didn't seem dangerous or malign now. He stood there patiently—a plain face, a high forehead threatening to recede and sweating from the fierce sun, a body soft around the waist from years of sitting behind administrative desks. He let her stare, let her search his gaze unflinchingly. Sara found that she couldn't imagine him killing or hurting. A person who enjoyed pain in the way she'd imagined would show it somewhere: in his body language, his eyes, his voice. There was none of it in Hartmann. He had a presence, yes, a charisma, but he didn't feel dangerous

Would he have told you about Succubus if he hadn't cared? Would a murderer have opened himself that far to

someone he didn't know, a hostile reporter? Doesn't violence follow everyone through life? Give him that much credit.

"I . . . I have to think about this," she said.

"That's all I ask," he answered softly. He took a deep breath, looking around the sun-baked ruins. "I should get back to the others before everyone starts talking, I suppose. The way Downs is snooping around me, he'll have all sorts of rumors started." He smiled sadly.

Hartmann moved toward the temple stairs. Sara watched him, frowning at the contradictory thoughts swirling inside her. As the senator passed her, he stopped.

His hand touched her shoulder.

His touch was gentle, warm, and his face was full of sympathy. "I put Andrea's face on Succubus and I'm sorry that caused you anguish. It's also plagued me." His hand dropped; her shoulder was cool where he'd been. He glanced at the serpent's heads to either side. "Pellman killed Andrea. No one else. I'm just a person accidentally caught up in your story. I think we'd make better friends than enemies."

He seemed to hesitate for a moment, as if waiting for a reply. Sara was looking out to the pyramid, not trusting herself to say anything. All the conflicting emotions that were Andrea surged in her: outrage, an aching loss, bitterness, a thousand others. Sara kept her gaze averted from Hartmann, not wanting him to see.

When she was sure he was gone, she sank down, sitting with her back against a serpent column. Her head on her knees, she let the tears come.

At the bottom of the steps Gregg looked upward at the temple. A grim satisfaction filled him. Toward the end he had felt Sara's hatred dissipate like fog in sunlight, leaving behind only a faint trace of its presence. *I did it without you*, he said to the power inside him. *Her hatred flung you away, but it didn't matter. She's Succubus, she's Andrea; I'll make her come to me by myself. She's mine. I don't need you to force her to me.*

Puppetman was silent.

BLOOD RIGHTS

Leanne C. Harper

The young Lacandon Maya coughed as the smoke followed him across the newly cleared field. Someone had to stay and watch the brush they had cut reduce to the ashes they would use to feed the ground of the *milpa*. The fire was burning evenly so he moved back out of range of the smoke. Everyone else was at home asleep in the afternoon, and the humid warmth made him drowsy too. Smoothing down his long white robe over his bare legs, he ate the cold tamales that were his dinner.

Lying in the shade, he began to blink and fall under his dream's spell once more. His dreams had taken him to the realm of the gods ever since he had been a boy, but it was rare that he remembered what the gods had said or done. José, the old shaman, became so angry when all he could recall were feelings or useless details from his latest vision. The only hope in it all was that the dream became more and more clear each time he had it. He had been denying to José that the dream had returned, waiting for the time when he could remember enough to impress even José, but the shaman knew he lied.

The dream took him to Xibalba, the domain of Ah Puch, the Lord of Death. Xibalba always smelled of smoke and blood. He coughed as the atmosphere of death entered his lungs. The coughing awakened him, and it took him a moment to realize that he was no longer in the underworld. Eyes watering, he backed away from the fire, out of range of the smoke that the wind had sent to follow him. Maybe his ancestors were angry with him too.

He stared at the flames, now slowly dying down, and moved a little closer to the bonfire in the center of the *milpa*. Wild-eyed, he slid into a crouch before the fire and watched it closely. José had told him again and again to trust what he felt and go where his intuition led him. This time, frightened but glad there was no one to see him, he would do it.

With both hands he pushed his black hair back behind his ears and reached forward to pull a short leafy branch from the edge of the brush pile and put it on the ground before him. Slowly, left hand trembling slightly, he drew the machete from its stained leather scabbard at his side. Flexing his right hand, he held it chest-high in front of him. He clenched his jaws and turned his head slightly up and away from looking at his hand. The sweat from his forehead fell into his eyes and dripped off his aristocratic nose as he brought the machete down across the palm of his right hand.

He made no sound. Nor did he move as the bright blood ran down his fingers to fall on the deep green of the leaves. Only his eyes narrowed and his chin lifted. When the branch was covered with his blood, he picked it up with his left hand and threw it into the flames. The air smelled of Xibalba again and of his ancestors' ancient rituals, and he returned to the underworld once more.

As always, a rabbit scribe greeted him, speaking in the ancient language of his people. Clutching the bark paper and brush to its furry chest, it told him in an odd, low voice to follow. Ahau Ah Puch awaited him.

The air was scented by burning blood.

The man and the rabbit had walked through a village of abandoned thatch huts, much like those of his own village. But here patches of thatch were missing from the roofs. The uncovered doorways gaped like the mouths of skulls, while the mud and grass of the walls fell away like the flesh from a decaying body.

The rabbit led him between the high, stone walls of a ball court with carved stone rings set on the walls above his head. He did not remember ever having been in a ball court before, but he knew he could play here, had played here, had scored here. He felt again the hard rubber ball strike the cotton padding on his elbow and arc toward the serpent's coils carved into the stone ring.

He drew his eyes back from the serpent to the face of the Lord of Death, seated on a reed mat on the dais in front of him at the end of the ball court. Ah Puch's eyes were black pits set in the white band across his skull. The Ahau's mouth and nose opened on eternity, and the smells of blood and rotting flesh were strong upon him.

"Hunapu. Ballplayer. You have returned to me."

The man knelt and put his forehead to the floor before Ah Puch, but he felt no fear. He felt nothing in this dream.

"Hunapu. Son." The man raised his head at the sound of the old woman's voice to his left. Ix Chel and her even older husband, Itzamna, sat cross-legged on reed mats attended by the rabbit scribe. Their dais was supported by twin, huge turtles whose intermittently blinking eyes were all that showed they lived.

"The cycle ends." The grandmother continued to speak. "Change comes for the *hach winik*. The white stickmen have created their own downfall. You, Hunapu, brother to Xbalanque, are the messenger. Go to Kaminaljuyu and meet your brother. Your path will become clear, ballplayer."

"Do not forget us, ballplayer." Ah Puch spoke and his voice was vicious and hollow as if he spoke through a mask. "Your blood is ours. Your enemies' blood is ours."

For the first time real fear broke through Hunapu's numbness. His hand throbbed in pain to the rhythm of Ah Puch's words, but despite his fear he rose from his kneeling position. His eyes met the endless black of Ah Puch's.

Before he could speak, a ball whose every edge was a razor-sharp blade cut through the air toward him. Then Xibalba was gone and he was back at the dead fire, hearing the old god speak but one word.

"Remember."

The stocky Mayan worker stood in the shadows of one of the work tents as he watched the last group of archaeological students and professors break up. As they wandered into their sleeping tents, he withdrew even farther into the protection of the tent. His classic Maya profile marked him as a pure-blood Indian, the lowest class in Guatemala's social hierarchy; but here among the blonde students, it marked him as a conquest. It was rare that a student of the past got to sleep with a living example of a race of priest-kings. The worker, dressed in overlarge blue jeans and a filthy University of Pennsylvania T-shirt, saw no reason to discourage this impression. But he made himself as unattractive as possible to watch their simultaneous desire and repulsion. He walked carefully down the short passage between the tents to the sheet-metal storage shed.

The Indian once again assured himself that there were no observers before grasping the padlock and thrusting his pick into the keyhole. Squinting against the flickering firelight, he probed a few times and the lock was open. He flashed bright teeth in a contemptuous look back at the professors' tent. Slipping the lock into a pocket of his jeans, he opened the door and eased himself sideways into the shed. Unlike the archaeologists, he didn't need to stoop.

He waited a moment for his eyes to adjust before tugging a flashlight from his back pocket. The end of the light was covered by a torn piece of cloth secured by a rubber band. The dim circle of light roamed around the room almost at random until it froze on a shelf crowded with objects taken from the tombs and trenches dug around the city. The thief moved sideways along the narrow center aisle, careful not to disturb the pots, statues, and other partially cleaned arti- facts on the shelves to either side. The small man pulled half a dozen small pots and miniature statutes off the shelves. None were located at the front of a shelf nor were they the finest examples, but all were intact, if somewhat the worse for their long burial. He put them into a cotton drawstring sack.

Sneering at the rows of ceramics and jade carvings, he wondered why the *norteamericanos* could curse the grave- robbers of the past when they were so efficient at the same thing. He sidled back up the aisle, catching a red-and-black- painted pot as his movement caused it to rock dangerously near the edge. Quick hands picked up a battered jade earplug and he paused, running the flashlight beam around the narrow room once more. Two things caught his eyes, a stingray spine and a bottle of Tanqueray gin kept locked up away from the workers.

Clutching the bottle and the spine against his chest, he listened, head leaned against the door, for any stray noises. All he heard was the muffled sound of lovemaking from a nearby tent. It sounded like the tall redhead. Satisfied that no one would observe him, he slid outside and replaced the lock.

He waited to open the gin until he had climbed up one of the larger hills. The professors said the hills were all temples. He had seen their drawings of what this place had once been. He didn't believe what he had been shown: plazas and tall temples with roof combs, all painted in yellow and red. He especially didn't believe the tall, thin men who presided over the temples. They didn't look like him, anyone he knew, or even much like the murals painted on some of the temple walls, but the professors said that they were his ancestors. It was typical of the *norteamericanos*. But it meant that he was only stealing his inheritance.

Something poked his side as he leaned over to open the bottle. He pulled the stingray spine out of his pocket. One of the blondes, no, the redhead, had told him what the old kings had done. Guh-ross, she had said. He had privately agreed. The *norteamericano* women with whom he slept always asked lots of questions about the ways of the old ones. They seemed to think that he should have the knowledge of a *brujo* just because he was an Indian. *Gringas*. He learned more from them than anyone in his family. They had taught him what was valuable, and more important, what would be immediately missed. He had a nice little collection now. He would be rich after he sold them in Guatemala.

The gin was good. He leaned back against a convenient tree trunk and watched the moon. Ix Chel, the Old Woman, was the moon goddess. The old ones' gods were ugly, not like the Virgin Mary or Jesus or even God in the Church where he had been raised. He picked up the stingray spine. Someone had brought it long ago up to this city in the Highlands. It was carved with intricate designs along its entire length. He held it beside his leg, measuring it against his thigh. It ran the full length. All those stories. He reached out for the gin bottle, but he missed and fell forward, catching himself with his free hand. He was drunk.

The moonlight shone off his sweating torso as he pulled off his T-shirt and folded it none too neatly into a pad. He put the shirt on his right shoulder. Closing his eyes, he weaved to the left and reopened them, blinking rapidly. He tried to pull his legs up into the position he had seen in so many paintings. It took maneuvering. He had to brace himself against the rock and hold his legs in place with his right hand. He secured the shirt with his jaw and his raised shoulder.

With a sureness that belied his intoxication, he brought
up the spine and pierced his right ear.

He gasped and swore at the pain. It swept through him,
driving out the alcohol and bringing on a euphoria as the
blood flowed from his shredded earlobe and was absorbed by
the T-shirt. The high made him tremble. It was better than
the gin, better than the marijuana the graduate students had,
better than the professor's cocaine he had once stolen and
snorted.

Penetrating his shadowed mind was the impression that
he was no longer alone on the temple. He opened his eyes,
not realizing that he had closed them. For just a moment the
temple as it had once stood glowed in the moonlight. The
bright reds were muted by the dim light. His wife knelt
before him with a rope of thorns drawn through her tongue.
Attendants surrounded them. His heavy ornamental headdress covered his eyes. He blinked.

The temple was a pile of stone covered by the jungle.
There was no wife wearing jade, no attendants. He was
wearing dirty jeans again. He shook his head sharply to clear
away the last of the vision. That hurt, *aiee,* did it hurt. It
must have been the gin and listening to those women.
According to what they had said, he'd messed up the old rites
anyway. The power was supposed to be in the *burning*
blood.

The shirt had fallen from his shoulder. It was bright red
and sodden with his blood. He thought about it a moment,
then pulled out a cigarette lighter he had stolen from one of
the professors and tried to burn the shirt. It was too wet; the
flames kept going out. Instead he made a fire with some
sticks he picked up off the ground. When he finally had a
small fire going, he threw on the shirt. The burning blood
gave off smoke and a stench that nearly made him sick.
Mostly in jest he sat in front of the blaze and aped the
cross-legged position he had seen on so many pots, one hand
extended toward the flames. He was starting to get very tired
and staring at the fire mesmerized him.

What little he knew of Xibalba led him to believe that it
was a place of darkness and flames, like the hell the fathers
warned him about as a child. It wasn't. It most resembled a
remote village where they still lived by the old ways. No
television antennas, no radios blaring the latest in rock and
roll from Guatemala. All was silent. He saw no one as he

walked about the small group of huts. The only movement
he saw was a bat flying out of the low doorway of one of the
thatch-roofed houses. The roofs were pitched like the
ceilings of the temple rooms, high and narrow, rising
almost to a point. He felt as if he were walking through a
mural on a temple wall. It was all so familiar. He remembered that none of his usual drunken dreams had this
clarity.

A rhythmic *ga-pow, ga-pow* brought him through the
quiet to a ball court. Three human figures sat on the platform
on top of the walls. He recognized them as Ah Puch, Itzamna,
and Ix Chel—the Death God, the Old Man, and the Old
Woman, supreme in the Mayan pantheon, or as supreme as
any of the many deities were. The three were surrounded by
animals who assisted them as scribes and servants. Drawing
his gaze back down the stone walls to the packed-dirt court
itself, he saw the source of the noise. Not deigning to notice
him, a creature that was half-human, half-jaguar repeatedly
attempted to knock a ball through one of the intricately
carved stone hoops high on the walls of the court. The
creature never used its paws. Instead it used head, hips,
elbows, and knees to send the ball bouncing up the wall
toward the ring. The jaguar-man and its fangs frightened him.
Since the dream had begun, it was the first thing he had felt
besides curiosity and wondering how he could steal those
stone rings. He watched the muscles beneath the black spots
bunch and release as he considered why none of this seemed
strange in the least. He lifted his head and stared up at the
watchers.

From one corner of his eye he saw the ball coming
toward him. Moving in patterns that seemed as familiar as the
village, he swung away from it before bringing his elbow up
and under the ball and launching it toward the nearest ring.
It arched through the goal without touching the stone. The
watchers gasped and murmured to each other. He was just as
surprised, but he decided that discretion was the best course
here.

"Ai! Not bad!" He yelled up at them in Spanish. Lord
Death shook his head and glared at the old couple. Itzamna
spoke to him in pure Maya. Although he had never spoken
the language before in his life, he recognized it and understood it.

"Welcome, Xbalanque, to Xibalba. You are as fine a ballplayer as your namesake."

"My name's not Xbalanque."

"From this time, it is." The black death-mask of Ah Puch glared down at him and he swallowed his next comment.

"*Sí*, this is a dream and I am Xbalanque." He spread his hands and nodded. "Whatever you say."

Ah Puch looked away.

"You are different; you have always known this." Ix Chel smiled down at him. It was the smile of a crocodile, not a grandmother. He grinned up at her, wishing he'd wake up. Now.

"You are a thief."

He began thinking about how he was going to get out of this dream. He had remembered the more troublesome parts of the ancient myths—the decapitations, the houses of multiple horrors . . .

"You should use your abilities to gain power."

"Hey, I'll do that. You're right. No problem. Just as soon as I get back." One of the rabbits who was attending the three gods watched him intently with head canted to one side and nostrils twitching. Occasionally it wrote frantically on an odd, folded piece of paper with a brushlike pen. He was reminded of a comic book he had once read, *Alice in Wonderland*. There had been rabbits in her dream too. And he was getting hungry.

"Go to the city, Xbalanque." Itzamna's voice was squeaky, pitched even higher than his wife's.

"Hey, isn't there a brother in this somewhere?" He was remembering even more of the myth.

"You'll find him. Go." The ball court began to quiver in front of his eyes, and the jaguar's paw struck him in the back of the head.

Xbalanque grunted in pain as his head slid off the rock he had apparently been using as a pillow. He pulled himself upright, shoving his bare back against the rough limestone. The dream was still with him, and he couldn't seem to focus on anything. The moon had gone down while he'd been passed out. It was very dark. The uncovered stones of the ruin glowed with their own light, like bones disturbed in a grave. The bones of his people's past glory.

He bent over to pick up his stolen treasures and fell to one knee. Unable to stop himself, he vomited the gin

and tortillas he had eaten. *Madre de Dios,* he felt bad.
Body empty and shaking, he staggered up again to begin
the descent from the pyramid. Maybe that dream was
right. He should leave, go to Guatemala City now. Take
what he had. It was enough to let him live comfortably for
a while.

Christ, his head hurt. Hungover and still drunk. It
wasn't fair. The last thing he picked up was the stingray
spine. Its barbs were still coated with his blood. Xbalanque
reached up to touch his ear gingerly. He fingered the hole
in the lobe with pain and disgust. His hand came away
bloody. That was definitely not part of the dream. Swaying,
he searched through his pockets until he found the earplug. He tried to insert it into his earlobe, but it hurt too
much and the torn flesh would not support it. He was
almost sick again.

Xbalanque tried to remember the strange dream. It was
fading. For the moment all he recalled was that the dream
recommended a retreat to the city. It still sounded like a good
idea. As he alternately tripped and slid down the side of the
hill, he decided to steal a jeep and go in style. Maybe they
wouldn't miss it. He couldn't walk all the way with this
headache anyway.

Inside the dark, smoke-filled thatch house José listened
gravely to Hunapu's tale of his vision. The shaman nodded
when Hunapu spoke of his audience with the gods. When he
finished, he looked to the old man for interpretation and
guidance.

"Your vision is a true one, Hunapu." He straightened
up and slid from his hammock to the dirt floor. Standing
before the crouching Hunapu, he threw copal incense on
his fire. "You must do as the gods tell you or bring us all
misfortune."

"But where am I to go? What is Kaminaljuyu?" Hunapu
shrugged in his confusion. "I do not understand. I have no
brother, only sisters. I do not play this ball game. Why
me?"

"You have been chosen and touched by the gods. They
see what we do not." José put his hand on the young man's
shoulder. "It is very dangerous to question them. They anger
easily.

"Kaminaljuyu is Guatemala City. That is where you must

go. But first we must prepare you." The shaman looked past him. "Sleep tonight. Tomorrow you will go."

When he returned to the shaman's home in the morning, most of the village was there to share in the magical thing that had happened. When he left them, José walked with him into the rain forest, carrying a package. Out of sight of the village, the shaman wrapped Hunapu's elbows and knees with the cotton padding he had brought with him. The old man told him that this was how he had been dressed in José's dream the night before. It too was a sign that Hunapu's vision was true. José warned him to tell those he met of his quest only if they could be trusted and were Lacandones like himself. The *Ladinos* would try to stop him if they knew.

Xepon was small. Perhaps thirty multicolored houses clustered around the church on the square. Their pink, blue, and yellow paint was faded, and they looked as though they crouched with their backs to the rain that had begun earlier. As Xbalanque bounced down the mountain road into the village, he was happy to see the cantina. He had decided to take the most isolated roads he could find on the worn road map under the driver's seat to get into the city.

He started to park in front of the cantina, but instead decided to park around the side, away from curious eyes. He thought it was strange that he had seen no one since entering town, but the weather was fit for no one, especially him and his hangover. His Reeboks, another gift from the *norteamericanos,* flopped against the wet wood walkway that ran in front of the cantina before he entered the open doorway. It was a disconcerting sound amid a silence broken only by dripping water and the rain on the tin roofs. Even the dimness outside had not prepared him for the darkness within, or the years of tobacco smoke still trapped between the narrow walls. A few tattered and faded *Feliz Navidad* banners hung down from the gray ceiling.

"What do you want?" He was assaulted in Spanish from behind the long bar that lined the wall to his left. The force and hostility behind the question hurt his head. A stooped old Indian woman glared at him from behind the bar.

"*Cerveza.*"

Unconcerned for his preferences, she removed a bottle from the cooler behind the bar and flipped off the cap as he walked toward her. She set it on the stained and pitted wood of the bar. When Xbalanque reached for it, she put a small gnarled hand around the bottle and nodded her chin at him. He pulled some crumpled quetzals from his pocket and laid them on the bar. There was a crash of nearby thunder and they both tensed. He realized for the first time that the reason she was so hostile might not have anything to do with an early customer. She snatched the money off the bar as if to deny her fear and put it into the sash around her stained huipil.

"What do you have to eat?" Whatever was going on certainly had nothing to do with him. The beer tasted good, but it was not what he really needed.

"Black bean soup." The woman's answer was a statement, definitely not an invitation. It was accompanied by more thunder rolling up the valley.

"What else?" Looking around, Xbalanque belatedly realized that something was extremely wrong. Every cantina he had ever been in, no matter where or how large, had some old drunks sitting around waiting to try to pick up a free drink. And women, even old women such as this one, rarely worked in bars in these small villages.

"Nothing." Her face was closed to him as he looked for a clue to what was happening.

Another peal of thunder turned into the low growling of truck engines. Both their heads swung toward the door. Xbalanque stepped back from the bar and looked for a back way out. There was none. When he turned again to the old woman, she had her back to him. He ran for the door.

Green-clad soldiers piled off the backs of the two army transports parked in the middle of the square. The paths of the trucks were marked by the broken benches and shrubs they had run over on their way across the tiny park. As the soldiers hit the ground, they pulled their machine guns into firing position. Two-man teams immediately left the central area to search the houses lining the square. Other armed men moved out of the square through the rest of the village.

Palms spread against the plaster, Xbalanque slid along the outside wall of the cantina for the safety of the side street.

If he could get to the jeep, he had a chance to escape. He had made it to the corner of the building when one of the soldiers spotted him. At the soldier's order to halt, he jumped for the street, sliding in the mud, and dashed for the jeep.

Shots into the ground in front of him splashed him with mud. Xbalanque threw his hand up to protect his eyes and fell to his knees. Before he could get back up, a sullen-faced soldier grabbed his arm and hauled Xbalanque back to the square, his feet slipping in the thick mud as he scrambled to stand up and walk.

One of the young *Ladino* soldiers stood with his Uzi pointed at Xbalanque's head while he was shoved facedown in the mud and searched. Xbalanque had hidden the artifacts in the jeep, but the soldiers found the stash of quetzals in his Reeboks. One of them held the wad of money up to the army lieutenant in charge. The lieutenant looked disgusted at the condition of the bills, but he put them in his own pocket anyway. Xbalanque did not protest. Through the excruciating pain in his head that had begun when he fled the soldiers, he was trying to decide what he could say to get out of this. If they knew the jeep was stolen, he was dead.

The sound of more gunfire made him wince into the mud. He raised his head slightly, knocking it into the barrel of the gun above him. The soldier holding it pulled back enough for him to see another man being dragged from inside the dilapidated yellow school on the west side of the square. He heard children crying inside the small building. The second prisoner was also an Indian, tall with eyeglasses knocked askew on his narrow face. The two soldiers escorting him allowed him to regain his feet before presenting him to the lieutenant.

The schoolteacher straightened his glasses before staring directly into the lieutenant's mirrored sunglasses. Xbalanque knew he was in trouble; the schoolteacher was deliberately trying to anger the army officer. It could only result in worse consequences than they already faced.

The lieutenant brought up his swagger stick and knocked the teacher's glasses off his face. When the teacher bent down to pick them up, the officer struck him across the side of the head. With blood dripping down his face onto his white European shirt, the teacher replaced his glasses. The right lens was shattered. Xbalanque began looking for an escape

route. He hoped that his guard might be sufficiently distracted. Looking sideways up at the young man with the Uzi, he
saw that the boy had not taken his eyes off him.

"You are a communist." The lieutenant made it a statement, not a question, directed to the teacher. Before the
teacher could reply, the officer glanced toward the school-
house with annoyance. The children inside were still crying.
He swung his swagger stick toward the school and nodded at
a soldier to his left. Without aiming, the soldier panned his
machine gun across the building, breaking windows and
pocking the plaster. A few screams erupted from inside, then
silence.

"You are a traitor and an enemy to Guatemala." He
brought the stick up across the other side of the teacher's
head. There was more blood, and Xbalanque began to feel
sick and somehow *wrong*.

"Where are the other traitors?"

"There are no other traitors." The teacher shrugged and
smiled.

"Fernandez, the church." The lieutenant spoke to a
soldier smoking a cigarette leaning against one of the trucks.
Fernandez tossed away the cigarette and picked up the thick
tube propped beside him against the truck. While he aimed,
another of the men around the trucks shoved a rocket into
the launcher.

Turning toward the old colonial church, Xbalanque saw,
for the first time, the village priest standing outside arguing with one of the search teams as the soldiers stood there
holding silver candlesticks. There was an explosion from
the rocket launcher, followed a split second later by the
blast as the church fell in on itself. The soldiers standing
outside had seen it coming and fallen to the ground. The
priest collapsed, from shock or injuries, Xbalanque could
not tell. By now he was feeling the pain in every joint and
muscle.

The rain mixed with the blood on the teacher's face and,
as it dripped down, stained his shirt pink. Xbalanque didn't
see any more. The pain had grown until he curled up in the
mud, clutching his knees to his chest. Something was happening. It must be because he had never felt such fear
before. He knew that he was going to die. The damned old
gods had led him to this.

He barely heard the order given to move him up against

the school wall with the teacher. The lieutenant didn't even care who he was. For some reason the fact that the officer hadn't even bothered to question him seemed the worst indignity of all.

Xbalanque shook as he stood with his back against the already bullet-marked wall. The soldiers left them there alone and backed off, out of the line of fire. The pain had begun to come in waves, driving out his fear, driving out everything except the enormous weight of the agony in his body. He stared through the soldiers gathering for the firing squad at the rainbow forming between the bright, jade green mountains as the sun finally came out. The teacher patted him on the shoulder.

"Are you all right?" His companion actually looked concerned. Xbalanque was silent as he gathered sufficient energy not to collapse to the ground.

"See, God has a sense of humor." The madman smiled at him as if at a crying child. Xbalanque cursed him in the language of his Quiche grandmother, a tongue he had not spoken before his dream of Xibalba.

"We die for the lives of our people." The schoolteacher lifted his head proudly and faced the soldiers' guns as they were raised to aim.

"No. Not again!" Xbalanque rushed the guns as they fired. His force knocked the other man to his knees. As he moved, Xbalanque realized in one small part of his brain that the exquisite agony had gone. As the bullets sped to meet his charge, he felt only stronger, more powerful than he ever had before. The bullets reached him.

Xbalanque hesitated as they struck. He waited an instant for the inevitable pain and final darkness. They didn't come. He looked at the soldiers; they stared back wide-eyed. Some ran for the trucks. Others dropped their guns and simply ran. A few held their ground and kept firing, looking to the lieutenant, who was backing up slowly toward the trucks and calling for Fernandez.

The warrior scooped up a brick from the street and, crying out his name in a mixture of fear and exhilaration, threw it with all his strength at one of the trucks. As it flew, it struck a soldier, crushing his head and splattering blood and brains across his fleeing companions before flying on toward the vehicle. The soldier had slowed its momentum. It was dropping as it streaked toward the truck. The brick struck the gas tank and the transport exploded.

Xbalanque stopped his rush toward the soldiers and stared at the fiery scene. Men in flames—soldiers who had made the shelter of the troop carrier—screamed. The scene was right out of one of the American movies he had watched in the city. But the movies hadn't had the smell of petrol, burning canvas and rubber, and underneath everything else the stench of burning flesh. He began backing away.

Remotely, as if through heavy padding, he felt someone grab his arm. Xbalanque turned to strike his enemy. The teacher was staring down at him through the shattered glasses.

"*Se habla español?*" The taller man was guiding him away from the square up a side street.

"*Sí, sí.*" Xbalanque was beginning to have time to wonder what was happening. He knew he had never before been able to do anything such as this. Something was not right. What had that vision done to him? He was involuntarily relaxing and he felt the strength draining from him. He began to lean against the wall of a peeling pale-red house.

"*Madre de Dios*—we have to keep moving." The teacher hauled at him. "They'll bring up the artillery. You're good with bullets, but can you fend off rockets?"

"I don't know. . . ." Xbalanque stopped to think about this for a moment.

"We'll figure it out later. Come *on.*"

Xbalanque realized that the man was right, but it was so difficult. With the fear of death gone, he felt as though he had lost not only the new power but also his regular strength. He looked up the street toward the forested mountainside so far away above the houses. The trees were safety. The soldiers would never follow them into the forest where guerrillas could be waiting to ambush them. The flat sound of a shot brought him back.

The teacher pulled him away from the house and, keeping his hand underneath Xbalanque's arm, steered him toward the green refuge ahead. They cut left between two small houses and moved sideways along the narrow, muddy alley that divided the clapboard and plaster buildings. Xbalanque was moving now, sliding and skidding in the slippery brown mud. Past rear gardens, the alley turned to a path leading up the steep hillside into the trees. The open ground was at least fifteen meters of utter exposure.

He ran into his compatriot as the other man stopped and peered around the corner of the house on the left.

"Clear." The teacher had not relinquished his grip on Xbalanque's arm. "Can you run?"

"*Sí.*"

After a frightened dash Xbalanque collapsed a few yards into the forest. The rain forest was thick enough to prevent their being spotted if they stayed still and quiet. They heard the soldiers arguing below until a sergeant came by and ordered them back to the square. Someone in the village would die in their place. The teacher was sweating and nervous. Xbalanque wondered if it was for their unwitting victim or his own unexpected survival. A bullet in the back was not as romantic as a firing squad.

As they trudged deeper into the wet mountains seeking to avoid the soldiers, Xbalanque's companion introduced himself. The teacher was Esteban Akabal, a devoted communist and freedom fighter. Xbalanque listened without comment to a long lecture on the evils of the existing government and the coming revolution. He only wondered at where Akabal found the energy to go on. When Akabal at last slowed down, panting as they worked their way up a difficult trail, Xbalanque asked him why he worked with *Ladinos*.

"It is necessary to work together for the greater good. The divisions between Quiché and *Ladino* are created and encouraged by the repressive regime under which we labor. They are false and, once removed, will no longer hamper the worker's natural desire to join with his fellow worker." At a level section of the path both men paused to rest.

"The *Ladinos* will use us, but nothing will change their feelings or mine." Xbalanque shook his head. "I have no desire to join your workers' army. How do I get a road to the city?"

"You can't take a main road. The soldiers will shoot you on sight." Akabal looked at the cuts and bruises Xbalanque had incurred on their climb. "Your talent seems very selective."

"I don't think it's a talent." Xbalanque wiped off some of the dried blood on his jeans. "I had a dream about the gods.

They gave me my name and my powers. After the dream I could do—what I did in Xepon."

"The *norteamericanos* gave you your powers. You are what they call an ace." Akabal examined him closely. "I know of few others this far south of the United States.

"It's a disease actually. A red-haired alien from outer space brought it to Earth. Or so they claim, since biological warfare has been outlawed. Most of those who caught it died. Some were changed."

"I have seen them begging in the city. It was bad sometimes." Xbalanque shrugged. "But I'm not like that."

"A very few become something more than they were. The *norteamericanos* worship these aces." Akabal shook his head. "Typical exploitation of the masses by fascist media masters.

"You know, you could be very important to our fight." The schoolteacher leaned forward. "The mythic element, a tie to our people's past. It would be good, very good, for us."

"I don't think so. I'm going to the city." Chagrined, Xbalanque remembered the treasure he had left in the jeep. "After I return to Xepon."

"The people *need* you. You could be a great leader."

"I've heard this before." Xbalanque was uncertain. The offer was attractive, but he wanted to be more than the people's-army figurehead. With his power he wanted to *do* something, something with money in it. But first he had to get to Guatemala City.

"Let me help you." Akabal had that intense look of desire that the graduate students had when they wanted to sleep with the Mayan priest-king, or as one of them had said, a reasonable facsimile thereof. Combined with the blood now caked on his face, it made Akabal appear to be the devil himself. Xbalanque backed off a couple steps.

"No, thank you. I'm just going to go back to Xepon in the morning, get my jeep, and leave." He started back down the trail. Over his shoulder he spoke to Akabal. "Thanks for your help."

"Wait. It's getting dark. You'll never make it back down at night." The teacher sat back down on a rock beside the trail. "We're far enough in that, even with more men, they would not dare follow us. We'll stay here tonight, and tomorrow morning we'll start back for the village. It will be safe. It will take the lieutenant at least a day to explain the loss of his truck and get reinforcements."

Xbalanque stopped and turned back.

"No more talk about armies?"

"No, I promise." Akabal smiled and gestured for Xbalanque to take another rock.

"Do you have anything to eat? I'm very hungry." Xbalanque could not remember ever having been this hungry, even in the worst parts of his childhood.

"No. But if we were in New York, you could go to a restaurant called Aces High. It is just for people like you. . . ."

As Akabal told him about life in the United States for the aces, Xbalanque gathered some branches to protect against the wet ground and lay down on them. He was asleep long before Akabal ended his speech.

In the morning before dawn they were on the trail back down. Akabal had found some nuts and edible plants for food, but Xbalanque remained ravenous and in pain. Still, they made it back to the village in much less time than it had taken them to toil up the trail the day before.

Hunapu found that wearing the heavy cotton padding while he was walking was clumsy and hot, so he wrapped it up and tied it to his back. He had walked a day and a night without sleep when he came to a small Indian village only slightly larger than his own. Hunapu stopped and wrapped the padding around himself as José had done it. The dress of a warrior and a ballplayer, he thought proudly, and held his head high. The people here were not Lacandones and they looked at him suspiciously as he entered with the sunrise.

An old man walked out into the main path that led between the thatched houses. He called out a greeting to Hunapu in a tongue that was similar but not quite the same as that of his people. Hunapu introduced himself to the *t'o'ohil* as he walked up to him. The village guardian stared at the young man for a full minute of contemplation before inviting him into his home, the largest house Hunapu had ever entered.

While most of the village waited outside for the guardian to tell them about this morning apparition, the two men spoke and drank coffee. It was a difficult conversation at first, but Hunapu soon understood the old man's pronunciations and was able to make himself and his mission known. When Hunapu was finished, the *t'o'ohil* sat back and called his three sons to him. They stood behind him and waited while he spoke to Hunapu.

"I believe that you are Hunapu returned to us. The end of the world comes soon, and the gods have sent messengers to us." The *t'o'ohil* gestured to one of his sons, a dwarf, to come forward. "Chan K'in will go with you. As you see, the gods touched him and he speaks to them directly for us. If you are *hach*, true, he will know it. If you are not, he will know that also."

The dwarf went to stand by Hunapu and looked back at his father and nodded.

"Bol will also go with you." At this, the youngest son started and glared down at his father. "He dislikes the old ways and he will not believe you. But he honors me and he will protect his brother in your travels. Bol, get your gun and pack whatever you need. Chan K'in, I will speak to you. Stay." The old man put down his coffee and stood. "I will tell the village of your vision and your journey. There may be those who wish to accompany you."

Hunapu joined him outside and stood silently while the *t'o'ohil* told his people that the young man followed a vision and was to be respected. Most of the people left after that, but a few remained and Hunapu spoke to them of his quest. Although they were Indian, he felt uncomfortable speaking to them because they wore pants and shirts like the *Ladinos*, not the long tunics of the Lacandones.

When Chan K'in and Bol, dressed for travel in the village's traditional clothing and carrying supplies, came for him, only three men were left to hear him. Hunapu rose and the other men walked away, talking among themselves. Chan K'in was calm. His composed face showed nothing of what he felt or if he was reluctant to embark on a journey that would undoubtedly bring his twisted body pain. Bol, though, showed his anger at his father's order. Hunapu wondered if the tall brother would simply shoot him in the back of the head at the first opportunity and return to his life. It did not matter. He had no choice; he had to continue on the path that the gods had chosen for him. He did feel a certain misgiving that the gods would have chosen him to have the company of such garishly dressed men. Used to the simple shifts of his people, he considered the bright red-and-purple embroidery and sashes of these men to be more like the clothing of the *Ladinos* than to be proper dress for real men. No doubt he would see much that he had not seen before on his travels to meet his brother. He hoped that his brother knew how to dress.

It took much less time to get out of the mountains than it had to climb up into them. A few hours walking that began at dawn brought Xbalanque and Akabal back into Xepon. This time the town was crowded with people. Looking at the remains of the truck in the square where most of the activity was centered made Xbalanque proud. Too late he began thinking about the price the town had paid for his escape. Perhaps these people would not be as impressed with him as Akabal. Akabal led him past the angry stares of some of the townsmen and the tearstained hate of many of the women. With so many people and Akabal's firm grip on his arm, he had no chance to make a break for the jeep and escape. They ended up back at the cantina, today the site of a town meeting.

Their entry caused an uproar as some of the men called for his death and others proclaimed him a hero. Xbalanque said nothing. He was afraid to open his mouth. He stood to one side, back against the hard wooden edge of the bar, as Akabal climbed up and began speaking to the groups of men circulating beneath him. It took several moments of mutual shouts and insults in Quiché and Spanish to gain the attention of all the men.

He was so busy watching the men watching him for signs of violence that it took a while for what Akabal was saying to make sense to him. Akabal was again mixing Maya and Spanish in a speech that centered on Xbalanque and his "mission." Akabal had taken what Xbalanque had said to him and linked it to a Christian second coming and the end of the world as prophesied by the ancient priests.

Xbalanque, the morning star, was the herald of a new age in which the Indians would take back their lands and become the rulers of their land as they had been centuries before. The coming doom was that of the *Ladinos* and *norteamericanos*, not the Maya, who would inherit the Earth. No longer should the Quiché follow the lead of outsiders, socialist, communist, or democratic. They had to follow their own or lose themselves forever. And Xbalanque was the sign.

He had been given his powers by the gods. Confused, Xbalanque remembered Akabal's explanation of his powers as the result of a disease. But even this son of a god could not win alone against the fascist invaders. He was sent here to gain followers, warriors who would fight at his side until they had taken back all that the *Ladinos* and the centuries had stolen from them.

When he had finished, Akabal hauled Xbalanque up onto the bar and jumped down, leaving the stocky man in filthy T-shirt and blue jeans alone above the packed room. Turning to face Xbalanque, Akabal raised his fist into the air and began chanting Xbalanque's name over and over again. Slowly, and then with increasing fervor, every man in the room followed the teacher's lead, many raising their rifles in their fists.

Faced with a chant of his name that shook the room, Xbalanque swallowed nervously, his hunger forgotten. He almost wished that he had only the army to worry about. He was not yet ready to become the leader about which the gods had spoken to him. This was not at all how he had imagined it. He wasn't wearing the splendid uniform he had designed in his mind, and this was not the well trained and directed army that would bring him to power and the presidential palace. They were all staring at him with an expression in their faces that he had never seen before. It was worship and trust. Slowly, trembling, he raised his own fist and saluted them and the gods. He silently prayed to those gods that he would not screw the whole thing up.

A dirty little man, the nightmare of the *Ladinos* come to life, he knew that he was not what these people had seen in their dreams either. But he also knew that he was their only hope now. And whether he was the accidental creation of the *norteamericanos*' sickness or the child of the gods, he swore to all the deities he recognized, Mayan and European, Jesus, Mary, and Itzamna, that he would do everything he could for his people.

But his brother Hunapu had to be having an easier time than he was.

Just outside the village, as Hunapu had been removing his cotton armor, one of the men he had spoken to had joined them. Silently they walked on through the Peten forests, each man with his own thoughts. They moved slowly because

of Chan K'in, but not as slowly as Hunapu had expected. The
dwarf was clearly used to making his own way with little help
from others. There had been no dwarves in Hunapu's village,
but they were known to bring good luck and to be the voice
of the gods. The little men were revered. José had often said
that Hunapu was meant to be a dwarf since he had been
touched by the gods. Hunapu looked forward to learning
from Chan K'in.

At the height of the sun they took a break. Hunapu was
staring at the sun, his namesake, at the center of the sky
when Chan K'in hobbled over to him. The dwarf's face still
showed nothing. They sat together in silence for some minutes before Chan K'in spoke.

"Tomorrow, at dawn, a sacrifice. The gods wish to make
sure that you are worthy." Chan K'in's huge black eyes were
turned on Hunapu, who nodded in agreement. Chan K'in
stood up and walked back to sit by his brother. Bol still
looked as if he wanted Hunapu dead.

It was a long, hot afternoon for walking. The insects
were bad and nothing worked to keep them away. It was
nearly dark by the time they had trudged to Yalpina. Chan
K'in entered first and spoke to the village elders. When he
had gained permission for them to enter, he sent a child out
to the waiting party in the forest. Wearing his armor, Hunapu
strode into the tiny town square. Everyone had gathered to
hear Chan K'in and Hunapu speak. It was plain that they
knew Chan K'in, and his reputation gave weight to Hunapu's
claims. Until they were hushed by their mothers, the children giggled and made fun of Hunapu's cotton armor and bare
legs. But when Hunapu began speaking of his quest to find
his brother and join him in a revival of their own Indian
culture, the people fell under the spell of his dream. They
had their own portents.

Fifteen years earlier a child had been born who had the
brilliant feathers of a jungle bird. The girl was thrust forward
through the crowd. She was beautiful, and the feathers that
replaced her hair only made her more so. She said that she
had been waiting for one to come and that Hunapu was
surely the one. Hunapu took her hand and she stood at his
side.

That night many of the people from the town came to
the home of the girl's parents, where Hunapu and Chan
K'in were staying, and spoke to them about the future. The

girl, Maria, never left Hunapu. When the last villager had left and they curled up by the fire, Maria watched them sleep.

Before dawn Chan K'in woke Hunapu and they trekked out to the forest, leaving Maria behind to get ready to leave. Hunapu had only his machete, but Chan K'in had a slim European knife. Taking the dwarf's knife, Hunapu knelt, holding his hands out in front of him palm up. In the left was the knife. The right, already healed from the machete cut three days before, trembled in anticipation. Without flinching or hesitating Hunapu drove the knife through the palm of his right hand, holding it there while his head dropped back and his body quivered in ecstasy.

With no movement except for a momentary widening of his huge eyes, Chan K'in watched the other man gasping, blood dripping from his hand. He roused himself from his revery to put a piece of hand-loomed cotton cloth on the ground beneath Hunapu's hands. He moved to Hunapu's side and pulled his head over toward him, staring into Hunapu's open, blind eyes as if seeking to peer into his mind itself.

After several minutes Hunapu collapsed to the ground and Chan K'in snatched up the blood-drenched cloth. Using flint and steel, he lit a small fire. As Hunapu returned to consciousness, he threw the offering onto the fire. Hunapu crawled over and both men watched the smoke rise to heaven to meet the rising sun.

"What did you see?" Chan K'in spoke first, his immobile face giving no clue to his own thoughts.

"The gods are pleased with me, but we must move faster and gather more people. I think . . . I saw Xbalanque leading an army of people." Hunapu nodded to himself and clasped his hands. "That is what they want."

"It is beginning now. But we still have far to go and much to do before we succeed." Hunapu looked over at Chan K'in.

The dwarf sat with his stunted legs spread out before him with his chin propped up on his hand.

"For now, we will go back to Yalpina and eat." He struggled to his feet. "I saw some trucks. We will take one and travel on the roads from now on."

Their discussion was interrupted by Maria, who ran into the clearing, panting.

"The cacique, he wants to speak to you now. A runner has come in from another village. The army is sweeping the area looking for rebels. You must leave at once." Her feathers shown in the early morning light as she looked at him in entreaty.

Hunapu nodded to her.

"I will meet you in the village. Prepare to go with us. You will be a sign to others." Hunapu turned back toward Chan K'in and closed his eyes in concentration. The trees in the background of the clearing began turning into the houses of Yalpina. The village seemed to grow toward him. The last thing he saw was Chan K'in's surprise and Maria falling to her knees.

By the time Chan K'in and Maria got back to Yalpina, transportation had been arranged. They had time for a quick breakfast, then Hunapu and his companions left in an old Ford pickup truck that carried them south on the road that connected with the capital. Maria joined them as well as half a dozen men from Yalpina. Others who had joined their cause were on their way to the other Indian villages in the Peten and north to Chiapas in Mexico, where tens of thousands of Indians driven from their homes by the *Ladinos* waited.

Xbalanque's army grew larger as he traveled down toward Guatemala City. So did the tales of his feats in Xepon. When he wanted to stop the stories, Akabal explained to him how important it was for his people to believe the fantastic rumors. Reluctantly Xbalanque accepted Akabal's judgment. It seemed to him now that he was constantly accepting Akabal's decisions. Being a leader of his people was not what he had expected.

His jeep and his cache had been intact. He and Akabal rode at the front of the column of old and creaking vehicles of all kinds. By now they had collected several hundred followers, all of whom were armed and ready to fight. In Xepon they had given him the pants and shirt of their village, but each town they rode into had another style and design. When they gave him their own clothes along with their husbands and sons, he felt obligated to wear them.

There were women now. Most had come to follow their men and take care of them, but there were many who had come to fight. Xbalanque was not comfortable with this, but

Akabal welcomed them. Most of Xbalanque's time was spent trying to feed his army or worrying about when the government would strike them. Both Xbalanque and Akabal agreed that they had come too far too easily.

Akabal had become obsessed with attempting to get television, radio, and newspaper reporters to join the march. Whenever they entered a town that had a telephone, Akabal began placing calls. As a result, the opposition press was sending out as many people as they could without arousing undue suspicion from the secret police. They counted on a few making it to Xbalanque without being arrested.

Outside Zacualpa that word came. A young boy told them that the army had set up a roadblock with two tanks and five armored troop carriers. Two hundred heavily armed soldiers stood ready to stop their advance with light artillery and rockets.

Xbalanque and Akabal called a meeting with the guerrilla leaders who had had combat experience. Their weapons, old rifles and shotguns, could not compete with the army's M-16's and rockets. Their only chance was to use the guerrilla experience they had to their advantage. Their troops were split up into teams and sent into the hills around Zacualpa. Messengers were sent to the town beyond Zacualpa in an effort to bring fighters in from behind the government army, but that would take time for the runners to take remote paths and circle back. Xbalanque would be the main defense and their inspiration. This would be his true test. If he won, he was suitable to be their leader. If he lost, he had led them only to death.

Xbalanque went back to his jeep and got the stingray spine out of the compartment under the driver's seat. Akabal tried to go with him into the jungle, but Xbalanque told him to stay. The soldiers could have snipers and both of them should not be at risk.

It was mainly an excuse. Xbalanque was terrified that the power would not return. He needed the time to sacrifice again, anything that might help him focus on the strength he had had before and had not felt since. He knew that Akabal would almost certainly have him followed, but he had to be alone.

Xbalanque found a tiny clearing formed by a circle of trees and sat down on the ground. He tried to regain the feeling he had had just before the other dream. He could not find a way to get even a bottle of beer out of the camp. What if being drunk was the key? It had to be the way the graduate students had explained it to him or everyone with him was dead. He had brought with him one of the white cotton shirts he had been given on the way. The intricate designs on it were done solely in bright red thread. It seemed appropriate. He put it on the dirt between his legs.

His ear had healed very quickly and he had been wearing the earplug for a couple of days. Where could he get blood this time? He mentally went through a list of the sacred sites on his body that were traditionally used. Yes, that would do well. He cleaned off the carved spine with the shirt and then pulled out his lower lip. Praying to every sacred name he could remember, he thrust the stingray spine down through his lip, brought it up part way, barbs tearing his flesh, and plunged it through again. Then he leaned over the shirt and let the blood course down the black spine onto the white shirt, making new designs as it flowed.

When only drops of his blood were falling onto the shirt, he pushed the spine all the way through and out of his body. The sickening, copper taste of the blood flooded his mouth and he gagged. Closing his eyes and clenching his fists, he controlled himself and tried to close his throat to the blood in his mouth. Using the same lighter, he set fire to the shirt, starting flames from the four sides of the stained cloth packet.

There weren't any dreams of Xibalba this time. Or any dreams at all that he remembered. But the smoke and the loss of blood made him pass out again. When he awoke, the moon was high above and the night was more than half gone. This time he had no hangover, no pain as his muscles adjusted to forces they were not used to carrying. He felt good, he felt wonderful.

He got up and crossed the clearing to the largest tree and struck the trunk with his bare fist. It exploded, showering the ground with splinters and branches as it fell. He lifted his face to the stars and thanked the gods.

Xbalanque stopped on the trail back to the camp as a man stepped out from behind a tree onto the bare earth. For a moment he was afraid the army had found him, but the man bowed to him. Gun held high, the guard led Xbalanque back down to the others.

For the rest of the night the sounds of the soldiers' preparations kept all but the most experienced of his people awake. Akabal paced beside the jeep, listening to the roaring engines of the tanks as they shifted position or swung their guns to bear on another phantom target. The sounds echoed up into the mountains. Xbalanque watched him in silence for a while.

"I can take them. I feel it." Xbalanque tried to encourage Akabal. "All I have to do is hit them with the stones."

"You can't protect everyone. You probably can't even protect yourself. They've got rockets, lots of them. They have tanks. What are you going to do against a tank?"

"I am told that the treads are the point of weakness. So I will first destroy the treads." Xbalanque nodded at the teacher.

"Akabal, the gods are with us. I am with you."

"*You* are with us. Since when are you a god?" Akabal glared at the man leaning on the jeep's steering wheel.

"I think I always have known it. It's just taken some time for others to recognize my power." Xbalanque looked dreamily up at the sky. "The morning star. That's me, you know."

"Mary, Mother of God! You've gone mad!" Akabal stopped pacing long enough to shake his head at Xbalanque.

"I don't think any of us should say that anymore. It's not . . . proper. All things considered."

"All things considered? You—" They were interrupted by a runner coming in from the town and the sounds of more activity from below.

There was another quick consultation among the guerrilla leaders. Akabal went over Xbalanque's part in the plan.

"You're going to be followed up to the bridge by the empty trucks. They'll draw the army fire." The former schoolteacher stared down into the impassive and calm face before him. Xbalanque felt no fear. There was only a euphoria that masked any other emotion. "But after the first few moments they will need more active opposition. That's you. Your fire will protect our snipers in the hills."

His stones had been loaded onto rough sledges that he

tied to the back of the jeep and the next truck back in line. As the campsite grew lighter, everyone went into position. The guerrilla drivers started their engines. Akabal walked up to the jeep.

"Try not to get yourself killed. We need you." He put out his hand in farewell.

"Stop worrying. I'll be fine." Xbalanque touched Akabal's shoulder. "Get into the hills."

Xbalanque's move forward was the signal for the column, single-wide on the narrow road, to begin its short journey. Rounding the corner, Xbalanque could see the bridge ahead and the tanks on either side with their guns pointed at him. As they fired, he jumped from the jeep, the increased weight of his body pounding dents into the pavement as he rolled away. The fragments of the jeep exploded toward him. He felt the power in every part of his body and the metal shrapnel bounced off. Still, he kept his head down as he scrambled for the sledge with his ammunition. Grabbing the first stone, he threw it into the air and batted it with his empty hand, sending it screaming through the air and into the hillside above the army. It threw dirt on the soldiers, but that was all. Better aim. The next rock was painstakingly aimed and it broke the tread on the left-hand tank. The one after jammed the turret so that it could not turn. The Indian fighters had started firing now, and the soldiers were beginning to fall. He threw more stones into the ranks of the army and saw men go down. There was blood, more blood than he could ever give by himself. They brought up a rocket and he saw the man shot by an Indian sniper before the soldier could fire. He was throwing as fast and as hard as he could.

Bullets occasionally struck him, but they were stopped by his skin. Xbalanque grew more reckless and stood facing his enemy without taking cover. His missiles were causing some damage, but most of the deaths were from the Indians on the slopes above the soldiers. The men in charge had seen this and were directing most of their fire up the hillsides. Great holes were appearing in the forest where the tanks and rockets had reached. Despite his strength, Xbalanque could not stop the second tank. The angle was wrong. Nothing he threw could reach it.

A new sound entered the battle. A helicopter was coming. Xbalanque realized that it could give the army the aerial spotting advantage that could get his people killed. It came in low and fast above the battle. Xbalanque reached for a stone and found that only a few small pieces of rock were left. He searched the ground frantically for something to throw. Giving up, he tugged a piece of twisted metal from the wreckage of the jeep and sent it flying toward the chopper. The helicopter met the chunk of metal in midair and exploded. Both sides were hit with debris. The fireball that had been a machine fell into the ravine and flames shot up higher than the bridge.

The engine on the remaining tank revved up and it started to back up. Soldiers moved out of the way and began retreating as well. Xbalanque could now get clear aim at the troop carriers. Using more pieces of metal he tore from the jeep, he destroyed two of them. Then he saw something that stopped all his fantasies of being a great warrior. A boy leapt down off the mountain onto the retreating tank. He swung open the hatch from the outside, and before he was shot, dropped a grenade within. There was an instant before the tank blew when the boy's body was draped across the hatch's opening like a flag across a coffin. Then the flames engulfed them both.

As the fighting at the bridge died down with the soldiers' retreat, the Indians began coming down out of the forest and moving toward the bridge. It became quiet. The moaning of the wounded broke the silence and was joined by the sounds of the birds who returned to their nests with the peace.

Akabal leapt down the road cut to join Xbalanque. He was laughing.

"We won! It worked! You were magnificent." Akabal grabbed Xbalanque and tried to shake him, only to find that the smaller man was immovable.

"Too much blood." With the boy's death Xbalanque had lost his desire to celebrate their victory.

"But it was *Ladino* blood. That is what matters." One of their lieutenants had come up to join them.

"Not all of it."

"But *enough* of it." The lieutenant looked more closely at Xbalanque. "You have not seen anything like this before, have you? You must not let our people see you this way. You are a hero. That is your duty."

"The old gods will feed well today." Xbalanque stared

across the expanse of the bridge to the bodies on the other side. "Perhaps that is all they were after."

Xbalanque was caught up in the rush across the bridge. He didn't have time to stop for the body of the boy who really had destroyed a tank. This time his people were taking him along.

The press found them before the army did. Hunapu, Chan K'in, and Bol stood outside their tent in the early morning chill and watched the two helicopters come in over the hills to the south. One landed in the open area where, last night, the dances and speeches had been held. The other set down near the horses. Hunapu had seen the occasional *Ladino* airplane, but never these strange machines. Another *Ladino* perversion of nature in an attempt to gain the level of gods.

Crowds began to gather around the two helicopters. The camp consisted of a few tents and some old and decrepit trucks, but there were now hundreds of people living there. Most slept on the ground. Many of his people were god-touched and had to be helped to the groups by others. It was sad to see so much pain, but it was clear that the gods had begun taking a greater role in the people's lives even before he had been chosen. With so many who were so close to the gods accompanying him, he felt strong and determined. He had to be following the gods' ways.

Maria came up to him and laid her hand on his arm, the tiny feathers covering her brushing lightly against his skin.

"What do they want with us?" Maria was uneasy. She had seen the *Ladino* reaction to the god-touched before.

"They want to make us into one of their circuses, a show for their amusement," Chan K'in angrily replied. This intrusion into their march toward Kaminaljuyu was unwanted.

"We will find out what they want, Maria. Do not fear them. They are stickmen without strength or true souls." Hunapu stroked the woman's shoulder. "Stay here and help keep the people calm."

Hunapu and Chan K'in began walking toward the helicopter at the center of the encampment. Bol followed, as silent as usual, carrying his rifle and watching the men with cameras as they piled out of the helicopter and stood staring at the quiet mass of people who faced them. When the helicopter's blades swung to a halt, there was almost no noise.

The three men made their way through the crowd slowly. They were careful not to move forward more quickly than someone could get out of their way. Hands, paws, wings, twisted limbs reached out to Hunapu as he passed. He tried to touch them all, but he could not pause to speak or he knew he would never get to the helicopter.

When they reached the machine, painted with a large, hand-lettered PRESS on each side and the bottom, the reporters were huddled against the helicopter. There was fear and revulsion in their eyes. When one of the god-touched moved forward, they all drew back. They did not understand that the god-touched were truer men than themselves. It was typical of the *Ladinos* to be so blind to the truth.

"I am Hunapu. Who are you and why have you come here?" Hunapu spoke first in Maya, then repeated his question in Spanish. He wore the cotton armor as he stood before the reporters and cameramen. The cameras had begun filming as soon as they could pick him out of the crowd.

"Christ, he really does think he's one of those Hero Twins." The comment in bad Spanish had come from one of the men in front of him. He looked across the huddled group. Not even having the man they wanted in front of them lessened their uneasiness.

"I am Hunapu," he repeated.

"I'm Tom Peterson from NBC, Central American bureau. We've heard that you have a joker crusade out here. Well, jokers and Indians. That's obviously true." The tall, blond man looked over Hunapu's shoulder at the crowd. His Spanish had an odd accent. He spoke slowly and drawled in a way Hunapu had never heard before. "I take it you're in charge. We'd like to talk to you about your plans. Maybe there's someplace where it would be more quiet?"

"We will speak to you here." Chan K'in stared up at the man dressed in a white cotton European suit. Peterson had ignored the dwarf at Hunapu's side. Their eyes met and it was the blond man who backed down.

"Right. Here is just fine. Joe, make sure you get good sound on this." Another man moved between Peterson and

Hunapu and held a microphone pointed at Peterson, waiting for his next words. But Hunapu's attention had been drawn away.

The reporters from the second helicopter had caught on to what was happening in the center and had begun shoving their way through the people to get to Hunapu. He turned to the men and women holding their equipment up out of the reach of his people as if they were crossing a river.

"Stop." He spoke in Maya, but his voice caught the attention of the reporters as well as his own people. Everything halted and all eyes turned toward him. "Bol, bring them here."

Bol glanced down at his brother before starting for the reporters. The crowd parted for him as he moved forward and again as he brought the journalists to join their fellows. He motioned them to stay put with his rifle before returning to Hunapu and Chan K'in.

Peterson began his questions again.

"What is your destination?"

"We go to Kaminaljuyu."

"That's right outside Guatemala City, isn't it? Why there?"

"I will meet my brother there."

"Well, what are you going to do when you meet your brother?"

Before Hunapu could answer the question, one of the women from the second helicopter interrupted.

"Maxine Chen, CBS. What are your feelings about your brother Xbalanque's victory over the soldiers sent to stop him?"

"Xbalanque is fighting the army?"

"You hadn't heard? He's coming through the Highlands and pulling in every Indian revolutionary group that exists. His army has defeated the government every time they've clashed. The Highlands are in a state of emergency and that hasn't even slowed Xbalanque down." The Oriental woman was no taller than Hunapu. She looked around at his followers.

"There's a rebel behind every tree in the Highlands, has been for years. Down here in the Peten, it's always been quiet. Before now. What's your goal?" Her attention shot back to him.

"When I see my brother Xbalanque, we will decide what we want."

"In the meantime, what do you plan to do about the army unit sent to stop *you*?"

Hunapu exchanged a glance with Chan K'in.

"Don't you know about that either? Jesus, they're just hours away. Why do you think all of us were so hot to get to you? You may not be here by sundown."

The dwarf began questioning Maxine Chen.

"How many and how far away?" Chan K'in fixed his impassive black eyes on hers.

"Maybe sixty men, a few more; they don't keep any real forces down here—"

"Maxine!" Peterson had lost his journalistic detachment. "Stay out of this, for God's sake. You'll get us all arrested."

"Stuff it, Peterson. You know as well as I do that they've been committing genocide here for years. These people are finally fighting back. Good for them." She knelt in the dirt and began drawing a map on the ground for Hunapu and Chan K'in.

"I'm getting out of here." Peterson waved his hand in the air and the helicopter's rotors began turning. The reporters and cameramen climbed back into the helicopter or began running for the one in the horse paddock.

Maxine looked up from the map toward her cameraman.

"Robert, stay with me and we'll have an exclusive."

The cameraman grabbed sound equipment off a technician ready to bolt and strapped it on.

"Maxine, you're gonna get me killed one day, and I'm gonna come back and haunt you."

Maxine was already back at the map.

"But not yet, Robert. Did you see any heavy artillery with the government troops?"

It had taken only a little while to get their people organized and to find out what weapons they had. There were some rifles and shotguns, nothing heavier. Most people had machetes. Hunapu called Chan K'in and Bol to him. Together they determined the best course of action. Bol led the discussion, and Hunapu was surprised at his expertise. Although they were facing only a few soldiers, they were at a disadvantage in weapons and experience. Bol recommended attacking the army troops when they came down from the canyons into the savanna. By splitting up their people into two groups, they could best use the terrain. Hunapu had begun to wonder where Bol had gained his knowledge. He suspected the tall, quiet man of having been a rebel.

After instructing his people in the planned defense, Hunapu left the drilling to Bol and made another blood sacrifice. He hoped the sincerity of his prayers would give him the strength he needed to use his god-given power and save his people. The gods would have to be on their side or they would all be destroyed.

When he returned to the camp, Hunapu found it broken down and the half of his warriors who would face the army already mounted. After he climbed up on his own horse, he swung Chan K'in up behind him. He spoke briefly to waiting Indian warriors, encouraging them and enjoining them to fight well for the gods.

Seeing the men on horseback riding toward them, the soldiers had stopped their trucks just outside the mouth of the canyon and unloaded. As the soldiers piled off the troop carrier and the jeeps preceding and following it, they were picked off by the snipers Bol had sent into the bush. Only a ragged line of men faced Hunapu's charge. They were distracted by their fellow soldiers falling to the left and right at the mercy of the snipers. A few of the older men ignored the deaths and stood their ground against the screaming men bearing down on them. The sergeant swore at them to hold ranks and fire at the filthy Indians.

Hunapu's horsemen were unused to firing from the moving animals and were barely able to hold on and shoot. They couldn't aim at the same time. Once the army men realized this, they began taking the horsemen down, one at a time. By now Hunapu was close enough to the soldiers to see the fear and confusion start to evaporate and discipline take over. One man stood up and followed Hunapu with his Uzi aimed squarely at the Lacandon's head. Chan K'in cried out a warning and Hunapu was gone. Chan K'in was alone on the horse, now uncontrolled, and facing the soldier's bullet. As the shot split Chan K'in's skull, Hunapu reappeared behind the soldier and slashed his throat with the obsidian blade, splashing blood over the soldier's companions before vanishing again.

Hunapu brought his rifle butt down on the helmet of a

man with a rocket launcher before he could fire into the bush where the snipers hid. Before any of the other soldiers reacted, he reversed the rifle and shot him. Grabbing the rocket launcher, he disappeared and came back almost immediately, without the launcher. This time he killed the sergeant.

Covered with blood and vanishing almost as soon as he appeared, Hunapu was the devil to the soldiers. They could not fight this apparition. No matter where they aimed, he would be somewhere else. They turned their backs on Hunapu's warriors to try to kill Hunapu himself. It was useless. Praying to the Virgin Mary and the saints that they would not be next, the men threw down their guns and knelt on the ground. Not all the kicks and threats of the lieutenant could get them to keep fighting.

Hunapu took thirty-six prisoners, including the lieutenant. Twenty soldiers had been killed. He had lost seventeen men and Chan K'in. The *Ladinos* had been defeated. They were not invincible.

That night while his people celebrated their victory, Hunapu mourned Chan K'in. He was dressed again in the long white tunic of his Lacandon people. Bol had come to him to claim the body of his brother. The tall Indian told him that Chan K'in had seen his death in a vision and knew his fate. Chan K'in's body had been wrapped in white cloth that was now stained by the dwarf's blood. Bol stood holding the small bundle and stared at Hunapu's tired, saddened face across the fire.

"I will see you at Kaminaljuyu." Hunapu looked up in surprise. "My brother saw me there, but even if he had not, I would go. May both our journeys go their way in peace, or in death to our enemies."

Despite the early victories both brothers suffered many losses during the rest of the march to Guatemala City. Xbalanque had been wounded in an assassination attempt, but he had healed with supernatural speed. The attempt had killed two of the guerrilla leaders who had followed and taught him. Word had come down from the north that Guatemalan air force planes were strafing and bombing the lines of Indians who were leaving the refugee camps of Chiapas in Mexico to join their fellows in Guatemala City. Hundreds were reported killed, but thousands kept coming.

The elite, highly trained police and military squads took a constant toll. Xbalanque was slowed, but the mass of people who followed him would not be stopped. At every firefight they took weapons from dead soldiers and armed themselves. Now they had rockets and even a tank, deserted by its frightened crew.

Hunapu fared less well. His people from the Peten had less experience. Many died in each clash with the army. After a battle in which neither side could actually claim a victory and ended only when he finally located the commander and could teleport in to kill him, Hunapu decided that it had become foolish to oppose the army and police directly. He dispersed his followers. They were to make their way singly or in small groups to Kaminaljuyu. Otherwise it seemed inevitable that the government would be able to muster sufficient forces to stop them.

Xbalanque arrived first. A truce had been declared as his army closed in on Guatemala City. Akabal had given interviews over and over again that declared their purpose was not to topple the Guatemalan government. Faced with questioning by the press and the imminent visit from the UN Wild Card tour, the general in charge ordered the army to escort Xbalanque and his followers but not to fire on them unless attacked. Xbalanque and Akabal made sure that the army had no excuses. The country's leader allowed Xbalanque access to Kaminaljuyu.

The ruins of Kaminaljuyu were filled with the followers of the brothers. They had put tents and rough shelters up on the low mounds. Looking over the soldiers, trucks, and tanks that guarded the perimeter of Kaminaljuyu, they could look down on the Guatemala City suburbs that surrounded them. The camp already held five thousand, and more were coming all the time. Besides the Guatemalan Mayas and the refugees from Mexico, others were traveling up from Honduras and El Salvador.

The world was watching to see what would happen in Guatemala City this Christmas. Maxine Chen's coverage of the battle between Hunapu's Indian and joker followers and the Guatemalan army had been an hour-long special report on *60 Minutes*. The meeting between the Hero Twins themselves was to be covered by all the major U.S. networks, cable, and European channels.

Hunapu had never before seen so many people together in one place. As he walked into the camp past the soldiers guarding the perimeter and then past the Maya sentries, he was amazed at the size of the gathering. He and Bol had taken a long and circuitous route to avoid trouble, and it had been a long walk. Unlike the people of the Peten, these followers of Xbalanque dressed in hundreds of different ways, all bright and festive. The atmosphere of celebration didn't seem proper to Hunapu. These people did not appear to be worshiping the gods who had prepared their way and led them here. They looked as though they were at a carnival—some of them looked as though they were the carnival.

Hunapu walked through a third of the crowded camp without being recognized. Sunlight glinting off opalescent feathers caught his eye just as Maria turned and saw him. She called out his name and ran to meet him. At the sound of the name of the other Hero Twin, people began to gather around him.

Maria took his hand and held it for a moment, smiling at him happily.

"I was so worried. I was afraid..." Maria looked down and away from Hunapu.

"The gods are not finished with us yet." Hunapu reached out to stroke the down on the side of her face. "And Bol came most of the way with me after getting back from his village."

Maria looked down at the hand she was clutching and released it in embarrassment.

"You will wish to see your brother. He has a house at the center of Kaminaljuyu. I would be honored to lead you there." She stepped back and gestured through the crowd down the rows of tents. Hunapu followed her as she parted the gathered people before him. As he passed, the Indians murmured his name and fell in behind him.

Within a few steps they were accosted by reporters. TV camera lights blazed on, and questions were shouted in English and Spanish. Hunapu glanced up at Bol, who began fending off those who came too close to his charge. They ignored the questions, and the camera crews withdrew after a few minutes of what Maxine called stock shots of Hunapu walking and occasionally greeting someone he recognized.

While most of the structures in Kaminaljuyu were tents or houses built out of whatever scrap material people could find, the large, twin wooden huts built on a plaza at the center of the ruins were impressive, permanent buildings. Their roofs were adorned with vertical roof combs like those on temple ruins, and banners and charms hung from these.

After they reached the open area of the plaza, the crowd stopped following him. Hunapu could hear the cameras and sense the shoving for position as he, Bol, and Maria walked alone to the house on the left. Before they reached it, a man dressed in a mix of red and purple Highland clothing stepped out. He was followed by a tall, thin Highland Maya wearing glasses and dressed in European clothing, except for the sash at his waist.

Hunapu recognized Xbalanque from his dreams of Xibalba, but he had looked younger in them. This man appeared more serious, but he noticed the expensive European watch on his wrist and the *Ladino* leather "running" shoes on his feet. It seemed a sharp contrast with the jade earplug he wore. Hunapu wondered about the earplug. Had the gods given it to him? Hunapu was caught in his examination of his brother by Xbalanque's companion. The other man took Hunapu by the shoulders and turned him toward the bank of cameras. Xbalanque rested his hand on Hunapu's left shoulder. In the Highland Maya that Hunapu loosely understood, Xbalanque spoke to him softly.

"The first thing we're going to do is get you some real clothes. Wave to the cameras." Xbalanque followed his own suggestion. "Then we have to work on ways to get more food into the camp."

Xbalanque turned him so that they faced each other and then clasped his hand.

"Hold that so they can get our profiles. You know, sun, I was beginning to get worried about you."

Hunapu looked into the eyes of the man across from him. For the first time since meeting this stranger who was his brother, he saw in Xbalanque's eyes the same shadows of Xibalba that he knew existed in his own. It was obvious that Xbalanque had much to learn about the proper worship of the gods, but it was also clear that he was chosen, like Hunapu, to speak for them.

"Come inside. Akabal will make his statement that *our*

statement will be issued later. *Ko'ox*." The last words Xbalanque
spoke were in Lacandon Maya. Hunapu began to think that
this Highland quetzal might be a worthy partner. Remembering Maria and Bol, he caught a glimpse of them melting into
the crowd as he walked into Xbalanque's house. His brother
seemed to catch his thought.

"She's beautiful and very devoted to you, isn't she? She'll
take care of your bodyguard and keep the press away until he
can get some rest. We've got plans to discuss. Akabal has
some wonderful ideas for helping our people."

For the next several days the brothers held private
conferences, lasting long after dark. But on the morning of
the third day Esteban Akabal stepped outside to announce
that a statement would be read at noon outside the compound where their prisoners were being held.

With the sun directly overhead, Xbalanque, Hunapu,
and Akabal walked out of Xbalanque's hut toward the prisoners' compound. As they moved, surrounded by their followers
and the reporters, Hunapu's shoulders tensed when he heard
the midday army flyover. The sound of the helicopters always
made him nervous. Once there, they waited until the sound
equipment was tested. Several of the technicians were wearing Hero Twin T-shirts. Akabal explained that the statement
would be read in two parts, the first by Hunapu and the
second by Xbalanque. They would speak in Maya and he,
Akabal, would translate them into Spanish and English.
Hunapu clutched his piece of paper nervously. Akabal had
been aghast to learn that he couldn't read, so he had had to
memorize the speech the teacher had written. He thanked
the gods for José's training in remembering rituals and
spells.

Hunapu stepped closer to his microphone and saw Maxine
wave in encouragement. Mentally he asked the gods not to
make him look foolish. When he began to speak, his nervousness
vanished, drowned in his anger.

"Since the time of your first coming to our lands, you
have murdered our children. You have sought to destroy our
beliefs. You stole our land and our sacred objects. You enslaved
us. You have allowed us no voice in the destruction of our
homes. If we spoke out, you kidnapped us, tortured us, and
killed us for being men and not the malleable children you
wanted.

"It is now that the cycle ends. We *hach winik*, true men,

will be free again to live as we wish to live. From the ice of the far north to the fire-lands of the south, we will see the coming of a new world in which all our people can be free.

"The gods are watching us now and they wish to be worshiped in the old, proper ways. In return they will give us the strength we need to overcome those who will try to defeat us again. My brother and I are the signs of this new world to come."

As he stepped back, Hunapu heard his name being cried out by the thousands of Maya in Kaminaljuyu. He looked over the ruined city in pride, soaking in the strength that his people's worship gave him. Maria had made it to the front of the gathered followers. She raised her arms to him in praise and hundreds of people around her did the same. The gesture spread through the crowd. When it seemed that everyone had lifted their hands to implore his help, Hunapu lifted his face and his arms toward heaven. The noise swelled until he dropped his hands and gazed over the people. Silence fell.

Xbalanque stepped forward.

"We are not *Ladino*. We do not want a war or more death. We seek only what is ours by right: a land, a country, that is ours. This land will be the homeland of any American Indian, no matter where in the Americas he was born. It is our intent to meet the WHO Wild Card delegation while it is in Guatemala City. We will ask for their aid and support in founding a *hach winik* homeland. The god-touched among our people are especially in need of immediate help.

"We do not ask now. We are telling you. *Ko'ox!* Let us go!"

Xbalanque raised his fist in the air and chanted the Lacandon phrase over and over until every Indian in the camp joined him. Hunapu joined the chant and felt the rush of power once again. Watching Xbalanque, he knew his brother felt it as well. It felt right. It was clear that the gods were with them.

Hunapu and Xbalanque flanked Akabal as he translated what they had said. The Hero Twins stood immobile and silent as the teacher refused to answer any other questions. Their people faced them, as silent and stoic now as themselves. When Akabal led the way back to their houses, where

they would wait for word from the WHO delegation, their
followers parted without a sound to allow them to pass, but
closed in before the press could get through.

"Well, one can't accuse them of lacking political savvy."
Senator Gregg Hartmann uncrossed his legs and got up out of
the colonial reproduction chair to turn off the hotel room
television set.

"A little chutzpah never hurts, Gregg." Hiram Worchester
leaned his head on his hand and looked over at Hartmann.
"But what do you think our response should be?"

"Response! What response can we possibly make?" Senator Lyons interrupted Hartmann's answer. "We are here to
help the victims of the wild card virus. I see no connection
whatsoever. These . . . revolutionaries or whatever they are
are simply trying to use us. We have a responsibility to ignore
them. We can hardly afford to become involved in some petty
nationalistic squabble!"

Lyons crossed his arms and walked over to the window.
Unobtrusively a young Indian maid was let into the room to
pick up the remains of their room-service lunch. Head down,
she glanced at each of them before silently carrying her
heavily loaded tray out the door. Hartmann shook his head at
Senator Lyons.

"I understand your point, but did you look at the people
out there? A lot of the people who are following these 'Hero
Twins' are jokers. Don't we have a responsibility toward
them?" Hartmann relaxed back into his chair and rolled his
back in an attempt to get comfortable. "Besides, we can't
afford to ignore them. It would compromise our own mission
if we pretended they, and their problems, didn't exist. The
world here is very different from what you're used to seeing,
even on the reservations. There are different attitudes. The
Indians have been suffering since the Conquest. They take
the long view. To them the wild card virus is just another
cross to bear."

"'Sides, Senator, you think those boys are aces, like the
reporters say?" Mordecai Jones looked across the hotel room
at the Wyoming senator. "Got to say, I've got some sympathy
for what they're tryin' to do. Slavery, whatever they call it
down here, ain't right."

"It's obvious that we are involved because of the wild
card victims, if nothing else. If meeting with them will help

them to get aid, we have a responsibility to do what we can."
Tachyon spoke from his chair. "On the other hand, I hear lots
of talk about homelands and I see very little commitment to
working on practical problems. Problems such as the subsist-
ence level of the victims here. You can see that they need
medical help. What do you think, Hiram?"

"Gregg's right. We can't avoid a meeting. There's been
too much publicity. Beyond that, we are here to see how
jokers are treated in other countries. Judging by what
we've seen, we could help out down here by leaning on the
government a little. This would appear to be a good way to
do it. We don't have to endorse their actions, just express
our concern."

"That sounds reasonable. I'll let you deal with the politics. I need to get to that hospital tour." Tachyon massaged
one temple. "I'm tired of talking to the government. I want
to see what's going on."

The door to the sitting room opened and Billy Ray
peered in. "The phones are ringing off the hooks, and we've
got reporters coming up the fire stairs. What are we supposed to tell them?"

Hartmann nodded to Tachyon before answering. "Those
of us who can spare the time from our carefully timed
schedules will see these 'Hero Twins.' But make it clear that
we are doing this in the interests of the wild card victims, not
for political reasons."

"Great. The Father, Chrysalis, and Xavier ought to be
back soon. They went out to see the camp and talk to the
jokers there." Anticipating Tachyon's next question, he smiled
at the doctor. "Your car's waiting downstairs. But the sooner
you can give me an official statement for the press, the
better."

"I'll have my people start drafting one immediately,
Billy." Hartmann was obviously on familiar ground. "You'll
have it within the hour."

In the morning everyone gathered, hungover and bleary
from the previous night's celebrations, but ready to march off
to see the United Nations tour. When Hunapu and Xbalanque
came out of their houses, the crowd became quiet. Xbalanque
looked out over the people and wished that it were possible
to have them follow him into the city. It would look great on
film, but Akabal was convinced that it might just be the

excuse the government was looking for to open fire. He jumped up onto the hood of the bus that had been chosen to take them into the city. He spoke for almost half an hour before the people appeared to agree that they would stay in Kaminaljuyu.

They arrived at the Camino Real without incident. The only surprise had come from the crowds of Indians lining the streets as they passed. The watchers were silent and impassive, but both Hunapu and Xbalanque were strengthened by their presence. At the Camino Real they jumped down from the truck and were escorted within the building by two of their own guards and almost a score of UN security people.

Xbalanque and Hunapu wore their closest approximation of the dress of the ancient kings. Hair tied up in warrior's knots on top of their heads, they were dressed in cotton tunics and dyed-cotton wrapped skirts. Hunapu was used to wearing only his *xikul,* a knee-length tunic. He felt at home in the ancient style. Xbalanque had spent the early morning tugging on his skirt and feeling self-conscious about his exposed legs. As he looked curiously around the hotel, he saw himself in a wall mirror. He almost stopped in wonder at the vision of a Mayan warrior looking back at him. Xbalanque straightened and raised his head, showing off his jade earplug.

Hunapu's eyes darted from one side of the lobby to the other. He had never seen a building this big with so many strange decorations and oddly dressed people. A fat man in a shiny white shirt and brightly colored, flowered short pants stared at them. The tourist grabbed his wife, who wore a dress that was made on the same loom as the man's pants, by the arm and pointed at them. Catching a glimpse of Xbalanque walking proudly alongside steadied Hunapu.

But it was all he could do not to cry out prayers to the gods when they walked into a room slightly smaller than his family's house and the doors slid shut without a human touch. The room moved under him, and only Xbalanque's calm face kept him from believing he was about to die. He slid his glance toward Akabal. The Maya in Western dress was clenching and releasing his fists rhythmically. Hunapu wondered if he was praying too.

Despite his outward impassivity Xbalanque was the first one out the opening doors when the elevator reached its destination. The entire group walked down the carpeted hall to a door flanked by two more UN soldiers. There were a few moments of discussion before it was agreed that, once the Indian guards had inspected the meeting room, they would retire outside the door until the conference was over. The Hero Twins would be allowed to keep their ceremonial stone knives, however. During this, Xbalanque and Hunapu said nothing, allowing Akabal to make the arrangements. Hunapu watched everything while he attempted to look like a warrior-king. Being in these enclosed spaces made him nervous. He repeatedly looked to his brother for guidance.

Inside the hotel room, the WHO delegates waited for them. Akabal immediately noticed Peregrine's cameraman. "Out. No cameras, no tapes." The tall Indian turned to Hartmann. "It was agreed. At your insistence."

"Peregrine, the lady with the wings, is one of us. She is only interested in making a historical record—"

"Which you can edit to suit your own purposes. No."

Hartmann smiled and shrugged at Peregrine. "Perhaps it would be better if. . ."

"Sure, no problem." She flapped her wings lazily and directed her cameraman to leave.

Xbalanque noted that Akabal seemed to be thrown off by the ease at which he had gotten his wish. He turned to look at his brother. Hunapu appeared to be communing directly with the gods. It was clear from looking at him that nothing here was of interest. Xbalanque tried to capture the same assurance.

"Good. Now, we are here to discuss—" Akabal began his prepared introduction, but was interrupted by Hartmann.

"Let's be informal here. Everyone please have a seat. Mr. Akabal, why don't you sit beside me since I believe you'll be doing the translating here?" Hartmann sat down at the head of a table apparently brought into the room for the meeting since the furniture around it had been moved against the walls. "Do the other gentlemen speak English?"

Xbalanque was about to reply when he caught Akabal's warning glance. Instead he guided Hunapu to a chair.

"No, I'll be translating for them as well."

Hunapu stared earnestly at the tentacled priest and the man with the nose like Chac, the long-nosed rain god. He was pleased that the god-touched would travel with this group. It was an auspicious sign. But he was also surprised to see a Father who was so blessed by the gods. Perhaps there was more to what the priests had tried to teach him than he had previously believed. He mentioned his thoughts to Akabal, who spoke in English to Hartmann.

"Among our people, the victims of the wild card virus are regarded as being favored by the gods. They are revered, not persecuted."

"And that's what we're here to talk about, isn't it? Your people." Hartmann had not stopped smiling since they'd entered the room. Xbalanque did not trust a man who showed his teeth so much.

The man with the elephant's trunk spoke next. "This new country of yours, would it be open to all jokers?"

Xbalanque pretended to listen to Akabal's translation. He replied in Maya, knowing that Akabal would change his words anyway.

"This homeland takes back only a tiny part of what has been stolen from us. It is for our people, whether god-touched or not. The god-touched of the *Ladinos* have other places to go for help."

"But why do you feel a separate nation is necessary? It seems to me that your show of political power would impress the Guatemalan government with your strength. They're bound to introduce the reforms you want." Hartmann brought the conversation back to Akabal, which didn't displease Hunapu. He could feel hostility in this room and a lack of understanding. Whatever else they were, they were also *Ladinos*. He looked over at Akabal as the man replied to one of the *norteamericano*'s questions.

"You aren't listening. We don't want reforms. We want our land back. But only a small part of it, at that. Reforms have come and gone for four hundred years. We are tired of waiting." Akabal was vehement. "Do you know that to most Indians this wild card virus is just another smallpox? Another white disease brought to us to kill as many as possible."

"That's ridiculous!" Senator Lyons was enraged at the accusation. "Humans had nothing to do with the wild card virus.

"We came here to help you. That is our only purpose. In order to help we feel we have to have the cooperation of the government." Senator Lyons seemed to be on the defensive.

"We spoke to the general. He's planning to put clinics in the outlying provinces and to bring serious cases of the wild card outbreak here to the city for treatment."

The brothers exchanged glances. It was clear to each man that these strangers from the north were not about to do anything for them. Hunapu was getting impatient. There were too many things they could be doing in Kaminaljuyu. He wanted to start teaching the uninformed about the old gods and the means of worshiping them.

"We can't change the past. We both know that. So what's the point? Why are you here?" Hartmann had stopped smiling.

"We are going to form an Indian nation. But we will need help." Akabal spoke firmly. Xbalanque approved of his lack of tolerance for distraction, even though he wasn't altogether sure about Akabal's plans for a socialist government.

"Do you have no idea of what the United Nations is? Surely you cannot expect us to provide weapons for your war." Senator Lyons's mouth was ringed with white from his anger.

"No, no weapons. But if you had come out to see our followers, you would have seen how many have been untreated by the *Ladino* doctors in the hope that they would not survive. And yes, I know what the general told you. We will need much medical aid, initially, to care for these people. After that we will need aid for schools, roads, transportation, agriculture. All the things a real country must provide."

"You understand we're only on a fact-finding tour? We don't have any real authority with the UN or even with the U.S. government, for that matter." Hartmann leaned back in his seat and spread his hands. "Sympathy is about all we can offer at this time."

"We are not about to jeopardize our standing in the international community for your military adventures!" Senator Lyons's eyes swept the three Indians. Hunapu was not impressed. Women should stay out of serious decisions.

"This is a peaceful mission. There is nothing political about suffering, and I don't intend to see you try to make the wild card virus a pawn in your bid for attention," Lyons said.

"I doubt if the European Jews of the Holocaust would agree that suffering is apolitical, Senator." Akabal watched Lyons's expression change to chagrin. "The wild card virus has affected my people. That is a truth. My people face active genocide. That too is truth. If you don't want the wild card virus involved, that's nice, but it's not really possible, is it?

"What do we want from you? Just two things. Humanitarian aid and recognition." For the first time Akabal looked a little unsure of himself. "Soon the Guatemalan government is going to try to destroy us. They'll wait until you are gone, you and the reporters following you. We don't intend to allow them to succeed. We have certain... advantages."

"They're aces, then?" Hartmann had grown suddenly quiet and introspective.

Some of the reporters had used that term and Akabal had mentioned it, but this was the first time Xbalanque felt that it would fit. He felt like an ace. He and his brother, the little Lacandon, could take anyone. They were the incarnations of the priest-kings of their fathers, favored by the gods or an alien disease. It didn't matter. They would lead their people to victory. He turned to Hunapu and saw that it was as if his brother shared his thoughts.

"To them, they have been called to serve the old gods and be the heralds of the new age, the beginning of the next cycle. By our calendar that will be in your year 2008. They are here to prepare the way over the next *katun*." Akabal looked back at the *norteamericanos*. "But yes, I believe that they are aces. The evidence fits. It is hardly unusual for an ace to exhibit powers that appear to be drawn from his cultural heritage, is it?"

There were three short raps on the door. Xbalanque saw the security chief, the one they called Carnifex, look in. He wondered for a moment if this was all an elaborate trap.

"The plane's ready and we need to leave within the next hour."

"Thanks." Hartmann put his hand under his chin in thought. "Speaking simply as a U.S. senator here, I'd like to see what we could work out, Mr. Akabal. Why don't we speak privately for a moment?"

Akabal nodded. "Perhaps the Father would like to talk to Xbalanque and Hunapu? The brothers speak Spanish, if there is a translator available."

When Hartmann and Akabal ended their huddle and rejoined them, Xbalanque was ready to leave. Listening to

Hunapu, he was becoming afraid that his brother was going to demonstrate calling on the gods right then and there. He knew that wasn't a good idea.

Xbalanque was trying to explain this as Hartmann shook Akabal's hand in farewell. To Xbalanque it seemed as though he held onto the teacher's hand too long. North American customs. He went back to dissuading Hunapu from pulling his obsidian knife and began leading his brother out.

When they were back in the elevator, escorted again by the UN security people, Xbalanque asked Akabal in Maya what Hartmann had said.

"Nothing. He will 'attempt' to set up a 'committee' to 'study' the matter. He talks like all the Yankees. At least they saw us. It gives us legitimacy in the eyes of the world. That much was useful."

"They do not believe that we serve the will of the gods, do they?" Hunapu was much more angry than he had allowed himself to show. Xbalanque watched him warily. He looked his brother in the eyes. "We will show them the power of the gods. They will learn."

Over the following twenty-four hours they lost half the journalists covering them as the reporters went on with the UN tour. And the army moved more units into place and, more ominously, began to evacuate the surrounding suburbs. Finally all travel into the camp was cut off. The peace from the anthropologists was welcome, but the intent was clear to everyone in Kaminaljuyu. No noncombatants in the camp.

At sunrise and noon for each of the three days since the visit to Hartmann and the tour, Hunapu had sacrificed his own blood on the highest of the temple mounds of the city. Xbalanque had joined him at the last two sunrises. Akabal's pleas for common sense were ignored. As the tension within Kaminaljuyu increased, the brothers grew more insular. Discussing their plans only with each other, they ignored most of the planning sessions held by Akabal and the rebel leaders. Maria spent all her time at Hunapu's side when she was not preparing an altar for a sacrifice. Bol constantly drilled the warriors.

Xbalanque and Hunapu stood atop the ruined temple surrounded by their followers. It was nearly dawn on the fourth day. An ornate decorated bowl was held between them by Maria. Each man held his obsidian blade to the palm of his hand. At the rising of the sun they would cut their flesh and let the blood pour down and mix together in the bowl before they burned it on the altar Maria had arranged with effigies and flowers. The sun was still behind the eastern volcano that loomed over Guatemala City and puffed smoke into the air as if constantly offering sacred tobacco to the gods.

First light. Knives flashed black, shining. Blood flowed, mingled, filled the bowl. Hands, covered with red, lifted to the sun. Thousands of voices raised in a chant welcoming the day with a plea for mercy from the gods. Two thatched huts exploded as the rays of the sun touched them.

The dirt and debris rained down on the people. Those closest to the huts were the first to see that a government rocket had blown the shelters apart. The fighters ran for the perimeter to try to stop the invasion, while those who were unable to defend the camp drew together in a great mass at its center. The government rockets targeted the central plaza where several thousand people knelt and prayed or screamed as the rockets arced overhead to fall nearby.

Maxine Chen was one of the few top journalists left to cover the Hero Twins' crusade. She and her crew had taken shelter behind one of the temple mounds where Maxine taped an introduction to the attack. An Indian girl, seven- or eight-years-old, ran around the side of the mound and in front of Maxine's camera. Her face and her embroidered white huipil were covered with blood, and she was crying out in fear as she ran. Maxine tried to grab her but missed, and the girl was gone.

"Robert..." Maxine looked across at her cameraman. He ducked out from under his camera and shoved it at the sound man, who barely caught it. Then they were both running into the crowd, getting them up and moving toward the small shelter of the mounds.

On the edge of the ruins the Hero Twins' people were firing down into the soldiers, causing some confusion but not enough damage. The rockets were coming from well behind the front lines of the army. The tank engines rumbled, but they held their ground and fired into the defenders, killing some and destroying the ruins that were their protection.

Struggling against the flow of people into the center of

Kaminaljuyu, Xbalanque and Hunapu managed to make their way to the front lines. They were cheered as their people spotted them. Standing out in the open, Xbalanque began throwing whatever he could get his hands on at the army. It had effect. The troops in front of his attack tried to move back, only to be stopped and ordered forward. Bullets ricocheted off his skin. The defending Indians saw this and drew strength from it. Aiming more carefully, they began to take a toll. But the rockets kept coming, and they could always hear the screams of the people trapped in the center of the camp.

Hunapu flipped back and forth, using his knife to slit the throats of the nearest soldiers before returning to his own place. He targeted officers, as Akabal had warned him to do. But with the press of men behind them, the frontline troops could not flee even when they wanted to escape the demon.

Xbalanque ran out of missiles and retired behind one of the mounds. He was joined by two of the experienced guerrilla leaders. They were frightened by the mass carnage. It was different from a jungle war. When they saw Hunapu shift back, Xbalanque caught him before he could return. Hunapu's cotton armor was soaked with the soldiers' blood. The smell gagged even the rebels. The blood and the smoke from the guns took Xbalanque back to the first time he had experienced it.

"Xibalba." He spoke only to his brother.

"Yes." Hunapu nodded. "The gods have grown hungry. Our blood was not enough. They want more blood, blood with power. A king's blood."

"Do you think they would accept a general's blood? A war captain's?" Xbalanque looked over his shoulder at the army on the other side of the dirt mound.

The guerrillas were following the exchange closely, looking for a reason to hope for victory. Both nodded at the thought.

"If you can take the general, things will fall apart down the line. They're draftees out there, not volunteers." The man wiped dusty black hair out of his eyes and shrugged. "It's the best idea I've heard."

"Where is the war captain?" Hunapu's eyes fixed on a distant goal. "I will bring him back. It must be done correctly or the gods will not be pleased."

"He'll be in the rear. I saw a truck back there with lots of antennas, a communications center. Over to the east." Xbalanque looked at his brother uneasily. Something felt wrong about him. "Are you all right?"

"I serve my people and my gods." Hunapu walked a few steps away and vanished with a soft *clok*.

"I'm not so sure that this was a good idea." Xbalanque wondered what Hunapu had in mind.

"Got a better one? He'll be okay." The rebel started to shrug but was stopped with shoulders lifted by the sound of helicopters.

"Xbalanque, you've got to take them. If they can attack from the air, we're dead." Before the other man had finished, Xbalanque was running back toward the helicopters and the middle of Kaminaljuyu. As the brace of Hueys came into sight, he picked up a rock the size of his head and launched it. The helicopter to the left exploded in flames. Its companion pulled up and away from the camp. But Xbalanque hadn't realized the position of the helicopter he had destroyed. Burning debris fell on his huddled followers, causing as much death and pain as a government rocket.

Xbalanque turned away, cursing himself for being oblivious to his people, and saw Hunapu atop the tallest mound. His brother held a limp figure, half-sprawled on the ground, beside Maria's altar. Xbalanque ran toward the temple.

From the other side Akabal had seen Hunapu appear with his captive. Akabal had been separated from the Twins in the melee following the first mortar strike. Now he turned his back to the mass of followers jammed together around the central dirt mounds. Maxine Chen's tug on his arm stopped him. She joined him, her face filthy and sweating and her two-man crew looking haggard. Robert had reclaimed his camera and filmed everything he could get as he moved around Kaminaljuyu.

"What's going on?" She had to shout to be heard over the crowd and the guns. "Who's that with Hunapu? Is it Xbalanque?"

Akabal shook his head and kept moving, followed by Chen. When she saw that Akabal intended to climb the mound in the open, she and Robert hesitated and followed him. The sound man shook his head and crouched at the base of the temple. Xbalanque had been met by Maria, and they scrambled up the other side. The cameraman stepped back and began filming as soon as all six had made it to the top.

Seeing Xbalanque, Hunapu lifted his face and began to chant to the sky. He no longer had his knife, and the dried blood that covered much of his face looked like ceremonial paint. Xbalanque listened for a moment and then shook his head. In an archaic Maya he argued with Hunapu, who continued his chant, oblivious to Xbalanque's interruption. Maxine asked Akabal what was happening, but he shook his head in confusion. Maria had hauled the Guatemalan general onto the earthen altar and began to strip off his uniform.

The guns ceased firing at the same moment Hunapu ended his chant and held out his hand to Xbalanque. In the silence Maxine put her hands to her ears. Maria knelt beside the general, holding the offering bowl in front of her. Xbalanque backed away, shaking his head. Hunapu sharply thrust his arm out at Xbalanque. Looking over Hunapu's shoulder, Xbalanque saw the government tanks roll forward, tearing apart the fence and crushing the Indians under their treads.

As Xbalanque hesitated, the general woke up. Finding himself stretched out on an altar, he cursed and tried to roll off. Maria shoved him back onto it. Noting her feathers, he held himself away from her as if he could be contaminated. He began haranguing Hunapu and Xbalanque in Spanish.

"What the hell do you think you are doing? The Geneva convention clearly states that officer prisoners of war are to be treated with dignity and respect. Give me back my clothes!"

Xbalanque heard the tanks and screams behind him as the Guatemalan army officer cursed him. He tossed his obsidian knife to Hunapu and grabbed the general's flailing arms.

"Let me go. What do you savages think you're doing?" As Hunapu raised the knife, the man's eyes widened. "You can't do this! Please, this is 1986. You're all mad. Listen, I'll stop them; I'll call them off. Let me up. Please, Jesus, let me up!"

Xbalanque pinned the general back against the altar and looked up as Hunapu brought the knife down.

"Hail, Mary, full of g—"

The obsidian blade cut through flesh and cartilage, spraying the brothers and Maria with blood. Xbalanque watched in horrified fascination as Hunapu decapitated the general, bearing down with the knife against the spine and severing the final connections before lifting the *Ladino*'s head to the sky.

Xbalanque released the dead man's arms and trembling, took the bowl filled with blood from Maria. Shoving the body off the altar, he set fire to the blood as Maria lit copal incense. He threw back his head and called the names of his gods to the sky. His voice was echoed by his people, gathered below with arms thrust into the air toward the temple. Hunapu placed the head, its eyes open and staring into Xibalba, on the altar.

The tanks stopped their advance and began a lumbering retreat. The foot soldiers dropped their guns and ran. A few shot officers that tried to stop them, and the officers joined the flight. The government forces disbanded in chaos, scattering into the city, abandoning their equipment and weapons.

Maxine had vomited at the sight of the sacrifice, but her cameraman had it all on tape. Shaking and pale, she asked Akabal what was happening. He looked down at her with wide eyes.

"It *is* the time of the Fourth Creation. The birth of Huracan, the heart of heaven, our home. The gods have returned to us! Death to the enemies of our people!" Akabal knelt and stretched his hands toward the Hero Twins. "Lead us to glory, favored of the gods."

In room 502 of the Camino Real a tourist in flowered shorts and a pale blue polyester shirt stuffed the last souvenir weaving into his suitcase. He looked around the room for his wife and saw her at the window.

"Next time, Martha, don't buy anything that won't fit into your suitcase." He leaned his considerable weight on the bag and slid the catches closed. "Where is that boy? We must have called half an hour ago. What's so interesting out there?"

"The people, Simon. It's some kind of procession. I wonder if it's a religious occasion."

"Is it a riot? With all this unrest we've been hearing about, the sooner we get out of here the better I'm going to feel."

"No, they just seem to be going somewhere." His wife

continued to peer down at the streets filled with men, women, and children. "They're all Indians too. You can tell by the costumes."

"My god, we're going to miss our plane if they don't get a move on." He glared at his watch as if it was responsible. "Call again, will you? Where the hell can he be?"

FROM *THE JOURNAL OF XAVIER DESMOND*

DECEMBER 15, 1986/EN ROUTE TO LIMA, PERU:

I have been dilatory about keeping up my journal—no entry yesterday or the day before. I can only plead exhaustion and a certain amount of despondence.

Guatemala took its toll on my spirit, I'm afraid. We are, of course, stringently neutral, but when I saw the televised news reports of the insurrection and heard some of the rhetoric being attributed to the Mayan revolutionaries, I dared to hope. When we actually met with the Indian leaders, I was even briefly elated. They considered my presence in the room an honor, an auspicious omen, seemed to treat me with the same sort of respect (or lack of respect) they gave Hartmann and Tachyon, and the way they treated their own jokers gave me heart.

Well, I am an old man—an old *joker* in fact—and I tend to clutch at straws. Now the Mayan revolutionaries have proclaimed a new nation, an Amerindian homeland, where *their* jokers will be welcomed and honored. The rest of us need not apply. Not that I would care much to live in the jungles of Guatemala—even an autonomous joker homeland down here would scarcely cause a ripple in Jokertown, let alone any kind of significant exodus. Still, there are so few places in the world where jokers are welcome, where we can make our homes in peace . . . the more we travel on, the more we see, the more I am forced to conclude that Jokertown is the best place for us, our only true home. I cannot express how much that conclusion saddens and terrifies me.

Why must we draw these lines, these fine distinctions, these labels and barriers that set us apart? Ace and nat and joker, capitalist and communist, Catholic and Protestant, Arab and Jew, Indian and *Ladino*, and on and on everywhere, and of course true humanity is to be found only on *our* side of the line and we feel free to oppress and rape and kill the "other," whoever he might be.

There are those on the *Stacked Deck* who charge that the Guatemalans were engaged in conscious genocide against their own Indian populations, and who see this new nation as a very good thing. But I wonder.

The Mayas think jokers are touched by the gods, specially blessed. No doubt it is better to be honored than reviled for our various handicaps and deformities. No doubt.

But...

We have the Islamic nations still ahead of us ... a third of the world, someone told me. Some Moslems are more tolerant than others, but virtually all of them consider deformity a sign of Allah's displeasure. The attitudes of the true fanatics such as the Shi'ites in Iran and the Nur sect in Syria are terrifying, Hitlerian. How many jokers were slaughtered when the Ayatollah displaced the Shah? To some Iranians the tolerance he extended to jokers and women was the Shah's greatest sin.

And are we so very much better in the enlightened USA, where fundamentalists like Leo Barnett preach that jokers are being punished for their sins? Oh, yes, there is a distinction, I must remember that. Barnett says he hates the sins but loves the sinners, and if we will only repent and have faith and love Jesus, surely we will be cured.

No, I'm afraid that ultimately Barnett and the Ayatollah and the Mayan priests are all preaching the same creed— that our bodies in some sense reflect our souls, that some divine being has taken a direct hand and twisted us into these shapes to signify his pleasure (the Mayas) or displeasure (Nur al-Allah, the Ayatollah, the Firebreather). Most of all, each of them is saying that jokers are *different*.

My own creed is distressingly simple—I believe that jokers and aces and nats are all just men and women and ought to be treated as such. During my dark nights of the soul I wonder if I am the only one left who still believes this.

Still brooding about Guatemala and the Mayas. A point I failed to make earlier—I could not help noticing that this glorious idealistic revolution of theirs was led by two aces and a nat. Even down here, where jokers are supposedly kissed by the gods, the aces lead and the jokers follow.

A few days ago—it was during our visit to the Panama Canal, I believe—Digger Downs asked me if I thought the U.S. would ever have a joker president. I told him I'd settle for a joker congressman (I'm afraid Nathan Rabinowitz, whose district includes Jokertown, heard the comment and took it for some sort of criticism of his representation). Then Digger wanted to know if I thought an ace could be elected president. A more interesting question, I must admit. Downs always looks half asleep, but he is sharper than he appears, though not in a class with some of the other reporters aboard the *Stacked Deck*, like Herrmann of AP or Morgenstern of the *Washington Post*.

I told Downs that before this last Wild Card Day it might have been possible . . . barely. Certain aces, like the Turtle (still missing, the latest NY papers confirm), Peregrine, Cyclone, and a handful of others are first-rank celebrities, commanding considerable public affection. How much of that could translate to the public arena, and how well it might survive the rough give-and-take of a presidential campaign, that's a more difficult question. Heroism is a perishable commodity.

Jack Braun was standing close enough to hear Digger's question and my reply. Before I could conclude—I wanted to say that the whole equation had changed this September, that among the casualties of Wild Card Day was any faint chance that an ace might be a viable presidential candidate—Braun interrupted. "They'd tear him apart," he told us.

What if it was someone they loved? Digger wanted to know.

"They loved the Four Aces," Braun said.

Braun is no longer quite the exile he was at the beginning of the tour. Tachyon still refuses to acknowledge his existence and Hiram is barely polite, but the other aces don't seem to know or care who he is. In Panama he was often in Fantasy's company, squiring her here and there, and I've heard rumors of a liaison between Golden Boy and Senator Lyons's press secretary, an attractive young blonde. Undoubtedly, of the male aces, Braun is by far the most attractive in the conventional sense, although Mordecai Jones has a certain brooding presence. Downs has been struck by those two also. The next issue of *Aces* will feature a piece comparing Golden Boy and the Harlem Hammer, he informs me.

THE TINT OF HATRED

Part Three

TUESDAY, DECEMBER 23, 1986, RIO:

Sara detested Rio.

From her room in the Luxor Hotel on Atlantica, the city looked like a curving Miami Beach: a display of gleaming, white high-rise hotels arrayed before a wide beach and gentle blue-green surf, all fading into a sun-hazed distance on either side.

The majority of the junket had fulfilled their obligations quickly and were using the Rio stopover for R&R. After all, it was almost the holidays; a month on the tour had worn the idealism off most of them. Hiram Worchester had gone on a binge, eating and drinking his way through the city's myriad *restaurante*. The press had opted for the local *cervezaria* and were sampling the native beers. American dollars exchanged into handfuls of *cruzados* and prices were low. The wealthier of the contingent had invested in the Brazilian gem market—there seemed to be a jewelry stall in every hotel.

And yet Sara was aware of the reality. The standard tourist warnings were indication enough: Don't wear any jewelry on the streets; don't get on the buses, don't trust the taxi drivers; be careful around children or any jokers; don't go out alone, especially if you're a woman; if you want to keep something, lock it up or stay with it. Beware. To Rio's multitudes of poor, any tourist was rich and the rich were fair game.

And reality intruded as, bored and restless, she left the hotel that afternoon, deciding to go see Tachyon at a local clinic. She hailed one of the ubiquitous black-and-yellow VW Beetle cabs. Two blocks in from the ocean, glittering Rio turned dark, mountainous, crowded, and miserable. Through the narrow alleys between buildings she could glimpse the old landmark, Corcovado, the gigantic statue of Christ the Redeemer atop a central peak of the city. Corcovado was a reminder of how the Wild Card had devastated this country. Rio had suffered a major outbreak in 1948. The city had always been wild and poor, with a downtrodden population simmering under the veneer. The virus had let loose months of panic and violence. No one knew which disgruntled ace was responsible for Corcovado. One morning the figure of Christ had simply "changed," as if the rising sun were melting a wax figurine. Christ the Redeemer became a joker, a misshapen, hunchbacked *thing*, one of his outstretched arms gone completely, the other twisted around to support the distorted body. Father Squid had celebrated a mass there yesterday; two hundred thousand people had prayed together under the deformed statue.

She'd told the taxi driver to take her to Santa Theresa, the old section of Rio. There, the jokers had gathered as they had gathered in New York's Jokertown, as if taking solace in their mutual afflictions in the shadow of Corcovado. Santa Theresa had been in the warnings too. Near Estrada de Redentor she tapped the driver on the shoulder. "Stop here," she said. The driver said something in rapid Portuguese, then shook his head and pulled over.

Sara found that this taxi driver was no different than the rest. She'd forgotten to insist that he turn on his meter when they'd left the hotel. *"Quanto custa?"* It was one of the few phrases she knew: How much? He insisted loudly that the fare was a thousand cruzados, forty dollars. Sara, exasperated and tired of constant small ripoffs, argued back in English. Finally she threw a hundred-cruzado bill at him, still far more than he should have received. He took it, then drove off with a screech of tires. *"Feliz Natal!"* he called sarcastically: Merry Christmas.

Sara flipped him the finger. It gave her little satisfaction. She began looking for the *clínica*.

It had rained that afternoon, the usual rainy-season squall that drenched the city for a few hours and then gave way to sunshine again. Even that hadn't managed to quell the stench of Rio's antiquated sewage system. Walking up the steeply inclined street, she was pursued by fetid oders. Like the others, she walked in the center of the narrow street, moving aside only if she heard a car. She quickly felt conspicuous as the sun began to fall behind the hills. Most of those around her were jokers or those too poor to live anywhere else. She saw none of the police patrols here that routinely swept the tourist streets. A fox-furred snout leered at her as someone jostled past, what looked to be a man-size snail slithered along the sidewalk to her right, a twin-headed prostitute loitered in a doorway. She'd sometimes felt paranoid in Jokertown, but the intensity was nothing like she felt here. In Jokertown she would have at least understood what the voices around her were saying, she would have known that two or three blocks over lay the relative security of Manhattan, she would have been able to call someone from a corner phone booth. Here there was nothing. She had only a vague notion of where she was. If she disappeared, it might be hours before anyone knew she was missing.

It was with distinct relief that she saw the clinic ahead and half ran to its open door.

The place hadn't changed since yesterday when the press corps had visited. It was a crowded, chaotic lunacy. The clinic smelled vile, a combination of antiseptics, disease, and human waste. The floors were filthy, the equipment antiquated, the beds mere cots packed together as closely as possible. Tachyon had howled at the appearance, then had immediately thrown himself into the fray.

He was still there, looking as if he'd never left. "*Boatarde*, Ms. Morgenstern," he said. His satin jacket missing, his shirt-sleeves rolled halfway up his lanky arms, he was drawing a blood sample from a comatose young girl whose skin was scaled like a lizard's. "Did you come to work or watch?"

"I thought it was a samba club."

That gained her a small, weary smile. "They can use help in back," he said. "*Felicidades.*" Sara waved to Tachyon and slid between the rows of cots. Near the rear of the clinic she halted in surprise, frowning. Her breath caught.

Gregg Hartmann was crouched beside one of the cots. A joker sat there, bristling with stiff, barbed quills like those of a porcupine. A distinct animal musk came from the man. The Senator, in hospital blues, was carefully cleaning a wound on the joker's upper arm. Despite the odor, despite the patient's appearance, Sara could see only concern on his face as he worked. Hartmann saw Sara and smiled. "Ms. Morgenstern. Hello."

"Senator."

He shook his head. "You don't need to be so damn formal. It's Gregg. Please." She could see fatigue in the lines around his eyes, in the huskiness of his voice; he'd evidently been here for some time. Since Mexico, Sara had avoided situations that might leave the two of them alone. But she'd watched him, wishing she could sort out her feelings, wishing that she didn't feel a confused liking for the man. She'd observed how he interacted with others, how he responded to them, and she wondered. Her mind told her that she may have misjudged him; her emotions tore her in two directions at once.

He was looking at her, patient and genial. She ran her hand through her short hair and nodded. "Gregg, then. And I'm Sara. Tachyon sent me back here."

"Great. This is Mariu, who was on the wrong end of somebody's knife." Gregg indicated the joker, who stared at Sara with unblinking, feral intensity. His pupils were reddish, and his lips were drawn back in a snarl. The joker said nothing, either unwilling or unable to talk.

"I guess I should find something to do." Sara looked around, wanting to leave.

"I could use an extra pair of hands with Mariu here."

No, she wanted to say. *I don't want to know you. I don't want to have to say I was wrong.* Belatedly Sara shook her head. "Umm, okay. Sure. What do you want me to do?"

They worked together silently. The wound had been stitched earlier. Gregg cleaned it gently as Sara held the prickly barbs away. He smeared antibiotic ointment on the long wound, pressed gauze to it. Sara noticed most that his touch was gentle, if clumsy. He bound the dressing and stepped back. "Okay, you're done, Mariu." Gregg patted the joker carefully on the shoulder. The spiny face nodded slightly, then Mariu padded away without a word. Sara found Gregg looking at her, sweating in the heat of the clinic. "Thanks."

"You're welcome." She took a step back from him, uncomfortable. "You did a good job with Mariu."

Gregg laughed. He held out his hands, and Sara saw angry red scratches scattered over them. "Mariu gave me lots of problems until you showed up. I'm strictly amateur help here. We made a good team, though. Tachyon wanted me to unload supplies; want to give me a hand with that?"

There wasn't a graceful way to say no. They worked in silence for a time, restocking shelves. "I didn't expect to find you here," Sara commented as they wrestled a packing crate into a storage room.

Sara saw that he noted her unspoken words and hadn't taken offense. "Without making sure a video camera was recording my good works, you mean?" he said, smiling. "Ellen was out shopping with Peregrine. John and Amy had a stack of paperwork this big they wanted me to tackle." Gregg held his hands two feet apart. "Coming here seemed a lot more useful. Besides, Tachyon's dedication can give you a guilt complex. I left a note for Security saying I was 'going out.' I imagine Billy Ray's probably having a fit by now. Promise not to tell on me?"

His face was so innocently mischievous that she had to laugh with him. With the laughter a little more of the brittle hatred flaked away. "You're a constant surprise, Senator."

"Gregg, remember?" Softly.

"Sorry." Her smile faded. For a moment she felt a strong pull to him. She forced the feeling down, denied it. *It's not what you want to feel. It's not real. If anything, it's a backlash reaction for having detested him for so long.* She looked around at the barren, dusty shelves of the storeroom and viciously tore open the carton.

She could feel his eyes watching her. "You still don't believe what I said about Andrea." His voice wavered halfway between statement and question. His words, so close to what she'd been thinking, brought sudden heat to her face.

"I'm not sure about anything."

"And you still hate me."

"No," she said. She pulled Styrofoam packing from the box. And then, with sudden, impulsive honesty: "To me that's probably more scary."

The admission left her feeling vulnerable and open. Sara was glad that she couldn't see his face. She cursed herself for the confession. It implied attraction for Gregg; it suggested that, far from hating him, she'd come nearly full circle in her feelings, and that was simply something she didn't want him to know. Not yet. Not until she was certain.

The atmosphere between them was charged with tension. She searched for some way to blunt the effect. Gregg could wound her with a word, could make her bleed with a look.

What Gregg did then made Sara wish that she'd never

seen Andrea's face on Succubus, that she hadn't spent years loathing the man.

He did nothing.

He reached over her shoulder and handed her a box of sterile bandages. "I think they go on the top shelf," he said.

"I think they go on the top shelf."

Puppetman was screaming inside him, battering at the mindbars that held him in. The power ached to be loose, to tear into Sara's opened mind and feed there. The hatred that had rebuffed him in New York was gone, and he could *see* Sara's affection; he tasted it, like blood-salt. Radiant, warm vermilion.

So easy, Puppetman moaned. *It would be easy. It's rich, full. We could make that an overwhelming tide. You could take her here. She would beg you for release, she would give you whatever you asked of her—pain, submission, anything, Please . . .*

Gregg could barely hold back the power. He'd never felt it so needy, so frantic. He'd known this would be the danger of the trip. Puppetman, that power inside him, would have to feed, and Puppetman only fed on torment and suffering, all the black-red and angry emotions. In New York and Washington it was easy. There were always puppets there, minds he'd found and opened so that he could use them later. Cattle, fodder for the power. There it was easy to slip away unseen, to stalk carefully and then pounce.

Not here. Not on this trip. Absences were conspicuous and needed explanations. He had to be cautious; he had to let the power go hungry. He was used to feeding weekly; since the plane had left New York, he'd managed to feed only once: in Guatemala. Too long ago.

Puppetman was famished. His need could not be held back much longer.

Later, Gregg pleaded. *Remember Mariu? Remember the rich potency we saw in him? We touched him, we opened him. Reach out now—see, you can still feel him, only a block away. A few hours and we feed. But not with Sara. I wouldn't let you have Andrea or Succubus; I won't let you have Sara.*

Do you think she'd love you if she knew? Puppetman mocked. *Do you think she'd still feel affection if you told her? You think she would embrace you, kiss you, let you enter her warmth? If you really want her to love you for yourself, then tell her everything.*

Shut up! Gregg screamed back. *Shut up! You can have Mariu. Sara is mine.*

He forced the power back down. He made himself smile. It was three hours before he found an excuse to leave; he was pleased when Sara decided to stay at the clinic. Shaking from the exertion of keeping Puppetman inside, he went into the night streets.

Santa Theresa, like Jokertown, was alive at night, still vibrant with dark life. Rio herself never seemed to sleep. He could look down into the city and see a deluge of lights flowing in the valleys between the sharp mountains and spilling halfway up the slopes. It was a sight to make one stop for a moment and ponder the small beauties that, unwittingly, a sprawling humanity had made.

Gregg hardly noticed it. The lashing power inside drove him. *Mariu. Feel him. Find him.*

The joker who had brought in the bleeding Mariu had spoken a little English. Gregg overheard the story he'd told Tachyon. Mariu was crazy, he said. Ever since Cara was nice to him, he'd been bothering her. Cara's husband, João, he told Mariu to stay away, told him he was just a fucking joker. Said he'd kill Mariu if Mariu didn't leave Cara alone. Mariu wouldn't listen. He kept following Cara, scaring her. So João cut him.

Gregg had offered to dress Mariu's wound after Tachyon had stitched it up, feeling Puppetman yammering inside. He'd touched the loathsome Mariu, let the power open his mind to feel the raging boil of emotions. He'd known immediately—this would be the one.

He could sense the emanations of the open mind at the edge of his range, perhaps a half mile away. He moved through narrow, twisting streets, still dressed in the blues. Some of his intensity must have shown for he wasn't bothered. Once a crowd of children surrounded him, pulling at his pockets, but he'd looked at them and they'd gone silent, scattering into darkness. He'd moved on, closer to Mariu, until he saw the joker.

Mariu was standing outside a ramshackle, three-story apartment building, watching a window on the second floor. Gregg felt the pulsing, black rage and knew João was there. Mariu's feelings for João were simple, bestial; those for Cara were more complex—a shifting, metallic respect; an azure affection laced through with veins of repressed lust. With his barbed skin Mariu had probably never had a willing lover, Gregg knew, but he could sense the fantasies in his mind. *Now, please*. Gregg took a shuddering breath. He let down the barriers. Puppetman laughed.

He stroked the surface of Mariu's mind possessively, cooing softly to himself. He removed the few restraints an uncaring society and church had put on Mariu. *Yes, be angry,* he whispered to Mariu. *Be full of devout rage. He keeps you from her. He insulted you. He hurt you. Let the fury come, let it blind you until you see nothing but its burning heat.* Mariu was moving restlessly in the street, his arms waving as if to some inner debate. Gregg watched as Puppetman amplified the frustration, the hurt, the anger, until Mariu screamed hoarsely and ran into the building. Gregg closed his eyes, leaning against a shadowed wall. Puppetman rode with Mariu, not seeing with Mariu's eyes but *feeling* with him. He heard shouts in angry Portuguese, the splintering of wood, and suddenly the rage flared up higher than before.

Puppetman was feeding now, taking sustenance from the rampant emotions. Mariu and João were struggling, for he could sense, deep underneath, a sensation of pain. He damped the pain down so Mariu would not notice it. The screams of a woman accompanied the shouts now, and from the twisting of Mariu's mind, Gregg knew that Cara was there too. Puppetman increased Mariu's anger until the glare of it nearly blinded him. He knew Mariu could feel nothing else now. The woman screamed louder; there was a distinct dull thud audible even in the street below. Gregg heard the sound of breaking glass and a wail: he opened his eyes to see a body strike the hood of a car and topple into the street. The body was bent at an obscene angle, the spine broken. Mariu was looking down from the window above.

Yes, that was good. That was tasty. This will taste good as well.

Puppetman let the rage slowly fade as Mariu ducked back inside. Now he toyed with the feelings for Cara. He diluted the binding respect, let the affection dim. *You need her. You've always wanted her. You looked at those hidden breasts as she walked by and wondered how they would feel, all silken and warm. You wondered at the hidden place between her legs, how it would taste, how it would feel. You*

*knew it would be hot, slick with desire. You'd stroke youself
at night and think of her writhing underneath you, moaning
as you thrust.*

Now Puppetman turned derisive, mocking, modifying
passion with the residue of Mariu's anger. *And you knew that
she'd never want you, not looking the way you do, not the
joker with the needled quills. No. Her body couldn't be for
you. She'd laugh about you, making coarse jokes. When João
possessed her, he'd laugh and say, "This would never be
Mariu; Mariu would never take pleasure from me."*

Cara screamed. Gregg heard cloth tear and felt Mariu's
uncontrolled lust. He could imagine it. He could imagine him
bearing her down roughly, uncaring that his barbs gouged
her unprotected skin, looking only for release and imagined
vengeance in the violent, agonizing rape.

Enough, he thought, quietly. *Let it be enough.* But
Puppetman only laughed, staying with Mariu until orgasm
threw his mind into chaos. Then Puppetman, sated himself,
withdrew. He laughed hilariously, letting Mariu's emotions
drop to normal, let the joker look in horror at what he'd
done.

Already there were more shouts from the building, and
Gregg heard the sirens in the distance. He opened his
eyes—gasping, blinking—and ran.

Inside, Puppetman eased himself into his accustomed
place and quietly let Gregg place the bars around him.
Satisfied, he slept.

FRIDAY, DECEMBER 26, 1986, SYRIA:

Misha sat bolt upright, sweat-drenched from the dream.
She had evidently cried out in fear, for Sayyid was struggling
to sit up in his own bed.

"*Wallah,* woman! What is it?" Sayyid was hewn from a
heroic mold, fully ten foot tall and muscled like a god. In
repose he was inspiring: a dark, Egyptian giant, a myth given
life. Sayyid was the weapon in Nur al-Allah's hands; terrorists
such as al-Muezzin were the hidden blades. When Sayyid
stood before the faithful, towering over all, they could see in
Nur al-Allah's general the visible symbol of Allah's protection.

In Sayyid's keen mind were the strategies that had
defeated the better-armed and supplied Israeli troops in the
Golan Heights, when the world had thought Nur al-Allah and

his followers hopelessly outnumbered. He had orchestrated the rioting in Damascus when al-Assad's ruling Ba'th Party had tried to move away from Qu'ranic law, allowing the Nur sect to forge an alliance with the Sunni and Alawite sects. He craftily advised Nur al-Allah to send the faithful into Beirut when the Christian Druze leaders had threatened to overthrow the reigning Islamic party. When the Swarm Mother had sent her deadly offspring to Earth the year before, it was Sayyid who had protected Nur al-Allah and the faithful. In his mind was victory. For the *jihad* Allah had given Sayyid *hikma*, divine wisdom.

It was a well-kept secret that Sayyid's heroic appearance was also a curse. Nur al-Allah had decreed that jokers were sinners, branded by God. They had fallen from *shari'a*, the true path. They were destined to be slaves of the true faithful at best; at worst they would be exterminated. It would not have been wise for anyone to see that Nur al-Allah's brilliant strategist was nearly a cripple, that Sayyid's mighty, rippling thews could barely support the crushing weight of his body. While his height had doubled, his mass had increased nearly fourfold.

Sayyid was always carefully posed. He moved slowly if at all. When he must go any distance, he rode.

Men who had seen Sayyid in the baths whispered that he was as heroically proportioned everywhere. Misha alone knew that his manhood was as crippled as the rest of him. For the failure of his appearance Sayyid could only blame Allah, and he did not dare. For his inability to stay aroused more than a few moments, he blamed Misha. Tonight, as often, her body bore the livid bruises of his heavy fists. But at least the beatings were quick. There were times when she thought his awful, suffocating weight would never rise from her.

"It is nothing," she whispered. "A dream. I didn't mean to wake you."

Sayyid rubbed at his eyes, staring groggily toward her. He had brought himself to a sitting position, and he panted from the effort. "A vision. Nur al-Allah has said—"

"My *brother* needs his sleep, as does his general. Please."

"Why must you always oppose me, woman?" Sayyid frowned, and Misha knew that he remembered his earlier embarrassment, when in frustration he had battered her, as if he could find release in her pain. "Tell me," he insisted. "I must know if it's something to tell the prophet."

I am Kahina, she wanted to say. *I'm the one Allah has gifted. Why must* you *be the one to decide whether to wake Najib? It was not your vision.* But she held back the words, knowing that they led to more pain. "It was confused," she told him. "I saw a man, a Russian by his dress, who handed Nur al-Allah many gifts. Then the Russian was gone, and another man—an American—came with more gifts and laid them at the prophet's feet." Misha licked dry lips, remembering the panic of the dream. "Then there was nothing but a feeling of terrible danger. He had gossamer strings knotted to his long fingers, and from each string dangled a person. One of his creatures came forward with a gift. The gift was for me, and yet I feared it, dreading to open the package. I ripped it open, and inside . . ." She shuddered. "I . . . I saw only myself. I know there was more to the dream, but I woke. Yet I know, I *know* the gift-bearer is coming. He will be here soon."

"An American?" Sayyid asked.

"Yes."

"Then I know already. You dream of the plane carrying the Western infidels. The prophet will be ready for them: a month, perhaps more."

Misha nodded, pretending to be reassured, though the terror of the dream still held her. *He was coming, and he held out his gift for her, smiling.* "I'll tell Nur al-Allah in the morning," she said. "I'm sorry I disturbed your rest."

"There's more I would talk about," Sayyid answered.

She knew. "Please. We're both tired."

"I'm entirely awake now."

"Sayyid, I wouldn't want to fail you again. . . ."

She had hoped that would end it, yet had known it would not. Sayyid groaned to his feet. He said nothing; he never did. He lumbered across the room, breathing loudly at the exertion. She could see his huge bulk beside her bed, a darker shade against the night.

He fell more than lowered himself atop her. "This time," he breathed. "This time."

It was not this time. Misha didn't need to be Kahina to know that it would never be.

FROM *THE JOURNAL OF XAVIER DESMOND*

DECEMBER 29, 1986/BUENOS AIRES:

Don't cry for Jack, Argentina....

Evita's bane has comes back to Buenos Aires. When the musical first played Broadway, I wondered what Jack Braun must have thought, listening to Lupone sing of the Four Aces. Now that question has even more poignance. Braun has been very calm, almost stoic, in the face of his reception here, but what must he be feeling inside?

Peron is dead, Evita even deader, even Isabel just a memory, but the Peronistas are still very much a part of the Argentine political scene. They have not forgotten. Everywhere the signs taunt Braun and invite him to go home. He is the ultimate *gringo* (do they use that word in Argentina, I wonder), the ugly but awesomely powerful American who came to the Argentine uninvited and toppled a sovereign government because he disapproved of its politics. The United States has been doing such things for as long as there has been a Latin America, and I have no doubt that these same resentments fester in many other places. The United States and even the dread "secret aces" of the CIA are abstract concepts, however, faceless and difficult to get a fix on— Golden Boy is flesh and blood, very real and very visible, and *here*.

Someone inside the hotel leaked our room assignments, and when Jack stepped out onto his balcony the first day, he was showered with dung and rotten fruit. He has stayed inside ever since, except for official functions, but even there he is not safe. Last night as we stood in a receiving line at the Casa Rosada, the wife of a union official—a beautiful young woman, her small dark face framed by masses of lustrous black hair—stepped up to him with a sweet smile, looked straight into his eyes, and spit in his face.

It caused quite a stir, and Senators Hartmann and Lyons have filed some sort of protest, I believe. Braun himself was remarkably restrained, almost gallant. Digger was hounding him ruthlessly after the reception; he's cabling a write-up on the incident back to *Aces* and wanted a quote. Braun finally gave him something. "I've done things I'm not proud of," he said, "but getting rid of Juan Peron isn't one of them."

"Yeah, yeah," I heard Digger tell him, "but how did you feel when she spit on you?"

Jack just looked disgusted. "I don't hit women," he said. Then he walked off and sat by himself.

Downs turned to me when Braun was gone. "I don't hit women," he echoed in a singsong imitation of Golden Boy's voice, then added, "What a weenie..."

The world is too ready to read cowardice and betrayal into anything Jack Braun says and does, but the truth, I suspect, is more complex. Given his youthful appearance, it's hard to recall at times how old the Golden Boy really is—his formative years were during the Depression and World War II, and he grew up listening to the NBC Blue Network, not MTV. No wonder some of his values seem quaintly old-fashioned.

In many ways the Judas Ace seems almost an innocent, a bit lost in a world that has grown too complicated for him. I think he is more troubled than he admits by his reception here in Argentina. Braun is the last representative of a lost dream that flourished briefly in the aftermath of World War II and died in Korea and the HUAC hearings and the Cold War. They thought they could reshape the world, Archibald Holmes and his Four Aces. They had no doubts, no more than their country did. Power existed to be used, and they were supremely confident in their ability to tell the good guys from the bad guys. Their own democratic ideals and the shining purity of their intentions were all the justification they needed. For those few early aces it must have been a golden age, and how appropriate that a golden boy be at its center.

Golden ages give way to dark ages, as any student of history knows, and as all of us are currently finding out.

Braun and his colleagues could do things no one else had ever done—they could fly and lift tanks and absorb a man's mind and memories, and so they bought the illusion that they could make a real difference on a global scale, and when that illusion dissolved beneath them, they fell a very long way indeed. Since then no other ace has dared to dream as big.

Even in the face of imprisonment, despair, insanity, disgrace, and death, the Four Aces had triumphs to cling to, and Argentina was perhaps the brightest of those triumphs. What a bitter homecoming this must be for Jack Braun.

As if this was not enough, our mail caught up with us just before we left Brazil, and the pouch included a dozen copies of the new issue of *Aces* with Digger's promised feature story. The cover has Jack Braun and Mordecai Jones in profile, scowling at each other (All cleverly doctored, of course. I don't believe the two had ever met before we all got together at Tomlin) over a blurb that reads, "The Strongest Man in the World."

The article itself is a lengthy discussion of the two men and their public careers, enlivened by numerous anecdotes about their feats of strength and much speculation about which of the two is, indeed, the strongest man in the world.

Both of the principals seem embarrassed by the piece, Braun perhaps more acutely. Neither much wants to discuss it, and they certainly don't seem likely to settle the matter anytime soon. I understand that there has been considerable argument and even wagering back in the press compartment since Digger's piece came out (for once, Downs seems to have had an impact on his journalistic colleagues), but the bets are likely to remain unresolved for a long time to come.

I told Downs that the story was spurious and offensive as soon as I read it. He seemed startled. "I don't get it," he said to me. "What's *your* beef?"

My beef, as I explained to him, was simple. Braun and Jones are scarcely the only people to manifest superhuman strength since the advent of the wild card; in fact, that particular power is a fairly common one, ranking close behind telekinesis and telepathy in Tachyon's incidence-of-occurrence charts. It has something to do with maximizing the contractile strength of the muscles, I believe. My point is, a number of prominent jokers display augmented strength as well—just off the top of my head, I cited Elmo (the dwarf bouncer at the

Crystal Palace), Ernie of Ernie's Bar & Grill, the Oddity, Quasiman . . . and, most notably, Howard Mueller. The Troll's strength does not perhaps equal that of Golden Boy and the Harlem Hammer, but assuredly it approaches it. None of these jokers were so much as mentioned in passing in Digger's story, although the names of a dozen other superstrong aces were dropped here and there. Why was that? I wanted to know.

I can't claim to have made much of an impression unfortunately. When I was through, Downs simply rolled his eyes and said, "You people are so damned *touchy*." He tried to be accommodating by telling me that if this story went over big, maybe he'd write up a sequel on the strongest *joker* in the world, and he couldn't comprehend why that "concession" made me even angrier. And they wonder why we people are touchy. . . .

Howard thought the whole argument was vastly amusing. Sometimes I wonder about him.

Actually my fit of pique was nothing compared to the reaction the magazine drew from Billy Ray, our security chief. Ray was one of the other aces mentioned in passing, his strength dismissed as not being truly "major league." Afterward he could be heard the length of the plane, suggesting that maybe Downs would like to step outside with him, seeing as how he was so minor league. Digger declined the offer. From the smile on his face I doubt that Carnifex will be getting any good press in *Aces* anytime soon.

Since then, Ray has been grousing about the story to anyone who will listen. The crux of his argument is that strength isn't everything; he may not be as strong as Braun or Jones, but he's strong enough to take either of them in a fight, and he'd be glad to put his money where his mouth is.

Personally I have gotten a certain perverse satisfaction out of this tempest in a teapot. The irony is, they are arguing about who has the most of what is essentially a minor power. I seem to recall that there was some sort of demonstration in the early seventies, when the battleship *New Jersey* was being refitted at the Bayonne Naval Supply Center over in New Jersey. The Turtle lifted the battleship telekinetically, got it out of the water by several feet, and held it there for almost half a minute. Braun and Jones lift tanks and toss automobiles about, but neither could come remotely close to what the Turtle did that day.

The simple truth is, the contractile strength of the human musculature can be increased only so much. Physical limits apply. Dr. Tachyon says there may also be limits to what the human mind can accomplish, but so far they have not been reached.

If the Turtle is indeed a joker, as many believe, I would find this irony especially satisfying.

I suppose I am, at base, as small a man as any.

THE TINT OF HATRED

Part Four

THURSDAY, JANUARY 1, 1987, SOUTH AFRICA:

The evening was cool. Beyond the hotel's wide veranda, the crumpled landscape of the Bushveld Basin seemed pastoral. The last light of the day edged grassy hills with lavender and burnt orange; in the valley the sluggish Olifants's brown waters were touched with gold. Among the stand of acacias lining the river monkeys settled to sleep with occasional hooting calls.

Sara looked at it and felt nausea. It was so damn beautiful, and it hid such a sickness.

There had been enough trouble even keeping the delegation together in the country. The planned New Year's celebration had been wrecked by jet lag and the hassles of getting into South Africa. When Father Squid, Xavier Desmond, and Troll had tried to eat with the others in Pretoria, the head waiter had refused to seat them, pointing to a sign in both English and Afrikaans: WHITES ONLY. "We don't serve blacks, coloreds, or jokers," he insisted.

Hartmann, Tachyon, and several of the other high-ranking members of the delegation had immediately protested to the Botha government; a compromise had been reached. The delegation was given the run of a small hotel on the Loskop Game Preserve; isolated, they could intermingle if they wished. The government had let it be known that they also found the idea distasteful.

When they had finally popped the champagne corks, the wine had tasted sour in all their mouths.

The junket had spent the afternoon at a ramshackle kraal, actually little more than a shantytown. There they'd seen firsthand the double-edged sword of prejudice: the new apartheid. Once it had been a two-sided struggle, the Afrikaners and the English against the blacks, the colored, and the Asians. Now the jokers were the new Uitlanders, and both white and black spat upon them. Tachyon had looked at the filth and squalor of this jokertown, and Sara had seen his noble, sculptured face go white with rage; Gregg had looked ill. The entire delegation had turned on the National Party officials who had accompanied them from Pretoria and begun to rail at the conditions here.

The officials spouted the approved line. This is why we have the Prohibition of Mixed Marriages Act, they said, pointedly ignoring the jokers among the group. Without strict separation of the races we will only produce *more* jokers, *more* colored, and we're sure none of you want that. This is why there's an Immorality Act, a Prohibition of Political Interference Act. Let us do things our way, and we will take care of our own problems. Conditions are bad, yes, but they are getting better. You've been swayed by the African/Jokers National Congress. The AJNC is outlawed, their leader Mandela is nothing more than a fanatic, a troublemaker. The AJNC has steered you to the worst encampment they could find—if the doctor, the senators, and their colleagues had only stayed with *our* itinerary, you would have seen the other side of the coin.

All in all, the year had begun like hell.

Sara put a foot up on the railing, lowered her head until it rested on her hands, and stared at the sunset. *Everywhere. Here you can see the problems so easily, but it's not really different. It's been horrible everywhere whenever you look past the surface.*

She heard footsteps, but didn't turn around. The railing shuddered as someone stood next to her. "Ironic, isn't it, how lovely this land can be." Gregg's voice.

"Just what I was thinking," Sara said. She glanced at him, and he was staring out at the hills. The only other person on the veranda was Billy Ray, reclining against the railing a discreet distance away.

"There are times when I wish the virus were more deadly, that it had simply wiped the planet clean of us and started over," Gregg said. "That town today . . ." He shook his head. "I read the transcript you phoned in. It brought back everything. I started to get furious all over again. You've a gift for making people respond to what you're feeling, Sara. You'll do more in the long run that I will. Maybe you can do something to stop prejudice; here, and with people like Leo Barnett back home."

"Thanks." His hand was very near hers. She touched it softly with her own; his fingers snared hers and didn't let her go. The emotions of the day, of the entire trip, were threatening to overwhelm her; her eyes stung with tears. "Gregg," she said very softly, "I'm not sure I like the way I feel."

"About today? The jokers?"

She took a breath. The failing sun was warm on her face. "That, yes." She paused, wondering if she should say more. "And about you too," she added at last.

He didn't say anything. He waited, holding her hand and watching the nightfall. "It's changed so fast, the way I've seen you," Sara continued after a time. "When I thought that you and Andrea . . ." She paused, her breath trembling. "You care, you hurt when you see the way people are treated. God, I used to detest you. I saw everything that Senator Hartmann did in that light. I saw you as false and empty of compassion. Now that's gone, and I watch your face when you talk about the jokers and what we have to do to change things, and . . ."

She pulled him around so that they faced each other. She looked up at him, not caring that he'd see that she'd been crying. "I'm not used to holding things inside. I like it when everything's out in the open, so forgive me if this isn't something I should say. Where you're concerned, I think I'm very vulnerable, Gregg, and I'm afraid of that."

"I don't intend to hurt you, Sara." His hand came up to her face. Softly he brushed moisture from the corner of her eyes.

"Then tell me where we're heading, you and I. I need to know what the rules are."

"I . . ." He stopped. Sara, watching his face, saw an inner conflict. His head came down; she felt his warm, sweet breath on her cheek. His hand cupped her chin. She let him lift her face up, her eyes closing.

The kiss was soft and very gentle. Fragile. Sara turned her face away, and he brought her to him, pressing her body to his. "Ellen . . ." Sara began.

"She knows," Gregg whispered. His fingers brushed her hair. "I've told her. She doesn't mind."

"I didn't want this to happen."

"It did. It's okay," he told her.

She pushed away from him and was glad when he simply let her go. "So what do we do about it?"

The sun had gone behind the hills; Gregg was only a shadow, his features barely visible to her. "It's your decision, Sara. Ellen and I always take a double suite; I use the second room as my office. I'm going there now. If you want, Billy will bring you up. You can trust him, no matter what anyone's told you about him. He knows how to be discreet."

For a moment, his hand stroked her cheek. Then he turned, walking quickly away. Sara watched him speak briefly to Ray, and then he went through the doors into the hotel's lobby. Ray remained outside.

Sara waited until full darkness had settled over the valley and the air had begun to cool from the day's heat, knowing that she'd already made the decision but not certain she wanted to follow it through. She waited, half looking for some sign in the African night. Then she went to Ray. His green eyes, set disturbingly off-line in an oddly mismatched face, seemed to look at her appraisingly.

"I'd like to go upstairs," she said.

FROM *THE JOURNAL OF XAVIER DESMOND*

JANUARY 16/ADDIS ABABA, ETHIOPIA:

A hard day in a stricken land. The local Red Cross representatives took some of us out to see some of their famine relief efforts. Of course we'd all been aware of the drought and the starvation long before we got here, but seeing it on television is one thing, and being here amidst it is quite another.

A day like this makes me acutely aware of my own failures and shortcomings. Since the cancer took hold of me, I've lost a good deal of weight (some unsuspecting friends have even told me how good I look), but moving among these people made me very self-conscious of the small paunch that remains. They were *starving* before my eyes, while our plane waited to take us back to Addis Ababa...to our hotel, another reception, and no doubt a gourmet Ethiopian meal. The guilt was overwhelming, as was the sense of helplessness.

I believe we all felt it. I cannot conceive of how Hiram Worchester must have felt. To his credit he looked sick as he moved among the victims, and at one point he was trembling so badly he had to sit in the shade for a while by himself. The sweat was just pouring off him. But he got up again afterward, his face white and grim, and used his gravity power to help them unload the relief provisions we had brought with us.

So many people have contributed so much and worked so hard for the relief effort, but here it seems like nothing. The only realities in the relief camps are the skeletal bodies with their massive swollen bellies, the dead eyes of the children, and the endless heat pouring down from above onto this baked, parched landscape.

Parts of this day will linger in my memory for a long time—or at least as long a time as I have left to me. Father Squid gave the last rites to a dying woman who had a Coptic cross around her neck. Peregrine and her cameraman recorded much of the scene on film for her documentary, but after a short time she had had enough and returned to the plane to wait for us. I've heard that she was so sick she lost her breakfast.

And there was a young mother, no more than seventeen or eighteen surely, so gaunt that you could count every rib, with eyes incredibly ancient. She was holding her baby to a withered, empty breast. The child had been dead long enough to begin to smell, but she would not let them take it from her. Dr. Tachyon took control of her mind and held her still while he gently pried the child's body from her grasp and carried it away. He handed it to one of the relief workers and then sat on the ground and began to weep, his body shaking with each sob.

Mistral ended the day in tears as well. En route to the refugee camp, she had changed into her blue-and-white flying costume. The girl is young, an ace, and a powerful one; no doubt she thought she could help. When she called the winds to her, the huge cape she wears fastened at wrist and ankle ballooned out like a parachute and pulled her up into the sky. Even the strangeness of the jokers walking between them had not awakened much interest in the inward-looking eyes of the refugees, but when Mistral took flight, most of them—not all, but most—turned to watch, and their gaze followed her upward into that high, hot blueness until finally they sank back into the lethargy of despair. I think Mistral had dreamed that somehow her wind powers could push the clouds around and make the rains come to heal this land. And what a beautiful, vainglorious dream it was. . . .

She flew for almost two hours, sometimes so high and far that she vanished from our sight, but for all her ace powers, all she could raise was a dust devil. When she gave up at last, she was exhausted, her sweet young face grimy with dust and sand, her eyes red and swollen.

Just before we left, an atrocity underscored the depth of the despair here. A tall youth with acne scars on his cheeks attacked a fellow refugee—went berserk, gouged out a woman's eye, and actually *ate* it while the people watched without comprehension. Ironically we'd met the boy briefly when we'd first arrived—he'd spent a year in a Christian school and had a few words of English. He seemed stronger and healthier than most of the others we saw. When Mistral flew, he jumped to his feet and called out after her. "Jetboy!" he said in a very clear, strong voice. Father Squid and Senator Hartmann tried to talk to him, but his English-language skills were limited to a few nouns, including "chocolate," "television," and "Jesus Christ." Still, the boy was more alive than most—his eyes went wide at Father Squid, and he put out a hand and touched his facial tendrils wonderingly and actually smiled when the senator patted his shoulder and told him that we were here to help, though I don't think he understood a word. We were all shocked when we saw them carrying him away, still screaming, those gaunt brown cheeks smeared with blood.

A hideous day all around. This evening back in Addis Ababa our driver swung us by the docks, where relief shipment stand two stories high in some places. Hartmann was in a cold rage. If anyone can make this criminal government take action and feed its starving people, he is the one. I pray for him, or would, if I believed in a god . . . but what kind of god would permit the obscenities we have seen on this trip. . . .

Africa is as beautiful a land as any on the face of the earth. I should write of all the beauty we have seen this past month. Victoria Falls, the snows of Kilimanjaro, a thousand zebra moving through the tall grass as if the wind had stripes. I've walked among the ruins of proud ancient kingdoms whose very names were unknown to me, held pygmy artifacts in my hand, seen the face of a bushman light up with curiosity instead of horror when he beheld me for the first time. Once during a visit to a game preserve I woke early, and when I looked out of my window at the dawn, I saw that two huge African elephants had come to the very building, and Radha stood between them, naked in the early morning light, while they touched her with their trunks. I turned away then; it seemed somehow a private moment.

Beauty, yes—in the land and in so many of the people, whose faces are full of warmth and compassion.

Still, for all that beauty, Africa has depressed and saddened me considerably, and I will be glad to leave. The camp was only part of it. Before Ethiopia there was Kenya and South Africa. It is the wrong time of year for Thanksgiving, but the scenes we have witnessed these past few weeks have put me more in the mood for giving thanks than I've ever felt during America's smug November celebration of football and gluttony. Even jokers have things to give thanks for. I knew that already, but Africa has brought it home to me forcefully.

South Africa was a grim way to begin this leg of the trip. The same hatreds and prejudices exist at home of course, but whatever our faults we are at least civilized enough to maintain a facade of tolerance, brotherhood, and equality under the law. Once I might have called that mere sophistry, but that was before I tasted the reality of Capetown and Pretoria, where all the ugliness is out in the open, enshrined by law, enforced by an iron fist whose velvet glove has grown thin and worn indeed. It is argued that at least South Africa hates openly, while America hides behind a hypocritical facade. Perhaps, perhaps... but if so, I will take the hypocrisy and thank you for it.

I suppose that was Africa's first lesson, that there are worse places in the world than Jokertown. The second was that there are worse things than repression, and Kenya taught us that.

Like most of the other nations of Central and East Africa, Kenya was spared the worst of the wild card. Some spores would have reached these lands through airborne diffusion, more through the seaports, arriving via contaminated cargo in holds that had been poorly sterilized or never sterilized at all. CARE packages are looked on with deep suspicion in much of the world, and with good reason, and many captains have become quite adept at concealing the fact that their last port of call was New York City.

When one moves inland, wild card cases become almost nonexistent. There are those who say that the late Idi Amin was some kind of insane joker-ace, with strength as great as Troll or the Harlem Hammer, and the ability to transform into some kind of were-creature, a leopard or a lion or a hawk. Amin himself claimed to be able to ferret out his enemies telepathically, and those few enemies who survived say that he was a cannibal who felt human flesh was necessary to maintain his powers. All this is the stuff of rumor and propaganda, however, and whether Amin was a joker, an ace, or a pathetically deluded nat madman, he is assuredly dead, and in this corner of the world, documented cases of the wild card virus are vanishingly hard to locate.

But Kenya and the surrounding nations have their own viral nightmare. If the wild card is a chimera here, AIDS is an epidemic. While the president was hosting Senator Hartmann and most of the tour, a few of us were on an exhausting visit to a half-dozen clinics in rural Kenya, hopping from one village to another by helicopter. They assigned us only one battered chopper, and that at Tachyon's insistence. The government would have much preferred that we spend our time lecturing at the university, meeting with educators and political leaders, touring game preserves and museums.

Most of my fellow delegates were only too glad to comply. The wild card is forty years old, and we have grown used to it—but AIDS, that is a new terror in the world, and one that we have only begun to understand. At home it is thought of as a homosexual affliction, and I confess that I am guilty of thinking of it that way myself, but here in Africa, that belief is given the lie. Already there are more AIDS victims on this continent alone than have ever been infected by the Takisian xenovirus since its release over Manhattan forty years ago.

And AIDS seems a crueler demon somehow. The wild card kills ninety percent of those who draw it, often in ways that are terrible and painful, but the distance between ninety percent and one hundred is not insignificant if you are among the ten who live. It is the distance between life and death, between hope and despair. Some claim that it's better to die than to live as a joker, but you will not find me among their number. If my own life has not always been happy, nonetheless I have memories I cherish and accomplishments I am proud of. I am glad to have lived, and I do not want to die. I've accepted my death, but that does not mean I welcome it. I have too much unfinished business. Like Robert Tomlin, I have not yet seen *The Jolson Story*. None of us have.

In Kenya we saw whole villages that are dying. Alive, smiling, talking, capable of eating and defecating and making love and even babies, alive to all practical purposes—and yet dead. Those who draw the Black Queen may die in the agony of unspeakable transformations, but there are drugs for pain, and at least they die quickly. AIDS is less merciful.

We have much in common, jokers and AIDS victims.

Before I left Jokertown, we had been planning for a JADL fund-raising benefit at the Funhouse in late May—a major event with as much big-name entertainment as we could book. After Kenya I cabled instructions back to New York to arrange for the proceeds of the benefit to be split with a suitable AIDS victims' group. We pariahs need to stick together. Perhaps I can still erect a few necessary bridges before my own Black Queen lies face up on the table.

DOWN BY THE NILE

Gail Gerstner-Miller

The torches in the temple burned slowly, steadily, occasionally flickering when someone passed by. Their light illuminated the faces of the people gathered in a small antechamber off the main hall. They were all present, those who looked like ordinary people, and the others who were extraordinary: the cat woman, the jackal-headed man, those with wings, crocodile skin, and bird heads.

Osiris the far-seer spoke. "The winged one comes."

"Is she one of us?"

"Will she help us?"

"Not directly," Osiris answered. "But within her is that which will have the power to do great things. For now we must wait."

"We have waited a very long time," said Anubis the jackal. "A little longer will not make a difference."

The others murmured in agreement. The living gods settled back to patiently wait.

The room in Luxor's Winter Palace Hotel was sweltering, and it was still only morning. The ceiling fan stirred the sluggish air tiredly and sweat ran in tickling rivulets over Peregrine's rib cage and breasts as she lay propped up in bed, watching Josh McCoy slip a new film cassette into his camera. He looked at her and smiled.

"We'd better get going," he said.

She smiled back lazily from the bed, her wings moving gently, bringing more coolness into the room than the slow-moving fan.

"If you say so." She stood, stretched lithely, and watched McCoy watch her. She walked by him, dancing out of his way as he reached for her. "Haven't you had enough yet?" she asked teasingly as she took a clean pair of jeans from her suitcase. She wiggled into them, batting her wings to keep her balance. "The hotel laundry must have washed these in boiling water." She took a deep breath and pulled on the stubborn zipper. "There."

"They look great, though," McCoy said. He put his arms around her from behind, and Peregrine shivered as he kissed the back of her neck and caressed her breasts, still sensitive from their morning lovemaking.

"I thought you said we had to get going." She settled back against him.

McCoy sighed and pulled away reluctantly. "We do. We have to meet the others in"—he checked his wristwatch—"three minutes."

"Too bad," Peregrine said, smiling mischievously. "I think I could be coaxed into spending all day in bed."

"Work awaits," McCoy said, rummaging for his clothes as Peregrine put on a tank top. "And I'm anxious to see if these self-proclaimed living gods can do all they claim."

She watched him as he dressed, admiring his lean, muscular body. He was blond and fit, a documentary filmmaker and cameraman, and a wonderful lover.

"Got everything? Don't forget your hat. The sun's fierce, even if it is winter."

"I've got everything I need," Peregrine said with a sidelong glance. "Let's go."

McCoy turned the DO NOT DISTURB sign hanging on the door handle to the other side, then closed and locked the door. The hotel corridor was quiet and deserted. Tachyon must have heard their muffled footsteps, because he poked his head out as they passed his room.

"Morning, Tachy," Peregrine said. "Josh, Father Squid, Hiram, and I are going to catch the afternoon ceremony at the Temple of the Living Gods. Want to come along?"

"Good morning, my dear." Tachyon, looking resplendent in a white brocade dressing gown, nodded distantly to McCoy. "No, thank you. I'll see everything I need to see at the meeting tonight. Right now it's much too hot to venture out." Tachyon looked closely at her. "Are you feeling all right? You look pale."

"I think the heat's getting to me too," Peregrine replied. "That and the food and water. Or rather the microbes that live in them."

"We don't need you getting sick," Tachyon said seriously. "Come in and let me do a quick examination." He fanned his face. "We'll find out what's bothering you, and it will give me something useful to do with my day."

"We don't have the time right now. The others are waiting for us—"

"Peri," McCoy interrupted, a concerned look on his face, "it'll only take a few minutes. I'll go downstairs and tell Hiram and Father Squid you've been delayed." She hesitated. "Please," he added.

"Oh, all right." She smiled at him. "I'll see you downstairs."

McCoy nodded and continued down the hallway as Peregrine followed Tachyon into his ornately appointed suite. The sitting room was spacious, and much cooler than the room she shared with McCoy. Of course, she reflected, they had generated a lot of heat themselves that morning.

"Wow," she commented, glancing around the luxuriously decorated room. "I must have gotten the servants' quarters."

"It's really something, isn't it? I especially like the bed." Tachyon pointed to a large four-poster draped with white netting that was visible through the bedroom's open door. "You have to climb steps to get into it."

"What fun!"

He glanced at her mischievously. "Want to try it out?"

"No, thanks. I've already had my morning sex."

"Peri," Tachyon complained in a teasing tone, "I don't understand why you're attracted to that man." He retrieved his red leather medical bag from the closet. "Sit there," he said, indicating a plush velvet wingback chair, "and open your mouth. Say *ahhh*."

"*Ahh*," Peregrine repeated obediently after seating herself.

Tachyon peered down her throat. "Well, that looks nice and healthy." He swiftly examined her ears and looked into her eyes. "Seems okay. Tell me about your symptoms." He removed his stethoscope from his bag. "Nausea, vomiting, dizziness?"

"Some nausea and vomiting."

"When? After you eat?"

"No, not really. Anytime."

"Do you get sick every day?"

"No. Maybe a couple times a week."

"*Hmmmm*." He lifted her shirt up and held his stethoscope against her left breast. She jumped at the touch of cold steel against her warm flesh. "Sorry...heartbeat is strong and regular. How long has this vomiting been occurring?"

"A couple of months, I guess. Since before the tour started. I thought it was stress related."

He frowned. "You've been vomiting for a couple of months, and you didn't see fit to consult me? I am your doctor."

She squirmed uncomfortably. "Tachy, you've been so busy. I didn't want to bother you. I think it's all the traveling, the food, different water, different standards of hygiene."

"Allow *me* to make the diagnosis, if you please, young lady. Are you getting enough sleep, or is your new boyfriend keeping you up all hours?"

"I'm getting to bed early every night," she assured him.

"I'm certain you are," he said drily. "But that wasn't what I asked. Are you getting enough sleep?"

Peregrine blushed. "Of course I am."

Tachyon replaced his equipment in his bag. "How's your menstrual cycle? Any problems?"

"Well, I haven't had a period in a while, but that's not unusual, even though I'm on the pill."

"Peri, please try to be a little more precise. How long is 'a while'?"

She bit her lip and waved her wings gently. "I don't know, a couple of months, I guess."

"*Hmmmmm.* Come here." He led her into his bedroom, and her wings instinctively curled over her body. The air conditioner was going full blast and it felt about twenty degrees cooler. Tachyon gestured at the bed. "Take off your jeans and lie down."

"Are you sure this is a medical examination?" she asked him teasingly.

"Do you want me to call a chaperon?"

"Don't be silly. I trust you!"

"You shouldn't," Tachyon leered. He raised an eyebrow as Peregrine kicked off her Nikes and peeled off her jeans. "Don't you wear underwear?"

"Never. It gets in the way. Do you want me to take off my shirt too?"

"If you do, you may never leave this room!" Tachyon threatened.

She laughed and kissed his cheek. "What's the big deal? You've examined me a million times."

"In the proper surroundings, with you in a medical gown and a nurse in the room," he retorted. "Never with you naked, almost naked," he corrected, "in my bedroom." He tossed her a towel. "Here, cover yourself."

Tachyon admired her long, tanned legs and shapely buttocks as she arranged herself on his bed, draping the towel discreetly over her hips. The blast of refrigerated air coming from the laboring air conditioner raised goosebumps all over her, but Tachyon ignored them.

"Your hands better be warm," Peregrine warned as he knelt next to her.

"Just like my heart," Tachyon said, palpating her stomach. "Does this hurt?"

"No."

"Here? Here?"

She shook her head.

"Don't move," he ordered. "I need my stethoscope." This time he warmed the metal head with his hand before placing it on her stomach. "Have you had much indigestion?"

"Some."

A strange expression crossed Tachyon's foxy face as he assisted her off the bed. "Get your jeans on. I'll take a blood sample, and then you can go play tourist with the others."

He got the syringe ready while she finished tying her track shoes. Peregrine held out her arm, winced as he expertly raised the vein, swabbed the skin above it, inserted the syringe, and withdrew the blood. She watched in fascination and suddenly realized that the sight of blood was making her ill.

"Shit." She ran into the bedroom, leaving behind a flurry of feathers, and leaned over the toilet vomiting up her room service breakfast and what was left of last night's dinner and champagne.

Tachyon held her shoulders while she was sick, and as she sagged against the tub, exhausted, wiped her face with a warm, wet washcloth.

"Are you all right?"

"I think so." He helped her to her feet. "It was the blood. Although the sight of blood has never bothered me before."

"Peregrine, I don't think that you should go sight-seeing this morning. The place for you is bed, alone, with a cup of hot tea."

"No," she protested. "I'm fine. It's just all this traveling. If I feel sick, Josh will bring me back here."

"I'll never understand women." He shook his head sadly. "To prefer a mere human when you could have me. Come here and I'll bandage that hole I put in your arm." He busied himself with sterile gauze and tape.

Peregrine smiled gently. "You're sweet, Doctor, but your heart is buried in the past. I'm getting to the point now that I'm ready for a permanent relationship, and I don't think you would give me that."

"And he can?"

She shrugged, her wings moving with her shoulders. "I hope so. We'll see, won't we?"

She picked up her bag and hat from the chair and walked to the door.

"Peri, I wish you would reconsider."

"What? Sleeping with you or sight-seeing?"

"Sight-seeing, wicked one."

"I'm fine now. Please stop worrying. Honestly, I've never had so many people worrying about me as on this trip."

"That's because, my dear, under your New York glamour, you're incredibly vulnerable. You make people want to protect you." He opened the door for her. "Be careful with McCoy, Peri. I don't want you to get hurt."

She kissed him as she left the room. Her wings brushed the doorway and a flurry of fine feathers fell to the floor.

"Damn," she said, stooping and picking one up. "I seem to be losing a lot of these lately."

"Indeed?" Tachyon looked curious. "No, don't bother with them. The maid will clean them up."

"Okay. Good-bye. Have fun with your tests."

Tachyon's eyes were worried as they followed Peregrine's graceful body down the hallway. He closed the door, one of her feathers in his hand.

"This doesn't look good," he said aloud as he tickled his chin with her feather. "Not good at all."

Peregrine spotted McCoy in the lobby talking to a stocky, dark man in a white uniform. Her two other companions were lounging nearby. Hiram Worchester, she reflected, was looking a little haggard. Hiram, one of Peregrine's oldest and dearest friends, was dressed in one of his custom-made tropical-weight suits, but it hung loosely on him, almost as if he had lost some of his three hundred plus pounds. Perhaps he was feeling the strain of constant traveling as much as she

was. Father Squid, the kindly pastor of the Church of Jesus
Christ, Joker, made Hiram look almost svelte. He was as tall
as a normal man and twice as broad. His face was round and
gray, his eyes were covered by nictitating membranes, and a
cluster of tentacles hung down over his mouth like a constantly
twitching mustache. He always reminded her of one of
Lovecraft's fictional Deep Ones, but he was actually much
nicer.

"Peri," said McCoy. "This is Mr. Ahmed. He's with the
Tourist Police. Mr. Ahmed, this is Peregrine."

"This is a pleasure," said the guide, bending to kiss her
hand.

Peregrine responded with a smile and then greeted
Hiram and the priest. She turned to Josh, who was watching
her closely. "You okay?" Josh asked. "You look awful. What
did Tachyon do, take a quart of blood?"

"Of course not. I'm fine," she said, following Ahmed and
the others to the waiting limo. And if I keep saying that, she
said to herself, maybe I'll even believe it.

"What on earth?" exclaimed Peregrine as they stopped
in front of a metal-and-glass guard station. There were two
heavily armed men inside the box, which stood next to a high
wall that surrounded several acres of desert that was the
Temple of the Living Gods. The whitewashed wall was topped
with strands of barbed wire and patrolled by men dressed in
blue and armed with machine guns. Video cameras tirelessly
surveyed the perimeter. The effect of the pure white wall
against the shining sand and bright blue Egyptian sky was
dazzling.

"Because of the Nur," explained Ahmed, pointing to the
line of tourists waiting to enter the temple grounds, "everyone
has to pass through two detectors, one for metal and the
other for nitrates. These fanatics are determined to destroy
the temple and the gods. They have already made several
attacks against the temple, but so far they've been stopped
before doing much damage."

"Who are the Nur?" Father Squid asked.

"They are the followers of Nur al-Allah, a false prophet
determined to unite all Islamic sects under himself," Ahmed
said. "He has decided that Allah desires the destruction of all
those deformed by the wild card virus, and so the Temple of
the Living Gods has become one of his sect's targets."

"Do we have to wait in line with the tourists?" Hiram broke in peevishly. "After all, we are here by special invitation."

"Oh, no, Mr. Worchester," Ahmed hurriedly answered. "The VIP gate is this way. You will go right through. If you please..."

As they lined up behind Ahmed, McCoy whispered to Peregrine, "I've never been through a VIP gate, only press gates."

"Stick with me," she promised. "I'll take you lots of places you've never been before."

"You already have."

The VIP gate had its own metal and nitrate detectors. They passed through, watched closely by security guards dressed in the blue robes worn by adherents of the living gods, who thoroughly examined Peregrine's bag and McCoy's camera. An elderly man approached as McCoy's equipment was being returned. He was short, deeply tanned and healthy looking, with gray eyes, white hair, and a magnificent white beard that contrasted nicely with his flowing blue robes.

"I am Opet Kemel," he announced. His voice was deep, mellifluous, and he knew how to use it to demand attention and respect. "I am the head priest of the Temple of the Living Gods. We are gratifed that you could grace us with your presence." He looked from Father Squid to Peregrine, Hiram, and McCoy, and then back to Peregrine. "Yes, my children will be glad that you have come."

"Do you mind if we film the ceremony?" asked Peregrine.

"Not at all." He gestured expansively. "Come this way and I'll show you the best seats in the house."

"Can you give us some background on the temple?" Peregrine asked.

"Certainly," Kemel replied as they followed him. "The Port Said wild card epidemic of 1948 caused many 'mutations,' I believe they're called, among them of course, the celebrated *Nasr*—Al Haziz, Khôf and other great heroes of past years. Many men of Luxor were working on the Said docks at the time and were also affected by the virus. Some passed it on to their children and grandchildren.

"The true meaning of these mutations struck me over a decade ago when I saw a young boy make clouds drop much-needed rain over his father's fields. I realized that he was an incarnation of Min, the ancient god of crops, and that his presence was a harbinger of the old religion.

"I was an archaeologist then and had just discovered an intact temple complex"—he pointed at their feet—"beneath the ground right where we stand. I convinced Min of his destiny and found others to join us: Osiris, a man pronounced dead who returned to life with visions of the future; Anubis, Taurt, Thoth . . . Through the years they have all come to the Temple of the Living Gods to listen to the prayers of their petitioners and perform miracles."

"Exactly what kind of miracles?" Peregrine asked.

"Many kinds. For example, if a woman with child is having a difficult time, she will pray to Taurt, goddess of pregnancy and childbirth. Taurt will assure that all will be fine. And it will be. Thoth settles disputes, knowing who tells the truth and who lies. Min, as I have said, can make it rain. Osiris sees bits of the future. It's all quite simple."

"I see." Kemel's claims seemed reasonable, given the abilities that Peregrine knew the virus could waken in people. "How many gods are there?"

"Perhaps twenty-five. Some cannot really do anything," Kemel said in confiding tones. "They are what you call jokers. However, they look like the old gods—Bast, for example, is covered with fur and has claws—and they give great comfort to the people who come to pray to them. But see for yourselves. The ceremony is almost ready to begin."

He led them past groups of tourists posing next to statues of the gods, booths that sold everything from Kodak film, key rings, and Coca-Cola to replicas of antique jewelry and little statuettes of the gods themselves. They went past the booths, through a narrow doorway into a sandstone block wall set flush against a cliff face, and then down worn stone steps. Goosebumps rose on Peregrine's skin. It was cool inside the structure, which was lit by electric lights that resembled flickering torches. The stairwell was beautifully decorated with bas-relief carvings of everyday life in ancient Egypt, intricately detailed hieroglyphic inscriptions, and representations of animals, birds, gods, and goddesses.

"What a wonderful job of restoration!" Peregrine exclaimed, enchanted by the beautiful freshness of the reliefs they passed.

"Actually," Kemel explained, "everything here is just as it was when I discovered it twenty years ago. We added some modern conveniences, like the electricity, of course." He smiled.

They entered a large chamber, an amphitheater with a stage faced by banked stone benches. The walls of the chamber were lined with glass cases displaying artifacts that, Kemel said, had been discovered in the temple.

McCoy meticulously recorded them, shooting several minutes of footage of painted wooden statues that looked as fresh as if they had been painted the day before, necklaces, collars, and pectorals of lapis lazuli, emerald, and gold, chalices carved of translucent alabaster, unguent jars of jade intricately carved in the shapes of animals, elaborately inlaid tiny chests, and gaming boards, and chairs... The exquisite treasures of a dead civilization were displayed before them, a civilization that, Peregrine reflected, Opet Kemel seemed, with his Temple of the Living Gods, to restore.

"Here we are." Kemel indicated a group of benches at the front of the amphitheater close to the stage, bowed slightly, and departed.

It didn't take long for the amphitheater to fill. The lights dimmed and the theater became silent. A spotlight shone on the stage, strange music that sounded as old and eerie as the temple itself softly played, and the procession of the living gods began. There was Osiris, the god of death and resurrection, and his consort Isis. Behind him came Hapi, carrying a golden standard. Thoth, the ibis-headed judge, followed with his pet baboon. Shu and Tefnut, brother and sister, god and goddess of the air, floated above the floor. Sobek followed them with his dark, cracked crocodile skin and snoutlike mouth. Hathor, the great mother, had the horns of a cow. Bast, the cat-goddess, moved delicately, her face and body covered with tawny fur, claws protruding from her fingers. Min looked like an ordinary man, but a small cloud hovered above him, following him like an obedient puppy wherever he went. Bes, the handsome dwarf, did cartwheels and walked on his hands. Anubis, the god of the underworld, had the head of a jackal. Horus had falconlike wings....

On and on they came, crossing the stage slowly and then seating themselves on gilded thrones as they were presented to the audience in English, French, and Arabic.

After the introductions the gods began to demonstrate their abilities. Shu and Tefnut were gliding in the air, playing tag with Min's cloud, when the unexpected, deafening sound of gunfire shattered the peaceful scene, evoking screams of terror from the spectators trapped in the amphitheater. Hundreds of tourists leapt up and milled about like terrified cattle. Some bolted for the doors at the back, and the stairways soon became clogged by panicked, shrieking people. McCoy, who had pushed Peregrine to the ground and covered her with his body at the first sound of gunfire, dragged her behind one of the large, elaborately carved stone pillars flanking the stage.

"You okay?" he gasped, peering around the column at the sounds of madness and destruction, his camera whirring.

"Uh-huh. What is it?"

"Three guys with machine guns." His hands were steady and there was an edge of excitement in his voice. "They don't seem to be shooting at the people, just the walls."

A bullet whined off the pillar. The sound of shattering glass filled the air as the terrorists destroyed the cases filled with the priceless artifacts and raked the beautifully carved walls with machine-gun fire.

The living gods had fled when the first shot sounded. Only one remained behind, the man who had been introduced as Min. As Peregrine peeked around the pillar, a cloud appeared from nowhere to hang over the terrorists' heads. It started to rain torrents upon them, and slipping and sliding on the wet stone floor, they scattered, trying to find cover from the blinding cloudburst. Peregrine, digging in her bag for her metal talons, noticed Hiram Worchester standing alone, a look of fierce concentration on his face. One of the attackers gave a distressed shout as his gun slipped from his hands and landed on his foot. He collapsed, screaming, blood spattering from his shattered limb. Hiram turned his gaze to the second terrorist as Peregrine pulled on her gauntlets.

"I'm going to try to get above them," she told McCoy.

"Be careful," he said, intent on filming the action.

She flexed her fingers, now encased in leather gauntlets tipped with razor-edged titanium claws. Her wings quivered in anticipation as she took a half-dozen running steps, then beat thunderously as she hurled herself forward and launched herself into the air—

—and fell jarringly to the floor.

She caught herself on her hands and knees, skinning her palms on the rough stones and banging her left knee so hard that it went numb after an initial stab of excruciatingly sharp pain.

For a long second Peregrine refused to believe what had

happened. She crouched on the floor, bullets whining around her, then sood and beat her wings again, hard. But nothing happpened. She couldn't fly. She stood in the middle of the floor, ignoring the gunfire around her, trying to figure out what was happening, what she was doing wrong.

"Peregrine," McCoy shouted, "get down!" The third terrorist aimed at her, screaming incoherently. A look of horror suddenly contorted his face and he swooped toward the ceiling. His gun slipped out of his hand and smashed to the floor. Hiram casually let the man drop thirty feet as the other terrorists were clubbed to the floor by temple security guards. Kemel bustled up, a look of incredulous horror on his face.

"Thank the Merciful Ones you weren't injured!" he cried, rushing to Peregrine, who was still dazed and confused at what had hapened to her.

"Yeah," she said distantly, then her eyes focused on the walls of the chamber. "But look at all the damage!"

A small wooden statue, gilded and inlaid with faience and precious stones, lay in fragments at Peregrine's feet. She stopped and picked it up gently, but the fragile wood turned to dust at her touch, leaving behind a twisted shell of gold and jewels. "It survived for so long, only to be destroyed by this madness. . . ." she murmured softly.

"Ah, yes." Kemel shrugged. "Well, the walls can be restored, and we have more artifacts to put into display cases."

"Who were those people?" Father Squid asked, imperturbably brushing dust off of his cassock.

"The Nur," Kemel said. He spat on the floor. "Fanatics!"

McCoy rushed up to them, his camera slung over his shoulder. "I thought I told you to be careful," he reproached Peregrine. "Standing in the middle of a room with idiots blazing away with machine guns is not my idea of careful! Thank God that Hiram was watching that guy."

"I know," Peregrine said, "but it shouldn't have happened that way. I was trying to get airborne, but I couldn't. Nothing like this has ever happened to me before. It's strange." She pushed her long hair out of her eyes, looking troubled. "I don't know what it is."

The chamber was still in turmoil. The terrorists could have slaughtered hundreds if they had chosen to shoot people rather than the symbols of the old religion, but as it was, several score of tourists had been hit by stray bullets or injured themselves trying to escape. Temple security guards were trying to help those who were hurt, but there were so many of them lying crumpled on the stone benches, wailing, crying, screaming, bleeding...

Peregrine turned from McCoy and the others, nauseated to the point of vomiting, but there was nothing in her stomach to throw up. McCoy held her as she was racked by dry heaves. When she stopped shuddering, she leaned against him gratefully.

He took her hand gently. "We'd better get you to Dr. Tachyon."

On the way back to the Winter Palace Hotel, McCoy put his arm around her and drew her to him. "Everything is going to be okay," he soothed. "You're probably just tired."

"What if it isn't that? What if something is really wrong with me? What," she asked in a horror-striken whisper, "if I'll never fly again?" She buried her face against McCoy's shoulder as the others looked on in mute sympathy. Her tears soaked through his shirt as he stroked her long brown hair.

"Everything will be all right, Peri. I promise."

"Hmmm, I should have expected that," Tachyon said as Peregrine tearfully told him her story.

"What do you mean?" asked McCoy. "What's wrong with her?"

Tachyon eyed Josh McCoy coldly. "It's rather private. Between a woman and her physician. So..."

"Anything that concerns Peri concerns me."

"It's that way, is it?" Tachyon looked at McCoy hostilely.

"It's all right, Josh," said Peregrine. She hugged him.

"If that's the way you want it." McCoy turned to go. "I'll wait for you in the bar."

Tachyon closed the door behind him. "Now, sit down and wipe your eyes. It's nothing serious, really. You're losing your feathers because of hormonal changes. Your mind has recognized your condition and has blocked your power as a means of protection."

"Condition? Protection? What's wrong with me?"

Peregrine perched on the edge of the sofa. Tachyon sat next to her and took her cold hands in his.

"It's nothing that won't be cleared up in a few months."

His lilac eyes looked straight into her blue ones. "You're pregnant."

"What!" Peregrine sank back against the sofa cushions. "That's impossible! How can I be pregnant? I've been on the pill forever!" She sat up again. "What will NBC say? I wonder if this is covered in my contract?"

"I suggest you stop taking the pill and all other drugs, including alcohol. After all, you want a happy, healthy baby."

"Tachy, this is ridiculous! I can't be pregnant! Are you sure?"

"Quite. And judging from your symptoms, I'd say you were about four months along." He nodded at the door. "How will your lover feel about being a father?"

"Josh isn't the father. We've only been together for a couple of weeks." Her mouth dropped open. "Oh, my God!"

"What is it?" Tachyon asked, concern in his voice and on his face.

She got off the sofa and began walking around the room, her wings fluttering absently. "Doctor, what would happen to the baby if both parents carried the wild card? Joker mother, ace father, that sort of thing?" She stopped by the marble mantel and fiddled with the dusty knickknacks set on it.

"Why?" Tachyon asked suspiciously. "If McCoy isn't the father, who is? An ace?"

"Yeah."

"Who?"

She sighed and put aside the figurine she was playing with. "I don't think it really matters. I'll never see him again. It was just one night." She smiled in recollection. "What a night!"

Tachyon suddenly remembered the dinner at Aces High on Wild Card Day. Peregrine had left the restaurant with— "Fortunato?" he shouted. "Fortunato's the father? You went to bed with that, that pimp? Have you no taste? You won't sleep with me, but you'll lay with him!" He stopped shouting and took several deep breaths. He walked to the room's bar and poured himself a brandy. Peregrine looked at him in amazement.

"I cannot believe it," Tachyon repeated, swallowing most of the glass. "I have so much more to offer."

Right, she thought. *Another notch on your bedpost. But then maybe I was just that for Fortunato too.*

"Let's face it, Doctor," Peregrine said flippantly, angered

by his self-centeredness. "He's the only man I've ever screwed that made me glow. It was absolutely incredible." She smiled inside at the furious look on Tachyon's face. "But that's not important now. What about the baby?"

A multitude of thoughts dashed through her mind. *I'll have to redo my apartment*, she thought. *I hope they've fixed the roof. A baby can't live in a house without a roof. Maybe I should move upstate. That would probably be better for a child.* She smiled to herself. *A big house with a large lawn, trees, and a garden. And dogs. I never thought about having a baby. Will I be a good mother? This is a good time to find out. I'm thirty-two and the old biological clock is ticking away.*

But how did it happen? The pill had always worked before. Fortunato's powers, she realized, *are based on his potent sexuality. Perhaps they somehow circumvented the contraceptives. Fortunato . . . and Josh! How would he react to the news? What would he think?*

Tachyon's voice broke into her reverie. "Have you heard a word I've said?" he demanded.

Peregrine blushed. "I'm sorry. I was thinking about being a mother."

He groaned. "Peri, it's not that simple," he said gently.

"Why not?"

"Both you and that man have the wild card. Therefore the child will have a ninety percent chance of dying before or at birth. A nine percent chance of being a joker, and one percent, *one percent*," he emphasized, "of being an ace." He drank more brandy. "The odds are terrible, terrible. The child has no chance. None at all."

Peregrine began pacing back and forth. "Is there something you can do, some sort of test, that can tell if the baby is all right now?"

"Well, yes, I can do an ultrasound. It's abysmally primitive, but it'll tell if the child is developing normally or not. If the baby is not, I suggest—no, I urge you, very strongly, to have an abortion. There are already enough jokers in this world," he said bitterly.

"And if the baby is normal?"

Tachyon sighed. "The virus often doesn't express itself until birth. If the child survives the birth trauma without the virus manifesting, then you wait. Wait and wonder what will happen, and when it will happen. Peregrine, if you allow the child to be born, you will spend your whole life in agony, worrying and trying to protect it from everything. Consider the stresses of childhood and adolescence, any one of which might trigger the virus. Is that fair to you? To your child? To the man waiting for you downstairs? Providing," Tachyon added coldly, "he still wants to be a part of your life when he learns of this."

"I'll have to take my chances with Josh," she said swiftly, coming again to the thought that dominated her mind. "Can you do the ultrasound soon?"

"I'll see if I can make arrangements at the hospital. If we can't do it in Luxor, then you'll have to wait until we get back to Cairo. If the child is abnormal, you must consider an abortion. Actually you should have an abortion, regardless."

She stared at him. "Destroy what may be a healthy human being? It might be like me," she argued. "Or Fortunato."

"Peri, you don't know how good the virus was to you. You've parlayed your wings into fame and financial success. You are one of the fortunate few."

"Of course I am. I mean, I'm pretty, but nothing special. Pretty girls are a dime a dozen. Actually I have you to thank for my success."

"This is the first time anyone has thanked me for helping to destroy the lives of millions of people," Tachyon said grimly.

"You tried to stop it," she said reassuringly. "It's not your fault Jetboy screwed up."

"Peri," Tachyon said grimly, changing the subject as if the failures of the past were too painful to dwell upon, "if you don't terminate the pregnancy, you'll be showing very shortly. You'd better start thinking about what you're going to tell people."

"Why, the truth of course. That I'm going to have a baby."

"What if they ask about the father?"

"That's nobody's business but mine!"

"And, I would submit," Tachyon said, "McCoy's."

"I guess you're right. But the world doesn't have to know about Fortunato. Please don't tell anyone. I'd hate for him to read it in the papers. I'd rather tell him myself." If I ever see him again, she added silently. "Please?"

"It is not my place to inform him," Tachyon said coldly. "But he must be told. It is his right." He frowned. "I don't know what you saw in that man. If it had been me, this would have never happened."

"You've said that before," Peregrine said, annoyance showing on her face. "But it's a little too late for might-have-beens. Eventually everything will be fine."

"Everything is *not* going to be fine," said Tachyon firmly. "The odds are the child will die or be a joker, and I don't think that you're strong enough to deal with either of those possibilities."

"I'll have to wait and see," Peregrine said pragmatically. She turned to leave. "I guess I'd better break the news to Josh. He'll be glad it's nothing serious."

"And that you're carrying the child of another man?" asked Tachyon. "If you can maintain your relationship through this, then McCoy is a very unusual man."

"He is, Doctor," she assured him, and herself. "He is."

Peregrine walked slowly to the bar, remembering the day she and McCoy had met. He had made his interest in her evident from the very first when they were introduced at the NBC offices in November. A talented cameraman and freelance documentary maker, he had jumped at the chance to film the tour, and as he later confessed to Peregrine, the opportunity to meet her up close and personal. Peregrine was almost over her obsession with Fortunato and McCoy's attentions had helped. They had teased and tantalized each other until they finally ended up in bed together in Argentina. They'd shared a room ever since.

But McCoy couldn't arouse in her the sexual passion that Fortunato had. She doubted if any man could. Peregrine had wanted him again after that wild night they'd had together. He was like a drug she craved. Every time the phone had rung or there was a knock at the door, she'd hoped it was Fortunato. But he'd never come back. With Chrysalis's help she had found his mother and learned that the ace had left New York and was somewhere in the Orient, probably Japan.

The realization that he had left her so casually helped her get over him, but now he rushed back into her mind. She wondered how he would feel about her pregnancy, about being a father. Would he ever even know? She sighed.

Josh McCoy, she told herself sternly, *is a wonderful man, and you love him. Don't blow it over a man you'll probably never see again. But if I did see him again, what would it be like?* For the millionth time she relived her hours with Fortunato. Just thinking about it made her want him. Or McCoy.

Josh was drinking a Stella beer. As he saw her, he signaled the waiter and they arrived at his table together.

"I'll have another beer," McCoy told the waiter. "Some wine, Peri?"

"Uh, no thanks. Do you have any bottled water?" she asked the waiter.

"Certainly, madam. We have Perrier."

"That'll be fine."

"Well?" McCoy asked. "What did Tachyon have to say? Are you okay?"

I'm not as brave about telling him this as I thought I'd be, Peregrine said to herself. *What if he can't deal with it?* It was best, she decided, to simply tell him the truth.

"There's nothing wrong with me. Nothing that time won't cure." She took a sip of the drink the waiter placed in front of her and murmured, "I'm going to have a baby."

"What?" McCoy almost dropped his beer. "A baby?"

She nodded, looking at him directly for the first time since she had sat down. *I really love you*, she said silently. *Please don't make this any harder on me than it already is.*

"Mine?" he inquired calmly.

This was going to be the hard part. "No," she admitted.

Josh downed the rest of his beer and picked up the second bottle. "If I'm not the father, who is? Bruce Willis?" Peregrine made a face. "Keith Hernandez? Bob Weir? Senator Hartmann? Who?"

She arched an eyebrow at him. "Regardless of what the supermarket tabloids, and apparently you, think, I do not sleep with every man my name is linked with." She drank some Perrier. "In fact, I happen to be rather particular about choosing bedmates." She grinned mischievously. "I picked you, after all."

"Don't try to change the subject," he warned. "Who's the father?"

"Do you really want to know?"

Josh nodded curtly.

"Why?"

"Because," he sighed, "I happen to love you and I think it's important that I know who is the father of your baby. Does he know yet?"

"How can he? I just found out myself."

"Do you love him?" McCoy asked, frowning. "Why did you break off your relationship? Was it him?"

"Josh," Peregrine explained patiently. "There was no relationship. It was one night. I met this man, we went to bed. I never saw him again." *Although not,* she silently added, *for lack of trying.*

McCoy's frown deepened. "Are you in the habit of going to bed with anybody who catches your fancy?"

Peregrine flushed. "No. I just told you I'm not." She laid her hand on his. "Please understand. I had no idea you were in my future when I met him. You knew you weren't my first the first time we made love, and after all," she challenged, "I'm surely not the first woman you've slept with, am I?"

"No, but I was hoping you'd be the last." McCoy ran his hand through his hair. "This really puts a cramp into my plans."

"What do you mean?"

"Well, what about the father? Is he going to just stand quietly by while I marry the mother of his kid?"

"You want to marry me?" For the first time Peregrine felt that everything would work out right.

"Yeah, I do! What's so strange about that? Is this guy going to be a problem? Who is it anyhow?"

"It's an ace," she said slowly.

"Who?" McCoy insisted.

Oh, hell, she thought. *Josh knows a lot about the New York scene. He's sure to have heard of Fortunato. What if he has the same attitude Tachyon has? Maybe I shouldn't tell him, but maybe he has the right to know.* "His name's Fortunato—"

"*Fortunato!*" exploded McCoy. "That guy with all the hookers? Geishas, he calls them! You slept with *him!*" He gulped down more beer.

"I really don't see that it matters now. It happened. And if you must know, he's very charming."

"Okay, okay." McCoy glowered.

"If you're going to be jealous of every man I ever slept with, then I don't give us very much of a chance. And marriage is out of the question."

"Come on, Peri, give me a break. This is kind of unexpected."

"Well, it's a shock to me too. This morning I thought I was tired. This afternoon I find out I'm pregnant."

A shadow fell over their table. It was Tachyon in a lilac silk suit that matched his eyes. "Do you mind if I join you?" He pulled out a chair without awaiting a reply. "Brandy," he snapped to the waiter, who was hovering nearby. They all stared at each other until the waiter made a precise little bow and left. "I've spoken to the local hospital," Tachyon said finally. "We can do the test tomorrow morning."

"What test?" McCoy asked, looking from Peregrine to Tachyon.

"Did you tell him?" Tachyon asked.

"I didn't have a chance to tell him about the virus," Peregrine said in a barely audible whisper.

"Virus?"

"Because both Peregrine and For—the father, that is— carry the wild card, the child will have it," Tachyon said crisply. "An ultrasound must be performed as soon as possible to determine the status of the fetus. If the child is developing abnormally, Peregrine must have an abortion. If the child is growing normally, I still advise termination, but that will, of course, be her decision."

McCoy stared at Peregrine. "You didn't tell me that!"

"I didn't have a chance," she said defensively.

"There is a one in one hundred chance that the child will be an ace, but a nine in one hundred chance that it will be a joker," added Tachyon relentlessly.

"A joker! You mean like one of those awful things that lives in Jokertown, something horrible, an atrocity?"

"My dear young man," began Tachyon angrily, "not all jokers—"

"Josh," Peregrine interrupted softly, "I'm a joker."

Both men turned to her. "I am," she insisted. "Jokers have physical deformities." Her wings fluttered. "Like these. I'm a *joker*."

"This discussion is getting us nowhere," said Tachyon after a long silence. "Peri, I'll see you tonight." He walked away without touching his brandy.

"Well," said McCoy. "Tachyon's little piece of news certainly puts a different light on the subject."

"What do you mean," she asked, a chill seizing her.

"I hate jokers," McCoy burst out. "They give me the creeps!" His knuckles were white on the beer bottle. "Look,

I can't go on with this. I'll call New York and tell them to
send you another cameraman. I'll get my gear out of your
room."

"You're leaving?" Peregrine asked, stunned.

"Yeah. Look, it's been a lot of fun," he said deliberately,
"and I've really enjoyed you. But I'll be damned if I'm going
to spend my life raising some pimp's bastard! Especially," he
added as an afterthought, "one that's going to develop into
some kind of monster!"

Peregrine winced as if she'd been slapped. "I thought
you loved me," she said, her voice and wings quivering. "You
just asked me to marry you!"

"I guess I was wrong." He finished his beer and stood
up. "Bye, Peri."

Peregrine couldn't face him as he left. She stared down
at the table, cold and shaken, and didn't notice the intense,
lingering look McCoy gave her as he left the bar.

"Ahem."

Hiram Worchester seated himself across from her in the
chair McCoy had just vacated. Peregrine shuddered. *It's true,
he's gone,* she thought. *I will never, never,* she told herself
fiercely, *get involved with another man. Never!*

"Where's McCoy? Father Squid and I want to know if
the two of you will join us for dinner. Of course," he added
when she didn't respond, "if you have other plans . . ."

"No," she said dully, "no other plans. It will be just me,
I'm afraid. Josh is, ahhh, out filming some local color." She
wondered why she lied to one of her oldest friends.

"Of course." Hiram beamed. "Let's get Father Squid and
retire to the dining room. Using my power always makes me
hungry." He stood and pulled out her chair.

Dinner was excellent, but she hardly tasted it. Hiram
wolfed down huge portions and waxed poetical about the
batarikh—Egyptian caviar—and lamb shish kebab served with
a wine called *rubis d'Égypte*. He loudly urged Tachyon to try
some when he joined them, but Tachyon declined with a
shake of his head.

"Are you ready for the meeting?" he asked Peregrine.
"Where's McCoy?"

"Out filming," answered Hiram. "I suggest we go without him."

Peregrine murmured her agreement.

"He wasn't invited anyway," Tachyon sniped.

*   *   *

Dr. Tachyon, Hiram Worchester, Father Squid, and Peregrine met with Opet Kemel in a small antechamber off the amphitheater that had been so severely damaged in the terrorist attack earlier that day.

"There must be Nur spies among us," Kemel exclaimed, glancing around the room. "That is the only way those dogs could have gotten through security. Or else they bribed one of my people. We are trying to ferret out the traitor now. The three assassins killed themselves after they were captured," Kemel said, the hatred in his voice making Peregrine doubt the strict truth of his words. "They are now *shahid,* martyrs for Allah at the instigation of that madman, Nur al-Allah, may he die a most painful and lingering death." Kemel turned to Tachyon. "You see, Doctor, that is why we need your assistance to protect ourselves. . . ."

His voice dragged on and on. Occasionally Peregrine heard Hiram or Father Squid or Tachyon chime in, but she wasn't really listening. She knew the expression on her face was polite and inquisitive. It was the face she wore when she had boring guests on her show who blathered on and on about nothing. She wondered how Letterman was doing with *Peregrine's Perch*. Probably fine. Her mind refused to stay on unimportant topics and wandered back to Josh McCoy. What could she have done to make him stay? Nothing. Perhaps it was better that he left if that was his real attitude toward those stricken with the wild card. She thought back to Argentina, their first night together. She had summoned up her courage, put on her sexiest dress, and gone to his room with a bottle of champagne. McCoy had been occupied with a woman he'd picked up in the hotel bar. Peregrine, extremely embarrassed, had slunk back to her room and begun drinking the champagne. Fifteen minutes later McCoy had appeared. It had taken so long, he explained, because he had to get rid of the woman.

Peregrine was impressed by his supreme confidence. He was the first man she'd been with since Fortunato, and his touch was wonderful. They'd spent every night since then together, making love at least once a day. Tonight she'd be alone. He hates you, she told herself, because you're a joker. She placed her left hand across her abdomen. *We don't need him,* Peregrine told the baby. *We don't need anyone*.

Tachyon's voice broke through her reverie. "I'll report

this to Senator Hartmann, the Red Cross, and the UN. I'm sure we can assist you somehow."

"Thank you, thank you!" Kemel reached across the table to take Tachyon's hands in gratitude. "Now," he said, smiling at the others, "perhaps you would like to meet my children? They have expressed a desire to talk to you all, especially you." He directed his penetrating stare at Peregrine.

"Me?"

Kemel nodded and stood. "Come this way."

They passed between the long golden curtains that separated the antechamber from the auditorium, and Kemel led them to another room where the living gods were waiting for them.

Min was there, and bearded Osiris, bird-headed Thoth, and the floating brother and sister, as were Anubis and Isis and a dozen others whose names Peregrine couldn't remember. They immediately surrounded the Americans and Dr. Tachyon, everyone talking at once. Peregrine found herself face-to-face with a large woman who smiled and spoke to her in Arabic.

"I'm sorry," Peregrine said, smiling back. "I don't understand."

The woman gestured to the bird-headed man standing close by, who immediately joined them.

"I am Thoth," he said in English, his beak giving him a strange clacking accent. "Taurt has asked me to tell you that the son you bear will be born strong and healthy."

Peregrine looked from one to the other, incredulity on her face. "How did you know I'm pregnant?" she demanded.

"Ah, we have known since we heard you were coming to the temple."

"But this trip was decided upon months ago!"

"Yes. Osiris is cursed by knowing pieces of the future. Your future, your child, was in one of those pieces."

Taurt said something and Thoth smiled. "She says not to worry. You will be a very good mother."

"I will?"

Taurt handed her a small linen pouch with hieroglyphs embroidered on it. Peregrine opened it and found a small amulet made of red stone. She examined it curiously.

"It is an *achet*," Thoth clacked. "It represents the sun rising in the east. It will give you the strength and power of Ra the Great. It is for the child. Keep it until the boy is old enough to wear it."

"Thank you. I will." She impulsively hugged Taurt, who returned the gesture and then disappeared into the crowded room.

"Come now," said Thoth, "the others wish to meet you."

As Peregrine and Thoth circulated among the gods, she was greeted with great affection by each.

"Why are they acting like this?" she asked after a particularly bone-crushing embrace from Hapi, the bull.

"They are happy for you," Thoth told her. "The birth of a child is a wonderous thing. Especially to one with wings."

"I see," she said, though she didn't. She had the feeling that Thoth was holding something back, but the bird-headed man slipped back into the crowd before she could question him.

Amid the greetings and extemporaneous speeches she suddenly realized that she was exhausted. Peregrine caught Tachyon's eye where he stood conversing with Anubis. She pointed to her watch and Tachyon beckoned to her. As she joined them, she heard him ask Anubis about the threat of the Nur. Father Squid was close by, discussing theology with Osiris.

"The gods will protect us," replied Anubis, lifting his eyes upward. "And from what I understand, security around the temple has been strengthened."

"Excuse me for interrupting," Peregrine apologized, addressing Tachyon, "but don't we have that appointment early tomorrow morning?"

"Burning sky, I'd almost forgotten. What time is it?" He lifted his eyebrows when he saw it was after one. "We'd best go. It will take us an hour to get back to Luxor, and you, young lady, need your sleep."

Peregrine entered her room at the Winter Palace Hotel with apprehension. McCoy's things were gone. She sank into a large armchair, and the tears that had been threatening all night came. She cried until she had no more tears left and her head ached with the strain. *Go to bed*, she told herself. *It's been a long day. Someone tries to shoot you, you find out you're pregnant, and the man you love leaves you. Next you'll find out that NBC's canceled* Peregrine's Perch. *At least you know your baby is going to be all right*, she thought as she undressed. She turned off the light and slipped into the lonely double bed.

But her brain woundn't turn off. *What if Taurt is wrong? What if the ultrasound reveals a deformity? I'll have to have an abortion. I don't want one, but I can't bring another joker into the world. Abortion is against everything I was brought up to believe.*

But do you want to spend the rest of your life taking care of a monster? Can you take the life of a baby, even if it's a joker?

Back and forth she went, until she finally dropped off to sleep. Her last coherent thought was of Fortunato. *What would he want,* she wondered?

She was awakened by Tachyon banging at her door.

"Peregrine," she foggily heard him call. "Are you there? It's seven-thirty."

She rolled out of bed, wrapped herself in the sheet, and opened the locked door. Tachyon stood there, annoyance written all over his face.

He glared at her. "Do you know what time it is? You were supposed to meet me downstairs a half hour ago."

"I know, I know. Yell at me while I get dressed."

She picked up her clothes and headed toward the bathroom. Tachyon closed the door behind him and eyed her sheet-clad body appreciatively.

"What happened here?" he asked. "Where's your paramour?"

Peregrine poked her head around the bathroom door and spoke around her toothbrush. "Gone."

"Do you want to tell me about it?"

"No!" She glanced in the mirror as she quickly brushed her hair and frowned at her exhausted face and swollen, red eyes. *You look like hell,* she told herself. She pulled on her clothes, pushed her feet into a pair of sandals, grabbed her bag, and joined Tachyon, who was waiting by the door.

"I'm sorry I overslept," she apologized as they hurried through the lobby and to the waiting cab. "It took me forever to fall asleep."

Tachyon watched her intently as he helped her into the cab. They rode in silence, her mind full of the baby, McCoy, Fortunato, motherhood, her career. Suddenly she asked, "If the baby... if the test..." She took a deep breath and began again. "If the test shows that there is some abnormality, will they be able to do the abortion today?"

Tachyon took her cold hands in his. "Yes."

Please, she prayed, *please don't let anything be wrong with my baby.* Tachyon's voice broke into her thoughts. "What?"

"Peri, what happened with McCoy?"

She stared out the window and withdrew her hand from Tachyon's. "He's gone," she said dully, twisting her fingers together. "I guess he went back to New York." She blinked away tears. "Everything seemed okay, I mean, about my being pregnant and Fortunato and all. But after he heard that if the baby lived, it would probably be a joker, well . . ." Her tears began again. Tachyon handed her his lace-trimmed silk handkerchief. Peregrine took it and wiped her eyes. "Well," she said, continuing her story, "when Josh heard that, he decided he didn't want to have anything to do with me or the baby. So he left." She rolled Tachyon's handkerchief into a small, damp ball.

"You truly love him, don't you?" Tachyon asked gently.

Peregrine nodded and pushed away more tears.

"If you have an abortion, will he come back?"

"I don't know and I don't care," she flared. "If he can't accept me the way I am, then I don't want him."

Tachyon shook his head. "Poor Peri," he said softly. "McCoy is a jackass."

It seemed like an eternity before the cab rolled up in front of the hospital. As Tachyon went to consult with the receptionist, Peregrine leaned against the cool, white wall of the waiting room and shut her eyes. She tried to make her mind go blank, but she couldn't stop thinking about McCoy. *If he did come to you, you'd take him back,* she accused herself. *You know you would. He won't, though, not with me carrying Fortunato's child.* She opened her eyes as someone touched her arm.

"Are you sure you're all right?" Tachyon asked.

"Just tired." She tried to smile.

"Scared?" he asked.

"Yes," she admitted. "I'd never really thought about having children, but now that I'm pregnant, I want to have a baby more than anything." Peregrine sighed and folded her arms protectively over her abdomen. "But I hope that the baby is all right."

"They're paging the doctor who'll perform the procedure," Tachyon said. "I hope you're thirsty. You have to drink several quarts of water." He removed a pitcher and a glass from a tray held by the nurse standing beside him. "You can start now."

Peregrine began drinking. She'd finished six glasses before a short man in a white coat hurried up to them.

"Dr. Tachyon?" he asked, grasping Tachyon's hand. "I am Dr. Ali. It is a great pleasure to meet you and welcome you to my hospital." He turned to Peregrine. "Is this the patient?"

Tachyon performed the introductions.

Dr. Ali rubbed his hands together. "Let's get on with it," he said, and they followed him to the OB-GYN section of the hospital.

"You, young lady, into that room." He pointed. "Remove all your clothing and put on the gown you'll find there. Keep drinking water. When you've changed, come back here and we'll perform the sonography."

When Peregrine rejoined Tachyon, now wearing a white coat over his silken finery, and Dr. Ali, she was told to lie on an examining table. She followed their directions, clutching Taurt's amulet in her hand. A nurse raised the robe up and rubbed a clear gel on Peregrine's stomach.

"Conductive jelly," Tachyon explained. "It helps carry the sound waves."

The nurse began to move a small instrument that looked like a microphone over Peregrine's belly.

"The transducer," said Tachyon as he and Ali studied the image on the video screen in front of them.

"Well, what do you see?" Peregrine demanded.

"A moment, Peri."

Tachyon and Ali conferred in low tones.

"Can you print that?" Peregrine heard Tachyon ask. Dr. Ali gave the nurse instructions in Arabic, and very shortly a computer printout of the image appeared.

"You can climb down now," said Tachyon. "We've seen everything there is to see."

"Well?" Peregrine asked anxiously.

"Everything looks fine . . . so far," said Tachyon slowly. "The child appears to be developing normally."

"That's wonderful!" She hugged him as he helped her down from the table.

"If you intend to go through with this pregnancy, I insist

on an ultrasound every four to five weeks to monitor the baby's growth."

Peregrine nodded. "These sound waves won't hurt the baby, will they?"

"No," said Tachyon. "The only thing that can injure the child already exists within it."

Peregrine looked at Tachyon. "I know you feel you have to keep telling me that, but the baby is going to be just fine, I know it."

"Peregrine, this is not a fairy tale! You are not going to live happily ever after! This could ruin your life!"

"Growing wings when I was thirteen could have ruined my life, but it didn't. This isn't going to either."

Tachyon sighed. "There is no reasoning with you. Go put your clothes on. It's time we got back to Cairo."

Tachyon was waiting for her outside the dressing room.

"Where's Dr. Ali?" she asked, looking around. "I wanted to thank him."

"He had other patients to attend to." Tachyon steered her down the corridor with his arm around her shoulders. "Let's get back..." his voice broke off. Coming down the hallway toward them was Josh McCoy. Peregrine was pleased to see that he looked as awful as she felt. He must not have gotten much sleep either. He stopped in front of them.

"Peri," he began, "I've been thinking—"

"Good for you," Peregrine said crisply. "Now if you will excuse us—"

McCoy reached out and grabbed her upper arm. "No. I want to talk to you and I intend to do it now." He pulled her away from Tachyon.

She had to talk to him, she told herself. Maybe everything could be straightened out. She hoped.

"It's all right," she said shakily to Tachyon. "Let's get this over with."

Tachyon's voice followed them. "McCoy. You are undoubtedly a fool. And I warn you, if you harm her—in any way—you will regret it for a very long time."

McCoy ignored him and continued to pull Peregrine down the hall, opening doors until he found an empty room. He dragged her in and slammed the door behind them. He let go of her arm and began pacing back and forth.

Peregrine stood against the wall, rubbing her arm where the marks of his fingers were visible.

McCoy stopped pacing and stared at her. "I'm sorry if I hurt you."

"I think it's going to bruise," she said, inspecting her arm.

"We can't have that," McCoy said mockingly. "Bruises on America's sex symbol!"

"That's pretty rotten," she said, her voice dangerously quiet.

"True, though," he shot back. "You are a sex symbol. There's your *Playboy* centerfold, that nude ice sculpture of you at Aces High. And what about that naked poster, 'Fallen Angel,' that Warhol did?"

"There's nothing wrong with posing nude! I'm not ashamed to show my body or to have other people look at it."

"No kidding! You strip for anyone who asks you!"

She went white with fury. "Yes, I do! Including you!" She slapped McCoy's face and turned to the door, her wings quivering. "I don't have to stand here and take any more abuse from you."

She reached for the door handle, but McCoy shoved in front of her and held it closed. "No. I need to talk to you."

"You're not talking, you're being abusive," Peregrine retorted, "and I don't like it one bit."

"You don't know what abuse is," he told her, brown eyes glittering angrily. "Why don't you scream? Tachyon's probably right outside. He'd love to rush in and rescue you. You could fuck him in gratitude."

"How dare you?" Peregrine shouted. "I don't need him to protect me! Him or you or anyone! Let me go!" she demanded angrily.

"No." He pressed her body to the wall. She felt like a butterfly pinned on velvet. She could feel his heavy warmth against her. "Is this what it's going to be like," he raged, "men always wanting to protect you? Men wanting to fuck you just because you're Peregrine? I don't want anyone else touching you. No one but me.

"Peri," he said more gently. "Look at me." When she refused, he forced her chin up until she looked him in the eyes, tears rolling down her cheeks. "Peri, I'm sorry for everything I said yesterday. And for everything I said just now. I didn't intend to lose my temper, but when I saw that overdressed quiche-eater with his hands on you, I just lost it. The thought of anyone but me touching you makes me furious." The fingers on her chin tightened. "Yesterday when you said that Fortunato was the baby's father, all I could see was him in bed with you, holding you, loving you." He let her go and walked to the window of the small room, staring out unseeing, his hands clenching and unclenching. "It was then," he continued, "that I realized exactly what I was up against. You're famous and beautiful and sexy and everyone wants you. I don't want to be Mr. Peregrine. I don't want to compete with your past. I want your future.

"What I said yesterday about jokers wasn't true. It was the first excuse that I could think of. I wanted to hurt you as bad as I was hurting." He ran a hand through his blond hair. "It really hurt me when you told me about the baby, because it's not mine. I don't hate jokers. I like kids and I'll love yours and try to be a good father. If Fortunato shows up, well, I'll deal with it the best I can. Hell, Peri, I love you. Last night without you was terrible. It showed me what the future would be like if I let you go. I love you," he repeated, "and I want you to be my life."

Peregrine put her arms around him and leaned against his back. "I love you too. Last night was about the worst night of my life. I realized what you meant to me, and also what this baby means. If I can only have one of you, I want my baby. I'm sorry to say that, but I had to tell you. But I want you too."

McCoy turned and took her hands. He kissed them. "You sound awfully determined."

"I am."

McCoy laughed. "No matter what happens when the baby is born, we'll do the best we can." He smiled down at her. "I have a bunch of nieces and nephews, so I even know how to change diapers."

"Good. You can teach me."

"I will," he promised, his lips touching hers as he pulled her closer.

The door opened. A white-clad figure looked at them disapprovingly. After a moment Doctor Tachyon peered in. "Are you quite finished?" he asked icily. "They need this room."

"We're done with the room, but we're not finished. We're just starting," Peregrine said, smiling radiantly.

"Well, as long as you're happy," Tachyon said slowly.

"I am," she assured him.

They left the hospital with Tachyon. He got into a cab by himself, while McCoy and Peregrine settled into the horse-drawn carriage waiting at the curb behind the taxi.

"We have to get back to the hotel," Peregrine said.

"Are you propositioning me?"

"Of course not. I have to pack so we can rejoin the tour in Cairo."

"Today?"

"Yes."

"Then we'd better hurry."

"Why?"

"Why?" McCoy trailed kisses over her face and neck. "We have to make up for last night, of course."

"Oh." Peregrine spoke to the driver and the carriage picked up speed. "We don't want to waste any more time."

"Enough has already been wasted," McCoy agreed. "Are you happy?" he asked softly as she settled in his arms, her head on his chest.

"Happier than I've ever been!" But a little voice in the back of her mind kept reminding her of Fortunato.

His arms tightened around her. "I love you."

FROM *THE JOURNAL OF XAVIER DESMOND*

JANUARY 30/JERUSALEM:

The open city of Jerusalem, they call it. An international metropolis, jointly governed by commissioners from Israel, Jordan, Palestine, and Great Britain under a United Nations mandate, sacred to three of the world's great religions.

Alas, the apt phrase is not "open city" but "open sore." Jerusalem bleeds as it has for almost four decades. If this city is sacred, I should hate to visit one that was profane.

Senators Hartmann and Lyons and the other political delegates lunched with the city commissioners today, but the rest of us spent the afternoon touring this free international city in closed limousines with bulletproof windshields and special underbody armor to withstand bomb blasts. Jerusalem, it seems, likes to welcome distinguished international visitors by blowing them up. It does not seem to matter who the visitors are, where they come from, what religion they practice, how their politics lean—there are enough factions in this city so that everyone can count on being hated by someone.

Two days ago we were in Beirut. From Beirut to Jerusalem, that is a voyage from day to night. Lebanon is a beautiful country, and Beirut is so lovely and peaceful it seems almost serene. Its various religions appear to have solved the problem of living in comparative harmony, although there are of course incidents—nowhere in the Middle East (or the world, for that matter) is completely safe.

But Jerusalem—the outbreaks of violence have been endemic for thirty years, each worse than the one before. Entire blocks resemble nothing so much as London during the Blitz, and the population that remains has grown so used to the distant sound of machine-gun fire that they scarcely seem to pay it any mind.

We stopped briefly at what remains of the Wailing Wall (largely destroyed in 1967 by Palestinian terrorists in reprisal

for the assassination of al-Haziz by Israeli terrorists the year
before) and actually dared to get out of our vehicles. Hiram
looked around fiercely and made a fist, as if daring anyone to
start trouble. He has been in a strange state of late; irritable,
quick to anger, moody. The things we witnessed in Africa
have affected us all, however. One shard of the wall is still
fairly imposing. I touched it and tried to feel the history.
Instead I felt the pocks left in the stone by bullets.

Most of our party returned to the hotel afterward, but
Father Squid and I took a detour to visit the Jokers' Quarter.
I'm told that it is the second-largest joker community in the
world, after Jokertown itself . . . a distant second, but second
nonetheless. It does not surprise me. Islam does not view my
people kindly, and so jokers come here from all over the
Middle East for whatever meager protection is offered by UN
sovereignty and a small, outmanned, outgunned, and demor-
alized international peacekeeping force.

The Quarter is unspeakably squalid, and the weight of
human misery within its walls is almost palpable. Yet ironically the streets of the Quarter are reputed safer than any other
place in Jerusalem. The Quarter has its own walls, built in
living memory, originally to spare the feelings of decent
people by hiding we living obscenities from their sight, but
those same walls have given a measure of security to those
who dwell within. Once inside I saw no nats at all, only
jokers—jokers of all races and religions, all living in relative
peace. Once they might have been Muslims or Jews or
Christians, zealots or Zionists or followers of the Nur, but
after their hand had been dealt, they were only jokers. The
joker is the great equalizer, cutting through all other hatreds
and prejudices, uniting all mankind in a new brotherhood of
pain. A joker is a joker is a joker, and anything else he is, is
unimportant.

Would that it worked the same way with aces.

The sect of Jesus Christ, Joker has a church in Jerusalem,
and Father Squid took me there. The building looked more
like a mosque than a Christian church, at least on the
outside, but inside it was not so terribly different from the
church I'd visited in Jokertown, though much older and in
greater disrepair. Father Squid lit a candle and said a prayer,
and then we went back to the cramped, tumbledown rectory
where Father Squid conversed with the pastor in halting
Latin while we shared a bottle of sour red wine. As they were

talking, I heard the sound of automatic weaponry chattering off in the night somewhere a few blocks away. A typical Jerusalem evening, I suppose.

No one will read this book until after my death, by which time I will be safely immune from prosecution. I've thought long and hard about whether or not I should record what happened tonight, and finally decided that I should. The world needs to remember the lessons of 1976 and be reminded from time to time that the JADL does not speak for all jokers.

An old joker woman pressed a note into my hand as Father Squid and I were leaving the church. I suppose someone recognized me.

When I read the note, I begged off the official reception, pleading illness once again, but this time it was a ruse. I dined in my room with a wanted criminal, a man I can only describe as a notorious international joker terrorist, although he is a hero inside the Jokers' Quarter. I will not give his real name, even in these pages, since I understand that he still visits his family in Tel Aviv from time to time. He wears a black canine mask on his "missions" and to the press, Interpol, and the sundry factions that police Jerusalem, he is variously known as the Black Dog and the Hound of Hell. Tonight he wore a completely different mask, a butterfly-shaped hood covered with silver glitter, and had no problem crossing the city.

"What you've got to remember," he told me, "is that nats are fundamentally stupid. You wear the same mask twice and let your picture get taken with it, and they start thinking it's your face."

The Hound, as I'll call him, was born in Brooklyn but emigrated to Israel with his family at age nine and became an Israeli citizen. He was twenty when he became a joker. "I traveled halfway around the world to draw the wild card," he told me. "I could have stayed in Brooklyn."

We spent several hours discussing Jerusalem, the Middle East, and the politics of the wild card. The Hound heads what honesty forces me to call a joker terrorist organization, the Twisted Fists. They are illegal in both Israel and Palestine, no mean trick. He was evasive about how many members they had, but not at all shy about confessing that virtually all of their financial support comes from New York's Jokertown.

"You may not like us, Mr. Mayor," the Hound told me, "but your people do." He even hinted slyly that one of the joker delegates on our tour was among their supporters, although of course he refused to supply a name.

The Hound is convinced that war is coming to the Middle East, and soon. "It's overdue," he said. "Neither Israel or Palestine have ever had defensible borders, and neither one is an economically viable nation. Each is convinced that the other one is guilty of all sorts of terrorist atrocities, and they're both right. Israel wants the Negev and the West Bank, Palestine wants a port on the Mediterranean, and both countries are still full of refugees from the 1948 partition who want their homes back. Everyone wants Jerusalem except the UN, which has it. Shit, they *need* a good war. The Israelis looked like they were winning in '48 until the *Nasr* kicked their asses. I know that Bernadotte won the Nobel Peace Prize for the Treaty of Jerusalem, but just between you and me, it might have been better if they'd fought it out to the bitter end . . . any kind of end."

I asked him about all the people who would have died, but he just shrugged. "They'd be dead. But maybe if it was over, really *over*, some of the wounds would start to heal. Instead we got two pissed-off half-countries that share the same little desert and won't even recognize each other, we've got four decades of hatred and terrorism and fear, and we're still going to get the war, and soon. It beats me how Bernadotte pulled off the Peace of Jerusalem anyway, though I'm not surprised that he got assassinated for his troubles. The only ones who hate the terms worse than the Israelis are the Palestinians."

I pointed out that, unpopular as it might be, the Peace of Jerusalem had lasted almost forty years. He dismissed that as "a forty-year stalemate, not real peace. Mutual fear was what made it work. The Israelis have always had military superiority. But the Arabs had the Port Said aces, and you think the Israelis don't remember? Every time the Arabs put up a memorial to the *Nasr*, anywhere from Baghdad to Marrakesh, the Israelis blow it up. Believe me, they remember. Only now the whole thing's coming unbalanced. I got sources say Israel has been running its own wild card experiments on volunteers from their armed forces, and they've come up with a few aces of their own. Now that's fanaticism for you, to *volunteer* for the wild card. And on the Arab side, you've got

Nur al-Allah, who calls Israel a 'bastard joker nation' and has vowed to destroy it utterly. The Port Said aces were pussycats compared to his bunch, even old Khôf. No, it's coming, and soon."

"And when it comes?" I asked him.

He was carrying a gun, some kind of small semiautomatic machine pistol with a long Russian name. He took it out and laid it on the table between us. "When it comes," he said, "they can kill each other all they want, but they damn well better leave the Quarter alone, or they'll have us to deal with. We've already given the Nur a few lessons. Every time they kill a joker, we kill five of them. You'd think they'd get the idea, but the Nur's a slow learner."

I told him that Senator Hartmann was hoping to set up a meeting with the Nur al-Allah to begin discussions that might lead to a peaceful solution to this area's problems. He laughed. We talked for a long time, about jokers and aces and nats, and violence and nonviolence and war and peace, about brotherhood and revenge and turning the other cheek and taking care of your own, and in the end we settled nothing. "Why did you come?" I finally asked him.

"I thought we should meet. We could use your help. Your knowledge of Jokertown, your contacts in nat society, the money you could raise."

"You won't get my help," I told him. "I've seen where your road leads. Tom Miller walked that road ten years ago."

"Gimli?" He shrugged. "First, Gimli was crazy as a bedbug. I'm not. Gimli wants the world to kiss it and make it all better. I just fight to protect my own. To protect you, Des. Pray that your Jokertown never needs the Twisted Fists, but if you do, we'll be there. I read *Time*'s cover story on Leo Barnett. Could be the Nur isn't the only slow learner. If that's how it is, maybe the Black Dog will go home and find that tree that grows in Brooklyn, right? I haven't been to a Dodger game since I was eight."

My heart stopped in my throat as I looked at the gun on the table, but I reached out and put my hand on the phone. "I could call down to our security right now and make certain that won't happen, that you won't kill any more innocent people."

"But you won't," the Hound said. "Because we have so much in common."

I told him we had nothing in common.

"We're both jokers," he said. "What else matters?" Then he holstered his gun, adjusted his mask, and walked calmly from my room.

And God help me, I sat there alone for several endless minutes, until I heard the elevator doors open down the hall—and finally took my hand off the phone.

THE TINT OF HATRED

Part Five

SUNDAY, FEBRUARY 1, 1987, THE SYRIAN DESERT:

Najib struck her down with one quick blow, but Misha persisted. "He's coming," Misha said. "Allah's dreams tell me that I must go to Damascus to meet him."

In the darkness of the mosque Najib glowed like a green beacon from near the *mihrab*, the jeweled prayer niche. It was at night that Nur al-Allah was the most impressive, a fiery vision of a prophet, gleaming with Allah's own fury. He said nothing to Misha's pronouncement, looking first at Sayyid, resting his great bulk against one of the tiled pillars.

"No," Sayyid grumbled. "No, Nur al-Allah." He looked at Misha, kneeling in supplication before her brother, and his eyes were full of a smoldering rage because she would not submit to her brother's will or Sayyid's suggestions. "You've often said that the abominations are to be killed. You've said that the only way to negotiate with the unbeliever is with the edge of a sword. Let me fulfill those words for you. The entire Ba'th government can do nothing to stop us; al-Assad trembles when Nur al-Allah speaks. I'll take some of the faithful to Damascus. We'll cleanse the abominations and those who bring them with purifying fire."

Najib's skin flared for a moment, as if Sayyid's advice had excited him. His lips had pulled back in a fierce grimace. Misha shook her head. "Brother," she implored. "Listen also to Kahina. I've had the same dream for three nights. I see the two of us with the Americans. I see the gifts. I see a new, untrodden path."

"Also tell Nur al-Allah that you woke screaming from the dream, that you felt the gifts were dangerous, that this Hartmann had more than one face in your dreams."

Misha looked back at her husband. "A new way is always

dangerous. Gifts always obligate the one who receives them. Will you tell the Nur al-Allah that there's no danger in *your* way, the way of violence? Is Nur al-Allah so strong already that he can defeat the entire West? The Soviets won't help in this; they'll want their hands to be clean."

"*Jihad* is struggle," Sayyid grated out.

Najib nodded his head. He raised a brilliant hand before his face, turning it as if marveling at the soft light it radiated. "Allah smote the unbelievers with His hand," he agreed. "Why shouldn't I do the same?"

"Because of Allah's dream," Misha insisted.

"Allah's dream or *yours,* woman?" Sayyid asked. "What will the infidels do if Nur al-Allah does as I've asked? The West has done *nothing* about the hostages Islam has taken, they've done nothing about other killings. Will they complain to Damascus and al-Assad? Nur al-Allah rules Syria in all but title; Nur al-Allah has united half of all Islam behind him. They'll complain, they'll bluster. They'll cry and moan, but they won't interfere. What will they do—refuse to trade with us? *Ptah!*" Sayyid spat on the intricate tiles at his feet. "They will hear Allah's laughter in the wind."

"These Americans have their own guards," Misha countered. "They have the ones they call aces."

"We have Allah. His strength is all we need. Any of my people would be honored to become *shahid,* a martyr for Allah."

Misha turned to Najib, still looking at his hand as Sayyid and Misha argued. "Brother, what Sayyid asks ignores the gifts that Allah has given us. His way ignores the gift of dreams, and it ignores *kuwwa nuriyah,* the power of light."

"What do you mean?" Najib's hand fell.

"Allah's power is in your voice, your presence. If you meet with these people, they would be swayed the way the faithful are swayed when you speak. *Any* of Allah's people could kill them, but only Nur al-Allah can actually bring the infidels to the faith of Allah. Which of the two is the greater honor to Allah?"

Najib didn't answer. She could see his luminescent face furrowed in a deep frown, and he turned to walk away a few paces. She knew then that she had won. *Praise Allah! Sayyid will beat me again for this, but it's worth it.* Her cheek throbbed where Najib had struck her, but she ignored the pain.

"Sayyid?" Najib asked. He looked from a slitted window to the village. Faint voices hailed the glowing visage.

"It is Nur al-Allah's decision. He knows my counsel," Sayyid said. "I'm not a *kahin*. My foresight is limited to war. Nur al-Allah is strong—I think we should demonstrate that strength."

Najib came back to the *mihrab*. "Sayyid, will you allow the Kahina to go to Damascus and meet with the Americans?"

"If that's what Nur al-Allah wishes," Sayyid answered stiffly.

"It is," Najib said. "Misha, go back to your husband's house and make yourself ready to travel. You'll meet this delegation, and you'll tell me of them. Then Nur al-Allah will decide how to deal with them."

Misha bowed, her head to the cool tiles. She kept her eyes down, feeling the heat of Sayyid's gaze as she passed him.

When she had gone, Najib shook his head at Sayyid's sullen posture. "You think I ignore you for yur wife, my friend? Are you insulted?"

"She is your sister, and she is Kahina," Sayyid replied, his voice neutral.

Najib smiled, and the darkness of his mouth was like a hole in his bright face. "Let me ask you, Sayyid, are we truly strong enough to do as you suggested?"

"*In sha'Allah*, of course, but I wouldn't have said so if I didn't think it true."

"And would your plan be easier to execute in Damascus, or here—in our own place, at our own time?"

Comprehension made Sayyid grin. "Why, *here*, of course, Nur al-Allah. *Here*."

TUESDAY, FEBRUARY 3, 1987, DAMASCUS:

The hotel was near the Suq al-Hamidiyah. Even through the chatter of the air conditioner's ancient compressor, Gregg could hear the market's boisterous energy. The *suq* was swirling with a thousand brightly hued *djellaba*, interspersed with the dull black of the *chador*. The crowds filled the narrow lanes between the stalls' colorful awnings and spilled out into the streets. On the nearest corner a water-seller called his wares: "*Atchen, taa saubi!*"—if you thirst, come to me.

Everywhere there were crowds, from the *suq* to the white minarets of 1200-year-old Umayyad Mosque. "You'd think the wild card never existed. Or the twentieth century, for that matter," Gregg commented.

"That's because Nur al-Allah has made sure that no joker dares to walk the streets. They kill jokers here." Sara, on the bed, laid her orange on the peels littering the copy of *al Ba'th*, the official Syrian newspaper. "I remember one tale we got from the *Post* stringer here. A joker had the misfortune of being caught stealing food in the *suq*. They buried him in the sand so that only his head showed, then they stoned him to death. The judge—who belonged to the Nur sect, by the way—insisted that only small stones be thrown, so the joker would have sufficient time to contemplate his many sins before he died."

Gregg laced his fingers in her tousled hair, gently pulled her head back, and kissed her deeply. "That's why we're here," he said. "That's why I hope to meet this Light of Allah."

"You've been edgy since Egypt."

"I think this is an important stop."

"Because the Middle East is going to be one of the main concerns of the next president?"

"You're an impertinent little bitch."

"I'll take the 'little' as a compliment. A 'bitch,' though, is a female dog, you sexist pig. And I *can* smell a story." She wrinkled her nose up at him.

"Does that mean I get your vote?"

"It depends." Sara threw back the sheet, scattering *al-Ba'th*, orange, and peels to the floor, and took Gregg's hand. She kissed his fingers lightly and then moved his hand lower on her body. "What kind of incentives were you thinking of offering?" she asked.

"I'll do whatever I have to do." *And that's true.* Puppetman stirred slightly, impatient. *If I make Nur al-Allah a puppet, I influence his action. I can sit down at the table with him and get him to sign whatever I want: Hartmann the Great Negotiator, the world's humanitarian. Nur al-Allah is the key to this region. With him and a few other leaders . . .* The thought made him smile. Sara laughed throatily.

"No sacrifice is too great, huh?" She laughed again and pulled him on top of her. "I like a man with a sense of duty.

Well, start earning your vote, Senator. And this time, *you* get the wet spot."

A few hours later there was a discreet knock on the outer door. Gregg was standing by the window, knotting his tie as he looked out on the city. "Yes?"

"It's Billy, Senator. Kahina and her group are here. I've told the others. Should I send her on to the conference room?"

"Just a second."

Sara called quietly from the open door of the bathroom, "I'll go down to my own room."

"You might as well stay here for a bit. Billy will make sure no one sees you leave. There'll be a press conference after, so you might want to head down in half an hour." Gregg went to the door, opened it slightly, and spoke to Billy. Then he stepped quickly to the door leading to the adjoining suite and knocked. "Ellen? Kahina's on her way."

Ellen came in as Gregg was putting on his jacket; Sara was brushing her hair. Ellen smiled automatically at Sara, nodding. Gregg could feel a mild annoyance in his wife, a glimmer of jealousy; he let Puppetman smooth that roughness, lathing it with cold blue. He needed very little effort; she had had no delusions about their marriage from the start—they had married because she was a Bonestell, and the New England Bonestells had always been involved in politics in one way or another. She understood how to play the supportive spouse: when to stand beside him; what to say and how to say it. She accepted that "men had needs" and didn't care as long as Gregg didn't flaunt it in public or stop her from having her own affairs. Ellen was among the most pliable of his puppets.

Deliberately, just for the small pleasure that Ellen's hidden distaste would give him, he hugged Sara. He could feel Sara holding back in Ellen's presence. *I can change that,* Puppetman murmured in his head. *See, there's so much affection in her. Just a twist, and I could . . .*

No! The depth of his response surprised Gregg. *We don't force her. We never touched Succubus; we won't touch Sara.*

Ellen watched the embrace blandly, and the smile never left her lips. "The two of you slept well, I hope." There was nothing in the tone beyond the mere words. Glacial, distant, her gaze left Sara; she smiled at Gregg. "Darling, we should go. And I want to talk to you about that reporter Downs—

he's been asking me the strangest questions, and he's talking to Chrysalis as well. . . ."

The meeting wasn't what he'd expected, though John Werthen had briefed him on the necessary protocol. The Arab guards along the wall, armed with a mixture of Uzis and Soviet-made automatic weapons, were unnerving. Billy Ray had carefully beefed up their own security. Gregg, Tachyon, and the other political members of the junket were in attendance. The aces and (especially) jokers were elsewhere in Damascus, as President al-Assad toured the city with them.

Kahina herself was a surprise. She was a small, petite woman. The ebony eyes above the veils were bright, inquisitive, and searching; her dress was plain except for a line of turquoise beads above her forehead. Translators accompanied her. In addition, a trio of burly men in bedouin dress sat nearby, watching.

"Kahina's a woman in a very conservative Islamic society, Senator," John had said. "I can't stress that enough. Her even *being* here is a break with tradition, allowed only because she's the prophet-twin of her brother and because they think she has magic, *sihr.* She's married to Sayyid, the general who masterminded Nur al-Allah's military victories. She might be the Kahina, and she's had a liberal education, but she's *not* a Westerner. Be careful. These people are quick to be insulted and very long on holding a grudge. And—Jesus, Senator— tell Tachyon to tone it down."

Gregg waved to Tachyon, dressed outrageously as usual, but with a new twist. Tachyon had abandoned the satins, too hot for him in this climate. Instead he looked as if he'd raided a bazaar in the *suq,* emerging as a movie-cliché vision of a sheikh: red, baggy silk trousers, a loose linen shirt and jacket with intricate brocade, bead and bangles jingling everywhere. His hair was hidden under an elaborate headdress; the long toes of his slippers turned up and curled back. Gregg decided not to comment. He shook hands with the others and seated Ellen as everyone found chairs. He nodded to Kahina and her entourage, who tore their gazes away from Tachyon.

"*Marhala,*" Gregg said: greetings.

Her eyes gleamed. She inclined her head. "I speak only a little English," she said slowly in a heavily accented, quiet voice. "It will be easier if my translator, Rashid, speaks for me."

Headsets had been provided; Gregg put his on. "We're delighted that Kahina would come to make arrangements for us to meet with Nur al-Allah. This is more honor than we deserve."

Her translator was speaking softly into his headset. Kahina nodded. She spoke in a stream of rapid Arabic. "The honor is that you have even gotten this close to meeting him, Senator," Rashid's husky voice translated. "The Qur'an says: 'For those who disbelieve in Allah and His apostle. We have prepared a blazing fire.'"

Gregg glanced toward Tachyon, who raised his eyebrows slightly under the headdress and shrugged. "We'd like to believe that we share a vision of peace with Nur al-Allah," Gregg answered slowly.

Kahina seemed almost amused by that. "Nur al-Allah, for this once, has chosen *my* vision. On his own, he might have stayed in the desert until you were gone . . ." Kahina was still speaking, but Rashid's voice had trailed into silence. Kahina glared at the man, saying something that made him grimace. One of the men with Kahina gestured harshly; Rashid cleared his throat and resumed.

"Or . . . or perhaps Nur al-Allah might have followed the advice of Sayyid and slain you and the abominations you bring with you."

Tachyon pressed back in his chair in shock; Lyons, the Republican senator, blustered, leaning over to Gregg to whisper, "And I thought *Barnett* was sick."

Inside Gregg, Puppetman stirred hungrily. Even without a direct mindlink, the surging emotions could be felt. Kahina's attendants were frowning, obviously upset by her candor but afraid to interfere with someone who was, after all, part of the twinned prophet. The guards around the wall tensed. The UN and Red Cross representatives consulted in whispers.

Kahina sat calmly in the middle of the turmoil, her hands folded on the tabletop, her regard on Gregg. The intensity of her stare was unnerving; he found himself struggling not to look away.

Tachyon leaned forward, his long fingers interlaced. "The 'abominations' are blameless," he said bluntly. "If anything, the responsibility should be laid at *my* feet. Your people would better serve the jokers with kindness than scorn and brutality. They were infected by a blind, horrible, and undiscriminating disease. So were you; you were simply lucky."

Her attendants muttered at that, darting angry stares at the alien, but Kahina answered calmly, "Allah is supreme. The virus might be blind, but Allah is not. Those who are worthy, He rewards. Those who are not, He strikes down."

"And what of the aces we brought with us, who worship another version of God, or perhaps none at all?" Tachyon persisted. "What of the aces in other countries who worship Buddha or Amaterasu or a Plumed Serpent or no gods at all?"

"The ways of Allah are subtle. I know that what He has spoken in the Qur'an is truth. I know that the visions He grants me contain truth. I know that when Nur al-Allah speaks in His voice, it is truth. Beyond that, it's folly to claim to understand Allah." Her voice now held an undertone of irritation, and Gregg knew Tachyon had hit a nerve with her.

Tachyon shook his head. "And I would claim that the ultimate folly is attempting to understand humans, who have made these gods," he retorted.

Gregg had listened to the exchange with growing excitement. To have Kahina for a puppet: she might be nearly as useful to him as Nur al-Allah himself. Until now he had dismissed Kahina's influence. He'd thought that a woman within this fundamentalist Islamic movement could wield no real power. Now he saw that his evaluation might have been wrong.

Kahina and Tachyon had locked gazes. Gregg held up his hand, making his voice reasonable, soothing.

"Please. Doctor, let me answer. Kahina, none of us have any intention of insulting your beliefs. We're here only to help your government deal with the problems of the wild card virus. My country has had to cope with the virus for the longest time; we've had the largest affected population. We're also here to learn, to see other techniques and resolutions. We can do that best by meeting with those who have the most influence. Throughout the Middle East we have heard that this person is Nur al-Allah. No one holds more power than he."

Kahina's gaze now flicked back to Gregg. The resentment had still not left the mahogany pupils. "You were in Allah's dreams," she said. "I saw you. Strings ran from your fingertips. As you tugged, the people held at the other ends moved."

My God! The shock and panic almost brought Gregg out of his seat. Puppetman snarled like a cornered dog in his head. His pulse pounded against his temples, and he could feel heat on his cheeks. *How could she know . . . ?*

Gregg made himself laugh, forced a smile to his lips. "That's a common dream of politicians," he said, as if she'd made a joke. "I was probably trying to make the voters check the right box on the ballot." There were chuckles around his side of the table at that. Gregg let his voice drift back to seriousness. "If I *could* control people, aside from being president already, I'd be pulling those strings that would make your brother meet with us. Could that be the meaning of your dream?"

Unblinking, she looked at him. "Allah *is* subtle."

You must take her. No matter that Tachyon is here or that it's dangerous because she's an ace. You must take her because of what she might say. You must take her because you may never meet Nur al-Allah. She is here, now.

The power in Gregg was impatient, eager; he forced it back down. "What will convince Nur al-Allah, Kahina?"

A burst of Arabic; Rashid's voice spoke in Gregg's ear. "Allah will convince him."

"And you. You're his adviser too. What will you tell him?"

"We argued when I said Allah's dreams told me to come to Damascus." Her escorts were muttering again. One of them touched her shoulder and whispered into her ear fiercely. Kahina shook her head. "I will tell my brother what Allah's dreams tell me to say. Nothing more. My own words have no weight."

Tachyon pushed his chair back. "Senator, I suggest that we waste no further time with this. I want to see the few clinics the Syrian government has bothered to set up. Maybe *there* I can accomplish something."

Gregg looked around the table; the others were nodding. Kahina's own people looked impatient. Gregg rose. "Then we'll wait for word from you, Kahina. Please, I beg you, tell your brother that sometimes when you know an enemy, you find that he is no enemy at all. We're here to help. That's all."

As Kahina stood, taking off her headset, Gregg casually held out his hand to her, ignoring the contempt the gesture elicited from her escorts. When Kahina didn't respond by taking his hand, he kept his hand extended. "We have a saying that, in Rome, one is supposed to act Roman," he commented, hoping she would understand the words or that Rashid would translate. "Still, the first step in understanding someone is to know their customs. One of ours is that peers shake hands to show understanding."

He thought for a moment that the ploy had failed, that the opportunity would pass. He was almost glad. Opening the mind and will of an ace who had already terrified him with her unknowing perception, and doing so with Tachyon standing alongside him, watching...

Then her hand, surprisingly white against the midnight darkness of her robes, brushed against his fingers.

You must ...

Gregg slid along the curving, branching tendrils of the nervous system, watching for blocks and traps, watching especially for any sign of awareness of his presence. Had he felt that, he would have fled as quickly as he'd entered. He'd always been extremely cautious with aces, even with those who he knew had no mental powers. Kahina seemed unaware of his penetration.

He opend her, setting up the entrances he would use later. Puppetman sighed at the swirling maelstrom of emotion he found there. Kahina was rich, complicated. The hues of her mind were saturated and strong. He could sense her attitude toward him: a brilliant gold-green hope, the ocher of suspicion, a vein of marbled pity/disgust for his world. And yet there was glimmering envy underneath as well, and a yearning that seemed tied to her feelings for her brother.

He followed that trail backward and was surprised at the pure, bitter gall he found there. It had been carefully concealed, layered under safer, more benign emotions and sealed with respect for Allah's favoring of Nur al-Allah, but it was there. It throbbed at his touch, alive.

It took only a moment. Her hand had already withdrawn, but the contact was established. He stayed with her for a few more seconds to be sure, and then he came back to himself.

Gregg smiled. It was done, and he was still safe. Kahina hadn't noticed; Tachyon hadn't suspected.

"We're all grateful for your presence," Gregg said. "Tell Nur al-Allah that all we wish is understanding. Doesn't the

Qur'an itself begin with the exordium 'In the name of Allah, the Compassionate, the Merciful'? We've come out of a sense of that same compassion."

"Is that the gift you bring, Senator?" she asked in English, and Gregg could feel the wistfulness surging from her opened mind.

"I think," he told her, "it's the same gift you would give yourself."

WEDNESDAY, FEBRUARY 4, 1987, DAMASCUS:

The knock on her hotel door woke Sara from sleep. Groggy, she glanced first at her travel clock: 1:35 A.M. local time—it felt much later. *Still jet lagged. Too early for Gregg, though.*

She put a robe on, rubbing her eyes as she went to the door. The security people had been very definite about the risks here in Damascus. She didn't stand directly in front of the door, but leaned over toward the central peephole. Glancing through, she saw the distorted face of an Arabic woman, swathed in the *chador*. The eyes, the fine structure of the face were familiar, as were the sea-blue beads sewn in the *chador*'s headpiece. "Kahina?" she queried.

"Yes," came the muffled voice from the hallway. "Please. I would talk."

"Just a minute." Sara ran a hand through her hair. She exchanged the thin, lacy robe she'd put on for a heavier, more concealing one. She unchained the door, opened it a crack.

A heavy hand threw the door entirely open, and Sara stifled a shout. A burly man scowled at her, a handgun gripped in his large fist. He ignored Sara after an initial glance and prowled through her room, opening the closet door, peering into the bathroom. He grunted, then went back to the door. He spoke something in Arabic, and then Kahina entered. Her bodyguard shut the door behind her and stationed himself near it.

"I'm sorry," Kahina said. Her voice struggled with the English, but her eyes seemed kind. She gestured in the direction of the guard. "In our society, a woman..."

"I think I understand," Sara said. The man was staring rudely at her; Sara tightened the robe's sash and tugged the neckline higher. Involuntarily she yawned. Kahina seemed to smile under her veil.

"Again I am sorry I woke you, but the dream..." She shrugged. "May I sit?"

"Please." Sara waved toward two chairs by the window. The guard grunted. He spoke in rapid-fire syllables. "He says not by the window," Kahina translated. "Too unsafe."

Sara dragged the chairs to the center of the room; that seemed to satisfy the guard, who leaned back against the wall. Kahina took one of the chairs, the dark cloth of her robes rustling. Sara seated herself carefully on the other.

"You were at the meeting?" Kahina asked when they were settled.

"At the press conference afterward, you mean? Yes."

Kahina nodded. "I saw you there. I knew your face from Allah's dreams. I come here now because of tonight's dream."

"You say *my* face was in your dreams?"

Kahina nodded. Sara found that the *chador* made it nearly impossible to read the hidden face. There were only Kahina's piercing eyes above the veils. Yet there seemed to be a deep kindness in them, an empathy. Sara felt herself warming to the woman. "At the... *conference*"—Kahina stumbled over the word—"I said that Nur al-Allah waited to hear of my dreams before he would decide to meet with your people. I've just had his dream."

"Then why come to me instead of your brother?"

"Because in the dream I was told to come to you."

Sara shook her head. "I don't understand. We don't know each other; I was just one of a dozen or more reporters there."

"You're in love with *him*."

She knew who Kahina meant. She knew, but the protest was automatic. "Him?"

"The one with a double face. The one with strings. Hartmann." When Sara didn't answer, Kahina reached out and touched her hand gently. The gesture was sisterly and strangely knowing. "You love the one you once hated," Kahina said. Her hand had not left Sara's.

Sara found that she could not lie, not to Kahina's open, vulnerable eyes. "I suppose so. You're the Seer; can you tell me how it turns out?" Sara said it jokingly, but Kahina either missed the inflection or chose to ignore it.

"You are happy for the moment, even though you are not his wife, even though you sin. I understand that." Kahina's fingers pressed against Sara's. "I understand how hate can be a blunted sword, how it can be beat upon until you begin to think it something else."

"You're confusing me, Kahina." Sara sat back, wishing she were completely awake, wishing that Gregg were there. Kahina withdrew her hand.

"Let me tell the dream." Kahina closed her eyes. She folded her hands in her lap. "I . . . I saw Hartmann, with his two faces, one pleasant to see, the other twisted like an abomination of Allah. *You* were beside him, not his wife, and the face that was pleasant smiled. I could see your feelings for him, how your hatred had been turned. My brother and I were there also, and my brother pointed to the abomination within Hartmann. The abomination spat, and the spittle fell upon me. I saw myself, and *my* face was yours. And I saw that I too had another face within my veils, an abomination-face ugly with spite. Hartmann reached out and twisted my head until only the abomination could be seen.

"For a time the images of the dream were confused. I thought I saw a knife, and I saw Sayyid, my husband, struggling with me. Then the images cleared, and I saw a dwarf, and the dwarf spoke. He said: 'Tell her that underneath the hate still lives. Tell her to remember that. The hate will protect you.' The dwarf laughed, and his laugh was evil. I did not like him."

Her eyes opened, and there was a distant terror in them.

Sara started to speak, stopped, began again. "I . . . Kahina, I don't know what any of that means. It's just random images, no better than the dreams I have myself. Does it mean something to you?"

"It's Allah's dream," Kahina insisted, her voice harsh with intensity. "I could feel His power in it. I understand this: My brother will meet with your people."

"Gregg—Senator Hartmann—and the others will be glad to know that. Believe me, we mean only to help your people."

"Then why is the dream so fearful?"

"Maybe because there's always fear in change."

Kahina blinked. Suddenly the openness was gone. She was isolated, as hidden as her face behind the *veils*. "I said something very like that to Nur al-Allah once. He did not like the thought any more than I do now." She rose swiftly to her feet. The guard came to attention by the door. "I am glad we met," she said. "I will see you again in the desert." She went to the door.

"Kahina—"

She turned, waiting.

"Was that all you wanted to tell me?"

The shadow of her veils hid her eyes. "I wanted to tell you one thing only," she said. "I wore your face in the dream. I think we are very alike; I feel we are . . . like kin. What this man you love would do to me, he might also do to you."

She nodded to the guard. They stepped quickly into the hallway and were gone.

WEDNESDAY, FEBRUARY 4, 1987, IN THE SYRIAN DESERT:

It was the most barren landscape Gregg had ever seen. The windows were thick with grime kicked up by the 'copter's blades. Below them, the land was desolate. The vegetation was sparse and dry, clinging to life in the volcanic rock of the desert plateau. The land around the coast had been relatively lush, but the date palms and arable farmland had given way to pines as the trio of helicopters left the mountains of Jabal Duriz. Then there were only hawthorns and bristly scrub. The only life they saw was in the occasional settlement, where robed and turbaned men looked up from goat herds with suspicious eyes.

The ride was long, noisy, and distinctly uncomfortable. The air was turbulent, and the faces around Gregg were sour. He glanced back at Sara; she gave him a halfhearted smile and shrug. The choppers began to descend toward a small town that seemed under siege by brightly colored tents, set in the folds of a prehistoric river valley. The sun was setting behind the barren, purpled hills; the lights of campfires dotted the area.

Billy Ray came back as the helicopter threw swirling gales of dust through the canvas. "Joanne said it's okay to land, Senator," Billy half-shouted through the clamor of the engines, cupping his mouth. "I want you to know that I still don't like it."

"We're safe enough, Billy," Gregg shouted back. "The man would have to be crazy to do anything to us."

Billy gave him a sidelong look. "Uh-huh. He's a fanatic. The Nur sect has been linked to terrorism everywhere in the

Middle East. Going to *his* headquarters, at *his* beck and call, and with the limited resources I have is cutting Security's throat."

He sounded more excited than worried—Carnifex *enjoyed* fighting—but Gregg could feel a faint, cold undercurrent of fear under Ray's swelling anticipation. He reached into Billy's mind and tweaked that fear, enjoying the sensation as the feeling heightened. Gregg told himself that it wasn't simply for enjoyment, but because paranoia would make Ray even more effective if there was trouble. "I appreciate your concerns, Billy," he said. "But we're here. Let's see what we can do."

The 'copters landed in a central square near the mosque. They filed out, all but Tachyon shivering in the evening chill. Only a portion of the delegation had taken the flight from Damascus. Nur al-Allah had forbidden any "loathsome abominations" to come to this place; the list had excluded all obvious jokers such as Father Squid or Chrysalis; Radha and Fantasy had decided on their own to remain in Damascus. Most of the spouses and much of the scientific team had remained behind as well. The haughtiness of Nur al-Allah's "invitation" had angered many of the contingent; there had been a bitter debate over whether they should go at all. Gregg's insistence had finally won out.

"Look, I find his demands as distasteful as anyone. But the man's a legitimate force here. He rules Syria and a good portion of Jordan and Saudi as well. It doesn't matter who the elected leaders are—Nur al-Allah has united the sects. I don't like his teachings or his methods, but I can't deny his power. If we turn our backs on him, we change *nothing*. His prejudice, his violence, his hatred will continue to spread. If we *do* meet him, well, at least there's a chance we can get him to temper his harshness."

He'd laughed self-deprecatingly, shaking his head at his own argument. "I don't think we have a prayer, really. Still . . . it's something we're going to face, if not with Nur al-Allah, then back home with fundamentalists such as Leo Barnett. Prejudice isn't going to go away because we ignore it."

Puppetman, reaching out, had made certain that Hiram, Peregrine, and the others open to him murmured agreement. The rest had reluctantly withdrawn their objections, even if most decided to remain behind in protest.

In the end the aces willing to meet with Nur al-Allah had been Hiram, Peregrine, Braun, and Jones. Senator Lyons had decided to go at the last minute. Tachyon, to Gregg's dismay, insisted on being included. Reporters and security people swelled the ranks further.

Kahina stepped out from the mosque as the *chuff* of the blades slowed and the steps were let down from the doors of the helicopters. She bowed to them as they disembarked. "Nur al-Allah bids you welcome," she said. "Please, follow me."

Gregg heard Peregrine's sudden intake of breath as Kahina motioned to them. In the same moment he felt a surge of indignation and panic. He glanced over his shoulder to see Peregrine's wings folded protectively around herself, her gaze fixed on the ground near the mosque. He followed her stare.

A fire had flared up between the buildings. In its flickering light they could all see three flyblown bodies crumpled against the wall, rocks scattered around them. The nearest body was unmistakably a joker, the face elongated into a furry snout and the hands hornlike claws. The smell hit them then, ripe and foul; Gregg could feel the swelling of shock and disgust. Lyons was being desperately and loudly sick; Jack Braun muttered a curse. Inside, Puppetman grinned gleefully while Gregg frowned.

"What is this outrage?" Tachyon demanded of Kahina.

Gregg let himself drift into her mind and found shifting hues of confusion. She'd looked back at the bodies herself, and Gregg felt the quick stab of betrayal within her. Yet when Kahina looked back, she'd covered it with the placid emerald of faith, and her voice was a careful monotone, her gaze flat. "They were . . . abominations. Allah placed the mark of their unworthiness on them, and their death is nothing. That is what Nur al-Allah has decreed."

"Senator, we are *leaving*," Tachyon declared. "This is an intolerable insult. Kahina, tell Nur al-Allah that we will protest most strongly to your government." His aristocratic face was tight with controlled fury, his hands clenched at his sides. But before any of them could move, Nur al-Allah stepped from the arched entrance to the mosque.

Gregg had no doubt that Nur al-Allah had chosen the time to best display himself. In the darkening night he appeared like a medieval painting of Christ, a holy radiance speading out from him. He wore a thin *djellaba* through which his skin gleamed, his beard and hair dark against the glow. "Nur al-Allah is Allah's prophet," he said in accented English. "If Allah would let you go, you may go. If He would bid you stay, you will stay."

Nur al-Allah's voice was a cello—a glorious, rich instrument. Gregg knew that he should answer, but couldn't. Everyone in the party was silent; Tachyon froze halfway in his turn back to the helicopters. Gregg had to fight to make his mouth work. His mind was filled with cobwebs, and it was only Puppetman's strength that allowed him to break those bonds. When he did reply, his own voice sounded thin and harsh. "Nur al-Allah allows the murder of innocents."

"Nur al-Allah allows the murder of innocents. That's not the power of Allah. That's only the failing of a man," Gregg rasped.

Sara wanted to shout agreement, but her voice wouldn't obey. Everyone stood as if stunned. Alongside Sara, Digger Downs had been scribbling frantically in his notebook; he'd stopped, the pencil forgotten in his hand.

Sara felt quick fright—for herself, for Gregg, for everyone. *We shouldn't have come. That voice* . . . They'd known Nur al-Allah was an accomplished orator; they'd even suspected that some ace power rode in it, but no reports had said that it was this powerful.

"Man fails when he fails Allah," Nur al-Allah answered placidly. His voice wove a soft spell, a blanketing numbness. When he spoke, his words seemed filled with truth. "You think me deranged; I'm not. You think me a threat; I threaten only Allah's enemies. You think me harsh and cruel; if that's so, then it's only because Allah is harsh with sinners. Follow me."

He turned, walking quickly back into the mosque. Peregrine and Hiram were already moving to follow; Jack Braun looked dazed as he strode after the prophet; Downs brushed past Sara. Sara fought the compulsion, but her legs were possessed. She shambled forward with the rest. Of the party, only Tachyon was immune to Nur al-Allah's power. His features strained, he stood stiffly immobile in the middle of the court. As Sara passed him, he looked back at the helicopters; then, with a glare, let himself be drawn with her into the interior of the mosque.

Oil lamps lit shadowed recesses among the pillars. In the front, Nur al-Allah stood on the dais of the *minbar*, the pulpit. Kahina stood at his right hand, and Sara recognized the gargantuan figure of Sayyid at his left. Guards with automatic weapons moved to stations around the room as Sara and the others milled around the *minbar* in confusion.

"Hear the words of Allah," Nur al-Allah intoned. It was as if some deity were speaking, for his voice thundered and roared. Its fury and scorn made them tremble, wondering that the very stones of the mosque didn't fall as the power throbbed. "'As for the unbelievers, because of their misdeeds, ill fortune shall not cease to afflict them or crouch at their very doorstep.' And He also says: 'Woe to the lying sinner! He heard the revelations of Allah recited to Him and then, as though he never heard them, persists in scorn. Those that deride Our revelations when they have scarcely heard them shall be put to a shameful punishment. Those that deny the revelations of their Lord shall suffer the torment of a hideous scourge.'"

Sara found unbidden tears streaking down her cheeks. The quotations seemed to burn, etching her soul like acid. Though a part of her struggled, she wanted to shout to Nur al-Allah and beg him for forgiveness. She looked for Gregg and saw him near the *minbar*. Tendons corded in his neck; he seemed to be reaching out for Nur al-Allah, and there was no repentance in his face. *Can't you see?* she wanted to say. *Can't you see how wrong we've been?*

And then, though Nur al-Allah's voice was still deep and resonant, the energy was gone from it. Sara wiped away tears angrily as his bright, sardonic face smiled. "You see? You feel the power of Allah. You came here to know your enemy—then know that he is strong. His strength is God's, and you could no more defeat that than you could crack the spine of the world itself." He lifted his hand, fisted it before them. "Allah's power is here. With it I will sweep all unbelievers from this land. Do you think I need guards to hold you?" Nur al-Allah spat. *"Ptah!* My voice alone is your prison; should I want you to die, I'll simply command it of you and you'll place the barrel in your own mouth. I'll raze Israel to the very ground; I will take the ones marked by the Scourge of Allah and make them slaves; those with power that refuse to give themselves to Allah I will kill. That is what I offer to you. No parley, no compromise, only the fist of Allah."

"And that we cannot allow." The voice was Tachyon's, from the back of the mosque. Sara allowed herself to feel a desperate hope.

"And that we cannot allow." Gregg heard the words as his fingers strained toward Nur al-Allah's sandals. Puppetman added his strength, but it was as if Nur al-Allah stood atop a mountain and Gregg were reaching vainly up from the foot. Beads of sweat stood out on his forehead. Sayyid glanced down scornfully, not even deigning to kick Gregg's hand away from his master.

Nur al-Allah laughed at Tachyon's words. "You'd challenge me, you who do not believe in Allah? I can feel you, Dr. Tachyon. I can feel your power prying at my mind. You believe that my mind can be broken the way you might break the mind of one of your companions. That's not so. Allah protects me, and Allah will punish those who attack him."

Yet even as he spoke, Gregg saw the strain on Nur al-Allah's face. His radiance seemed to dim, and the barriers holding Gregg loosened. Whatever the prophet's boast, Tachyon's mental attack was getting through. Gregg felt a quick hope.

At that moment, with Nur al-Allah's attention on Tachyon, Gregg managed to touch the shimmering flesh of the prophet's foot. The emerald radiance burned hot; he ignored it. Puppetman shouted in triumph.

And then quickly recoiled. Nur al-Allah was *there*. He was aware, and Gregg could sense Tachyon's presence as well. *Too dangerous*, Puppetman cried. *He knows, he knows*. From behind, there was a thud and strangled cry, and Gregg looked back over his shoulder at the doctor.

One of the guards had come up behind Tachyon, clubbing the alien on the head with the butt of his Uzi. Tachyon was on his knees, his hands covering his head, moaning. He struggled to rise, but the guard struck him down brutally. Tachyon lay unconcious on the tiled mosaic of the floor, his breathing labored.

Nur al-Allah laughed. He looked down at Gregg, whose hand still reached futilely toward the foot of the prophet. "There, you see? I am protected: by Allah, by my people. What about *you*, Senator Hartmann, you with Kahina's strings? Do you still want me now? Perhaps I should show you the strings of Allah and make you dance for His pleasure. Kahina

said you are a danger, and Sayyid wants you killed. So
perhaps you should be the first sacrifice. How would your
people react if they saw you confess your crimes and then,
begging Allah's forgiveness, kill yourself? Would that be
effective, do you think?"

Nur al-Allah pointed a finger at Gregg. "Yes," he said. "I
think it would."

Puppetman yammered in fear.

"Yes, I think it would."

Misha listened to her brother's words with unease. Everything he had done was a slap in her face: the flaunting of
the stoned jokers, the attack on Tachyon, his haughty threats
now. Najib betrayed her with every word.

Najib had used her and lied to her, he and Sayyid. He'd
let her go to Damascus thinking that she was representing
them, that if she brought the Americans, there might be a
chance of some agreement. But Najib hadn't cared. He hadn't
listened to her warnings that he overreached himself. A slow
festering rose inside her, leaching away her faith. *Allah. I
believe in Your voice within Najib. But now he shows his own
second face. Is it Yours, as well?*

The doubt diluted the magic of Najib's voice, and she
dared to speak and interrupt him.

"You move too fast, Najib," she hissed. "Don't destroy us
with your pride."

His glowing face contorted, his speech halting in mid-
sentence. "*I* am the Prophet," he snapped. "Not you."

"Then at least listen to me, who sees our future. This is a
mistake, Najib. This way leads away from Allah."

"Be *silent!*" he roared, and his fist lashed out. A
red-hued dizziness blinded her. In that moment, with
Najib's voice dulled by pain, something in her mind gave
way, some barrier that had been holding back all the
venom. This fury was cold and deadly, poisonous with
every insult and abuse Najib had given her over the years,
laced with frustration and denial and subjugation. Najib
had turned away from her, expecting her obedience. He
resumed his tirade, the power of the voice coiling out over
the crowd once more.

It could not touch her, not through what spilled from the
bitter pool.

She saw the knife in his sash and knew what she had

to do. The compulsion was too great for her to resist. She leapt at Najib, screaming wordlessly.

Sara saw Nur al-Allah point his glowing finger toward Gregg. Yet in following that gesture, her attention was snagged by Kahina. Sara frowned even under the spell of Nur al-Allah's words, for Kahina was trembling—she stared at her brother and there was nothing in her eyes but acid. She shouted something to him in Arabic, and he swung around to her, still pulsing with flaring power. They exchanged words; he struck her.

It was as if that blow had driven her into a divine madness. Kahina leapt at Nur al-Allah like some predatory cat, screaming as she clawed at him with bare hands. Dark rivulets of blood dimmed the moon of his face. She tugged at the long, curved knife in his sash, pulling it from the bejeweled scabbard. In the same motion she slashed across his throat with the keen edge. Nur al-Allah clutched at his neck, blood pouring between his fingers as a strangled, wet gasping came from him. He toppled backward.

For a moment the horror held everyone in suspension, then the room erupted into shouts. Kahina was standing in shock above Nur al-Allah, the knife dangling from white fingers. Sayyid bellowed in disbelief, swinging a huge arm that sent Kahina tumbling to the floor. Sayyid took a clumsy step forward—Sara realized with a start that the giant was a cripple. Two of the guards seized Kahina, dragging her to her feet as she struggled. Other men crouched beside the stricken Nur al-Allah, trying to stanch the flow of blood.

Sayyid had reached Kahina. He picked up the dagger she'd dropped, staring at the dark stains on it. He wailed, his eyes raised to heaven, and then drew the blade back to stab her.

But he moaned, the blade still raised. He sagged, his knees buckling as if some great weight were pressing down on him from above, crushing him. Sayyid screamed in agony, dropping the weapon. His massive body collapsed in on itself, the skeleton no longer able to support the flesh. Everyone heard the dry, sickening crack of snapping bones. Sara glanced around and saw Hiram sweating, his right fist squeezing into a white-knuckled fist.

Sayyid whimpered, a shapeless mass on the tiles. The guards let go of Kahina in confusion.

Kahina ran. One of the guards brought his Uzi to bear,

but he was slammed against the wall by Mordecai Jones. Jack
Braun, glowing golden, picked up another of the Nur al-
Allah's guards and tossed him bodily across the room. Peregrine, her feathers molting, was unable to take to the air.
Still, she slipped on her taloned gloves and slashed at a
guard. Billy Ray, with an exultant whoop, spun and kicked
the knees of the gunman alongside him.

Kahina ducked through an archway and was gone.

Sara found Gregg in the confusion. He was safe; a wave
of relief flooded through her. She began to run toward him,
and the relief turned frigid.

There was no more fright on *his* face, no concern at all.
He seemed calm. He almost seemed to smile.

Sara gaped. She felt nothing but a yawning emptiness.
"No," she whispered to herself.

What he would do to me, he would also do to you.

"No," she insisted. "That can't be."

Nur al-Allah had pointed his accusing finger at Gregg,
and Gregg had known that his only hope lay in the bitterness
within Kahina. Nur al-Allah was beyond his control, he knew
now, but Kahina was his. Gregg's rape of her mind was brutal
and ruthless. He'd stripped everything from her but that
underlying hate, letting it flood and swell. It had worked
beyond his expectations.

But he'd wanted Kahina dead. He'd wanted her silenced. It must have been Hiram that had stopped Sayyid—
too chivalrous to give Kahina to Islamic justice and strangely
brutal with his power. Gregg berated himself for not having
foreseen that; he could have controlled Hiram, long a puppet,
even with the strange hues he'd seen in the man lately. Now
the moment was gone, the spell broken with the loss of Nur
al-Allah's voice. Gregg let himself touch Hiram's mind and
saw that faint, odd coloring there again. He had no time to
muse on it.

People were shouting. An Uzi chattered, deafening.

In the midst of chaos Gregg felt Sara. He swung about to
find her staring at him. Emotions were shifting wildly inside
her. Her love was tattered, stretched thin under swelling
ocher suspicion. "Sara," he called, and her gaze slid sharply
away, looking at the press of people around Nur al-Allah.

There was fighting all around him. He thought he saw
Billy, glee on his face, dive bodily at a guard.

Let me have Sara or you've lost her. Puppetman sounded oddly sad. *There's nothing you can say to undo the damage. She's all you can salvage from this. Give her to me, or she's gone too.*

No, she can't know. It's not possible that she knows. Gregg protested, but he knew that he was wrong. He could see the damage in her mind. No lie could repair that.

Grieving, he entered her mind and caressed the torn azure fabric of her affection. Gregg watched as—slowly, carefully—Puppetman buried her distrust under bright and soft ribbons of false love.

He hugged her quickly. "Come on," he said gruffly. "We're leaving."

Out in the room Billy Ray stood over an unconscious guard. His strident voice ordered his security people into position. "Move! You—get the doctor. Senator Hartmann—now! Let's get out of here!" There was still some resistance on the floor, but Nur al-Allah's people were in shock. Most knelt around Nur al-Allah's prone body. The prophet was still alive: Gregg could sense his fright, his pain. Gregg wanted Nur al-Allah dead, too, but there was no opportunity for that.

Gunfire erupted near Gregg. Braun, glowing intensely now, stepped in front of the hidden gunman; they could hear the whine of the slugs ricocheting from his body. Gregg grunted in shock even as Braun tore the weapon away from the man. A lancing fire slammed into his shoulder, the impact staggering him. "Gregg!" he heard Sara cry.

On his knees, he groaned. He pulled his hand away from his shoulder and saw his fingers bright with blood. The room spun around him; Puppetman cowered.

"Joanne, get 'em out! The Senator's hit!" Billy Ray moved Sara aside and crouched beside Gregg. He carefully stripped the bloodstained jacket from the senator to examine the wound. Gregg could feel relief flood through the man. "You'll be okay—a good, long graze, that's all. Let me give you a hand—"

"I can make it," he grated through clenched teeth, struggling to his feet. Sara took his good arm, helping him up. He gulped air—there was violence all around him, and Puppetman was too dazed to even feed. He forced himself to think, to ignore the throbbing pain. "Billy, go on. Get the others." There was little to do. The remainder of Nur al-Allah's people were tending to their prophet; Peregrine had slipped outside; Jones and Braun were shepherding Lyons and the other dignitaries. Hiram had turned Tachyon nearly weightless and was assisting him outside as the doctor shook his head groggily. No one resisted their retreat.

Sara let Gregg lean against her as they fled. As they tumbled into seats in the helicopter, she hugged him softly.

"I'm glad you're safe," she whispered. She took his hand as the chopper's blades tore the night air.

It was as if Gregg grasped a doll's wooden hand. It meant nothing. Nothing at all.

FROM *THE JOURNAL OF XAVIER DESMOND*

FEBRUARY 7/KABUL, AFGHANISTAN:

I am in a good deal of pain today. Most of the delegates have gone on a day trip to various historic sights, but I elected to stay at the hotel once again.

Our tour... what can I say? Syria has made headlines around the world. Our press contingent has doubled in size, all of them eager to get the inside story of what happened out in the desert. For once, I am not unhappy to have been excluded. Peri has told me what it was like....

Syria has touched all of us, myself included. Not all of my pain is caused by the cancer. There are times when I grow profoundly weary, looking back over my life and wondering whether I have done any good at all, or if all my life's work has been for nothing. I have tried to speak out on behalf of my people, to appeal to reason and decency and the common humanity that unites us all, and I have always been convinced that quiet strength, perseverance, and nonviolence would get us further in the long run. Syria makes me wonder... how do you reason with a man like the Nur al-Allah, compromise with him, talk to him? How do you appeal to his humanity when he does not consider you human at all? If there is a God, I pray that he forgives me, but I find myself wishing they had killed the Nur.

Hiram has left the tour, albeit temporarily. He promises to rejoin us in India, but by now he is back in New York City, after jetting from Damascus to Rome and then catching a Concorde back to America. He told us that an emergency had arisen at Aces High that demanded his personal attention, but I suspect the truth is that Syria shook him more than he cared to admit. The rumor has swept round the plane that Hiram lost control in the desert, that he hit General Sayyid with far more weight than was necessary to stop him. Billy Ray, of course, doesn't think Hiram went far enough. "If it'd been me, I would have piled it on till he was just a brown and red stain on the floor," he told me.

Worchester himself refused to talk about it and insisted that he was taking this brief leave of us simply because he was "sick unto death of stuffed grape leaves," but even as he made the joke, I noticed beads of sweat on his broad, bald forehead and a slight tremor in his hand. I hope a short respite restores him; the more we have traveled together, the more I have to come to respect Hiram Worchester.

If clouds do indeed have a silver lining, however, then perhaps one good did come out of the monstrous incident in Syria: Gregg Hartmann's stature seems to have been vastly enhanced by his near brush with death. For a decade now his political fortunes have been haunted by the specter of the Great Jokertown Riot in 1976, when he "lost his head" in public. To me his reaction was only human—he had just witnessed a woman being torn to pieces by a mob, after all. But presidential candidates are not allowed to weep or grieve or rage like the rest of us, as Muskie proved in '72 and Hartmann confirmed in '76.

Syria may finally have put that tragic incident to rest. Everyone who was there agrees that Hartmann's behavior was exemplary—he was firm, cool-headed, courageous, a pillar of strength in the face of the Nur's barbarous threats. Every paper in America has run the AP photo that was taken as they pulled out: Hiram helping Tachyon into the helicopter in the background, while in the foreground Senator Hartmann waited, his face streaked with dust, yet still grim and strong, his blood soaking through the sleeve of his white shirt.

Gregg still claims that he is not going to be a presidential candidate in 1988, and indeed all the polls show that Gary Hart has an overwhelming lead for the Democratic nomination, but Syria and the photograph will surely do wonders for his name recognition and his standing. I find myself desperately hoping that he will reconsider. I have nothing against Gary Hart, but Gregg Hartmann is something special, and perhaps for those of us touched by the wild card, he is our last best hope.

If Hartmann fails, all my hopes fail with him, and then what choice will we have but to turn to the Black Dog?

I suppose I should write something about Afghanistan, but there is little to record. I don't have the strength to see what sights Kabul has to offer. The Soviets are much in evidence here, but they are being very correct and courteous. The war is being kept at arm's length for the duration of our short stopover. Two Afghan jokers have been produced for our approval, both of whom swear (through Soviet interpreters) that a joker's life is idyllic here. Somehow I am not convinced. If I understand correctly, they are the only two jokers in all of Afghanistan.

The *Stacked Deck* flew directly from Baghdad to Kabul. Iran was out of the question. The Ayatollah shares many of the Nur's views on wild cards, and he rules his nation in name as well as fact, so even the UN could not secure us permission to land. At least the Ayatollah makes no distinctions between aces and jokers—we are all the demon children of the Great Satan, according to him. Obviously he has not forgotten Jimmy Carter's ill-fated attempt to free the hostages, when a half-dozen government aces were sent in on a secret mission that turned into a horrid botch. The rumor is that Carnifex was one of the aces involved, but Billy Ray emphatically denies it. "If I'd been along, we would have gotten our people out and kicked the old man's ass for good measure," he says. His colleague from Justice, Lady Black, just pulls her black cloak more tightly about herself and smiles enigmatically. Mistral's father, Cyclone, has often been linked to that doomed mission as well, but it's not something she'll talk about.

Tomorrow morning we'll fly over the Khyber Pass and cross into India, a different world entirely, a whole sprawling subcontinent, with the largest joker population anywhere outside the United States.

FEBRUARY 12/CALCUTTA:

India is as strange and fabulous a land as any we have seen on this trip... if indeed it is correct to call it a land at all. It seems more like a hundred lands in one. I find it hard to connect the Himalayas and the palaces of the Moguls to the slums of Calcutta and Bengali jungles. The Indians themselves live in a dozen different worlds, from the aging Britishers who try to pretend that the Viceroy still rules in their little enclaves of the Raj, to the maharajas and nawabs who are kings in all but name, to the beggars on the streets of this sprawling filthy city.

There is so *much* of India.

In Calcutta you see jokers on the streets everywhere you go. They are as common as beggars, naked children, and corpses, and too frequently one and the same. In this quasi-nation of Hindu and Moslem and Sikh, the vast majority of jokers seem to be Hindu, but given Islam's attitudes, that can hardly be a surprise. The orthodox Hindu has invented a new caste for the joker, far below even the untouchable, but at least they are allowed to live.

Interestingly enough, we have found no jokertowns in India. This culture is sharply divided along racial and ethnic grounds, and the enmities run very deep, as was clearly shown in the Calcutta wild card riots of 1947, and the wholesale nationwide carnage that accompanied the partition of the subcontinent that same year. Despite that, today you find Hindu and Muslim and Sikh living side by side on the same street, and jokers and nats and even a few pathetic deuces sharing the same hideous slums. It does not seem to have made them love each other any more, alas.

India also boasts a number of native aces, including a few of considerable power. Digger is having a grand time dashing about the country interviewing them all, or as many as will consent to meet with him.

Radha O'Reilly, on the other hand, is obviously very unhappy here. She is Indian royalty herself, it appears, at least on her mother's side ... her father was some sort of Irish adventurer. Her people practice a variety of Hinduism built around Gonesh, the elephant god, and the black mother Kali, and to them her wild card ability makes her the destined bride of Gonesh, or something along those lines. At any rate she seems firmly convinced that she is in imminent danger of being kidnapped and forcibly returned to her homeland, so except for the official receptions in New Delhi and Bombay, she has remained closely closeted in the various hotels, with Carnifex, Lady Black, and the rest of our security close at hand. I believe she will be very happy to leave India once again.

Dr. Tachyon, Peregrine, Mistral, Fantasy, Troll, and the Harlem Hammer have just returned from a tiger hunt in the Bengal. Their host was one of the Indian aces, a maharaja blessed with a form of the midas touch. I understand that the gold he creates is inherently unstable and reverts to its original state within twenty-four hours, although the process of transmutation is still sufficient to kill any living thing he touches. Still, his palace is reputed to be quite a spectacular place. He's solved the traditional mythic dilemma by having his servants feed him.

Tachyon returned from the expedition in as good a spirit as I've seen him since Syria, wearing a golden nehru jacket and matching turban, fastened by a ruby the size of my thumb. The maharaja was lavish with his gifts, it seems. Even the prospect of the jacket and turban reverting to common cloth in a few hours does not seem to have dampened our alien's enthusiasm for the day's activities. The glittering pageant of the hunt, the splendors of the palace, and the maharaja's harem all seem to have reminded Tach of the pleasures and prerogatives he once enjoyed as a prince of the Ilkazam on his home world. He admitted that even on Takis there was no sight to compare to the end of the hunt, when the maneater had been brought to bay and the maharaja calmly approached it, removed one golden glove, and transmuted the huge beast to solid gold with a touch.

While our aces were accepting their presents of fairy gold and hunting tigers, I spent the day in humbler pursuits, in the unexpected company of Jack Braun, who was invited to the hunt with the others but declined. Instead Braun and I made our way across Calcutta to visit the monument the Indians erected to Earl Sanderson on the site where he saved Mahatma Gandhi from assassination.

The memorial resembles a Hindu temple and the statue inside looks more like some minor Indian deity than an American black who played football for Rutgers, but still . . . Sanderson has indeed become some sort of god to these people; various offerings left by worshipers were strewn about the feet of his statue. It was very crowded, and we had to wait for a long time before we were admitted. The Mahatma is still universally revered in India, and some of his popularity seems to have rubbed off on the memory of the American ace who stepped between him and an assassin's bullet.

Braun said very little when we were inside, just stared up at the statue as if somehow willing it to come to life. It was a moving visit, but not entirely a comfortable one. My obvious deformity drew hard looks from some of the higher-caste Hindus in the press of the people. And whenever someone brushed against Braun too tightly—as happened frequently among such a tightly packed mass of people—his biological force field would begin to shimmer, surrounding him with a ghostly golden glow. I'm afraid my nervousness got the better of me, and I interrupted Braun's reveries and got us out of there hastily. Perhaps I overreacted, but if even one person in that crowd had realized who Jack Braun was, it might have triggered a vastly ugly scene. Braun was very moody and quiet on the way back to our hotel.

Gandhi is a personal hero of mine, and for all my mixed feelings about aces I must admit that I am grateful to Earl Sanderson for the intervention that saved Gandhi's life. For the great prophet of nonviolence to die by an assassin's bullet would have been too grotesque, and I think India would have torn itself apart in the wake of such a death, in a fratricidal bloodbath the likes of which the world has never seen.

If Gandhi had not lived to lead the reunification of the subcontinent after the death of Jinnah in 1948, would that strange two-headed nation called Pakistan actually have endured? Would the All-India Congress have displaced all the petty rulers and absorbed their domains, as it threatened to do? The very shape of this decentralized, endlessly diverse patchwork country is an expression of the Mahatma's dreams. I find it inconceivable to imagine what course Indian history might have taken without him. So in that respect, at least, the Four Aces left a real mark on the world and perhaps demonstrated that one determined man can indeed change the course of history for the better.

I pointed all this out to Jack Braun on our ride home, when he seemed so withdrawn. I'm afraid it did not help much. He listened to me patiently and when I was finished, he said, "It was Earl who saved him, not me," and lapsed back into silence.

True to his promise, Hiram Worchester returned to the tour today, via Concorde from London. His brief sojourn in New York seems to have done him a world of good. His old ebullience was back, and he promptly convinced Tachyon, Mordecai Jones, and Fantasy to join him on an expedition to find the hottest vindaloo in Calcutta. He pressed Peregrine to join the foraging party as well, but the thought seemed to make her turn green.

Tomorrow morning Father Squid, Troll, and I will visit the Ganges, where legend has it a joker can bathe in the sacred waters and be cured of his afflictions. Our guides tell us there are hundreds of documented cases, but I am frankly dubious, although Father Squid insists that there have been miraculous joker cures in Lourdes as well. Perhaps I shall succumb and leap into the sacred waters after all. A man dying of cancer can ill afford the luxury of skepticism, I suppose.

Chrysalis was invited to join us, but declined. These days she seems most comfortable in the hotel bars, drinking amaretto and playing endless games of solitaire. She has become quite friendly with two of our reporters, Sara Morgenstern and the ubiquitous Digger Downs, and I've even heard talk that she and Digger are sleeping together.

Back from the Ganges. I must make my confession. I took off my shoe and sock, rolled up my pants legs, and put my foot in the sacred waters. Afterward, I was still a joker, alas . . . a joker with a wet foot.

The sacred waters are filthy, by the way, and while I was fishing for my miracle, someone stole my shoe.

THE TEARDROP OF INDIA

Walton Simons

The people of Colombo had been waiting for the ape since early morning, and the police were having trouble keeping them away from the docks. A few were getting past the wooden barricades, only to be quickly caught and hustled into the bright yellow police vans. Some sat on parked cars; others had children perched on their shoulders. Most were content to stand behind the cordons, craning their necks for a look at what the local press called "the great American monster."

Two massive cranes lifted the giant ape slowly off the barge. It hung bound and limp, dark fur poking out from inside the steel mesh. The only indication of life was the slow rising and falling of its fifteen-foot-wide chest. There was a grinding squeal as the cranes pivoted together, swinging the ape sideways until it was over the freshly painted, green railway car. The flatcar groaned as the ape settled onto its broad steel bed. There was scattered cheering and clapping from the crowd.

It was the same as the vision he'd had only a few months ago—the crowd, the calm sea, and clear sky, the sweat on the back of his neck—all the same. The visions never lied. He knew exactly what would happen for the next fifteen minutes or so; after that he could go back to living again.

He adjusted the collar of his nehru shirt and flashed his government ID card to the policeman nearest him. The officer nodded and stepped out of his way. He was a special assistant to the Secretary of the Interior, which gave him a particularly wide range of responsibilities. Sometimes what he did was little more than nursemaid rich, visiting foreigners. But it was preferable to the twenty-plus years he'd spent in embassies overseas.

There was a group of twenty or thirty Americans around

the train. Most wore light gray security uniforms and were busy chaining the beast down to the railway car. They kept an eye on the ape while going about their business but didn't act afraid. A tall man in a Hawaiian print shirt and plaid Bermuda shorts was standing well away, talking to a girl in a light blue cotton sundress. They were both wearing red and black "King Pongo" visors.

He walked over to the tall man and tapped him on the shoulder.

"Not now." The man didn't even bother to turn and look at him.

"Mr. Danforth?" He tapped him on the shoulder again, harder. "Welcome to Sri Lanka. I'm G. C. Jayewardene. You telephoned me last month about your film." Jayewardene spoke English, Sinhalese, Tamil, and Dutch. His position in the government required it.

The film producer turned, his face blank. "Jayewardene? Oh, right. The government guy. Nice to meet you." Danforth grabbed his hand and pumped it a few times. "We're real busy right now. Guess you can see that."

"Of course. If it's not too much trouble, I'd like to ride along while you're transporting the ape." Jayewardene could not help but be impressed with its size. The monster was even taller than the forty-foot Aukana Buddha. "It seems much larger when you see it up close."

"No joke. But it'll be worth all the blood, sweat, and tears it took to get it here when the film comes out." He jerked his thumb toward the monster. "That baby is great pub."

Jayewardene put his hand over his mouth, trying to hide his puzzled expression.

"Publicity." Danforth smiled. "Have to watch the industry slang, I guess. Sure, G. C., you can ride in the VIP car with us. It's the one in front of our hairy friend."

"Thank you."

The giant ape exhaled, stirring the dust and dirt by its open mouth into a small cloud.

"Great pub," said Jayewardene.

The rhythmic clacking of the train's wheels on the old railway track relaxed him. Jayewardene had ridden the island trains on countless trips in the forty-odd years since he'd boarded one for the first time as a boy. The girl in the blue dress, who'd finally introduced herself as Paula Curtis, was staring out the window at the terraced tea fields. Danforth was working over a map with a red felt-tip pen.

"Okay," he said, putting the handle end of the pen to his lips. "We take the train to the end of the line, which is around the headwaters of the Kalu Ganga." He flattened the map onto his knees and pointed to the spot with his pen. "That puts us at the edge of the Udu Walawe National Park, and Roger has supposedly scouted out some great locations for us there. Right?"

"Right," Paula answered. "If you trust Roger."

"He's the director, my dear. We have to trust him. Too bad we couldn't afford somebody decent, but the effects are going to take up most of the budget."

A steward walked over to them, carrying a tray with plates of curried rice and string hoppers, small steamed strands of rice flour dough. Jayewardene took a plate and smiled. "*Es-thu-ti*," he said, thanking the young steward. The boy had a round face and broad nose, obviously Sinhalese like himself.

Paula turned from the window long enough to take a plate. Danforth waved the boy away.

"I'm not sure I understand." Jayewardene took a mouthful of the rice, chewed briefly, and swallowed. There was too little cinnamon in the curry for his taste. "Why spend money on special effects when you have a fifty-foot ape?"

"Like I said earlier, the monster's great pub. But it would be hell trying to get the thing to perform on cue. Not to mention being prohibitively dangerous to everyone around him. Oh, we may use him in a couple of shots, and definitely for sound effects, but most of the stuff will be done with miniatures." Danforth grabbed a fingerful of rice from Paula's plate and dropped it into his mouth, then shrugged. "Then, when the movie opens, the critics will say they can't tell the real ape from the model, and people take that as a challenge, see. Figure they can be the one to spot it. It sells tickets."

"Surely the publicity value is less than the money it took to get the beast from the City of New York and bring it halfway around the world." Jayewardene dabbed at the corner of his mouth with a cloth napkin.

Danforth looked up, grinning. "Actually we got the ape for nothing. See, it gets loose every now and then and starts tearing things up. The city is up to its ass in lawsuits every time that happens. If it's not in New York, it can't do any damage. They almost paid us to take the thing off their hands. Of course we have to make sure nothing happens to it, or the zoo would lose one of its main attractions. That's what those boys in gray are for."

"And if the ape escapes here, your film company will be liable." Jayewardene took another bite.

"We've got it doped up all the time. And frankly it doesn't seem much interested in anything."

"Except blond women." Paula pointed to her short, brown hair. "Lucky for me." She looked back out the window. "What's that mountain?"

"Sri Pada. Adam's Peak. There is a footprint at the top said to be made by the Buddha himself. It is a very holy place." Jayewardene made the pilgrimage to the top every year. He planned to do so in the near future, as soon as his schedule allowed it. This time with hopes of cleansing himself spiritually so that there were no more visions.

"No kidding." Paula elbowed Danforth. "We going to have time to do any sight-seeing?"

"We'll see," Danforth said, reaching over for more rice.

Jayewardene set his plate down. "Excuse me." He got up and walked to the rear of the car, slid the door open, and stepped out onto the platform.

The giant ape's head was only about twelve feet from where he stood. Its eyes fluttered, then stared up at the rounded top of Adam's Peak. The ape opened its mouth; lips pulled back, revealing the huge yellow-white teeth. There was a rumble, louder than the train engine, from the back of the monster's throat.

"It's waking up," he yelled at the security men riding at the back of the flatcar.

They walked forward carefully, steadying themselves on the car's side railing, avoiding the ape's manacled hands. One watched the monster, rifle centered on its head. The other changed the plastic bottle hooked up to the IV in the ape's arm.

"Thanks." One of the guards waved at Jayewardene. "It'll be okay now. This stuff will put him out for hours."

The ape twisted its head and looked directly at him, then turned back to Adam's Peak. It sighed and closed its eyes.

There was something in the monster's brown eyes that

he couldn't identify. He paused, then went back into the car.
The curry aftertaste was sour in the back of his throat.

They reached the camp at dusk. Actually it was more of a
hastily thrown together city of tents and portable buildings.
There was less activity than Jayewardene had expected. Most
of the crew sat around talking or playing cards. Only the zoo
security people were busy, carefully unloading the ape onto a
broadbed truck. It was still unconscious from the drug.

Danforth told Paula to introduce Jayewardene around.
The director, Roger Winters, was busy making changes in the
shooting script. He wore a Frank S. Buck outfit, complete
with pith helmet to hide his thinning hair. Paula guided
Jayewardene away from the director.

"You wouldn't like him," she said. "Nobody does. At
least nobody I know. But he can bring them in on schedule.
Here's somebody you'll be more interested in. You're not
married, are you?"

"Widowed."

"Oh, sorry." She waved at a blond woman sitting on the
bare wooden steps of the camp's main building. The woman
wore a black and red "King Pongo" T-shirt, tight blue jeans,
and leather walking boots.

"Hi, Paula," said the blonde, tossing her hair. "Who's
your friend?"

"Robyn Symmes, meet Mr. G. C. Jayewardene," Paula
said. Robyn extended her hand. Jayewardene lightly shook it.

"Nice to meet you, Miss Symmes." Jayewardene bowed,
embarrassingly aware of the tightness of his shirt across his
oversize stomach. He was flattered to be in the company of
the only two women he'd seen in the camp. They were both
attractive, in a foreign way. He wiped the sweat from his
brow and wondered how they would look in saris.

"Look, I have to go settle Danforth in. Why don't you
two entertain each other for a while." Paula was walking away
before either of them had time to answer.

"Your name is Jayewardene? Any relation to President
Junius Jayewardene?"

"No. It's a common name. How do you like it here?" He
sat down next to her. The steps were uncomfortably hot.

"Well, I've only been here a few days, but it's a beautiful
place. A bit too hot for my taste, but I'm from North Dakota."
He nodded. "We have every kind of beauty imaginable

here. Beaches, mountains, jungle, cities. Something for everyone. Except cold weather of course."

There was a pause. "So." Robyn slapped her hands on
her thighs. "What is it you do that your government decided
to stick you out here with us?"

"I'm a diplomat of sorts. My job is to make foreign
visitors happy here. Or at least to try. We like to maintain a
reputation as a friendly country."

"Well, I sure haven't seen anything to contradict that.
The people I've met practically kill you with kindness." She
pointed to the line of trees at the edge of the camp. "The
animals are something again, though. You know what they
found this morning?"

He shrugged.

"A cobra. Right over there. *Ŭffdä*. That's something that
you definitely don't get in North Dakota." She shuddered.
"Most animals I can handle, but snakes . . ." She made a face.

"Nature is complete and harmonious here." He smiled.
"But I must be boring you."

"No. Not really. You're certainly more interesting than
Roger, or the gaffers and grips. How long will you be here? I
mean, with the film company."

"Off and on for your entire stay, although I'll be going
back to Colombo tomorrow for a few days. Dr. Tachyon, the
alien, and a large party from your country will be arriving
here then. To study the effect of the virus in my country." A
shiver eased up his spine.

"You are a busy little bee, aren't you?" She looked up.
The light was beginning to dim around the swaying treetops.
"I'm going to go get some sleep. You might want to do the
same. Paula will show you where. She knows everything.
Danforth wouldn't ever finish a film without her."

Jayewardene watched her walk away, sighing at the
memory of pleasure he thought best forgotten, then got up
and headed in the direction Paula had gone. He would need
sleep to be fresh for the trip back tomorrow. But sleep never
came easily to him. And he was afraid to dream. He'd learned
to be afraid.

He woke up biting his right hand hard enough to draw
blood. His breathing was ragged and his nightshirt was
bathed in sweat. The world around him shimmered and then
came into focus. Another vision, snatched from the future.

They were happening more and more often in spite of his prayers and meditation. It was only a small comfort that this one wasn't about him. Not directly anyway.

He pulled on his pants and shoes, unzipped his tent, and stepped outside. Jayewardene walked quietly toward the truck where the ape was chained. Two men were on guard. One was leaning against the cab; the other was sitting with his back to one of the huge, mud-covered tires. Both had rifles and lit cigarettes. They were speaking softly to each other.

"What's up?" asked the man by the cab as Jayewardene approached. He didn't bother to raise his rifle.

"I wanted to look at the ape again."

"In the middle of the night? You'll see more tomorrow morning when it's light."

"I couldn't sleep. And I'll be returning to Colombo tomorrow." He walked up next to the monster. "When did the ape first appear?"

"Blackout of '65 in New York City," said the seated man. "Showed up in the middle of Manhattan. Nobody knows where it came from, though. Probably had something to do with the wild card. At least that's what people say."

Jayewardene nodded. "I'm going to walk around to the other side. To look at his face."

"Just don't put your head in its mouth." The guard flicked his cigarette butt onto the ground. Jayewardene crushed it out with his shoe as he walked past.

The ape's breath was hot, organic, but not foul. Jayewardene waited, hoping that the beast would open its eyes again. The vision had told him what was behind them, but he wanted another look. The dreams had never been wrong before, but his reputation would be destroyed if he went to the authorities with this story and it proved wrong. And there would be questions about how he could have known. He would have to answer them without revealing his unusual abilities. Not an easy problem to solve in so little time.

The ape's eyes stayed shut.

The jungle's night sounds were more distant than usual. The animals were staying far away from the camp. Jayewardene hoped it was because they sensed the ape. Sensed the wrongness about it. He glanced at his watch. It would be dawn in a couple of hours. He would speak to Danforth first thing in the morning, then go back to Colombo. Dr. Tachyon had the reputation of being able to work wonders. It would be his task to transform the ape. The vision made that very clear. Perhaps the alien could even help him. If his pilgrimage failed.

He walked back to his tent and spent the next few hours praying to the Buddha for a little less enlightenment.

It was past nine o'clock when Danforth emerged, bleary-eyed, from the main portable building. Jayewardene was on his second cup of tea but was still moving slowly, as if his body were encased in mud.

"Mr. Danforth. I must speak to you before leaving this morning."

Danforth yawned and nodded. "Fine. Look, before you get away, I want to take some pictures. You know, the entire crew and the ape. Something to give to the wire services. I'd appreciate it if you'd be in it too." Danforth yawned again, even wider. "God, got to get some coffee in me. The boys are supposed to have everything set up by now. I'll be free for a few minutes after that, and we can talk about it then."

"I think it would be best to discuss it now, privately." He looked out into the jungle. "Perhaps take a walk away from the camp."

"In the jungle? I heard they killed a cobra yesterday. No way." Danforth backed away. "I'll talk to you after we get our publicity shots done, not before."

Jayewardene took another sip of tea and walked over to the truck. He wasn't surprised or disgusted at Danforth's attitude. The man had the weight of a multimillion dollar project on his shoulders. That kind of pressure could skew anyone's values; make him fear the wrong things.

Most of the crew were already assembled in front of the giant ape. Paula was sitting in front, chewing on her fingernails while looking over the production schedule. He knelt down next to her.

"I see his majesty hooked you into doing this just like the rest of us," Paula said without looking up.

"I'm afraid so. You don't look like you slept very well."

"It's not that I didn't sleep well. I didn't sleep period. I was up with Roger and Mr. D. all last night. But it comes with the territory." She leaned her head back and rotated it in a slow, circular motion. "Well, as soon as Roger, Robyn, and the boss get here, we can get this fun over with."

Jayewardene downed the rest of his tea. Later in the day a busload of extras, most Sinhalese with a few Tamils and Muslims, was scheduled to arrive. All those selected to be in the film spoke English, which was not uncommon, given the island's history of British involvement.

Danforth showed up with Roger in tow. The producer looked at the group and squinted. "The ape's facing the wrong way. Somebody get that truck turned around."

A gray-clad guard waved, jumped up into the cab, and started the truck up.

"Okay. Everybody out of the way so we can get this done quickly." Danforth motioned them toward him.

Somebody whistled and Jayewardene turned. Robyn was walking toward the group. She was wearing a long, skintight silver dress. She wasn't smiling.

"Why do I have to wear this now? It's going to be bad enough during shooting. I'll probably get heat stroke." Robyn put her hands on her hips and frowned.

Danforth shrugged. "Jungle shooting is a pain in the butt. You knew that when you took the part."

Robyn pressed her lips tightly together and was quiet.

The truck backed into position and Danforth clapped his hands. "All right. Everybody back where you were before. We'll get this over as quickly as possible."

One of the guards walked over to Danforth. Jayewardene moved in close enough to hear.

"I think we woke it up when we moved the truck, sir. Want me to dope him up again before you take your pictures?"

"No. It'll look better if there's a little life in the damned thing." Danforth stroked his chin. "And feed it when we're done. Then you can knock it out again."

"Right, sir."

Jayewardene took his place in front of the truck. The ape's breathing was irregular. He turned. The ape's eyes fluttered and opened. Its pupils were dilated. The eyes moved about slowly, looked at the cameras, and stopped at Robyn. They became bright and purposeful. Jayewardene felt his skin go cold.

The ape took a deep breath and roared, a sound like a hundred lions. Jayewardene started to run but tripped over somebody who'd reacted away from the ape and into him. The ape was rocking back and forth on the truck. One of the tires blew out. The monster continued to roar and pull at the chains. Jayewardene struggled to his feet. He heard the high-pitched squeal of metal straining against metal, then a loud pinging noise as the chains snapped. Steel shrapnel from the broken chains flew in all directions. One piece hit a guard. The man fell, screaming. Jayewardene ran to the man and helped him to his feet. The ground was shaking right behind them. He turned to look back, but the ape was already past them. Jayewardene turned to the injured man.

"Broken rib, I think. Maybe two," said the guard through gritted teeth. "I'll be okay."

A woman screamed. Jayewardene left the man and rushed ahead. He could see most of the ape over the tin tops of the portable buildings. It bent down and picked up something in its right hand. It was Robyn. He heard a gunshot and tried to move faster. His sides ached already.

The ape snatched up a tent and threw it at one of the guards, whose rifle was raised for another shot. The canvas drifted down over the man, spoiling his aim.

"No. No," Jayewardene yelled. "You might hit the woman."

The monster looked over the camp briefly, then waved its free arm disdainfully at the humans and shouldered into the jungle. Robyn Symmes was limp and pale against the huge darkness of its chest.

Danforth sat on the ground, head in hands. "Oh, shit. What the hell do we do now. This wasn't supposed to happen. Those chains were made of titanium steel. It can't be happening."

Jayewardene put his hand on the producer's shoulder. "Mr. Danforth, I'll need your fastest car and your best driver. And it might be better if you came along with us."

Danforth looked up. "Where are we going?"

"Back to Colombo. A group of your aces is arriving there in a few hours." He smiled thinly. "Long ago our island was called Serendib. The land of fortunate coincidence."

"Thank god. There's a chance then." He stood up, the color returning to his face. "I'll get things moving."

"Need any help?" Paula dabbed at a cut over her eye with her shirtsleeve.

"Only all I can get," Danforth said.

The ape roared again. It already seemed impossibly far away.

*   *   *

The car sped along down the road, jolting them at every
bump and pothole. They were still a few miles outside
Ratnapura. Jayewardene was in the front seat, directing the
driver. Paula and Danforth sat silently in the back. As they
rounded a corner, he saw several saffron-robed Buddhist
priests ahead. "Stop," he yelled as the driver braked the car.
They went into a skid and off the road, sliding to a stop. The
priests, who had been working on the dirt road with shovels,
stood to one side and motioned them through.

"Who are they?" asked Paula.

"Priests. Members of an appropriate technologist group,"
Jayewardene said as the driver pulled back onto the road. He
bowed to the priests as he went past. "Much of their time is
spent doing such work."

He planned to call ahead from Ratnapura. Let the government know the situation and discourage the military from
attacking the creature. That would be difficult, given the
amount of damage it could cause. Tachyon and the aces would
be the answer. They had to be. His stomach burned. It was
dangerous to hinge his plans on people he'd never met, but
he had no other choice.

"I wonder what set him off?" Danforth asked, his voice
almost too soft to hear.

"Well"—Jayewardene turned to speak to them—"he looked
at the cameras, then at Miss Symmes. It was as if something
clicked in his brain, brought him right out of the stupor."

If anything happens to her, it'll be my fault." Danforth
looked at the muddy floorboard. "My fault."

"Then we'll all have to work hard to make sure nothing
does happen to her," Paula said. "Okay?"

"Right," Danforth said weakly.

"Remember," she said, patting his shoulder. "It's beauty
that kills the beast. Not the other way around."

"Hopefully we can resolve the situation and keep both
beauty and beast alive." Jayewardene turned to look back at
the road. He spotted the buildings of Ratnapura ahead. "Slow
down when you get to town. I'll direct you where we need to
go." He intended to inform the military of the situation and
then return to Colombo. Jayewardene sank back into the car
seat. He wished he had slept better the night before. Today's
work was going to spill into tomorrow and maybe even the
next day.

*   *   *

They arrived back in Colombo a little after noon and went directly to Jayewardene's home. It was a large white stucco residence with a red-tiled roof. Even when his wife had been alive, it had been more space than they needed. Now he rattled around in it like a coconut in an empty boxcar. He called his office and found out the American delegation of aces had arrived and was staying at the Galadari Meridien Hotel. After settling Danforth and Paula in, he went to his garden shrine and reaffirmed his pledge of the Five Precepts.

Afterward he hurriedly put on a clean white shirt and pair of pants and ate a few fingerfuls of cold rice.

"Where are you going now?" Paula asked as he opened the door to leave.

"To speak to Dr. Tachyon and the Americans about the ape." He shook his head as she got up off the couch. "It would be better for you to rest now. Whatever develops, I'll call you."

"Okay."

"Is it all right if we get something to eat?" Danforth already had the refrigerator door open.

"Certainly. Help yourselves."

Traffic was heavy, even on the Sea Beach Road, which Jayewardene had instructed the driver to take. The car's air conditioner was broken and his clean clothes were soaked with sweat before they were even halfway to the hotel.

The film company driver, his name was Saul, was slowing to stop in front of the Galadari Meridien when the engine died. He turned the key several times, but there was only a clicking sound.

"Look." Jayewardene pointed toward the hotel entrance. People were scattering around the main doorway as something rose into the air. Jayewardene shaded his eyes as they flew over. One was a full-grown Indian elephant. A common enough sight, but this one was flying. Seated on its back was a well-muscled man. The elephant's ears were extended and appeared to help the creature steer while flying.

"Elephant Girl," said Saul. Crowds stopped up and down the street, pointing in silence as the aces flew by overhead.

"Do what you can with the car," he told Saul, who already had the hood up.

Jayewardene walked quickly to the hotel's main entrance. He pushed past the doorman, who was sitting on the sidewalk shaking his head, and into the darkness inside. Hotel employees were busy lighting candles and reassuring the guests in the bar and restaurant.

"Waiter, get those drinks over here." The male voice came from the bar. He spoke English with an American accent.

Jayewardene let his eyes adjust to the dim lighting, then made his way carefully into the bar. The bartender was setting lamps up next to the mirror behind the bar. Jayewardene pulled out his handkerchief and wiped his sweaty forehead.

They were seated together in a booth. There was a large man with a dark spade-shaped beard, wearing a tailored blue three-piece suit. Across from him was another man. He was middle-aged, but trim, and sat in the booth as if it were a throne. Although he thought he knew the men, the woman sitting between them was instantly recognizable. She was wearing a low-cut, shoulderless black dress, trimmed with sequins. Her skin was transparent. He quickly looked away from her. Her bone and muscles reflected the light in a disturbing manner.

"Pardon me," he said, walking over to them. "My name is Jayewardene. I'm with the Department of the Interior."

"And what do you want?" The large man took a skewered cherry from his drink and rolled it between his manicured thumb and forefinger.

The other man stood, smiled, and shook Jayewardene's hand. The gesture was studied, a political greeting refined by years of practice. "I'm Senator Gregg Hartmann. Pleased to meet you."

"Thank you, Senator. I hope your shoulder is better." Jayewardene had read about the incident in the newspapers.

"It wasn't as bad as the press made it sound." Hartmann looked at the other end of the booth. "The man torturing that cherry is Hiram Worchester. And the lady is—"

"Chrysalis, I believe." Jayewardene bowed. "May I join you."

"Certainly," Hartmann said. "Is there something we can do for you?"

Jayewardene sat down next to Hiram, whose bulk partially obscured Chrysalis. He found her profoundly disturbing to look at. "Several things perhaps. Where were Elephant Girl and that man going just now?"

"To catch the ape, of course." Hiram looked at him as

one might at an embarrassing relative. "And rescue the girl. We just found out about it. Catching the beast is something of a tradition." He paused. "For aces."

"Is that possible? I don't think Elephant Girl and one man can manage that." Jayewardene turned to Hartmann.

"The man with her was Jack Braun," Chrysalis said. Her accent was more British than American. "Golden Boy. He can handle almost anything, up to and including the giant ape. Although he hasn't been getting his rest lately. His glow's been a little on the feeble side." She nudged Hiram. "Don't you think?"

"Personally I don't really care what happens to Mr. Braun." Hiram twirled the small, red plastic sword from his drink. "And I think the feeling's mutual."

Hartmann coughed. "At the very least they should be able to rescue the actress. That should simplify matters for your government."

"Yes. One would hope." Jayewardene folded and unfolded a cloth napkin. "But such a rescue should be carefully planned out."

"Yes, they did rather fly off the handle," Chrysalis said, taking a sip of brandy.

Jayewardene thought he caught a glint of mischief in Hartmann's eyes, but dismissed it as the lighting. "Could you tell me where to find Dr. Tachyon?"

Hiram and Chrysalis both laughed. Hartmann maintained his poise and gave them a disapproving look. "He's unavailable right now."

Chrysalis motioned to the waiter and pointed to her glass. "Which one of the stewardesses is he trying this time?"

"Upstairs, trapped in the darkness together. If anything will help Tachy get over his problem, this is it. The doctor's not to be disturbed right now." Hiram held the plastic sword above the table and made a fist with his other hand. The sword fell and stuck in the tabletop. "Get the point?"

"Could we give him a message for you?" Hartmann asked, ignoring Hiram.

Jayewardene pulled out his snakeskin wallet and handed Hartmann one of his business cards. "Please have him contact me as soon as possible. I may be busy the rest of the afternoon, but he can reach me at my home. It's the bottom number."

"I'll do what I can," Hartmann said, standing to shake hands again. "I hope we see you again before we leave."

"Nice meeting you, Mr. Jayewardene," Chrysalis said. He thought perhaps she was smiling, but couldn't be sure.

Jayewardene turned to leave but stopped short as two people entered the bar. One was a man whom Jayewardene judged to be in his late thirties. He was tall and muscular with blond hair and a camera slung over his shoulder. The woman with him was as stunningly beautiful as any of the photographs Jayewardene had seen of her. Even without the wings she would have attracted attention.

Peregrine was a vision he would willingly linger on. Jayewardene stepped out of their way as they joined the others in the booth.

They were still lighting candles and lamps in the lobby when he left.

It was hard to arrange for a helicopter with the ape on the loose, but the base commander owed him more than one favor. The pilot, headgear under his arm, was waiting for Jayewardene at the chopper. He was dark-skinned, a Tamil, part of the military's new plan to try to integrate the armed forces. The aircraft itself was a large, outdated model, lacking the sleek aerodynamics of the newer attack ships. Olive paint was peeling from the chopper's metal skin and the tires were balding.

Jayewardene nodded to the pilot and spoke to him in Tamil. "I had requested a bullhorn be put on board."

"Already done, sir." The pilot opened the door and crawled up into the cockpit. Jayewardene followed.

The young Tamil was going through a checklist, flipping switches, examining gauges.

"I've never been in a helicopter before," Jayewardene said, buckling his seat belt. He pulled against the belt, testing it, not exactly happy that it was fraying around the edges.

The pilot shrugged and put on his helmet, then cranked the engine, took the stick, and engaged the rotor. The blades whopped noisily and the helicopter lifted slowly into the sky. "Where are we going, sir?"

"Let's head down toward Ratnapura and Adam's Peak." He coughed. "We'll be looking for a man on a flying elephant. American aces."

"Do you want to engage them, sir?" The pilot's tone was cool and professional.

"No. No, nothing like that. Just observe them. They're after the ape that escaped."

The pilot took a deep breath and nodded, then flipped on the radio and picked up the mouthpiece. "Lion base, this is Shadow One. Can you give us any information on a flying elephant? Over."

There was a pause and crackle of static before the base answered. "Your target reported heading due east from Colombo. Approximate speed one five zero kilometers per hour. Over."

"Acknowledged. Over and out." The pilot checked his compass and adjusted his course.

"Hopefully we can find them before they locate the ape. I don't think they have any real idea where to look, but the country isn't that large." Jayewardene pointed to dark clouds ahead. As he did there was a flash of lightning. "Are we safe from bad weather?"

"Fairly safe. Do you think these Americans would be stupid enough to fly into a storm?" He pointed the chopper toward a thin spot in the wall of clouds.

"Hard to say. I don't know these people. They've handled the creature before, though." Jayewardene looked down. The land beneath was rising steadily upward. The jungle was broken here and there with tea and rice fields or water reservoirs. From the air the flooded rice paddies looked like the shards of a broken mirror, the pieces reassembled so that they almost touched each other.

"Something ahead, sir." The pilot reached under his seat and handed over a pair of binoculars. Jayewardene took them, wiped off the lenses with the tail of his shirt, and looked in the direction the pilot was pointing. There was something. He rotated the adjusting knob and brought it into focus. The man on the elephant was pointing toward the ground.

"It's them," Jayewardene said, setting the binoculars on his lap. "Get in close enough for this to be heard." He raised the bullhorn.

"Yes, sir."

Jayewardene's mouth and throat were dry. He opened his window as they got closer in. The aces didn't seem to have noticed them yet. He switched on the bullhorn and set the volume control near the top. He saw the ape's shoulders and head above the treetops and knew why the Americans were paying no attention to the helicopter.

He stuck the bullhorn out the window as the chopper moved in. "Elephant Girl. Mr. Braun." Jayewardene thought Golden Boy was inappropriate for a grown man. "My name is Jayewardene. I'm an official with the Sri Lankan government. Do you understand what I am saying?" He spoke each word slowly and carefully. The bullhorn vibrated in his sweaty hand.

Jack Braun waved and nodded. The monster had stopped to look up and bare its teeth. It stripped the foliage off the top of a tree and set Robyn in a crook between two bare branches.

"Rescue the woman if you can, but do not harm the ape." Jayewardene's voice sounded almost unintelligible from inside the helicopter, but Braun made a thumbs-up signal to show he understood. "We'll stand by," Jayewardene said.

The ape reached down, scooped up a handful of dirt, and crushed the contents down with its palms. The creature roared and threw the dirtball at the aces. The flying elephant dropped out of its path. The missile continued upward. Jayewardene saw it was going to hit the chopper and gripped the seat as tightly as possible. The earth thudded against the side of the aircraft. The helicopter began to spin, but the pilot quickly brought it back under control and pulled up sharply.

"Better keep a safe distance," the pilot said, making sure the ape stayed in view. "If the momentum hadn't been spent on that, I don't think we'd still be in the air."

"Right." Jayewardene slowly exhaled and wiped his brow. A few scattered raindrops began to dot the windshield.

The Elephant Girl had moved about fifty yards away from the ape and down to treetop level. Braun jumped off her and disappeared into the undergrowth. The elephant gained height again and trumpeted, moving back toward the monster. The ape snarled and beat its chest, the sound like an explosion underground.

The standoff lasted a minute or two, then the ape rocked backward, catching its balance just at the point of falling over. Elephant Girl swooped down quickly toward the woman in the tree. The ape swung his arms at her. The flying elephant banked away, wobbling a bit.

"Did it hit her?" Jayewardene turned to the pilot. "Should we move in and try to help?"

"I don't think there's much we can do. Possibly distract it. But that could get us knocked down." The pilot put the stick between his knees and wiped the sweat from his palms.

The ape roared and reached down to pick up something. Jack Braun struggled in the creature's hand, trying to push the giant fingers open. The ape lifted him up to its open mouth.

"No," Jayewardene said, turning his head away.

The beast roared again and Jayewardene looked back. The monster rubbed its mouth with its free hand. Braun, apparently unhurt, was bracing his back against the ape's fingers and pushing the thumb open. The monster flipped its arm like a baseball pitcher, sending Braun cartwheeling through the air. He came down in heavy jungle several seconds and several hundred yards away.

The Tamil sat with his mouth slightly open, then put the helicopter into a turn toward the spot where Braun had disappeared into the trees. "It tried to eat him, but he wouldn't go down. I think he broke one of the devil's teeth."

The Elephant Girl followed behind them. The ape picked Robyn out of the tree and after a final triumphant roar, began wading through the jungle again. Jayewardene bit his lip and looked at the treetops for broken limbs to show where Braun had fallen through.

The rain grew heavier and the pilot switched on the wipers. "There he is," the Tamil said, slowing to a hover. Braun was climbing up a large coconut palm tree. His clothes were in tatters, but he didn't appear hurt. Elephant Girl moved in, curled her trunk around his waist, and lifted him onto her back. Braun bent over and held on to her ears.

"Follow us," Jayewardene said, using the bullhorn again. "We'll lead you back to the airbase. Are you all right, Mr. Braun?"

The golden ace made a thumbs-up again, this time without looking at them.

Jayewardene said nothing for several minutes. Perhaps his vision had been wrong. The beast appeared so vicious. A normal person would have been crushed to a paste between the monster's teeth. No. The dream had to be true. He couldn't allow any self-doubt, or the ape would have no chance at all.

They outraced the storm back to Colombo.

*   *   *

Jayewardene paused outside Tachyon's door. He'd been sleeping when the alien called. Tachyon had apologized for taking so long to get back to him and began listing the reasons. Jayewardene had interrupted and asked if he could come over immediately. The doctor had said yes with little enthusiasm.

He knocked and waited, then raised his hand again before he heard footfalls from the other side. Tachyon opened the door, wearing a puffy-sleeved white shirt and blue velvet pants sashed with a large red scarf. "Mr. Jayewardene? Please come in." Jayewardene bowed and went in.

Tachyon sat down on the bed, underneath an oil painting of Dunhinda Falls. A scarlet-plumed hat and a partially eaten plate of rice were on the bedside table. "You are the same Mr. Jayewardene from the helicopter? The one Radha told me about."

"Yes." Jayewardene lowered himself into the lounger next to the bed. "I hope Mr. Braun wasn't injured."

"Only his already battered pride." Tachyon closed his eyes for a moment, as if trying to gather strength, then reopened them. "Please tell me how I can help you, Mr. Jayewardene."

"The military is planning on attacking the ape tomorrow. We must stop them and subdue the creature ourselves." Jayewardene rubbed his eyes. "But I'm not starting at the beginning. The military deals with harsh reality. But you, Doctor, work in the context of the extraordinary on a daily basis. I don't know you, but I am in a position of needing to trust you."

Tachyon placed his dangling feet firmly on the floor and straightened his shoulders. "I've spent most of my life here trying to live up to the trust of others. I only wish I could believe the trust was warranted. But you say we must stop the military and subdue the ape ourselves. Why? Surely they're better equipped—"

Jayewardene interrupted. "The virus doesn't affect animals, if I understand correctly."

"I know the virus doesn't affect animals," Tachyon replied with a shake of his curly, red hair. "I helped develop the virus. Every child knows..." He covered his mouth. "Ancestors forgive me." He slid off the bed and walked to the window. "For twenty years it's been staring me in the face, and I *missed* it. By my own blind stupidity I've sentenced some individual to a living hell. I've failed one of mine again. The trust isn't warranted." Tachyon pressed his fists against his temples and continued berating himself.

"Your pardon, Doctor," Jayewardene said. "I think your energies would be more beneficial if we applied them to the problem at hand." Tachyon turned, a pained expression on his face. "I meant no offense, Doctor," he added, sensing the depth of the alien's guilt.

"No. No, of course not. Mr. Jayewardene, how did you know?"

"Not many of our people have been touched by the virus. I'm one of the very few. I suppose I should be grateful to be alive and whole, but it's in our nature to complain. My ability gives me visions of the future. Always about someone or some place I know, usually myself. And so detailed and vivid." He shook his head. "My most recent one showed me the ape's true nature."

Tachyon sat back down on the bed, tapping his fingertips together. "What I don't understand is the primitive behavior exhibited by the creature."

"I'm sure that most of our questions can be answered once he's a man again."

"Of course. Of course." Tachyon popped up off the bed again. "And your ability. Temporal displacement of the cognitive self during dreamstate. This was what my family had in mind when they created the virus. Something that transcends known physical values. Amazing."

Jayewardene shrugged. "Yes, amazing. But it's a burden I would gladly give up. I want to view the future from its proper perspective, the here and now. This—power—destroys the natural flow of life. After the ape is restored, I plan to make my pilgrimage to Sri Pada. Perhaps through spiritual purity I may be rid of it."

"I've had some success reversing the effects at my clinic." Tachyon twisted his sash. "Of course the success rate isn't what I'd hoped. And the risk would be yours to take."

"We must deal with the ape first. After that my path may become more clear."

"If only we had more time here," Tachyon complained. "The tour is supposed to leave for Thailand day after tomorrow. That leaves us little margin for error. And we can't all go chasing out after the creature."

"I don't think the government would allow it in any case. Not after today. The fewer of your people we involve, the better."

"Agreed. I can't believe the others went off like that. Sometimes I think we're all suffering from some kind of creeping insanity. Hiram especially." Tachyon walked to the window and opened the mini-blinds. Lightning flashed on the horizon, briefly silhouetting the wall of towering thunderclouds. "Obviously I must be included in this little adventure. Radha can give me maneuverability. She's half-Indian. There have been problems between your country and India lately, I believe?"

"Sadly, yes. The Indians support the Tamils, since they have the same cultural heritage. The Sinhalese majority looks at this as support for the Tamil Tigers, a terrorist group." Jayewardene looked down at the floor. "It is a conflict with no winners and too many victims."

"So we must have a cover story. That Radha was hiding out, afraid for her life. She might present the answer to some other problems." Tachyon closed the blinds. "What weaponry will be used against the ape?"

"Two waves of helicopters. The first will move in with steel nets. The second, if needed, will be fully armed attack ships."

"Could you slip us onto their base before the second wave gets off the ground?" Tachyon rubbed his palms together.

"Possibly. Yes, I think I could."

"Good." The alien smiled. "And Mr. Jayewardene, in my own defense, there's been so much in my life, the founding of the clinic, unrest in Jokertown, the Swarm invasion—"

Jayewardene cut him off. "Doctor, you owe me no explanation."

"But I will owe him one."

They'd stopped the car a couple of miles from the gate to put Radha into the trunk. Jayewardene took a sip of tea from his Styrofoam cup. It was thick, coppery, and hot enough to help ward off the predawn chill. Since the road to the air base was bumpy, he had only partially filled his cup. There was a cold ache inside him that even the tea could not reach. Even in his best case scenario he would be forced to resign his post. He was overstepping his authority in an unforgivable manner. But he couldn't worry about what might happen to him; the ape was his first concern. He and Tachyon had stayed up most of the night, trying to cover all the things that might go wrong and what to do if the worst happened.

Jayewardene was in the front seat with Saul. Tachyon was in back between Danforth and Paula. No one spoke. Jayewardene reached for his government ID as they approached the well-lit front gate.

The gate guard was a young Sinhalese. His shoulders were as straight as the creases in his khaki uniform. His eyes were bright and he moved with measured steps to Jayewardene's side of the car.

Jayewardene rolled down his window and handed the guard his ID. "We wish to speak with General Dissanayake. Dr. Tachyon and two representatives of the American film company are in our party as well as myself."

The guard looked at the ID, then at the people in the car. "One moment," he said, then headed over to the small booth beside the gate and picked up the phone. After speaking for a few moments he walked back and handed the ID back with five laminated visitor badges. "The general will see you. He's in his office. Do you know the way, sir?"

"Yes, thank you," Jayewardene said, rolling his window back up and clipping one of the badges onto his shirt pocket.

The guard opened the gate and motioned them past with his red-tipped flashlight. Jayewardene sighed as they drove through and the gate closed behind them. He directed Saul to the officers' complex and patted the driver on the shoulder. "You know what to do?"

Saul eased the car to a stop between two faded yellow stripes and removed the keys, holding them between his thumb and forefinger. "As long as the trunk opens, you don't have to worry about my screwing up."

They got out of the car and walked down the sidewalk toward the building. Jayewardene heard helicopter rotors cutting the air overhead. Once inside, Tachyon stayed at Jayewardene's side as he guided them down the linoleum hallways. The alien was fussing with the cuffs of his coral-pink shirt. Paula and Danforth followed closely behind them, whispering to each other.

The corporal in the general's outer office looked up from his cup of tea and waved them in. The general was sitting behind his desk in a large swivel chair. He was a man of average height and compact build with dark, deep-set eyes and an expression that seldom changed. Some in the military community felt that, at fifty-four, Dissanayake was too young to be a general. But he had been both firm and controlled in his dealing with the Tamil Tigers, a militant separatist group. He had managed to avoid a bloodbath without appearing weak. Jayewardene respected him. The general nodded as they entered, pointing to the group of chairs opposite his cluttered desk.

"Please, sit down," Dissanayake said, tightening his lips into a half-smile. His English was not as good as Jayewardene's, but was still easily understandable. "Always a pleasure to see you, Mr. Jayewardene. And of course to welcome our other distinguished visitors."

"Thank you, General." Jayewardene waited for the others to seat themselves before continuing. "We know that you're quite busy now and appreciate your time."

Dissanayake looked at his gold watch and nodded. "Yes, I'm supposed to be up at operations right now. The first wave is scheduled to be taking off as we speak. So," he said, clasping his hands, "if you could be as brief as possible."

"We don't think you should attack the ape," Tachyon said. "To my knowledge it's never harmed anyone. Are there any reports of casualties so far?"

"None have been reported, Doctor." Dissanayake leaned back in his chair. "But the monster is headed for Adam's Peak. If unchecked, there will almost certainly be fatalities."

"But what about Robyn?" Paula said. "You go after the ape with attack choppers and she's likely to be killed."

"And if we do nothing, hundreds could be killed. Possibly thousands if it reaches a city." Dissanayake bit his lip. "It is my duty to prevent that from happening. I do understand what it means to have a friend in danger. And be assured, we will do everything possible to rescue Miss Symmes. My men will sacrifice their own lives to save hers, if need be. But to me her safety is no more important than the others who are threatened. Please, try to understand my position."

"And nothing we can say will persuade you even to postpone the attack?" Tachyon hand-combed his hair back out of his eyes.

"The ape is very near to Adam's Peak. There are many pilgrims at this time of year, and there is no time for a

successful evacuation. Delay will almost certainly cost lives."
Dissanayake stood and picked up his cap from the desktop.
"And now I must see to my duties. You're welcome to monitor
the operation from here if you like."

Jayewardene shook his head. "No, thank you. We do
appreciate your taking time to see us."

The general extended his palms. "I wish I could have
been more helpful. Good luck to us all, even the ape."

The sky was beginning to brighten when they got back to
the car. Saul was leaning against the door, an unlit cigarette in
his mouth. Tachyon and Jayewardene walked over to him as
Danforth and Paula got into the car.

"Everything proceeding according to plan?" Jayewardene
asked.

"She's out and hidden. Nobody seems to have noticed a
thing." Saul pulled out a plastic lighter. "Now?"

"Now or never," said Tachyon, sliding into the backseat.

Saul flicked the lighter and stared a moment at the flame
before starting up his cigarette. "Let's get the hell out of
Dodge."

"Five minutes," said Jayewardene, walking quickly to
the other side of the car.

They pulled up next to the front gate. The guard walked
slowly over and extended his hand. "Your badges, please."

Jayewardene unclipped his and handed it over as the
guard collected them.

"Shit," said Danforth. "I dropped the damn thing."

Saul flipped on the car's interior lights. Jayewardene
glanced at his watch. They didn't have time for this. Danforth
reached into the crack between the edge of the seat and the
door, made a face, and pulled out the badge. He handed it
quickly to the guard, who took the badges back to his post
before swinging the gate open.

The gate creaked closed behind them with less than two
minutes left. Saul pushed the accelerator quickly up to fifty,
doing his best to avoid the larger potholes.

"I hope Radha can manage this. She's never extended
her powers over such a large area before." Tachyon drummed
his fingers on the vinyl car seat. He turned to look back.
"We're far enough away, I think. Stop here."

Saul pulled over and they all got out and looked back
toward the base.

"I don't get it." Danforth crouched down next to the rear

of the car. "I mean, all she can do is turn into an elephant. I don't see where this gets us."

"Yes, but the mass has to come from somewhere, Mr. Danforth. And electrical energy is the most easily convertible source." Tachyon looked at his watch. "Twenty seconds."

"You know, if you could make your movies this exciting, Mr D. . . ." Paula shook her head. "Come on, Radha."

The entire base went silently dark. "Hot damn." Danforth popped up and bounced on his toes. "She did it."

Jayewardene looked at the gray sky above the horizon. A dark shape lifted itself up out of the larger blackness and moved toward them, throwing off occasional blue sparks.

"I think she may be a bit overcharged," said Tachyon. "But no gunfire. I'm sure they don't know what hit them."

"That's fine," said Danforth. "Because I'm not really sure what did either."

"What I understand," said Saul, leaning into the front seat and starting up the car, "is that no more choppers are taking off from there for a while. And Miss Elephant Girl owes me a new battery from yesterday."

Radha flew in and landed next to the car, sparks igniting from each foot as she touched the ground. Jayewardene thought she looked a little bigger than she had the day before. Tachyon walked over and stepped onto her front leg, his hair standing out like a clown's wig as he touched her. Radha lifted him up onto her back.

"We'll see you soon, with luck," the alien said, waving.

Jayewardene nodded. "The drive to Adam's Peak should take us about an hour from here. Fly northwest as quickly as you can."

The elephant rose noiselessly into the air and they were gone before anything else could be said.

The road was narrow. Dense trees grew to its edge and stretched ahead endlessly. They had been alone except for a bus and a few horse-drawn carts. Jayewardene explained to them what the ape really was and how he had come by the knowledge. Discussing his ace ability passed the time during the drive. Saul was pushing as hard as he could on the mud-slicked roads, making better time than Jayewardene had thought possible.

"I don't understand one thing, though," said Paula, leaning forward from the backseat to put her head next to his.

"If these visions are always true, why are you working so hard to see that things turn out?"

"For myself there is no choice," Jayewardene said. "I cannot let the visions dictate how I lead my life, so I try to act as I would have without such knowledge. And a little knowledge of the future is very dangerous. The final outcome is not my only concern. What happens in the interim is equally as important. If anyone was killed by the ape because I knew it would ultimately have its humanity restored, I would be guilty of having caused that death."

"I think you're being a little hard on yourself." Paula gave his shoulder a light squeeze. "There's only so much anyone can do."

"Those are my beliefs." Jayewardene turned around and looked into her eyes. She returned the look for an instant, then sank back next to Danforth.

"Something going on up ahead," Saul said in a level, almost disinterested tone.

They were at the top of a hill. The trees had been cleared away from the roadside for a hundred yards or so on either side, giving them an unobstructed view.

Sri Pada's peak was still shrouded in the early morning mist. Helicopters circled something unseen near the base of the mountain.

"Think it's our boy they're after?" asked Danforth.

"Almost certainly." Jayewardene wished he had brought along field glasses. One of the circling shapes might be Radha and Tachyon, but from this distance there was no way to tell. The clearing ended, and they were again surrounded by jungle.

"Want me to jack it up a little?" Saul crushed out his cigarette in the ashtray.

"As long as we get there alive," Paula said, fastening her seat belt.

Saul pushed the accelerator down a little farther, leaving a spray of mud behind them.

They parked behind a pair of abandoned buses that blocked off the road. No one was visible other than the beast and its attackers. The pilgrims had either fled up the mountain or back down the road into the valley. Jayewardene walked as quickly as he could up the stone steps, the others following behind him. The helicopters had kept the ape from making it very far up the mountain.

"Any sign of our elephant?" asked Danforth.

"Can't see them from here." Jayewardene's sides already hurt from the exertion. He paused to rest a moment and looked up as one of the choppers dropped a steel net. There was an answering roar, but they couldn't tell if the net had found its target.

They worked their way up the steps for several hundred yards, passing through an empty but undamaged rest station. The helicopters were still pressing their attack, although they appeared to be fewer in number now. Jayewardene slipped on one of the wet flagstones and smashed his knee against a step edge. Saul grabbed him by the armpits and lifted him up. "I'm all right," he said, painfully straightening his leg. "Let's keep on."

An elephant trumpeted in the distance.

"Hurry," said Paula, taking the stairs in twos.

Jayewardene and the others trotted up after her. After another hundred-yard climb he stopped them. "We have to cut across the mountain's face here. The footing is very dangerous. Hold on to the trees when you can." He stepped out onto the moist soil and steadied himself against a coconut palm, then began working slowly toward the direction of the battle.

They were slightly higher than the ape when they got close enough to see what was going on. The monster had a steel net in one hand and a stripped tree in the other. It was holding Radha and the two remaining helicopters at bay like a gladiator with a net and trident. Jayewardene couldn't see Robyn but assumed that the beast had her in the top of a tree again.

"Well, now that we're here, what the hell do we do?" Danforth leaned against a jak tree, breathing hard.

"We go get Robyn." Paula wiped her muddy hands on her shorts and took a step toward the ape.

"Wait." Danforth grabbed her hand. "I can't afford to lose you too. Let's see what Tachyon can do."

"No," Paula said, twisting away. "We have to get her out while the ape's distracted."

The pair stared hard at each other for a moment, then Jayewardene came between them. "Let's get a bit closer and see what's possible."

They half-slid, half-walked down the slope, then hit a ledge that was deep mud. Jayewardene felt it slip uncomfortably into his shoes. Robyn was still nowhere in sight, but the ape hadn't noticed them.

The last helicopter moved into position over the ape and dropped its net. The ape caught it on the end of the tree and deflected it to one side, then tossed the tree at the retreating chopper, which had to bank away sharply to avoid being hit. The ape beat its chest and roared.

Radha and Tachyon moved in from behind at treetop level. The ape reached down, picked up one of the steel nets, and swung it in a blur of motion. There was a pinging thwack as the edge of the net caught Radha on the foreleg. Tachyon slipped off her back and was left dangling from her ear. Radha gained height and pulled Tachyon back up onto her shoulders.

The ape pounded the earth and bared its teeth, then stood there clutching and unclutching its huge, black hands.

"I don't see what they can do," said Danforth. "That thing is just too strong."

"We shall see," Jayewardene said.

Tachyon leaned in close to one of Radha's immense ears. The elephant dropped down like a stone for a distance, then began circling rapidly around the ape's head. The ape lifted its arms and twisted around, trying to keep its enemy in sight. After a few moments the creature was half a turn behind the elephant. Radha dove directly for the ape's back. Tachyon jumped onto the ape's neck, and the flying elephant moved away quickly to a safe distance. The ape hunched down, then reached back for Tachyon, who was clinging to the thick fur on its shoulder. The beast plucked the alien off easily and held him up for inspection, then roared and brought Tachyon toward its mouth.

"Holy shit," said Danforth, restraining Paula.

The monster had Tachyon almost into its mouth when it froze, jerked convulsively for a moment, and toppled over backward. The impact jarred water from the trees, streaking the mud on the faces of Jayewardene and his companions. Jayewardene hurried downhill toward the ape, trying to ignore the pain in his knee.

Tachyon was squirming out of the ape's rigid fingers when they arrived at the creature's side. He slid down quickly off the giant body and steadied himself against Jayewardene.

"Burning sky! You were right, Mr. Jayewardene." He took several deep breaths. "There is a man inside the beast."

"How did you stop it?" Danforth asked, staying a few steps farther away than the others. "And where's Robyn?"

"Headed back to North Dakota," came a weak voice from a nearby treetop. Robyn waved and began picking her way down.

"I'll see if she's okay," Paula said, running over.

"To answer your first question, Mr. Danforth," Tachyon said, counting the missing buttons on his shirt, "the main portion of the brain is simian and consists mostly of an old black-and-white film. But there is also a human personality, completely subordinate to the ape mentality. I have temporarily given them equal control, thus providing a stasis that has paralyzed it."

Danforth nodded uncomprehendingly. "So what do we do now?"

"Dr. Tachyon will now restore the ape to human form." Jayewardene rubbed his leg. "The military isn't likely to stay away for long. There isn't much time to do what must be done." As if to punctuate his remark, one of the helicopters appeared and hovered over them for a moment before turning away.

Tachyon nodded and looked at Jayewardene. "You saw the transformation in your vision. Was I injured? Just out of curiosity."

Jayewardene shrugged. "Would it matter?"

"No. I suppose not." Tachyon chewed on a fingernail. "Matter. That's the real problem. When we restore the human mind to dominance, he'll shed all that excess matter as energy. Anyone near, including myself, is likely to be killed."

Jayewardene pointed to Radha, who was helping Robyn down out of the tree. "Perhaps if you were held in the air, ungrounded so to speak, the danger would be minimized. And if the energy was channeled into something like a lightning bolt . . ." Jayewardene looked up at the overcast sky.

"Yes. That idea has possibilities." Tachyon nodded and yelled to Radha. "Don't change back yet."

A few minutes later everyone was in position. Jayewardene sat next to Paula, who held Robyn's head in her lap. Saul and Danforth stood a few yards away. Radha, some ten feet off the ground, held Tachyon in her trunk a few feet from the ape's head. Saul had torn his shirt into blindfolds for Elephant Girl and Tachyon. They could hear the beast's labored breathing from where they sat.

"You'd better close your eyes or turn away," said Jayewardene. They did as he suggested.

The vision took over and Jayewardene felt all the air go out of him. He smelled the damp jungle. Heard birds singing and the faraway flap of helicopter rotors. The sun went behind a cloud. An ant crawled up his leg. He shut his eyes. Even through his closed lids the flash was magnesium bright. There was a single deafening boom of thunder. He jumped involuntarily, then waited a moment and opened his eyes.

Through the white streak in his vision caused by the flash, he saw Tachyon kneeling next to a thin, naked, Caucasian man. Radha was stomping out small fires that had broken out in a circle around them.

"How am I going to explain this to the Central Park Zoo?" asked Danforth, his expression dazed.

"Oh, I don't know," said Jayewardene, moving slowly back down the mountainside toward Tachyon. "It sounds like great pub to me."

Tachyon helped the naked man to his feet. He was of average height with plain features. He moved his mouth but made no sound.

"I think he's come through it intact," said Tachyon, getting his shoulder under the man's armpit. "Thanks to you."

Jayewardene shook his head and pulled three identical envelopes out of his pants pocket. "What happened had to happen. When the military shows up, and they will, I want you to deliver these to them. Say they are from me. One goes to the president, one the Minister of State, the last to the Minister of the Interior. It is my letter of resignation."

Tachyon took the envelopes and tucked them away. "I see."

"As for me, I intend to make the pilgrimage to the top of Sri Pada. Perhaps it will help me achieve my goal. To be rid of these visions." Jayewardene headed back toward the stone steps.

"Mr. Jayewardene," Tachyon said. "If your pilgrimage is not successful, I would be willing to do anything possible to help you. Perhaps try to put some mental damper to keep you out of touch with your ability. We leave tomorrow. I

suspect your government will be glad to see us go. But you'd
be more than welcome to come with us."

Jayewardene bowed and moved over toward Paula and
Robyn.

"Mr. Jayewardene," Robyn said in a rasping voice. Her
blond hair was tangled and matted with mud. Her clothes
were in shreds. Jayewardene tried not to look. "Thank you for
helping save me."

"You're most welcome. But you should be gotten to a
hospital as soon as possible. Just for observation." He turned
to Paula. "I plan to make the pilgrimage up the mountain
now, if you'd like to come."

"I don't know," said Paula, looking down at Robyn.

"Go ahead," Robyn said. "I'll be fine."

Paula smiled and looked back at Jayewardene. "I'd love
to."

*The multicolored neon reflects brokenly from the wet
pavement. The Japanese are all around us, mostly men. They
stare at Peregrine, who has her beautiful, banded wings
folded tight around her. She looks ahead, ignoring them.*

*We have been walking a long way. My sides burn and my
feet ache. She stops at an alleyway and turns to me. I nod.
She walks slowly into the darkness. I follow, afraid of making
a noise that will attract attention. I feel useless, like a
shadow. Peregrine stretches her wings. They almost touch the
cold stone on either side of the alleyway. She folds them back.*

*A door opens and the alley is filled with light. A man
steps out. He is thin, tall, with dark skin, almond eyes, and a
high forehead. He cranes his head forward to look at us.*

"Fortunato?" she asks.

Jayewardene crouched next to the dying embers of the
campfire. A few other pilgrims sat wordlessly next to him.
The vision had awakened him. Even here there was no
escape. Although the pilgrimage was not officially complete
until he returned home, he knew that the visions would
continue. He was tainted with the wild card virus, perhaps
tainted by the years he'd spent in foreign countries. Spiritual
purity and completeness was impossible to attain. At least for
the present.

Paula came up behind him and put her hands lightly on
his shoulders. "It's beautiful up here, really."

The others around the campfire looked up at her suspiciously. Jayewardene guided her away. They stood at the edge of the peak, staring out into the dark mist down the mountain.

"Each religion had its own belief about the footprint," he said. "We believe it was made by Buddha. The Hindus say it was made by Shiva. Moslems argue that it is where Adam stood for a thousand years, atoning for the loss of paradise."

"Whoever it was, they had a big foot," Paula said. "That print was three feet long."

The sun came up over the horizon, slowly bringing light to the swirling mists below them. Their shadows grew huge in the grayness. Jayewardene caught his breath. "The Specter of the Brocken," he said, closing his eyes in prayer.

"Wow," said Paula. "I guess it's my week for things giant."

Jayewardene opened his eyes and sighed. His fantasies about Paula had been as unrealistic as those about his hope of destroying his power through the pilgrimage. They were like two wheels in a clockwork whose teeth meshed but whose centers forever remained at a distance. "What you have seen is the rarest of wonders here. One can come here every day for a year and not witness what we have."

Paula yawned, then smiled weakly. "Sounds like it's time to go down."

"Yes. It's time."

Danforth and Paula met him at the airport. Danforth was shaved and in clean clothes, almost the same cocksure producer he'd met only a few days ago. Paula wore shorts and a tight, white T-shirt. She seemed ready to get on with her life. Jayewardene envied her.

"How's Miss Symmes?" he asked.

Danforth rolled his eyes. "Well enough to have called her lawyer three times in the last twelve hours. I'm really in the soup now. I'll be lucky to stay in the business at all."

"Offer her a five-picture deal and plenty of points," said Jayewardene, cramming his entire knowledge of film jargon into one sentence.

"Sign this guy up, Mr. D." Paula grinned and took Jayewardene by the arm. "He might be able to get you out of some jams even I couldn't."

Danforth stuck his thumbs through his belt loops and

rocked back and forth. "That's really not a bad idea. Not bad at all." He took Jayewardene's hand and shook it. "I really don't know what we would have done without you."

"Gone right down the drain." Paula gave Jayewardene a one-shoulder hug. "I guess this is where we have to say good-bye."

"Mr. Jayewardene." A young government courier shouldered his way through the crowd to their side. He was breathing hard, but took time to straighten his uniform before handing Jayewardene an envelope. It bore the presidential seal.

"Thank you," he said, popping it open with his thumb. He read it silently.

Paula leaned in to look, but the writing was Sinhalese. "What does it say?"

"That my resignation has not been accepted and I am considered to be on an extended leave of absence. Not exactly the safest thing he could have done, but much appreciated." He bowed to Danforth and Paula. "I'll look for the film when it comes out."

"*King Pongo*," Danforth said. "It'll be a monster hit for sure."

The plane was more crowded than he had expected. People had been wandering around since after takeoff, chatting, complaining, getting drunk. Peregrine was standing in the aisle, talking to the tall, blond man who'd been with her in in the bar. They were keeping their voices low, but Jayewardene could tell from the looks on their faces that it was not a pleasant conversation. Peregrine turned away from the man, took a deep breath, and walked over to Jayewardene.

"May I sit next to you?" she asked. "I know everyone else on this plane. Some considerably better than I'd like."

"I'm flattered and delighted," he said. And it was true. Her features and fragrance were beautiful but intimidating. Even to him.

She smiled, her lips curving in an almost inhumanly attractive manner. "That man you and Tach saved. He's sitting right over there." She indicated him with the arch of an eyebrow. "His name's Jeremiah Strauss. Used to be a minor league ace named the Projectionist. I guess we're all bozos on this bus. Ah, here he comes now."

Strauss wandered over, his hands clutching the backs of

seats as he went. He was pale and afraid. "Mr. Jayewardene?" He said it as if he'd been practicing the pronunciation for the last ten minutes. "My name is Strauss. I've been told all that you did for me. And I want you to know that I never forget a favor. If you need a job when we get to New York, U Thant's a friend of the family. We'll work something out."

"That's very kind of you, Mr. Strauss, but I would have done it in any case." Jayewardene reached up and shook his hand.

Strauss smiled, straightened his shoulders, and clutched his way back to his seat.

"I'd say he's going to need quite a while to readjust," Peregrine said in a whisper. "Twenty-plus years is a lot to lose."

"I can only wish him a speedy recovery. It's difficult to feel sorry for myself considering his circumstances."

"Feeling sorry for oneself is an inalienable right." She yawned. "I can't believe how much I'm sleeping. Should have time for a nice long nap before we get to Thailand. Do you mind if I use your shoulder?"

"No. Please think of it as your own." He looked out the window. "Australia. Then where?"

She rested her head against him and closed her eyes. "Malaysia, Vietnam, Indonesia, New Zealand, Hong Kong, China, Japan. Fortunato." She said the last word almost too quietly for him to hear. "I doubt we'll be running into him."

"But you will." He said it hoping to please her, but she looked at him as if she'd caught him going through her underwear.

"You know this? You've had one of those visions about me?" Someone had obviously told her about his power.

"Yes. I'm sorry. I really have no control over them." He looked back out the window, feeling ashamed.

She rested her head back onto his shoulder. "It's not your fault. Don't worry. I'm sure Tach will be able to do something for you."

"I hope so."

She'd been asleep for over an hour. He'd eaten one-handed to keep from waking her up. The roast beef he'd had was like a ball of lead in his stomach. He knew he would

survive Western food at least until they reached Japan. The
air was a low rumble as it rushed by the plane's metal skin.
Peregrine breathed softly next to his ear. Jayewardene closed
his eyes and prayed for dreamless sleep.

DOWN IN THE DREAMTIME

Edward Bryant

Cordelia Chaisson had dreamed about the murder less frequently during the month past. It surprised her she still thought of it even that much; after all, she had seen far worse. Work consumed her; the job with Global Fun & Games sufficiently exhausted her days; laboring on the AIDS/WCV benefit to be held in May at Xavier Desmond's Jokertown Funhouse took up much of the nights. Most evenings she went to sleep long after the eleven o'clock news. Five in the morning came all too early. There was little time for diversion.

But there were still the occasional bad nights of dreaming:

—Coming up out of the Fourteenth Street station, heels clicking smartly on the dirty concrete, traffic muttering down from above. Hearing the voice a few steps up at street level saying, "Just give us the purse, bitch!" Hesitating, then going ahead anyway. Fearing, but—

She heard the second voice, the Aussie accent: "G'day, mates. Some problem here?"

Cordelia emerged from the stairwell into the sweltering night. She saw the instant tableau of two unshaven white punks backing a middle-aged woman into the space between the short row of phone carrels and the plywood butt of a shuttered newsstand. The woman had tight hold of both a yapping black poodle and her handbag.

Sun-burnt and rangy, the man Cordelia assumed was an Aussie faced down the two youths. He wore a sand-colored outfit that looked like a rougher, more authentic version of a Banana Republic ensemble. There was a bright, well-cared-for knife in one hand.

"A problem, sonny?" he repeated.

"No, no problem, dick-head," said one of the punks. He pulled out a short-barreled pistol from his jacket and shot the Aussie in the face.

It simply happened too quickly for Cordelia to react. As

the man fell to the sidewalk, the assailants ran. The woman
with the poodle screamed, momentarily harmonizing with
the cries of the dog.

Cordelia ran to the man and knelt beside him. She felt
for the pulse in his neck. Almost imperceptible. It was
probably too late for CPR. She averted her gaze from the
blood pooling beneath the man's head. The hot metallic smell
of blood nauseated her. A siren wailed up the scale less than a
block away.

"I've still got my purse!" the woman cried.

The man's face twitched. He died. "Shit," said Cordelia
softly, helplessly. There wasn't a damned thing she could do.

Some kind of trouble now, Cordelia thought, as a dark-
suited man she didn't recognize waved her into one of
GF&G's executive offices. Deep shit, maybe. The two wom-
en standing by the desk examined a stack of printouts.
Red-haired and tough, Polly Rettig was marketing chief for
the GF&G satellite service. She was Cordelia's immediate
boss. The other woman was Luz Alcala, vice president for
programming and Rettig's boss. Neither Rettig nor Alcala
smiled as they usually did. The man in black stepped back by
the door and stood there with his arms folded. Security?
Cordelia speculated. "Good morning, Cordelia," Rettig said.
"Please have a seat. We'll be with you in just a moment." She
turned her attention back to Alcala and pointed out something on the sheet in her hand.

Luz Alcala slowly nodded. "Either we buy it first, or
we're dead in the water. Maybe hire someone good—"

"Don't even think it," said Rettig, frowning slightly.

"It might become necessary," Alcala said. "He's dangerous."

Cordelia tried to keep the bewildered look off her face.

"He's also too powerful." Folding her hands, Rettig
turned toward Cordelia. "Tell me what you know about
Australia."

"I've seen everything Peter Weir ever directed," Cordelia
said, momentarily hesitating. What was going on here?

"You've never been there?"

"New York is the farthest I've ever been from home."
Home was Atelier Parish, Louisiana. Home was a place she'd
rather not think about. In most respects it didn't exist.

Rettig was looking at Alcala. "What do you think?"

"I think yes." The older woman picked up a thick

envelope and handed it across the desk to Cordelia. "Open it, please." She found a passport, a sheaf of airline tickets, an American Express card, and a hefty folder of traveler's checks. "You'll need to sign those." Alcala indicated the checks and the credit card.

Cordelia looked silently up from the smiling image affixed to the first page of the passport. "Nice photo," she said. "I don't remember applying."

"There was little time," said Polly Rettig apologetically. "We took liberties."

"The point is," said Alcala, "you're leaving this afternoon for the other side of the world."

Cordelia felt stunned, then recognized the excitement growing. "All the way to Australia?"

"Commercial flight," said Alcala. "Brief stops for fuel in L.A., Honolulu, and Auckland. In Sydney you'll catch an Ansett flight to Melbourne and another plane up to Alice Springs. Then you'll rent a Land-Rover and drive to Madhi Gap. You're going to have a full day," she added dryly.

A thousand things crowded into Cordelia's mind. "But what about my job here? And I can't just abandon the benefit—I want to go to New Jersey this weekend to check out Buddy Holley."

"He can wait till you're back. The whole benefit can wait," said Rettig firmly. "PR is fine, but the JADL and the Manhattan AIDS Project don't pay your salary. This is Global Fun & Games business."

"But—"

"It is important." Voice smoothly modulated, Alcala made it sound like a pronouncement.

"But what *is* it?" She felt as if she were listening to Auntie Alice on Radio Wonderland. "What's all this about?"

Alcala seemed to be picking her words carefully. "You've seen the PR flacking GF&G's plan to inaugurate a worldwide entertainment service via satellite."

Cordelia nodded. "I thought that was years down the road."

"It was. The only thing holding back the plan was the investment capital."

"We've got the money," Rettig said. "We have the help of allied investors. Now we need the satellite time and the ground stations to pipe our programming down to the earth."

"Unfortunately," said Alcala, "we have sudden competition for securing the services of the commercial facility in the telecommunications complex in Madhi Gap. A man named Leo Barnett."

"The TV evangelist?"

Alcala nodded.

"The ace-baiting, intolerant, psychotic, species-chauvinist son of a bitch," said Rettig with sudden passion. "*That* TV evangelist. Fire-breather, some call him."

"And you're sending *me* to Madhi Gap?" said Cordelia excitedly. Incredible, she thought. It was too good to be true. "Thank you! Thank you very much. I'll do a terrific job."

Rettig and Alcala glanced at each other. "Hold on," said Alcala. "You're going along to assist, but you're not going to be negotiating."

It *was* too good to be true. Shit, she thought.

"Meet Mr. Carlucci," said Alcala.

"Marty," said a nasal voice from behind Cordelia.

"*Mr.* Carlucci," Alcala repeated.

Cordelia turned and took another, closer look at the man she had dismissed as some kind of hired help. Medium height, compact build, styled black hair. Carlucci smiled. He looked like a thug. An amiable one, but still a thug. His suit didn't look as if it had come off the rack. Now that she looked more closely, the coat looked expensively tailored to a T.

Carlucci extended his hand. "It's Marty," he said. "We got to spend a day and a night on a plane, we might as well be friendly about it, you know?"

Cordelia sensed disapproval from the two older women. She took Carlucci's hand. She was no jock, but she knew she had a firm grip. Cordelia felt that the man could have squeezed her fingers a *lot* harder had he wished to. Behind his smile, she sensed a glint of something feral. Not a man to cross.

"Mr. Carlucci," said Alcala, "represents a large investors' group that has entered into partnership with us in the matter of acquiring a major share in global satellite entertainment. They are providing a portion of the capital with which we expect to set up the initial satellite net."

"A lot of bucks," said Carlucci. "But we'll all make it back and probably ten times as much in about five years. With our resources and your ability to"—he grinned—"acquire talent, I figure there's no way we can lose. Everybody makes out."

"But we do wish to saturate the Australian market," said

Alcala, "and the ground station is already in place. All we need is a signed letter of intent to sell."

"I can be very persuasive." Carlucci grinned again. To Cordelia the expression looked like a barracuda showing its teeth. Or maybe a wolf. Something predatory. And definitely persuasive.

"You'd better go pack, dear," said Alcala. "Try for one carry-on bag. Enough clothes to last a week. One sophisticated outfit; a more comfortable one for the outback. Anything else you need you can buy there. Alice Springs is isolated, but it is not an uncivilized place."

"It ain't Brooklyn," said Carlucci.

"No," said Alcala. "No, it isn't."

"Be at Tomlin," said Rettig, "by four."

Cordelia glanced from Carlucci to Rettig to Alcala. "I meant it before. Thank you. I'll do a good job."

"I know you will, dear," said Alcala, her dark eyes suddenly looking tired.

"I hope so," Rettig said.

Cordelia knew she was dismissed. She turned and headed for the door.

"See you on the plane," said Carlucci. "First class all the way. Hope you don't mind smoking."

She hesitated only momentarily, then said firmly, "I do."

For the first time Carlucci frowned. Polly Rettig grinned. Even Luz Alcala smiled.

Cordelia lived in an apartment with a single roommate in a high rise on Maiden Lane near the Woolworth Building and Jetboy's Tomb. Veronica wasn't home, so Cordelia scrawled a brief note. It took her about ten minutes to pack what she thought she'd need on the trip. Then she called Uncle Jack and asked whether he could meet her before she hopped the Tomlin Express. He could. It was one of his days off.

Jack Robicheaux was waiting for her in the diner when she entered from the avenue. No surprise. He knew the transit system below Manhattan better than anyone else.

Every time Cordelia saw her uncle, she felt as if she were looking into a mirror. True, he was male, twenty-five years older, sixty pounds heavier. But the dark hair and eyes were the same. So were the cheekbones. The family resemblance was undeniable. And then there was the less tangible similarity. Both had despaired of any kind of normal growing up in Louisiana; each in young adulthood had fled Cajun country and run away to New York City.

"Hey, Cordie." Jack rose to his feet when he saw her, gave her a firm hug and a kiss on the cheek.

"I'm going to Australia, Uncle Jack." She hadn't meant to give away the surprise, but it burst out anyway.

"No kidding." Jack grinned. "When?"

"Today."

"Yeah?" Jack sat down and leaned back in the green Naugahyde seat. "How come?"

She told him about the meeting.

Jack frowned at the mention of Carlucci. "You know what I think? Suzanne—Bagabond—has been hanging around Rosemary and the DA's office, feeding me a little spare-time work. I don't hear everything, but I catch enough. I think maybe we're talking about Gambione cash here."

"GF&G wouldn't go for that," said Cordelia. "They're legitimate, even if they do funnel money from the skin mags."

"Desperation breeds a special blindness. Especially if the money's been laundered through Havana. I know Rosemary's been trying to steer the Gambiones into legitimate enterprise. I guess satellite TV qualifies."

"That's my job you're talking about," said Cordelia.

"Better than hooking for the big F."

Cordelia knew her cheeks were coloring. Jack looked repentant. "Sorry," he said. "I wasn't trying to be bitchy."

"Listen, this was really a big day for me. I just wanted to share it."

"I appreciate that." Jack leaned across the Formica table. "I know you're gonna do just fine down under. But if you need any help, if you need anything at all, just call."

"Halfway around the world?"

He nodded. "Doesn't matter how far. If I can't be there in person, maybe I can suggest something. And if you really need a fourteen-foot 'gator in the flesh"—he grinned—"give me about eighteen hours. I know you can hold any fort *that* long."

She knew he meant it. That was why Jack was the only person in the Robicheaux clan who meant anything at all to her. "I'll be okay. It's going to be terrific." She got up from the booth.

"No coffee?"

"No time." She hefted the soft leather carry-on case. "I need the next train to Tomlin. Please tell C.C. good-bye for me. Bagabond and the cats too."

Jack nodded. "Still want the kitten?"

"You better believe it."

"I'll walk you to the station." Jack got up and took her case. She resisted only a moment before smiling and allowing him.

"There's something I want you to remember," said Jack.

"Don't talk to strangers? Take my pill? Eat green vegetables?"

"Shut up," he said fondly. "Your power and mine, they may be related, but they're still different."

"I'm not as likely to get turned into a suitcase," said Cordelia.

He ignored her. "You've used the reptile level in your brain to control some pretty violent situations. You killed folks to protect yourself. Don't forget you can use the power for life too."

Cordelia felt bewildered. "I don't know how. It scares me. I just would rather ignore it."

"But you can't. Remember what I'm saying." Braving cabs, they crossed the avenue to the subway entrance.

"Ever see much Nicolas Roeg?" Cordelia said.

"Everything," said Jack.

"Maybe this will be my 'walkabout.'"

"Just make it back in one piece."

She smiled. "If I can deal with a bull alligator here, I figure I can handle a bunch of crocodiles in Australia just fine."

Jack smiled too. It was a warm, friendly expression. But it showed all his teeth. Jack was a shape-shifter and Cordelia wasn't, but the family resemblance was unmistakable.

When she found Marty Carlucci at the United terminal at Tomlin, Cordelia discovered the man was carrying an expensive alligator overnight bag and a similarly appointed attaché case. She was less than pleased, but there wasn't much she could say.

The woman working the computer at the ticketing counter gave them seats one row apart in first class—smoking and nonsmoking. Cordelia suspected it wouldn't make much of a difference to her lungs, but felt she had won a moral deci-

sion. Also she suspected she'd feel more comfortable not
having to sit with her shoulder rubbing up against his.

A good deal of the excitement of travel had worn off by
the time the 747 set down at LAX. Cordelia spent much of
the next two hours looking out at the early evening darkness
and wondering if she'd ever get to see the La Brea Tar Pits,
Watts Towers, Disneyland, Giant Insect National Monument,
the Universal tour. She bought some paperbacks in the gift
shop. Finally Carlucci and she were called for the Air New
Zealand flight. As with the first leg, they had requested
first-class seats on either side of the terminator dividing
active smoke from passive.

Carlucci snored much of the way to Honolulu. Cordelia
couldn't sleep at all. She divided her time between the new
Jim Thompson mystery and staring out the window at the
moonlit Pacific thirty-six thousand feet below.

Both Carlucci and she converted some of their traveler's
checks into Australian dollars on the concourse in Honolulu.
"The numbers are good." Carlucci gestured at the conversion
chart taped to the window of the change booth. "I checked
the paper before we left the States."

"We're still in the States."

He ignored her.

Just to make conversation, she said, "You know a lot
about finance?"

Pride filled his voice. "Wharton School of Finance and
Commerce. Full ride. Family paid for it."

"You've got rich parents?"

He ignored her.

The Air New Zealand jumbo loaded and took off, and the
stewards fed the passengers one last time in preparation for
tucking into the long night to Auckland. Cordelia switched on
her reading light when the cabin illumination dimmed. Finally she heard Carlucci grumble from the row ahead, "Get
some sleep, kiddo. Jet lag's gonna be bad enough. You got a
lotta Pacific to cross yet."

Cordelia realized the man had a valid point. She waited
a few more minutes so that it would look more like it was her
own idea, then switched off the light. She pulled the blanket
tight around her and scrunched into the seat so she could
look out the port. The travel excitement was almost all gone
now. She realized she was indeed exhausted.

She saw no clouds. Just the shining ocean. She found it

astonishing that anything could be so apparently endless. So enigmatic. It occurred to her that the Pacific could swallow up a 747 without more than the tiniest ripple.

Eer-moonans!
The words meant nothing to her.
Eer-moonans.
The phrase was so soft it could have been a whisper in her mind.

Cordelia's eyes clicked open. Something was very wrong. The reassuring vibration of the jumbo's engines was somehow distorted, blended with the sigh of a rising wind. She tried to throw the suddenly strangling blanket away and clawed her way up the back of the seat ahead, nails biting into the cool leather.

When she looked down the other side, Cordelia sharply drew in her breath. She was staring into the wide, surprised, dead eyes of Marty Carlucci. His body still faced forward. But his head had been screwed around 180 degrees. Viscid blood slowly dripped from his ears, his mouth. It had pooled at the bottom of his eyes and was oozing down over his cheekbones.

The sound of her scream closed in around Cordelia's head. It was like crying out in a barrel. She finally struggled free of the blanket and stared unbelievingly down the aisle.

She still stood in the Air New Zealand 747. And she stood in the desert. One was overlaid on the other. She moved her feet and felt the gritty texture of the sand, heard its rasp. The aisle was dotted with scrubby plants moving as the wind continued to rise.

The jumbo's cabin stretched into a distance her eye couldn't quite follow, diminishing endlessly into perspective as it approached the tail section. Cordelia saw no one moving.

"Uncle Jack!" she cried out. There was, of course, no answer.

Then she heard the howling. It was a hollow ululation rising and falling, gaining in volume. Far down the cabin, in the tunnel that was also the desert, she saw the shapes leaping toward her. The creatures bounded like wolves, first in the aisle, then scrambling across the tops of the seats.

Cordelia smelled a rank, decaying odor. She scrambled into the aisle, recoiling until her spine was flush against the forward bulkhead.

The creatures were indistinct in the half-light. She couldn't even be sure of their numbers. They *were* like wolves, claws clicking and tearing on the seats, but their heads were all wrong. The snouts were blunted off, truncated. Ruffs of shining spines ringed their necks. Their eyes were flat black holes deeper than the surrounding night.

Cordelia stared at the teeth. There were just too many long needle fangs to fit comfortably into those mouths. Teeth that champed and clashed, throwing out a spray of dark saliva.

The teeth reached for her.

Move, goddamnit! The voice was in her head. It was her own voice. Move!

—as teeth and claws sought her throat.

Cordelia hurled herself to the side. The lead wolf-creature smashed into the steel bulkhead, howled in pain, staggered upright confusedly as the second leaping monster rammed into its ribs. Cordelia scrambled past the confusion of horrors into the narrow galleyway.

Focus! Cordelia knew what she had to do. She wasn't Chuck Norris nor did she have an Uzi at hand. In her instant of respite as the wolf-creatures snarled and spat at one another, she wished again that Jack were here. But he wasn't. Concentrate, she told herself.

One of the blunted muzzles poked around the corner of the galley. Cordelia stared into the pair of deadly matte-black eyes. "Die, you son of a bitch," she cried aloud. She sensed the power uncoiling from the reptile level of her brain, felt the force flow into the alien mind of the monster, striking directly for the brain stem. She shut off its heart and respiration. The creature struggled toward her, then collapsed forward on its clawed paws.

The next monster appeared around the corner. How many of them were there? She tried to think. Six, eight, she wasn't sure. Another blunt muzzle protruded. Another set of claws. More gleaming teeth. Die! She felt the power draining from her. This was no feeling she'd known before. It was like trying to jog in quicksand.

The bodies of the wolf-creatures piled up. The surviving monsters scrambled over the barrier, lunging at her. The final one made it all the way into the galley.

Cordelia tried to shut down its brain, felt the power waning as the creature launched itself down the heap of corpses. As the toothy jaws reached for her throat, she swung a double fist and tried to smash them aside. One of the spines from the thing's ruff slid into the back of her left hand. Steaming spittle spattered her face.

She felt the staccato rhythm of the wolf-creature's breathing hesitate and cease as its body slumped onto her feet. But now she felt a chill spreading across her hand and up her arm. Cordelia grasped the spine with her right hand and wrenched it free. The shaft came loose and she hurled it from her, but the coldness didn't abate.

It'll reach my heart, she thought, and that was the last thing that passed through her mind. Cordelia felt herself collapsing, falling across the crazy-quilt arrangement of monstrous bodies. The wind filled up her ears; the darkness took her eyes.

"Hey! You okay, kid? Whattsa matter?" The accent was all New York. It was Marty Carlucci's voice. Cordelia struggled to open her eyes. The man bent over her, breath minty with recent toothpaste. He grasped her shoulders and shook her slightly.

"*Eer-moonans*," Cordelia said weakly.

"Huh?" Carlucci looked baffled.

"You're . . . dead."

"Damn straight," he said. "I don't know how many hours I slept, but I feel like shit. How about you?"

Memories of the night slammed back. "What's going on?" Cordelia said.

"We're landing. Plane's about half an hour out of Auckland. You wanna use the can, get cleaned up and all, you better do it quick." He took his fingers away from her shoulders. "Okay?"

"Okay." Cordelia sat up shakily. Her head felt as if it were stuffed with sodden cotton. "Everybody's okay? The plane isn't full of monsters?"

Carlucci stared at her. "Just tourists. Hey, you have some bad dreams? Want some coffee?"

"Coffee. Thanks." She grabbed her bag and struggled past him into the aisle. "Right. Nightmares. Bad ones."

In the restroom she alternated splashing cold and hot water on her face. Brushing her teeth helped. She slugged down three Midol and unsnarled her hair. Cordelia did her best with makeup. Finally she stared at herself in the mirror and shook her head. "Shit," she told herself, "you look thirty."

Her left hand itched. She raised it in front of her face and stared at the inflamed puncture wound. Maybe she had caught her hand on something when she'd moved in her sleep, and that had translated into the dream. Perhaps it was stigmata. Either story sounded equally implausible. Maybe this was some weird new menstrual side effect. Cordelia shook her head. Nothing made sense. Weakness flooded over her and she had to sit down on the lid of the toilet. The inside of her skull felt scoured. Maybe she *had* spent much of the night battling monsters.

Cordelia realized someone was knocking on the door of the restroom. Others wanted to get ready for New Zealand. So long as they weren't wolf-creatures . . .

The morning was sunny. The North Island of New Zealand was intensely green. The 747 touched down with scarcely a bump and then sat at the end of the runway for twenty minutes until the agriculture people climbed on board. Cordelia hadn't expected that. She watched bemusedly as the smiling young men in their crisp uniforms walked down the aisles, an aerosol jet of pest-killer fogging from the can in each hand. Something about this reminded her perversely of what she'd read of the final moments of Jetboy.

Carlucci must have been thinking something similar. Having promised not to smoke, he'd moved into the seat beside her. "Sure hope it's pesticide," he said. "Be a really nasty joke if it was the wild card virus."

After the passengers had murmured, griped, wheezed, and coughed, the jumbo taxied to the terminal and everyone debarked. The pilot told them they had two hours before the plane left on the thousand-mile leg to Sydney.

"Just time to stretch our legs, buy some cards, make some phone calls," said Carlucci. Cordelia welcomed the thought of getting some exercise.

In the main terminal Carlucci went off to place his trans-Pacific calls. The terminal seemed extraordinarily crowded. Cordelia saw camera crews in the distance. She headed for the doors to the outside.

From behind her she heard, "Cordelia! Ms. Chaisson!" The voice wasn't Carlucci's. Who the hell? She turned and saw a vision of flowing red hair framing a face that looked vaguely like Errol Flynn's in *Captain Blood*. But Flynn had never worn such bright clothing, not even in the colorized *Adventures of Captain Fabian*.

Cordelia stopped and smiled. "So," she said. "Do you like new wave music any better these days?"

"No," said Dr. Tachyon. "No, I'm afraid I do not."

"I fear," said the tall, winged woman standing beside Tachyon, "that our good Tacky will never progress much beyond Tony Bennett." A simply cut, voluminous blue silk dress whispered softly around her. Cordelia blinked. Peregrine was hard to mistake.

"Unfair, my dear." Tachyon smiled at his companion. "I have my favorites among contemporary performers. I'm rather fond of Placido Domingo." He turned back toward Cordelia. "I'm forgetting my manners. Cordelia, have you formally met Peregrine?"

Cordelia took the proffered hand. "I've had a call in to your agent for weeks now. Nice to see you." Shut up, she said to herself. Don't be rude.

Peregrine's dazzling blue eyes regarded her. "I'm sorry," she said. "Is this about the benefit at Dez's club? I'm afraid I've been incredibly busy tidying up other projects in the midst of getting ready for this trip."

"Peregrine," said Tachyon, "this young woman is Cordelia Chaisson. We know each other from the clinic. She's come frequently with friends to visit C.C. Ryder."

"C.C.'s going to be able to do the Funhouse," said Cordelia.

"That would be fabulous," said Peregrine. "I've admired her work for a long time."

"Perhaps we could all sit down over a drink," said Tachyon. He smiled at Cordelia. "There has been a delay with arranging the senator's ground transport into Auckland. I'm afraid we're stranded at the airport for a bit." The man glanced back over his shoulder. "As well, I'm afraid we are trying to avoid the rest of the party. The aircraft does get a bit close."

Cordelia felt the tempting proximity of fresh air starting to drift away. "I've got just about two hours," she said, hesitating. "Okay, let's have a drink." As they walked toward the restaurant, Cordelia didn't see Carlucci. He could get along fine by himself. What she did notice was the number of stares following them. No doubt some of the attention was being paid to Tachyon—his hair and wardrobe always ensured that. But mostly people were looking at Peregrine. Probably the New Zealanders weren't all that accustomed to seeing a tall, gorgeous woman with functional wings folded against her back. She *was* spectacular, Cordelia admitted to herself. It would be great to have the looks, the stature, the presence. At once Cordelia felt very young. Almost like a kid. Inadequate. Damn it.

Cordelia ordinarily took her coffee with milk. But if black would help clear her head, then she'd give it a try. She insisted that the three of them wait for a window table. If she wasn't going to breathe the outside air, at least she could sit within inches of it. The colors of the unfamiliar trees reminded her of photos she'd seen of the Monterey Peninsula.

"So," she said after they'd given orders to the waitress, "I guess I should say something about a small world. How's the junket? I saw some pictures of the Great Ape on the eleven o'clock news before I left."

Tachyon rambled on about Senator Hartmann's round-the-world tour. Cordelia remembered reading about it interminably in the *Post* on the subway, but had been so busy with the Funhouse benefit, she hadn't paid much attention. "Sounds like a backbreaker," she said when Tachyon finished his gloss.

Peregrine smiled wanly. "It hasn't exactly been a vacation. I think Guatemala was my favorite. Have your people thought of climaxing the benefit with a human sacrifice?"

Cordelia shook her head. "I think we're going for a little more festive tone, even considering the occasion."

"Listen," Peregrine said. "I'll do what I can with my agent. In the meantime maybe I can introduce you to a few folks who'll do you some good. Do you know Radha O'Reilly? Elephant Girl?" At Cordelia's head shake she continued, "When she turns into a flying elephant, it's smoother than anything Doug Henning's dreamed of. You ought to talk to Fantasy too. You could use a dancer like her."

"That'd be terrific," Cordelia said. "Thank you." She felt the frustration of wanting to do everything herself—*showing* everyone—and yet knowing when to accept the aid that was being graciously extended.

"So," Tachyon said, breaking in on her thoughts. "And

what are *you* doing here so far from home?" His expression looked expectant; his eyes gleamed with honest curiosity.

Cordelia knew she couldn't get away with claiming she'd won the trip for selling Girl Scout cookies. She opted for honesty. "I'm going to Australia with a guy from GF&G to try and buy a satellite ground station before it gets scarfed up by a TV preacher."

"Ah," said Tachyon. "Would that evangelist be Leo Barnett, by chance?"

Cordelia nodded.

"I hope you succeed." Tachyon frowned. "Our friend Fire-breather's power is growing at a dangerously exponential rate. I, for one, would prefer to see the growth of his media empire retarded."

"Just yesterday," said Peregrine, "I heard from Chrysalis that some of Barnett's youth-group thugs are hanging out in the Village and beating the stuffing out of anybody they think is both a joker and vulnerable."

"*Die Juden,*" Tachyon murmured. The two women glanced questioningly at him. "History." He sighed, then said to Cordelia, "Whatever help you need in competing with Barnett, let us know. I think you'll find a great deal of support from both aces and jokers."

"Hey," said an overly familiar voice from behind Cordelia's scapula. "What's happening?"

Without looking around Cordelia said, "Marty Carlucci, meet Dr. Tachyon and Peregrine." To the latter she said, "Marty's my chaperon."

"Hiya." Carlucci took the fourth chair. "Yeah, I know you," he said to Tachyon. He stared at Peregrine, frankly surveying her. All of her. "You I've seen a lot. I got tapes of every show you've done for years." His eyes narrowed. "Say, you pregnant?"

"Thank you," said Peregrine. "Yes." She stared him down.

"Uh, right," said Carlucci. He turned to Cordelia. "Kid, come on. We gotta get back on the plane." More firmly, "Now!"

Good-byes were said. Tachyon volunteered to pay for the coffee. "Good luck," Peregrine said, aimed specifically at Cordelia. Carlucci seemed preoccupied, not noticing.

As the two of them walked toward the boarding gate, he said, "Dumb fuckin' bitch."

Cordelia stopped dead still. *"What?"*

"Not you." Carlucci took her elbow roughly and propelled her toward the security checkpoint. "That joker who sells info—Chrysalis. I ran into her by the phones. I figured I'd save the price of a call."

"So?" said Cordelia.

"One of these days she's gonna get her invisible tits caught in the wringer and there's going to be real bright blood all over the laundry room wall. I told New York that too."

Cordelia waited, but he didn't elaborate. "So?" she said again.

"What did you tell those two geeks?" said Carlucci. His voice sounded dangerous.

"Nothing," said Cordelia, listening to the internal warning bells. "Nothing at all."

"Good." Carlucci grimaced. He mumbled, "She's gonna be fish food, I swear it."

Cordelia stared at Carlucci. The sheer conviction in his voice kept him from appearing a comic-opera gangster. She thought he meant what he was saying. He reminded her of the wolf-creatures in last night's maybe-dream. All that was missing was the dark spittle.

Carlucci's mood didn't improve on the flight to Australia. In Sydney they cleared customs and transferred to an A-300 Airbus. In Melbourne, Cordelia finally got to stick her head out of doors for a few minutes. The air smelled fresh. She admired the DC-3 suspended from a cable in front of the terminal. Then her companion fussed at her to get to the proper Ansett gate. This time they were seated on a 727. Cordelia was glad she wasn't trusting her bag to checked luggage. Part of Marty Carlucci's gloom involved speculation that *his* checked bag was going to get missent to Fiji or some other improper destination.

"So why didn't you carry everything on?" Cordelia had said.

"There's some stuff you *can't* carry on."

The 727 droned north, away from the coastal greenery. Cordelia had the window seat. She stared down at the apparently unending desert. She squinted, looking for roads, railroad tracks, any other sign of human intervention. Noth-

ing. The flat brownish-tan wasteland was dotted with cloud
shadows.

When word crackled over the cabin speakers that the
plane was approaching Alice Springs, Cordelia realized only
after she'd performed the actions that she had stowed the tray
table, cinched her seat belt, and shoved her bag back under
the seat ahead. It had all become utterly automatic.

The airport was busier than she'd expected. Somehow
she had anticipated a single dusty runway with a galvanized
tin shack beside it. A TAA flight had landed minutes before
and the terminal was crowded with people who clearly resembled tourists.

"We rent the Land-Rover now?" she asked Carlucci. The
man was leaning impatiently over the luggage belt.

"Uh-uh. We go into town. I've got us reservations at the
Stuart Arms. We're both getting a good night's sleep. I don't
want to be any nastier than I *have* to be tomorrow at the
meeting. It's all set up for three o'clock," he added as an
apparent afterthought. "The lag's gonna catch up with us real
fast. I suggest you get a good supper with me when we get to
Alice. Then it's beddy-bye till ten or eleven tomorrow morning. If we pick up the rental and get out of Alice by noon, we
should hit the Gap in plenty of time. *There*, you son of a
bitch!" He grabbed his alligator case from the conveyor.
"Okay, let's go."

They took an Ansett coach into Alice. It was half an hour
into town and the air-conditioning labored hard against the
baking heat outside. Cordelia stared out the window as the
bus approached downtown Alice Springs. At first glance it
didn't look terribly different from a small, arid American city.
Certainly Baton Rouge was more alien than this, Cordelia
thought. It didn't look at all as she'd expected from seeing
both versions of *A Town Like Alice*.

The air transit terminal turned out to be across the street
from the turn-of-the-century architecture of the Stuart Arms,
a fact for which Cordelia was grateful. It was getting dark as
the passengers climbed down to the pavement and claimed
their bags. Cordelia glanced at her watch. The numbers
meant absolutely nothing. She needed to reset to local time.
And change the date as well, she reminded herself. She
wasn't even sure what day of the week it was now. Her head
had started to throb when she plunged into the heat that
lingered even while the dark was falling. She thought longingly

of being able to lie straight, stretched out on clean sheets. *After* she'd had a long bath. She checked that. The bath could wait until she'd slept for twenty or thirty hours. At least.

"Okay, kiddo," said Carlucci. They were standing in front of the antique registration desk. "Here's your key." He paused. "Sure you wouldn't like to shave expenses for GF&G and stay in my room?"

Cordelia didn't have the energy to smile wanly. "Nope," she said, taking the key from his hand.

"You wanna know something? You're not on this picnic just because the Fortunato broads think you're such hot shit."

What was he talking about? She used enough energy to glance at him.

"I've seen you around the GF&G offices. I liked what I saw. I put in the word."

Cordelia sighed. Aloud.

"Okay," he said. "Hey, no offense. I'm bushed too." Carlucci picked up the alligator bag. "Let's get the stuff stowed and catch supper." There was a LIFT OUT OF ORDER sign on the elevator. He turned wearily toward the staircase.

"Second floor," said Carlucci. "At least that's a goddamn blessing." They passed a mimeographed poster in the stairwell advertising a band called Gondwanaland. "Maybe after we eat, you wanna go dancing?" Even he didn't sound all that enthusiastic.

Cordelia didn't bother to reply.

The landing opened out into a hallway lined with dark wood trim and some unobtrusive glass cases containing aboriginal artifacts. Cordelia glanced at the boomerangs and bull roarers. Doubtless she'd be able to work up a little more interest tomorrow.

Carlucci looked at his key. "The rooms are next to each other. God, I'm looking forward to bagging it. I really am dead."

A door slammed open behind them. Cordelia caught a quick flash of two dark figures leaping. They were monsters. Later she decided they must have been wearing masks. *Ugly* masks.

Tired as she was, her reflexes still worked. She'd started to duck to the side when a stiffened forearm caught her across the chest and drove her into one of the glass cases. Glass shattered, shards spraying. Cordelia flailed her arms, trying to keep her equilibrium, as someone or something tried to grapple with her. She thought she heard Marty Carlucci screaming.

Her fingers closed on something hard—the end of a boomerang—as she sensed rather than saw her assailant spin around and spring for her again. She brought the boomerang forward in a whistling arc. Instinct. All instinct. *Shit*, she thought. *I'm going to die*.

The sharp edge of the boomerang sliced into the face of her attacker with the sound of a carving knife slicing into a watermelon. Outstretched fingers slapped her neck and dropped away. A body rolled to the floor.

Carlucci! Cordelia turned and saw a dark figure crouched over her colleague. It straightened, stood, started for her, and she realized it was a man. But now she had a little time. Think! she said to herself. Think think think. Focus. It was as though the power had been blanketed by the smothering layers of fatigue. But it was still there. She concentrated, felt the lowest level of her brain engage and strike out.

Stop, goddamn you!

The figure stopped, staggered, started forward again. And fell. Cordelia knew she'd shut down everything in his autonomic system. The smell as his bowels released made it even worse.

She edged around him and knelt down by Marty Carlucci. He lay on his stomach, looking upward. His head had been screwed around completely, just as it had been in the maybe-dream. Slightly walleyed, his dead eyes stared past her.

Cordelia rocked back on her heels against the wall, putting her fists to her mouth, feeling her incisors bite into the knuckles. She felt the epinephrine still prickling in her arms and legs. Every nerve seemed raw.

Christ! she thought. *What am I gonna* do? She looked both ways along the hall. There were no more attackers, no witnesses. She could call Uncle Jack in New York. Or Alcala or Rettig. She could even try to find Fortunato in Japan. If the number she had was still good. She could attempt to locate Tachyon in Auckland. It came home to her. She was many thousands of miles from anyone she trusted, anyone she even *knew*.

"What am I gonna do?" This time she muttered it aloud.

She scrambled over to Carlucci's alligator case and clicked the catches open. The man had affected an icy calm at customs. She had no doubt there was a reason. Cordelia tore through the clothing, searching for the weapon she knew had to be there. She opened the case marked "shaver and converter set." The gun was blued steel and ugly, some kind of snubbed-off, scaled-down automatic weapon. It felt reassuringly heavy in her hand.

Floorboards creaked down in the stairwell. On some level Cordelia caught the scattered words: "... by now he and the bitch should both be dead..."

She forced herself to get up and step over Marty Carlucci's corpse. Then she ran.

At the end of the hallway farthest from the main staircase, a window overlooked a fire-stairs. Cordelia slid it open, softly cajoling the window when the pane momentarily stuck in the casement. She skinned through, then turned to shut the window after her. She saw shadows writhing at the other end of the hall. Cordelia ducked and scuttled crabwise to the steps down.

She momentarily wished she'd grabbed her overnight bag. At least she had the passport case with the Amex card and traveler's checks in the small handbag slung around her shoulder. Cordelia realized she still had the room key clutched in her left hand. She maneuvered it in her fist so that the key thrust out from between her index and middle fingers.

The steps were metal, but they were old and they creaked. Quick and stealthy, Cordelia discovered, were mutually contradictory here.

She saw she was descending into an alley. The noise from the street, about twenty yards distant, was loud and boisterous. At first she thought it sounded like a party. Then she detected undercurrents of anger and pain. The crowd noise rose. Cordelia heard the flat sounds of what she guessed were fists on flesh.

"Terrific," she muttered. Then it occurred to her that a riot would provide good cover for her escape. She had already started mulling contingency plans. First, stay alive. Get out of here. Then call Rettig or Alcala and let them know what had happened. They would send someone to replace Carlucci while she stayed out of sight. Wonderful. A brand-new guy in a tailored suit to sign his company's name on a contract. What was so difficult about that? *She* could do it. But not if she was dead.

With both key and gun at the ready Cordelia eased down from the bottom step of the fire-stairs and started toward the mouth of the alley. Then she froze. She *knew* someone was standing directly behind her.

She whirled, driving her left hand forward, aiming the key at a spot she hoped would be right beneath the intruder's chin. Someone was indeed there. Strong fingers clamped around her wrist, easily soaking up all the forward momentum of her thrust.

The figure pulled her forward into what little light spilled down from the Stuart Arms through the stair gratings. Cordelia brought the gun up and stuck the barrel into her assailant's belly. It didn't go far. She pulled the trigger.

Nothing happened.

She caught a glimpse of dark eyes catching hers. The figure reached forward with its free hand and clicked something on the side of the weapon. A male voice said, "Here, little missy, you left on the safety. Now it will work."

Cordelia was too astonished to pull the trigger. "Okay, I get the point. Who are you, and can we get out of here?"

"You can call me Warreen." Sudden light flooded down from above them, bursting through the gratings, painting quagga stripes of illumination.

Cordelia stared at the bars of light falling across the man's face. She registered the wild, curly black hair, the hooded eyes as dark as hers, the broad flat nose, the high, sharp cheekbones, the strong lips. He was, her mama would have called him, a man of some color. He was, she also realized, the most striking man she had ever seen. Her daddy would have whipped her for that thought alone.

Footsteps clattered down the fire-stairs.

"Now we get out of here," Warreen said, steering her toward the alley mouth.

Naturally it wasn't as easy as that. "There are men there," said Cordelia. She saw an indeterminate number of men holding what seemed to be sticks. They were waiting, silhouetted against the light from the street.

"So there are." Warreen grinned and Cordelia caught the flash of white teeth. "Shoot at them, little missy."

Sounds good to me, Cordelia thought, bringing up the weapon in her right hand. When she pulled the trigger, there was a sound like ripping canvas and bullets screamed off brick. The ragged muzzle flash showed her the men in the alley were now flat in the dirt. She didn't think she had hit any of them.

"Later we worry about marksmanship," said Warreen. "Now we go." He enclosed her left hand in his right, not seeming to notice the key still in place in her fist.

She wondered if they were going to jump from back to back of the prostrate men like Tarzan hopscotching crocodiles in lieu of stepping stones.

They didn't *go* anywhere.

Something akin to heat washed over her. It felt like energy flooding through Warreen's fingers and into her body. The heat seared from the inside out—just like, she thought, a microwave oven.

The world seemed to move sharply two feet to the left and then drop a foot more. The air rotated around her. The night funneled into a blazing speck centered in her chest.

Then it was no longer night.

Warreen and she stood on a reddish-brown plain that joined the distant sky in a far, flat horizon. There were occasional hardy-looking plants and a bit of a breeze. The wind was hot and it eddied the dust.

She realized this was the same plain that had overlaid the cabin of the Air New Zealand jumbo in her nightmare between Honolulu and Auckland.

Cordelia staggered slightly and Warreen caught her arm. "I've seen this place before," she said. "Will the wolf-creatures come?"

"Wolf-creatures?" Warreen looked momentarily puzzled. "Ah, little missy, you mean the Eer-moonans, the long-toothed ones from the shadows."

"I guess so. Lots of teeth? Run in packs? They've got rows of quills around their necks." Holding the gun loosely, Cordelia massaged the inflamed place on the back of her left hand.

Warreen frowned and examined the wound. "Pierced by a quill? You're very fortunate. Their venom is usually fatal."

"Maybe us 'gator types have natural immunity," Cordelia said, smiling wanly. Warreen looked politely puzzled. "Never mind. I guess I'm just lucky."

He nodded. "Indeed so, little missy."

"What's this 'little missy' crap?" Cordelia said. "I didn't want to take time to ask back in the alley."

Warreen looked startled, then grinned widely. "The European ladies seem to like it. It feeds those delicious colonial impulses, you know? Sometimes I still talk like I'm a guide."

"I'm not European," said Cordelia. "I'm a Cajun, an American."

"Same thing to us." Warreen continued to grin. "Yank's same as a European. No difference. You're all tourists here. So what should I call you?"

"Cordelia."

His expression became serious as he leaned forward and took the gun from her hand. He examined it closely, gingerly working the action, then clicking the safety back on. "Scaled down H and K full auto. Pretty expensive hardware, Cordelia. Going shooting dingos?" He gave her back the weapon.

She let it dangle from her hand. "It belonged to the guy I came to Alice Springs with. He's dead."

"At the hotel?" said Warreen. "The minions of the Murga-muggai? Word was out, she was going to ice the agent of the evangelist."

"Who?"

"The trap-door spider woman. Not a nice lady. She's tried to kill me for years. Since I was a kid." He said it matter-of-factly. Cordelia thought he still looked like a kid.

"Why?" she said, involuntarily shivering. If she had any phobia, it was spiders. She coughed as the wind kicked red dust up into her face.

"Started as clan vengeance. Now it's something else." Warreen seemed to reflect, then added, "She and I both have some powers. I think she feels there is space in the outback for only one such. Very shortsighted."

"What kind of powers?" said Cordelia.

"You are full of questions. So am I. Perhaps we can trade knowledge on our walk."

"Walk?" said Cordelia a bit stupidly. Once again events threatened to outstrip her ability to comprehend them. "Where?"

"Uluru."

"Where's that?"

"There." Warreen pointed toward the horizon.

The sun was directly overhead. Cordelia had no idea which compass direction was indicated. "There's nothing there. Just a lot of countryside that looks like where they shot *Road Warrior.*"

"There will be." Warreen had started walking. He was already a dozen paces away. His voice drifted back on the wind. "Shake a pretty leg, little missy."

Deciding she had little choice, Cordelia followed. "Agent of the evangelist?" she muttered. That wasn't Marty. Somebody had made a bad mistake.

"Where are we?" said Cordelia. The sky was dotted with small cumulus, but none of the cloud-shadows ever seemed to shade her. She wished mightily that they did.

"The world," said Warreen.

"It's not my world."

"The desert, then."

"I *know* it's the desert," said Cordelia. "I can see it's the desert. I can feel it. The heat's a dead giveaway. But what desert is it?"

"It is the land of Baiame," said Warreen. "This is the great Nullarbor Plain."

"Are you sure?" Cordelia scrubbed sweat from her forehead with the strip of fabric she had carefully torn away from the hem of her Banana Republic skirt. "I looked at the map on the plane all the way up from Melbourne. The distances don't make sense. Shouldn't this be the Simpson Desert?"

"Distances are different in the Dreamtime," Warreen said simply.

"The Dreamtime?" *What am I in, a Peter Weir movie?* she thought. "As in the myth?"

"No myth," said her companion. "We are now where reality was, is, and will be. We are in the origin of all things."

"Right." *I am dreaming,* Cordelia thought. *I'm dreaming— or I'm dead and this is the last thing my brain cells are creating before everything flares and goes black.*

"All things in the shadow world were created here first," said Warreen. "Birds, creatures, grass, the ways of doing things, the taboos that must be observed."

Cordelia looked around her. There was little to see. "These are the originals?" she said. "I've only seen the copies before?"

He nodded vigorously.

"I don't see any dune buggies," she said a bit petulantly,

feeling the heat. "I don't see any airliners or vending machines full of ice-cold Diet Pepsi."

He answered her seriously. "Those are only variations. Here is where everything begins."

I'm dead, she thought glumly. "I'm hot," she said. "I'm tired. How far do we have to walk?"

"A distance." Warreen kept striding along effortlessly.

Cordelia stopped and set hands to hips. "Why should I go along?"

"If you don't," Warreen said back over his shoulder, "then you shall die."

"Oh." Cordelia started walking again, having to run a few steps in order to catch up with the man. The image she couldn't get out of her head was that of cold cans of soda, the moisture beading on the aluminum outsides. She ached to hear the click and hiss as the tabs peeled back. And the bubbles, the taste . . .

"Keep walking," said Warreen.

"How long have we been walking?" said Cordelia. She glanced up and shaded her eyes. The sun was measurably closer to the horizon. Shadows stretched in back of Warreen and her.

"Are you tired?" said her companion.

"I'm exhausted."

"Do you need to rest?"

She thought about that. Her own conclusion surprised her. "No. No, I don't think I do. Not yet, anyway." Where was the energy coming from? She *was* exhausted—and yet strength seemed to rise up into her, as though she were a plant taking nourishment from the earth. "This place is magical."

Warreen nodded matter-of-factly. "Yes, it is."

"However," she said, "I *am* hungry."

"You don't need food, but I'll see to it."

Cordelia heard a sound apart from the wind and the padding of her own feet on the dusty soil. She turned and saw a brownish-gray kangaroo hopping along, easily pacing them. "I'm hungry enough to eat one of those," she said.

The kangaroo stared at her from huge chocolate eyes. "I should hope not," it said.

Cordelia closed her mouth with a click. She stared back. Warreen smiled at the kangaroo and said courteously,

"Good afternoon, Mirram. Will we shortly find shade and water?"

"Yes," said the kangaroo. "Sadly, the hospitality is being hoarded by a cousin of the Gurangatch."

"At least," said Warreen, "it is not a bunyip."

"That is true," agreed the kangaroo.

"Will I find weapons?"

"Beneath the tree," said the kangaroo.

"Good," Warreen said with relief. "I wouldn't relish wrestling a monster with only my hands and teeth."

"I wish you well," said the kangaroo. "And you," it said to Cordelia, "be at peace." The creature turned at right angles to their path and bounded into the desert where it soon was lost to sight.

"Talking kangaroos?" said Cordelia. "Bunyips? Gurnagatches?"

"Gurangatch," Warreen corrected her. "Something of both lizard and fish. It is, of course, a monster."

She was mentally fitting pieces together. "And it's hogging an oasis."

"Spot on."

"Couldn't we avoid it?"

"No matter what trail we follow," Warreen said, "I think it will encounter us." He shrugged. "It's just a monster."

"Right." Cordelia was glad she still had tight hold of the H and K mini. The steel was hot and slippery in her hand. "Just a monster," she mumbled through dry lips.

Cordelia had no idea how Warreen found the pond and the tree. So far as she could tell, they followed a perfectly straight path. A dot appeared in the sunset distance. It grew as they approached it. Cordelia saw a tough-looking desert oak streaked with charcoal stripes. It seemed to have been struck by lightning more than once and looked as if it had occupied this patch of hardscrabble soil for centuries. A belt of grass surrounded the tree. A gentle slope led down to reeds and then the edge of a pool about thirty feet across.

"Where's the monster?" said Cordelia.

"Hush." Warreen strode up to the tree and began to strip. His muscles were lean and beautifully defined. His skin shimmered with sweat, glowing almost a dark blue in the dusk. When he skinned out of the jeans, Cordelia at first turned away, then decided this was not an occasion for politeness, whether false or otherwise.

God, she thought. *He's gorgeous.* Depending on gender, her kin would have been either scandalized or triggered to a lynching impulse. Even though she had been reared to abhor such a thought, she wanted to reach and lightly touch him. This, she abruptly realized, was not like her at all. Although she was surrounded in New York by people of other colors, they still made her nervous. Warreen was engendering that reaction, yet it was vastly different in nature and intensity. She *did* want to touch him.

Naked, Warreen neatly folded his clothes and set them in a pile beneath the tree. In turn, he picked up a variety of objects from the grass. He inspected a long club, then set it back down. Finally he straightened with a spear in one hand, a boomerang in the other. He looked fiercely at Cordelia. "I can be no more ready."

She felt a chill like ice water run through her. It was a sensation both of fear and of excitement. "Now what?" She tried to keep her voice low and steady, but it squeaked slightly. God, she hated that.

Warreen didn't have a chance to answer. He gestured toward the dark pool. Ripples had appeared on the far side. The center of those ripples seemed to be moving toward them. A few bubbles burst on the surface.

The water was shrugged aside. What surveyed the couple on the bank was a figure out of a nightmare. *Looks meaner than any joker I've ever seen,* Cordelia thought. As it lifted more of its body from the water, she decided the creature must possess at least the mass of Bruce the Shark. The froglike mouth gaped, revealing a multitude of rust-colored teeth. It regarded the humans with slitted, bulging lizard eyes.

"It is equally sired of fish and lizard," said Warreen conversationally, as though guiding a European tourist through a wild-game park. He stepped forward and raised his spear. "Cousin Gurangatch!" he called out. "We would drink from the spring and rest beneath the tree. We would do this in peace. If we cannot, then I must treat you in the manner employed by Mirragen the Cat-man against your mighty ancestor."

Gurangatch hissed like a freight train bleeding its brakes. Without hesitation it lunged forward, slamming down on the wet bank with the slap of a ten-ton eel. Warreen lightly leapt back, and the stained teeth clashed together just in front of his face. He poked Gurangatch's snout with the spear. The fish-lizard hissed even louder.

"You are not so lithe as Mirragen," it said with the voice of a steam hose. Gurangatch jerked away as Warreen pulled loose the spear and stabbed again. This time the pointed end jammed under the shining silver scales surrounding the monster's right eye. The creature twisted, tugging the spear loose from Warreen's fingers.

The monster reared high, gazing at Warreen from ten feet, fifteen, twenty. The man looked up, expectant, the boomerang cocked in his right hand. The hiss was almost a sigh. "Time to die again, little cousin!" Gurangatch's bull neck flexed, dipped. Jaws gaped.

This time Cordelia remembered to click off the safety. This time she braced herself by holding the H and K with both hands. This time the bullets went exactly where she wished.

She saw the slugs stitch a line down Gurangatch's throat. She released the trigger, raised the gun, fired a quick burst at the monster's face. One of the creature's eyes burst like a balloon full of dye. It cried out in pain, green jelly sloshing down across its snout. The wounds in the neck were oozing crimson. *Christmas colors*, Cordelia thought. *Get a grip, girl. Don't go hysterical.*

As Gurangatch writhed in the water, Warreen swung his arm in a short, tight arc and set the end of the boomerang into the creature's remaining eye. At this, the monster bellowed so loudly, Cordelia winced and recoiled back a step. Then Gurangatch doubled over in the water and dove. Cordelia had a quick impression of a thick, gilalike tail disappearing through the spray. Then the pool was quiet, small wavelets still splashing up on the banks. The ripples flattened and were gone.

"He has dived into the earth," said Warreen, squatting and peering into the water. "He will be gone a long time."

Cordelia put the H and K back on safety.

Hands free of weapons, Warreen turned away from the pool and stood. Cordelia couldn't help herself. She stared. Warreen glanced down, then met her eyes again. With little apparent embarrassment he said, "It is the excitement of the contest." Then he smiled and said, "This wouldn't happen under ordinary circumstances if I were guiding a European lady in the outback."

It occurred to Cordelia to pick up his folded clothing and hold it out to him.

With dignity Warreen accepted the garments. Before turning away to dress he said, "If you're ready, it would be a good time for a refreshing drink and some rest. I'm sorry I'm a bit short of tea."

Cordelia said, "I'll manage."

The desert was slow to cool with the sunset. Cordelia continued to feel the heat rise out of the ground beneath her. Warreen and she lay back against the gnarled, semiexposed roots of the tree. The air felt as though it were a quilted comforter pulled up over her face. When she moved, the motion seemed to be at half speed.

"The water was delicious," she said, "but I'm still hungry."

"Your hunger here is an illusion."

"Then I'll fantasize a pizza."

"Mmph," Warreen said. "Very well." With a sigh he raised himself to his knees and ran his fingers over the rough bark of the tree. When he found a loose patch, he tugged it away from the trunk. His right hand darted forward, fingers scrambling to catch something Cordelia couldn't see. "Here." He displayed his find to her.

Her first impression was of something snakelike and squirming. She saw the pasty color, the segments and the many legs. "What *is* that?" she said.

"Witchetty grub." Warreen smiled. "It's one of our national cuisines." He thrust his hand forward like a mischievous little boy. "Does it turn your stomach, little missy?"

"Goddamnit. No," she said with a flash of anger. "Don't call me that." *What are you doing?* she said to herself as she reached for the creature. "Do I have to eat it live?"

"No. It is not necessary." He turned and cracked the creature against the desert oak. The witchetty grub convulsed once and ceased struggling.

Forcing herself just to *do* it and not think about the act, she took the witchetty, popped it into her mouth, and started chewing. *God*, she thought, *why do I do these things?*

"How do you find it?" said Warreen with a solemn face.

"Well," said Cordelia, swallowing, "it doesn't taste like chicken."

*   *   *

The stars came out, spangling a belt across the entire
sky. Cordelia lay with fingers plaited behind her head. She
realized she had lived in Manhattan for close to a year and
never looked for the stars at all.

"Nurunderi is up there," said Warreen, pointing at the
sky, "along with his two young wives, placed there by Nepelle,
the ruler of the heavens, after the women ate the forbidden
food."

"Apples?" said Cordelia.

"Fish. Tukkeri—a delicacy given only to the men." His
hand moved, the fingers pointing again. "There, farther
on—you can make out the Seven Sisters. And there is
Karambal, their pursuer. You call him Aldebaran."

Cordelia said, "I have a lot of questions."

Warreen paused. "Not about the stars."

"Not about the stars."

"What, then?"

"All of this." She sat up and spread her arms to the night.
"How am I here?"

"I brought you."

"I know. But how?"

Warreen hesitated for a long time. Then he said, "I am of
Aranda blood, but was not raised within the tribe. Do you
know of the urban aborigines?"

"Like in *The Last Wave*," Cordelia said. "I saw *The
Fringe Dwellers* too. There aren't really tribal aborigines in
the cities, right? Just sort of like individuals?"

Warreen laughed. "You compare almost everything to
the cinema. That is likening everything to the shadow world.
Do you know anything of reality?"

"I think so." In this place she wasn't so sure, but she
wasn't about to admit it.

"My parents sought work in Melbourne," Warreen said.
"I was born in the outback, but cannot recall any of that. I
was a boy in the city." He laughed bitterly. "My walkabout
seemed destined to lead me only among drunken diggers
chundering in the gutter."

Cordelia, listening raptly, said nothing.

"When I was an infant, I nearly died of a fever. Nothing
the wirinun—the medicine man—could do helped. My parents, despairing, were ready to take me to the white doctor.
Then the fever broke. The wirinun shook his medicine stick

over me, looked into my eyes, and told my parents I would
live and do great things." Warreen paused again. "The other
children in the town had taken ill with the same sort of fever.
All of them died. My parents told me their bodies shriveled
or twisted or turned into unspeakable things. But they all
died. Only I survived. The other parents hated me and hated
my parents for bearing me. So we left." He fell silent.

It dawned in Cordelia's mind like a star, rising. "The
wild card virus."

"I know of it," said Warreen. "I think you are right. My
childhood was as normal as my parents could make it until I
grew the hair of an adult. Then . . ." His voice trailed off.

"Yes?" Cordelia said eagerly.

"As a man, I found I could enter the Dreamtime at will. I
could explore the land of my ancestors. I could even take
others with me."

"Then this truly is the Dreamtime. It isn't some kind of
shared illusion."

He turned on his side and looked at her. Warreen's eyes
were only about eighteen inches from hers. His gaze was
something she could feel in the pit of her stomach. "There is
nothing more real."

"The thing that happened to me on the airplane. The
Eer-moonans?"

"There are others from the shadow world who can enter
the Dreamtime. One is Murga-muggai, whose totem is the
trap-door spider. But there is something . . . wrong with her.
You would call her psychotic. To me she is an Evil One, even
though she claims kinship with the People."

"Why did she kill Carlucci? Why try to kill me?"

"Murga-muggai hates European holy men, especially the
American who comes from the sky. His name is Leo Barnett."

"Fire-breather," said Cordelia. "He is a TV preacher."

"He would save our souls. In doing so he will destroy us
all, as kin and as individuals. No more tribes."

"Barnett . . ." Cordelia breathed. "Marty wasn't one of
his people."

"Europeans look much like one another. It doesn't matter that he didn't work for the man from the sky." Warreen
regarded her sharply. "Aren't you here for the same purpose?"

Cordelia ignored that. "But how did I survive the
Eer-moonans?"

"I believe Murga-muggai underestimated your own power." He hesitated. "And possibly was it your time of the moon? Most monsters will not touch a woman who bleeds."

Cordelia nodded. She began to be very sorry her period had ended in Auckland. "I guess I'll have to depend on the H and K." After a time she said, "Warreen, how old are you?"

"Nineteen." He hesitated. "And you?"

"Going on eighteen." They both were quiet. A very mature nineteen, Cordelia thought. He wasn't like any of the boys she remembered at home in Louisiana, or in Manhattan either.

Cordelia felt a chill plummeting both in the desert air and inside her mind. She knew the coldness growing within her was because she now had time to think about her situation. Not just thousands of miles from home and among strangers, but also not even in her own world.

"Warreen, do you have a girlfriend?"

"I am alone here."

"No, you're not." Her voice didn't squeak. Thank God. "Will you hold me?"

Time stretched out. Then Warreen moved close and clumsily put his arms around her. She accidentally elbowed him in the eye before they both were comfortable. Cordelia greedily absorbed the warmth of his body, her face tucked against his. Her fingers wound through the surprising softness of his hair.

They kissed. Cordelia knew her parents would kill her if they knew what she was doing with this black man. First, of course, they would have lynched Warreen. She surprised herself. It was no different touching him than it had been touching anyone else she'd liked. There hadn't been many. Warreen felt much better than any of them.

She kissed him many times more. He did the same to her. The night chill deepened and their breathing pulsed faster.

"Warreen . . ." she finally said, gasping. "Do you want to make love?"

He seemed to go away from her, even though he was still there in her arms. "I shouldn't—"

She guessed at something. "Uh, are you a virgin?"

"Yes. And you?"

"I'm from Louisiana." She covered his mouth with hers.

"Warreen is only my boy's name. My true name is Wyungare."

"What does that mean?"

"He who returns to the stars."

The moment came when she raised herself to take him and felt Wyungare driving deep within her. Much later she realized she hadn't thought of her mama and what her family would think. Not even once.

The giant first appeared as the smallest nub on the horizon.

"That's where we're going?" said Cordelia. "Uluru?"

"The place of greatest magic."

The morning sun rose high as they walked. The heat was no less pressing than it had been the previous day. Cordelia tried to ignore her thirst. Her legs ached, but it was not from trudging. She welcomed the feeling.

Various creatures of the outback sunned themselves by the path and inspected the humans as they passed.

An emu.

A frilled lizard.

A tortoise.

A black snake.

A wombat.

Wyungare acknowledged the presence of each with a courteous greeting. "Cousin Dinewan" to the emu; "Mungoongarlie" to the lizard; "Good morning, Wayambeh" to the tortoise, and so on.

A bat circled them three times, squeaked a greeting, and flew off. Wyungare waved politely. "Soar in safety, brother Narahdarn."

His greeting to the wombat was particularly effusive. "He was my boy-totem," he explained to Cordelia. "Warreen."

They encountered a crocodile sunning itself beside their trail.

"He is your cousin as well," said Wyungare. He told her what to say.

"Good morning, cousin Kurria," said Cordelia. The reptile stared back at her, moving not an inch in the baking heat. Then it opened its jaws and hissed. Rows of white teeth flashed in the sun.

"A fortunate sign," said Wyungare. "The Kurria is your guardian."

As Uluru grew in the distance, fewer were the creatures that came to the path to look upon the humans.

Cordelia realized with a start that for an hour or more she had been dwelling within her own thoughts. She glanced aside at Wyungare. "How was it that you were in the alley at just the right time to help me?"

"I was guided by Baiame, the Great Spirit."

"Not good enough."

"It was a sort of a corroboree that night, a get-together with a purpose."

"Like a rally?"

He nodded. "My people don't usually engage in such things. Sometimes we have to use European ways."

"What was it about?" Cordelia shaded her eyes and squinted into the distance. Uluru had grown to the size of a fist.

Wyungare also narrowed his eyes at Uluru. Somehow he seemed to be gazing much farther. "We are going to drive the Europeans out of our lands. Especially we are not going to allow the men-who-preach to seize further footholds."

"I don't think that's going to be very easy. Aren't the Aussies pretty well entrenched?"

Wyungare shrugged. "Have you no faith, little missy? Just because we are outnumbered forty or fifty to one, own no tanks or planes, and know that few care about our cause? Just because we are our own worst enemies when it comes to organizing ourselves?" His voice sounded angry. "Our way of life has stretched unbroken for sixty thousand years. How long has *your* culture existed?"

Cordelia started to say something placating.

The young man rushed on. "We find it hard to organize effectively in the manner of the Maori in New Zealand. They are great clans. We are small tribes." He smiled humorlessly. "You might say the Maori resemble your aces. We are like the jokers."

"The jokers can organize. There are people of conscience who help them."

"We will not need help from Europeans. The winds are rising—all around the world, just as they are here in the outback. Look at the Indian homeland that is being carved with machetes and bayonets from the American jungle. Consider Africa, Asia, every continent where revolution lives." His voice lifted. "It's time, Cordelia. Even the white Christ recognizes the turning of the great wheel that will groan and move again in little more than a decade. The fires already burn, even if your people do not yet feel the heat."

Do I know him? thought Cordelia. She knew she did not. She had suspected none of this. But within her heart she recognized the truth of what he said. And she did not fear him.

"Murga-muggai and I are not the only children of the fever," said Wyungare. "There are others. There will be many more, I fear. It will cause a difference here. *We* will make a difference."

Cordelia nodded slightly.

"The whole world is aflame. All of us are burning. Do your Dr. Tachyon and Senator Hartmann and their entire party of touring Europeans know this?" His black eyes stared directly into hers. "Do they truly know what is happening outside their limited sight in America?"

Cordelia said nothing. No, she thought. Probably not. "I expect they don't."

"Then that is the message you must bear them," said Wyungare.

"I've seen pictures," said Cordelia. "This is Ayers Rock."

"It is Uluru," said Wyungare.

They stared up at the gigantic reddish sandstone monolith. "It's the biggest single rock in the world," said Cordelia. "Thirteen hundred feet up to the top and several miles across."

"It is the place of magic."

"The markings on the side," she said. "They look like the cross section of a brain."

"Only to you. To me they are the markings on the chest of a warrior."

Cordelia looked around. "There should be hundreds of tourists here."

"In the shadow world there are. Here they would be fodder for Murga-muggai."

Cordelia was incredulous. "She eats people?"

"She eats anyone."

"God, I hate spiders." She stopped looking up the cliff. Her neck was getting a crick. "We have to climb this?"

"There is a slightly gentler trail." He indicated they should walk farther along the base of Uluru.

Cordelia found the sheer mass of the rock astonishing—

and something more. She felt an awe that large stones did not ordinarily kindle. *It's gotta be magic,* she thought.

After a twenty-minute hike Wyungare said, "Here." He reached down. There was another cache of weapons. He picked up a spear, a club—nullanulla, he called it—a flint knife, a boomerang.

"Handy," Cordelia said.

"Magic." With a leather strap Wyungare tied the weapons together. He shouldered the packet and pointed toward the summit of Uluru. "Next stop."

To Cordelia the proposed climb looked no easier than it had at the first site. "You're sure?"

He gestured at her handbag and the H and K. "You should leave those."

She shook her head, surveying first his weapons, then hers. "No way."

Cordelia lay flat on her belly, peering up the rocky slope. Then she looked down. *I shouldn't have done that,* she thought. It might only have been a few hundred yards, but it was like leaning over an empty elevator shaft. She scrambled for a purchase. The H and K in her left hand didn't help.

"Just let it go," said Wyungare, reaching back to secure her free hand.

"We might need it."

"Its power will be slight against the Murga-muggai."

"I'll risk it. When it comes to making magic, I need all the help I can get." She was out of breath. "You're sure this is the easiest ascent?"

"It is the only one. In the shadow world there is a heavy chain fixed to the rock for the first third of this journey. It is an affront to Uluru. Tourists use it to pull themselves up."

"I'd settle for the affront," said Cordelia. "How much farther?"

"Maybe an hour, maybe less. It depends whether Murga-muggai decides to hurl boulders down upon us."

"Oh." She considered that. "Think there's a good chance?"

"She knows we are coming. It depends on her mood."

"I hope she doesn't have PMS."

"Monsters don't bleed," said Wyungare seriously.

They reached the broad, irregular top of Uluru and sat on a flat stone to rest. "Where is she?" said Cordelia.

"If we don't find her, she'll find us. Are you in a hurry?"

"No." Cordelia looked around apprehensively. "What about the Eer-moonans?"

"You killed them all on the shadow plane. There is not an endless supply of such creatures."

Oh, God, thought Cordelia. *I killed off an endangered species.* She wanted to giggle.

"Got your breath?"

She groaned and got up from the slab.

Wyungare was already up, his face angled at the sky, gauging the temperature and the wind. It was a great deal cooler on top of the rock than it had been on the desert floor. "It is a good day to die," he said.

"You've seen too many movies too."

Wyungare grinned.

They trudged along nearly the entire diameter of the top of Uluru before coming to a wide, flat area about a hundred yards across. A sandstone cliff fell away to the desert only a few yards beyond. "This looks promising," said Wyungare. The surface of scoured sandstone was not completely bare. Football-size bits of rock were littered about like grains of sand. "We are very close."

The voice seemed to come from everywhere around them. The words grated like two chunks of sandstone rubbing together. "This is my home."

"It is not your home," said Wyungare. "Uluru is home to us all."

"You have intruded..."

Cordelia looked around apprehensively, seeing nothing other than rock and a few sparse bushes.

"...and will die."

Across the rocky clearing, a sheet of sandstone about ten feet across flipped over, slamming into the surface of Uluru and shattering. Bits of stone sprayed across the area, and Cordelia reflexively stepped back. Wyungare did not move.

Murga-muggai, the trap-door spider woman, heaved herself up out of her hole and scrabbled into the open air.

For Cordelia it was like suddenly leaping into her worst nightmares. There were big spiders at home in the bayous, but nothing of this magnitude. Murga-muggai's body was dark brown and shaggy, the size of a Volkswagen. The bulbous body balanced swaying on eight articulated legs. All her limbs were tufted with spiky brown hair.

Glittering faceted eyes surveyed the human interlopers.

A mouth opened wide, papillae moving gently, a clear, viscid liquid dripping down to the sandstone. Mandibles twitched apart.

"Oh, my God," Cordelia said, wanting to take another step backward. Many more steps. She wished to wake up from this dream.

Murga-muggai moved toward them, legs shimmering as they seemed to slip momentarily in and out of phase with reality. To Cordelia it was like watching well-done stop-motion photography.

"Whatever else she is," said Wyungare, "Murga-muggai is a creature of grace and balance. It is her vanity." He unslung the packet of weapons, unwinding the leather strap.

"Your flesh will make a fine lunch, cousins," came the abrasive voice.

"You're no relation of mine," said Cordelia.

Wyungare hefted the boomerang as though considering an experiment, then fluidly hurled it toward Murga-muggai. The honed wooden edge caressed the stiff hairs on top of the spider-creature's abdomen and sighed away into the open sky. The weapon swung around and started to return, but didn't have sufficient altitude to clear the rock. Cordelia heard the boomerang shatter on the stone below Uluru's rim.

"Bad fortune," said Murga-muggai. She laughed, an oily, sticky sound.

"Why, cousin?" said Wyungare. "Why do you do any of this?"

"Silly boy," said Murga-muggai, "you've lost hold of tradition. It will be the death of you, if not the death of our people. You are so wrong. I must remedy this."

Apparently in no hurry to eat, she slowly closed the distance between them. Her legs continued to strobe. It was dizzying to watch. "My appetite for Europeans is growing," she said. "I will enjoy today's varied feast."

"I will have only one chance," Wyungare said in a low voice. "If it doesn't work—"

"It will," said Cordelia. She stepped even with him and touched his arm. "*Laissez les bon temps rouler.*"

Wyungare glanced at her.

"Let the good times roll. My daddy's favorite line."

Murga-muggai leapt.

The spider-creature descended over them like a wind-torn umbrella with spare, bent struts flexing.

Wyungare jammed the butt of the spear into the un-
yielding sandstone and lifted the fire-hardened head toward
the body of the monster. Murga-muggai cried out in rage and
triumph.

The spear-head glanced off one mandible and broke. The
supple shaft of the spear at first bent, then cracked into
splinters like the shattering of a spine. The spider-creature
was so close, Cordelia could see the abdomen pulse. She
could smell a dark, acrid odor.

Now we're in trouble, she thought.

Both Wyungare and she scrambled backward, attempting
to avoid the seeking legs and clashing mandibles. The nullanulla
skittered across the sandstone.

Cordelia scooped up the flint knife. It was suddenly like
watching everything in slow motion. One of Murga-muggai's
hairy forelegs lashed out toward Wyungare. The tip fell across
the man's chest, just below his heart. The force of the blow
hurled him backward. Wyungare's body tumbled across the
stone clearing like one of the limp rag dolls Cordelia had
played with as a girl.

And just as lifeless.

"No!" Cordelia screamed. She ran to Wyungare, knelt
beside him, felt for the pulse in his throat. Nothing. He was
not breathing. His eyes stared blindly toward the empty sky.

She cradled the man's body for just a moment, realizing
that the spider-creature was patiently regarding them from
twenty yards away. "You are next, imperfect cousin," came
the ground-out words. "You are brave, but I don't think you
can help the cause of my people any more than the Wombat."
Murga-muggai started forward.

Cordelia realized she was still clinging to the gun. She
aimed the H and K mini at the spider-creature and squeezed
the trigger. Nothing happened. She clicked the safety on,
then off again. Pulled the trigger. Nothing. Damn. It was
finally empty.

Focus, she thought. She stared at Murga-muggai's eyes
and willed the creature to die. The power was still there
within her. She could feel it. She strained. But nothing
happened. She was helpless. Murga-muggai was not even
slowed.

Evidently the reptile-level had nothing to say to spiders.

The spider-thing rushed toward her like a graceful,
eight-legged express train.

Cordelia knew there was nothing left to do. Except the one thing she dreaded most.

She wondered if the image in her mind would be the last thing she would ever know. It was the memory of an old cartoon showing Fay Wray in the fist of King Kong on the side of the Empire State Building. A man in a biplane was calling out to the woman, "Trip, him, Fay! Trip him!"

Cordelia summoned all the hysterical strength left within her and hurled the empty H and K at Murga-muggai's head. The weapon hit one faceted eye and the monster shied slightly. She leapt forward, wrapping arms and legs around one of the pistoning spider-creature's forelegs.

The monster stumbled, started to recover, but then Cordelia jammed the flint knife into a leg joint. The extremity folded and momentum took over. The spider-thing was a ball of flailing legs rolling along with Cordelia clinging to one hairy limb.

The woman had a chaotic glimpse of the desert floor looming ahead and below her. She let go, hit the stone, rolled, grabbed an outcropping and stopped.

Murga-muggai was propelled out into open space. To Cordelia the monster seemed to hang there for a moment, suspended like the coyote in the Roadrunner cartoons. Then the spider-creature plummeted.

Cordelia watched the flailing, struggling thing diminish. A screech like nails on chalkboard trailed after.

Finally all she could see was what looked like a black stain at the foot of Uluru. She could imagine only too well the shattered remains with the legs splayed out. "You deserved it!" she said aloud. "Bitch."

Wyungare! She turned and limped back to his body.

He was still dead.

For a moment Cordelia allowed herself the luxury of angry tears. Then she realized she had her own magic. "It's only been a minute," she said, as if praying. "Not longer. Not long at all. Only a minute."

She bent close to Wyungare and concentrated. She felt the power draining out of her mind and floating down around the man, insulating the cold flesh. The thought had been a revelation. In the past she had tried only to shut autonomic nervous systems down. She had never tried to start one up. It had never occurred to her.

Jack's words seemed to echo from eight thousand miles away: "You can use it for life too."

The energy flowed.

The slightest heartbeat.

The faintest breath.

Another.

Wyungare began to breathe.

He groaned.

Thank God, thought Cordelia. Or Baiame. She glanced around self-consciously at the top of Uluru.

Wyungare opened his eyes. "Thank you," he said faintly but distinctly.

The riot swirled past them. Police clubs swung. Aboriginal heads cracked. "Bloody hell," said Wyungare. "You'd think this was bloody Queensland." He seemed restrained from joining the fray only by Cordelia's presence.

Cordelia reeled back against the alley wall. "You've brought me back to Alice?"

Wyungare nodded.

"This is the same night?"

"All the distances *are* different in the Dreamtime," said Wyungare. "Time as well as space."

"I'm grateful." The noise of angry shouts, screams, sirens, was deafening.

"Now what?" said the young man.

"A night's sleep. In the morning I'll rent a Land-Rover. Then I'll drive to Madhi Gap." She pondered a question. "Will you stay with me?"

"Tonight?" Wyungare hesitated as well. "Yes, I'll stay with you. You're not as bad as the preacher-from-the-sky, but I must find a way to talk you out of what you want to do with the satellite station."

Cordelia started to relax just a little.

"Of course," said Wyungare, glancing around, "you'll have to sneak me into your room."

Cordelia shook her head. *It's like high school again*, she thought. She put her arm around the man beside her.

There were so many things she needed to tell people. The road south to Madhi Gap stretched ahead. She still hadn't decided whether she was going to call New York first.

"There is one thing," said Wyungare.

She glanced at him questioningly.

"It has always been the custom," he said slowly, "for European men to use their aboriginal mistresses and then abandon them."

Cordelia looked him in the eye. "I am not a European man," she said.

Wyungare smiled.

FROM *THE JOURNAL*
OF XAVIER DESMOND

MARCH 14/HONG KONG:

I have been feeling better of late, I'm pleased to say. Perhaps it was our brief sojourn in Australia and New Zealand. Coming close upon the heels of Singapore and Jakarta, Sydney seemed almost like home, and I was strangely taken with Auckland and the comparative prosperity and cleanliness of its little toy jokertown. Aside from a distressing tendency to call themselves "uglies," an even more offensive term than "joker," my Kiwi brethren seem to live as decently as any jokers anywhere. I was even able to purchase a week-old copy of the *Jokertown Cry* at my hotel. It did my soul good to read the news of home, even though too many of the headlines seem to be concerned with a gang war being fought in our streets.

Hong Kong has its jokertown too, as relentlessly mercantile as the rest of the city. I understand that mainland China dumps most of its jokers here, in the Crown Colony. In fact a delegation of leading joker merchants have invited Chrysalis and me to lunch with them tomorrow and discuss "possible commercial ties between jokers in Hong Kong and New York City." I'm looking forward to it.

Frankly it will be good to get away from my fellow delegates for a few hours. The mood aboard the *Stacked Deck* is testy at best at present, chiefly thanks to Thomas Downs and his rather overdeveloped journalistic instincts.

Our mail caught up with us in Christchurch, just as we were taking off for Hong Kong, and the packet included advance copies of the latest issue of *Aces*. Digger went up and down the aisles after we were airborne, distributing complimentary copies as is his wont. He ought to have read them first. He and his execrable magazine hit a new low this time out, I'm afraid.

The issue features his cover story of Peregrine's pregnancy. I was amused to note that the magazine obviously feels that Peri's baby is the big news of the trip, since they devoted twice as much space to it as they have to any of Digger's previous stories, even the hideous incident in Syria, though perhaps that was only to justify the glossy four-page fotospread of Peregrine past and present, in various costumes and states of undress.

The whispers about her pregnancy started as early as India and were officially confirmed while we were in Thailand, so Digger could hardly be blamed for filing a story. It's just the sort of thing that *Aces* thrives on. Unfortunately for his own health and our sense of camaraderie aboard the *Stacked Deck*, Digger clearly did not agree with Peri that her "delicate condition" was a private matter. Digger dug too far.

The cover asks, "Who Fathered Peri's Baby?" Inside, the piece opens with a double-page spread illustrated by an artist's conception of Peregrine holding an infant in her arms, except that the child is a black silhouette with a question mark instead of a face. "Daddy's an Ace, Tachyon Says," reads the subhead, leading into a much larger orange banner that claims, "Friends Beg Her to Abort Monstrous Joker Baby." Gossip has it that Digger plied Tachyon with brandy while the two of them were inspecting the raunchier side of Singapore's nightlife, managing to elicit a few choice indiscretions. He did not get the name of the father of Peregrine's baby, but once drunk enough, Tachyon displayed no reticence in sounding off about all the reasons why he believes Peregrine ought to abort this child, the foremost of which is the nine percent chance that the baby will be born a joker.

I confess that reading the story filled me with a cold rage and made me doubly glad that Dr. Tachyon is not my personal physician. It is at moments such as this that I find myself wondering how Tachyon can possibly pretend to be my friend, or the friend of any joker. *In vino veritas*, they say; Tachyon's comments make it quite clear that he thinks abortion is the only choice for any woman in Peregrine's position. The Takisians abhor deformity and customarily "cull" (such a polite word) their own deformed children (very few in number, since they have not yet been blessed with the virus that they so generously decided to share with Earth) shortly after birth. Call me oversensitive if you will, but the clear implication of what Tachyon is saying is that death is preferable to jokerhood, that it is better that this child never live at all than live the life of a joker.

When I set the magazine aside I was so livid that I knew I could not possibly speak to Tachyon himself in any rational manner, so I got up and went back to the press compartment to give Downs a piece of my mind. At the very least I wanted to point out rather forcefully that it was grammatically permissible to omit the adjective "monstrous" before the phrase "joker baby," though clearly the copy editors at *Aces* feel it compulsory.

Digger saw me coming, however, and met me halfway. I've managed to raise his consciousness at least enough so that he knew how upset I'd be, because he started right in with excuses. "Hey, I just wrote the article," he began. "They do the headlines back in New York, that and the art, I've got no control over it. Look, Des, next time I'll talk to them—"

He never had a chance to finish whatever promise he was about to make, because just then Josh McCoy stepped up behind him and tapped him on the shoulder with a rolled-up copy of *Aces*. When Downs turned around, McCoy started swinging. The first punch broke Digger's nose with a sickening noise that made me feel rather faint. McCoy went on to split Digger's lips and loosen a few teeth. I grabbed McCoy with my arms and wrapped my trunk around his neck to try to hold him still, but he was crazy strong with rage and brushed me off easily, I'm afraid. I've never been the physical sort, and in my present condition I fear that I'm pitifully weak. Fortunately Billy Ray came along in time to break them up before McCoy could do serious damage.

Digger spent the rest of the flight back in the rear of the plane, stoked up with painkillers. He managed to offend Billy Ray as well by dripping blood on the front of his white Carnifex costume. Billy is nothing if not obsessive about his appearance, and as he kept telling us, "those fucking bloodstains don't come out." McCoy went up front, where he helped Hiram, Mistral, and Mr. Jayewardene console Peri, who was considerably upset by the story. While McCoy was assaulting Digger in the rear of the plane, she was tearing into Dr. Tachyon up front. Their confrontation was less physical but equally dramatic, Howard tells me. Tachyon kept apologizing over and over again, but no amount of apologies seemed to stay Peregrine's fury. Howard says it was a good thing that her talons were packed away safely with the luggage.

Tachyon finished out the flight alone in the first-class lounge with a bottle of Remy Martin and the forlorn look of a puppy dog who has just piddled on the Persian rug. If I had been a crueler man, I might have gone upstairs and explained my own grievances to him, but I found that I did not have the heart. I find that very curious, but there is something about Dr. Tachyon that makes it difficult to stay angry with him for very long, no matter how insensitive and egregious his behavior.

No matter. I am looking forward to this part of the trip. From Hong Kong we travel to the mainland, Canton and Shanghai and Peking and other stops equally exotic. I plan to walk upon the Great Wall and see the Forbidden City. During World War II I'd chosen to serve in the Navy in hopes of seeing the world, and the Far East always had a special glamour for me, but I wound up assigned to a desk in Bayonne, New Jersey. Mary and I were going to make up for that afterward, when the baby was a little older and we had a little more in the way of financial security.

Well, we made our plans, and meanwhile the Takisians made theirs.

Over the years China came to represent all the things I'd never done, all the far places I meant to visit and never did, my own personal Jolson story. And now it looms on my horizon, at last. It's enough to make one believe the end is truly near.

ZERO HOUR

Lewis Shiner

The store had a pyramid of TV sets in the window, all tuned to the same channel. They tracked a 747 landing at Narita Airport, then pulled back to show an announcer in front of a screen. Then the airport scene switched to a graphic featuring a caricature of Tachyon, a cartoon jet, and the English words *Stacked Deck*.

Fortunato stopped in front of the store. It was just getting dark, and all around him the neon ideograms of the Ginza blazed into red and blue and yellow life. He couldn't hear anything through the glass, so he watched helplessly while the screen flashed pictures of Hartmann and Chrysalis and Jack Braun.

He knew they were going to show Peregrine an instant before she flashed on the screen, lips slightly parted, her eyes starting to look away, the wind in her hair. He didn't need wild card powers to have predicted it. Even if he'd still had them. He knew they'd show her because it was the thing he feared. Fortunato watched his reflected image superimposed over hers, faint, ghostlike.

He bought a *Japanese Times*, Tokyo's biggest English-language paper. "Aces Invade Japan," the headline said, and there was a special pullout section with color photographs. The crowds surged around him, mostly male, mostly in business suits, mostly on autopilot. The ones that noticed him gave him a shocked glance and looked away again. They saw his height and thinness and foreignness. If they could tell he was half-Japanese, they didn't care; the other half was black American, *kokujin*. In Japan, as in too many other parts of the world, the whiter the skin the better.

The paper said the tour would be staying at the newly remodeled Imperial Hotel, a few blocks from where Fortunato stood. And so, Fortunato thought, the mountain has come to Muhammad. Whether Muhammad wants it or not.

It was time, Fortunato thought, for a bath.

*   *   *

Fortunato crouched by the tap and soaped himself all over, then carefully rinsed it off with his plastic bucket. Getting soap into the *ofuro* was one of two breaches of etiquette the Japanese would not tolerate, the other being the wearing of shoes on tatami mats. Once he was clean, Fortunato walked over to the edge of the pool, his towel hanging to cover his genitals with the casual skill of a native Japanese.

He slipped into the 115-degree water, giving himself over to the agonizing pleasure. A mixture of sweat and condensation immediately broke out across his forehead and ran down his face. His muscles relaxed in spite of himself. Around him the other men in the *ofuro* sat with their eyes shut, ignoring him.

He bathed about this time every day. In the six months he'd spent in Japan he'd become a creature of habit, just like the millions of Japanese around him. He was up by nine in the morning, an hour he'd seen only half a dozen times back in New York City. He spent the mornings in meditation or study, going twice a week to a zen *Shukubo* across the bay in Chiba City.

In the afternoons he was a tourist, seeing everything from the French Impressionists at the Bridgestone to the woodcuts at the Riccar, walking in the Imperial Gardens, shopping in the Ginza, visiting the shrines.

At night there was the *mizu-shōbai*. The water business.

It was what they called the huge underground economy of pleasure, everything from the most conservative of geisha houses to the most blatant of prostitutes, from the mirror-walled nightclubs to the tiny red-light bars where, late at night, after enough saki, the hostess might be talked into dancing naked on the Formica counter. It was an entire world catering to the carnal appetite, unlike anything Fortunato had ever seen. It made his operations back in New York, the string of high-class hookers that he'd naively called geishas, seem puny in comparison. In spite of everything that had happened to him, in spite of the fact that he was still trying to push himself toward leaving the world entirely and shutting himself in a monastery, he couldn't stay away from these women. The *jo-san*, the play-for-pay hostesses. If only to look at them and talk to them and then go home alone to mastur-

bate in his tiny cubicle, in case his burned-out wild card
ability had started to come back, in case the tantric power
was beginning to build inside his Muladhara chakra.

When the water wasn't painful anymore, he got up and
soaped and rinsed again and got back into the *ofuro*. It was
time, he thought, for a decision. Either to face Peregrine and
the others at the hotel, or leave town entirely, maybe stay a
week at the *Shukubo* in Chiba City so he wouldn't run into
them by accident.

Or, he thought, the third way. Let fate decide. Go on
about his business, and if he was meant to find them, he
would.

It happened five days later, just before sunset on Tuesday
afternoon, and it was not an accident at all. He'd been talking
to a waiter he knew in the kitchen of the Chikuyotei, and
he'd taken the back door into an alley. When he looked up,
she was there.

"Fortunato," she said. She held her wings straight out
behind her. Still, they nearly touched the walls of the alley.
She wore a deep blue off-the-shoulder knit dress that clung to
her body. She looked to be about six months pregnant.
Nothing he'd seen had mentioned it.

There was a man with her, from India or somewhere
near it. He was about fifty, thick in the middle, losing his
hair.

"Peregrine," Fortunato said. She looked upset, tired,
relieved—all at once. Her arms came up and Fortunato went
to her and held her gently. She rested her forehead on his
shoulder for a second and then pulled away.

"This . . . this is G. C. Jayewardene," Peregrine said. The
man put his palms together, elbows out, and ducked his
head. "He helped me find you."

Fortunato bowed jerkily. Christ, he thought, I'm turning
Japanese. Next I'll be stammering nonsense syllables at the
beginning of every sentence, not even be able to talk anymore.
"How did you know . . ." he said.

"The wild card," Jayewardene said. "I saw this moment a
month ago." He shrugged. "The visions come without my
asking. I don't know why or what they mean. I'm their
prisoner."

"I know the feeling," Fortunato said. He looked at
Peregrine again. He reached out and put a hand on her

stomach. He could feel the baby moving inside her. "It's mine. Isn't it?"

She bit her lip, nodded. "But that's not the reason I'm here. I would have left you alone. I know it's what you wanted. But we need your help."

"What kind of help?"

"It's Hiram," she said. "He's disappeared."

Peregrine needed to sit down. In New York or London or Mexico City there would have been a park within walking distance. In Tokyo the space was too valuable. Fortunato's apartment was a half-hour train ride away, a four-tatami room, six feet by twelve, in a gray-walled complex with narrow halls and communal toilets and no grass or trees. Besides, only a lunatic would try to ride a train at rush hour, when white-gloved railroad employees stood by to shove people into already-packed cars.

Fortunato took them around the corner to a cafeteria-style sushi bar. The decor was red vinyl, white Formica, and chrome. The sushi traveled the length of the room on a conveyor belt that passed all the booths.

"We can talk here," Fortunato said. "But I wouldn't try the food. If you want to eat, I'll take you someplace else—but it'd mean waiting in line."

"No," Peregrine said. Fortunato could see that the sharp vinegar and fish smells weren't sitting well on her stomach. "This is fine."

They'd already asked each other how they'd been, walking over here, and both of them had been pleasant and vague in their answers. Peregrine had told him about the baby. Healthy, she said, normal as far as anyone could tell. Fortunato had asked Jayewardene a few polite questions. There was nothing left but to get down to it.

"He left this letter," Peregrine said. Fortunato looked it over. The handwriting seemed jagged, unlike Hiram's usual compulsive penmanship. It said he was leaving the tour for "personal reasons." He assured everyone he was in good health. He hoped to rejoin them later. If not, he would see them in New York.

"We know where he is," Peregrine said. "Tachyon found him, telepathically, and made sure he wasn't hurt or anything. But he refuses to go into Hiram's brain and find out what's wrong. He says he doesn't have the right. He won't let any of us talk to Hiram, either. He says if somebody wants to leave the tour it's not our business. Maybe he's right. I know if I tried to talk to him, it wouldn't do any good."

"Why not? You two always got along."

"He's different now. He hasn't been the same since December. It's like some witch doctor put a curse on him while we were in the Caribbean."

"Did something specific happen to set him off?"

"Something happened, but we don't know what. We were having lunch at the Palace Sunday with Prime Minister Nakasone and all these other officials. Suddenly there's this man in a cheap suit. He just walks in and hands Hiram a piece of paper. Hiram got very pale and wouldn't say anything about it. That afternoon he went back to the hotel by himself. Said he wasn't feeling good. That must have been when he packed and moved out, because Sunday night he was gone."

"Do you remember anything else about the man in the suit?"

"He had a tattoo. It came out from under his shirt and went down his wrist. God knows how far up his arm it went. It was really vivid, all these greens and reds and blues."

"It probably covered his whole body," Fortunato said. He rubbed his temples, where his regular daily headache had set in. "He was *yakuza*."

"*Yakuza* . . ." Jayewardene said.

Peregrine looked from Fortunato to Jayewardene and back. "Is that bad?"

"Very bad," Jayewardene said. "Even I have heard of them. They're gangsters."

"Like the Mafia," Fortunato said. "Only not as centralized. Each family—they call them clans—is on its own. There's something like twenty-five hundred separate clans in Japan, each with its own *oyabun*. The *oyabun* is like the don. It means 'in the role of parent.' If Hiram's in trouble with the *yak*, we may not even be able to find out which clan is after him."

Peregrine took another piece of paper out of her purse. "This is the address of Hiram's hotel. I . . . told Tachyon I wouldn't see him. I told him somebody should have it in case of emergency. Then Mr. Jayewardene told me about his vision . . . ."

Fortunato put his hand on the paper but didn't look at it.

"I don't have any power left," he said. "I used everything I had fighting the Astronomer, and there isn't anything left."

It had been back in September, Wild Card Day in New York. The fortieth anniversary of Jetboy's big fuckup, when the spores had fallen on the city and thousands had died, Jetboy among them. It was the day a man named the Astronomer chose to get even with the aces who had hounded him and broken his secret society of Egyptian Masons. He and Fortunato had fought it out with blazing fireballs of power over the East River. Fortunato had won, but it had cost him everything.

That had been the night he had made love to Peregrine for the first and last time. The night her child had been conceived.

"It doesn't matter," Peregrine said. "Hiram respects you. He'll listen to you."

In fact, Fortunato thought, he's afraid of me and he blames me for the death of a woman he used to love. A woman Fortunato had used as a pawn against the Astronomer, and lost. A woman Fortunato had loved too. Years ago.

But if he walked away now he wouldn't see Peregrine again. It had been hard enough to stay away from her, knowing that she was so close by. It was a whole other order of difficult to get up and walk away from her when she was right there in front of him, so tall and powerful and overflowing with emotions. The fact that she carried his child made it even harder, made just one more thing he wasn't ready to think about.

"I'll try," Fortunato said. "I'll do what I can."

Hiram's room was in the Akasaka Shanpia, a businessman's hotel near the train station. Except for the narrow hallways and the shoes outside the doors, it could have been any middle-price hotel in the U.S. Fortunato knocked on Hiram's door. There was a hush, as if all noises inside the room had suddenly stopped.

"I know you're in there," Fortunato said, bluffing. "It's Fortunato, man. You might as well let me in." After a couple of seconds the door opened.

Hiram had turned the place into a slum. There were clothes and towels all over the floor, plates of dried-out food and smudged highball glasses, stacks of newspapers and magazines. It smelled faintly of acetone and a mixture of sweat and old booze.

Hiram himself had lost weight. His clothes sagged around him like they were still on hangers. After he let Fortunato in, he walked back to the bed without saying anything. Fortunato shut the door, dumped a dirty shirt off a chair, and sat down.

"So," Hiram said at last. "It would seem I've been ferreted out."

"They're worried. They think you might be in some kind of trouble."

"It's nothing. There's absolutely nothing for them to be concerned about. Didn't they get my note?"

"Don't bullshit me, Hiram. You've gotten messed up with the *yakuza*. Those are not the kind of people you take chances with. Tell me what happened."

Hiram stared at him. "If I don't tell you, you'll just come in and get it, won't you?" Fortunato shrugged, another bluff. "Yeah. Right."

"I just want to help," Fortunato said.

"Well, your help is not required. It's a small matter of money. Nothing else."

"How much money?"

"A few thousand."

"Dollars, of course." A thousand yen were worth a little over five dollars U.S. "How did it happen? Gambling?"

"Look, this is all rather embarrassing. I'd prefer not to talk about it, all right?"

"You're saying this to a man who was a pimp for thirty years. Do you think I'm going to come down on you? Whatever you did?"

Hiram took a deep breath. "No. I suppose not."

"Talk to me."

"I was out walking Saturday night, kind of late, over on Roppongi Street. . . ."

"By yourself?"

"Yes." He was embarrassed again. "I'd heard a lot about the women here. I just wanted to . . . tantalize myself, you know? The mysterious Orient. Women who would fulfill your wildest dreams. I'm a long way from home. I just . . . wanted to see."

It wasn't that different from what Fortunato had been doing the last six months. "I understand."

"I saw a sign that said 'English-speaking hostesses.' I

went in and there was a long hallway. I must have missed the place the sign was for. I went back into the building a long way. There was a padded kind of a door at the end, no sign or anything. When I got inside, they took my coat and went away with it somewhere. Nobody spoke English. Then these girls more or less dragged me over to a table and got me buying them drinks. There were three of them. I had one or two drinks myself. More than one or two. It was a sort of a dare. They were using sign language, teaching me some Japanese. God. They were so beautiful. So... delicate, you know? But with huge dark eyes that would look at you and then skitter away. Half shy and half... I don't know. Challenging. They said nobody had ever drunk ten jars of saki there before. Like no one had ever been quite man enough. So I did. By then they had me pretty well convinced I would get all three of them for a reward."

Hiram started to sweat. The drops ran down his face and he wiped them off with the cuff of a stained silk shirt. "I was . . . well, very aroused, shall we say. And drunk. They kept flirting and touching me on the arm, so lightly, like butterflies landing on my skin. I suggested we go somewhere. They kept putting me off. Ordering more drinks. And then I just lost control."

He looked up at Fortunato. "I haven't been... quite myself lately. Something just came over me in that bar. I guess I grabbed one of the girls. Sort of tried to take her dress off. She started screaming and all three of them ran away. Then the bouncer started hustling me toward the door, waving a bill in my face. It was for fifty thousand yen. Even drunk I knew there was something wrong. He pointed at my coat and then at a number. Then the jars of saki and more numbers. Then the girls and more numbers. I think that was what really got to me. Paying so much money just to be flirted with."

"They were the wrong girls," Fortunato said. "Christ, there's a million women for sale in this town. All you have to do is ask a taxi driver."

"Okay. Okay. I made a mistake. It could happen to anybody. But they went too far."

"So you walked out."

"I walked out. They tried to chase me and I glued them to the floor. Somehow I got back to the hotel. It took me forever to find a cab."

"Okay," Fortunato said. "Where exactly was this place? Could you find it again?"

Hiram shook his head. "I tried. I've spent two days looking for it."

"What about the sign? Do you remember anything about it? Could you sketch any of the characters?"

"The Japanese, you mean? No way."

"There must have been something."

Hiram closed his eyes. "Okay. Maybe there was a picture of a duck. Side view. Looked like a decoy, back home. Just an outline."

"Okay. And you've told me everything that happened at the club."

"Everything."

"And the next day the *kobun* found you at lunch."

"*Kobun?*"

"The *yakuza* soldier."

Hiram blushed again. "He just walked in. I don't know how he got past the security. He stood right across the table from where I was sitting. He bowed from the waist with his legs spread; his right hand is out like this, palm up. He introduced himself, but I was so scared I couldn't remember the name. Then he handed me a bill. The amount was two hundred and fifty thousand yen. There was a note in English at the bottom. It said the amount would double every day at midnight until I paid it."

Fortunato worked the figures out in his head. In U.S. money the debt was now close to seven thousand dollars.

Hiram said, "If it's not paid by Thursday they said . . ."

"What?"

"They said I would never even see the man who killed me."

Fortunato phoned Peregrine from a pay phone, color-coded red for local calls only. He fed it a handful of ten-yen coins to keep it from beeping at him every three minutes.

"I found him," Fortunato said. "He wasn't a lot of help."

"Is he okay?" Peregrine sounded sleepy. It was all too easy for Fortunato to picture her stretched out in bed, covered only by a thin white sheet. He had no powers left. He couldn't stop time or project his astral body or hurl bolts of *prana* or move around inside people's thoughts. But his senses were still acute, sharper than they'd ever been before the virus, and he could remember the smell of her perfume and her hair and her desire as if they were there all around him.

"He's nervous and losing weight. But nothing's happened to him yet."

"Yet?"

"The *yakuza* want money from him. A few thousand. It's basically a misunderstanding. I tried to get him to back down, but he wouldn't. It's a pride thing. He sure picked the country for it. People die from pride here by the thousands, every year."

"You think it's going to come to that?"

"Yes. I offered to pay the money *for* him. He refused. I'd do it behind his back, but I can't find out which clan is after him. What scares me is it sounds like they're threatening him with some kind of invisible killer."

"You mean, like an ace?"

"Maybe. In all the time I've been here I've only heard about one actual confirmed ace, a zen *rōshi* up north on Hokkaido Island. For one thing, I think the spores had pretty much settled out before they could get here. And even if any did, you might never hear about them. We're talking about a culture here that makes self-effacement into a religion. Nobody wants to stand out. So if we're up against some kind of ace, it's possible nobody's even heard of him."

"Can I do anything?"

He wasn't sure what she was offering and he didn't want to think too hard about it. "No," he said. "Not now."

"Where are you?"

"A pay phone, in the Roppongi district. The club where Hiram got in trouble is somewhere around here."

"It's just . . . we never really had a chance to talk. With Jayewardene there and everything."

"I know."

"I went looking for you after Wild Card Day. Your mother said you were going to a monastery."

"I was. Then when I got here I heard about that monk, the one up on Hokkaido."

"The ace."

"Yeah. His name is Dogen. He can create mindblocks, a little like the Astronomer could, but not as drastic. He can make people forget things or take away worldly skills that might interfere with their meditation or—"

"Or take away somebody's wild card power. Yours, for instance."

"For instance."

"Did you see him?"

"He said he'd take me in. But only if I gave up my power."

"But you said your power was gone."

"So far. But I haven't given it a chance to come back. And if I go in the monastery, it could be permanent. Sometimes the block wears off and he has to renew it. Sometimes it doesn't wear off at all."

"And you don't know if you want to go that far."

"I want to. But I still feel . . . responsible. Like the power isn't entirely *mine*, you know?"

"Kind of. I never wanted to give mine up. Not like you or Jayewardene."

"Is he serious about it?"

"He sure seems to be."

"Maybe when this is over," Fortunato said, "him and me can go see Dogen together." Traffic was picking up around him; the daytime buses and delivery vans had given way to expensive sedans and taxis. "I have to go," he said.

"Promise me," Peregrine said. "Promise me you'll be careful."

"Yeah," he said. "Yeah. I promise."

The Roppongi district was about three kilometers southwest of the Ginza. It was the one part of Tokyo where the clubs stayed open past midnight. Lately it was overrun with *gaijin* trade, discos and pubs and bars with Western hostesses.

It had taken Fortunato a long time to get used to things closing early. The last trains left the center of the city at midnight, and he'd walked down to Roppongi more than once during his first weeks in Tokyo, still looking for some elusive satisfaction, unwilling to settle for sex or alcohol, not ready to risk the savage Japanese punishment for being caught with drugs. Finally he'd given it up. The sight of so many tourists, the loud, unceasing noise of their languages, the predictable throb of their music, were not worth the few pleasures the clubs had to offer.

He tried three places and no one remembered Hiram or recognized the sign of the duck. Then he went into the north Berni Inn, one of two in the district. It was an English pub, complete with Guinness and kidney pie and red velvet everything. About half the tables were full, either of foreign tourists in twos and threes, or large tables of Japanese businessmen.

Fortunato slowed to watch the dynamics at one of the Japanese tables. Expense accounts kept the water trade alive. Staying out all night with the boys from the office was just part of the job. The youngest and least confident of them talked the loudest and laughed the hardest. Here, with the excuse of alcohol, was the one time the pressure was off, their only chance to fuck up and get away with it. The senior men smiled indulgently. Fortunato knew that even if he could read their thoughts there wouldn't be much there to see. The perfect Japanese businessman could hide his thoughts even from himself, could efface himself so completely that no one would even know he was there.

The bartender was Japanese and probably new on the job. He looked at Fortunato with a mixture of horror and awe. Japanese were raised to think of *gaijin* as a race of giants. Fortunato, over six feet tall, thin, his shoulders hunched forward like a vulture's, was a walking childhood nightmare.

"Genki desu-ne?" Fortunato asked politely, with a little bow of the head. "I'm looking for a nightclub," he went on in Japanese. "It has a sign like this." He drew a duck on one of the red bar napkins and showed it to the bartender. The bartender nodded, backing away, a rigid smile of fear on his face.

Finally one of the foreign waitresses ducked behind the bar and smiled at Fortunato. "I have a feeling Tosun is not going to do well here," she said. Her accent was Northern England. Her hair was dark brown and pinned up with chopsticks, and her eyes were green. "Can I help?"

"I'm looking for a nightclub somewhere around here. It's got a duck on the sign, like this one. Small place, doesn't do a lot of *gaijin* trade."

The woman looked at the napkin. For a second she had the same look as the bartender. Then she worked her face around into a perfect Japanese smile. It looked horrible on her European features. Fortunato knew she wasn't afraid of him. It had to be the club. "No," she said. "Sorry."

"Look. I know the *yakuza* are mixed up in this. I'm not a cop, and I'm not looking for any trouble. I'm just trying to pay a debt for somebody. For a friend of mine. Believe me, they *want* to see me."

"Sorry."

"What's your name?"

"Megan." The way she thought before saying it told Fortunato she was lying.

"What part of England are you from?"

"I'm not, actually." She casually crumpled the napkin and threw it under the bar. "I'm from Nepal." She gave him the brittle smile again and walked away.

He'd looked at every bar in the district, most of them twice. At least it seemed that way. Hiram could, of course, have been half a block farther on in the wrong direction, or Fortunato could simply have missed it. By four A.M. he was too tired to look anymore, too tired even to go home.

He saw a love hotel on the other side of the Roppongi Crossing. The hourly rates were on the high, windowless walls by the entrance. After midnight it was actually something of a bargain. Fortunato went in past the darkened garden and slipped his money through a blind slot in the wall. A hand slid him out a key.

The hall was full of size-ten foreign men's shoes paired off with tiny *zōri* or doll-sized spike heels. Fortunato found his room and locked the door behind him. The bed was freshly made with pink satin sheets. There were mirrors and a video camera on the ceiling, feeding a big-screen TV in the corner. By love hotel standards the room was pretty tame. Some featured jungles or desert islands, beds shaped like boats or cars or helicopters, light shows and sound effects.

He turned out the light and undressed. All around him his oversensitive hearing picked up tiny cries and shrill, stifled laughter. He folded the pillow over his head and lay with his eyes open to the darkness.

He was forty-seven years old. For twenty of those years he'd lived inside a cocoon of power and never noticed himself aging. Then the last six months had begun to teach him what he'd missed. The dreadful fatigue after a long night like this one. Mornings when his joints hurt so badly it was hard to get up. Important memories beginning to fade, trivia haunting him obsessively. Lately there were the headaches, and indigestion and muscle cramps. The constant awareness of being human, being mortal, being weak.

Nothing was as addictive as power. Heroin was a glass of flat beer in comparison. There had been nights, watching an endless throng of beautiful women move down the Ginza or the Shinjuku, virtually all of them for sale, when he'd thought he couldn't go on without feeling that power again. He'd talked to himself like an alcoholic, promising himself he'd wait just one more day. And somehow he'd held out. Partly because the memories of his last night in New York, of his final battle with the Astronomer, were still too fresh, reminding him of the pain the power had cost him. Partly because he was no longer sure the power was there, whether Kundalini, the great serpent, was dead or just asleep.

Tonight he'd watched helplessly as a hundred or more Japanese lied to him, ignored him, even humiliated themselves rather than tell him what they so obviously knew. He'd started to see himself through their eyes: huge, clumsy, sweaty, loud, and uncivilized, a pathetic barbarian giant, a kind of oversized monkey who couldn't even be held accountable for common politeness.

A little tantric magick would change all that.

Tomorrow, he told himself. *If you still feel this way tomorrow then you can go ahead, try to get it back.*

He closed his eyes and finally fell asleep.

He woke up with an erection for the first time in months. It was fate, he told himself. Fate that brought Peregrine to him, that provided the need for him to use his power again.

Was that the truth? Or did he just want an excuse to make love to her again, an outlet for six months of sexual frustration?

He dressed and took a cab to the Imperial Hotel. The tour took up an entire floor of the new thirty-one-story tower, and everything inside was scaled up for Europeans. The halls and the insides of the elevators seemed huge to Fortunato now. By the time he got off on the thirtieth floor his hands were shaking. He leaned against Peregrine's door and knocked quietly. A few seconds later he knocked again, harder.

She answered the door in a loose nightgown that touched the floor. Her feathers were ruffled and she could hardly open her eyes. Then she saw him.

She took the chain off the door and stood aside. He shut the door behind him and took her in his arms. He could feel the tiny creature in her belly moving as he held her. He kissed her. Sparks seemed to be crackling around them, but it could have been just the strength of his desire, breaking out of the chains he'd kept it in for so long.

He pulled the straps of her nightgown down along her arms. It fell to her waist and revealed her breasts, their nipples dark and puffy. He touched one with his tongue and tasted the chalky sweetness of her milk. She put her arms around his head and moaned. Her skin was soft and fragrant as the silk of an antique kimono. She pulled him toward the unmade bed and he broke away from her long enough to take off his clothes.

She lay on her back. The pregnancy was the summit of her body, where all the curves ended. Fortunato knelt next to her and kissed her face and throat and shoulders and breasts. He couldn't seem to get his breath. He turned her on her side, facing away from him, and kissed the small of her back. Then he reached up between her legs and held her there, feeling the warmth and wetness against his palm, moving his fingers slowly through the tangle of her pubic hair. She undulated slowly, clutching a pillow in both hands.

He lay down behind her and went into her from behind. The soft flesh of her buttocks pressed into his stomach and his eyes went out of focus. "Oh, God," he said. He began to move slowly inside her, his left arm under her and cupping one breast, his right hand lightly touching the curve of her stomach. She moved with him, both of them in slow motion, her breath coming harder and faster until she cried out and ground her hips against him.

At the last possible moment he reached down and blocked his ejaculation at the perineum. The hot fluid flooded back into his groin and lights seemed to flash around him. He relaxed, ready to feel his astral body come loose from his flesh.

It didn't happen.

He put his arms around Peregrine and held onto her fiercely. He buried his face in her neck, let her long hair cover his head.

Now he knew. The power was gone.

He had a single bright moment of panic, then exhaustion carried him on into sleep.

*   *   *

He slept for an hour or so and woke up tired. Peregrine was on her back, watching him.

"You okay?" she said.

"Yeah. Fine."

"You're not glowing."

"No," he said. He looked at his hands. "It didn't work. It was wonderful. But the power didn't come back. There's nothing there."

She turned on her side, facing him. "Oh, no." She stroked his cheek. "I'm sorry."

"It's okay," he said. "Really. I've spent the last six months going back and forth, afraid the power would come back, then afraid it wouldn't. At least now I know." He kissed her neck. "Listen. We need to talk about the baby."

"We can talk. But it's not like I expect anything from you, okay? I mean, there's some things I should probably have told you. There's a guy on the tour name of McCoy. He's the cameraman for this documentary we're doing. It looks like it could get serious with us. He knows about the baby and he doesn't care."

"Oh," Fortunato said. "I didn't know."

"We had a big fight couple of days ago. And seeing you again—well, that really was something, that night back in New York. You're quite a guy. But you know there couldn't ever be anything permanent between us."

"No," Fortunato said. "I guess not." His hand moved reflexively to stroke her swollen stomach, tracing blue veins against the pale skin. "It's weird. I never wanted kids. But now that it's happened, it's not like I thought it would be. It's like it doesn't really matter what I want. I'm responsible. Even if I never see the kid, I'm still responsible, and I always will be."

"Don't make this harder than it has to be. Don't make me wish I hadn't come to you with this."

"No. I just want to know that you're going to be okay. You and the baby both."

"The baby's fine. Other than the fact that neither one of us has a last name to give it."

There was a knock at the door. Fortunato tensed, feeling suddenly out of place. "Peri?" said Tachyon's voice. "Peri, are you in there?"

"Just a minute," she said. She put on a robe and handed

Fortunato his clothes. He was still buttoning his shirt when she opened the door.

Tachyon looked at Peregrine, at the rumpled bed, at Fortunato. "You," he said. He nodded like his worst suspicions had just proved out. "Peri told me you were . . . helping."

Jealous, little man? Fortunato thought. "That's right," he said.

"Well, I hope I didn't interrupt." He looked at Peregrine. "The bus for the Meiji Shrine is supposed to leave in fifteen minutes. If you're going."

Fortunato ignored him, went to Peregrine, and kissed her gently. "I'll call you," he said, "when I know something."

"All right." She squeezed his hand. "Be careful."

He walked past Tachyon and into the hall. A man with an elephant's trunk instead of a nose was waiting there.

"Des," Fortunato said. "It's good to see you." That was not entirely true. Des looked terribly old, his cheeks sunken, the bulk of his body melting away. Fortunato wondered if his own pains were as obvious.

"Fortunato," Des said. They shook hands. "It's been a long time."

"I didn't think you'd ever leave New York."

"I was due to see a little of the world. Age has a way of catching up with one."

"Yeah," Fortunato said. "No kidding."

"Well," Des said. "I have to make the tour bus."

"Sure," Fortunato said. "I'll walk you."

There was a time when Des had been one of his best customers. It looked like those times were over.

Tachyon caught up with them at the elevator. "What do you *want?*" Fortunato said. "Can't you just leave me alone with this?"

"Peri told me about your powers. I came to tell you I'm sorry. I know you hate me. Though I don't really know why. I suppose the way I dress, the way I behave, is some kind of obscure threat to your masculinity. Or at least you've chosen to see it that way. But it's in your mind, not mine."

Fortunato shook his head angrily.

"I just want one second." Tachyon closed his eyes. The elevator chimed and the doors opened.

"Your second's up," Fortunato said. Still he didn't move. Des got on, giving Fortunato a mournful look, and the elevator closed again. Fortunato heard the cables creaking behind bamboo-patterned doors.

"Your power is still there."

"Bullshit."

"You're shutting it inside yourself. Your mind is full of conflicts and contradictions, holding it in."

"It took everything I had to fight the Astronomer. I hit empty. The bottom of the barrel. Cleaned out. Nothing left to recharge. Like running a car battery dry. It won't even jumpstart. It's over."

"To take up your metaphor, even a live battery won't start when the ignition key is turned off. And the key," Tachyon said, pointing at his forehead, "is inside." He walked away and Fortunato slammed the elevator button with the flat of his hand.

He called Hiram from the lobby.

"Get over here," Hiram said. "I'll meet you out front."

"What's wrong?"

"Just get over here."

Fortunato took a cab and found Hiram pacing back and forth in front of the plain gray facade of the Akasaka Shanpia. "What happened?"

"Come in and see," Hiram said.

The room had looked bad before, but now it was a disaster. The walls were spattered with shaving cream, the dresser drawers had been thrown into the corner, the mirrors were shattered and the mattress ripped to shreds.

"I didn't even see it happen. I was here the whole time and I didn't see it."

"What are you talking about? How could you not see it?"

Hiram's eyes were frantic. "I went to the bathroom about nine this morning and got a glass of water. I know everything was okay then. I came back in here and put the TV on and watched for maybe half an hour. Then I heard something that sounded like the door slamming. I looked up and the room was like you see it. And this note was in my lap."

The note was in English. "Zero hour comes tomorrow. You can die this easy. Zero man."

"Then it is an ace."

"It won't happen again," Hiram said. He obviously didn't

even believe himself. "I'll know what to look for. He couldn't fool me twice."

"We can't risk it. Leave everything. You can buy some new clothes this afternoon. I want you to hit the street and keep moving. Around ten o'clock go into the first hotel you see and get a room. Call Peregrine and tell her where you are."

"Does she . . . does she know what happened?"

"No. She knows it's money trouble. That's all."

"Okay. Fortunato, I . . ."

"Forget it," Fortunato said. "Just keep moving."

The shade of the banyan tree had saved a little coolness from the morning. Overhead the milk-colored sky was thick with smog. *Sumoggu*, they called it. It was easy to see what the Japanese thought of the West by the words they borrowed: *rashawa*, rush hour; *sarariman*, salary man, executive; *toire*, toilet.

It helped to be here in the Imperial Gardens, an oasis of calm in the heart of Tokyo. The air was fresher, though the cherry blossoms wouldn't be blooming for another month. When they did, the entire city would turn out with cameras. Unlike New Yorkers, the Japanese could appreciate the beauty that was right in front of them.

Fortunato finished the last piece of boiled shrimp from his *bentō*, the box lunch he'd bought just outside the park, and tossed the box away. He couldn't seem to settle down. What he wanted was to talk to the *rōshi*, Dogen. But Dogen was a day and a half away, and he would have to travel by airplane, train, bus, and foot to get there. Peregrine was grounded by her pregnancy, and he doubted Mistral was strong enough for a twelve-hundred-mile round trip. There was no way he could get to Hokkaido and back in time to help Hiram.

A few yards away an old man raked the gravel in a rock garden with a battered bamboo rake. Fortunato thought of Dogen's harsh physical discipline: the 38,000-kilometer walk, equivalent to a trip all the way around the earth, lasting a thousand days, around and around Mt. Tanaka; the constant sitting, perfectly still, on the hard wooden floors of the temple; the endless raking of the master's stone garden.

Fortunato walked up to the old man. *"Sumi-masen,"* he said. He pointed to the rake. "May I?"

The old man handed Fortunato the rake. He looked like he couldn't decide if he was afraid or amused. There were advantages, Fortunato thought, to being an outsider among the most polite people on earth. He began to rake the gravel, trying to raise the least amount of dust possible, trying to form the gravel into harmonious lines through the strength of his will alone, channeled only incidentally through the rake. The old man went to sit under the banyan tree.

As he worked, Fortunato pictured Dogen in his mind. He looked young, but then most Japanese looked young to Fortunato.' His head was shaved until it glistened, the skull formed from planes and angles, the cheeks dimpling when he spoke. His hands formed *mudras* apparently of their own volition, the index fingers reaching to touch the ends of the thumbs when they had nothing else to do.

Why have you called me? said Dogen's voice inside Fortunato's head.

Master! Fortunato thought.

Not your master yet, said Dogen's voice. *You still live in the world.*

I didn't know you had the power to do this, Fortunato thought.

It is not my power. It is yours. Your mind came to me.

I have no power, Fortunato thought.

You are filled with power. It feels like Chinese peppers inside my head.

Why can't I feel it?

You have hidden yourself from it, the way a fat man tries to hide himself from the yakitori *all around him. This is how it is in the world. The world demands that you have power, and yet the use of it makes you ashamed. This is the way Japan is now. We have become very powerful in the world, and to do it we gave up our spiritual feelings. You have to make the decision. If you want to live in the world you must admit your power. If you want to feed your spirit, you must leave the world. Right now you are pulling yourself into pieces.*

Fortunato knelt in the gravel and bowed low. *Domo arigatō, o sensei. Arigatō* meant "thank you," but literally it meant "it hurts." Fortunato felt the truth inside the words. If he hadn't believed Dogen, it wouldn't have hurt so much. He looked up and saw the old gardener staring at him in abject fear, but at the same time making a series of short, nervous bows from the waist so as not to seem rude. Fortunato smiled at him and bowed low again. "Don't worry," he said in Japanese. He stood up and gave the old man back his rake. "Just another crazy *gaijin*."

His stomach hurt again. It wasn't the *bentō*, he knew. It was the stress inside his own mind, eating his body up from within.

He was back on Harumi-Dori, heading toward the Ginza corner. He'd been wandering for hours, while the sun had set and the night had flowered around him. The city seemed like an electronic forest. The long vertical signs crowded each other down the entire length of the street, flashing ideograms and English characters in blazing neon. The streets were crowded with Japanese in jogging outfits or jeans and sport shirts. Packed in with the regular citizens were the *sararimen* in plain gray suits.

Fortunato stopped to lean against one of the graceful f-shaped streetlights. Here it is, he thought, in all its glory. There was no more worldly a place on the planet, no place more obsessed with money, gadgets, drinking, and sex. And a few hours away were wooden temples in pine forests where men sat on their heels and tried to turn their minds into rivers or dust or starlight.

Make up your mind, he told himself. You have to make up your mind.

"*Gaijin-san!* You like girl? Pretty girl?"

Fortunato turned around. It was a tout for a *Pinku Saron*, a unique Japanese institution where the customer paid by the hour for a bottomless saki cup and a topless *jo-san*. She would sit passively in his lap while he fondled her breasts and drank himself into a state where he was prepared to go home to his wife. It was, Fortunato decided, an omen.

He paid three thousand yen for half an hour and walked into a darkened hallway. A soft hand took his and led him downstairs into a completely dark room filled with tables and other couples. Fortunato heard business being discussed all around him. His hostess led him to one end of the room and sat him with his legs pinned under a low table, his back supported by a legless wooden chair. Then she gracefully moved into his lap. He heard her kimono rustle as she opened it to free her breasts.

The woman was tiny and smelled of face powder, sandal-wood soap, and, faintly, of sweat. Fortunato reached up with both hands and touched her face, his fingers tracing the lines of her jaw. She paid no attention. "Saki?" she asked.

"No," Fortunato said. *"I-ie, domo."* His fingers followed the muscles of her neck down to her shoulders, out to the edges of her kimono, then down. His fingertips brushed lightly over her small, delicate breasts, the tiny nipples hardening at his touch. The woman giggled nervously, raising one hand to cover her mouth. Fortunato laid his head between her breasts and inhaled the aroma of her skin. It was the smell of the world. It was time either to turn away or surrender, and he had backed himself into a corner, left himself without the strength to resist.

He gently pulled her face down and kissed her. Her lips were tight, nervous. She giggled again. In Japan they called kissing *suppun*, the exotic practice. Only teenagers and foreigners did it. Fortunato kissed her again, feeling himself stiffening, and the electricity went through him and into the woman. She stopped giggling and began to tremble. Fortunato was shaking too. He could feel the serpent, Kundalini, begin to wake up. It moved around in his groin and began to uncoil through his spine. Slowly, as if she didn't understand what she was doing or why, the woman touched him with her little hands, putting them behind his neck. Her tongue touched him lightly on his lips and chin and eyelids. Fortunato untied her kimono and opened it up. He lifted her easily by the waist and sat her on the edge of the table, putting her legs over his shoulders, bending to open her up with his tongue. She tasted spicy, exotic, and in seconds she had come alive under him, hot and wet, her hips moving involuntarily.

She pushed his head away and leaned forward, working at his trousers. Fortunato kissed her shoulders and neck. She moaned softly. There didn't seem to be anyone else in the hot, crowded room, no one else in the world. It was happening, Fortunato thought. Already he could see a little in the darkness, see her plain, square face, the lines beginning to show under her eyes, seeing how her looks had consigned her to the darkness of the *Pinku Saron*, wanting her even more for the desire he could see hidden inside her. He lowered her onto him. She gasped as he went into her, her fingers digging into his shoulders, and his eyes rolled back in his head.

Yes, he thought. Yes, yes, yes. The world. I surrender. The power rose inside him like molten lava.

*   *   *

It was a little after ten when he walked into the Berni Inn. The waitress, the one who'd told him her name was Megan, was just coming out of the kitchen. She stopped dead when she saw Fortunato. The waitress behind her nearly ran into her with a tray of meat pies.

She stared at his forehead. Fortunato didn't have to see himself to know that his forehead had swollen again, bulging with the power of his *rasa*. He walked across the room to her. "Go away," she said. "I don't want to talk to you."

"The club," Fortunato said "The one with the sign of the duck. You know where it is."

"No. I never—"

"Tell me where it is," he ordered.

All expression left her face. "Across Roppongi. Right at the police box, down two blocks, then left half a block. The bar in front is called Takahashi's."

"And the place in back? What's it called?"

"It hasn't got a name. It's a *yak* hangout. It's not the Yamaguchi-gumi, none of the big gangs. Just this one little clan."

"Then why are you so afraid of them?"

"They've got a *ninja*, a shadow-fighter. He's one of those what-you-call-thems. An ace." She looked at Fortunato's forehead. "Like you, then, isn't he? They say he's killed hundreds. Nobody's ever seen him. He could be in this room right now. If not now, then he will be later. He'll kill me for having told you this."

"You don't understand," Fortunato said. "They want to see me. I've got just the thing they want."

It was the way Hiram had described it. The hallway was raw gray plaster and the door at the end of it was padded in turquoise Naugahyde with big brass nailheads. Inside, one of the hostesses came up to take Fortunato's jacket. "No," he said in Japanese. "I want to see the *oyabun*. It's important."

She was still a little stunned just by the way he looked. His rudeness was more than she could deal with. "*W-w-wakarimasen*," she stammered.

"Yes, you do. You understand me perfectly well. Go tell your boss I have to speak to him. Now."

He waited next to the doorway. The room was long and narrow, with a low ceiling and mirrored tiles on the left-hand wall, above a row of booths. There was a bar along the other wall, with chrome stools like an American soda fountain. Most of the men were Koreans, in cheap polyester suits and wide ties. The edges of tattoos showed around their collars and cuffs. Whenever they looked at him, Fortunato stared back and they turned away.

It was eleven o'clock. Even with the power moving through him, Fortunato was a little nervous. He was a foreigner, out of his depth, in the middle of the enemy's stronghold. I'm not here for trouble, he reminded himself. I'm here to pay Hiram's debt and get out.

And then, he thought, everything will be okay. It was not even midnight Wednesday, and Hiram's business was nearly settled. Friday the 747 would be off for Korea and then the Soviet Union, taking Hiram and Peregrine with it. And then he would be on his own, able to think about what came next. Or maybe he should get on the plane himself, go back to New York. Peregrine said they had no future together, but maybe that wasn't true.

He loved Tokyo, but Tokyo would never love him back. It would see to all his needs, give him enormous license in exchange for even the smallest attempt at politeness, dazzle him with its beauty, exhaust him with its exquisite sexual pleasures. But he would always be a *gaijin*, a foreigner, never have a family in a country where family was more important than anything.

The hostess crouched by the last booth, talking to a Japanese with long permed hair and a silk suit. The little finger of his left hand was missing. The *yakuza* used to cut their fingers off to atone for mistakes. The younger kids, Fortunato had heard, didn't hold much with the idea. Fortunato took a breath and walked up to the table.

The *oyabun* sat next to the wall. Fortunato figured him to be about forty. There were two *jo-san* next to him, and another across from him between a pair of heavyset bodyguards. "Leave us," Fortunato ordered the hostess. She walked away in the middle of her protest. The first bodyguard got up to throw Fortunato out. "You too," Fortunato said, making eye contact with each of them and each of the girls.

The *oyabun* watched it all with a quiet smile. Fortunato bowed to him from the waist. The *oyabun* ducked his head and said, "My name is Kanagaki. Will you sit down?"

Fortunato sat across from him. "The *gaijin* Hiram Worchester has sent me here to pay his debt." Fortunato took out his checkbook. "The amount, I believe, is two million yen."

"Ah," Kanagaki said. "Another 'ace.' You have provided us with much amusement. Especially the little red-haired fellow."

"Tachyon? What does he have to do with this?"

"With this?" He pointed to Fortunato's checkbook. "Nothing. But many *jo-san* have tried to bring him pleasure these past few days. It seems he is having trouble performing as a man."

Tachyon? Fortunato thought. Can't get it up? He wanted to laugh. It certainly explained the little man's rotten mood at the hotel. "This has nothing to do with aces," Fortunato said. "This is business."

"Ah. Business. Very well. We shall settle this in a businesslike way." He looked at his watch and smiled. "Yes, the amount is two million yen. In a few minutes it will become four million. A pity. I doubt you will have time to bring the *gaijin* Worchester-*san* here before midnight."

Fortunato shook his head. "There is no need for Worchester-*san* to be here in person."

"But there is. We feel there is some honor at stake here."

Fortunato held the man's eyes. "I am asking you to do the needful." He made the traditional phrase an order. "I will give you the money. The debt will be canceled."

Kanagaki's will was very strong. He almost managed to say the words that were trying to get out of his throat. Instead he said in a strangled voice, "I will honor your face."

Fortunato wrote the check and handed it to Kanagaki. "You understand me. The debt is canceled."

"Yes," Kanagaki said. "The debt is canceled."

"You have a man working for you. An assassin. I think he calls himself Zero Man."

"Mori Riishi." He gave the name in Japanese fashion, family name first.

"No harm will come to Worchester-*san*. He is not to be harmed. This Zero Man, Mori, will stay away from him."

Kanagaki was silent.

"What is it?" Fortunato asked him. "What is it you're not saying?"

"It's too late. Mori has already left. The *gaijin* Worchester dies at midnight."

"Christ," Fortunato said.

"Mori comes to Tokyo with a great reputation, but we have no proof. He was very concerned to make a good impression."

Fortunato realized he hadn't checked with Peregrine. "What hotel? What hotel is Worchester-*san* staying in?"

Kanagaki spread his hands. "Who knows?"

Fortunato started to get up. While he'd been talking to Kanagaki, the bodyguards had come back with reinforcements. They surrounded the table. Fortunato couldn't be bothered with them. He formed a wedge of power around himself and sprinted for the door, pushing them aside as he ran.

Outside, the Roppongi was still crowded. Over at Shinjuku station the late-night drinkers would be trying to push their way onto the last trains of the night. On the Ginza they would be lining up at the cab stands. It was ten minutes to midnight. There wasn't time.

He let his astral body spring loose and rocket through the night toward the Imperial Hotel. The neon and mirrored glass and chrome blurred as he picked up speed. He didn't slow until he was through the wall of the hotel and hovering in Peregrine's room. He let himself become visible, a glowing, golden-rose image of his physical body.

Peregrine, he thought.

She rolled over in bed, opened her eyes. Fortunato saw, with a small, distant sort of pang, that she was not alone.

I need to know where Hiram is.

"Fortunato?" she whispered, then saw him. "Oh my God."

Hurry. The name of the hotel.

"Wait a minute. I wrote it down." She walked naked over to the phone. Fortunato's astral body was free of lust and hunger, but still the sight of her moved him. "The Ginza Dai-Ichi. Room eight oh one. He says it's a big H-shaped building by the Shimbashi station—"

I know where it is. Meet me there as fast as you can. Bring help.

He couldn't wait for her answer. He snapped back to his physical body and lifted it into the air.

He hated the spectacle of it. Being in Japan had made him even more self-conscious than he ever had been in New York. But there was no choice. He levitated straight up into the sky, high enough that he couldn't make out the faces turned up to stare at him, and arced toward the Dai-Ichi Hotel.

He got to the door of Hiram's room at twelve midnight. The door was locked, but Fortunato wrenched the bolts back with his mind, splintering the wood around them.

Hiram sat up in bed. "Wha—"

Fortunato stopped time.

It was like a train grinding to a halt. The countless tiny sounds of the hotel slowed to a bass growl, then hung in the silence between beats. Fortunato's own breathing had stopped.

There was nobody in the room but Hiram. It hurt Fortunato to make his head turn; to Hiram it would have seemed like he was moving in a blur of speed. The sliding doors to the bathroom were open. Fortunato couldn't see anyone in there either.

Then he remembered how the Astronomer had been able to hide from him, to make Fortunato not see him. He let time begin to trickle past him again. He brought up his hands, fighting the heavy, clinging air, and framed the room, making an empty square bordered by his thumbs and index fingers. Here was the closet, the doors open. Here was a stretch of bamboo-patterned wall with nothing in it. Here was the foot of the bed, and the edge of a samurai sword moving slowly toward Hiram's head.

Fortunato threw himself forward. His body seemed to take forever to rise into the air and float toward Hiram. He opened his arms and knocked Hiram to the floor, feeling something hard scrape the bottoms of his shoes. He rolled onto his back and saw the sheets and mattress slowly splitting in two.

The sword, he thought. Once he convinced himself it was there, he could see it. Now the arm, he thought, and slowly the entire man took shape in front of him, a young Japanese in a white dress shirt and gray wool pants and bare feet.

He let time start again before the strain wore him out completely. He heard footsteps in the hall. He was afraid to look away, afraid he might loose the killer again. "Drop the sword," Fortunato said.

"You can see me," the man said in English. He turned to look toward the door.

"Put it down," Fortunato said, making it an order now,

but it was too late. He no longer had eye contact and the man resisted him.

Without thinking, Fortunato looked at the doorway. It was Tachyon, in red silk pajamas, Mistral behind him. Tachyon was charging into the room, and Fortunato knew the little alien was about to die.

He looked back for Mori. Mori was gone. Fortunato went cold with panic. The sword, he thought. Find the sword. He looked where the sword would have to be if it were slicing toward Tachyon and slowed time again.

There. The blade, curved and impossibly sharp, the steel dazzling as sunlight. Come to me, Fortunato thought. He pulled at the blade with his mind.

He only meant to take it from Mori's hands. He misjudged his own power. The blade spun completely around, missing Tachyon by inches. It whirled around ten or fifteen times and finally buried itself in the wall behind the bed.

Somewhere in there it had sliced off the top of Mori's head.

Fortunato shielded them with his power until they were on the street. It was the same trick Zero Man had used. No one saw them. They left Mori's corpse in the room, his blood soaking into the carpet.

A taxi pulled up and Peregrine got out. The man who'd been in bed with her got out behind her. He was a bit shorter than Fortunato, with blond hair and a mustache. He stood next to Peregrine and she reached out and took his hand. "Is everything okay?" she said.

"Yeah," Hiram said. "It's okay."

"Does this mean you're back on the tour?"

Hiram looked around at the others. "Yeah. I guess I am."

"That's good," Peregrine said, suddenly noticing how serious everyone was. "We were all worried about you."

Hiram nodded.

Tachyon moved next to Fortunato. "Thank you," he said quietly. "Not only for saving my life. You probably saved the tour as well. Another violent incident—after Haiti and Guatemala and Syria—well, it would have undone everything we were trying to accomplish."

"Sure," Fortunato said. "We probably shouldn't hang around here too long. No point in taking chances."

"No," Tachyon said. "I guess not."

"Uh, Fortunato," Peregrine said. "Josh McCoy."

Fortunato shook his hand and nodded. McCoy smiled and gave his hand back to Peregrine. "I've heard a lot about you."

"There's blood on your shirt," Peregrine said. "What happened?"

"It's nothing," Fortunato said. "It's all over now."

"So much blood," Peregrine said. "Like with the Astronomer. There's so much violence in you. It's scary sometimes."

Fortunato didn't say anything.

"So," McCoy said. "What happens now?"

"I guess," Fortunato said, "me and G. C. Jayewardene will go see a man about a monastery."

"You kidding?" McCoy said.

"No," Peregrine said. "I don't think he is." She looked at Fortunato for a long time, and then she said, "Take care of yourself, will you?"

"Sure," Fortunato said. "What else?"

"There it is," Fortunato said. The monastery straggled across the entire hillside, and beyond it were stone gardens and terraced fields. Fortunato wiped the snow from a rock next to the path and sat down. His head was clear and his stomach quiet. Maybe it was just the clean mountain air. Maybe it was something more.

"It's very beautiful," Jayewardene said, crouching on his heels.

Spring wouldn't get to Hokkaido for another month and a half. The sky was clear, though. Clear enough to see, for instance, a 747 from miles and miles away. But the 747s didn't fly over Hokkaido. Especially not the ones headed for Korea, almost a thousand miles to the southwest.

"What happened Wednesday night?" Jayewardene asked after a few minutes. "There was all kind of commotion, and when it was over Hiram was back. Do you want to talk about it?"

"Not much to tell," Fortunato said. "People fighting over money. A boy died. He'd never actually killed anybody, as it turned out. He was very young, very afraid. He just wanted to do a good job, to live up to the reputation he'd invented for himself." Fortunato shrugged. "It's the way of the world. That kind of thing is always going to happen in a place like

Tokyo." He stood up, brushing at the seat of his pants. "Ready?"

"Yes," Jayewardene said. "I've been waiting for this a long time."

Fortunato nodded. "Then let's get on with it."

FROM *THE JOURNAL*
OF XAVIER DESMOND

MARCH 21/EN ROUTE TO SEOUL:

A face out of my past confronted me in Tokyo and has preyed on my mind ever since. Two days ago I decided that I would ignore him and the issues raised by his presence, that I would make no mention of him in this journal.

I've made plans to have this volume to be offered for publication after my death. I do not expect a best-seller, but I would think the number of celebrities aboard the *Stacked Deck* and the various newsworthy events we've generated will stir up at least a little interest in the great American public, so my volume may find its own audience. Whatever modest royalties it earns will be welcomed by the JADL, to which I've willed my entire estate.

Yet, even though I will be safely dead and buried before anyone reads these words, and therefore in no position to be harmed by any personal admissions I might make, I find myself reluctant to write of Fortunato. Call it cowardice, if you will. Jokers are notorious cowards, if one listens to the jests, the cruel sort that they do not allow on television. I can easily justify my decision to say nothing of Fortunato. My dealings with him over the years have been private matters, having little to do with politics or world affairs or the issues that I've tried to address in this journal, and nothing at all to do with this tour.

Yet I have felt free, in these pages, to repeat the gossip that has inevitably swirled about the airplane, to report on the various foibles and indiscretions of Dr. Tachyon and Peregrine and Jack Braun and Digger Downs and all the rest. Can I truly pretend that their weaknesses are of public interest and my own are not? Perhaps I could . . . the public has always been fascinated by aces and repelled by jokers . . . but I will not. I want this journal to be an honest one, a true one. And I want the readers to understand a little of what it has been like to live forty years a joker. And to do that I must talk of Fortunato, no matter how deeply it may shame me.

Fortunato now lives in Japan. He helped Hiram in some obscure way after Hiram had suddenly and quite mysteriously left the tour in Tokyo. I don't pretend to know the details of that; it was all carefully hushed up. Hiram seemed almost himself when he returned to us in Calcutta, but he has deteriorated rapidly again, and he looks worse every day. He has become volatile and unpleasant, and secretive. But this is not about Hiram, of whose woes I know nothing. The point is, Fortunato was embroiled in the business somehow and came to our hotel, where I spoke to him briefly in the corridor. That was all there was to it . . . now. But in years past Fortunato and I have had other dealings.

Forgive me. This is hard. I am an old man and a joker, and age and deformity alike have made me sensitive. My dignity is all I have left, and I am about to surrender it.

I was writing about self-loathing.

This is a time for hard truths, and the first of those is that many nats are disgusted by jokers. Some of these are bigots, always ready to hate anything different. In that regard we jokers are no different from any other oppressed minority; we are all hated with the same honest venom by those predisposed to hate.

There are other normals, however, who are more predisposed to tolerance, who try to see beyond the surface to the human being beneath. People of good will, not haters, well-meaning generous people like . . . well, like Dr. Tachyon and Hiram Worchester to choose two examples close to hand. Both of these gentlemen have proven over the years that they care deeply about jokers in the abstract, Hiram through his anonymous charities, Tachyon through his work at the clinic. And yet both of them, I am convinced, are just as sickened by the simple physical deformity of most jokers as the Nur al-Allah or Leo Barnett. You can see it in their eyes, no matter how nonchalant and cosmopolitan they strive to be. Some of their best friends are jokers, but they wouldn't want their sister to marry one.

This is the first unspeakable truth of jokerhood.

How easy it would be to rail against this, to condemn men like Tach and Hiram for hypocrisy and "formism" (a hideous word coined by a particularly moronic joker activist and taken up by Tom Miller's Jokers for a Just Society in their heyday). Easy, and wrong. They are decent men, but still only men, and cannot be thought less because they have normal human feelings.

Because, you see, the second unspeakable truth of jokerhood is that no matter how much jokers offend nats, we offend ourselves even more.

Self-loathing is the particular psychological pestilence of Jokertown, a disease that is often fatal. The leading cause of death among jokers under the age of fifty is, and always has been, suicide. This *despite* the fact that virtually every disease known to man is more serious when contracted by a joker, because our body chemistries and very shapes vary so widely and unpredictably that no course of treatment is truly safe.

In Jokertown you'll search long and hard before you'll find a place to buy a mirror, but there are mask shops on every block.

If that was not proof enough, consider the issue of names. Nicknames, they call them. They are more than that. They are spotlights on the true depths of joker self-loathing.

If this journal is to be published, I intend to insist that it be titled *The Journal of Xavier Desmond*, not *A Joker's Journal* or any such variant. I am a man, a particular man, not just a generic joker. Names are important; they are more than just words, they shape and color the things they name. The feminists realized this long ago, but jokers still have not grasped it.

I have made it a point over the years to answer to no name but my own, yet I know a joker dentist who calls himself Fishface, an accomplished ragtime pianist who answers to Catbox, and a brilliant joker mathematician who signs his papers "Slimer." Even on this tour I find myself accompanied by three people named Chrysalis, Troll, and Father Squid.

We are, of course, not the first minority to experience this particular form of oppression. Certainly black people have been there; entire generations were raised with the belief that the "prettiest" black girls were the ones with the lightest skins whose features most closely approximated the Caucasian ideal. Finally some of them saw through that lie and proclaimed that *black* was beautiful.

From time to time various well-meaning but foolish

jokers have attempted to do the same thing. Freakers, one of the more debauched institutions of Jokertown, has what it calls a "Twisted Miss" contest every year on Valentine's Day. However sincere or cynical these efforts are, they are surely misguided. Our friends the Takisians took care of that by putting a clever little twist on the prank they played on us.

The problem is, every joker is unique.

Even before my transformation I was never a handsome man. Even after the change I am by no means hideous. My "nose" is a trunk, about two feet long, with fingers at its end. My experience has been that most people get used to the way I look if they are around me for a few days. I like to tell myself that after a week or so you scarcely notice that I'm any different, and maybe there's even a grain of truth in that.

If the virus had only been so kind as to give *all* jokers trunks where their noses had been, the adjustment might have been a good deal easier, and a "Trunks Are Beautiful" campaign might have done some real good.

But to the best of my knowledge I am the only joker with a trunk. I might work very hard to disregard the aesthetics of the nat culture I live in, to convince myself that I am one handsome devil and that the rest of them are the funny-looking ones, but none of that will help the next time I find that pathetic creature they call Snotman sleeping in the dumpster behind the Funhouse. The horrible reality is, my stomach is as thoroughly turned by the more extreme cases of joker deformity as I imagine Dr. Tachyon's must be—but if anything, I am even more guilty about it.

Which brings me, in a roundabout way, back to Fortunato. Fortunato is . . . or was at least . . . a procurer. He ran a high-priced call girl ring. All of his girls were exquisite; beautiful, sensual, skilled in every erotic art, and by and large pleasant people, as much a delight out of bed as in it. He called them geishas.

For more than two decades I was one of his best customers.

I believe he did a lot of business in Jokertown. I know for a fact that Chrysalis often trades information for sex, upstairs in her Crystal Palace, whenever a man who needs her services happens to strike her fancy. I know a handful of truly wealthy jokers, none of whom are married, but almost all of whom have nat mistresses. The hometown papers we've seen tell us that the Five Families and the Shadow Fists are warring in the streets, and I know why—because in Jokertown prostitution is big business, along with drugs and gambling.

The first thing a joker loses is his sexuality. Some lose it totally, becoming incapable or asexual. But even those whose genitalia and sexual drives remain unaffected by the wild card find themselves bereft of sexual identity. From the instant one stabilizes, one is no longer a man or a woman, only a joker.

A normal sex drive, abnormal self-loathing, and a yearning for the thing that's been lost . . . manhood, femininity, beauty, whatever. They are common demons in Jokertown, and I know them well. The onset of my cancer and the chemotherapy have combined to kill all my interest in sex, but my memories and my shame remain intact. It shames me to be reminded of Fortunato. Not because I patronized a prostitute or broke their silly laws—I have contempt for those laws. It shames me because, try as I did over the years, I could never find it in me to desire a joker woman. I knew several who were worthy of love; kind, gentle, caring women, who needed commitment and tenderness and yes, sex, as much as I did. Some of them became my cherished friends. Yet I could never respond to them sexually. They remained as unattractive in my eyes as I must have been in theirs.

So it goes, in Jokertown.

The seat belt light has just come on, and I'm not feeling very well at present, so I will sign off here.

FROM *THE JOURNAL OF XAVIER DESMOND*

APRIL 10/STOCKHOLM:

Very tired. I fear my doctor was correct—this trip may have been a drastic mistake, insofar as my health is concerned. I feel I held up remarkably well during the first few months, when everything was fresh and new and exciting, but during this last month a cumulative exhaustion has set in, and the day-to-day grind has become almost unbearable. The flights, the dinners, the endless receiving lines, the visits to hospitals and joker ghettos and research institutions, it is all threatening to become one great blur of dignitaries and airports and translators and buses and hotel dining rooms.

I am not keeping my food down well, and I know I have lost weight. The cancer, the strain of travel, my age...who can say? All of these, I suspect.

Fortunately the trip is almost over now. We are scheduled to return to Tomlin on April 29, and only a handful of stops remain. I confess that I am looking forward to my return home, and I do not think I am alone in that. We are all tired.

Still, despite the toll it has taken, I would not have forfeited this trip for anything. I have seen the Pyramids and the Great Wall, walked the streets of Rio and Marrakesh and Moscow, and soon I will add Rome and Paris and London to that list. I have seen and experienced the stuff of dreams and nightmares, and I have learned much, I think. I can only pray that I survive long enough to use some of that knowledge.

Sweden is a bracing change from the Soviet Union and the other Warsaw Pact nations we have visited. I have no strong feelings about socialism one way or the other, but I grew very weary of the model joker "medical hostels" we were constantly being shown and the model jokers who occupied them. Socialist medicine and socialist science would undoubtedly conquer the wild card, and great strides were already being made, we were repeatedly told, but even if one credits these claims, the price is a lifetime of "treatment" for the handful of jokers the Soviets admit to having.

Billy Ray insists that the Russians actually have thousands of jokers locked away safely out of sight in huge gray "joker warehouses," nominally hospitals but actually prisons in all but name, staffed by a lot of guards and precious few doctors and nurses. Ray also says there are a dozen Soviet aces, all of them secretly employed by the government, the military, the police, or the party. If these things exist—the Soviet Union denies all such allegations, of course—we got nowhere close to any of them, with Intourist and the KGB carefully managing every aspect of our visit, despite the government's assurance to the United Nations that this UN-sanctioned tour would receive "every cooperation."

To say that Dr. Tachyon did not get along well with his socialist colleagues would be a considerable understatement. His disdain for Soviet medicine is exceeded only by Hiram's disdain for Soviet cooking. Both of them do seem to approve of Soviet vodka, however, and have consumed a great deal of it.

There was an amusing little debate in the Winter Palace, when one of our hosts explained the dialectic of history to Dr. Tachyon, telling him feudalism must inevitably give way to capitalism, and capitalism to socialism, as a civilization matures. Tachyon listened with remarkable politeness and then said, "My dear man, there are two great star-faring civilizations in this small sector of the galaxy. My own people, by your lights, must be considered feudal, and the Network is a form of capitalism more rapacious and virulent than anything you've ever dreamed of. Neither of us shows any signs of maturing into socialism, thank you." Then he paused for a moment and added, "Although, if you think of it in the right light, perhaps the Swarm might be considered communist, though scarcely civilized."

It was a clever little speech, I must admit, although I think it might have impressed the Soviets more if Tachyon had not been dressed in full cossack regalia when he delivered it. Where does he *get* these outfits?

* * *

Of the other Warsaw Bloc nations there is little to report. Yugoslavia was the warmest, Poland the grimmest, Czechoslovakia seemed the most like home. Downs wrote a marvelously engrossing piece for *Aces*, speculating that the widespread peasant accounts of active contemporary vampires in Hungary and Rumania were actually manifestations of the wild card. It was his best work, actually, some really excellent writing, and all the more remarkable when you consider that he based the whole thing on a five-minute conversation with a pastry chef in Budapest. We found a small joker ghetto in Warsaw and a widespread belief in a hidden "solidarity ace" who will shortly come forth to lead that outlawed trade union to victory. He did not, alas, come forth during our two days in Poland. Senator Hartmann, with greatest difficulty, managed to arrange a meeting with Lech Walesa, and I believe that the AP news photo of their meeting has enhanced his stature back home. Hiram left us briefly in Hungary—another "emergency" back in New York, he said—and returned just as we arrived in Sweden, in somewhat better spirits.

Stockholm is a most congenial city, after many of the places we have been. Virtually all the Swedes we have met speak excellent English, we are free to come and go as we please (within the confines of our merciless schedule, of course), and the king was most gracious to all of us. Jokers are quite rare here, this far north, but he greeted us with complete equanimity, as if he'd been hosting jokers all of his life.

Still, as enjoyable as our brief visit has been, there is only one incident that is worth recording for posterity. I believe we have unearthed something that will make the historians around the world sit up and take notice, a hitherto-unknown fact that puts much of recent Middle Eastern history into a new and startling perspective.

It occurred during an otherwise unremarkable afternoon a number of the delegates spent with the Nobel trustees. I believe it was Senator Hartmann they actually wanted to meet. Although it ended in violence, his attempt to meet and negotiate with the Nur al-Allah in Syria is correctly seen here for what it was—a sincere and courageous effort on behalf of peace and understanding, and one that makes him to my mind a legitimate candidate for next year's Nobel Peace Prize.

At any rate, several of the other delegates accompanied Gregg to the meeting, which was cordial but hardly stimulating. One of our hosts, it turned out, had been a secretary to Count Folke Bernadotte when he negotiated the Peace of Jerusalem, and sadly enough had also been with Bernadotte when he was gunned down by Israeli terrorists two years later. He told us several fascinating anecdotes about Bernadotte, for whom he clearly had great admiration, and also showed us some of his personal memorabilia of those difficult negotiations. Among the notes, journals, and interim drafts was a photo book.

I gave the book a cursory glance and then passed it on, as did most of my companions. Dr. Tachyon, who was seated beside me on the couch, seemed bored by the proceedings and leafed through the photographs with rather more care. Bernadotte figured in most of them, of course—standing with his negotiating team, talking with David Ben-Gurion in one photo and King Faisal in the next. The various aides, including our host, were seen in less formal poses, shaking hands with Israeli soldiers, eating with a tentful of bedouin, and so on. The usual sort of thing. By far the single most arresting picture showed Bernadotte surrounded by the *Nasr*, the Port Said aces who so dramatically reversed the tide of battle when they joined with Jordan's crack Arab Legion. Khôf sits beside Bernadotte in the center of the photograph, all in black, looking like death incarnate, surrounded by the younger aces. Ironically enough, of all the faces in that photo, only three are sill alive, the ageless Khôf among them. Even an undeclared war takes it toll.

That was not the photograph that caught Tachyon's attention, however. It was another, a very informal snapshot, showing Bernadotte and various members of his team in some hotel room, the table in front of them littered with papers. In one corner of the photograph was a young man I had not noticed in any of the other pictures—slim, dark-haired, with a certain intense look around the eyes, and a rather ingratiating grin. He was pouring a cup of coffee. All very innocent, but Tachyon stared at the photograph for a long time and then called our host over and said to him privately, "Forgive me if I tax your memory, but I would be very interested to know if you remember this man." He pointed him out. "Was he a member of your team?"

Our Swedish friend leaned over, studied the photograph, and chuckled. "Oh, him," he said in excellent English. "He was...what is the slang word you use, for a boy who runs errands and does odd jobs? An animal of some sort..."

"A gofer," I supplied.

"Yes, he was a *gopher*, as you put it. Actually a young journalism student. Joshua, that was his name. Joshua... something. He said he wanted to observe the negotiations from within so he could write about them afterward. Bernadotte thought the idea was ridiculous when it was first put to him, rejected it out of hand in fact, but the young man was persistent. He finally managed to corner the Count and put his case to him personally, and somehow he talked him around. So he was not officially a member of the team, but he was with us constantly from that point through the end. He was not a very efficient gopher, as I recall, but he was such a pleasant young man that everyone liked him regardless. I don't believe he ever wrote his article."

"No," Tachyon said. "He wouldn't have. He was a chess player, not a writer."

Our host lit up with remembrance. "Why, yes! He played incessantly, now that I recall. He was quite good. Do you know him, Dr. Tachyon? I've often wondered whatever became of him."

"So have I," Tachyon replied very simply and very sadly. Then he closed the book and changed the topic.

I have known Dr. Tachyon for more years than I care to contemplate. That evening, spurred by my own curiosity, I managed to seat myself near to Jack Braun and ask him a few innocent questions while we ate. I'm certain that he suspected nothing, but he was willing enough to reminisce about the Four Aces, the things they did and tried to do, the places they went, and more importantly, the places they did *not* go. At least not officially.

Afterward, I found Dr. Tachyon drinking alone in his room. He invited me in, and it was clear that he was feeling quite morose, lost in his damnable memories. He lives as much in the past as any man I have ever known. I asked him who the young man in the photograph had been.

"No one," Tachyon said. "Just a boy I used to play chess with." I'm not sure why he felt he had to lie to me.

"His name was not Joshua," I told him, and he seemed

startled. I wonder, does he think my deformity affects my mind, my memory? "His name was David, and he was not supposed to be there. The Four Aces were never officially involved in the Mideast, and Jack Braun says that by late 1948 the members of the group had gone their own ways. Braun was making movies."

"Bad movies," Tachyon said with a certain venom.

"Meanwhile," I said, "the Envoy was making peace."

"He was gone for two months. He told Blythe and me that he was going on a vacation. I remember. It never occurred to me that he was involved."

No more has it ever occurred to the rest of the world, though perhaps it should have. David Harstein was not particularly religious, from what little I know of him, but he was Jewish, and when the Port Said aces and the Arab armies threatened the very existence of the new state of Israel, he acted all on his own.

His was a power for peace, not war; not fear or sandstorms or lightning from a clear sky, but pheromones that made people like him and want desperately to please him and agree with him, that made the mere presence of the ace called Envoy a virtual guarantee of a successful negotiation. But those who knew who and what he was showed a distressing tendency to repudiate their agreements once Harstein and his pheromones had left their presence. He must have pondered that, and with the stakes so high, he must have decided to find out what might happen if his role in the process was carefully kept secret. The Peace of Jerusalem was his answer.

I wonder if even Folke Bernadotte knew who his gopher really was. I wonder where Harstein is now, and what he thinks of the peace that he so carefully and secretly wrought. And I find myself reflecting on what the Black Dog said in Jerusalem.

What would it do to the fragile Peace of Jerusalem if its origins were revealed to the world? The more I reflect on that, the more certain I grow that I ought tear these pages from my journal before I offer it for publication. If no one gets Dr. Tachyon drunk, perhaps this secret can even be kept.

Did he ever do it again, I wonder? After HUAC, after prison and disgrace and his celebrated conscription and equally celebrated disappearance, did the Envoy ever sit in on any other negotiations with the world's being none the wiser? I wonder if we'll ever know.

I think it unlikely and wish it were not. From what I have seen on this tour, in Guatemala and South Africa, in Ethiopia and Syria and Jerusalem, in India and Indonesia and Poland, the world today needs the Envoy more than ever.

PUPPETS

Victor W. Milán

MacHeath had a jackknife, so the song went.

Mackie Messer had something better. And it was ever so much easier to keep out of sight.

Mackie blew into the camera store on a breath of cool air and diesel farts from the Kurfürstendamm. He left off whistling his song, let the door hiss to behind him, and stood with his fists rammed down in his jacket pockets to catch a look around.

Light slamdanced on countertops, the curves of cameras, black and glassy-eyed. He felt the humming of the lights down beneath his skin. This place got on his tits. It was so clean and antiseptic it made him think of a doctor's office. He hated doctors. Always had, since the doctors the Hamburg court sent him to see when he was thirteen said he was crazy and penned him up in a *Land* juvie/psych ward, and the orderly there was a pig from the Tirol who was always breathing booze and garlic over him and trying to get him to jerk him off. . . and then he'd turned over his ace and walked on out of there, and the thought brought a smile and a rush of confidence.

On a stool by the display counter lay a *Berliner Zeitung* folded to the headline: "Wild Card Tour to Visit Wall Today." He smiled, thin.

Yeah. Oh, yeah.

Then Dieter came in from the back and saw him. He stopped dead and put this foolish smile on his face. "Mackie. Hey. It's a little early, isn't it?"

He had a narrow, pale head with dark hair slicked back in a smear of oil. His suit was blue and ran to too much padding in the shoulders. His tie was thin and iridescent. His lower lip quivered just a little.

Mackie was standing still. His eyes were the eyes of a shark, cold and gray and expressionless as steel marbles.

"I was just, you know, putting in my appearance here, Dieter said." A hand jittered around at the cameras and the neon tubing and the sprawling shiny posters showing the tanned women with shades and too many teeth. The hand glowed the white of a dead fish's belly in the artificial light. "Appearances are important, you know. Got to lull the suspicions of the bourgeoisie. Especially today."

He tried to keep his eyes off Mackie, but they just kept rolling back to him, as if the whole room slanted downward to where he stood. The ace didn't look like much. He was maybe seventeen, looked younger, except for his skin—that had a dryness to it, a touch of parchment age. He wasn't much more than a hundred seventy centimeters tall, even skinnier than Dieter, and his body kind of twisted. He wore a black leather jacket that Dieter knew was scuffed to gray along the canted line of his shoulders, jeans that were tired before he fished them out of a trash can in Dahlem, a pair of Dutch clogs. A brush of straw hair stuck up at random above the drawn-out face of an El Greco martyr, oddly vulnerable. His lips were thin and mobile.

"So you stepped up the timetable, came for me early," Dieter said lamely.

Mackie flashed forward, wrapped his hand in shiny tie, hauled Dieter toward him. "Maybe it's too late for you, comrade. Maybe maybe."

The camera salesman had a curious glossy-pale complexion, like laminated paper. Now his skin turned the color of a sheet of the *Zeitung* after it had spent the night blowing along a Budapesterstrasse curb. He'd seen what that hand could do.

"M-mackie," he stammered, clutching at the reed-thin arm.

He collected himself then, patted Mackie affectionately on a leather sleeve. "Hey, hey now, brother. What's the matter?"

"You tried to sell us, motherfucker!" Mackie screamed, spraying spittle all over Dieter's after-shave.

Dieter jerked back. His arm twitched with the lust to wipe his cheek. "What the fuck are you talking about, Mackie? I'd never try—"

"Kelly. That Australian bitch. Wolf thought she was

acting funny and leaned on her." A grin winched its way across Mackie's face. "She's never going to the fucking *Bundeskriminalamt* now, man. She's *Speck*. Lunchmeat."

Dieter's tongue flicked bluish lips. "Listen, you've got it wrong. She was nothing to me. I knew she was just a groupie, all along—"

His eyes informed on him, sliding ever so slightly to the right. His hand suddenly flared up from below the register with a black snub revolver in it.

Mackie's left hand whirred down, vibrating like the blade of a jigsaw. It sheared through the pistol's top strap, through the cylinder and cartridges, and slashed open the trigger guard a piece of a centimeter in front of Dieter's forefinger. The finger clenched spastically, the hammer came back and clicked to, and the rear half of the cylinder, its fresh-cut face glistening like silver, fell forward onto the countertop. Glass cracked.

Mackie grabbed Dieter by the face and hauled him forward. The camera salesman put down his hands to steady himself, shrieked as they went through the countertops. The broken glass raked him like talons, slashing through blue coat sleeve and blue French shirt and fishbelly skin beneath. His blood streamed over Zeiss lenses and Japanese import cameras that were making inroads in the Federal Republic despite chauvinism and high tariffs, ruining their finish.

"We were comrades! Why? *Why?*" Mackie's whole skinny body was shaking in hurt fury. Tears filled his eyes. His hands began to vibrate of their own accord.

Dieter squealed as he felt them rasping at the post-shave stubble he could never get rid of, the only flaw in his neo-sleek grooming. "I don't know what you're talking about," he screamed. "I never meant to do it—I was playing her along—"

"Liar!" Mackie yelled. The anger jolted through him like a blast from the third rail, and his hands were buzzing, buzzing, and Dieter was flopping and howling as the flesh began to come off his cheeks, and Mackie gripped him harder, hands on cheekbones, and the rising vibration of his hands was transmitted through bone to the wet mass of Dieter's brain, and the camera salesman's eyes rolled and his tongue came out and the violent agitation flash-boiled the fluids in his skull and his head exploded.

Mackie dropped him, danced back howling like a man on

fire, swiping at the clotted stuff that filled his eyes and clung to his cheeks and hair. When he could see, he went around the counter and kicked the quivering body. It slid onto the cuffed linoleum floor. The cash register was flashing orange error-condition warnings, the display case swam with blood, and there were lumps of greasy yellow-gray brains all over everything.

Mackie dabbed at his jacket and screamed again when his hands came away slimy. "You bastard!" He kicked the headless corpse again. "You got this shit all over me, you asshole. Asshole, asshole, *asshole!*"

He hunkered down, pulled up the tail of Dieter's suit coat, and wiped the worst lumps off his face and hands and leather jacket. "Oh, Dieter, Dieter," he sobbed, "I wanted to *talk* to you, stupid son of a bitch—" He picked up a cold hand, kissed it, tenderly rested it on a spattered lapel. Then he went back to the john to wash down as best he could.

When he came out, anger and sorrow both had faded, leaving a strange elation. Dieter had tried to fuck with the Fraction and he'd paid the price, and what the hell did it matter if Mackie hadn't been able to find out why? It didn't matter, nothing mattered. Mackie was an ace, he was MacHeath made flesh, invulnerable, and in a couple of hours he was going to show the cocksuckers—

The glass doors up front opened and somebody came in. Laughing to himself, Mackie changed phase and walked through the wall.

Rain jittered briefly on the roof of the Mercedes limo. "We'll be meeting a number of influential people at this luncheon, Senator," said the young black man with the long narrow face and earnest expression, riding with his back to the driver. "It's going to be an excellent opportunity to show your commitment to brotherhood and tolerance, not just for jokers, but for members of oppressed groups of all persuasions. Really excellent."

"I'm sure it will, Ronnie." Chin on hand, Hartmann let his eyes slide away from his junior aide and out the condensation-fogged window. Blocks of apartments rolled by, tan and anonymous. This close to the Wall Berlin seemed always to be holding its breath.

"Aide et Amitié has an international reputation for its work to promote tolerance," Ronnie said. "The head of the

Berlin chapter, Herr Prahler, recently received recognition for his efforts to improve public acceptance of the Turkish 'guest workers,' though I understand he's a rather, ah, controversial personality—"

"Communist bastard," grunted Möller from the front seat. He was a strapping blond kid plainclothesman with big hands and prominent ears that made him resemble a hound pup. He spoke English out of deference to the American senator, though between a grandmother from the Old Country and a few college courses, Hartmann knew enough German to get by.

"Herr Prahler's active in *Rote Hilfe*, Red Help," explained Möller's opposite number, Blum, from the backseat. He was sitting on the other side of Mordecai Jones, who sometimes and with poor grace responded to the nickname Harlem Hammer. Jones was concentrating on *The New York Times* crossword puzzle and acting as if no one else were there. "He's a lawyer, you know. Been defending radicals since Andy Baader's salad days."

"Helping damned terrorists get off with a slap on the wrists, you mean."

Blum laughed and shrugged. He was leaner and darker than Möller, and he wore his curly black hair shaggy enough to push even the notoriously liberal standards of the Berlin *Schutzpolizei*. But his brown artist's eyes were watchful, and the way he held himself suggested he knew how to use the tiny machine pistol in the shoulder holster that bulked out his gray suit coat in a way not even meticulous German tailoring could altogether conceal.

"Even radicals have a right to representation. This is Berlin, *Mensch*. We take freedom seriously here—if only to set an example for our neighbors, *ja?*" Möller made a skeptical sound low in his throat.

Ronnie fidgeted on the seat and checked his watch. "Maybe we could go a little faster? We don't want to be late."

The driver flashed a grin over his shoulder. He resembled a smaller edition of Tom Cruise, though more ferret faced. He couldn't have been as young as he looked. "The streets are narrow here. We don't want to have an accident. Then we'd be even later."

Hartmann's aide set his mouth and fussed with papers in the briefcase open on his lap. Hartmann slid another glance toward the bulk of the Hammer, who was still stolidly ignoring everybody. Puppetman was amazingly quiescent, given his gut dread of aces. Maybe he was even feeling a certain thrill at Jones's proximity.

Not that Jones looked like an ace. He appeared to be a normal black man in his mid to late thirties, bearded, balding, solidly built, looking none too well at ease knotted into coat and tie. Nothing out of the ordinary.

As a matter of fact he weighed four hundred and seventy pounds and had to sit in the center of the Merc so it wouldn't list. He might be the strongest man in the world, stronger than Golden Boy perhaps, but he refused to engage in any kind of competition to settle the issue. He disliked being an ace, disliked being a celebrity, disliked politicians, and thought the entire tour was a waste of time. Hartmann had the impression he'd only agreed to come along because his neighbors in Harlem got such a kick out of his being in the spotlight, and he hated to let them down.

Jones was a token. He knew it. He resented it. That was one reason Hartmann had goaded him into coming to the Aide et Amitié luncheon; that and the fact that for all their pious pretensions of brotherhood, most Germans didn't like blacks and were uncomfortable around them; they pretended, but that wasn't the sort of thing you could hide from Puppetman. *He* found the Hammer's pique and the discomfort of their hosts amusing; almost worthwhile to take Jones on as a puppet. But not quite. The Hammer was known primarily as a musleman ace, but the full scope of his powers was a mystery. Any chance of discovery was too much for Puppetman.

Beyond the minor titillations poking everyone off balance provided, Hartmann was getting fed up with Billy Ray. Carnifex had fumed and blustered when Hartmann ditched him with the rest of the tour back at the Wall—detailed to escort Mrs. Hartmann and the senator's two senior aides back to the hotel—but he couldn't say much without offending their hosts, whose security men were on the job. And anyway, with the Hammer along, what could possibly happen?

"*Scheisse*," the driver said. He had turned a corner to find a gray and white telephone van parked blocking the street next to an open manhole. He braked to a halt.

"Idiots," said Möller. "They're not supposed to do that." He unlocked the passenger door.

Beside Hartmann, Blum flicked his eyes to the rearview

mirror. "Uh-oh," he said softly. His right hand went inside his coat.

Hartmann craned his neck. A second van had cranked itself across the street not thirty feet behind them. Its doors were open, spilling people onto pavement wet from the rain spasm. They held weapons. Blum shouted a warning to his partner.

A figure loomed up beside the car. A terrible metal screeching filled the limousine. Hartmann's breath turned solid in his throat as a hand cut through the roof of the car in a shower of sparks.

Möller winced away. He drew his MP5K from its shoulder holster, pressed it to the window, and fired a burst. Glass exploded outward.

The hand snapped back. "Jesus *Christ*," Möller shouted, "the bullets went right through him!"

He threw open the door. A man with a ski mask over his face fired an assault rifle from the rear of the telephone van.

The noise rattled the car's thick windows, on and on. It sounded oddly remote. The windshield starred. The man who'd cut through the roof screamed and went down. Möller danced back three steps, fell against the Mercedes's fender, collapsed to the pavement squirming and screaming. His coat fell open. Scarlet spiders clung to his chest.

The assault rifle ran dry. The sudden silence was thunderous. Puppetman's fingers were clenched on the padded handle of the door as Möller's mindscream jolted into him like speed hitting the main line. He gasped, at the hot mad pleasure of it, at the cold rush of his own fear.

"*Hände hoch!*" shouted a figure beside the van that had boxed them from behind. "Hands up!"

Mordecai Jones put a big hand on Hartmann's shoulder and pushed him to the floor. He clambered over him, careful not to squash him, put his weight against the door. Metal wailed and it came away with him as Blum, more conventional, pulled the lever on his own door to disengage the latching mechanism, twisted, and shouldered it open. He brought his MP5K up with his left hand clutching the vestigial foregrip, aimed the stubby machine pistol back around the frame as Hartmann yelled, "*Don't shoot!*"

The Hammer was racing toward the telephone van. The terrorist who'd shot Möller pointed his weapon at him, pumped his finger on the empty weapon's trigger in a comic pantomime of panic. Jones backhanded him gently. He sailed backward to rebound off the front of a building and land in a heap on the sidewalk.

The moment hung in air like a suspended chord. Jones squatted, got his hands under the phone van's frame. He strained, straightened. The van came up with him. Its driver screamed in terror. The Hammer shifted his grip and pressed the vehicle over his head as if it were a not-particularly-heavy barbell.

A burst of gunfire stuttered from the second van. Bullets shredded open the back of Jones's coat. He teetered, almost lost it, swung in a ponderous circle with the van still balanced above his head. Then several terrorists fired at once. He grimaced and fell backward.

The van landed right on top of him.

The limo driver had his door open and a little black P7 in his hand. As the Hammer fell, Blum blazed a quick burst at the van behind. A man ducked back as 9mm bullets punched neat holes in thin metal—a joker, Hartmann realized. *What the hell's going on here?*

He ducked his head below window level and grabbed at Blum's coattail. He felt the vehicle shudder on its suspension as bullets struck it. The driver gasped and slumped out of the car. Hartmann heard somebody yelling in English to cease fire. He shouted for Blum to quit shooting.

The policeman turned toward him. "Yes, sir," he said. Then a burst punched through his opened door and sugared the glass in the window and threw him against the senator.

Ronnie was plastered against the back of the driver's seat. "Oh, God," he moaned. "Oh, dear God!" He jumped out the door the Hammer had torn from its hinges and ran, with papers scattered from his briefcase swooping around him like seagulls.

The terrorist Mordecai Jones had brushed aside had recovered enough to come to one knee and stuff another magazine into his AKM. He brought it to his shoulder and emptied it at the senator's aide in a juddering burst. A scream and mist of blood sprayed from Ronnie's mouth. He fell and skidded.

Hartmann huddled on the floor in fugue, half-terrified, half-orgasmic. Blum was dying, holding on to Hartmann's arm, the holes in his chest sucking like lamia mouths, his life-force surging into the senator like arrhythmic surf.

"I'm hurt," the policeman said. "Oh, mama, mama please—" He died. Hartmann jerked like a harpooned seal as the last of the man's life gushed into him.

Out by the street Hartmann's young aide was dragging himself along with his arms, glasses askew, leaving a snail-trail of blood on the sidewalk. The slightly built terrorist who had shot him ambled up, stuffing a third magazine into his weapon. He positioned himself in front of the wounded man.

Ronnie blinked up at him. Disjointedly Hartmann remembered he was desperately nearsighted, virtually blind without his glasses.

"Please," Ronnie said, and blood rolled from his mouth. "Please."

"Have a *Negerkuss*," the terrorist said, and fired a single shot into his forehead.

"Dear God," Hartmann said. A shadow fell across him, heavy as a corpse. He looked up with inhuman eyes at a figure black against the gray-cloud sky beyond. A hand gripped him by the arm, electricity blasted through him, and consciousness exploded in ozone convulsion.

Substantial again, Mackie bounced to his feet and tore off his ski mask. "You shot at me! You could have killed me," he shrieked at Anneke. His face was almost black.

She laughed at him.

The world seemed to come on to Mackie in Kodachrome colors. He started for her, hand beginning to buzz, when a commotion behind him brought his head around.

The dwarf had grabbed Ulrich's rifle by the still-hot muzzle brake and spun him round, echoing Mackie's theme, with variations. "You stupid bastard, you could have killed him!" he screamed. *"You could have offed the fucking senator!"*

Ulrich had fired the final burst that downed the cop in the back of the limousine. Weight lifter though he was, he was only just hanging on to his piece against the dwarf's surprising strength. The two were orbiting each other out there on the street, spitting at one another like cats.

Mackie had to laugh.

Then Mólniya was beside him, touching his shoulder with a gloved hand. "Let it go. We have to move quickly."

Mackie arched like a cat to meet the touch. Comrade Mólniya was worried he was still mad at Anneke for shooting at him and then laughing about it.

But that was forgotten. Anneke was laughing too, over the body of the man she'd just finished off, and Mackie had to laugh with her.

"A *Negerkuss*," he said. "You said did he want a *Negerkuss*. Huh huh. That was pretty good." It meant *Negro Kiss*, a small chocolate-covered cake. It was especially funny since they'd told him Negro Kisses were a trademark of the group from back in the old days, back when all of them but Wolf were kids.

It was nervous laughter, relieved laughter. He'd thought he'd lost it when the pig shot at him; he'd just seen the gun come up in time to phase out, and the anger burned black within him, the desire to make his hand vibrate till it was hard as a knife blade and drive it into that fucking cop, to make sure he felt the buzz, to feel the hot rush of blood along his arm and spraying in his face. But the bastard was dead, it was too late now. . . .

He'd worried again when the black man picked up the van, but then Comrade Ulrich shot him. He was strong, but he wasn't immune to bullets. Mackie liked Comrade Ulrich. He was so self-assured, so handsome and muscular. Women liked him; Anneke could hardly keep her hands off him. Mackie might have envied him, if he hadn't been an ace.

Mackie didn't have a gun himself. He hated them, and anyway he didn't need a weapon—there wasn't any weapon better than his own body.

The American joker called Scrape was fumbling Hartmann's limp body out of the limousine. "Is he dead?" Mackie called in German, caught up by sudden panic. The dwarf let go of Ulrich's rifle and stared wildly at the car. Ulrich almost fell over.

Scrape looked up at Mackie, face frozen into immobility by its exoskeleton, but his lack of understanding clear from the tilt of his head. Mackie repeated the question in the halting English he'd learned from his mother before the worthless bitch had died and deserted him.

Comrade Mólniya pulled his other glove back on. He wore no mask, and now Mackie noticed he looked a little green at the sight of the blood spilled all over the street. "He's fine," he replied for Scrape. "I just shocked him unconscious. Come now, we must hurry."

Mackie grinned and bobbed his head. He felt a certain satisfaction at Mólniya's squeamishness, even though he wanted to please the Russian ace almost as much as he did his own cell leader Wolf. He went to help Scrape, though he hated being so close to the joker. He feared he might touch him accidentally; the thought made his flesh crawl.

Comrade Wolf stood by with his own unfired Kalashnikov dangling from one huge hand. "Get him in the van," he ordered. "Him too." He nodded to Comrade Wilfried, who'd stumbled from the driver's seat of the telephone van and was on his knees pitching breakfast on the wet asphalt.

It started to rain again. Broad pools of blood on the pavement began to fray like banners whipped by the wind. In the distance sirens commenced their hair-raising chant.

They put Hartmann into the second van. Scrape got behind the wheel. Mólniya slid in beside him. The joker backed up onto the sidewalk, turned, and drove away.

Mackie sat on the wheel well, drumming a heavy-metal beat on his thighs. *We did it! We captured him!* He could barely sit still. His penis was stiff inside his jeans.

Out the back window he saw Ulrich spraying letters on a wall in red paint: RAF. He laughed again. That would make the bourgeoisie shit their pants, that was for sure. Ten years ago those initials had been a synonym for terror in the Federal Republic. Now they would be again. It gave Mackie happy chills to think about it.

A joker wrapped head to toe in a shabby cloak stepped up and sprayed three more letters beneath the first with a hand wrapped in bandages: JJS.

The other van heeled way over to the side as its wheels rolled over the supine body of the black American ace, and they were gone.

With her NEC laptop computer tucked under one arm and a a bit of her cheek caught between her small side teeth, Sara strode across the lobby of the Bristol Hotel Kempinski with briskness that an outside observer would probably have taken for confidence. It was a misapprehension that had served her well in the past.

Reflexively she ducked into the bar of Berlin's most luxurious hotel. *The tour proper's long since been mined out, at least of stuff we can print,* she thought, *but what the heck?* She felt heat in her ears at the thought that she was the star of one of the tour's choicer unprintable vignettes.

Inside was dark, of course. All bars are the same song;

the polished wood and brass and old pliable leather and elephant ears were grace notes to set apart this particular refrain. She tipped her sunglasses up on top of her nearly white hair, drawn back this afternoon in a severe ponytail, and let her eyes adjust. They always adjusted to dark more quickly than light.

The bar wasn't crowded. A pair of waiters in arm garters and starched highboy collars worked their way among the tables as if by radar. Three Japanese businessmen sat at a table chattering and pointing at a newspaper, discussing either the exchange rates or the local tit bars, depending.

In the corner Hiram was talking shop, in French of course, with the Kempinski's *cordon bleu*, who was shorter than he was but at least as round. The hotel chef had a tendency to flap his short arms rapidly when he spoke, which made him look like a fat baby bird that wasn't getting the hang of flight.

Chrysalis sat at the bar drinking in splendid isolation. There was no joker chic here. In Germany, Chrysalis found herself discreetly avoided rather than lionized.

She caught Sara's eye and winked. In the poor light Sara only knew it because of the way Chrysalis's mascaraed eyelashes tracked across a staring eyeball. She smiled. Professional associates back home, sometime rivals in the bartering of information that was the meta-game of Jokertown, they'd grown to be friends on this trip. Sara had more in common with Debra-Jo than her nominal peers who were along.

At least Chrysalis was dressed. She was showing a different face to Europe than she did the country she pretended wasn't her native one. Sometimes Sara envied her, secretly. People looked at her and saw a joker, an exotic, alluring and grotesque. But they didn't see *her*.

"Looking for me, little lady?"

Sara started, turned. Jack Braun sat at the end of the bar, hardly five feet from her. She hadn't noticed him. She had a tendency to edit him out; the force of him made her uncomfortable.

"I'm going out," she said. She slapped the computer, a touch harder than necessary, so her fingers stung. "Down to the main post office to file my latest material by modem. It's the only place you can get a transatlantic connection that won't scramble all your data."

"I'm surprised you're not off pushing cookies with Senator Gregg," he said, eyeing her cantwise from beneath bushy eyebrows.

She felt color come to her cheeks. "Senator *Hartmann* attending a banquet may be a hot item for my colleagues with the celebrity-hunting glossies. But it's not exactly hard news, is it, Mr. Braun?"

It was an open afternoon. There wasn't much hard news here, not the kind to interest readers following the WHO tour. The West German authorities had blandly assured the visitors there was no wild card problem in *their* country, and used the tour as a counter in whatever game they were playing with their Siamese twin to the east—that damp, dreary ceremony this morning, for instance. Of course they were right: even proportionally, the number of German wild card victims was minuscule. The most pathetic or unsightly couple of thousand were kept discreetly tucked away in state housing or clinics. Much as they'd sneered at Americans for their treatment of jokers during the Sixties and Seventies, the Germans were embarrassed by their own.

"Depends on what gets said at the banquet, I guess. What's on your schedule after you file your piece, little lady?" He was grinning that B-movie leading-man grin at her. Golden highlights glimmered on the planes and contour edges of his face. He was flexing his muscles to bring on the glow that gave him his ace name. Irritation tightened the skin at the outskirts of her eyes. He was either coming on to her for real or teasing her. Either way she didn't like it.

"I have work to do. And I could use a little time to catch my breath. Some of us have had a busy time on this tour."

Is that really the reason you were relieved when Gregg dropped the hint that it might not be discreet to tag along to the banquet with him? she wondered. She frowned, surprised at the thought, and turned crisply away.

Braun's big hand closed on her arm. She gasped and spun back to him, angry and starting to panic. What could she do against a man who could lift a bus? That detached observer inside her, the journalist within, reflected on the irony that Gregg, whom she'd come to hate, yes, obsessively, should be the first man in years whose touch she'd come to welcome—

But Jack Braun was frowning past her, into the lobby of the hotel. It was filling up with purposeful, husky young men in suit coats.

One of them came into the bar, looked hard at Braun, consulted a piece of paper in his hand. "Herr Braun?"

"That's me. What can I do you for?"

"I am with the Berlin *Landespolizei*. I'm afraid I must ask you not to leave the hotel."

Braun pushed his jaw forward. "And why might that be?"

"Senator Hartmann has been kidnapped."

Ellen Hartmann shut the door with eggshell care and turned away. The flowered vines fading in the carpet seemed to twine about her ankles as she walked back into the suite and sat down on the bed.

Her eyes were dry. They stung, but they were dry. She smiled slightly. It was hard to let her emotions go. She had so much experience controlling her emotions for the cameras. And Gregg—

I know what he is. But what he is is all I have.

She picked up a handkerchief from the bedside table and methodically began to tear it to pieces.

"Welcome to the land of the living, Senator. For the moment at least."

Slowly Hartmann's mind drained into consciousness. There was a tinny taste in his mouth and a singing in his ears. His right upper arm ached as if from sunburn. Someone hummed a familiar song. A radio muttered.

His eyes opened to darkness. He felt the obligatory twinge of blindness anxiety, but something pressed his eyeballs, and from the small stinging pull at the back of his head he guessed it was taped gauze. His wrists were bound behind the back of a wooden chair.

After the awareness of captivity, what struck hardest was the smells: sweat, grease, mildew, dust, sodden cloth, unfamliar spices; ancient urine and fresh gun oil, crowding his nostrils clear to his sinuses.

He inventoried all these things before permitting himself to recognize the rasping voice.

"Tom Miller," he said. "I wish I could say it's a pleasure."

"Ah, yes, Senator. But *I* can." He could feel Gimli's gloating as he could smell his stinking breath—toothpaste and mouthwash belonged to the surface-worshiping nat world. "I could also say you have no idea how long I've waited for this, but of course you do. You know full well."

"Since we know each other so well, why don't you undo my eyes, Tom." As he spoke he probed with his power. It had been ten years since he'd last had physical contact with the dwarf, but he didn't think the link, once created, ever decayed. Puppetman feared loss of control more than anything but discovery; and being discovered itself represented the ultimate loss of power. If he could get his hooks back into Miller's soul, Hartmann could at the very least be sure of holding down the panic that bubbled like magma low in his throat.

"*Gimli!*" the dwarf shouted. His spittle sprayed Hartmann's lips and cheeks.

Instantly Hartmann dropped the link. Puppetman reeled. For a moment he'd felt Gimli's hatred blazing like an incandescent wire. *He suspects!*

Most of what he'd sensed was the hate. But beneath that, beneath the conscious surface of Gimli's mind lay awareness that there was something out of the ordinary about Gregg Hartmann, something inextricably tied to the bloody shambles of the Jokertown Riots. Gimli wasn't an ace, Hartmann was sure of that. But Gimli's natural paranoia was itself something of a sixth sense.

For the first time in his life Puppetman faced the possibility he had lost a puppet.

He knew he blanched, knew he flinched, but fortunately his reaction passed for squeamishness at being spat on.

"Gimli," the dwarf repeated, and Hartmann sensed he was turning away. "That's my name. And the mask stays on, Senator. You know me, but the same doesn't apply to everybody here. And they'd like to keep it that way."

"That's not going to work too well, Gimli. You think a ski mask is going to disguise a joker with a furry snout? I—that is, if anybody saw you grab me, they'll have little enough trouble identifying you and your gang."

He was saying too much, he belatedly realized—he didn't want Miller dwelling too much on the fact that Hartmann could make him and some of his accomplices. Whatever had put him out had stirred his brains like omelette batter.

—an electrical shock of some sort, he thought. Back in the Sixties he'd been a freedom rider briefly—it was an up-and-coming New Frontier sort of thing to do, and there was always the hatred, heady as wine, the possibility of lovely violence, crimson and indigo. A peckerwood state trooper had nailed him with a cattle prod during the Selma protests, which was too firsthand for his taste and sent him back north in a hurry. But it had felt like that, back in the limousine.

"Come now, Gimli," said a gritty baritone voice in accented but clear English. "Why not have the mask off? The whole world will know us soon enough."

"Oh, all right," Gimli said. Puppetman could taste his resentment without having to reach. Tom Miller was having to share stage with someone, and he didn't like it. Little bubbles of interest began to well up through the seethe of Hartmann's incipient panic.

Hartmann heard the scrape of feet on bare floor. Someone fumbled briefly, cursed, and then he caught his breath involuntarily as the tape was unwound, pulling reluctantly away from his hair and skin.

The first thing he saw was Gimli's face. It still looked like a bagful of rotten apples. The look of exultation didn't improve it any. Hartmann pushed his gaze past the dwarf to the rest of the room.

It was a shitty little tenement, like shitty little tenements pretty much everywhere in the world. The wooden floor was stained and the striped wallpaper had patches of damp like a workman's armpits. From the general scatter of crunchy and crinkly trash underfoot, Hartmann guessed the place was derelict. Still, a lightbulb glared in a busted-globe fixture overhead, and he felt a radiator drumming out too much heat the way every radiator in Germany did until it came down June.

For all he knew he could be in the Eastern sector, which was a hell of a cheery thought. On the other hand, he'd been in German homes before. This one smelled *wrong*, somehow.

There were three other overt jokers in the room, one swathed from head to feet in a dusty-looking cowled robe, one covered with yellowish chitin dotted with tiny red pimples, a third the furry one he'd seen next to the van. The three young nats in Hartmann's field of vision looked offensively normal by comparison.

His power felt others behind him. That was strange. He wasn't usually able to taste another's emotions, unless that one was broadcasting strongly, or was a puppet. He sensed a peculiar squirming in the power inside him.

He glanced back. Two more back there, nats to the eye, though the scrawny youth leaning on the stained wall next to

the radiator had an odd look to him. A man in his mid-thirties
sat next to him in a gaudy plastic chair with his hands in the
pockets of an overcoat. Hartmann thought the older man was
subconsciously straining away from the younger; when their
eyes met he caught a quick impression of sadness.

That's odd, he thought. Maybe tension had heightened
his normal perceptions; maybe he was imagining things. But
something was coming off that kid as he grinned at Hartmann,
something that prickled all around the edges of his awareness.
Again he had that evasive feeling from Puppetman.

A shoe crunched debris. He turned, found himself looking
up at an enormous nat dressed in suit coat and trousers of an
odd tan-green, almost military. The man had no tie; his shirt
collar hung unbuttoned around a thick neck, open to a spray
of grizzled blond chest hair. Big hands rested on his hips with
the coattails swept up behind, like something out of a little
theater production of *Inherit the Wind*. His long hair lay
combed back from a high forehead.

He smiled. He had one of those rugged ugly faces
women fall for and men believe.

"A very great pleasure to meet you, Senator." It was the
rolling sea swell of the voice he'd heard urge Gimli to remove
his blindfold.

"You have the advantage."

"That's true. Oh, but I daresay my name won't be
unfamiliar to you. I am Wolfgang Prahler."

Behind Hartmann someone *tsked* in exasperation. Prahler
frowned, then laughed. "Ah, now, Comrade Mólniya, do I
break security? Well, did we not agree that we must come
out into the light of day to accomplish a task so important?"

Like many educated Berliners he spoke English with a
pronouncedly British cast. From behind, Puppetman felt a
flicker of agitation at the name *Mólniya*. It was Russian. It
meant *lightning;* the Soviets had a series of communications
satellites by that name.

"What exactly is going on here?" Hartmann demanded.
His heart lurched at the words. He didn't mean to take that
tone with cold-blooded killers who had him altogether at
their mercy. But Puppetman, coming suddenly into arrogance, had taken the bit in his teeth. "Couldn't you wait until
the *Aide et Amitié* banquet to make my acquaintance?"

Prahler's laugh resonated up from deep in his chest.
"Very good. But have you not figured it out? It was never

intended you should reach the banquet, Senator. You were, as you Americans say, set up."

"Drawn to the bait and trapped," said a slight redheaded woman who wore a black turtleneck and jeans. "Set cheese for a rat; set a fine banquet to catch a fine lord."

"Rats and lords," a voice repeated. "A fine rat. A fine lord." It giggled. It was a male voice, cracked and adolescent: the leather boy. Hartmann felt a tickle run along the cord of his scrotum like the fingers of a whore. No doubt about it. He was getting emotion from him like static on a line. A hint of something potent—something terrible. For once Puppetman felt no desire to probe further.

He feared this one. More than the others, Prahler, these casual youths with guns. Even Gimli.

"You went to all this trouble to help Gimli here settle an old, imaginary score?" he made himself say. "That's generous of you."

"We're doing this for the revolution," said a youthful nat with a blond flattop and a heat-lamp tan and the air of having worked hard to memorize the line. His turtleneck and jeans were molded around an athlete's figure. He stood by the wall caressing the muzzle brake of a Soviet assault rifle grounded by his foot.

"You're of no significance, Senator," the woman said. She flipped her square-cut bangs off her forehead. "Simply a tool. What your naive egotism tells you notwithstanding."

"Who the hell are you people?"

"We bear the sacred name of the Red Army Fraction," she told him. She hovered over a stocky youngster who sat cross-legged fiddling with a radio perched on a warped wooden nightstand. He wouldn't meet Hartmann's eyes.

"Comrade Wolf gave it to us," the blond boy said. "He used to hang out with Baader and Meinhof and them. They used to be close like this." He held up a clenched fist.

Hartmann sucked in his lips. Since the terrorist wars had gotten underway for true in the early Seventies, it wasn't uncommon for radical attorneys to come to involve themselves directly in the activities of those they represented in court, especially in Germany and Italy. Apparently, if what the kid said was true, Prahler had been a leader in the Baader-Meinhof group and the RAF all along, without the authorities ever getting wind of the fact.

Hartmann looked at Tom Miller. "I'll rephrase my question. How did *you* get mixed up in this, Gimli?"

"We just happened to be in the right place at the right time, Senator."

The dwarf smirked at him. Puppetman felt an urge to crush that smug face, to tear out the dwarf's guts and throttle him with them. The frustration was physical torment.

Sweat crawled down Hartmann's forehead like a centipede. His emotions were oddly distinct from Puppetman's. His other self whipsawed from rage to fear. What he mostly felt now was tired and annoyed.

And sad. *Poor Ronnie. He meant so well. He tried so hard.*

The redhead suddenly slapped the seated man on the shoulder. "You idiot, Wilfried, there it was! You went past it." He mumbled apology and dialed back.

"—captured by the Red Army Fraction, acting in concert with comrades from the Jokers for a Just Society who have fled persecution in Amerika." It was Comrade Wolf's voice, pouring like liquid amber from the cheap little radio. "The terms of his release are these: release of the Palestinian freedom fighter al-Muezzin. An airliner with sufficient fuel to take al-Muezzin to a country in the liberated Third World. Immunity from prosecution for members of this action team. We demand that the Jetboy memorial be torn down and in its place a facility built to provide shelter and medical attention to joker victims of Amerikan intolerance. And finally, just to poke the capitalist swine where it most hurts them, ten million dollars cash, which will be used to aid victims of Amerikan aggression in Central Amerika.

"If these terms are not met by ten o'clock tonight, Berlin time, Senator Gregg Hartmann will be executed.

"We return you now to regularly scheduled programming."

"We have to do something." Hiram Worchester tangled his fingers in his beard and gazed out the window at the patchy Berlin sky.

Digger Downs turned over a card. Trey of clubs. He grimaced.

Billy Ray paced the carpet of Hiram's suite like a tyrannosaurus with an itch. "If I'd been there, this shit would never have happened," he said, and aimed a green glare at Mordecai Jones.

The Hammer sat on the sofa. It was oak and flowered upholstery, and like many of the hotel's furnishings had survived the war. Fortunately they'd built stout furniture back in the 1890s.

Jones made a dirty-gearbox noise toward the center of him and stared at his big hands, which he was working into tangles between his knees.

The door opened and Peregrine flew into the room. Figuratively, at least, her wings jittering on her back. She wore a loose velour blouse and jeans that muted the advanced state of her pregnancy.

"I just heard on the radio—isn't it terrible?" Then she stopped and stared at the Hammer. "Mordecai—what on earth are *you* doing here?"

"Just like you, Ms. Peregrine. Won't let me out."

"But why aren't you in the hospital? The reports said you were terribly injured."

"Just shot a little." He slapped his gut. "Got me a pretty tough hide, kind of like that Kevlar stuff you read about in *Popular Science.*"

Downs turned up a new card. Red eight. "Shit," he muttered.

"But a *van* fell on you," Peregrine said.

"Yeah, but see, I got these funky heavy metals replacing the calcium in my bones, so they're like stronger and more flexible and all, and my innards and whatnot are a lot sturdier than most folks'. And I heal mighty fast—don't even get sick—since I turned up my ace. I'm a pretty durable sort of dude."

"Then why'd you let them get away?" Bill Ray challenged, almost shouting. "Goddamn, the senator was your responsibility. You could've kicked some *ass.*"

"To tell you the entire truth, Mr. Ray, it hurt like a sonofabitch. I wasn't good for much for a while there."

The *Mister* came out differently than *Ms.* had. Billy Ray cocked his head and looked hard at him. Jones ignored him.

"Lay off him, Billy," said Carnifex's partner, Lady Black, who sat to one side with her long legs crossed at the ankles before her.

Peregrine came and touched Mordecai on the shoulder. "It must have been awful. I'm surprised they let you out of the hospital."

"They didn't," Downs said, splitting open the deck in his

left hand to catch a peek inside. "He released himself. Smashed right through the wall. The public health people are kind of pissed about it."

Jones looked down at the floor. "Don't like doctors," he muttered.

Peregrine looked around. "Where's Sara? The poor thing. This must be hell for her."

"They let *her* go over to the crisis control center in City Hall. No other reporter from the tour. Just her." Downs made a face and went back to his solitaire game.

"Sara took over a statement from Mr. Jones about what he saw and heard during the abduction," Lady Black said. "He didn't give one before he left the hospital." After the accident that triggered his wild card virus, Jones had been held by the Oklahoma Department of Public Health as a lab specimen, a virtual prisoner. The experience had given him an almost pathological fear of medical science and all its appurtenances.

"Funny damn thing," Jones said, shaking his head. "I was lying there trying to breathe with this fu—with this van on my chest, and I keep hearing all these people yelling at each other. Like little kids fightin' on a playground."

Hiram turned from the window. The rings that had been sinking in around his eyes since the tour began were even more pronounced. "I understand," he said, bringing his hands up cupped before his chest. They were dainty hands, and fit oddly with his bulk. "I understand what's happening here. This has been a blow to all of us. Senator Hartmann isn't just the last best hope for jokers to get a fair shake—and maybe aces too, with this crazy Barnett fellow on the loose— he's our *friend*. We're trying to soften the blow by talking around the subject. But it won't do. We have to *do* something."

"That's what I say." Billy Ray slammed a fist into his palm. "Let's kick butts and take names!"

"Whose butt?" Lady Black asked tiredly. "Whose name?"

"That sawed-off little bastard Gimli for starters. We should have grabbed him when he was dicking around New York last summer—"

"Where are you going to find him?"

He flung out his arm. "Hell, that's why we ought to be looking for him, instead of sitting here on our duffs wringing our hands and saying how sorry we are the fucking senator's gone."

"There are ten thousand cops out there combing the streets," Lady Black said. "You think we'll find him quicker?"

"But what can we do, Hiram?" Peregrine asked. Her face was pale, and the skin stretched tight over her cheekbones. "I feel so helpless." Her wings opened slightly, then folded again.

Hiram's little pink tongue dabbed his lips. "Peri, I wish I knew. Surely there must be something—"

"They mentioned ransom," Digger Downs said.

Hiram punched his palm twice in unconscious imitation of Carnifex. "That's it. That's it! Maybe we can raise enough money to buy him back."

"Ten million's a lot of bread," Mordecai said.

"That's just a bargaining position," Hiram said, sweeping aside objections with his small hands. "Surely we can work them down."

"What about their demands this terrorist dude be released? We can't do nothing about that."

"Money talks," Downs said. "Nobody walks."

"Inelegantly put," Hiram said, beginning to drift here and there like an ungainly cloud, "but correct. Surely if we can scrape together sufficient funds, they'll leap at our offer."

"Now, wait a minute—" Carnifex began.

"I'm a man of not inconsiderable means," Hiram said, scooping up a handful of mints from a silver salver in passing. "I can contribute a fair amount—"

"I have money," Peregrine said excitedly. "I'll help."

Mordecai frowned. "I'm not crazy about politicians, but shoot, I feel I *lost* the man and shit. Count me in, for what it's worth."

"Hold on, dammit!" Billy Ray said. "President Reagan has already announced there will be no negotiating with these terrorists."

"Maybe he'll go for it if we throw in a Bible and a mess of rocket launchers," Mordecai said.

Hiram elevated his chin. "We're private citizens, Mr. Ray. We can do as we please."

"We'll by God see—"

The door opened. Xavier Desmond walked in. "I couldn't bear to sit alone any longer," he said. "I'm so worried—my God, Mordecai, what are you doing here?"

"Never mind that, Des," Hiram said. "We've got a plan."

*   *   *

The man from the Federal Criminal Office tapped his pack of cigarettes on the edge of the desk in the crisis center in City Hall, shook out a cigarette, and put it between his lips. "What on earth were you thinking of, permitting that to go over the air without consulting me!" He made no move to light the cigarette. He had a young man's face with an old man's wrinkles, and lynx yellow eyes. His ears stuck out.

"Herr Neumann," the mayor's representative said, trapping the phone receiver between his shoulder and a couple of chins and getting it quite sweaty, "here in Berlin our reflex is to shy away from censorship. We had enough of that in the bad old days, *na ja?*"

"I don't mean that. How are we to control this situation if we're not even *informed* when steps like this are taken?" He leaned back and stroked a finger down one of the furrows that bracketed his mouth. "This could turn into Munich all over again."

Tachyon studied the digital clock built into the high heel of one of the pair of boots he'd bought on the Ku'damn the day before. Aside from the clocks he was in full seventeenth-century regalia. *This tour was a political stunt*, he thought. *But still, we might have accomplished some good. Is this how it's going to end?*

"Who is this al-Muezzin?" he asked.

"Daoud Hassani is his name. He's an ace who can destroy things with his voice, rather like your own late ace Howler," Neumann said. If he noticed Tachyon's wince he gave no sign. "He's from Palestine. He's one of Nur al-Allah's people, works out of Syria. He claimed responsibility for the downing of that El Al jetliner at Orly last June."

"I'm afraid we've heard far from the last of the Light of Allah," Tachyon said. Neumann nodded grimly. Since the tour had left Syria, there had been three dozen bombings worldwide in retribution for its "treacherous attack" on the ace prophet.

If only that wretched woman had finished the job, Tach thought. He was careful not to speak it aloud. These Earthers could be sensitive about such things.

Sweat ran down the side of his neck and into the lace collar of his blouse. The radiator hummed and groaned with heat. *I wish they were less sensitive to cold. Why do these Germans insist on making their hot planet so much hotter?*

The door opened. Clamor spilled in from the international press corps crammed into the corridor outside. A political aide slipped inside and whispered to the mayor's man. The mayor's man petulantly slammed down his phone.

"Ms. Morgenstern has come from the Kempinski," he announced.

"Bring her in at once," Tachyon said.

The mayor's man jutted his underlip, which gleamed wet in the fluorescents. "Impossible. She's a member of the press, and we have excluded the press from this room for the duration."

Tachyon looked at the man down the length of his fine, straight nose. "I demand that Ms. Morgenstern be admitted at once," he said in that tone of voice reserved on Takis for grooms who tread on freshly polished boots and serving maids who spill soup on heads of allied Psi Lord houses who are guesting in the manor.

"Let her in," Neumann said. "She's brought Herr Jones's tape for us."

Sara was wearing a white trench coat with a hand-wide belt red as a bloody bandage. Tach shook his head. Like all fashion statements she made, this one jarred.

She came to him. They shared a brief, dry embrace. She turned away, unslinging her heavy handbag.

Tachyon wondered. Had that been a touch of metal in her watercolor eyes, or only tears?

"Did you hear that?" the redhead called Anneke warbled. "One of the pigs we got today was a Jew."

Early afternoon. The radio simmered with reports and conjectures about the kidnapping. The terrorists were exalted, strutting and puffing for each other's benefit.

"One more drop of blood to avenge our brothers in Palestine," said Wolf sonorously

"What about the nigger ace?" demanded the one who looked like a lifeguard and answered to Ulrich. "Has he died yet?"

"He's not going to anytime soon," Anneke said. "According to the news, he walked out of the hospital within an hour of being admitted."

"That's bullshit! I hit him with half a magazine. I saw that van fall on him."

Anneke sidled over from the radio and ran her fingers

along the line of Ulrich's jaw. "Don't you think if he can lift a van all by himself, he might be a little hard to hurt, sweetheart?"

She stood up on the toes of her sneakers and kissed him just behind the lobe of his ear. "Besides, we killed two—"

"Three," said Comrade Wilfried, who was still monitoring the airwaves. "The other, uh, policeman just died." He swallowed.

Anneke clapped her hands in delight. "You see?"

"I killed somebody too," said the boy's voice from behind Hartmann. Just the sound of it filled Puppetman with energy. *Easy, easy,* Hartmann cautioned his other half, wondering, *do I have this one? Is it possible to create a puppet without knowing it? Or is he constantly emoting at such a pitch that I can feel it without having the link?*

The power didn't answer.

The leather boy shuffled forward. Hartmann saw he was hunchbacked. A joker?

"Comrade Dieter," the teenager said. "I offed him— *brrr*—like *that!*" He held his hands up in front of him and suddenly they were vibrating like a powersaw blade, a blur of lethality.

An ace! Hartmann's own breath hit him in the chest.

The vibration stopped. The boy showed yellow teeth around at the others. They were very quiet.

Through the pounding in his ears Hartmann heard a scrape of tubular metal on wood as the man in the coat got up from his chair. "You killed someone, Mackie?" he asked mildly. His German was a touch too perfect to be natural. "Why?"

Mackie tucked his head down. "He was an informer, Comrade," he said sidelong. His eyes jittered between Wolf and the other. "Comrade Wolf ordered me to take him into custody. But he—he tried to kill me! That was it. He pulled a gun on me and I *buzzed* him off." He brandished a vibrating hand again.

The man came slowly forward where Hartmann could see him. He was medium height, dressed well but not too well, hair neat and blond. A man just on the handsome side of nondescriptness. Except for his hands, which were encased in what appeared to be thick rubber gloves. Hartmann watched them in sudden fascination.

"Why wasn't I told of this, Wolf?" The voice stayed level, but Puppetman could hear an unspoken shout of anger. There was sadness too—the power was pulling it in, no question now. And a hell of a lot of fear.

Wolf rolled heavy shoulders. "There was a lot going on this morning, Comrade Mólniya. I learned that Dieter planned to betray us, I sent Mackie after him, things got out of hand. But everything's all right now, everything's going fine."

Facts dropped into place like tumblers in a lock. *Mólniya—lightning.* Suddenly Hartmann knew what had happened to him in the limousine. The gloved man was an ace, who'd used some kind of electric power to shock him under.

Hartmann's teeth almost splintered from the effort it took to bite back the terror. *An unknown ace! He'll know me, find me out. . . .*

His other self was ice. *He doesn't know anything.*

But how can you know? *We don't know his powers.*

He's a puppet.

It was a fight to keep his face from matching his emotion. *How the hell can that be?*

I got him when he shocked me. Didn't even have to do anything; his own power fused our nervous systems for a moment. That's all it took.

Mackie squirmed like a puppy caught peeing on the rug. "Did I do right, Comrade Mólniya?"

Mólniya's lips whitened, but he nodded with visible effort. "Yes . . . under the circumstances."

Mackie preened and strutted. "Well, there it is. I executed an enemy of the Revolution. You're not the only ones."

Anneke clucked and brushed fingertips across Mackie's cheek. "Preoccupied with the search for individual glory, Comrade? You're going to have to learn to watch those bourgeois tendencies if you want to be part of the Red Army Fraction."

Mackie licked his lips and slunk away, flushing. Puppetman felt what was going on inside him, like the roil beneath the surface of the sun.

What about him? Hartmann asked.

Him too. And the blond jock as well. They both handled us after the Russian shocked you. That jolt made me hypersensitive.

Hartmann let his head drop forward to cover a frown. *How could all this happen without my knowledge?*

I'm your subconscious, remember? Always on the job.

*   *   *

Comrade Mólniya sighed and returned to his seat. He felt hairs rise on the back of his hands and neck as his hyperactive neurons fired off. There was nothing he could do about low-level discharges such as this; they happened of their own accord under stress. It was why he wore gloves— and why some of the more lurid tales they told around the Aquarium about his wedding night had damned near come to pass.

He had to smile. *What's there to be tense about?* Even if he were identified for what he was, after the fact, there would be no international repercussions; that was how the game was played, by us and by them. So his superiors assured him.

Right.

Good God, what did I do to deserve being caught up in this lunatic scheme? He wasn't sure who was crazier, this collection of poor twisted men and bloodthirsty political naïfs or his own bosses.

It was the opportunity of the decade, they'd told him. Al-Muezzin was in the vest pocket of the Big K. If we spring him, he'll fall into our hands out of gratitude. Work for us instead. He might even bring the Light of Allah along.

Was it worth the risk? he'd demanded. Was it worth blowing the underground contacts they'd been building in the Federal Republic for ten years? Was it worth risking the Big War, the war neither side was going to win no matter what their fancy paper war plans said? Reagan was president; he was a cowboy, a madman.

But there was only so far you could push, even if you were an ace and a hero, the first man into the Bala Hissar in Kabul on Christmas Day of '79. The gates had closed in his face. He had his orders. He needed no more.

It wasn't that he disagreed with the goals. Their archrivals, the *Komitet Gosudarstvennoi Bezopasnosti*—the State Security Committee—were arrogant, overpraised, and undercompetent. No good GRU man could ever object to taking those assholes down a peg. As a patriot he knew that Military Intelligence could make far better use of an asset as valuable as Daoud Hassani than their better-known counterparts the KGB.

But the method...

It wasn't for himself he worried. It was for his wife and

daughter. And for the rest of the world too; the risk was enormous, should anything go wrong.

He reached into a pocket for cigarettes and a lighter.

"A filthy habit," Ulrich said in that lumbering way of his.

Mólniya just looked at him.

After a moment Wolf produced a laugh that almost didn't sound forced. "The kids these days, they have different standards. In the old days—ah, Rikibaby, Comrade Meinhof, she was a smoker. Always had a cigarette going."

Mólniya said nothing, just kept staring at Ulrich. His eyes bore a trace of epicanthic fold, legacy of the Mongol Yoke. After a moment the blond youth found somewhere else to look.

The Russian lit up, ashamed of his cheap victory. But he had to keep these murderous young animals under control. What an irony it was that he, who had resigned from the *Spetsnaz* commandos and transferred to the Chief Intelligence Directorate of the Soviet General Staff because he could no longer stomach violence, should find himself compelled to work with these creatures for whom the shedding of blood had become addiction.

Oh, Milya, Masha, will I ever see you again?

"Herr Doktor."

Tach scratched the side of his nose. He was getting restive. He'd been cooped up here two hours, unsure of what he might be contributing. Outside . . . well, there was nothing to be done. But he might be with his people on the tour, comforting them, reassuring them.

"Herr Neumann," he acknowledged.

The man from the Federal Criminal Office sat down next to him. He had a cigarette in his fingers, unlit despite the layer of tobacco that hung like a fogbank in the thick air. He kept turning it over and over.

"I wanted to ask your opinion."

Tachyon raised a magenta eyebrow. He had long since realized the Germans wanted him here solely because he was the tour's leader in Hartmann's absence. Otherwise they would hardly have cared to have a medical doctor, and a foreigner at that, underfoot. As it was, most of the civil and police officials circulating through the crisis center treated him with the deference due his position of authority and otherwise ignored him.

"Ask away," Tachyon said with a hand wave that was only faintly sardonic. Neumann seemed honestly interested, and he had shown signs of at least nascent intelligence, which in Tach's compass was rare for the breed.

"Were you aware that for the past hour and a half several members of your tour have been trying to raise a sum of money to offer Senator Hartmann's kidnappers as ransom?"

"No."

Neumann nodded, slowly, as if thinking something through. His yellow eyes were hooded. "They are experiencing considerable difficulty. It is the position of your government—"

"Not *my* government."

Neumann inclined his head. "—of the United States government, that there will be no negotiation with the terrorists. Needless to say, American currency restrictions did not permit the members of the tour to take anywhere near a sufficient amount of money from the country, and now the American government has frozen the assets of all tour participants to preclude their concluding a separate deal."

Tachyon felt his cheeks turn hot. "That's damned high-handed."

Neumann shrugged. "I was curious as to what you thought of the plan."

"Why me?"

"You're an acknowledged authority on joker affairs—that's the reason you honor our country with your presence, of course." He tapped the cigarette on the table next to a curling corner of a map of Berlin. "Also, you come of a culture in which kidnapping is a not uncommon occurrence, if I do not misapprehend."

Tach looked at him. Though he was a celebrity, most Earthers knew little of his background beyond the fact that he was an alien. "I can't speak of the RAF, of course—"

"The *Rote Armee Fraktion* in its current incarnation consists primarily of middle-class youths—much like its previous incarnations, and for that matter most First World revolutionary groups. Money means little to them; as children of our so-called Economic Miracle, they've been raised always to assume a sufficiency of it."

"That's certainly not something you can say for the JJS," Sara Morgenstern said, coming over to join the conversation. An aide moved to intercept her, reaching a hand to shepherd her away from the important masculine conversation. She

shied away from him as if a spark had jumped between them
and glared.

Neumann said something brisk that not even Tachyon
caught. The aide retreated.

"Frau Morgenstern. I am also much interested in what
you have to say."

"Members of the Jokers for a Just Society are authenti-
cally poor. I can vouch for that at least."

"Would money tempt them, then?"

"That's hard to say. They are committed, in a way I
suspect the RAF members aren't. Still—" a butterfly flip of
the hand—"they haven't lost any Mideastern aces. On the
other hand, when they demand money to benefit jokers, I
believe them. Whereas that might mean less to the Red
Army people."

Tach frowned. The demand to knock down Jetboy's Tomb
and build a joker hospice rankled him. Like most New
Yorkers, he wouldn't miss the memorial—an eyesore erected
to honor failure, and one he'd personally prefer to forget. But
the demand for a hospice was a slap in his face: *When has a
joker been turned away from my clinic? When?*

Neumann was studying him. "You disagree, *Herr Doktor*?"
he asked softly.

"No, no. She's right. But Gimli—" he snapped his
fingers and extended a forefinger. "Tom Miller cares deeply
for jokers. But he has also an eye for what Americans call the
main chance. You might well be able to tempt him."

Sara nodded. "But why do you ask, Herr Neumann?
After all, President Reagan refuses to negotiate for the senator's
return." Her voice rang with bitterness. Still, Tach was
puzzled. As high-strung as she was, he'd thought that surely
worry for Gregg would have broken her down by now.

Instead she seemed to be growing steadier by the hour.

Neumann looked at her for a moment, and Tach wondered if he was in on the ill-kept secret of her affair with the
missing senator. He had the impression those yellow eyes—
red-rimmed now from the smoke—missed little.

"Your President has made his decision," he said softly.
"But it's my responsibility to advise my government on
what course to take. This is a German problem too, you
know."

*   *   *

At two-thirty Hiram Worchester came on the air reading a statement in English. Tachyon translated it into German during the pauses.

"Comrade Wolf—Gimli, if you're there," Hiram said, voice fluting with emotion, "we want the senator back. We're willing to negotiate as private citizens.

"Please, for the love of God—and for jokers and aces and all the rest of us—please call us."

Mólniya stared at the door. White enamel was coming away in flakes. Striae of green and pink and brown showed beneath the white, around gouges that looked as if someone had used the door for knife-throwing practice. He was all but oblivious to the others in the room. Even the mad boy's incessant humming; he'd long since learned to tune that out for sanity's sake.

I should never have let them go.

It took him aback when both Gimli and Wolf wanted to make the meet with the tour delegation. It was about the first thing they'd agreed on since this whole comic-opera affair had gotten underway.

He'd wanted to forbid them. He didn't like the smell of this rendezvous . . . but that was foolish. Reagan had closed the door on overt negotiation, but didn't the current Irangate hearings with which the Americans were currently amusing themselves prove he was not averse to using private channels to deal with terrorists against whom he'd taken a hard public line?

Besides, he thought, *I've long since learned better than to issue orders I doubt will be obeyed.*

It had been so different in *Spetsnaz*. The men he'd commanded were professionals and more, the elite of the Soviet armed forces, full of esprit and skilled as surgeons. Such a contrast to this muddle of bitter amateurs and murderous dilettantes.

If only he'd at least had someone trained back home, or in a camp in some Soviet client state, Korea or Iraq or Peru. Someone except Gimli, that is—he had the impression years had passed since anything but plastique would open the dwarf's mind enough to accept input from anyone else, nats in particular.

He wished at least he might have gone on the meet. But his place was here, guarding the captive. Without Hartmann they had nothing—except a worldful of trouble.

Does the KGB have this much trouble with its puppets?
Rationally he guessed they did. They'd fluffed a few big ones
over the years—the mention of Mexico could still make
veterans wince—and GRU had evidence of plenty of missteps
the Big K thought they'd covered up.

But the Komitet's publicists had done their job well, on
both sides of the quaintly named "Iron Curtain." Down
behind his forebrain not even Mólniya could shake the image
of the KGB as the omniscient puppet master, with its strings
wrapping the world like a spider's web.

He tried to envision himself as a master spider. It made
him smile.

*No. I'm not a spider. Just a small, frightened man whom
somebody once called* hero.

He thought of Ludmilya, his daughter. He shuddered.

*There are strings attached to me, right enough. But I'm
not the one who pulls them.*

I want him.

Hartmann looked around the squalid little room. Ulrich
was pacing, face fixed and sullen at having been left behind.
Stocky Wilfried sat cleaning an assault rifle with compulsive
care. He always seemed to be doing something with his
hands. The two remaining jokers sat by themselves saying
nothing. The Russian sat and smoked and stared at the wall.

He studiously didn't look at the boy in the scuffed
leather jacket.

Mackie Messer hummed the old song about the shark
and its teeth and the man with his jackknife and fancy gloves.
Hartmann remembered a mealymouthed version popular when
he was a teenager, sung by Bobby Darin or some such
teen-idol crooner. He also recalled a different version, one
he'd heard for the first time in a dim dope-fogged room on
Yale's Old Campus when antiwar activist Hartmann returned
to his alma mater to lecture in '68. Dark and sinister, a
straighter translation of the original, sung in the whisky
baritone of a man who, like old Bertolt Brecht himself,
delighted in playing Baal: Thomas Marion Douglas, Destiny's
doomed lead singer. Remembering the way the words went
down his spine on that distant night, he shuddered.

I want him.

No! his mind shouted. *He's insane. He's dangerous.*

He could be useful, once I get us out of here.

Hartmann's body clenched in rictus terror. *No! Don't do anything! The terrorists are negotiating right now. We'll get out of this.*

He felt Puppetman's disdain. Seldom had his alter ego seemed more discrete, more other. *Fools. What has Hiram Worchester ever been involved in that amounted to anything? It'll fall through.*

Then we just wait. Sooner or later something will be worked out. It's how these things go. He felt slimy vines of sweat twining his body inside his blood-spattered shirt and vest.

How long do you think we have to wait? How long before our jokers and their terrorists friends blow up in each other's faces? I have puppets. They're our only way out.

What can they do? I can't just make someone let me go. I'm not that little mind-twister Tachyon.

He felt a smug vibration within.

Don't forget 1976, he told his power. *You thought you could handle that too.*

The power laughed at him, until he closed his eyes and concentrated and forced it to quiescence.

Has it become a demon, possessing me? he wondered. *Am I just another of Puppetman's puppets?*

No. I'm the master here. Puppetman's just a fantasy. A personification of my power. A game I play with myself.

Inside the tangled corridors of his soul, the echo of triumphant laughter.

"It's raining again," Xavier Desmond said.

Tach made a face and refrained from a rejoinder commending the joker's firm grasp of the obvious. Des was a friend, after all.

He shifted his grip on the umbrella he shared with Desmond and tried to console himself that the squall would soon pass. The Berliners strolling the paths that veined the grassy Tiergarten park and hurrying along the sidewalks of the nearby Bundes Allee clearly thought so, and they should know. Old men in homburgs, young women with prams, intense young men in dark wool sweaters, a sausage vendor with cheeks like ripe peaches; the usual crowd of Germans taking advantage of anything resembling decent weather after the lengthy Prussian winter.

He glanced at Hiram. The big round restaurateur was resplendent in his pin-striped three-piece suit, hat at a jaunty angle, and black beard curled. He had an umbrella in one hand, a gleaming black satchel in the other, and Sara Morgenstern standing primly next to him, not quite making contact.

Rain was dripping off the brim of Tach's plumed hat, which swept beyond the coverage of the cheap plastic umbrella. A rivulet ran down one side of Des's trunk. Tach sighed.

How did I let myself get talked into this? he wondered for the fourth or fifth time. It was idle; when Hiram had called to say a West German industrialist who wished to remain nameless had offered to front them the ransom money, he'd known he was in.

Sara stood stiff. He sensed she was shivering, almost subliminally. Her face was the color of her raincoat. Her eyes were a paleness that somehow contrasted. He wished she hadn't insisted on coming along. But she was the leading journalist on this junket; they'd have had to lock her up to keep her from covering this meeting with Hartmann's kidnappers at first hand. And there was her personal interest.

Hiram cleared his throat. "Here they come." His voice was pitched higher than usual.

Tachyon glanced right without turning his head. No mistake; there weren't enough jokers in West Germany that it was likely to have two just happen along at this moment, even if there could be any doubt about the identity of the small bearded man who walked with the Toulouse-Lautrec roll beside a being who looked like a beige anteater on its hind legs.

"Tom," Hiram said, voice husky now.

"Gimli," the dwarf replied. He said it without heat. His eyes glittered at the satchel hanging from Hiram's hand. "You brought it."

"Of course . . . Gimli." He handed the umbrella to Sara and cracked the satchel. Gimli stood on tiptoe and peered in. His lips pursed in a soundless whistle. "Two million American dollars. Two more after you hand Senator Hartmann over to us."

A snaggletoothed grin. "That's a bargaining figure."

Hiram colored. "You agreed on the phone—"

"We agreed to consider your offer once you demonstrated your good faith," said one of the two nats who accompanied Gimli and his partner. He was a tall man made bulkier by his raincoat. Dark blond hair was slicked back and down from a balding promontory of forehead by the intermittent rain. "I am Comrade Wolf. Let me remind you, there is the matter of the freedom of our comrade, al-Muezzin."

"Just what is it that makes German socialists risk their lives and freedom on behalf of a fundamentalist Muslim terrorist?" Tachyon asked.

"We're all comrades in the struggle against Western imperialism. What brings a Takisian to risk his health in our beastly climate on behalf of a senator from a country that once whipped him from its shores like a rabid dog?"

Tach drew his head back in surprise. Then he smiled. "Touché." He and Wolf shared a look of perfect understanding.

"But we can only give you money," Hiram said. "We can't arrange for Mr. Hassani to be released. We *told* you that."

"Then it's no sale," said Wolf's nat companion, a red-headed woman Tach could have found attractive but for a sullen, puffy jut to her lower lip and a bluish cast to her complexion. "What use is your toilet-paper money to us? We merely demand it to make you pigs sweat."

"Now, wait a minute," Gimli said. "That money can buy a lot for jokers."

"Are you so obsessed with buying into consumption fascism?" sneered the redhead.

Gimli went purple. "The money's here. Hassani's in Rikers, and that's a long way away."

Wolf was frowning at Gimli in a speculative sort of way. Somewhere an engine backfired.

The woman spat like a cat and jumped back, face pale, eyes feral.

Motion tugged at the corner of Tach's eye.

The chubby sausage seller had flipped open the lid of his cart. His hand was coming out with a black Heckler & Koch mini-machine pistol in it.

Ever suspicious, Gimli traced his gaze. "It's a trap!" he shrieked. He whipped open his coat. He'd been holding one of those compact little Krinkov assault rifles beneath.

Tachyon kicked the foreshortened Kalashnikov from Gimli's hand with the toe of an elegant boot. The nat woman pulled out an AKM from inside her coat and stuttered a burst one-handed. The sound threatened to implode Tach's eardrums.

Sara screamed. Tach threw himself onto her, bore her

down to wet, fragrant grass as the female terrorist tracked her weapon from left to right, face a rictus of something like ecstasy.

There was motion all around. Old men in homburgs and young women with prams and intense young men in sweaters were whipping out machine pistols and rushing toward the party clumped around the two umbrellas.

"Wait," Hiram shouted, "hold on! It's all a misunderstanding."

The other terrorists had guns out now, firing in all directions. Bystanders screamed and scattered. The slick-soled shoes of a man waving a machine pistol with one hand lost traction on the grass and shot out from under him. A man with an MP5K and a business suit tripped over a baby carriage whose operator had frozen on the handle and fell on his face.

Sara lay beneath Tachyon, rigid as a statue. The clenched rump pressed against his crotch was firmer than he would have expected. *This is the only way I'm ever going to get on top of her,* he thought ruefully. It was almost physical pain to realize it was contact with him and not fear of the bullets crackling like static overhead that made her go stiff.

Gregg, you are a lucky man. Should you somehow survive this imbroglio.

Scrambling after his rifle, Gimli ran into a big nat who snatched at him. He picked him up by one leg with that disproportionate strength of his and pitched him into the faces of a trio of his comrades like a Scot tossing the caber.

Des was making love to the grass. *Smart man,* Tachyon thought. His head was full of burned powder and the green and brown aromas of wet turf. Hiram was wandering dazed through a horizontal firestorm, waving his arms and crying, "Wait, wait—oh, it wasn't supposed to happen like this."

The terrorists bolted. Gimli ducked between the legs of one nat who flailed his arms at him in a grab, came up and punched a second in the nuts and followed them.

Tach heard a squeal of pain. The snouted joker fell down with black ropy strands of blood unraveling from his belly. Gimli caught him up on the run and slung him over his shoulder like a rolled carpet.

A gaggle of Catholic schoolgirls scattered like blue quail, pigtails flying, as the fugitives stampeded through them.

Tachyon saw a man go to one knee, raise his machine pistol for a burst at the terrorists.

He reached out with his mind. The man toppled, asleep.

A van coughed into life and roared from the curb with Gimli thrashing for the handles of the open doors with his stubby arms.

Hiram sat on the wet grass, weeping into his hands. The black satchel wept bundled money beside him.

"The political police," Neumann said, as if trying to work a shred of spoiled food from inside his mouth. "They don't call them *Popo* for nothing."

"Herr Neumann—" the man in mechanic's coveralls began beseechingly.

"Shut up. Doctor Tachyon, you have my personal apology." Neumann had arrived within five minutes of the terrorists' escape, just in time to keep Tachyon from being arrested for screaming abuse at the police interlopers.

Tachyon sensed Sara beside and behind him like a whiteout shadow. She'd just finished narrating a sketch of what had just happened into the voice-actuated mike clipped to the lapel of her coat. She seemed calm.

He gestured at the ambulances crowded together like whales with spinning blue lights beyond the police cordon, with a hat still bedraggled from being jumped up and down on. "How many people did your madmen gun down?"

"Three bystanders were injured by gunfire, and one policeman. Another officer will require hospitalization but he, ah, was not shot."

"What were you *thinking* of?" Tachyon screamed. He thought he'd blasted all his fury out of him, all over the plainclothes officers who'd been stumbling across each other demanding to know how the terrorists could *possibly* have gotten away. But now it was back, filling him up to overflow. "Tell me, what did you people think you were doing?"

"It wasn't my people," Neumann said. "It was the political branch of the Berlin *Land* police. The *Bundeskriminalamt* had nothing to do with it."

"It was all a setup," Xavier Desmond said, stroking his trunk with leaden fingers. "That millionaire philanthropist who lent the ransom—"

"Was fronting for the political police."

"Herr Neumann." It was a *Popo* with grass stains on the

knees of his once sharply pressed trousers, pointing an accusing finger at Tachyon "He let the terrorists go. Pauli had a clear shot at them, and he—he knocked him down with that mind power of his."

"The officer was aiming his weapon at a crowd of people through whom the terrorists were fleeing," Tach said tautly. "He could not have fired without hitting innocent bystanders. Or perhaps I am confused as to who is the terrorist."

The plainclothesman turned red. "You interfered with one of my officers! We could have stopped them—"

Neumann reached out and grabbed a pinch of the man's cheek. "Go elsewhere," he said softly. "Really."

The man swallowed and walked away, sending hostile looks back over his shoulder at Tachyon. Tachyon grinned and shot him the bird.

"Oh, Gregg, my God, what have we done?" sobbed Hiram. "We'll never get him back."

Tachyon tugged on his elbow, more trying to encourage him to his feet than help him. He forgot about Hiram's gravity power; the fat man popped right up. "What do you mean, Hiram, my friend?"

"Are you out of your mind, Doctor? They'll kill him now."

Sara gasped. When Tach glanced to her she looked quickly away, as if unwilling to show him her eyes.

"Not so, my friend," Neumann said. "That's not how the game is played."

He stuck hands in the pockets of his trousers and gazed off across the misty park at the line of trees that masked the outer fences of the zoo. "But now the price will go up."

"The bastards!" Gimli turned, whipping rain from the tail of his raincoat, and beat fists on the mottled walls. "The cocksuckers. *They set us up!*"

Shroud and Scrape were huddled over the thin, filthy mattress on which Aardvark lay moaning softly. Everybody else seemed to be milling around a room crowded with heavy damp as well as bodies.

Hartmann sat with his head pulled protectively down inside his sweat-limp collar. He agreed with Gimli's character assessment. *Are those fools trying to get me killed?*

A thought went home like a whaler's bomb-lance: *Tachyon!*

Does that alien demon suspect? Is this a convoluted Takisian plot to get rid of me without a scandal?

Puppetman laughed at him. *'Never attribute to malice what may adequately be explained by stupidity,'* he said. Hartmann recognized the quote; Lady Black had said it to Carnifex once, during one of his rages.

Mackie Messer stood shaking his head. "This isn't right," he said, half-pleading. "We have the senator. Don't they know that?"

Then he was raging around the room like a cornered wolf, snarling and hacking air with his hands. People jostled to get out of the way of those hands.

"What do they think's going on?" Mackie screamed. "Who do they think they're fucking with? I'll tell you something. I'll tell you what. Maybe we should send them a few pieces of the Senator here, show them what's what."

He *buzzed* his hand inches from the tip of the captive's nose.

Hartmann yanked his head back. *Christ, he almost got me!* The intent had been there, for real—Puppetman had felt it, felt it waver at the final millisecond.

"Calm down, Detlev," Anneke said sweetly. She seemed exalted by the shootout in the park. She'd been fluttering around and laughing at nothing since the group's return, and red spots glowed like greasepaint on her cheeks. "The capitalists won't be eager to pay all we ask for damaged goods."

Mackie went white. Puppetman felt fresh anger burst inside him like a bomb. "Mackie! I'm Mackie Messer, you fucking bitch! Mackie the Knife, just like my song."

Detlev was slang for *faggot*, Hartmann remembered. He kept his last breath inside.

Anneke smiled at the youthful ace. From the side of his eye Hartmann saw Wilfried pale, and Ulrich picked up an AKM with an elaborate casualness he wouldn't have thought the blond terrorist could muster.

Wolf put his arm around Mackie's shoulders. "There, Mackie, there. Anneke didn't mean anything by it." Her smile made a liar of him. But Mackie pressed against the big man's side and allowed himself to be gentled. Mólniya cleared his throat, and Ulrich set the rifle down.

Hartmann let the breath go. The explosion wasn't coming. Quite yet.

"He's a good boy," Wolf said, giving Mackie another hug

and letting him go. "He's the son of an American deserter and a Hamburg whore—another victim of your imperialist venture in Southeast Asia, Senator."

"My father was a general," Mackie shouted in English.

"Yes, Mackie; anything you say. The boy grew up running the docks and alleys, in and out of institutions. Finally he drifted to Berlin, more helpless flotsam cast up by our own frenetic consumer culture. He saw posters, began to attend study groups at the Free University—he's barely literate, the poor child—and that's where I found him. And recruited him."

"And he's been *sooo* helpful," Anneke said, rolling her eyes at Ulrich, who laughed. Mackie glanced at them, then quickly away.

You win, Puppetman said.

What?

You're right. My control isn't perfect. And this one is too unpredictable, too . . . terrible.

Hartmann almost laughed aloud. Of all the things he'd come to expect from the power that dwelt within him, humility wasn't one.

Such a waste; he'd be such a perfect puppet. And his emotion, so furious, so lovely—like a drug. But a deadly drug.

So you've given up. Relief flooded him.

No. The boy just has to die.

—But that's all right. I've got it all worked out now.

Shroud squatted over Aardvark like a solicitous mummy, bathing his forehead with a length of his own bandage, which he'd dipped in water from one of the five-liter plastic cans stacked in the bedroom. He shook his head and murmured to himself.

Eyes malice-bright, Anneke danced up to him. "Thinking of all that lovely money you lost, Comrade?"

"Joker blood's been shed—again," Shroud said levelly. "It better not have been for nothing."

Anneke sauntered over to Ulrich. "You should have seen them, sweetheart. All ready to hand Senator *Schweinfleisch* over for a suitcase full of dollars." She pursed her lips. "I do believe they were so excited they forgot all about the frontline fighter we've sworn to liberate. They would have sold us all."

"Shut up, you bitch!" Gimli yelled. Spittle exploded from the center of his beard as he lunged for the redhead. With a scratch of chitin on wood Scrape interposed himself, threw his horny arms around his leader as guns came up.

A loud *pop* stopped them like a freeze-frame. Mólniya stood with a bare hand upturned before his face, fingers extended as if to hold a ball. An ephemeral blue flicker limned the nerves of his hand and was gone.

"If we fight among ourselves," he said calmly, "we play into our enemies' hands."

Only Puppetman knew his calm was a lie.

Deliberately Mólniya drew his glove back on. "We were betrayed. What more can we expect from the capitalist system we oppose?" He smiled. "Let us strengthen our resolve. If we stand together, we can make them pay for their treachery."

The potential antagonists fell back away from each other.

Hartmann feared.

Puppetman exulted.

The last of day lay across the Brandenburg plain west of the city like a layer of polluted water. From the next block tinny Near Eastern music skirled from a radio. Inside the little room it was tropical, from the heat billowing out of the radiator that the handy Comrade Wilfried had got going despite the building's derelict status, as well as electricity; from the humidity of bodies confined under stress.

Ulrich let the cheap curtains drop and turned away from the window. "Christ, it stinks in here," he said, doing stretches. "What do those fucking Turks do? Piss in the corners?"

Lying on the foul mattress next to the wall, Aardvark huddled closer around his injured gut and whimpered.

Gimli moved over beside him, felt his head. His ugly little face was all knotted up with concern. "He's in a bad way," the dwarf said.

"Maybe we oughta get him to a hospital," Scrape said.

Ulrich jutted his square chin and shook his head. "No way. We decided."

Shroud knelt down next to his boss, took Aardvark's hand, and felt the low fuzzy forehead. "He's got some fever."

"How can you tell?" Wilfried asked, his broad face concerned. "Maybe he's naturally got a higher temperature than a person, like a dog or something."

Quick as a teleport Gimli was across the room. He swept
Wilfried off his feet with a transverse kick and straddled his
chest, pummeling him. Shroud and Scrape hauled him off.

Wifried was holding his hands up before his face. "Hey,
hey, what did I do?" He seemed almost in tears.

"You stupid bastard!" Gimli howled, windmilling his
arms. "You're no better than the rest of the fucking nats!
None of you!"

"Comrades, please—" Mólniya began

But Gimli wasn't listening. His face was the color of raw
meat. He· sent his companions flying with a heave of his
shoulders and marched to Aardvark's side.

Puppetman hated to let Gimli off like this, walking away
clear. He'd have to kill the evil little fuck someday.

But survival surmounted even vengeance. Puppetman's
imperative was to shave the odds against him. This was the
quickest way.

Tears streamed over Gimli's lumpy cheeks. "That's enough,"
he sobbed. "We're taking him for medical attention, and
we're taking him *now.*" He bent down and looped a limp
furry arm over his neck. Shroud glanced around, eyes alert
above the bandage wrap, then joined him.

Comrade Wolf blocked the door. "Nobody leaves here."

"What the fuck are you talking about, little man?" Ulrich
said pugnaciously. "He's not hurt that badly."

"Who says he's not eh?" Shroud said. For the first time
Hartmann realized he had a Canadian accent.

Gimli's face twisted like a rag. "That's shit. He's hurting.
He's dying. Dammit, let us go."

Ulrich and Anneke were sidling for their weapons. "United
we stand, brother," Wolf intoned. "Divided we fall. As you
Amis say."

A double clack brought their heads around. Scrape stood
by the far wall. The assault rifle he'd just cocked was pointed
at the buckle of the blond terrorist's army belt. "Then maybe
we just fell, comrades," he said. "Because if Gimli says we're
going, we're gone."

Wolf's mouth crumpled in on itself, as if he were old and
had forgotten his false teeth. He glanced at Ulrich and
Anneke. They had the jokers flanked. If they all moved at
once . . .

Clinging to one of Aardvark's wrists, Shroud brought up an AKM with his free hand. "Keep it cool, nat."

Mackie felt his hands beginning to buzz. Only the touch of Mólniya's hand on his arm kept him from slicing some joker meat. *Ugly monsters! I knew we couldn't trust them.*

"What about the things we're working for?" the Soviet asked.

Gimli wrung Aardvark's hand. "*This* is what *we're* working for. He's a joker. And he needs help."

Comrade Wolf's face was turning the color of eggplant. Veins stood out like broken fingers on his temples. "Where do you think you're going?" he forced past grinding teeth.

Gimli laughed. "Right through the Wall. Where our friends are waiting for us."

"Then leave. Walk out on us. Walk out on the great things you were going to do for your fellow monsters. We still have the senator; we are going to win. And if we ever catch you—"

Scrape laughed. "You gonna have trouble catching your breath after this goes down. The pigs'll be crawling all over you, I guarantee. You're such total fuckups I can smell it."

Ulrich's eyes were rolling belligerently despite the rifle aimed at his midsection. "No," Mólniya said. "Let them go. If we fight everything is lost."

"Get out," Wolf said.

"Yeah," Gimli said. He and Shroud gently carried Aardvark out into the unlit hallway of the abandoned building. Scrape covered them until they were out of sight, then swiftly crossed the room. He paused, gave them as much of a smile as chitin would permit, and closed the door.

Ulrich hurled his Kalashnikov against the door. Fortunately it failed to go off. "Bastards!"

Anneke shrugged. Clearly she was bored with the psychodrama. "Americans," she said.

Mackie sidled over to Mólniya. Everything seemed wrong. But Mólniya would make it right. He knew he would.

The Russian ace was cake.

Ulrich swung around with his big hands tied into fists. "So what's going to happen? Huh?"

Wolf sat on a stool with his belly on his thighs and hands on his knees. He'd visibly aged as the thrill of high adventure ebbed. Perhaps the exploit he'd hoped to cap his double life with was going sour on his tongue.

"What do you mean, Ulrich?" the lawyer asked wearily.

Ulrich turned him a look of outrage. "Well, I mean it's our deadline. It's ten o'clock. You heard the radio. They still haven't met our demands."

He picked up an AKM, jacked a round into the chamber. "Can't we kill the son of a bitch now?"

Anneke laughed like a ringing bell. "Your political sophistication never ceases to amaze me, lover."

Wolf hiked up the sleeve of his coat and checked his wristwatch. "What happens now is that you, Anneke, and you, Wilfried, will go and telephone the message we agreed upon to the crisis center the authorities have so conveniently established. We've both proved we can play the waiting game; it's time to make things move a little."

And Comrade Mólniya said, "No."

The fear was gathering. Bit by bit it coalesced into a cancer, black and amorphous in the center of his brain. With each minute's passage it seemed Mólniya's heart gained a beat. His ribs felt as if they were vibrating from the speed of his pulse. His throat was dry and raw, his cheeks burned as though he stared into the open maw of a crematorium. His mouth tasted like offal. He had to get out. Everything depended on it.

Everything.

No, a part of him cried. *You've got to stay. That was the plan.*

Behind his eyes he saw his daughter Ludmilya sitting in a rubbled building with her melted eyes running down blister-bubbled cheeks. *This is at stake, Valentin Mikhailovich,* another, deeper voice replied, *if anything goes wrong. Do you dare entrust this errand to these adolescents?*

"No," he said. His parched palate would barely produce the word. "I'll go."

Wolf frowned. Then the ends of his wide mouth drew up in a smile. Doubtless it occurred to him that would leave him in complete control of the situation. *Fine. Let him think as he will. I've got to get* out of here.

Mackie blocked the door, Mackie Messer with tears thronging the lower lids of his eyes. Mólniya felt fear spike within him, almost ripped off a glove to shock the boy from his path. But he knew the young ace would never harm him, and he knew why.

He mumbled an apology and shouldered past. He heard a sob as the door shut behind him, and then only his footsteps, pursuing him down the darkened hall.

One of my better performances, Puppetman congratulated himself.

Cake.

Mackie beat his open palms on the door. Mólniya had abandoned him. He hurt, and he couldn't do anything about the hurt. Not even if he made his hands buzz so they'd cut through steel plate.

Wolf was still here. Wolf would protect him . . . but Wolf hadn't. Not really. Wolf had let the others laugh at him—him, Mackie the ace, Mackie the Knife. It had been Mólniya who'd stood up for him the last few weeks. Mólniya who had taken care of him.

Mólniya who was gone. Who wasn't supposed to go. Who was gone.

He turned, weeping, and slid slowly down the door to the floor.

Exhilaration swelled Puppetman. It was all working just as he had planned. His puppets cut the capers he directed and suspected nothing. And here he sat, at breath's distance, drinking their passions like brandy. Danger was no more than added poignance; he was Puppetman, and in control.

And finally the time had come to make an end of Mackie Messer and get himself out of here.

Anneke stood over Mackie, taunting: "Crybaby. And you call yourself a revolutionary?" He pulled himself upright, whimpering like a lost puppy.

Puppetman reached out for a string, and pulled.

And Comrade Ulrich said, "Why didn't you just go with the rest of the jokers, you ugly little queer?"

"Kreuzberg," Neumann said.

Slumped in his chair, Tachyon could barely muster the energy to lift his head and say, "I beg your pardon?" Ten o'clock was ancient history now. So, he feared, was Senator Gregg Hartmann.

Neumann grinned. "We have them. It took the Devil's own time, but we traced the van. They're in Kreuzberg. The Turkish ghetto next to the Wall."

Sara gasped and quickly looked away.

"An antiterrorist team from GSG-9 is standing by," Neumann said.

"Do they know what they're doing?" Tach asked, remembering the afternoon's fiasco.

"They're the best. They're the ones who sprang the Lufthansa 737 the Nur al-Allah·people hijacked to Mogadishu in 1977. Hans-Joachim Richter himself is in charge." Richter was the head of the Ninth Border Guards Group, GSG-9, especially formed to combat terrorism after the Munich massacre of '72. A popular hero in Germany, he was reputed to be an ace, though nobody knew what his powers might be.

Tach stood. "Let's go."

Mackie's left hand cut right down Comrade Ulrich's right side from the base of his neck to the hip. It felt good going through, and the kiss of bone thrilled him like speed.

Ulrich's arm fell off. He stared at Mackie. His lips peeled back away from perfect teeth, which clacked open and closed three times like something in the window of a novelty store.

He looked down at what had been his perfect animal body and shrieked.

Mackie watched in fascination. The scream made his exposed lung work in and out like a vacuum cleaner bag, all grayish purple and moist and veined with blue and red. Then his guts started to spill out the side of him, piling over his fallen rifle, and the blood rushing out of him carried away the strength that kept him standing, and he dropped.

"Holy Mary mother of God," Wilfried said. Puke slopped from a corner of his mouth as he backed away from the wreckage of his comrade. Then he looked past Mackie and yelled, "No—"

Anneke aimed her Kalashnikov at the small of the ace's back. Fear knotted her finger sphincter-tight.

Mackie phased out. The burst splashed Wilfried all over the wall.

Mólniya stood with hands on knees and his back against the side of a stripped Volvo, pulling in deep breaths of diesel-flavored Berlin night. It wasn't a part of town in which strangers cared to spend much time alone. That didn't concern him. What he feared was fear.

What came over me? I've never felt like that in my life.

He'd fled the apartment in a bright haze of panic. No sooner had he stepped outside than it evaporated like water spilled on a sun-heated rock in the Khyber. Now he was trying to collect himself, unsure for the moment whether to carry on with his errand or go back and send a couple of Wolf's vicious cubs.

Papertin was right, he told himself. *I've gotten soft. I—*

From above came a familiar heavy stutter. His blood ran like freon through his veins as he raised his head to see fireflashes dancing on chintz curtains two stories up.

It was all over.

If I'm not found here, he thought, *then maybe—conceivably—the Third World War won't happen tonight.*

He turned and walked away down the street, very fast.

Hartmann lay on his side with the floorboards throbbing against the bruise they'd made on his cheekbone. He'd kicked the chair over as soon as things started happening.

What in hell's name went wrong? he wondered desperately. *The bastard wasn't supposed to talk, just shoot.*

It was '76 all over again. Once again Puppetman in his arrogance had overreached himself. And it may just have cost him his ass.

His nostrils buzzed with the stink of hot lubricant and blood and fresh moist shit. Hartmann could hear the two surviving terrorists stumbling around the room shouting at each other. Ulrich was dying in wheezes a few feet away. He could feel the energy running from him like an ebb tide.

"Where is he? Where'd the fucker go?" Wolf was saying.

"He went through the wall," Anneke said. She was hyperventilating, tearing the words out of the air like pieces of cloth.

"Well, watch for him. Oh, holy Jesus."

Their terror was stark as crucifixion as they stood trying to cover all three interior walls with their guns. Hartmann shared it. The twisted ace had gone berserk.

Someone shrieked and died.

*   *   *

Mackie stood for a moment with his arm elbow-deep in Anneke's back. He took the buzz off, leaving his hand jutting from the woman's sternum like a blade. Blood oozed greasily around the leather sleeve on Mackie's arm where it vanished into her torso. He enjoyed the look of it, and the intimate way what remained of Anneke's heart kept hugging his arm. The fools hadn't even been looking his way when he slipped back through the wall from the bedroom, not that it would have helped them if they had. Three quick steps and that was it for redheaded little Comrade Anneke.

"Fuck you," he said, and giggled.

The heart convulsed one last time around Mackie's arm and was still. Putting a slight buzz on, Mackie pulled his arm free. He swung the corpse around as he did so.

Wolf was standing there with his cheeks quivering. He brought up his gun as Mackie turned. Mackie pushed the corpse at him. He fired. Mackie laughed and phased out.

Wolf emptied the magazine in a shivering ejaculation. Plaster dust filled the room. Anneke's corpse collapsed across the senator. Mackie phased back in.

Wolf screamed pleas, in German, in English. Mackie took the Kalashnikov away from him, pinned him against the door, and taking his time about it, sawed his head in two, right down the middle.

Riding in the armored van with the particolored lights of downtown Berlin washing over her and the faces and weapons of the GSG-9 men who sat facing her, Sara Morgenstern thought, *What's come over me?*

She wasn't sure whether she meant now or before—weeks before, when the affair with Gregg began.

How strange, how very strange. How could I have ever have thought I loved . . . him? I feel nothing for him now.

But that wasn't really true. Where love had left a vacuum an earlier emotion was seeping in. Tainted with a toxic flavor of betrayal.

Andrea, Andrea, what have I done?

She bit her lip. The GSG-9 commando riding across from her saw and grinned, his teeth startling in his blackened face. She was instantly wary, but there was no sex in that smile, only the self-distracting camaraderie of a man facing battle with both pleasure and fear. She made herself smile back and nestled closer against Tachyon, sitting by her side.

He put his arm around her. It wasn't just a brotherly gesture. Even the prospect of danger wasn't enough to drive sex wholly from his mind. Oddly she found she didn't mind the attention. Perhaps it was her acute awareness of how incongruous they were, a pair of small gaudy cockatoos riding among panthers.

And Gregg . . . did she really care what happened to him?

Or do I hope he never leaves that tenement alive?

The screaming had stopped, and the buzz-saw sounds. Hartmann had feared they might go on forever. He gagged on the reek of friction-burned hair and bone.

He felt like something from a medieval fable as painted by Bosch: a glutton presented with the fullest of feasts, only to have it turn to ashes in his mouth. Puppetman had drawn no nourishment from the terrorists' dying. He'd been nearly as terrified as they.

A humming, coming closer: Morität, *The Ballad of Mackie the Knife*. The mad ace was locked in killing frenzy now, stalking toward him with his terrible hand still dripping brains. Hartmann writhed in his bonds. The woman Mackie had impaled was a dead weight across his legs. He was going to die now. Unless . . .

Bile surged up his throat at what he was going to do. He choked it back, reached for a string, and pulled. Pulled *hard*.

The humming stopped. The soft tocking of clogs on wood stopped. Hartmann looked up. Mackie leaned over him with glowing eyes.

He pulled Anneke off Hartmann's legs. He was strong for his size. Or maybe inspired. He pulled Hartmann's chair upright. Hartmann winced, dreading contact, fearing death. Fearing the alternative almost as much.

His own breathing nearly deafened him. He could feel the emotion swelling within Mackie. He steeled himself and stroked it, teased it, made it grow.

Mackie went to his knees before the chair. He unfastened the fly of Hartmann's trousers, slipped fingers inside, tugged the senator's cock out into the humid air and fastened his lips around the glans. He began to pump his head up and down, slowly at first, then gaining speed. His tongue went caduceus round and round.

Hartmann moaned. He couldn't let himself enjoy this.

If you don't it's never going to end, Puppetman taunted.

What are you doing to me?

Saving you. And securing the best puppet of all.

But he's so powerful—so . . . unpredictable. Involuntary pleasure was breaking his thoughts into kaleidiscope fragments.

But I've got him now. Because he wants *to be my puppet. He loves you, the way that neurasthenic bitch Sara never could.*

God, God, am I still a man?

You're alive. And you're going to smuggle this creature back to New York. And anyone who stands in our way from now on will die.

—Now relax and enjoy it.

Puppetman took over. As Mackie sucked his cock, he sucked the boy's emotions with his mind. Hot-wet and salty, they gushed into him.

Hartmann's head went back. Involuntarily he cried out.

He came as he had not come since Succubus died.

Senator Gregg Hartmann pushed through a door from which the glass had long since been broken. He leaned against the cold metal frame and stared into a street that was empty except for gutted cars and weeds pushing up through cracks in the pavement.

White light drilled him from the rooftop opposite, fierce as a laser. He raised his head, blinking.

"My God," a German voice yelled, "it's the senator."

The street filled up with cars and whirling lights and noise. It didn't seem to take any time at all. Hartmann saw magenta highlights struck like sparks off Tachyon's hair, and Carnifex in his comic-book outfit, and from doorways and behind the automotive corpses appeared men totally encased in black, trotting warily forward with stubby machine pistols held ready.

Past them all he saw Sara, dressed in a white coat that was the defiant antithesis of camouflage.

"I . . . got away," he said, voice creaking like an unused door. "It's over. They—they killed each other."

Television spotlights spilled over him, hot and white as milk fresh from the breast. His gaze caught Sara's. He smiled. But her eyes drilled into his like iron rods.

Cold and hard. *She's slipped away!* he thought. With the thought came pain.

But Puppetman wasn't buying pain. Not tonight. He drove himself into her through the eyes.

And she came running for him, arms spread, her mouth a red hole through which love-words poured. And Hartmann felt his puppet wrap her arms around his neck and makeup-streaked tears gush onto his collar, and he hated that part of him that had saved his life.

And down away where light never was, Puppetman smiled.

MIRRORS OF THE SOUL

Melinda M. Snodgrass

April in Paris. The chestnut tress resplendent in their pink and white finery. The blossoms drifting like fragrant snow about the feet of the statues in the Tuileries Garden, and floating like colorful foam atop the muddy waters of the Seine.

April in Paris. The song bubbling incongruously through his head as he stood before a simple gravestone in the Cimetière Montmartre. So hideously inappropriate. He banished it only to have it return with greater intensity.

Irritably Tachyon hunched one shoulder, took a tighter grip on the simple bouquet of violets and lily of the valley. The crisp green florist's paper crackled loudly in the after-noon air. Away to his left he could hear the urgent bleat of horns as the bumper-to-bumper traffic crawled up the Rue Norvins toward Sacré-Coeur. With its gleaming white walls, cupolas, and dome the cathedral floated like an Arabian nights dream over this city of light and dreams.

The last time I saw Paris.

Earl, his face holding all the expression of an ebony statue. Lena, flushed, impassioned. "You must go!" Looking to Earl for help and comfort. The quiet; "it would probably be best." The path of least resistance. So strange from this of all men.

Tachyon knelt, brushed away the petals that littered the stone slab.

Earl Sanderson Jr.
"Noir Aigle"
1919–1974

You lived too long, my friend. Or so it was said. Those busy, noisy activists could have used you better if you'd had

the grace to die in 1950. No—even better—while liberating
Argentina or freeing Spain or saving Gandhi.

Laid the bouquet on the grave. A sudden breeze set the
delicate white bells of the lilies to trembling. Like a young
girl's lashes just before she was kissed. Or like Blythe's lashes
just before she wept.

The last time I saw Paris.

A cold, bleak December, and a park in Neuilly.

Blythe van Renssaeler, aka Brain Trust, died yesterday. . . .

Gracelessly he surged to his feet, dusted the knees of his
pants with a handkerchief. Gave his nose a quick, emphatic
blow. That was the trouble with the past. It never stayed
buried.

Straddling the slab was a large elaborate wreath. Roses
and gladiolas and yards of ribbon. A wreath for a dead hero.
A travesty. A small foot came up, sent the wreath tumbling.
Contemptuously Tachyon walked over it, grinding the fragile
petals beneath his heel.

*One cannot propitiate the ancestors, Jack. Their ghosts
will follow.*

His certainly were.

On the Rue Etex he hailed a cab, fished for the note,
read off the name of the Left Bank café in rusty French.
Settled back to watch the unlit neon signs flash past. *XXX, Le
Filles!* *"Les Sexy."* Strange to think of all this smut at the foot
of a hill whose name translated as the Mountain of Martyrs.
Saints had died on Montmartre. The Society of Jesus had
been founded on the hill in 1534.

They proceeded in noisy and profane lurches. Bursts of
heart-stopping speed followed by neck-wrenching stops. A
blare of horns, and an exchange of imaginative insults. They
shot through the Place Vendome past the Ritz where the
delegation was housed. Tachyon hunkered deeper into his
seat though it was unlikely he would be spotted. He was so
sick of them all. Sara, quiet, sleek, and secretive as a mon-
goose. She had changed since Syria, but refused to confide.
Peregrine flaunting her pregnancy, refusing to accept that she
might not beat the odds. Mistral, young and beautiful. She
had been tactful and understanding and kept his shameful
secret. Fantasy, sly and amused. She had not. Hot blood
washed his face. His humiliating condition was now public to
be sniggered at and discussed in tones ranging from the

sympathetic to the amused. His hand closed tightly on the note. There would be at least one woman he could face without embarrassment. One of his ghosts, but more welcome than the living right now.

She had chosen a café on the Boulevard Saint-Michel in the heart of the Latin Quarter. The area had always despised the bourgeoisie. Tachyon wondered if Danelle still did. Or had the years dampened her revolutionary ardor? One could only hope it had not dampened her other ardors. Then he remembered, and shrunk down once more.

Well, if he could no longer taste passion, he could at least remember it.

She had been nineteen when they'd met in August of 1950. A university student majoring in political philosophy, sex, and revolution. Danelle had been eager to comfort the shattered victim of a capitalist witch-hunt: the new darling of the French intellectual left. She took pride in his sufferings. As if the mystique of his martyrdom could rub off with bodily contact.

She had used him. But by the Ideal he had used her. As a shroud, a buffer against pain and memory. Drowned himself in cunt and wine. Nursing a bottle in Lena Goldoni's Champs-Élysées penthouse listening to the impassioned rhetoric of revolution. Caring far less for the rhetoric than the passion. Red-tipped nails meeting a slash of red for a mouth as Dani puffed inexpertly at larynx-stripping Gauloises. Black hair as smooth as an ebony helmet over her small head. Lush bosoms straining at a too tight sweater, and short skirts that occasionally gave him tantalizing glimpses of pale inner thigh.

God, how they had screwed! Had there ever been any emotion past mutual using? Yes, perhaps, for she had been one of the last to condemn and reject him. She had even seen him off on that frigid January day. That was when he'd still had luggage and a semblance of dignity. There on the platform of the Montparnasse railway station, she had pressed money and a bottle of cognac onto him. He hadn't refused. The cognac had been too welcome, and the money meant that another bottle would follow.

In 1953 he had called Dani when another fruitless visa battle with the German authorities had sent him careening back into France. Called her hoping for one more bottle of cognac, one more handout, one more round of desperate fornication. But a man had answered, and in the background he had heard a child crying, and when she had finally come to the phone, the message was clear. *Get fucked, Tachyon.* Tittering, he had suggested that was why he'd called. The unpleasant buzz of a disconnected phone.

Later in that cold park in Neuilly he'd read of Blythe's death, and nothing had seemed to matter anymore.

And yet when the delegation arrived in Paris, Dani had reached out. A note in his box at the Ritz. A meeting on the Left Bank as the silver-gray Parisian sky was turning to rose, and the Eiffel Tower became a web of diamond light. So maybe she had cared. And maybe, to his shame, he hadn't.

Dôme was a typical working-class Parisian café. Tiny tables squeezed onto the sidewalk, gay, blue, and white umbrellas, harried, frowning waiters in none-too-clean white smocks. The smell of coffee and *grillade*. Tach surveyed the handful of patrons. It was early yet for Paris. He hoped she hadn't chosen to sit inside. All that smoke. His glance kept flicking across a thickset figure in a rusty black coat. There was a watchful intensity about the raddled face, and—

Dear God, could it . . .NO!

"*Bon soir*, Tachyon."

"Danelle," he managed faintly, and groped for the back of a chair.

She smiled an enigmatic smile, sucked down some coffee, ground out a cigarette in the dirty ashtray, lit another, leaned back in a horrible parody of her old sexy manner, and eyed him through the rising smoke. "You haven't changed."

His mouth worked, and she laughed sadly. "The platitude a little hard to force out? Of course *I've* changed—it's been thirty-six years."

Thirty-six years. Blythe would be seventy-five.

Intellectually he had accepted the reality of their pitifully short lifespans. But it had not come home to him before. Blythe had died. Braun remained unchanged. David was lost, so like Blythe remained a memory of youth and charm. And of his new friends, Tommy, Angelface, and Hiram were just entering that uncomfortable stage of middle age. Mark was the merest child. Yet forty-one years ago it had been Mark's father who had impounded Tach's ship. *And Mark hadn't even been born yet!*

Soon (or at least as his people measured time), he would be forced to watch them pass from youth into inevitable decay and thence into death. The chair was a welcome support as his rump hit the cold wrought-iron.

"Danelle," he said again.

"A kiss, Tachy, for old times' sake?"

Heavy yellowish pouches hung beneath faded eyes. Gray brittle hair thrust into a careless bun, the deep gouges beside her mouth into which the scarlet lipstick had bled like a wound. She leaned in close, hitting him with a wave of foul breath. Strong tobacco, cheap wine, coffee, and rotting teeth combining in a stomach-twisting effluvium.

He recoiled, and this time when the laughter came it seemed forced. As if she hadn't expected this reaction and was covering the hurt. The harsh laugh ended in a long coughing jag that brought him out of his chair and to her side. Irritably she shrugged off his soothing hand.

"Emphysema. And don't you start, *le petit docteur*. I'm too damn old to give up my cigarettes, and too damn poor to get medical attention when the time comes to die. So I smoke faster hoping I'll die faster, and then it won't cost so much at the end."

"Danelle—"

"*Bon Dieu*, Tachyon! You are dull. No kiss for old times' sake, and apparently no conversation either. Though as I recall, you weren't much of a talker all those years ago."

"I was finding all the communication I needed in the bottom of a cognac bottle."

"It doesn't seem to have inconvenienced you any. Behold! A great man."

She saw the world-renowned figure, a slim figure dressed in brocade and lace, but he, gazing back at the reflections of a thousand memories, saw a cavalcade of lost years. Cheap rooms stinking of sweat, vomit, urine, and despair. Groaning in an alley in Hamburg, beaten almost to death. Accepting a devil's pact with a gently smiling man, and for what? Another bottle. Waking hallucinations in a cell in the Tombs.

"What are you doing, Danelle?"

"I'm a maid at the Hotel Intercontinental." She seemed to sense his thought. "Yes, an unglamorous end to all that revolutionary fervor. The revolution never came, Tachy."

"No."

"Which doesn't leave you brokenhearted."

"No. I never accepted your—all of your—versions of utopia."

"But you stayed with us. Until finally we threw you out."

"Yes, I needed you, and I used you."

"My God, such a soul-deep confession? At meetings like these it's supposed to be all '*bonjour*' and '*Comment allez-vous*,' and 'My, you haven't changed.' But we've already done that, haven't we?" The bitter mocking tone added a razor's edge to the words.

"What do you want, Danelle? Why did you ask to see me?"

"Because I knew it would bother you." The butt of the Gauloise followed its predecessor into a squashed and ashy death. "No, that's not true. I saw your little motorcade pull in. All flags and limousines. It made me think of other years and other banners. I suppose I wanted to remember, and alas as one grows older, the memories of youth become fainter, less real."

"I unfortunately do not share that kindly blurring. My kind do not forget."

"Poor little prince." She coughed again, a wet sound.

Tachyon reached into his breast pocket, pulled out his wallet, stripped off bills.

"What's that for?"

"The money you gave me and the cognac and thirty-six years interest."

She flinched away, eyes bright with unshed tears. "I didn't call you for charity or pity."

"No, you called to rip at me, hurt me."

She looked away. "No, I called you so I could remember another time."

"They weren't very good times."

"For you maybe. I loved them. I was happy. And don't flatter yourself. You weren't the reason."

"I know. Revolution was your first and final love. I find it hard to accept that you've given it up."

"Who says I have?"

"But you said . . . I thought . . ."

"Even the old can pray for change, perhaps even more fervently than the young. By the way"—she drained the last of her coffee with a noisy slurp—"why wouldn't you help us?"

"I couldn't."

"Ah, of course. The little prince, the dedicated royalist. You never cared about the people."

"Not as you use that phrase. You reduce them to slogans.

I was bred to lead and to protect and to care for them as individuals. Ours is a better way."

"You're a parasite!" And in her face he saw a fleeting shadow of the girl she had been.

An almost rueful smile touched his lips. "No, an aristocrat, which you would probably argue is synonymous." His long forefinger played among the little pile of francs. "Despite what you think, it really wasn't my aristocratic sensibilities that kept me from using my power on your behalf. What you were doing was harmless enough—unlike this new breed who think nothing of killing a man merely for being successful."

She hunched a shoulder. "Please, get to the point."

"I'd lost my powers."

"What? You never told us."

"I was afraid of losing my mystique if I had."

"I don't believe you."

"It's true. Because of Jack's cowardice." His face darkened. "The HUAC returned Blythe to the stand. They were demanding the names of all known aces, and because she had my mind, she knew. She was about to betray them, so I used my power to stop her and in so doing broke her mind and left the woman I loved a raving maniac." He raised trembling fingertips to his damp forehead. The retelling in this of all cities infused it with new power, new pain.

"It took years for me to overcome my guilt, and it was the Turtle who showed me how. I destroyed one woman, but saved another. Does that balance the scales?" He was speaking more to himself than to her.

But she was not interested in his ancient pain; her own memories were too intense. "Lena was so angry. She called you a disgusting user, taking and taking and giving nothing in return. Everyone wanted you out because you had so spoiled our beautiful plan."

"Yes, and not *one* person took my side! Not even Earl." His expression softened, as he looked past the ruin of age, to the beautiful girl he remembered. "No, that's not true. You defended me."

"Yes," she admitted gruffly. "Little good that it did. It took me years to regain the respect of my comrades." She stared blindly down at the tabletop.

Tachyon glanced at the watch in his boot heel, rose. "Dani, I must go. The delegation is due at Versailles by eight, and I must change. It's been..." He tried again. "I'm so glad that you contacted me." The words seemed stilted and insincere even to his own ears.

Her face crumpled, then stiffened into bitter lines. "That's it? Forty minutes and *au revoir,* you wouldn't even drink with me?"

"I'm sorry, Dani. My schedule—"

"Ah, yes, the great man." The pile of bills still lay between them on the table. "Well, I'll take these as an example of your noblesse oblige."

She lifted up a shapeless bag and fished out a billfold. Scooped up the francs and jammed them into the battered wallet. Then paused and stared at one photo. A cruel little smile played about her wrinkled lips.

"No, better yet. I'll give you value for your money." Gnarled, arthritic fingers pulled free the picture and tossed it onto the table.

It was a breathtaking still of a young woman. A river of red hair half masking the narrow, shadowed face. A mischievous, knowing look in the uptilted eyes. A delicate forefinger pressed against a full lower lip as if shushing the onlooker.

"Who is she?" Tach asked, but with a breath-stopping certainty that he knew the answer.

"My daughter." Their eyes locked. Dani's smile broadened. "And yours."

"Mine." The word emerged as a wondering, joyful sigh.

Suddenly all the weariness and anguish of the trip sloughed away. He had witnessed horrors. Jokers stoned to death in the slums of Rio. Genocide in Ethiopia. Oppression in South Africa. Starvation and disease everywhere. It had left him feeling hopeless and defeated. But if *she* walked this planet, then it could be borne. Even the anguish over his impotence faded. With the loss of his virility he had lost a major part of himself. Now it had been returned to him.

"Oh, Dani, Dani!" He reached across and gripped her hand. "Our daughter. What is her name?"

"Gisele."

"I must see her. Where is she?"

"Rotting. She's dead."

The words seemed to shatter in the air, sending ice fragments deep into his soul. A cry of anguish was torn from him, and he wept, tears dropping through his fingers.

Danelle walked away.

*   *   *

Versailles, the greatest tribute to the divine right of kings ever constructed. Tachyon, heels tapping on the parquet floor, paused and surveyed the scene through the distorting crystal of his champagne glass. For an instant he might have been home, and the longing that gripped him was almost physical in its intensity.

There is indeed no beauty to this world. I wish I could leave it forever.

No, not true, he amended as his gaze fell upon the faces of his friends. *There is much here still to love.*

One of Hartmann's polished aides was at his shoulder. Was this the one fortunate enough to have survived the kidnapping in Germany, or had he been flown in specially to serve as cannon fodder for this line-withering tour? Well, perhaps the increased security would keep this young man alive until they could reach home.

"Doctor, Monsieur de Valmy would like to meet you."

The young man forced a path for Tachyon while the alien studied France's most popular presidential candidate since de Gaulle. Franchot de Valmy, said by many to be the next president of the Republic. A tall, slim figure moving easily through the crowd. His rich chestnut hair was streaked with a single two-inch bar of white. Very striking. More striking, though far less evident, was the fact he was a wild card. An ace. In a country gone mad for aces.

Hartmann and de Valmy were shaking hands. It was an outstanding display of political soft soap. Two eager hunters using one another's power and popularity to catapult them into the highest offices in their lands.

"Sir, Dr. Tachyon."

De Valmy turned the full force of his compelling green-eyed gaze onto the Takisian. Tachyon, raised in a culture that put a high premium on charm and charisma, found that this man possessed both to an almost Takisian magnitude. He wondered if that was his wild card gift.

"Doctor, I am honored." He spoke in English.

Tach placed a small hand over his breast and replied in French, "The honor is entirely mine."

"I will be interested to hear your comments on our scientists' work on the wild card virus."

"Well, I have only just arrived." He fingered his lapel, raised his eyes, and pinned de Valmy with a sharp glance.

"And will I be reporting to *all* the candidates in the race? Will they also wish to hear my comments?"

Senator Hartmann took a small step forward, but de Valmy was laughing. "You are very astute. Yes, I am—how do you Americans say—counting my chickens."

"With reason," said Hartmann with a smile. "You've been groomed by the President as his heir apparent."

"Certainly an advantage," said Tachyon. "But your status as an ace hasn't hurt."

"No."

"I would be curious to know your power."

De Valmy covered his eyes. "Oh, Monsieur Tachyon, I'm embarrassed to speak of it. It's such a contemptible little power. Mere parlor tricks."

"You are very modest, sir."

Hartmann's aide glared, and Tach stared blandly back, though he regretted the momentary flash of sarcasm. It was ill bred of him to take out his weariness and unhappiness on others.

"I am not above using the advantage granted to me, Doctor, but I hope that it will be my policies and leadership that will give me the presidency."

Tachyon gave a small laugh and caught Gregg Hartmann's eye. "It is ironic, is it not, that in this country the wild card bestows a cachet to help a man into high office, while in our country that same information would defeat him."

The senator pulled a face. "Leo Barnett."

"I beg you pardon?" asked de Valmy in some confusion.

"A fundamentalist preacher who's gathering quite a following. He'd restore all the old wild card laws."

"Oh, worse than that, Senator. I think he would place them in detention camps and force mass sterilizations."

"Well, this is an unpleasant subject. But on another unpleasant subject I'd like a chance to talk to you, Franchot, about your feelings on the phaseout of medium-range missiles in Europe. Not that I have any standing with the current administration, but my colleagues in the Senate..." He linked arms with de Valmy and they drifted away, their various aides trailing several paces behind like hopeful pilot fish.

Tach gulped down champagne. The chandeliers glittered in the long line of mirrors, multiplying them a hundredfold and throwing back bright light like shards of glass into his aching head. He took another swallow of champagne, though he knew the alcohol was partly to blame for his present discomfort. That and the drilling hum of hundreds of voices, the busy scrape of bows on strings, and outside, the watching presence of an adoring public. Sensitive telepath that he was, it beat on him like an urgent, hungry sea.

As the motorcade had driven up the long chestnut-lined boulevard, they had passed hundreds of waving people all eagerly craning for a glimpse of the *les ases fantastiques*. It was a welcome relief after such hatred and fear in other countries. Still, he was glad that only one country remained, and then he would be home. Not that anything waited for him there but more problems.

In Manhattan, James Spector was on the streets. Death incarnate stalking free. Another monster created by my meddling. Once home I must deal with this. Trace him. Find him. Stop him. I was so stupid to abandon him in favor of pursuing Roulette.

And what of Roulette? Where can she be? Did I do wrong to release her? I am undoubtedly a fool where women are concerned.

"Tachyon." Peregrine's gay call floated on the strains of Mozart and pulled him from his introspective fog. "You've got to see this."

He pinned a smile firmly in place and kept his eyes strictly off the mound of her belly thrust aggressively front and center. Mordecai Jones, the Harlem auto repairman, looking uncomfortable in his tuxedo, nervously eyed a tall gold-and-crystal lamp as if expecting it to attack. The long march of mirrors brought back thoughts of the Funhouse, and Des, the fingers at the end of his elephant's trunk twitching slightly, heightened the memory. *The past.* It seemed to be hanging like a dead weight from his shoulders.

The knot of friends and fellow travelers parted, and a hunched, twisted figure was revealed. The joker lurched around and smiled up at Tach. The face was a handsome one. Noble, a little tired, lines about the eyes and mouth denoting past suffering, a kindly face—*his, in fact.* There was a shout of laughter from the group as Tach gaped down into his own features.

There was a shifting like clay being mashed or a sponge being squeezed, and the joker faced him with his own

features in place. A big square head, humorous brown eyes, a
mop of gray hair, set atop that tiny, twisted body.

"Forgive me, the opportunity was too enticing to pass
up," chuckled the joker.

"And your expression the best of all, Tachy," put in
Chrysalis.

"You can laugh, you're safe. He can't do you," harrumphed
Des.

"Tach, this is Claude Bonnell, *Le Miroir*. He's got this
great act at the Lido."

"Poking fun at the politicos," rumbled Mordecai.

"He does this hysterical skit with Ronald and Nancy
Reagan," giggled Peregrine.

Jack Braun, drawn by the laughing group, hovered at its
outskirts. His eyes met Tachyon's, and the alien looked
through him. Jack shifted until they were at opposite sides of
the circle.

"Claude's been trying to explain to us this alphabet soup
that's French politics," said Digger. "All about how de Valmy
has welded an impressive coalition of the RPR, the CDS, the
JJSS, the PCF—"

"No, no, Mr. Downs, you must not include my party
among the ranks of those who support Franchot de Valmy.
We communists have better taste, and our own candidate."

"Who won't win," ejected Braun, frowning down at the
tiny joker.

The features blurred, and Earl Sanderson Jr. said softly,
"There were some who supported the goals of world revolution."

Jack, face gone sickly white, staggered back. There was a
sharp *crack* as his glass shattered in his hands, and a flare of
gold as his biological force field came to life to protect him.
There was an uncomfortable silence after the big ace had left,
then Tachyon said coolly, "Thank you."

"My pleasure."

"You are here as a wild card representative?"

"Partly, but I also have an official capacity. I am a
member of the party congress."

"You are a big wheel with the commies," whistled Digger
with his usual lack of tact.

"Yes."

"How did you pick up Earl? Or have you just made it a
point to study those of us on the tour?" asked Chrysalis.

"I have a very low-level telepathy. I can pick up the faces of those who have deeply affected a person."

Hartmann's aide was once again at his side. "Doctor, Dr. Corvisart has arrived and wants to meet you."

Tachyon made a face. "Duty calls, so pleasure must be forgone. Gentlemen, ladies." He bowed and walked away.

An hour later Tach was standing by the small chamber orchestra, allowing the soothing strains of Mendelssohn's Trout quintet to work its magic. His feet were beginning to hurt, and he realized that forty years on Earth had robbed him of his ability to stand for hours. Recalling long-past deportment lessons, he tucked in his hips, pulled back his shoulders, and lifted his chin. The relief was immediate, but he decided that another glass would also help.

Flagging down a waiter, he reached for the champagne. Then staggered, and fell heavily against the man as a blinding, directionless mind assault struck his shields.

Mind control!

The source?

Outside . . . somewhere.

The focus?

He was dimly aware of crashing glasses as he slumped against his startled support. Forced up lids that seemed infinitely heavy. So distorting was the effect of his own psi search, and the screaming power of the mind control, that reality took on a strange shifting quality. The reception guests in their bright finery faded to gray. He could "see" the mind probe like a brilliant line of light. Becoming diffuse at its source, impossible to pinpoint. But haloing:

A man.

Uniform.

One of the security captains.

Attaché case.

BOMB!

He reached out with his mind and seized the officer. For a moment the man writhed and danced like a moth in a flame as his controller and Tach fought for supremacy. The strain was too much for his human mind, and consciousness left him like a candle being snuffed. The major went down spraddle-legged on the polished wood floor. Tach found his fingers closing about the edges of the black leather case, though he couldn't remember moving.

Controller knows he's lost focus. Time detonated or command detonated? No time to ponder on it.

The solution, when it came, almost wasn't conscious. He reached out, gripped the mind. Jack Braun stiffened, dropped his drink, and went running for the long windows overlooking the front garden and fountains. People flew like ninepins as the big ace came barreling through them. Tachyon cocked back his arm, prayed to the ancestors for aim and strength, and threw.

Jack, like a hero in a forties football film, leapt, plucked the spinning case from the air, tucked it tight into his chest, and launched himself out the window. Glass haloed his gold-glowing body. A second later, and a tremendous explosion blew out the rest of the windows lining the Hall of Mirrors. Women screamed as razor-edged glass shards bit deep into unprotected skin. Glass and gravel from the yard pattered like hysterical raindrops onto the wood floor.

People rushed to the window to check on Braun.

Tachyon turned his back on the windows and knelt beside the stentoriously breathing major. One should have priorities.

"Let's go over it again."

Tach eased his aching buttocks on the hard plastic chair, shifted until he could take a surreptitious glance at his watch. *12:10 A.M.* Police were definitely the same the world over. Instead of being grateful for his having averted a tragedy, they were treating him as if he were the criminal. And Jack Braun had been spared all this because the authorities had insisted on carting him off to the hospital. Of course he wasn't hurt, that was why Tachyon had selected him. No doubt by morning the papers would be filled with praise for the brave American ace, thought Tach sourly. *Never noticing my contributions.*

"*Monsieur?*" prodded Jean Baptiste Rochambeau of the French Sûreté.

"To what purpose? I've *told* you. I sensed a powerful, natural mind control at work. Because of the user's lack of training and control, I was unable to pinpoint the source. I could, however, pinpoint its victim. When I fought for control, I read through to the controller's mind, read the presence of the bomb, mind-controlled Braun, tossed him the bomb, he went out the window, the bomb exploded, with him no worse for the wear except perhaps wearing some of the topiary."

"There is no topiary beyond the windows of the Hall of Mirrors," sniffed Rochambeau's assistant in his nasal, high-pitched voice.

Tach swung around in the chair. "It was a little joke," he explained gently.

"Dr. Tachyon. We are not doubting your story. It's just that it's impossible. No such powerful . . . mentat?"—he looked to Tachyon for confirmation—"exists in France. As Dr. Corvisart has explained, we have every carrier, both latent and expressed, on file."

"Then one has slipped past you."

Corvisart, an arrogant gray-haired man with fat cheeks like a chipmunk's and a tiny pursed bud of a mouth, gave a stubborn headshake.

"Every infant is tested and registered at birth. Every immigrant is tested at the border. Every tourist must have the test before they can receive a visa. The only explanation is the one I have suspected for several years. The virus has mutated."

"That is patent and utter nonsense! With all due respect, Doctor, *I* am the foremost authority on the wild card virus on this or any other world."

Perhaps something of an exaggeration that, but surely it could be forgiven. He had been enduring fools with such patience for so many hours.

Corvisart was quivering with outrage. "Our research has been acknowledged as the best in the world."

"Ah, but *I* don't publish." Tachyon was on his feet. "*I* don't have to." A single-step advance. "*I* have a certain advantage." Another. "*I* helped develop the withering thing!" he bellowed down into the Frenchman's face.

Corvisart held stubbornly firm. "You are wrong. The mentat exists, he is not on file, ergo the virus has mutated."

"I want to see your notes, duplicate the research, look over these vaunted files." This he addressed to Rochambeau. He might have the soul of a policeman, but at least he wasn't an idiot.

The Sûreté officer cocked an eyebrow. "You have any objections, Dr. Corvisart?"

"I suppose not."

"You want to start now?"

"Why not? The night's ruined anyway."

*   *   *

They set him up in Corvisart's office with an impressive computer at his disposal, bulging hard-copy files of research, a foot-high stack of disks, and a cup of strong coffee that Tach liberally laced with brandy from his hip flask.

The research was good, but it was geared toward proving Corvisart's pet premise. The hope of fame in the form of a mutated form—Wild Cardus Corvisartus?—was subtly coloring the Frenchman's interpretations of the data he was collecting. The virus was *not* mutating.

Thank the gods and ancestors, Tach sent up as a heartfelt prayer.

He was scrolling idly through the wild card registry when an anomaly, something not quite right, caught his attention. It was five in the morning, hardly the time to scroll back several years to check if he'd seen what he'd thought he'd seen, but upbringing and his own curious nature could not be denied. After several minutes of fervid key tapping he had the screen divided and both documents called up side by side. He fell back in the chair, rumpling his already tumbled curls with nervous fingers.

"Well, I'll be damned," he said aloud to the silent room.

The door opened, and the adenoidal sergeant thrust in his head. "Monsieur? You require something?"

"No, nothing."

His hand shot out, and he erased the damning documents. What he discovered was for him alone. For it was political dynamite. It would create havoc with an election, cost a man the presidency, and shake the foundations of trust of the electorate should it get out.

Tach pressed his hands into the small of his back, stretched until vertebrae popped, and shook his head like a weary pony. "Sergeant, I am very much afraid that I have found nothing that is of any help. And I'm too tired to go on. May I please be returned to the hotel?"

But his bed at the Ritz had held no comfort or rest, so here he was leaning over the bridge railing on the Pont de la Concorde watching coal barges slip by, and snuffling eagerly at the smell of baking bread, which seemed to have permeated the city. Every part of his small body seemed to be suffering from some discomfort. His eyes felt like two burned holes in a blanket, his back still ached from that impossible chair, and his stomach was demanding to be fed. But worst of all was what he had dubbed his mental indigestion. He had seen or heard something of significance. And until he hit upon it, his brain was going to continue to seethe like jelly boiling on a stove.

"Sometimes," he told his mind severely, "I feel as if you have a mind of your own."

He began walking through the Place de la Concorde, where Marie Antoinette had lost her head, the spot now marked by a venerable Egyptian obelisk. There were plenty of restaurants to choose from: the Hotel de Crillon, the Hotel Intercontinental, just two blocks from the square, where Dani was no doubt hard at work, and beyond it the Ritz. He hadn't seen any of his companions since the dramatic events of the previous night. His entrance would be met with exclamations, congratulations... He decided to miss the whole mess.

He was still wearing his reception finery. Pale lavender and rose, and a foam of lace. He frowned when a taxi driver gaped and drove over a curb and almost into one of the central fountains. Embarrassed, Tachyon darted through the richly decorated iron railing and into the Tuileries Gardens. On either side loomed the Jeu de Paume and the Orangerie, ahead the neat rows of chestnut trees, fountains, and a riot of statues.

Tach dropped wearily onto the edge of a basin. The fountain squirted into life and sent a fine spray of mist across his face. For a moment he sat with eyes closed, savoring the cool touch of the water. Retreating to a nearby bench, he pulled out the picture of Gisele and again studied those delicate features. Why was it that whenever he came to Paris, he found only death?

And suddenly the piece fell into place. The puzzle lay complete before him. With a cry of joy he leapt to his feet and broke into a frantic run. The high heels of his formal pumps slipped on the gravel path. Cursing, he hopped along, pulling them off. Then with a shoe in each hand he flew up the stairs and onto the Rue de Rivoli. Horns blared, tires squealed, drivers shrieked. He ran on heedless of it all. Pulled up gasping before the glass and marble entrance to the Hotel Intercontinental. Met the bemused eyes of the doorman, slipped his feet into his shoes, straightened his coat, patted at his tumbled hair, trod casually into the quiet lobby.

"Bonjour."

The desk clerk's eyes widened in dawning wonder as he recognized the extravagant figure before him. He was a handsome man in his mid-thirties with sleek seal-brown hair and deep blue eyes.

"You have a woman working here. Danelle Moncey. It is vital that I speak with her."

"Moncey? No, Monsieur Tachyon. There is no one by—"

"Damn! She married. I forgot that. She's a maid, mid-fifties, black eyes, gray hair." His heart was thundering, setting up an answering pounding in his temples. The young man looked nervously down at Tachyon's hands, which had closed urgently about his lapels, pulling him half over the counter. Releasing the clerk, Tachyon rubbed his fingertips. "Forgive me. As you can see, this is very important . . . very important to me."

"I'm sorry, but there is no Danelle working here."

"She's a Communist," Tach added in desperation.

The man shook his head, but the pert blond behind the exchange counter suddenly said, "Ah, no, François. You know, Danelle."

"Then she is here?"

"Oh, *mais oui*. She is on the third floor—"

"Will you get her for me?" Tachyon gave the girl his best come-hither smile.

"Monsieur, she is working," protested the desk clerk.

"I only require a moment of her time."

"Monsieur, I cannot have a cleaning woman in the lobby of the Intercontinental." It was almost a wail.

"Blood's end! Then I'll go to her."

Danelle was bundling sheets into a hamper. Gasped when she saw him, tried to bull past him using her cleaning cart as a battering ram. He danced aside and caught her by the wrist.

"We must talk." He was grinning like a fool.

"I'm working."

"Take the day off."

"I'll lose my job."

"You're not going to need this job any longer."

"Oh, why not?"

A man and his wife stepped out of their room and stared curiously at the couple.

"This won't do."

She eyed him, checked her cheap wristwatch. "It's almost my break. I'll meet you at the Café Morens just down from the hotel on the Rue du Juillet. Buy me some cigarettes and my usual."

"Which is?"

"They'll know. I always take my break there."

He took her face between his hands and kissed her. Smiled at her confused expression.

"What has happened with you?"

"I'll tell you at the café."

As he hurried back through the lobby he saw the desk clerk just hanging up the phone in one of the public booths. The young blond woman waved and called, "Did you find her?"

"Oh, yes. Thank you very much."

Tachyon fidgeted at one of the tiny tables that had been squeezed out front of the café. The street was so narrow that the parked cars had two wheels cocked up on the sidewalks.

Dani arrived and lit a Gauloise. "So what is this all about?"

"You lied to me." He shook a finger coyly under her nose. "Our daughter is not dead. At Versailles . . . that was not a wild card, it was my blood kin. I don't blame you for wanting to hurt me, but let me make it up to you. I'll get you both back to America."

A small car was gunning down the street. As it swept past, the chatter of automatic weapon fire echoed off the gray stone buildings. Danelle jerked in the chair. Tachyon caught her, flung them both down behind one of the parked cars. A white-hot poker burned through his thigh, and his elbow hit the sidewalk with a jarring crack. He lay frozen, cheek pressed to the pavement, something warm running over his hand. His leg had gone numb.

Danelle's breath was rattling in her throat. Tachyon took her mind. Gisele appeared. Reflected a million times over in a million different memories. *Gisele*. A brilliant firefly presence.

Desperately he reached after her, but she was receding, a lost and elusive magic among the darkening pathways of her dying mother's mind.

Danelle died.

Gisele died.

But had left a part of herself. A son. Tach clung to her, violating every rule of advanced mentatics by holding to a dying mind. Panic seized him, and he fled back from that terrifying boundary.

In the physical world the air was filled with the undulating wail of sirens. *Oh, ancestors, what to do?* Be found here with a murdered hotel maid? Ludicrous. There would be questions to be answered. They would learn of his grandchild. And if wild cards were a national treasure, how much more a treasure was a part-blood Takisian?

The pain was beginning. Tachyon experimentally moved the leg and found that the bullet had missed the bone. The effort had popped sweat and filled the back of his throat with bile. How could he possibly reach the Ritz? He tightened his jaw. Because he was a prince of the house Ilkazam. *It's only two blocks*, he thought encouragingly.

He laid Danelle gently aside, folded her hands on her bosom, kissed her forehead. *Mother of my child*. Later he would mourn her properly. But first came vengeance.

The bullet had passed cleanly through the fleshy part of his thigh. There wasn't much blood. Yet. As he walked it began to pump. Camouflage, something to hide the wound just long enough to get past the desk and up to his room. He checked in parked cars. A folded newspaper. And the window was open. Not perfect, but good enough. Now he just had to find enough control not to limp those few steps from the front door to the elevator.

Piece of cake, as Mark would say. Training was everything. And blood. Blood would always tell.

He had taken a stab at sleeping, but it had been useless. Finally at six Jack Braun kicked aside the entangling bed clothes, stripped off sweat-soaked pajamas, dressed, and went in search of food.

Five months of hunched shoulders and nervous backward glances. Five months in which *he* had *never* spoken. Refused to grant him even eye contact. Had the hope of rehabilitation really been worth this amount of hell?

The Swarm invasion was to blame. It had pulled him back, out of the womb of real estate and California evenings and poolside sex. Here was a real crisis. No ace, no matter how tainted, would be unwelcome. And he'd done good, stomping all over monsters in Kentucky and Texas. And he'd

discovered something interesting. Most of the new young
aces didn't know who the hell he was. A few, Hiram Worchester,
the Turtle, had known and it had mattered. But it was
bearable. So maybe there was a way to come back. To be a
hero again.

Hartmann had announced the world tour.

Jack had always admired Hartmann. Admired the way
he'd led the fight to repeal certain parts of the Exotic Powers
Control Act. He'd called the senator and offered to foot part
of the bill. Money was always welcome to a politician, even if
it wasn't being used to finance a campaign. Jack found himself
on the plane.

And most of it hadn't been bad. There'd been plenty of
action with women—most notably with Fantasy. They had
lain in bed one night in Italy, and she'd told him with vicious
wit about Tachyon's impotency. And he'd laughed, too loud
and too long. Trying to diminish Tachyon. Trying to make him
less of a threat.

Over the years he'd absorbed a bit about Takisian culture
from the interviews he'd read. Vengeance was definitely part
of the code. So he'd watched his back and waited for Tachyon
to act. *And nothing had happened.*

The strain was killing him.

And then had come last night.

He smeared butter on the last roll in the bread basket,
washed down the hard crusted bite with a sip of the unbelievably
strong French coffee. He sure wished these Frenchies had a
concept of a real breakfast. He could order an American
breakfast of course, but the cost was as unbelievable as the
coffee. This basket of dry bread and coffee was costing him
ten dollars. Add in some eggs and bacon, and the cost soared
to near thirty dollars. For breakfast!

Suddenly the absurdity of the thought struck him. He
was a rich man, not a Depression farm boy from North
Dakota. His contribution to this tour had been big enough to
buy him a piece of the big 747, or at least the jet fuel to fly
it—

Tachyon was entering the hotel, and the hair on the nape
of Jack's neck prickled. The door of the small restaurant gave
him only a limited view, and soon the alien was out of sight.
Jack felt the muscles in his neck and shoulders relax, and
with a sigh he lifted a finger and ordered a full American
breakfast.

Tachyon had looked funny. Fork moved mechanically from plate to mouth. *Holding himself real stiff.* Folded newspaper along his thigh like a soldier on dress parade. None of his business what the bastard was getting up to.

But last night was his business.

Anger ate through his belly like a physical pain. Sure the bomb couldn't have hurt him, but *he took my mind.* Casually, like a man tasting a mint. Reducing him in an instant from man to object.

Jack mopped up the last of the yolk while anger and outrage grew. God damn it! It was stupid to be scared of a pint-size fairy in fancy dress.

Not scared, Jack's mind quickly amended. He'd stayed away from the alien out of politeness, an acknowledgment of how much Tachyon hated him. But now Tachyon had changed the rules. He'd taken his mind. That he wasn't going to allow to pass.

They looked like two little red mouths. Bullet in, bullet out. Tach, seated in his undershorts, jabbed in a hypodermic, depressed the plunger, waited for the painkiller to take effect. Just for good measure he'd given himself a tetanus shot and an injection of penicillin. Spent hypos littered the table, a gauze pad lay ready, a roll of cotton. But for the moment he would let it seep. And do some hard thinking.

So Danelle had not lied. She had just not told all. Gisele was dead. The question was, how? Or did that matter? Probably not. What mattered was that she had married and borne a son. *My grandson.* And he had to be found.

And the father? Well, what of him? Assuming he was still alive, he was no fit guardian for the boy. The father—or unknown others—were manipulating this Takisian gift to spread terror.

So where to start? Undoubtedly at Danelle's apartment. Then to the hall of records to search for the marriage license and birth certificate.

But that attack on Danelle and himself had been no accident. *They,* whoever they were, were watching. So, however distasteful, he was going to have to make an effort to blend in.

Braun spent a few moments dithering in the hall. But outrage won over prudence. He tested the door, found it locked, gave a hard twist, and broke the knob. Stepped over the threshold and froze in astonishment at the sight of Tachyon, scissors at the ready, seated in the midst of a circle of snipped red locks.

The Takisian gaped back, a final hank of that improbable hair clutched in a hand.

"How *dare* you!"

"What in the hell are you doing?"

As their first exchange in almost forty years, it seemed to lack something.

In quick flicks like the shuttering of a camera, the rest of the scene came into focus. Jack's forefinger shot out.

"That's a bullet wound."

"Nonsense." The gauze was laid quickly over the white thigh with its peppering of red-gold hairs. "Now get out of my room."

"Not until I have some answers out of you. Who the hell has been shooting at you?" He snapped his fingers. "The bomb at Versailles. You've got a line into the people—"

"NO!" Far too quick and far too strong.

"Have you told the authorities?"

"There is no need. This is not a bullet wound. I know nothing of the terrorists." The scissors sawed viciously through the last piece of hair. It fluttered to the floor, ironically forming a shape very reminiscent of a question mark.

"Why are you cutting your hair?"

"Because I feel like it! Now get out before I take your mind and make you go."

"You do, and I'll come back and break your damn neck. You've never forgiven me—"

"You have *that* right!"

"You threw a goddamm bomb at me!"

"Unfortunately I knew it wouldn't hurt you."

The long slender fingers played about his cropped head, fluttering among the curls until they clustered about his face. It had the effect of making him appear suddenly very young.

Braun stepped in on him, rested his hands on either arm of the chair, effectively trapping Tachyon. "This tour is important. If you get up to some crazy stunt, it could damage everybody's reputation. *You* I don't give a damn about, but Gregg Hartmann is important."

The alien looked away and gazed woodenly out the

window. Despite being clad only in shirt and shorts he managed to make it seem regal.

"I'll go to Hartmann."

There was a flicker of alarm deep in the lilac eyes, quickly suppressed. "Fine, go. Anything to be rid of you."

Silence stretched between them. Suddenly Braun asked, "Are you in trouble?" No reply. "If you are, tell me. Maybe I can help."

The long lashes lifted, and Tachyon looked him fully in the eyes. There was nothing young about the narrow face now. It looked as cold and old and as implacable as death.

"I've had enough of your help for one lifetime, thank you."

Jack almost ran from the room.

Tachyon pulled off the soft brown fedora and crumpled it agitatedly in his hands. The tiny two-room flat looked as if it had been struck by a cyclone. Drawers stood open, a cheap picture frame stood forlornly empty on a scarred table. What had it held that was so significant it had to be removed?

The police? he wondered. No, they would have been more careful. So Dani's killers had been here, and the police were yet to come, which meant Tach had to hurry. The newly purchased jeans felt stiff against his skin, and he tugged fretfully at the crotch while he riffled through the paperbacks that littered the front room.

A faint rasp sounded from the bedroom. Tachyon froze, crept cat-footed to the hot plate, and lifted the knife lying next to it. In a quick rush he crossed the room and pressed himself against the wall, ready to stab whatever came through the connecting door.

Careful, quiet footsteps, but enough vibration for Tach to tell that his opponent was big. Two sets of soft breaths from either side of the wall. Tach held his, waited. The man came through the door in a rush; Tachyon lunged in low, ready to drive the blade up beneath the ribs. The blade snapped, and gold light flashed across the dingy apartment walls. Jack Braun, forming his hand into a gun, placed his forefinger firmly between Tachyon's eyes, "Bang, bang, you're dead."

"GOD DAMN YOU!" In a blaze of temper he flung the broken knife against the wall. "What are you doing here?"

"I followed you."

"I never saw you!"

"I know. I'm pretty good at this." The implication was clear.

"Why can't you just leave ... me ... alone?"

"Because you're getting in way over your head."

"I can take care of myself."

A derisive snort.

"If it hadn't been you, I'd have taken you out," Tach cried.

"Yeah? And what if there'd been more than one? Or if they'd had guns?"

"I don't have time to discuss this with you. The police may be here any minute," the alien threw over his shoulder as he stormed into the bedroom and continued his search.

"Police! HOLD IT! What is going on? Why the police?"

"Because the woman who lived in this flat was murdered this morning."

"Oh, great. And why does this involve you?" Tachyon's mouth tightened mulishly. Braun gathered up the front of the alien's shirt, hefted him off the ground, and held him at eye level, noses almost touching. "Tachyon." It was a warning rumble.

"It's a private matter."

"Not if the police are involved it isn't."

"I can handle it myself."

"I don't think so. You couldn't even spot me." Tachyon sulked. "Tell me what's going on. I just might help you."

"Oh, very well," he snapped pettishly. "I'm searching for any clue as to the whereabouts of my grandson."

That took some explaining. Tachyon fired out the tale in quick staccato sentences while they finished pawing through the jumble, turning up absolutely nothing.

"So you see, I have to find him first and get him out of the country before the French authorities realize what they possess," he concluded, laying his hand on the doorknob. And heard a key rasp in the lock.

"Oh, shit," whispered Tach.

"Police?" mouthed Jack.

"Undoubtedly," the Takisian mouthed back.

"Fire escape." Jack pointed back over his shoulder.

They fled.

"Let's see what we've got." Braun paused to light a cigarette. Tachyon stopped wolfing down his enormous and

very belated lunch and fished the paper from his jeans.
Tossed it, only to have it land fluttering in the mustard jar.
"God damn it, be careful," said Jack, aggrieved, and mopped
at the paper with his napkin.

Tachyon continued to shovel it in. With an annoyed
grunt the ace pulled out a pair of reading glasses and peered
at the Takisian's florid hand:

*Gisele Bacourt wed François Andrieux in a civil ceremo-
ny on December 5th, 1971.*

One child, Blaise Jeannot Andrieux, born May 7, 1975.

*Gisele Andrieux killed in a shoot-out with industrialist
Simon de Montfort's personal bodyguard, November 28, 1984.*

*Both husband and wife were members of the French
Communist Party.*

*François Andrieux had been pulled in for questioning,
but was released when nothing conclusive could be found.*

They had tried the simple expedient of checking the
phone book, and—not surprisingly—Andrieux had not been
listed. Jack sighed, rocked back in his chair, and returned his
glasses to his shirt pocket. The Eiffel Tower cast an elongated
shadow across the outdoor café.

"It's getting late, and we've got that dinner at the Tour
Eiffel."

"I'm not going."

"Oh?"

"No, I'm going to go talk to Claude Bonnell."

"Who?"

"Bonnell, Bonnell! *Le Miroir,* you know?"

"Why?"

"Because he's a major figure in the Communist Party. He
may be able to obtain Andrieux's address for me."

"And if that fails?" The smoke from the cigarette formed
a loop in the air between them.

"I don't want to think about that."

"Well, you better, if you really want to find this guy."

"So what's your suggestion?"

"Try tracing the materials used in the bomb. They had to
buy the stuff somewhere."

Tach made a face. "Sounds slow and tedious."

"It is."

"Then I'll pin my hope on Bonnell."

"Fine, you hope, and I'll pursue my bomb idea. Of
course, how we're going to get that information I'm not

certain. I suppose you could always go to see Rochambeau and pick his brains. . . ."

Tachyon steepled his fingers before his face and peered speculatively over the top at Jack. "I have a better idea."

"What?"

"Don't sound so suspicious. You and Billy Ray could talk to Rochambeau about the bomb. Say that you think it was meant for the senator—it might have been for all we know—suggest that you pool information."

"Might work." Jack ground out the cigarette. "Billy Ray is a Justice Department ace, and Hartmann's bodyguard. 'Course he's bound to ask why I'm involved."

"Just tell him it's because you're *Golden Boy*." And the tone was undiluted acid.

Bonnell's dressing room backstage at the Lido was typical. The strong odor of cold cream, greasepaint, and hair spray overlaying the fainter scents of old sweat and stale perfume.

Tachyon straddled a chair, arms resting along the back, and watched the joker put the final touches on his makeup.

"Could you hand me my ruff?"

Bonnell clasped it about his neck, rose, took one final critical look at the black and white harlequin costume, and settled back into the battered wooden chair.

"All right, Doctor. I'm ready. Now tell me what I can do for you."

"I need a favor." They spoke in French.

"Which is?"

"Do you have membership lists—addresses—for your members?"

"I assume we're speaking of the Party."

"Oh, forgive me. Yes."

"And to answer you, yes, we do."

Bonnell was not helping him any. Tach plowed awkwardly on. "Could you obtain an address for me?"

"That would depend on what you want it for."

"Nothing nefarious, I assure you. A personal matter."

"*Hmmm.*" Bonnell straightened the already meticulously arranged pots and tubes on his dressing table. "Doctor, you presume a great deal. We have met only once, yet you come to me asking for private information. And if I were to ask you why?"

"I'd rather not say."

"I rather thought that would be your answer. So I'm afraid I really must refuse."

Exhaustion, tension, and the throbbing ache from his leg slammed down like a curling storm wave. Tach laid his head on his arms. Fought tears. Considered just giving up. A gentle but firm hand caught his chin and forced his head up.

"This really means a great deal to you, doesn't it?"

"More than you can know."

"So tell me so I will know. Can't you trust me? Just a little?"

"I lived in Paris long ago. Have you been a communist for long?" he asked abruptly

"Ever since I was able to comprehend politics."

"Then I'm surprised I didn't meet you all those long years ago. I knew them all. Thorenz, Lena Goldoni . . . Danelle."

"I wasn't in Paris then. I was still in Marseilles getting the crap beat out of me by my supposedly *normal* neighbors." His smile was bitter. "France has not always been so kind to her wild cards."

"I'm sorry."

"Why should *you* be?"

"Because it's my fault."

"That's an exceedingly silly and self-indulgent attitude."

"Thank you so very much."

"The past is dead, buried, and gone forever past recall. Only the present and the future matter, Doctor."

"And I think that's a silly and simplistic attitude. The actions of the past have consequences for the present and the future. Thirty-six years ago I came to this country broken and bitter. I slept with a young girl. Now I return to find that I left a more permanent mark on this place than I had thought. I sired a child who was born, lived, and died without my ever knowing of her existence. I could curse her mother for that, and yet perhaps she was wise. For the first thirteen years of Gisele's life her father was a drunken derelict. What could I have given her?" He paced away and stood rigidly regarding a wall. Then whirled and rested his shoulders against the cool plaster.

"I lost my chance with her, but the Ideal has granted me another. She had a son, my grandchild. And I want him."

"And the father?"

"Is a member of your party."

"You say you want him. What? You would steal him from his father?"

Tach rubbed wearily at his eyes. Forty-eight hours without sleep was taking its toll. "I don't know. I haven't thought that far ahead. All I want is to see him, to hold him, to look into the face of my future."

Bonnell slapped his hands onto his thighs and pushed up from the chair. "C'est bien, Doctor. A man deserves a chance to look upon the intersection of his past, present, and future. I will find you this man."

"Just give his address, there's no reason for you to be involved."

"He might take fright. I can reassure him, set up a meeting. His name—?"

"François Andrieux."

Bonnell noted it. "Very good. So, I will speak to this man, and then I will ring you at the Ritz—"

"I'm no longer staying there. You can reach me at the Lys on the Left Bank."

"I see. Any particular reason?"

"No."

"I must work on that innocent expression. It is very charming, if not terribly convincing." Tachyon flushed, and Bonnell laughed. "There, there, don't take offense. You've told me enough of your secrets tonight. I won't press you for any more."

The junket was dining at the expensive Tour Eiffel.

Tachyon, leaning on the rail of the observation deck, fidgeted and waited for Braun to emerge. Through the windows of the restaurant he could see that the party had reached the brandy-coffee-cigars-speeches stage. The door opened, and Mistral, giggling, darted out. She was followed by Captain Donatien Racine, one of France's more prominent aces. His sole power was flight, but that coupled with the fact he was career military had ensured that the press dubbed him Tricolor. It was a name he hated.

Gripping the American about her slender waist, Racine carried them over the protective railing. Mistral gave him a quick kiss, pushed free of his encircling arm, and floated away on the gentle breezes that sighed about the tower. Her great blue-and-silver cape spread around her until she resembled an exotic moth drawn by the glittering lights webbing the tower. Watching the couple darting and swooping in an intricate game of tag, Tachyon suddenly felt very weary and very old and very earthbound.

The restaurant doors flew open, and the delegation flowed out like water through a broken dam. After five months of formal dinners and endless speeches, it was no wonder they fled.

Braun, elegant in his white tie and tails, paused to light a cigarette. Tachyon touched him with a thread of telepathy.

Jack.

He stiffened, but gave no other outward sign.

Gregg Hartmann glanced back. "Jack, are you coming?"

"I'll catch up with you. Think I'll enjoy the air and the view and watch those crazy kids skydive." He pointed to Mistral and Racine.

A few moments later he joined Tachyon at the rail.

"Bonnell's going to set up a meeting."

Braun grunted, flicked ash. "The Sûreté were at the hotel when I got back. They tried to be subtle about questioning the delegation as to your whereabouts, but the news hounds are snuffling. They sense a story."

The Takisian shrugged it aside with a hunch of the shoulder. "Will you come with me? To the meeting?"

Ancestors, how it stuck in the throat to ask him for help!

"Sure."

"I may need help with the father."

"So you're going to do..."

"Whatever it takes. I want him."

Montmartre. Where artists, legitimate and otherwise, swarmed like locusts ready to fall upon the unwary tourist. *A portrait of your beautiful wife, monsieur.* The cost politely never mentioned, then when it was completed a charge sufficient to purchase an old master.

Tour buses groaned up the hill and disgorged their eager passengers. The Gypsy children, circling like vultures, moved in. The European travelers, wise to the ways of these innocent-faced thieves, drove them away with loud threats. The Japanese and Americans, lulled by sparkling black eyes in dark faces, allowed them to approach. Later they would rue it when they discovered the loss of wallets, watches, jewelry.

So many people, and one small boy.

Braun, hands on hips, gazed out across the plaza before

Sacré-Coeur. It was awash with people. Easels thrust up like masts from a colorful surging sea. He sighed, checked his watch.

"They're late."

"Patience."

Braun stared pointedly at his watch again. The Gypsy children attracted by the slim gold band of the Longines crept forward.

"Beat it!" Jack roared. "Jesus, where do they all come from? Is there a Gypsy factory the same way there's a hooker factory?"

"They're usually sold by their mothers to 'talent scouts' from France and Italy. They're then trained to steal and work like slaves for their owners."

"Jesus, sounds like something out of Dickens."

Tachyon shaded his eyes with one slim hand and searched for Bonnell.

"You know you were supposed to address a conference of researchers today."

"Yes."

"Well, did you call to cancel?"

"No, I forgot. I have more important things on my mind right now than genetic research."

"I'd say that's exactly what you have on your mind," came Braun's dry reply.

A taxi pulled up, and Bonnell struggled painfully out. He was followed by a man and a small boy. Tachyon's fingers dug deep into Jack's bicep.

"Look. Dear God!"

"What?"

"That man. He's the clerk from the hotel."

"Huh?"

"He was at the Intercontinental."

The trio were walking toward them. Suddenly the father froze, pointed at Jack, gestured emphatically, grabbed the child by the wrist, and hustled for the taxi.

"No, dear God, no." Tachyon ran forward a few steps. Reached out, his power closing about their minds like a vise. They froze. He walked slowly toward them. Felt his breath go short as he devoured the small, stubborn face beneath its cap of red hair. The boy was fighting with not insignificant power, and only a quarter Takisian. Pride surged through Tach.

Suddenly he was flung to the ground, fists and rocks raining down upon him. He clung desperately to the control while the Gypsy children plucked at him, removing wallet, watch, and all the time continuing the hysterical beating. Jack waded in and began plucking urchins off him.

"No no, catch *them*. Don't worry about me!" screamed Tach. With a leg sweep he brought two to the ground, lurched to one knee, stiffened his fingers, and jabbed them hard into one gangling teenager's throat. The boy fell back, choking.

Jack hesitated, turned toward Andrieux and the boy, broke into a run. Tachyon, distracted, watched his progress. Never even saw the boot come swinging in. Pain exploded in his temple. Distantly he heard someone shouting, then bitter darkness.

Bonnell was wiping his face with a damp handkerchief when he finally came around. Desperately Tachyon levered up onto his elbows, then fell back as the motion sent waves of pain through his head and filled the back of his throat with nausea.

"Did you get them?"

"No." Jack was holding a bumper like a man displaying a prize catch. "When you went under they ran for it and made it into the cab. I tried to grab the car, but could only get the bumper. It came off," he added unnecessarily. Jack eyed the interested crowd that had surrounded them and shooed them away.

"Then we've lost them."

"What did you expect? You turn up with the Judas Ace," said Bonnell angrily.

Jack flinched, murmured through stiff lips, "That was a long time ago."

"Some of us don't forget. And others of us shouldn't." He glared at Tachyon. "I thought I could trust you."

"Jack, go away."

"Well, fuck you too." Long, jerky strides carried him into the crowd and out of sight.

"It's funny, but I feel very badly about that." He gave himself a shake. "So what do we do now?"

"First I extract a promise from you that there will be no more stunts like today."

"All right."

"I'll reset the meeting for tonight. And this time *come alone*."

Jack wasn't sure why he did it. After the insult Tachyon had given him, he should have just washed his hands of the whole thing or told the Sûreté everything he knew. Instead he turned up at the Lys with an ice pack and aspirin.

"Thank you, but I do have a medical kit."

Jack tossed the bottle several times. "Oh, yeah? Well, then I'll take them. This whole thing is giving me a headache."

Tach lifted the pack from his eye. "Why you?"

"Lie down and leave that thing on your eye." He scratched at his chin. "Look, let me throw something out to you. Doesn't this whole thing strike you as just a little too convenient?"

"In what way?" But Jack could tell from the little alien's cautious tone that he'd struck a nerve.

"Instead of just giving you Andrieux's address, Bonnell insists on setting up a meeting. They tried to split—"

"Because you were there."

"Yeah, right. You mind control them, then you just happen to get attacked by a gang of Gypsy children. I've done a little checking around. They *never* do that kind of thing. I think somebody had this arranged ahead of time. To make certain you couldn't use your mind control. And what about Andrieux? You said he was the clerk at the hotel. Then why did he deny any knowledge of Danelle? She was his mother-in-law, for Christ's sake. This thing stinks to high heaven."

Tachyon flung the ice pack against the wall. "So what do you suggest I do?"

"Don't work with Bonnell anymore. Don't go to any more meetings. Let me see what I can do with the bomb fragments. Rochambeau has agreed to work with Ray."

"That could take weeks. We leave in a few days."

"You are fucking obsessed with this!"

"Yes!"

"Why? Is it because you're impotent? Is that the big deal here?"

"I don't wish to discuss this."

"I know you don't, but you've got to! You're not thinking this through, Tachyon. What it could do to the tour, to your reputation—to mine for that matter. We're withholding vital evidence pertaining to a murder."

"You didn't have to become involved."

"I know that, and sometimes I wish to Christ I hadn't. But I'm into it now, so I'll see it through to the end. So are you going to sit tight and see what I can find?"

"Yes, I'll wait to see what you find out."

Jack shot him a suspicious glance. "Well, I guess that'll have to do."

"Oh, Jack." The big ace paused, hand on the doorknob, and looked back. "I apologize for this afternoon. It was wrong of me to send you away."

It was obvious from the Takisian's expression what this was costing him. "Okay," Jack replied gruffly.

It was an old house, a very old house, in the university district. Cracks cut the dingy plaster walls, and the musty odor of mold hung in the air. Bonnell gave Tachyon's arm a hard squeeze.

"Remember not to expect too much. This child doesn't know you."

Tachyon barely heard him, certainly paid no attention. He was already heading up the stairs.

There were five people in the room, but Tachyon saw only the boy. Perched on a stool, he was swinging one foot, slamming his heel rhythmically into a battered wooden leg. His fine straight hair lacked the metallic copper fire of his grandsire's, but it was nonetheless a deep rich red. Tach felt a surge of pride at this evidence of his prepotence. Straight red brows gave Blaise an overly serious expression that set oddly on the narrow child's face. His eyes were a brilliant purple-black.

Standing behind, a hand possessively on his son's shoulder, was Andrieux. Tachyon studied him with the critical eye of a Takisian psi lord evaluating breeding stock. *Not bad, human of course, but not bad.* Definitely handsome, and he appeared intelligent. Still it was hard to tell. If only he could run tests.... He tried to close his mind to the unwelcome suspicion that this man had been instrumental in Dani's death.

He looked back to Blaise and found the boy studying him with equal interest. There was nothing shy about the gaze. Suddenly Tach's shields repelled a powerful mind assault.

"Trying to pay me back for yesterday?"

"*Mais oui.* You took my mind."

"You take people's minds."

"Of course. No one can stop me."

"I can." The brows snapped together in a thunderous frown. "I'm Tachyon. I'm your grandfather."

"You don't look like a grandfather."

"My kind live a very long time."

"Will I?"

"Longer than a human." The boy seemed pleased with this oblique reference to his alienness.

As they talked, Tach made a preliminary probe of his abilities. An unbelievable mind control aptitude for one so young. And all self-taught, that was the truly amazing thing. With proper instruction he would be a force to be reckoned with. No teke, no precog, and worst of all almost no telepathy. He was virtually mind blind.

That's what comes of unrestricted and unplanned breeding.

"Doctor," said Claude. "Won't you sit down?"

"First I would like to give Blaise a hug." He looked inquiringly at the boy, who made a face.

"I don't like hugs and kisses."

"Why not?"

"It makes me feel like ants are on me."

"A common mentat reaction. You will not feel that way with me."

"Why not?"

"Because I am your kin and kind. I understand you better than anyone else in the world can ever understand you." François Andrieux shifted angrily.

"Well, I'll try it," said Blaise decisively, and slid off his stool. Again Tachyon was pleased with his assurance.

As his arms closed about his grandson's small form, tears rushed into his eyes.

"You're crying," Blaise accused.

"Yes."

"Why?"

"Because I am so very happy to have found you. To know that you exist in the world."

Bonnell cleared his throat, a discreet little sound. "As loath as I am to interrupt this, I'm really afraid I must, Doctor." Tachyon stiffened warily. "We have to talk a little business."

"Business?" The word was dangerously low.

"Yes. I've given you what you want." He indicated Blaise with a flip of a tiny hand. "Now you have to give me what I want. François, take him."

Father and son left. Tachyon speculatively studied the remaining men.

"Please don't consider a mind-assisted escape. There are more of us waiting outside this room. And my companions are armed."

"I somehow assumed they would be." Tach settled onto a sagging sofa. It sent up a puff of dust under his weight. "So, you are a member of this little gang of galloping terrorists."

"No, sir, I lead it."

"Umm, and you had Dani killed."

"No. That was an act of blatant stupidity for which François has been . . . *chastised*. I disapprove of subordinates acting on their own initiative. They so often screw up. Don't you agree?"

Tachyon's late cousin Rabdan came instantly to mind, and he found himself nodding. Pulled himself up short. There was something very outré about this chatty little conversation, faced as he was with the man who had attempted to kill hundreds at Versailles.

"Oh, dear, and I had so hoped that Andrieux was bright," mused Tachyon, then he asked, "Is this a kidnapping for ransom?"

"Oh, no, Doctor, you're quite beyond price."

"So I've always thought."

"No, I need your help. In two days there will be a great debate between all the presidential candidates. We intend to kill as many of them as we can."

"Even your own candidate?"

"In a revolution sometimes sacrifice is necessary. But for your information, I have little loyalty to the Communist Party. They have betrayed the people, lost the will and the strength to make the difficult decisions. The mandate has passed to us."

Tach rested his forehead on a hand. "Oh, please, don't blurt slogans at me. It's one of the most tiresome things about you people."

"May I outline my plan?"

"I don't see any way I can prevent you."

"The security will undoubtedly be very tight."

"Undoubtedly." Bonnell shot him a sharp glance at the irony. Tachyon gazed innocently back.

"Rather than attempt to run this gauntlet with weapons of our own, we will use those already provided. You and Blaise will mind control as many guards as possible and have them rake the platform with automatic weapons fire. It should have the desired result."

"Interesting, but what can you possibly gain by this?"

"The destruction of France's ruling elite will throw the country into chaos. When that occurs, I won't need your esoteric powers. Guns and bombs will suffice. Sometimes the simplest things are often the best."

"What a philosopher you are. Perhaps you should set yourself up as a guide to the young."

"I already have. I'm Blaise's beloved Uncle Claude."

"Well, this has of course been instructional, but I very much regret that I must refuse."

"Not surprising. I had anticipated this. But consider, Doctor, I hold your grandson."

"You won't harm him, he's too precious to you."

"True. But my threat is not of death. If you refuse to accommodate me in this, I will be forced to have certain very unpleasant things done to you, being careful to ensure that you live. I will then disappear with Blaise. You might find it somewhat difficult to trace us when you are a bedridden cripple."

He smiled in satisfaction at the look of horror on Tachyon's face. "Jean will escort you to your room now. There you can reflect upon my offer and, I'm certain, see your way clear to help me."

"I doubt it," gritted Tachyon, regaining command of his voice, but it was hollow bravado, and Bonnell undoubtedly knew it.

The "room" turned out to be the very cold and dank basement of the house. Hours later Blaise arrived with his dinner.

"I have come to visit with you," he announced, and Tach sighed, again admiring and regretting Bonnell's cunning. The joker had obviously made a careful study of Tachyon, his attitudes and culture.

He ate while Blaise, chin resting in his cupped hands, gazed thoughtfully at him.

Tach set aside his fork. "You are very silent. I thought we were going to visit."

"I don't know what to say to you. It's very strange."

"What is?"

"Finding out about you. Now I'm not so special anymore, which bothers me, but it's also good to know..." He considered.

"That you're not alone," suggested Tach gently.

"Yes, that's it."

"Why do you help them?"

"Because they are right. The old institutions must fall."

"But people have died."

"Yes," he agreed sunnily.

"Doesn't that bother you?"

"Oh, no. They were bourgeois capitalist pigs and deserved to die. Sometimes killing is the only way."

"A very Takisian attitude."

"You will help us, won't you? It will be fun."

"Fun!"

It's his upbringing, Tach consoled himself. Endow any child with this kind of unsupervised power and they would react the same.

They talked. Tachyon pieced together a picture of unfettered freedom, virtually no formal schooling, the excitement of playing hide-and-seek with the authorities. More chilling was the realization that Blaise did not withdraw from his victims when they died. Rather he rode through the terror and pain of their final moment.

There will be time to correct this, he promised himself.

"So will you help?" Blaise asked, hopping down from the chair. "Uncle Claude said to be sure and ask you."

Seconds stretched into minutes as he considered. The noble course would be to tell Bonnell to go to hell. He considered Bonnell's gently worded threats and shuddered. He had been bred and trained to seize the opportunity, to turn defeat into victory. He would trust to that. Surely they could not guard him as closely at the rally.

"Tell Claude that I will help."

An exuberant hug.

Alone, Tachyon continued to reflect. He did have one other advantage. Jack... who would surely realize something had gone terribly wrong and alert the Sûreté. But his hope was founded on a man whose weakness was well known to him, and his fears on a man who, despite his civilized exterior, possessed no humanity.

Coming up on twenty-four hours since the little bastard had disappeared. Jack swung at the wall, pulled the punch just in time. Knocking out a wall at the Ritz wasn't going to help.

Was Tachyon in trouble?

Despite his promise, had he gone off with Bonnell? And did that necessarily mean trouble? Was it possible he was merely playing hooky with his grandkid?

If he was out visiting the zoo or whatever and Jack alerted the Sûreté, and they found out about Blaise, Tachyon would never forgive him. It would be another betrayal. Maybe his last one. The Takisian would find a way to get even this time.

But if he's really in trouble?

A knock pulled him from his distracted thoughts. One of Hartmann's interchangeable aides stood in the hall.

"Mr. Braun, the senator would like to invite you to join him at the debate tomorrow."

"Debate? What debate?"

"All one thousand and eleven"—a condescending little laugh—"or however many candidates there are in this crazy race, will be taking part in a round-robin debate in the Luxembourg Gardens. The senator would like as many of the tour as possible to be there. To show support for this great European democracy—such as it is. Mr. Braun . . . are you all right?"

"Fine, yeah, I'm fine. You tell the senator I'll be there."

"And Doctor Tachyon? The senator's very concerned by his continued absence."

"I think I can safely promise the senator that the doctor will be there too."

Closing the door, Jack quickly crossed to the phone and put in a call for Rochambeau. A probable terrorist attack on the candidates. No need to mention the child. Just an urgent need to call out the troops.

And a long night of praying he had guessed correctly. That he had made the right choice.

*   *   *

He should be sleeping, preparing mind and body for the morrow. His life and the future of his line depended upon his skill and speed and cunning.

And on Jack Braun. Ironic that.

If Jack had drawn the correct conclusion. *If* he had alerted the Sûreté. *If* there were sufficient officers. *If* Tachyon could stretch his talent beyond all limits and hold an unheard of number of minds.

He sat up on the rickety cot and hugged his stomach. Sank back and tried to relax. But it was a night for memories. Faces out of the past. Blythe, David, Earl, Dani.

I'm gambling my life and the life of my grandchild on the man who destroyed Blythe. Lovely.

But the possibility of dying can act as a spur for self-examination. Force a person to strip away the comforting, insulating little lies that buffer one from their most private guilts and regrets.

"Then give me those names!"

"All right . . . all right."

The power—lancing out—fragmenting her mind . . . her mind . . . her mind.

But they wouldn't have known but for Jack. And she wouldn't have absorbed their minds but for Holmes, and she wouldn't have been there but for the paranoia of a nation. *And no one would suffer had they not been born*, thought Tach, quoting a favorite adage of his father's. Sometime one must stop excusing, accept responsibility for actions taken.

Tisianne brant Ts'ara, Jack Braun didn't destroy Blythe, you *did.*

He flinched, prepared for it to hurt. Instead he felt better. Lighter, freer, at peace for the first time in so many, many years. He began to laugh, was not surprised when it turned to quiet tears.

They lasted for some time. When the storm ended, he lay back, exhausted but calm. Ready for tomorrow. After which he would return home and *make* a home and raise his child. Calmly and a little regretfully he turned his back on the past.

He was Tisianne brant Ts'ara sek Halima sek Ragnar sek Omian, a prince of the House Ilkazam, and tomorrow his enemies would learn to their pain and regret what it meant to stand against him.

* * *

Claude, Blaise, and a driver remained in a car almost a block from the gardens. Tachyon, linked through the barrel of a Beretta with a stone-faced Andrieux, hovered at the outskirts of an enormous crowd. Parisians were nothing if not enthusiastic about their politics. But spotted throughout this sea of humanity like an insidious infection were the other fifteen members of Bonnell's cell. Waiting. For blood to flow and nurture their violent dreams.

On the stand, the candidates—all seven of them. About half the delegation seated in chairs directly in front of the bunting-hung platform. There was no way they would escape without injury if Tach should fail and the shooting begin. Jack came into view. Hands thrust deep into pants pockets, he paced and frowned out over the throng.

Blaise was a rider in Tachyon's mind. Ready to sense the tiniest use of telepathy. His power might be slight, but he was sensitive enough to detect the shift in focus such mind communication required. His presence suited his grandsire just fine. It would make what was to come all the easier.

Carefully Tachyon constructed a mind-scrim of the scene. A false picture to lull his grandchild. He hedged it around with shields, presented it to Blaise. Then from beneath its protective cover he reached out, touched Jack's mind.

Don't jump, keep frowning.
Where are you?
Near gate, edge of trees.
Got it.
Sûreté?
Everywhere. Terrorists?
Likewise everywhere.
How . . .!?
They'll come to you.
Wha . . .???
Trust.

He withdrew and carefully constructed a trap. It was similar to the link he enjoyed with Baby when the ship boosted and amplified his own natural powers to allow for transspace communication, but much, much stronger. Its teeth were very deep. What might it do to Blaise? No. There was no time for doubts.

The mind snare snapped down. A mental scream of alarm from the boy. Desperate struggle, panting resignation. The rider had become the ridden.

Tachyon joined Blaise's power to his. It was like a bar of white-hot light. Carefully he split it into strands. Each tendril snapped out like a burning whip. Settled on his captors. They became frozen statues.

He was gasping with effort, sweat bursting from his forehead, running in rivulets into his eyes. He set them marching, a regiment of zombies. As Andrieux stepped from his side, Tachyon forced his hand to move, to close about the Beretta, to pull it from his slave's limp grasp.

Braun was leaping about, gesticulating, summoning help with great arm sweeps.

Hurry! Hurry!

He had to hold them. All of them. If he failed . . .

Blaise was struggling again. It was like being kicked over and over again in the gut. One thread snapped. To Claude Bonnell. With a cry Tachyon dropped the control, ran for the gate. Behind him there was the vicious snarl of an Uzi. Apparently one of his captives had tried to run and been cut down by the French security forces. Perhaps it had been Andrieux. More gunfire, punctuating screams. A torrent of people swept past, almost knocking him from his feet. He tightened his grip on the Beretta, pumped harder. Slid around the corner just as the dazed driver reached for the key. A blow from Tachyon's mind, and he collapsed onto the steering wheel, and the blare of the horn was added to the pandemonium.

Bonnell struggled from the car, gripping Blaise by the wrist. He went lurching and stumbling for a narrow, deserted side street.

Tach flew after them, caught Blaise by his free hand, and wrenched him free.

"LET ME GO! LET ME GO!"

Sharp teeth bit deep into his wrist. Tachyon silenced the boy with a crushing imperative. Supported the sleeping child with one arm. He and Bonnell regarded one another over the limp figure.

"Bravo, Doctor. You outfoxed me. But what a media event my trial will be."

"I'm afraid not."

"Eh?"

"I require a body. One infected with the wild card. Then the Sûreté will have their mysterious mentat ace and will look no further."

"You can't be serious! You can't mean to kill me in cold blood." He read the answer in Tachyon's implacable lilac gaze. Bonnell tottered back, came up short against a wall, moistened his lips. "I treated you fairly, kindly. You took no hurt from me."

"But others have not fared so well. You shouldn't have sent Blaise to me. He was quick to tell me of your other *triumphs*. An innocent banker, controlled by Blaise, sent into his bank carrying his own death. That bomb blast killed seventeen. Clearly a triumph."

Bonnell's face shifted, took on the aspect of Thomas Tudbury, the Great and Powerful Turtle. "Please, I beg you. At least grant me the opportunity for a trial."

"No," The features shifted again—Mark Meadows, Captain Trips blinked confusedly at the gun. "I think the outcome is fairly predictable." Danelle, but as she had been all those long years ago. "I merely hasten your execution."

A final transformation. Shoulder-length sable hair cascading over the shoulders, long sooty lashes brushing at her cheeks, lifting to reveal eyes of a profound midnight blue. *Blythe*.

"Tachy, please."

"I'm sorry, but you're dead."

And Tach shot him.

"Ah, Doctor Tachyon." Franchot de Valmy rose from his desk, hand outstretched. "France owes you a great debt of gratitude. How can we ever repay you?"

"By issuing me a passport and visa."

"I'm afraid I don't understand. You of course—"

"Not for me. For Blaise Jeannot Andrieux."

De Valmy fiddled with a pen. "Why not merely apply?"

"Because François Andrieux is currently in custody. Checks will be run, and I can't allow that."

"Aren't you being a bit forthright with me?"

"Not at all. I know what an expert you are on falsified documents." The Frenchman froze, then shifted slowly to the back of his chair. "I know you're not an ace, Monsieur de Valmy. I wonder, how would the French public react to news of such a cheat? It would cost you the election."

De Valmy forced past stiff lips, "I am a very capable public servant. I can make a difference for France."

"Yes, but none of that is half so alluring as a wild card."

"What you're asking is impossible. What if it's traced to me? What if—" Tachyon reached for the phone. "What are you doing?"

"Calling the press. I too can arrange press conferences at a moment's notice. One of the privileges of fame."

"You'll get your documents."

"Thank you."

"I'll find out why you're doing this."

Tachyon paused at the door, glanced back. "Then we'll each have a secret on the other, won't we?"

The big plane was darkened for the late-night hop to London. The first-class section was deserted save for Tach, Jack, and Blaise, sleeping soundly in his grandfather's arms. There was something about the little tableau that warned everyone to stay well away.

"How long are you gonna keep him under?" The single reading light pulled fire from the twin red heads.

"Until we reach London."

"Will he ever forgive you?"

"He won't know."

"About Bonnell maybe, but the rest he'll remember. You betrayed him."

"Yes." It was scarcely audible over the rumble of the engines. "Jack?"

"Yeah?"

"I forgive you."

Their eyes met.

The human reached down, softly pushed back a lock of silky hair from the child's forehead. "Then I guess maybe there's hope for you too."

LEGENDS

Michael Cassutt

The month of April brought little in the way of relief to
Muscovites staggered by an unusually cold winter. Following
a brief flurry of southern breezes, which sent boys into the
newly green football fields and encouraged pretty girls to
discard their overcoats, the skies had darkened again, and a
dreary, uninspired rain had begun to fall. To Polyakov the
scene was autumnal and therefore entirely appropriate. His
masters, bending in the new breeze from the Kremlin, had
decreed that this would be Polyakov's last Moscow spring.
The younger, less-tainted Yurchenko would move up, and
Polyakov would retire to a dacha far from Moscow.

Just as well, Polyakov thought, since scientists were
saying that weather patterns had changed because of the
Siberian airbursts. There might never be a decent Moscow
spring again.

Nevertheless, even in its autumn clothes Moscow had
the ability to inspire him. From this window he could see the
cluster of trees where the Moscow River skirted Gorky Park,
and beyond that, looking appropriately medieval in the mist,
were the domes of St. Basil's and the Kremlin. In Polyakov's
mind age equalled power, but then he was old.

"You wanted to see me?" The voice interrupted his
musings. A young major in the uniform of the Chief Intelligence Directorate of the General Staff—uncommonly known
as the GRU—had entered. He was perhaps thirty-five, a bit
old to still hold the rank of major, Polyakov thought, especially with the Hero of the Soviet Union medal. With his classic
White Russian features and sandy hair, the man looked like
one of those unlikely officers whose pictures appeared on the
cover of *Red Star* every day.

"Mólniya." Polyakov elected to use the young officer's
code name rather than Christian name and patronymic. Initial formality was one of the interrogator's tricks. He held out

his hand. The major hesitated, then shook it. Polyakov was pleased to note that Mólniya wore black rubber gloves. So far his information was correct. "Let's sit down."

They faced each other across the polished wood of the conference table. Someone had thoughtfully provided water, which Polyakov indicated. "You have a very pleasant conference room here."

"I'm sure it hardly compares with those at Dzerzhinsky Square," Mólniya shot back with just the proper amount of insolence. Dzerzhinsky Square was the location of KGB headquarters.

Polyakov laughed. "As a matter of fact it's identical, thanks to central planning. Gorbachev is doing away with that, I understand."

"We've been known to read the Politburo's mail too."

"Good. Then you know exactly why I'm here and who sent me."

Mólniya and the GRU had been ordered to cooperate with the KGB, and the orders came from the very highest places. That was the slim advantage Polyakov brought to this meeting . . . an advantage that, as the saying went, had all the weight of words written on water . . . since he was an old man and Mólniya was the great Soviet ace.

"Do you know the name Huntington Sheldon?"

Mólniya knew he was being tested and said tiredly, "He was CIA director from 1966 to 1972."

"Yes, a thoroughly dangerous man . . . and last week's issue of *Time* magazine has a picture of him standing right in front of the Lubiyanka—pointing up at the statue of Dzerzhinsky!"

"Maybe there's a lesson in that . . . cousin." *Worry about your own security and leave our operations alone!*

"I wouldn't be here if you hadn't had such a spectacular failure."

"Unlike the KGB's perfect record." Mólniya didn't try to hide his contempt.

"Oh, we've had our failures, cousin. What's different about our operations is that they've been approved by the Intelligence Council. Now, you're a Party member. You couldn't have graduated from the Kharkov Higher Engineering School without being at least slightly familiar with the principles of collective thought. Successes are shared. So are failures. This operation you and Dolgov cooked up—what were you doing, taking lessons from Oliver North?"

Mólniya flinched at the mention of Dolgov's name, a state secret and, more importantly, a GRU secret. Polyakov continued, "Are you worried about what we say, Major? Don't be. This is the cleanest room in the Soviet Union." He smiled. "*My* housekeepers swept it. What we say here is between us.

"So, now, tell me," Polyakov said, "what the hell went wrong in Berlin?"

The aftermath of the Hartmann kidnapping had been horrible. Though only a few right-wing German and American newspapers mentioned possible Soviet involvement, the CIA and other Western agencies made the connections. Finding the bodies, even mutilated as they were, of those Red Army Faction punks had allowed the CIA to backtrack through their residences, cover names, bank accounts, and contacts, destroying in a matter of days a network that had been in place for twenty years. Two military attachés, in Vienna and Berlin, had been expelled, and more were to follow.

The involvement of the lawyer Prahler in such a brutal and inept affair would make it impossible for other deep-cover agents of his stature to act... and make it difficult to recruit new ones.

And who knew what else the American senator was telling.

"You know, Mólniya, for years my service ran moles at the very heart of the British intelligence service... we even had one who acted as liaison with the CIA."

"Philby, Burgess, Maclean, and Blount. And old man Churchill, too, if you believe the Western spy novels. Is there a point to this anecdote?"

"I'm just trying to give you some idea of the damage you've done. Those moles paralyzed the British for over twenty years. That's what could happen to us... to both of us. Your GRU bosses will never admit it; if they do, they certainly won't discuss it with you. But that's the mess I've got to clean up.

"Now... if you know anything at all about me"—Polyakov was certain that Mólniya knew as much about him as the KGB, which meant that Mólniya did not know one very

important thing—"you know that I'm fair. I'm old, I'm fat,
I'm faceless... but I'm objective. I'm retiring in four months.
I have *nothing* to gain from causing a new war between our
two services."

Mólniya merely returned his gaze. Well, Polyakov expected
as much. The rivalry between the GRU and KGB had been
bloody. At various times in the past each service had managed to have the leaders of its rival shot. There is nothing
longer than institutional memory.

"I see." Polyakov stood up. "Sorry to have troubled you,
Major. Obviously the General Secretary was mistaken... you
have nothing to say to me—"

"Ask your questions!"

Forty minutes later Polyakov sighed and sat back in his
chair. Turning slightly, he could see out the window. GRU
headquarters was called the Aquarium because of its glass
walls. It fit. Polyakov had noticed, as he was driven by
another GRU officer past the Institute of Space Biology,
which, together with the little-used Frunze Central Airport,
surrounded the Aquarium, that this building—perhaps the
most inaccessible, indeed even invisible place in the city of
Moscow—appeared to be almost transparent. A fifteen-story
building with nothing but floor-to-ceiling windows!

To find it inviting was a mistake. Polyakov pitied the
theoretical casual visitor. Before even reaching the inner
circle, one had to penetrate an outer one consisting of three
secret aircraft design bureaus, the even more secret Chelomei
spacecraft design bureau, or the Red Banner Air Force
Academy.

At the far end of the courtyard below, nestled against the
impenetrable concrete wall that surrounded the Aquarium,
was a crematorium. The story was that, in the final interview
before acceptance into the GRU, every candidate was shown
this squat green building and a special film.

The film was of the 1959 execution of GRU Colonel
Popov, who had been caught spying for the CIA. Popov was
strapped to a stretcher with unbreakable wire and simply
fed—alive—into the flames. The process was interrupted so
that the coffin of another, substantially more honored GRU
employee could be consigned first.

The message was clear: *You leave the GRU only through
the crematorium. We are more important than family, than*

country. A man such as Mólniya, trained by such an organization, was not vulnerable to any of Polyakov's interrogator's tricks. In almost an hour all Polyakov had pried out of him were operational details... names, dates, places, events. Material that Polyakov already possessed. There was something more to be learned—a secret of some kind—Polyakov was sure of it. A secret no one else had been able to get out of Mólniya. A secret that, perhaps, no one but Polyakov knew existed. How could he get Mólniya to talk?

What could be more important to this man than that crematorium?

"It must be difficult being a Soviet ace."

If Mólniya was surprised by Polyakov's sudden statement, he didn't show it. "My power is just another tool to be used against the imperialists."

"I'm sure that's what your superiors would like to think. God forbid you should use it for yourself." Polyakov sat down again. This time he poured himself a glass of water. He held out the bottle to Mólniya, who shook his head. "You must be tired of the jokes by now. Water and electricity."

"Yes," Mólniya said tiredly. "I have to be careful when it rains. I can't take baths. The only water I like is snow.... Given the number of people who know about me, it's amazing how many jokes I've heard."

"They have your family, don't they? Don't answer. It's not something I know. It's just... the only way to control you."

The wild card virus was relatively dissipated by the time it reached the Soviet Union, but it was still strong enough to create jokers and aces, and to cause the creation of a secret state commission to deal with the problem. In typical Stalinist fashion aces were segregated from the population and "educated" in special camps. Jokers simply disappeared. In many ways it was worse than the Purge, which Polyakov had seen as a teenager. In the Thirties the knock on the door came for Party members... those with incorrect ambitions. But *everyone* was at risk during the Wild Card Purge.

Even those in the Kremlin. Even those at the very highest levels.

"I knew someone like you, Mólniya. I used to work for him, not far from here as a matter of fact."

For the first time Mólniya dropped his guard. He was genuinely curious. "Is the legend true?"

"Which legend? That Comrade Stalin was a joker and died with a stake driven through his heart? Or that it was Lysenko who had been affected?" Polyakov could tell that Mólniya knew them all. "I must say I'm shocked to think that such fabrications are circulated by officers of military intelligence!"

"I was thinking of the legend that there was nothing left of Stalin to bury... that the corpse displayed at the funeral was made up by the same geniuses who maintain Lenin's."

Very close, Polyakov thought. What *did* Mólniya know? "You're a war hero, Mólniya. Yet you ran from that building in Berlin like a raw recruit. Why?"

This was another one of the old tricks, the sudden segue back to more immediate business.

As Mólniya replied that he didn't honestly remember running, Polyakov went around the table and, sliding a chair closer, sat down right next to him. They were so close that Polyakov could smell the soap and, under that, the sweat... and something that might have been ozone. "Can you tell when someone is an ace?"

Finally Mólniya was getting nervous. "Not without some demonstration... no."

Polyakov lowered his voice and jabbed a finger at the Hero's medal on Mólniya's chest. "What do you think now?"

Mólniya's face flushed and tears formed in his eyes. One gloved hand slapped Polyakov's away. It only lasted an instant.

"I was burning up!"

"Within seconds, yes. Burnt meat."

"*You're* the one." There was as much fascination—after all, they had a lot in common—as fear in Mólniya's face. "That was another one of the legends, that there was a second ace. But you were supposed to be in the Party hierarchy, one of Brezhnev's people."

Polyakov shrugged. "The second ace belongs to no one. He's very careful about that. His loyalty is to the Soviet Union. To Soviet ideals and potential, not the pitiful reality." He remained close to Mólniya. "And now you know my secret. One ace to another... what do *you* have to tell *me?*"

It was good to leave the Aquarium. Years of institutional hatred had imbued the place with an almost physical barrier—

like an electrical charge—that repelled all enemies, especially
the KGB.

Polyakov should have been feeling elated: he had gotten
some very important information out of Mólniya. Even Mólniya
himself did not know how important. No one knew why the
Hartmann kidnapping had fallen apart, but what had happened
to Mólniya could best be explained by the presence of a
secret ace, one with the power to control men's actions.
Mólniya could not know, of course, that something much like
this had happened in Syria. But Polyakov had seen that
report. Polyakov was afraid he knew the answer.

*The man who might very well be the next president of
the United States was an ace.*

ii.

"The chairman will see you now."

To Polyakov's surprise the receptionist was a young
woman of striking beauty, a blonde straight out of an American movie. Gone was Seregin, Andropov's old gatekeeper, a
man with the physical appearance of a hatchet—appropriately
enough—and a personality to match. Seregin was perfectly
capable of letting a Politburo member cool his heels for
eternity in this outer office, or if necessary, physically ejecting
anyone foolish enough to make an unexpected call on the chairman of the Committee for State Security, the chief of the KGB.

Polyakov imagined that this lissome woman was potentially just as lethal as Seregin; nevertheless, the whole idea
struck him as ludicrous. An attempt to put a smile on the
face of the tiger. Meet your new, caring Kremlin. Today's
friendly KGB!

Seregin was gone. But then, so was Andropov. And
Polyakov himself was no longer welcome on the top floor . . . not
without the chairman's invitation.

The chairman rose from his desk to kiss him, interrupting
Polyakov's salute. "Georgy Vladimirovich, how nice to see
you." He was directed to a couch—another new addition,
some kind of conversational nook in the formerly Spartan
office. "You're not often seen in these parts." *By your choice,*
Polyakov wanted to say.

"My duties have kept me away."

"Of course. The rigors of field work." The chairman, who like most KGB chiefs since Stalin's day was essentially a Party political appointee, had served the KGB as a snitch—a *stukach*—not an operative or analyst. In this he was the perfect leader of an organization consisting of a million *stukachi*. "Tell me about your visit to the Aquarium."

Quickly to business. Another sign of the Gorbachev style. Polyakov was thorough to the point of tedium in his replay of the interrogation, with one significant omission. He counted on the chairman's famous impatience and wasn't disappointed.

"These operational details are all well and good, Georgy Vladimirovich, but wasted on poor bureaucrats, hmm?" A self-deprecating smile. "Did the GRU give you full and complete cooperation, as directed by the General Secretary."

"Yes . . . alas," Polyakov said, earning the chairman's equally famous laugh.

"Do you have enough information to salvage our European operations?"

"Yes."

"How will you proceed? I understand that the German networks are being rolled up. Every day Aeroflot brings our agents back to us."

"Those not held for trial in the West, yes," Polyakov said. "Berlin is a wasteland for us now. Most of Germany is barren and will be for years."

"Carthage."

"But we have other assets. Deep-cover assets that have not been utilized in years. I propose to activate one known as the Dancer."

The chairman drew out pen and made a note to have the Dancer file brought up from the registry. He nodded. "How much time will this . . . recovery take, in your honest estimation?"

"At least two years."

The chairman's gaze drifted off. "Which brings me to a question of my own," Polyakov persisted. "My retirement."

"Yes, your retirement." The chairman sighed. "I think the only course is to bring Yurchenko in on this as soon as possible, since he'll be the one who has to finish the job."

"Unless I postpone my retirement." Polyakov had said the unspeakable. He watched the chairman make an unaccustomed search for an unprogrammed response.

"Well. That would be a problem, wouldn't it? All the papers have been signed. Yurchenko's promotion is already approved. You will be promoted to general and will receive your third Hero's medal. We're prepared to announce it at the plenum next month." The chairman leaned forward. "Is it money, Georgy Vladimirovich? I shouldn't mention this, but there is often a pension bonus for extremely... valuable service."

It wasn't going to work. The chairman might be a political hack, but he was not without his skills. He had been ordered to clean house at the KGB and clean house he would. Right now he feared Gorbachev more than he feared an old spy.

Polyakov sighed. "I only want to finish my job. If that is not the... desire of the Party, I will retire as agreed."

The chairman had been anticipating a fight and was relieved to have won so quickly. "I understand the difficulty of your situation, Georgy Vladimirovich. We all know your tenacity. We don't have enough like you. But Yurchenko is capable. After all... you trained him."

"I'll brief him."

"I tell you what," the chairman said. "Your retirement doesn't take effect until the end of August."

"My sixty-third birthday."

"I see no reason why we should deprive ourselves of your talents until that date." The chairman was writing notes to himself again. "This is highly unusual, as you well know, but why don't you go with Yurchenko? Hmm? Where is this Dancer?"

"France, at the moment, or England."

The chairman was pleased. "I'm sure we can think of worse places for a business trip." He wrote another note with his pen. "I will authorize you to accompany Yurchenko... to assist in the transition. Charming bureaucratic phrase."

"Thank you."

"Nonsense, you've earned it." The chairman got up and went to the sideboard. That, at least, had not changed. He drew out a bottle of vodka that was almost empty, pouring two glasses full, which finished it. "A forbidden toast—the end of an era!" They drank.

The chairman sat down again. "What will happen to Mólniya? No matter how badly he bungled Berlin, he's too valuable to waste in that horrible furnace of theirs."

"He's teaching tactics now, here in Moscow. In time, if he's good, they may let him return to fieldwork."

The chairman shuddered visibly. "What a mess." His tight smile showed a pair of steel teeth. "Having a wild card working for you! I wonder, would one ever sleep?"

Polyakov drained his glass. "*I* wouldn't."

iii.

Polyakov loved the English newspapers. *The Sun . . . The Mirror . . . The Globe . . .* with their screaming three-inch headlines about the latest royal rows and their naked women, they were bread and circus rolled into one. At the moment some M P was on trial, accused of hiring a prostitute for fifty pounds and then, in *The Sun*'s typically restrained words, "Not getting his money's worth!" ("'It was over so *fast*,' tart claims!") Which was the greater sin? Polyakov wondered.

A tiny deck on that same front page mentioned that the Aces Tour had arrived in London.

Perhaps Polyakov's affection for the papers derived from professional appreciation. Whenever he was in the West, his legend or cover was that of a Tass correspondent, which had required him to master enough rudimentary journalistic skills to pass, though most Western reporters he met *assumed* he was a spy. He had never learned to write well—certainly not with the drunken eloquence of his Fleet Street colleagues— but he could hold his liquor and he could find a story.

At that level, at least, journalism and intelligence were not mutually exclusive.

Alas, Polyakov's old haunts were unsuitable for a rendezvous with the Dancer. Recognition of either of them would be disastrous for both. They could not, in fact, use a public house of any kind.

To make matters worse, the Dancer was an uncontrolled agent—a "cooperative asset" to use Moscow Center's increasingly bland jargon. Polyakov had not even seen him in over twenty years, and that had been an accidental encounter following even more years of separation. There were no prearranged signals, no message drops, no intermediaries, no channels to let the Dancer know that Polyakov had come to collect.

Though the Dancer's notoriety made certain kinds of contacts impossible, it made Polyakov's job easier in one respect: If he wanted to know how to find this particular asset—

—all he had to do was pick up a paper.

His assistant, and future successor, Yurchenko, was busy ingratiating himself with the London *rezident;* both men showed only a passing interest in Polyakov's comings and goings, joking that their soon-to-be- retired friend was spending his time with King's Cross whores—"Just be sure you don't wind up in the newspapers, Georgy Vladimirovich," Yurchenko had teased. "If you do . . . at *least* get your money's worth!"—since such behavior by Polyakov was not unprecedented. Well . . . he had never married. And years in Germany, particularly in Hamburg, had given him a taste for pretty young mouths at affordable prices. It was also quite true that the KGB did not trust an agent who possessed no notable weakness. One vice was tolerated, so long as it was one of the controllable ones—alcohol, money, or women—rather than, say, religion. A dinosaur such as Polyakov—who had worked for Beria, for God's sake!—having a taste for honey . . . well, that was considered rakish, even charming.

From the Tass office near Fleet, Polyakov went alone to the Grosvenor House Hotel, riding in one of the famous English black cabs—this one actually belonged to the Embassy— down Park Lane to Knightsbridge to Kensington Road. It was early on a work day and the cab crawled through a sea of vehicles and humanity. The sun was up, burning off the morning haze. It was going to be a beautiful London spring day.

At Grosvenor House, Polyakov had to talk his way past several very obvious guards while noting the presence of several discreet ones. He was allowed as far as the concierge station, where he found, to his annoyance, another young woman in place of the usual old scout. This one even looked like the chairman's new gatekeeper. "Will the house telephone put me through to the floors where the Aces Tour is staying?"

The concierge frowned and framed a reply. Clearly the tour's presence here was not common knowledge, but Polyakov preempted her questions, as he had gotten past the guards, by presenting his press credentials. She examined them—they were genuine in any case—then guided him to the telephones. "They might not be answering at this hour, but these lines are direct."

"Thank you." He waited until she had withdrawn, then asked the operator to ring through to the room number one of the Embassy's footmen had already provided.

"Yes?" Polyakov had not expected the voice to change, yet he was surprised that it had not.

"It's been a long time . . . Dancer."

Polyakov was not surprised by the long silence at the other end. "It's you, isn't it?"

He was pleased. The Dancer retained enough tradecraft to keep the telephone conversations bland. "Didn't I promise that I would give you a visit someday?"

"What do you want?"

"To meet, what else? To see you."

"This is hardly the place—"

"There's a cab waiting out front. It'll be easy to spot. It's the only one at the moment."

"I'll be down in a few minutes."

Polyakov hung up and hurried out to the cab, not forgetting to nod to the concierge again.

"Any luck?"

"Enough. Thank you."

He slipped into the cab and closed the door. His heart was pounding. *My God*, he thought, *I'm like a teenager waiting for a girl!*

Before long the door opened. Immediately Polyakov was awash in the Dancer's scent. He extended his hand in the Western fashion. "Dr. Tachyon, I presume."

The driver was a young Uzbek from the Embassy whose professional specialty was economic analysis, but whose greatest virtue was his ability to keep his mouth shut. His total lack of interest in Polyakov's activities and the challenge of navigating London's busy streets allowed Polyakov and Tachyon some privacy.

Polyakov's wild card had no face, so he had never been suspected of being an ace or joker. That, and the fact that he had only used his powers twice:

The first time was in the long, brutal winter of 1946–47, the winter following the release of the virus. Polyakov was a senior lieutenant then, having spent the Great Patriotic War as a *zampolit*, or political officer, at the munitions factories in the Urals. When the Nazis surrendered, Moscow Center assigned him to the counterinsurgency forces fighting Ukrainian nationalists—the "men from the forests" who had fought with the Nazis and had no intentions of giving up. (In fact they continued fighting until 1952.)

Polyakov's boss there was a thug named Suvin, who confessed drunkenly one night that he had been an executioner in the Lubiyanka during the Purge. Suvin had developed a real taste for torture; Polyakov wondered if that was the only possible response to a job that daily required one to shoot a fellow Party member in the back of the neck. One evening Polyakov brought in a Ukrainian teenager, a boy, for questioning. Suvin had been drinking and began to beat a confession out of the kid, which was a waste of time: the boy had already confessed to stealing food. But Suvin wanted to link him to the rebels.

Polyakov remembered, mostly, that he had been tired. Like everyone in the Soviet Union in that year, including those at the very highest levels, he was often hungry. It was the fatigue, he thought shamefully now, not human compassion, that made him leap at Suvin and shove him aside. Suvin turned on him and they fought. From underneath the other man, Polyakov managed to get his hands on his throat. There was no chance he could choke him . . . yet Suvin suddenly turned red—dangerously red—and literally burst into flames.

The young prisoner was unconscious and knew nothing. Since fatalities in the war zone were routinely ascribed to enemy action, the bully Suvin was officially reported to have died "heroically" of "extreme thoracic trauma" and "burns," euphemisms for being fried to a cinder. The incident terrified Polyakov. At first he didn't even realize what had happened; information on the wild card virus was restricted. But eventually he realized that he had a power . . . that he was an ace. And he swore never to use the power again.

He had only broken that promise once.

By the autumn of 1955, Georgy Vladimirovich Polyakov, now a captain in the "organs," was using the legend of a junior Tass reporter in West Berlin. Aces and jokers were much in the news in those days. The Tass men monitored the Washington hearings with horror—it reminded some of them of the Purge—and delight. The mighty American aces were being neutralized by their own countrymen!

It was known that some aces and their Takisian puppet master (as *Pravda* described him) had fled the U.S. following the first HUAC hearings. They became high-priority targets for the Eighth Directorate, the KGB department responsible for Western Europe. Tachyon in particular was a personal target for Polyakov. Perhaps the Takisian held some clue to the secret of the wild card virus...something to explain it...something to make it go away. When he heard that the Takisian was on the skids in Hamburg, he was off.

Since Polyakov had made prior "research" trips to Hamburg's red-light district, he knew which brothels were likely to cater to an unusual client such as Tachyon. He found the alien in the third establishment he tried. It was near dawn; the Takisian was drunk, passed out, and out of money. Tachyon should have been grateful: the Germans as a race had little liking for drunken indigents; masters of Hamburg whorehouses had even less. Tachyon would have been lucky to have been dumped in the canal...alive.

Polyakov had him taken to a safe house in East Berlin, where, after a prolonged argument among the *rezidenti,* he was supplied with controlled amounts of alcohol and women while he slowly regained his health...and while Polyakov and at least a dozen others questioned him. Even Shelepin himself took time out from his plotting back in Moscow to visit.

Within three weeks it was clear that Tachyon had nothing left to give. More likely, Polyakov suspected, the Takisian had regained sufficient strength to withstand any further interrogation. Nevertheless, he had supplied them with so much data on the American aces, on Takisian history and science, and on the wild card virus itself, that Polyakov half-expected his superiors to give the alien a medal and a pension.

They did almost as much. Like the German rocket engineers captured after the war, Tachyon's ultimate fate was to be quietly repatriated...in this case to West Berlin. They transferred Polyakov to the illegals residence there at the same time, hoping for residual contacts, and allowing both men a simultaneous introduction to the city. Because of East Berlin, they would never be friends. Because of their time in the western sector, they could never be total enemies.

"In forty years on this world I've learned to alter my expectations every day," Tachyon told him. "I honestly thought you were dead."

"Soon enough I will be," Polyakov said. "But you look better now that you did in Berlin. The years truly pass slowly for your kind."

"Too slowly at times." They rode in silence for a while,

each pretending to enjoy the scenery while each ordered his memories of the other.

"Why are you here?" Tachyon asked.

"To collect on a debt."

Tachyon nodded slightly, a gesture that showed how thoroughly assimilated he had become. "That's what I thought."

"You knew it would happen one day."

"Of course! Please don't misunderstand! My people honor their commitments. You saved my life. You have a right to anything I can give you." Then he smiled tightly. "This one time."

"How close are you to Senator Gregg Hartmann?"

"He's a senior member of this tour, so I've had some contact with him. Obviously not much lately, following that terrible business in Berlin."

"What do you think of him... as a man?"

"I don't know him well enough to judge. He's a politician, and as a rule I despise politicians. In that sense he strikes me as the best of a bad lot. He seems to be genuine in his support for jokers, for example. This is probably not an issue in your country, but it's a very emotional one in America, comparable to abortion rights." He paused. "I doubt very much he would be susceptible to any kind of... arrangement, if that's what you're asking."

"I see you've taken up reading spy novels," Polyakov said. "I'm more interested in... let's call it a political analysis. Is it possible that he will become president of the United States?"

"Very possible. Reagan has been crippled by his current crisis and is not, in my judgment, a well man. He has no obvious successor, and the American economy is likely to worsen before the election."

The first piece of the puzzle: There is one American politician who has left in his wake a series of mysterious deaths worthy of Beria or Stalin.... The second: The same politician is kidnapped—twice. And escapes under mysterious circumstances—twice.

"The Democrats have several candidates, none without major weaknesses. Hart is sure to eliminate himself. Biden, Dukakis, any of the others could disappear tomorrow. If Hartmann can put together a strong organization, and if the right opening occurs, he could win."

A recent Moscow Center briefing had predicted that

Dole would be the next U.S. president. Strategists at the American Institute were already creating an expert psychological model of the senator from Kansas. But these were the same analysts who predicted Ford over Carter and Carter over Reagan. On the principle that events never turn out the way experts say, Polyakov was inclined to believe Tachyon.

Even the theoretical possibility of a Hartmann presidency was important... if he was an ace! He needed to be watched, stopped if necessary, but Moscow Center would never authorize such a move, especially if it contradicted its expensive little studies.

The driver, by prearrangement, headed back toward Grosvenor House. The rest of the trip was spent in reminiscence of the two Berlins, even of Hamburg. "You aren't satisfied, are you?" Tachyon said finally. "You want more from me than a superficial political analysis, surely."

"You know the answer to that."

"I have no secret documents to give you. I'm hardly inconspicuous enough to work as a spy."

"You have your *powers*, Tachyon—"

"*And* my limitations! You know what I will and will not do."

"I'm not your enemy, Tachyon! I'm the only one who even remembers your debt, and in August I'll be retired. At this point I'm just an old man trying to put together the pieces of a puzzle."

"Then tell me about your puzzle—"

"You know better than that."

"Then how can I possibly help you?" Polyakov didn't answer. "You're afraid that by even asking me a direct question, I'll learn too much. Russians!"

For a moment Polyakov wished for a wild card power that would let him read minds. Tachyon had many human characteristics, but he was Takisian... all of Polyakov's years of training did not help him decide whether or not he was lying. Must he depend on Takisian honor?

The cab pulled up to the curb and the driver opened the door. But Tachyon didn't get out. "What's going to happen to you?"

What, indeed? Polyakov thought. "I'm going to become an honored pensioner, like Khrushchev, able to go to the front of a queue, spending my days reading and reliving my exploits over a bottle of vodka for men who will not believe them."

Tachyon hesitated. "For years I hated you...not for exploiting my weakness, but for saving my life. I was in Hamburg because I wanted to die. But now, finally, I have something to live for...it's only been very recent. So I *am* grateful, you know."

Then he got out of the cab and slammed the door. "I'll see you again," he said, hoping for a denial.

"Yes," Polyakov said, "you will." The driver pulled away. In the rearview mirror Polyakov saw that the Takisian watched them drive off before going into his hotel.

No doubt he wondered where and when Polyakov would turn up again. Polyakov wondered too. He was all alone now...mocked by his colleagues, discarded by the Party, loyal to some ideal that he only barely remembered. Like poor Mólniya in a way, sent out on some misguided mission and then abandoned.

The fate of a Soviet ace is to be betrayed.

He was scheduled to remain in London for several weeks yet, but if he could no longer extract useful information from a relatively cooperative source such as the Dancer, there was no point in staying. That night he packed for the return to Moscow and his retirement. After a dinner in which he was joined only by a bottle of Stolichnaya, Polyakov left the hotel and took a walk, down Sloane, past the fashionable boutiques. What did they call the young women who shopped here? Yes, Sloane Rangers. The Rangers, to judge from the stray samples still hurrying home at this hour, or from the bizarre mannequins in the windows, were thin, wraithlike creatures. Too fragile for Polyakov.

In any case, his ultimate destination...his farewell to London and the West...was King's Cross, where the women were more substantial.

On reaching Pont Street, however, he noticed an off-duty black cab following him. In moments he considered possible assailants, ranging from renegade American agents to Light of Allah terrorists to English hoodlums...until he read, in the reflection from a shop window, the license number of a vehicle belonging to the Soviet Embassy. Further examination revealed that the driver was Yurchenko.

Polyakov dropped his evasions and simply met the car.

In the back was a man he didn't know. "Georgy Vladimirovich," Yurchenko shouted. "Get in!"

"There's no need to yell," Polyakov said. "You'll draw attention." Yurchenko was one of those polished young men for whom tradecraft came so easily that, unless reminded, he often neglected to use it.

As soon as Polyakov was aboard in the front seat, the car jumped into traffic. They were quite obviously going for a ride.

"We thought we were losing you," Yurchenko said pleasantly.

"What's this all about?" Polyakov said. He indicated the silent man in the backseat. "Who's your friend?"

"This is Dolgov of the GRU. He's presented me with some very disturbing news."

For the first time in years Polyakov felt real fear. Was *this* to be his retirement? An "accidental" death in a foreign country?

"Don't keep me in suspense, Yurchenko. The last time I checked, I was still your boss."

Yurchenko couldn't look at him. "The Takisian is a double agent. He's working for the Americans and has for thirty years."

Polyakov turned toward the GRU man. "So now the GRU is *sharing* its precious intelligence. What a great day for the Soviet Union. I suppose I'm suspected of being an agent."

The GRU man spoke for the first time. "What did the Takisian give you?"

"I'm not talking to you. What my agents give me is KGB business—"

"The GRU will share with you, then. Tachyon has a grandson named Blaise, whom he found in Paris last month. Blaise is a new kind of ace ... potentially the most powerful and dangerous in the world. And he was snatched right out of our hands to be taken to America."

The car was crossing Lambeth Bridge, heading toward a gray and depressing industrial district, a perfect location for a safe house ... the perfect setting for an execution.

Tachyon had a grandson with powers! Suppose this child came into contact with Hartmann—the potential was horrifying. Life in a world threatened by nuclear destruction was safe compared to one dominated by a wild card Ronald Reagan. How could he have been so stupid?

"I didn't know," he said finally. "Dancer was not an active agent. There was no reason to place him under surveillance."

"But there was," Dolgov persisted. "He's a goddamned alien, for one thing! And if his presence on the tour itself wasn't enough, there was the situation in Paris!"

It was easy for the GRU to spy on someone in Paris: the embassy there was full of its operatives. Of course the sister service hadn't bothered to pass its vital information along to the KGB. Polyakov would have acted differently with Mólniya had he known about Blaise!

Now he needed time to think. He realized he had been holding his breath. A bad habit. "This is serious. We should obviously be working together. I'm ready to do whatever I can—"

"Then why are you packed?" Yurchenko interrupted, sounding genuinely anguished.

"You've been watching me?" He looked from Yurchenko to Dolgov. My God, they *actually* thought he was going to defect!

Polyakov turned slightly, his hand brushing Yurchenko, who recoiled as if slapped. But Polyakov didn't let go. The cab sideswiped a parked car and skidded back into traffic just as Polyakov saw Yurchenko's eyes roll up . . . the heat had already boiled his brain.

Dolgov threw himself into the front seat, grabbing for the wheel, and managed to steer right into another parked car, where they stopped. Polyakov had braced for the impact, which threw Yurchenko's smoking body off him . . . freeing him to reach out for Dolgov, who made the mistake of grabbing back.

For an instant Dolgov's face was the face of the Great Leader . . . the Benevolent Father of the Soviet People . . . himself turned into a murderous joker. Polyakov was just a young courier who carried messages between the Kremlin and Stalin's dacha—sufficiently trusted that he was allowed to know the secret of Great Stalin's curse—not an assassin. He had never intended to be an assassin. But Stalin had already ordered the execution of *all* wild cards. . . .

If it was his destiny to carry this power, it must also be his destiny to use it. As he had eliminated Stalin, so he eliminated Dolgov. He didn't allow the man to say a word, not even the final gesture of defiance, as he burned the life out of him.

The impact had jammed the two front doors, so Polyakov would have to crawl out the back. Before he did, he removed the silencer and the heavy service revolver Dolgov carried... the weapon he was to have pressed to the back of Polyakov's neck. Polyakov fired a round into the air, then put the revolver back where Dolgov carried it. Scotland Yard and the GRU could think what they liked... another unsolved murder with the murderers themselves the victims of an unlucky accident.

The fire from the two bodies reached the tiny trickle of gasoline spilled in the crash.... The crematorium would not get Dolgov.

The explosion and flames would attract attention. Polyakov knew he should go... yet there was something attractive in the flames. As if an aged, dutiful KGB colonel were dying, too, to be reborn as a superhero, the one true Soviet ace....

This would be a legend of his *own* creation.

iv.

There were many signs in Russian at the British Airways terminal at Robert Tomlin International Airport, placed there by members of Jewish Relief, headquartered in nearby Brighton Beach. For Jews who managed to emigrate from the Eastern bloc, even those who dreamed of eventually settling in Palestine, this was their Ellis Island.

Among those debarking this day in May was a stocky man in his early sixties, dressed like a typical middle-class émigré, in brown shirt buttoned to the neck and well-worn gray jacket. A woman from Relief stepped forward to help him. *"Strasvitye s Soyuzom Statom,"* she said in Russian, "Welcome to the United States."

"Thank you," the man replied in English.

The woman was pleased. "If you already speak the language, you will find things very easy here. May I help you?"

"No, I know what I'm doing."

Out there, in the city, waited Dr. Tachyon, living in fear of their next encounter, wondering what it would mean to his very special grandson. To the south, Washington, and Senator Hartmann, a formidable target. But Polyakov would not work alone. No sooner had he gone underground in England than he had managed to contact the shattered remains of Mólniya's network. Next week Gimli would be joining him in America. . . .

As he waited for customs to clear his meager luggage, Polyakov could see through the windows that it was a beautiful American summer day.

FROM *THE JOURNAL OF XAVIER DESMOND*

April 27/ SOMEWHERE OVER THE ATLANTIC:

The interior lights were turned out several hours ago, and most of my fellow travelers are long asleep, but the pain has kept me awake. I've taken some pills, and they are helping, but still I cannot sleep. Nonetheless, I feel curiously elated... almost serene. The end of my journey is near, in both the larger and smaller senses. I've come a long way, yes, and for once I feel good about it.

We still have one more stop—a brief sojourn in Canada, whirlwind visits to Montreal and Toronto, a government reception in Ottawa. And then home. Tomlin International, Manhattan, Jokertown. It will be good to see the Funhouse again.

I wish I could say that the tour had accomplished everything we set out to do, but that's scarcely the case. We began well, perhaps, but the violence in Syria, West Germany, and France undid our unspoken dream of making the public forget the carnage of Wild Card Day. I can only hope that the majority will realize that terrorism is a bleak and ugly part of the world we live in, that it would exist with or without the wild card. The bloodbath in Berlin was instigated by a group that included jokers, aces, and nats, and we would do well to remember that and remind the world of it forcefully. To lay that carnage at the door of Gimli and his pathetic followers, or the two fugitive aces still being sought by the German police, is to play into the hands of men like Leo Barnett and the Nur al- Allah. Even if the Takisians had never brought their curse to us, the world would have no shortage of desperate, insane, and evil men.

For me, there is a grim irony in the fact that it was Gregg's courage and compassion that put his life at risk, and hatred that saved him, by turning his captors against each other in that fratricidal holocaust.

Truly, this is a strange world.

I pray that we have seen the last of Gimli, but meanwhile I can rejoice. After Syria it seems unlikely that anyone could still doubt Gregg Hartmann's coolness under fire, but if that was indeed the case, surely all such fears have now been firmly laid to rest by Berlin. After Sara Morgenstern's exclusive interview was published in the *Post*, I understand Hartmann shot up ten points in the polls. He's almost neck and neck with Hart now. The feeling aboard the plane is that Gregg is definitely going to run.

I said as much to Digger back in Dublin, over a Guinness and some fine Irish soda bread in our hotel, and he agreed. In fact, he went further and predicted that Hartmann would get the nomination. I wasn't quite so certain and reminded him that Gary Hart still seems a formidable obstacle, but Downs grinned in that maddeningly cryptic way of his beneath his broken nose and said, "Yeah, well, I got this hunch that Gary is going to fuck up and do something really stupid, don't ask me why."

If my health permits, I will do everything I can to rally Jokertown behind a Hartmann candidacy. I don't think I'm alone in my commitment either. After the things we have seen, both at home and abroad, a growing number of prominent aces and jokers are likely to throw their weight behind the senator. Hiram Worchester, Peregrine, Mistral, Father Squid, Jack Braun... perhaps even Dr. Tachyon, despite his notorious distaste for politics and politicians.

Terrorism and bloodshed notwithstanding, I do believe we accomplished some good on this journey. Our report will open some official eyes, I can only hope, and the press spotlight that has shone on us everywhere has greatly increased public awareness of the plight of jokers in the Third World.

On a more personal level, Jack Braun did much to redeem himself and even buried his thirty-year emnity with Tachyon; Peri seems positively radiant in her pregnancy; and we did manage, however belatedly, to free poor Jeremiah Strauss from twenty years of simian bondage. I remember Strauss from the old days, when Angela owned the Funhouse and I was only the maître d', and I offered him a booking if and when he resumes his theatrical career as the Projectionist. He was appreciative, but noncommittal. I don't envy him his period of adjustment. For all practical purposes, he is a time traveler.

And Dr. Tachyon . . . well, his new punk haircut is ugly in the extreme, he still favors his wounded leg, and by now the entire plane knows of his sexual dysfunction, but none of this seems to bother him since young Blaise came aboard in France. Tachyon has been evasive about the boy in his public statements, but of course everyone knows the truth. The years he spent in Paris are scarcely a state secret, and if the boy's hair was not a sufficient clue, his mind control power makes his lineage abundantly clear.

Blaise is a strange child. He seemed a little awed by the jokers when he first joined us, particularly Chrysalis, whose transparent skin clearly fascinated him. On the other hand, he has all of the natural cruelty of an unschooled child (and believe me, any joker knows how cruel a child can be). One day in London, Tachyon got a phone call and had to leave for a few hours. While he was gone, Blaise grew bored, and to amuse himself he seized control of Mordecai Jones and made him climb onto a table and recite "I'm a Little Teapot," which Blaise had just learned as part of an English lesson. The table collapsed under the Hammer's weight, and I don't think Jones is likely to forget the humiliation. He didn't much like Dr. Tachyon to begin with.

Of course not everyone will look back on this tour fondly. The trip was very hard on a number of us, there's no gainsaying that. Sara Morgenstern has filed several major stories and done some of the best writing of her career, but nonetheless the woman is edgier and more neurotic with every passing day. As for her colleagues in the back of the plane, Josh McCoy seems alternately madly in love with Peregrine and absolutely furious with her, and it cannot be easy for him with the whole world knowing that he is not the father of her child. Meanwhile, Digger's profile will never be the same.

Downs is, at least, as irrepressible as he is irresponsible. Just the other day he was telling Tachyon that if he got an exclusive on Blaise, maybe he would be able to keep Tach's impotence off-the-record. This gambit was not well received. Digger has also been thick as thieves with Chrysalis of late. I overheard them having a very curious conversation in the bar one night in London. "I know he is," Digger was saying. Chrysalis told him that knowing it and proving it were two different things. Digger said something about how they *smelled* different to him, how he'd known ever since they met, and Chrysalis just laughed and said that was fine, but smells that no one else could detect weren't much good as proof, and even if they were, he'd have to blow his own cover to go public. They were still going at it when I left the bar.

I think even Chrysalis will be delighted to return to Jokertown. Clearly she loved England, but given her Anglophile tendencies, that was hardly a surprise. There was one tense moment when she was introduced to Churchill during a reception, and he gruffly inquired as to exactly what she was trying to prove with her affected British accent. It is quite difficult to read expressions on her unique features, but for a moment I was sure she was going to kill the old man right there in front of the Queen, Prime Minister, and a dozen British aces. Thankfully she gritted her teeth and put it down to Lord Winston's advanced age. Even when he was younger, he was never precisely reticent about expressing his thoughts.

Hiram Worchester has perhaps suffered more on this trip than any of us. Whatever reserves of strength were left to him burned out in Germany, and since then he has seemed exhausted. He shattered his special custom seat as we were leaving Paris—some sort of miscalculation with his gravity control, I believe, but it delayed us nearly three hours while repairs were made. His temper has been fraying too. During the business with the seat, Billy Ray made one too many fat jokes, and Hiram finally snapped and turned on him in a white rage, calling him (among other things) an "incompetent little guttermouth." That was all it took. Carnifex just grinned that ugly little grin of his, said, "For that you get your ass kicked, fat man," and started to get out of his seat. "I didn't say you could get up," Hiram replied; he made a fist and trebled Billy's weight, slamming him right back into the seat cushion. Billy was still straining to get up and Hiram was making him heavier and heavier, and I don't know where it might have ended if Dr. Tachyon hadn't broken it up by putting both of them to sleep with his mind control.

I don't know whether to be disgusted or amused when I see these world-famous aces squabbling like petty children, but Hiram at least has the excuse of ill health. He looks terrible these days: white-faced, puffy, perspiring, short of breath. He has a huge, hideous scab on his neck, just below the collar line, that he picks at when he thinks no one is watching. I would strongly advise him to seek out medical attention, but he is so surly of late that I doubt my counsel would be welcomed. His short visits to New York during the tour always seemed to do him a world of good, however, so we can only hope that homecoming restores his health and spirits.

And lastly, me.

Observing and commenting on my fellow travelers and what they've gained or lost, that's the easy part. Summing up my own experience is harder. I'm older and, I hope, wiser than when we left Tomlin International, and undeniably I am five months closer to death.

Whether this journal is published or not after my passing, Mr. Ackroyd assures me that he will personally deliver copies to my grandchildren and do everything in his power to make sure that they are read. So perhaps it is to them that I write these last, concluding words . . . to them, and all the others like them. . . .

Robert, Cassie . . . we never met, you and I, and the blame for that falls as much on me as on your mother and your grandmother. If you wonder why, remember what I wrote about self-loathing and please understand that I was not exempt. Don't think too harshly of me . . . or of your mother or grandmother. Joanna was far too young to understand what was happening when her daddy changed, and as for Mary . . . we loved each other once, and I cannot go to my grave hating her. The truth is, had our roles been reversed, I might well have done the same thing. We're all only human, and we do the best we can with the hand that fate has dealt us.

Your grandfather was a joker, yes. But I hope as you read this book you'll realize that he was something else as well—that he accomplished a few things, spoke up for his people, did some good. The JADL is perhaps as good a legacy as most men leave behind them, a better monument to my mind than the Pyramids, the Taj Mahal, or Jetboy's Tomb. All in all, I haven't done so badly. I'll leave behind some friends who loved me, many treasured memories, much unfinished business. I've wet my foot in the Ganges, heard Big Ben sound the hour, and walked on the Great Wall of China. I've seen my daughter born and held her in my arms, and I've dined with aces and TV stars, with presidents and kings.

Most important, I think I leave the world a slightly better place for my having been in it. And that's really all that can be asked of any of us.

Remember me to your children, if you will.

My name was Xavier Desmond, and I was a man.

FROM *THE NEW YORK TIMES*

JULY 17, 1987

Xavier Desmond, the founder and president emeritus of the Jokers' Anti-Defamation League (JADL) and a community leader among the victims of the wild card virus for more than two decades, died yesterday at the Blythe van Rensselaer Memorial Clinic, after a long illness.

Desmond, who was popularly known as the "Mayor of Jokertown," was the owner of the Funhouse, a well-known Bowery night spot. He began his political activities in 1964, when he founded the JADL to combat prejudice against wild card victims and promote community education about the virus and its effects. In time, the JADL became the nation's largest and most influential joker rights organization, and Desmond the most widely-respected joker spokesman. He sat on several mayors' advisory committees, served as a delegate on the recent global tour sponsored by the World Health Organization. Although he stepped down as president of the JADL in 1984, citing age and ill health, he continued to influence the organization's policies until his death.

He is survived by his former wife, Mary Radford Desmond, his daughter, Mrs. Joanna Horton, and his grandchildren, Robert Van Ness and Cassandra Horton.

THE STRANGE HISTORY OF
THE WILD CARDS

It all began in 1946 . . .

When a bizarre gene-altering virus was unleashed in the skies over New York City. It came from an alien planet, brought by scientists who regarded humanity as nothing more than useful guinea pigs. One of their number found the plan ignoble, unworthy of Takisians. In orbit above Earth, he battled against his fellows . . . but lost.

His spacecraft was crippled. The other—the ship carrying the virus—crashed, and its Takisian passengers were killed. Before any authorities could reach it, the deadly virus was released. . . .

The street was full of stopped cars now, for as far as Croyd could see in either direction. There were people on the tops of buildings and people at every window, most of them looking upward.

He rushed to the sidewalk and turned right. His home was six blocks to the south, in an anomalous group of row houses in the eighties. Joe's route took him half that way, then off to the east.

Before they reached the corner they were halted as a stream of people flowed from the side street to the right, cutting into their line of pedestrian traffic, some turning north and trying to push through, others heading south. The boys heard cursing and the sound of a fistfight from up ahead.

A man lay upon the pavement. He was having convulsions. His head and hands had swollen enormously, and they were dark red, almost purple in color. Just as they caught sight of him, blood began to rush from his nose and mouth; it trickled from his ears, it oozed from his eyes and about his fingernails.

"Holy Mary!" Joe said, crossing himself as he drew back. "What's he got?"

"I don't know," Croyd answered. "Let's not get too close."

Croyd saw a reptilian face through a windshield then, and scaly hands clutching at a steering wheel that had been torn loose from its column as the driver slowly slumped to the side. Looking away, he saw a rising tower of smoke from beyond buildings to the northeast.

When they reached the corner there was no place to descend. People stood packed and swaying. There were occasional screams. He wanted to cry, but he knew it would do no good. He clenched his teeth and shuddered.

"What're we going to do?" he called to Joe.

"If we're stuck here overnight we can bust the window on an empty car and sleep in it, I guess."

"I want to go home!"

"Me, too. Let's try and keep going as far as we can."

Croyd saw a man perform a series of dancelike movements, tearing at his clothing. Then he began to change shape. Someone back up the road started howling. There came sounds of breaking glass.

During the next half-hour the sidewalk traffic thinned to what might, under other circumstances, be called normal. The people seemed either to have achieved their destinations or to have advanced their congestion to some other part of town. Those who passed now picked their way among corpses. Faces had vanished from behind windows. No one was in sight atop the buildings. The sounds of auto horns had diminished to sporadic outbursts. The boys stood on a corner. They had covered three blocks and crossed the street since they had left school.

"I turn here," Joe said. "You want to come with me or you going ahead?"

Croyd looked down the street.

"It looks better now. I think I can make it okay," he said.

"I'll see you."

"Okay."

Joe hurried off to the left. Croyd watched him for a moment, then moved ahead. Far up the street, a man raced from a doorway screaming. He seemed to grow larger and his movements more erratic as he moved to the center of the street. Then he exploded. Croyd pressed his back against the brick wall to his left and stared, heart pounding, but there was no new disturbance. He heard a bullhorn from somewhere to the west. ". . . The bridges are closed to both auto and foot traffic. Do not attempt to use the bridges. Return to your homes. The bridges are closed. . . ."

An army truck rolled from the side street at the corner ahead of him. He ran to it. A helmeted face turned toward him from the passenger side.

"Why are you out, son?" the man asked.

"I'm going home," he answered.

"Where's that?"

He pointed ahead.

"Two blocks," he said.

"Go straight home," the man told him.

"What's happening?"

"We're under martial law. Everybody's got to get indoors. Good idea to keep your windows closed, too."

"Why?"

"It seems that was some kind of germ bomb that went off. Nobody knows for sure."

"Was it Jetboy that . . . ?"

"Jetboy's dead. He tried to stop them."

Croyd's eyes were suddenly brimming.

"Go straight home."

The truck crossed the street and continued on to the west. Croyd ran across and slowed when he reached the sidewalk. He began to shake. He was suddenly aware of the pain in his knees, where he had scraped them in crawling over vehicles. He wiped his eyes. He felt terribly cold. He halted near the middle of the block and yawned several times. Tired. He was incredibly tired. He began moving. His feet felt heavier than he ever remembered. He halted again beneath a tree. There came a moaning from over-head.

When he looked up he realized that it was not a tree. It was tall and brown, rooted and spindly, but there was an enormously elongated human face near its top and it was from there that the moaning came. As he moved away one of the limbs plucked at his shoulder, but it was a weak thing and a few more steps bore him out of its reach. He whimpered. The corner seemed miles away, and then there was another block. . . .

Now DR. TACHYON, the sole surviving Takisian, dedicates his life to the study of the Wild Card Virus and how it might be cured. Unfortunately, it's too late for thousands of people. Many of the survivors of Wild Card Day would be forever changed. Some were called Aces, gifted with extraordinary abilities; others were called Jokers, cursed with bizarre disfigurements.

Their progress through the decades of an everaltered Earth would not be easy. Aces and Jokers alike had to face disdain, jealousy, and fear as America struggled with the anticommunist hysteria of the 1950s, the summer-of-love '60s, and the '70s of Vietnam and Watergate.

Young Croyd, altered forever in the chaos of Wild Card Day, became known as THE SLEEPER. Trapped in an ever-changing form, he tries desperately to resist sleep . . . because every time he wakes he is something new, something strange, something frightening. . . .

Others you will meet in Volume I of the WILD CARDS series include:

GOLDEN BOY—a football hero and actor whose superhuman strength and power brought a meteoric rise and an equally rapid fall.

THE BLACK EAGLE—the powerful, thunderthrowing champion destroyed by the forces of fear in the hate-ridden '50s.

PUPPETMAN—who used his gifts to enslave.

THE GREAT AND POWERFUL TURTLE—a mild-mannered Ace who fought to become a true hero.

WILD CARDS II—ACES HIGH

The year—1979. The place—New York City, home of Aces High, glamorous lounge atop the

Empire State Building, and Jokertown, squalid residence of the city's underclass. The victims of the Wild Card Virus are no longer new and strange, but neither are they accepted by a world that still fears them.

But as the '80s dawn, all eyes are drawn to the skies and the Wild Cards may be the planet's only hope, as an abomination called the Swarm arrives to threaten Earth. . . .

A pillar of darkness rose over Princeton. The android saw it on radar and first thought it smoke, but then realized the cloud did not drift with the wind, but was composed of thousands of living creatures circling over the landscape like a flock of scavenger birds. The pillar was alive.

There was a touch of uncertainty in the android's macroatomic heart. His programming hadn't prepared him for this.

Emergency broadcasts crackled in his mind, questioning, begging for assistance, crying in despair. Modular Man slowed, his perceptions searching the dark land below. Large infrared signatures—more Swarm buds—crawled among tree-lined streets. The signatures were scattered but their movement was purposeful, heading toward the town. It seemed as if Princeton was their rallying point. The android dropped, heard tearing noises, screams, shots. The guns on his shoulders tracked as he dipped and increased speed.

The Swarm bud was legless, moving like a snail with undulating thrusts of its slick thirty-foot body. The head was armored, with dripping sideways jaws. A pair of giant boneless arms terminated in claws. The creature was butting its head into a two-story suburban colonial, punching holes, the arms questing through windows, looking for things that lived inside. Shots were coming from the second floor. Christmas lights blinked from the edges of the roof, the ornamental shrubs.

Modular Man hovered overhead, fired a precise burst from his laser. The pulsed microwave was invisible, silent. The creature quivered, rolled on its side, began to thrash. The house shuddered to mindless blows. The android shot again. The creature trembled, lay still. The android slipped feet first into the window where the shots had been coming from, saw a stark-naked fat man clutching a deer rifle, a teenage boy with a target pistol, a woman clutching two young girls. The woman was screaming. The two girls were too stunned even to tremble. "Jesus Christ," the fat man said.

"I killed it," the android said. "Can you get to your car?"

"I think so," the fat man said. He stuffed rounds into his rifle. His wife was still screaming.

"Head east, toward New York," Modular Man said. "They seem to be thickest around here. Maybe you can convoy with some neighbors."

"What's happening?" the man asked, slamming the bolt back and then forward. "Another Wild Card outbreak?"

"Monsters from space, apparently." There was a crashing sound from behind the house. The android spun, saw what looked like a serpent sixty feet long, moving in curving sidewinder pattern as it bowled down bushes, trees, power poles. The underside of the serpent's body writhed with ten-foot cilia. Modular Man sped out the window, fired another burst of microwave at the thing's head. No effect. Another burst, no success. Behind him, the deer rifle barked.

Other heroes and villains you'll meet in *Aces High* include:

JAMES SPECTOR—possessor of one of the deadliest Ace powers, he can kill with a mere look.

KID DINOSAUR—a starry-eyed teenaged boy whose strange powers earned him a place in the action.

CHRYSALIS—though her skin is transparent, no one can see through to the mysteries she hides within.

JUBE—the walrus who peddles newspapers and, on the side, masterminds an attempt to save the human race.

WILD CARDS III—JOKERS WILD

Every year on September 15, in remembrance of the original Wild Card Day, the streets of New York erupt in celebration. The anniversary is a time for excitement, for grief and joy, for remembering the dead and cherishing the living. It is a day for fireworks and street fairs and parades, for political rallies and memorial banquets, for drinking and fighting in the alleys. With each passing year, the festivities become larger and more fevered.

This year—1986, the fortieth anniversary—promises to be the biggest and best Wild Card Day ever. The media and the tourists have discovered the celebration, and taverns and restaurants expect record-setting business. But lurking in the background is a twisted mind which cares nothing for fun and festivity. The Astronomer has only one concern. Destruction. . . .

The Crystal Palace smelled like any other bar in the morning—like stale smoke and spilled beer and disinfectant. Fortunato found Chrysalis in a dark corner of the club, where her transparent skin made her nearly invisible. He and Brennan sat down across from her.

"You got the message, then," she said in her phony English-public-school accent.

"I got it," Fortunato said. "But the trail's cold. The Astronomer could be anywhere by now. I was hoping you might have something else for me."

"Perhaps. You know a yo-yo calls himself 'Demise'?"

"Yes," Fortunato said. His fingernails dug uselessly at the urethane finish on the table.

"He was in about an hour ago. Sascha got a reading off him, loud and clear. 'He's going to fucking kill me. That twisted old fuck.'"

"Meaning the Astronomer."

"Right you are. This Demise seemed completely round the bend. Had quite a lot on his mind, Sascha said."

"You mean there's more," Fortunato said.

"Yes, but the next bit's going to cost you."

"Cash or favors?"

"Blunt this morning, aren't we? Well, I'm inclined to say favors. And in honor of the holiday, I'll even extend you a line of credit."

"You know I'm good for it," Fortunato said. "Sooner or later."

"I don't like charging for bad news, in any event.

The other line Sascha heard was, 'Maybe he'll be too busy with the others.'"

"Christ," Fortunato said.

Brennan looked at him. "You think he's going on some kind of killing spree."

"The only thing that surprises me is that it took him this long. He must have been waiting for Wild Card Day."

Aces High introduces these Aces and Jokers:

BAGABOND—she commands armies of animals and can send them against predators, human and superhuman.

SEWER JACK—hidden deep in his mind is a monstrous reptile driven by a desperate hunger.

ROULETTE—she kills men with love.

FATMAN—he can command gravity itself.

WILD CARDS IV—ACES ABROAD

Though the Wild Cards Virus burst into existence over New York City, the plague that followed was not confined to the United States. It spawned Aces and Jokers in every country on Earth. Now a fact-finding mission seeks the truth about how Wild Cards are treated in other nations. From the jungles of Haiti to the Great Wall of China and behind the Iron Curtain, the Wild Cards team investigates the fate of their fellows everywhere.

My name is Xavier Desmond, and I am a joker. Jokers are always strangers, even on the street where they were born, and this one is about to visit a number of strange lands. In the next five months I will see veldts and mountains, Rio and Cairo, the Khyber Pass and the Straits of Gibraltar, the Outback and the Champs-Élysées—all very far from home for a man who has often been called the mayor of Jokertown. Jokertown, of course, has no mayor. It is a neighborhood, a ghetto neighborhood at that, and not a city. Jokertown is more than a place though. It is a condition, a state of mind. Perhaps in that sense my title is not undeserved.

I have been a joker since the beginning. Forty years ago, when Jetboy died in the skies over Manhattan and loosed the wild card upon the world, I was twenty-nine years of age, an investment banker with a lovely wife, a two-year-old daughter, and a bright future ahead of me. A month later, when I was finally released from the hospital, I was a monstrosity with a pink elephantine trunk growing from the center of my face where my nose had been. There are seven perfectly functional fingers at the end of my trunk, and over the years I have become quite adept with this "third hand." Were I suddenly restored to so-called normal humanity, I believe it would be as traumatic as if one of my limbs were amputated. With my trunk I am ironically somewhat more than human . . . and infinitely less.

My lovely wife left me within two weeks of my release from the hospital, at approximately the same time that Chase Manhattan informed me that my services would no longer be required. I moved to Jokertown nine months later, following my eviction from my Riverside Drive apartment for "health reasons." I last saw my daughter in 1948.

I am the founder and president emeritus of the

Jokers' Anti-Defamation League, or JADL, the oldest and largest organization dedicated to the preservation of civil rights for the victims of the wild card virus. The JADL has had its failures, but overall it has accomplished great good. I am also a moderately successful businessman. I own one of New York's most storied and elegant nightclubs, the Funhouse, where jokers and nats and aces have enjoyed all the top joker cabaret acts for more than two decades. The Funhouse has been losing money steadily for the last five years, but no one knows that except me and my accountant. I keep it open because it is, after all, the Funhouse, and were it to close, Jokertown would seem a poorer place.

Next month I will be seventy years of age.

Mary and I often talked of a trip around the world, in those days before the wild card when we were young and in love. I could never have dreamt that I would finally take that trip without her, in the twilight of my life, and at government expense, as a delegate on a fact-finding mission organized and funded by the Senate Committee on Ace Resources and Endeavors, under the official sponsorship of the United Nations and the World Health Organization. We will visit every continent but Antarctica and call upon thirty-nine different countries (some only for a few hours), and our official charge is to investigate the treatment of wild card victims in cultures around the world.

There are twenty-one delegates, only five of whom are jokers. I suppose my selection is a great honor, recognition of my achievements and my status as a community leader. I believe I have my good friend Dr. Tachyon to thank for it.

But then, I have my good friend Dr. Tachyon to thank for a great many things.

The heroes and villains of ACES ABROAD include:

PEREGRINE—the winged beauty whose talent is to drive men sexually mad—before she flies away.

FATHER SQUID—the kindly pastor of the Church of Jesus Christ, Joker. He delivers his moving sermons through the tentacles that hang over his mouth like a constantly twitching mustache.

FORTUNATO—the handsome half black/half Japanese ex-pimp whose special powers depend on his sexuality.

WILD CARDS V—DOWN AND DIRTY

When rival gangs stage a bitter war for control of the streets of Jokertown, District Attorney Rosemary Muldoon asks for Ace volunteers. But then Muldoon is exposed as Rosa Maria Gambione—a Mafia don—and all the Aces are under suspicion for connections with organized crime. In the meantime, the killings continue, and other events stir the lives of Aces and Jokers alike. . . .

♥ ♦ ♠ ♣

"Captain Ellis doesn't approve of this protection racket," Digger Downs bulled ahead. "She says somebody's going to get hurt and it ain't gonna be the bad guys."

"I would submit to the good captain that the protection rackets have all been coming from one direction. And she's being unduly pessimistic. I think we can look out for ourselves. Ideal knows we've had enough practice," Tachyon added dryly, recalling all the years when the police were curiously uninterested whenever a joker was beaten or killed, but Johnny-on-the-spot whenever a tourist howled. Things were better now, but it was still an uneasy relationship between New York's jokers and New York's finest.

Digger licked the tip of his ballpoint pen, a silly, affected gesture. "I know my readers will want to know why these patrols consist only of jokers. With you heading up this effort why not pull in some of the big guns? The Hammer for example, or Mistral or J.J. Flash or Starshine."

"This is a joker neighborhood. We can take care of ourselves."

"Meaning there's hostility between jokers and aces?"

"Digger, don't be an ass. Is it *so* surprising that these people choose to handle this themselves? They are viewed as freaks, treated like retarded children, and ignored in favor of their more fortunate and flamboyant brethren. May I point out that your magazine is titled *Aces*, and no one is panting to found a concomitant magazine entitled *Jokers*? Look around you. This is an activity born out of love and pride. How could I say to these people you're not tough enough or smart enough or strong enough to defend yourselves? Let me call in the aces."

Which was of course precisely what he had been going to do until Des had opened his eyes. But Digger didn't need to know that. Still, Tach had the grace to blush as he shamelessly appropriated Des's lecture and passed it on to the journalist.

"Comment on Leo Barnett?"

"He is a hate-mongering lunatic."

"Can I quote you on that?"

"Go ahead."

"So who's going to be the white knight? Hart-mann?"

"Maybe. I don't know."

"I thought you two were real tight."

"We're friends, but hardly intimates."

"Why do you think Hartmann's been such a friend to the jokers? Personal interest? His wife a carrier, or maybe an illegitimate joker baby hidden away somewhere?"

"I think he is a friend to the wild cards because he is a good man," replied Tachyon a little frigidly.

"Hey, speaking of monstrous joker babies, what's the latest poop on Peregrine's pregnancy?"

Tachyon went rigid with fury, then carefully uncoiled his fists, and relaxed. "No, Digger, you're not going to get me again. I will never stop regretting that I let slip that the father of Peregrine's child was an ace."

WILD CARDS VI—ACE IN THE HOLE

It's 1988, an election year. For the first time the victims of the Wild Card Virus have a candidate who isn't afraid to stand up for jokers' rights. And Greg Hartmann stands a good chance of winning the Democratic nomination, even against competition like Jesse Jackson, Michael Dukakis, and Leo Barnett, the fiery anti-Wild Cards preacher.

But there's more than speeches going on at Atlanta's Convention Center. Behind the scenes a killer ace is on the prowl, and several important lives are at stake. . . . *On sale now!*

Editors Gregory Benford and Martin H. Greenberg
ask the provocative question

What Might Have Been?

* if the Egyptian dynasties—and their Hebrew
  slaves—had survived until modern times?

* if Mahatma Gandhi used passive resistance
  when the Nazis invaded India during World
  War II?

* If Lawrence of Arabia faced Rommel in
  North Africa?

These star-studded anthologies include stories by
some of the most imaginative authors writing speculative
fiction today, including Poul Anderson, Gregory
Benford, George Alec Effinger, Harry Harrison, and
Tom Shippey, Barry Malzberg, James Morrow, Larry
Niven, Frederik Pohl, Robert Silverberg, and Judith
Tarr to name a few. Here are stories that will engage
the mind and challenge the imagination!

☐ Volume One: **Alternate Empires** (27845-2 • $4.50/
  $5.50 in Canada)
☐ Volume Two: **Alternate Heroes** (28279-4 • $4.50/
  $5.50 in Canada)

Buy **What Might Have Been?** on sale now wherever
Bantam Spectra Books are sold, or use this handy
page to order: